THE CHILD BRIDE AND THE OLD MAN OF ARABIA

PART ONE

DR. A. A. AHMED

PublishAmerica
Baltimore

First printing

Hardcover 9781462672417
PUBLISHED BY PUBLISHAMERICA, LLLP
www.publishamerica.com
Baltimore

Printed in the United States of America

DEDICATION

This story is dedicated to each and everyone battered and abused in what is known as the religion of Islam. To the female children, teenage girls and Muslim women all over the world—to those who are suffering in silence and hopelessness; we are your voices to bring to light a world hiding behind a lie. The truth cannot be ignored. Your suffering and abuse is not a responsibility to shelter. Let your light shine out of darkness and expose the fault of those guilty for your hardship, pain, struggle and devastation. You are not to blame.

This dedication is to all individuals from all reaches of the earth who cherish the gift God give in love, knowledge, wisdom and "freeness of speech". May we use these great gifts in spreading word of the detrimental affliction of our Muslim sisters, mothers, daughters, nieces, aunts, cousins, young and old, and all victims of abuse and helplessness. If we speak in their behalf and do not let up, perhaps they can take the first step in speaking up for themselves and walking out of this hellhole called Islam and a life that was never meant to be even from the beginning of time. Eph 6:19, 20.

Seth Bullock, "This story must be repeated and repeated over and over again. It must be sent to all Governments in the Free World. Please join in to do so."

ACKNOWLEDGEMENT

I would like to acknowledge the sincere and arduous efforts of all volunteer proofreaders for the extraordinary care they have taken in perfecting this story. Some have proofread 25 pages or more and some 50 pages or more. Some have agreed to be mentioned in this acknowledgement and some preferred to remain anonymous.

I would like to acknowledge and extend special thanks to Alan S. TAN who proofread, edited, and revised the entire manuscript, 950 pages. I would also like to thank J. Mercer who was exceptional in proofreading, editing and revising 500 pages of this publication.

1. Alan S. TAN
2. J. Mercer.
3. Susan Stickevers.
4. Rebecca Figone.
5. William Vaughan.
6. Cheryl Curtis.
7. Nancy von Minden.
8. Robin Hubbard.
9. Heather Scott.
10. Suzanne Fields.
11. Henrietta Netta.
12. Judith Westerfield.
13. Gloria Hodgson.
14. Author J. Forbes.
15. Ron Parrs.

16. Kevin Wright.
17. Lisa Wilson.
18. Darlene Enderby.
19. Ami Le Difni.
20. Anonymous Proofreaders-

BOOK I

RAYHANA KHAN

CHAPTER 1

RAYHANA

Life is a harsh reality for the majority of people in India. For the poor, every new morning brings with it the many struggles for survival, and the night shrouds in its darkness questions of life and death. The destitute go without food for days and it is not uncommon for some to starve and die in the streets like stray dogs abandoned by their owners. In big cities such as Bombay, Calcutta, Madras, and New Delhi many people are homeless, living on the streets, in railways stations or shanties of discarded packing material and rags. Many can ill-afford three meals in a day and for most, breakfast is a luxury. The Untouchables eat food by chance, whatever they can find, and those not adept at foraging will eventually meet their end in filthy gutters.

Poor Indians usually live in a slum, which isn't fit for the housing of animals. For this reason, the Oscar-winning movie, *Slum Dog Millionaire,* called the inhabitants of these slums, "Dogs." Of course, they aren't dogs, but dogs in the West live in better conditions than these living dead. There are no toilets or bathrooms inside the slum residence. Members of the family are left to use public washrooms, which are filthy as hell. Bathing is rare, and when it happens, women will bathe in the slums while the males would bathe either in an open public area or wait for the rainy season to rinse off their emaciated bodies. Their environment, for those used to the relative luxury of urban living, is unimaginable for those who have yet to walk the lanes of the slums. Of course, the condition of the slum dwellers is considerably superior to that of the Untouchables who have no shelter or roof over their heads. A typical small-sized slum shanty measures about four meters square. In this square box, you are likely to find a mother and a father with their six children, accompanied by all four of their grandparents. Imagine twelve people making a home in an area no larger than a typical western washroom. Slum abodes have no windows or plumbing. The sight of filthy rags and a cistern of water will greet anyone entering a slum abode. There are no televisions or radios and computers are unheard of.

Our report begins with one particular Indian Muslim family living in a multi-cultural slum area. In a small-sized slum dwelling of about two by two meters lived poor Indian Muslim family consisting of a mother and a father with their six children and all four of their grandparents. The slum in which they were living had no windows or washroom. It had nothing except filthy rags scattered everywhere and a small jar of water. They had no radio or television. Their immediate neighbor across the muddied lane was a Hindu family of eight. The hovel behind their shanty was occupied by a Buddhist family, which besides the lord Buddha, also deified Dr. Ambedkar, the father of the Indian Constitution. Their immediate neighbors were Hindus—each family revering a different god. One worshipped the goddesses Durga and Kali while the other centered their lives around the elephant-headed god Ganapati (in English Ganesha). In Hinduism there are thirty-three crores gods (i.e. three hundred and thirty million gods). The visitor to India would find in every city and every area a different god or goddess being worshiped. Hinduism is loosely used as an umbrella term to cover thousands of different religious beliefs among the Hindus. The only common factor uniting all these various beliefs is the Caste System, which has persisted to present day.

Most of the other dilapidated homes surrounding this poor Muslim family were inhabited by Hindus except for one. There was another Muslim family eking out a miserable existence not far from their home. These Muslims differed in their beliefs by virtue of their spiritual leader—Aga Khan. This sect believed that Aga Khan was a manifestation of Allah on earth and a ‘walking, talking Qur’an.’ The Aga Khan devotees lived decidedly better than their neighbors. Although both Muslim families lived in close proximity in the same slum, there was a remarkable difference between the two, and that difference will become clear as our story unfolds.

The father of the Indian family of six children and four grandparents committed suicide because he was burdened with a handicap and could no longer work to support his large family. His intention was to lessen the number of mouths to feed by one. Everyone, including his wife who was now the breadwinner of the family, felt that his sacrifice was honorable. When he became disabled, his wife started working in homes of the rich. Their situation did not get better after the death of the father. Being poor in India is more than just an unfortunate state of finances. Being poor is synonymous with many other negative social and religious connotations. Most religious followers in India believe that poverty is the curse of the gods. Some religious adherents on the other hand believe that poor people are reaping what they sowed in their previous lives. Abundance and richness are considered the fruits of good deeds and hence deserving of divine blessings. So, aside from wallowing in their misery and suffering, the poor are despised and considered to be divinely cursed, their lot in life entirely fitting and divinely ordained.

Hindus are especially prone to this line of thought. Slum dwellers have misfortune showered on them as a result of bad karma, accumulated through past lifetimes. Karma simply means deeds, in this life or another. If you were rich and well-to-do then you are enjoying the law of good karma, accumulated by your actions in a previous life. Such unfair ideologies justify the abject discrimination the well-to-do heap upon the destitute. Simply put, the man starving to death could have been Adolph Hitler in a previous life. This doctrine is based on the Hindu caste system comprising of four classes of people:—Brahmins (priests and gurus, also known as gods on earth), Ksatriyas (rulers and warriors), Vaisyas (merchants and farmers), and Sudras (servants). Centuries of belief in the caste system, has condemned many to a life of abject poverty and discrimination. Blighted lives without opportunity to change their lot, leaves countless millions to live lives of squalor, surviving on menial labor and the hopelessness of life in the slums.

Hindus not aggregated within the caste system are known as outcasts. They are treated by all as polluted servants and Untouchables. The Untouchables are treated like animals and rank even lower than livestock. They are considered defiled and sub-human. Mahatma Gandhi tried to reverse the trend by coining a new name for them—Hirijans, meaning Children of God. Sadly, a simple change of name alone cannot erase centuries of conditioning. Apart from the new name, they are exactly where the caste system has put them all this time. Given their social and cultural status, they are simply unclean and all castes avoid touching them. The Brahmins and the other castes do not allow the Hirijans to drink water when they come to work in their homes because they believe this would defile them. No one would marry an outcast. This is the ugly side of Hinduism. The damage done to these people are beyond remedy. Most of the dwellers of the slums are either low castes or untouchables. While it is predominantly a Hindu value, it matters not what their religious backgrounds are, they are all equally discriminated accordingly.

The slums themselves are very filthy and full of flies, mosquitoes, cockroaches, and lizards. Very narrow gutters separate rows upon rows of shanties. The footpaths double as garbage dumps, storm drains, sewage passages and toilets. Needless to say, one must tread carefully. Children and women too afraid to venture into public washrooms at night will use the alleys and footpaths. The resultant assault on a newcomer's sense of smell can be overpowering. There are many sad and disgusting details too innumerable to mention of the misery and plight of those unable to rise above their miserable existence and which causes the heart to search for answers and the eyes brim with tears in futility.

Let us return to the misfortunes of our first Muslim family. They had five sons and a daughter. The daughter was the oldest, at seven years old. Every child was younger to the one before him and older to the one after him by nine to ten months. In fact, slum people have no other means of entertainment or enjoyment other than sex. They cannot afford to go to the movie theater or visit a beach or any other place. The only recreation available to them is sex with each other or their neighbors. After all, it is free. Sex outside marriage is very common thing among the slum residents.

The day takes its toll on the inhabitants of the slums. A working day lasts from sunrise to sunset and rest is uppermost on the mind of one who has worked all day to earn a pittance. Usually parents of poor families work from early morning until late evening. When they return home overcome by the fatigue of the day, they quickly fall fast asleep. Desire however stirs a man or a woman sufficiently rested and despite the rigors of the day, a husband will find it in himself to satisfy the urge to make love to his wife. After sleeping for a few hours the husband might force his tired body out of sleep and crawl to the body of his wife to have sexual intercourse. Sometimes, the wife may not even realize this because she would be dead to the world. If lucky, she responds to him but more often than not, she lies exhausted from toil and the oppressive heat of the slum. Occasionally, the husband might stop half way when his son or daughter awakes due to the disturbance of this sexual activity. This is because all twelve members of the family sleep on the floor in this washroom-sized lodging. Privacy in this act is not afforded as families sleep together in the one room and any physical or vocal expression of their union is tempered by the proximity of three generations of the one family. Violation of one's privacy is an unheard-of concept. If you are a light sleeper, you are more than likely hear the sexual exploits of your neighbors as if they were right there beside you.

Anyway, the daughter of this poor Muslim family was named *Iffat, meaning chaste, pure, virtuous, and modest*. The first four sons were named after the first four successors of the prophet of Islam which are known as the rightly-guided caliphs; *Abu Bakr, Omar, Osman, and Ali*. The last son was named *Muhammad* after the prophet of Islam. The mother was called *Rayhana* after the Jewish female concubine of the prophet Muhammad. The father was called *Khan*. The family lived on the meager earnings of Mr. Khan before an accident at work rendered him incapacitated. This was a great tragedy for the family. At that time, Rayhana was not working because Mr. Khan would not allow his wife in her young age to go from house to house cleaning, cooking and working in the homes of the rich. He was afraid that his young wife might have to share her virtue among the lustful rich. As a matter of fact, Rayhana was a very beautiful woman. She was like a lotus flower growing out of a muddy swamp in a dense forest. For those not in the know, the lotus thrives in very muddy and dirty waters but the petals of the lotus are of the most lustrous white, which never seem to stain from the water of its sustenance.

After Mr. Khan's accident, which necessitated the amputation of both his legs, he was forced to allow Rayhana to seek employment in the homes of the rich. This set him into depression, as he could not bear the guilt and the shame of allowing his stunning wife running from house to house exposing herself to all kinds of abuse and harassment. His situation was made worse by the fact that no one in the family was strong enough to move him, even for a simple task of relieving oneself in the public washroom. The humiliation of not being able to exercise simple dignities let him to seek ways to end his life. At first Mr. Khan thought to immolate himself, saving his family the trouble and the expense of keeping him alive. He realized that that method might leave them without house and home, as his home was basically a fire hazard. He could not electrocute himself, as they had no supply. There was no medication he could take to pass away in his sleep or kill him painlessly. Not being well-informed, he did not know he could just cut his wrists and bleed to death. He had no rope to hang himself and even if he had a rope where would he fasten it? If he tied it up to the shaky roof, the slum might collapse without killing him. In that case, he would merely end up destroying his family's slum and live to face the consequences. That would be another unnecessary tragedy for his poor family.

Mr. Khan thought of many ways to kill himself but none was practical and would result in dire consequences for his already destitute family. At last, Mr. Khan took his life in a very painful and cruel way. He stabbed himself in the heart with his own knife and died. As he predicted, his wife had only to wash his blood off the floor of the slum after the government workers came to carry his corpse away. The government extends help to those who cannot afford to bury their dead due to their adversity. Mr. Khan died without a pension, for in India, only the families of government workers were entitled to collect pensions of a family member. Therefore, after his accident, Mr. Khan was not given any kind of workers' compensation or disability benefits. There was nothing of that sort in India. Like all other third world countries, India does not have a government-assisted welfare benefit program. If you don't work, you basically starve to death. In India, starving to death and dying on the streets is an everyday occurrence.

After her husband's selfless suicide, the entire responsibility of her six children and parents and her in-laws rested on her shoulders. Her parents and those of her late husband were aged, but ambulatory. The seven-year-old Iffat was the main caretaker of her four grandparents and five brothers while her mother was at work. Although merely a child, she had to babysit her brothers and mind her grandparents. She even learned to cook and did most of the work for her poor family. By the way, slum dwellers don't like to send their children to school. Of course, no one could blame them for that. Besides, education is not compulsory in India. The decision to educate their children or not is a choice left entirely to the parents. Children as young as six and seven years old are allowed to work in India. There is no such thing as child labor legislation or child abuse in this regard. As long as the child is strong enough to carry a tea tray full of six or seven cups of tea he can be put to work.

None of the six Khan children attended school. However, Mrs. Khan did not send her daughter Iffat to work in the houses of the rich Indians because of the fear of exposing her to sexual molestation, harassment, or even rape. Nonetheless, shortly after the death of her husband, Rayhana Khan allowed her six-year-old son, Abu Bakr to clean tables and serve water to customers of a nearby teashop. The owner of that shop was a Muslim man and that is why he agreed to allow Abu Bakr to do light jobs for him, and paying him the same as the other street urchins who did more advanced jobs like making, and pouring tea, and sweeping the floor.

Besides being young and beautiful, Rayhana was a smart woman. Although, she had never been to school and could not read and write, she learned from her employers how to draw out her name and signature. Moreover, her contact with those rich people helped her to learn things about the outside world. A constant worry she had was of being sexually harassed by the male members of these rich families, but she knew that if she had to leave every house because of that she would never find work to help her feed her own large family. The owners of those houses sometimes gave her their unwanted dresses and clothes for her children. She was very fortunate in that sometimes, she was allowed to take home leftover food and to eat food and drink water while in their employ. At least she was a Muslim and not a Hindu low caste or untouchable Hirijan, which saved her from the unnecessary trouble of being treated like filth. Besides that, her young age and beauty played a very important role in her being treated with slightly more decorum and allowed her to carry more favor.

Interacting with rich families, Rayhana learned that a woman's beauty could be used to earn more money and live a better life. She did not intend to sell her body but she came to realize that in the Middle East many young Indian women were working in wealthy Arab homes, earning good wages. Arabs loved Indian women because of their marvelous beauty and hard work. Rayhana became fully aware of her strong feminine attraction and gorgeous beauty only after her husband died and she began to work outside the home. Before that, her beauty was wasted, hidden in rubble like a beautiful flower growing amongst the tombs. Her late husband never allowed her to step out of her slum until his accident deprived him of his ability to work and support his family. Only after his accident was she at liberty to show her youth and beauty to the outside world.

Rayhana had her mind set on taking full advantage of her young age and beauty, being leveraging off her physique, working for wealthy Arabs. The money she earned would be pivotal in raising her family's standard of living. She came to know that wealthy Arabs come every year during the monsoon rains to spend time in Bombay because most of them live in desert countries and very rarely see rain. Some of them would bring work visas with them and sell them to recruitment agencies. However, agencies would usually demand no less than 500,000 rupees per visa, a princely sum for Rayhana. For that reason, she decided to go to Colaba area of downtown Bombay and try her luck. She knew that she was not educated and had no professional training; hence, she could not find a job nursing or other professional work. She could do other kinds of housework like cleaning, cooking, washing clothes, *et cetera*.

One day, Rayhana Khan pretended to be sick and informed her employers through her oldest son that she would not be able to come to work that day because she was going to the hospital. With so much hope in her heart, Rayhana put on one of those lovely dresses given to her by her rich employer and then took the local train and traveled to downtown Bombay. It took her an hour and a half to travel from the Dharavi slums to the Colaba area. Luckily, the local train had a special compartment for ladies only. However, as soon as she reached Churchgate station men began to tease and flirt with her. She ignored them and continued her trip to Colaba. She did not want to spend money on hiring a taxi so she asked some women to show her how to get to Colaba. The women pointed out the general direction and she began to walk to her destination. While she was walking from Churchgate to Colaba, Rayhana's head was turning like a table fan. She had never seen skyscrapers before. Looking at the tall, beautiful buildings of Nariman Point her head and neck swayed from left to right, back and forth, as if she was searching for her one lucky star amidst a sea of celestial bodies. She even collided a couple of times with people walking along the street and then stumbled over the pavement and fell off.

The asphalt street appeared to her as if she was walking on a road made of black glass. She had never seen such a beautiful street before. In her slum area, the roads were very rough, full of holes, stones and garbage. In fact, thousands of tons of garbage and containers littered the streets of the slums, always full and overflowing. Some people never bother to throw their garbage inside the containers because there was simply not enough room. Suddenly, she was far removed from the scattered, garbage-filled streets of the slums, teeming with mice, rats, lizards, flies and insects; roads crowded with human beings, and domestic animals such as cows, dogs, cats, chickens, and goats. Oh, but here in this beautiful world on this beautiful day Rayhana felt as if she was walking on the road to heaven.

When she arrived at the Gate of India in front of the Taj Mahal Hotel, Rayhana felt as if she had come out of the wretched world she had been engulfed in all her life and into the highest of heavens. She could almost hear the voices of angels welcoming her. This beautiful vision of paradise was also full of the realities of life when heaven suddenly became marred by a mass of beggars and loafers shocking her back to her senses. Hundreds of young Indian girls roamed about the crowd in front of the Taj Mahal Hotel. From the way those girls walked and talked Rayhana knew they were street girls or prostitutes. Then grabbing her attention, she could not believe her eyes when she saw young Indian boys and girls sitting on the beach lip kissing without so much as a word of caution from the passers-by. Rayhana had never been to a movie theater and had never seen lovers before. Married to her late husband in what Indians called *an arranged marriage,* her life had been devoid of love and romance. Although she spent seven years with her husband, she neither loved him nor felt loved by him.

In this magnificent place, half splendor, half hell, there were many foreigners, most of them Arabs from either Saudi Arabia or the Gulf countries. Rayhana knew they were Arabs because of their Islamic clothes, similar to the ones she had seen in pictures of pilgrims on their way to Mecca. Rayhana was a very simple, naive woman. She thought that if she just walked up to any one of those Arabs she would get a work visa to an Arab country and they would accept whatever little money she had in her pocket. She did not carry a purse for she didn't want to spend money on unnecessary things. After pacing up and down and roaming aimlessly for some time, Rayhana saw an old Arab man sitting all alone. He looked in his late sixties. She thought that such an old man would not be interested in women any more. With four hundred rupees on her person, she walked up to him and began to talk to him in Hindi. The old man understood nothing of what she was saying to him. He said to her in broken Hindi he did not speak her language. Rayhana understood the problem. She kept smiling and looking at him. The old man became very interested in this pretty young Indian woman whom he thought was a prostitute offering her services for the night. In his desire to have her he was sure he could strike a deal they both would be happy with. He waved his hand to a young Indian boy and requested he translate what the young woman was trying to tell him. The young boy spoke Arabic and told him that the young Indian woman was looking for a work visa to an Arab country. When informed of this by the young lad, the old man became disappointed that this pretty young thing wasn't a call girl and was looking for a work visa instead. Nevertheless, he ignored her request and asked the Indian boy to ask her how much she would charge for the night. The boy understood what the Arab man wanted and decided he could profit from this situation. He knew that Rayhana wasn't a prostitute; however he changed the question and asked her how much she was prepared to pay for a visa to Saudi Arabia. She told him that she had not so much to offer except four hundred rupees. The boy laughed loudly before he told her for that amount of money she could not hire a taxi to take her to the Bombay international airport. He then turned to the old man and told him that she said she would charge two thousand rupees for a full night. The old man could not believe his ears when he heard such a beautiful woman was prepared to sleep with an old man like him with such a small amount of money. He would easily spend two thousand rupees buying coffee or a soft drink in the expensive hotel he vacationed in. Therefore, the old wealthy man agreed to pay the young woman more than she asked for. He took out of his suitcase ten thousand rupees. He gave the young boy five hundred rupees and asked him to leave. The boy took the money and disappeared in an instant. Then, the old man stretched out his hand and tried to put the rest of the money in the Rayhana's hand. Rayhana quickly withdrew her hand and stepped back. The old man was surprised and kept repeating, *hotel, hotel, hotel!* Rayhana did not understand his meaning. She kept saying to him, *"Rayhana visa, Rayhana visa, Rayhana visa."*

The old man finally understood that the young woman wasn't a prostitute. He also understood that she wanted a visa to go to an Arab country. Moreover, he realized that her name was Rayhana and that revealed she was a Muslim like him. He also knew that the Indian boy had cheated him and used Rayhana to accomplish it. However, for him, five hundred rupees was nothing. He was thrilled upon discovering such a gorgeous young woman wanted him to offer her a visa and take her with him to his country, Saudi Arabia. He felt as if Allah had sent him a beautiful girl from heaven and offered her to him as an everlasting concubine. If Rayhana truly wanted to go with him to his country, he was determined to do everything within his power to make his dreams and hers come true. However, before he made this hasty step, he decided to find a reliable interpreter and get all the information he could about Rayhana and find out exactly what it was she wanted. He knew of a recruitment agency that he often sold visas to. He took out his cell phone, dialed the number of the recruitment agency, and requested they send a reliable interpreter and preferably someone other than an Indian. The agency told him that they had a Sudanese student working for them and that he would perform the interpretation quite well. The old Arab asked him to rush to the location as quickly as possible. He was afraid Rayhana might get fed up and leave so while waiting for the interpreter he kept repeating, *"Rayhana visa, Rayhana visa"*. Rayhana kept smiling and saying the same thing. The happiness on the face of the old man assured Rayhana that he was going to fulfill her dreams.

The old man anxiously counted the seconds. It took the interpreter over half an hour to arrive in a taxi at the place where his sills were urgently needed. As soon as the Sudanese boy showed up the old man asked him to tell the Indian woman that he was ready to give her a visa and take her with him to the Kingdom of Saudi Arabia as a maidservant. Rayhana was overjoyed when she heard those promising words. She said that she would love to go to the Arab country to work as a maidservant in the house of the old man. The Sudanese boy asked the old man how much he wanted Rayhana to pay for the work visa. The old man told him that he did not want her to pay a single rupee.

Further, he was prepared to give her the visa for free and also pay for her airfare. The Sudanese could not believe his ears when he heard the old man willing to make such a large and generous offer. He told Rayhana the words the old man had spoken to him.

The Sudanese boy soon realized why the Saudi man was making such a generous offer. Rayhana was extremely beautiful and the old man wanted to take her to his country to use her as a concubine. Rayhana did not expect such an old man to be interested in somebody like her. She was nobody to him. Besides, there were many other young Indian girls roaming the streets of Colaba ready and willing to offer their bodies for very little money. Why then should he favor her over and above all those other girls much younger than her? Therefore, she concluded that the old man favored her because she was a Muslim woman.

CHAPTER 2

CHRISTIE

Rayhana speculated correctly but arrived at a conclusion that was far from the truth. It was true that the old man was interested in her because she was a Muslim woman, but there was more to his favor than just her religion. Her marvelous beauty and young age were his main attraction. Yet, this in itself was not why his fondness for her was growing. Her refusal to offer her body for thousands of rupees was yet another important reason that assured him she wasn't lady of the night. But, this was not the only cause of his budding obsession. To understand the reason that led this old Saudi into a crazed longing for this radiant, vibrant young Indian woman, we need to go back a few years and dig out some pleasant and unpleasant memories of his life in India…

Sheikh Faiz bin Ahmed came to India for the first time five years before. At that time, he was just sixty-four years old and had four wives and many sons and daughters. In fact, he married more than four women in his life but the Islamic Shari'a law would not allow him to keep more than four wives at the same time. All of his wives were Saudi. In Saudi Arabia, it is forbidden for any citizen of that kingdom to marry an outsider, so citizens had to contend with Saudi wives. The law of his country would not allow him to marry an Arab from another Arab country even if she was a Muslim. Let us recall the case of a Saudi princess who fell in love with an Egyptian national, a man who happened to be one of her many foreign servants. She knew she could not marry him while they were in the Kingdom of Saudi

Arabia even though he was Muslim. For this reason, she decided to leave the country with him. She took on a male identity and dressed to suit the role. Unfortunately, she was caught at the airport and then summarily executed along with her Egyptian boyfriend. A movie of her story, called *The Death of a Princess* was banned in Saudi Arabia and all the Arab countries.

Anyway, when Sheikh Faiz bin Ahmed first came to India it was as a tourist. A famous Egyptian journalist rightly said that *the tourism of the Arab man is the woman*. Everywhere the Arab men went they always looked for women. Of course, there were many reasons for their obsession. No one should hastily conclude that the Arab man lusts after sex and women more than men of any other nationality or culture. Neither is the reason attributable to their sexual abilities to marry four women at the same time. The main reason for their sexual predation is their religious upbringing, imposed upon them from an early age; a total segregation of male and female. Arab males are not allowed to mix with the Arab females even as children. In their homes, segregation of genders is carried to an extreme with sections cordoned off for males and females. These two sections were separated from each other like public washrooms—men and women. It was strictly forbidden at any time and under any circumstances for either of the sexes to mix or set foot in the restricted areas. For this reason, the Arab male is not allowed to enjoy bonding with his baby sister as a little boy. The restrictions grew tighter as they grew older. Beginning at school age, the males attended an all boys' school and the females attended the all girls' school. Of course, this strict segregation between males and females has led to adverse social consequences for both men and women. The homosexuality rate in Saudi Arabia to date is alarming to say the least. Rape crimes are common in the kingdom of Saudi Arabia. Many young female children are raped by their uncles and cousins and brothers. Women sometimes get raped inside elevators. In the villages, whenever young boys find the chance, they would catch their own sisters and either sodomize them, or just dry hump them from behind until they ejaculate.

Sheikh Faiz bin Ahmed was neither a womanizer nor a sexual pervert. He was just another run of the mill Arab suffering from sexual frustration. If he had sex with a hundred women, he would still not be satisfied. By the way, in Colaba sometimes you can see an Arab man with as many as six Indian prostitutes in a hotel room. Many times whenever the Bombay police decide to crack down on prostitution, the front page of the newspapers would feature a story of an Arab man caught with half a dozen prostitutes in his hotel room. The funniest thing would be the fact that not all these prostitutes might be Indians. Some of them would be from Nepal. Although, Nepalese girls are not as pretty as Indian girls, Arabs still prefer them. The main reason is that Indian prostitutes for the most part will not allow their customers to sodomize them, even if they are offered thousands of rupees, while most Nepalese prostitutes do not mind anal sex at all. Besides, the backsides of Nepalese girls are much larger and wider than the Indian girls. Don't ask me why the Arabs like women with large backsides. I admit that I have no answer for that question although I could make a reasonable guess. It isn't only the Arab man, but the African male that also shares the same penchant. One can understand the problem of the African man. African women do not conform to the media ideal of beauty, and probably use their large backsides and spear-like breasts to attract men. On the other hand, the Arab girls were prettier than the African girls and should have had no problem attracting males. However, due to the segregation between sexes and the total concealment of her face and her other feminine qualities, the Arab woman was forced to develop other means to attract the opposite sex. She would deliberately gorge herself with food in order to develop a buxom physique, deemed desirable in the Middle East.

Sheikh Faiz bin Ahmed, on his first visit to India, desperately fell in love with a Christian girl that caught his eye. Of course, it was a one-sided love affair because he was sixty-four years old and the girl was only twenty. Sheikh Ahmed hated Hindu girls, and if you offered him the Bollywood superstar and former Miss World, Aishwariya Rai, he would not marry her because she was a polytheist. He would not mind to have sex with her but he would never ever marry her.

His Qur'an forbade marriage to a polytheist woman. It's funny how a Muslim man is allowed to commit adultery with a polytheist and even rape her but he's not allowed to marry her. The prophet Muhammad and his Companions did the same, according to "*Abu Sa'id al-Khudri: The Apostle of Allah (may peace be upon him) sent a military expedition to Awtas on the occasion of the battle of Hunain. They met their enemy and fought with them. They defeated them and took them captives. Some of the companions of the Apostle of Allah (may peace be upon him) were reluctant to have intercourse with the female captives in the presence of their husbands who were polytheists. So Allah, the Exalted, sent down the Qur'anic verse: "And all married women (are forbidden) unto you save those (captives) whom your right hands possess" (Sunnan Abu Dawud 2150).* Accordingly, in this way, a Muslim man is allowed to marry three types of women—Muslim women, Jewish women, and Christian women. In addition, he is permitted to have sex with any other female including a Hindu, Buddhist, Satanist, or even an atheist. Again, he just cannot marry her. Some schools of the Shari'a law state that these women should be possessed as war booties or bought from the slave market.

Now, five years ago, Sheikh Faiz bin Ahmed saw this pretty young Christian girl while he was staying in the Taj Mahal Hotel. The girl was working in the housekeeping department of the hotel. He saw her when she came along with another girl to clean up his luxurious suite. His soul clung to this lovely picture of perfection and he was determined to get her no matter how much it might cost him and no matter what the risk. He bribed the bellboy and asked him to convince the young lady to sleep with him. He promised to pay whatever the asking price. The bellboy returned with an answer from the young woman, "Not interested in your money." Moreover, the bellboy told the old man that the girl was a Christian and she was originally from Goa. Instead of being discouraged, Sheikh Ahmed's interest escalated. He claimed to have fallen in love with her at first sight. One good thing about him was that he had high respect for any woman who would not surrender her body no matter how much a man might offer her. Moreover, Sheikh Ahmed knew that his religion allowed him to marry a Christian girl, so he was determined to get as much information as he could about her. He told the bellboy to find out where she was staying in Bombay and whether she was married or not. In a short period of time, the bellboy was able to ascertain that she was still single. He also bribed someone in the housekeeping department and obtained her address from the application she filled out when she applied for the job at the hotel. The old man, of course, compensated the housekeeping manager amply for his treasure trove of information.

After that, Sheikh Ahmed went with the bellboy and met the parents of the girl and offered them many things in exchange for their daughter's hand in marriage. He promised to buy them a house in a very exclusive area. The girl's parents were poor and lived in a house little better than a slum shanty. There were houses in Bombay called *Chawls*. A chawl was neither a real house as people in the West would call a home, nor was it a slum where Rayhana and her children lived like eggs stuffed inside a carton. In the chawl you could have electricity and tap water and a few other necessities. However, in the chawl you would not have your own washroom. Chawls had common areas with public washrooms. The chawl dwellers were not rich people and they were not that poor, but they should not be confused with the middle class people of the West. Chawl residents are usually gainfully employed and generally educate their children. Only the rich send their children to private schools. The rich people do not send their children to public schools because children of rich families often get kidnapped for ransom by gangsters of the underworld.

Christina Loboz was the Christian girl Sheikh Ahmed had his eye on. Her family and friends called her Christie. She studied up to grade eleven. She was the eldest in her family and had four siblings after her. Her father was a drunkard and rarely went to work. He had been fired many times due to his heavy drinking. Because of the father's alcoholic binges, it was a daily struggle for Christie's mother, who was trying to raise her and her two brothers and two sisters. When Christie was in grade twelve her mother lost her eyesight and became blind. Therefore, Christie left school and began to work. At this young age, she had to contend with being sexually harassed wherever she worked.

Christie then fell in love with a Christian boy called Bobby. Although, Bobby was also from a poor family and living in the chawls, he was a very intelligent young man. He worked in small hotels and motels in Bombay before he finally went to work in the gulf country of Kuwait and worked there for two years. He could not marry Christie because he had a huge responsibility towards his large family. He had to take care of his four brothers, five sisters, and his parents. He made a promise to Christie that one day he would come back to India and marry her and bring her with him to live. Unfortunately, Saddam Hussein invaded Kuwait and Bobby, like many other foreign workers, had to run for their lives. He returned to India empty-handed and could not fulfill his promise to marry his dream girl, the one he cared for so deeply. Instead, he went back to his small job in a motel and continued to support his family.

Although Bobby was struggling to support his family, he still approached Christie's parents and expressed his love and proposal to marry her. Christie's parents strongly rejected this proposition and kicked him out of their chawl. About that same time, Christie had already started working housekeeping at the Taj Mahal Hotel. She was now the only breadwinner in the family. In India, if a girl married, she would become the property of her husband and in-laws. Her family therefore could not hope to see a single rupee of her wages. Nonetheless, the love between Bobby and Christie continued to grow. Bobby suggested they get married at the local court, run away together and just forget about their families. Christie strongly rejected this idea because both her parents were disabled—her mother was blind and her father was constantly in an alcohol-induced stupor. She decided to sacrifice her dreams of marriage and having a family of her own until God provide a way for them to be united in wedded bliss. As it seemed, God was indeed working out a miracle and in a most unexpected way. Her disabled parents felt as if God himself had come down from heaven through divine intervention when the wealthy business tycoon, Sheikh Ahmed, approached them and pleaded for their daughter's hand in marriage in exchange for all that riches could bring. He had much to offer and was willing to give the whole world to them when he fell in love with their beautiful Christina. Well, the parents were simply overjoyed and happy to accept this outstanding proposal. They promised Sheikh Ahmed they would convince their daughter to marry him. They were not in the least bothered about the old man's age. This didn't disturb them at all, nor did they consider their daughter's love for her boyfriend, Bobby. They imposed considerable pressure on their daughter until she succumbed to their demands.

At first, Christie refused and strongly rejected this marriage proposal. She threatened to burn herself alive if her parents tried to force her to marry him. However, she started to have second thoughts on the matter. She calculated and studied her options. She needed to wait for at least another ten years until all her siblings would finish their education and began to work and support themselves. At that time, her boyfriend might get tired of waiting and decide to marry someone else without all the hassle. Moreover, after ten years her age might be another factor for her boyfriend and his family to reject her. Christie then realized that Sheikh Ahmed could be a short cut to fulfill her dreams and marry her true love. Before she made a commitment to the old man, she talked to Bobby and disclosed to him her secret plan. Although hesitant, her boyfriend found her plan to be the only anchor that would snatch them from their desperate situation and move them closer to their goals of being together.

So the plan was set in motion. Christie would marry the old man but she established certain conditions. One of her conditions was she would stay in her own country to oversee the welfare of her parents and siblings. If he wanted to marry her, he had to agree to this term and she would accept his proposal. She would remain a resident of India and he could travel between the two countries to visit her. Not only did Sheikh Ahmed accept this condition but he was overjoyed to hear of it. It was exactly what he had in mind. He knew that the law of his country would not allow him to marry a non-Saudi woman and bring her to his country. Secondly, the kind of marriage that Christie asked for was called in the Shari'a law, Zawaj Al-Misyar. (Al-Misyar is an official marriage institution in Islam, which allows for a lesser form of relationship between a man and a woman other than the normal marriage arrangement. The regulations governing Al-Misyar do not require that a married couple live together, but Al-Misyar allows the man to have another wife in addition to his primary wives. The Misyar wife is expected to live with her parents, and her husband can visit her according to a predetermined schedule or agreement. Al-Misyar marriage has been practiced in Saudi Arabia and Egypt for many years).

Christie also demanded that Sheikh Ahmed should buy one house for her and one house for her parents and siblings. Moreover, he should give her a dowry of fifty lakhs of rupees (i.e. 5,000,000 Indian rupees). Sheikh Ahmed agreed to buy the two houses and give Christie five million rupees. However, he himself countered with an important stipulation; his requirement was for Christie to stop working immediately and be a housewife instead. Christie gladly accepted this condition because it would relieve her from the drudgery of working long, hard days for meager wages.

When both parties came to an amiable agreement of the terms that were beneficial to each, the marriage took place. Sheikh Ahmed spent only a couple of weeks with his new bride and then flew back to his country. As soon as he returned to his country, Christie had Bobby move into her beautiful home, courtesy of Sheikh Ahmed. This was more than she could have asked of her wonderful God and Creator, to be able to enjoy all that life had in store and the wealth supplied her by her rich Saudi husband. And what's more, she was enjoying every moment of it with her Indian boyfriend.

In those days, Sheikh Ahmed had four Saudi wives. He divorced one of them in order to make a room for his young Indian wife. He often boasted to his elite group of wealthy Saudi friends about his young pretty Indian wife. His friends did not blame him because Islam permitted him to marry four women at the same time and also he was allowed by Shari'a law to marry a Christian girl. His friends were quite envious of the prize he had acquired after seeing his wedding photos of his young Indian bride sitting by his side in her wedding gown. At the time of their marriage, Christie was twenty years old and one month. Sheikh Ahmed was sixty-four years old and eleven months. Although the difference between the two was forty-four years and ten months, none of his friends could judge him because the prophet Muhammad was fifty-four when he married his third wife, Aisha and it is recorded she was but six years old when he married her, forty-eight years difference between the two.

Every three to four months, Sheikh Ahmed visited his young Indian wife and spent a few weeks with her and then flew back to his country. Whenever, he decided to visit he would call in advance so that she could prepare for his stay with her. Every month he would send between twenty to thirty thousand rupees to her. In a short time, Christie was a very wealthy woman. Filthy rich and loving every minute of it, she shared her new fortune with her boyfriend who lived with her without the benefit of marriage. However, the secret lovers always felt there was something absent in their relationship and something preventing them from being truly happy. They did not belong to each other. Something was causing a terrible disturbance so much, so it was like a branding iron igniting over coals of fire burning deep down into their inner souls. Unless that person was removed, they would not feel free to belong to each other. The lovers wanted to start a family and have children of their own and enjoy a real family life. So after a year and a half the lovers decided Christie would file for divorce and cut all ties that bind with her Saudi husband, benefits and all. She felt she had already given him enough of her body and she did not want to be tormented forever by having sex with a man old enough to be her grandfather. Besides, she had no love or respect for him. He had used his money to buy her from her family in their desperation and, as far as she was concerned, the debt was paid.

Consequently, after eighteen months, Christie went to *Bandara* Court and filed for divorce from her Saudi husband. Her grounds for divorce were that her husband, Sheikh Ahmed, had cheated on her by marring two Arab women, thereby committing adultery. The court in India however, did not require any reason for the granting of a divorce. As long as one of the partners decided they wanted to leave the marriage, he/she could get a divorce from the other. Christie gave the court the address of her husband in Saudi Arabia. When Sheikh Ahmed received the divorce certificate from his Indian wife, his heart almost stopped. He thought he was going to have a heart attack. After he had overcome the initial shock and impact of this devastating news, he rushed back to India. He had never loved a woman more than Christie. She was young, pretty, and educated whereas his Saudi wives were all old and illiterate. Their children had all grown up and gotten married and had children of their own. He cared materially for his wives but Christie was his love. Among all his women, he called Christina Loboz his *beloved wife*.

From Bombay Sahara international airport, Sheikh Ahmed took a taxi and went to his ex-wife's villa in Ban Stand, Bandara. Only Bollywood film superstars and very wealthy Indians lived in Ban Stand. The place had a very beautiful view of the sea. The famous Sea Rock 5-star hotel was located in this beautiful paradise-like landscape. Many times, Sheikh Ahmed took his pretty Indian wife for dinner there and they would spend a few days at this magnificent hotel. Sometimes they visited other hotels like the Oberoi Towers and the Taj Mahal Hotel and stayed overnight. Whenever Christie came for dinner or stayed at the Taj Mahal Hotel, her ex-coworkers, especially the housekeepers, envied her. From being a servant working in this grand hotel, she was now elevated to a queen, thanks to her new status as wife of a rich Saudi Arab. Whatever she wanted the old man provided her; food, drink, entertainment, anything she wanted. Always arrayed in the most expensive attire that only film actresses or wives of wealthy Indians could afford, she was lavished in whatever she fancied from head to foot; gold, pearls, diamonds…

Whenever Sheikh Ahmed came to Bombay, his wife would usually pick him up in her expensive Mercedes Benz automobile to take him to her villa. Christie had two other smaller cars as well. All three cars were bought for her by her wealthy Saudi husband. She also had four maidservants and three menservants in her mansion-like house. Each servant had different duties. The first maidservant did the cooking.

The second maidservant washed the clothes and linens, and the third maidservant was the housekeeper and swept and cleaned the house. The fourth maidservant was a masseuse. Her duty was to massage Christie's body. The jobs of the menservants consisted of grounds keeping or gardening; another's job was to purchase necessities for the household; lastly, one was a secretary who took care of the bills and other accounts and expenses for the running of the household. Christie also had two male guards; one sat with his gun, guarding the house during the day, and the other during the night.

Christina Loboz strictly warned her servants not to tell her Arab husband about her Indian boyfriend. She was paying them extra money to keep their mouths shut and to avert their eyes to her affair with Bobby. Christie also had two German Shepherd dogs for guarding her villa. She had a smaller adorable dog, which was her favorite and special pet. She did not have any children because it was never her intention to have a child with her husband the Sheikh. His desire, however, was for her to become pregnant because he believed that a child would keep her attached to him. She was smart in making excuses as to why she was not yet with child while using contraception and lying to her husband and deceiving him. However, after her divorce, she married her Indian boyfriend and she became pregnant almost immediately. She was one month pregnant when her ex-husband, the Saudi, came back to claim his most prized possession.

When Sheikh Faiz bin Ahmed reached his ex-wife's villa, he tried to enter but the watchman stopped him. Then, the watchman called Christie and informed her that her ex-husband had arrived and he was trying to enter the villa by force. Christie and her new husband came at once and confronted the angry old man. Sheikh Ahmed's anger intensified when he saw another man holding his beloved wife's hand. In his Muslim country, if a man came to his house and found a male stranger with his wife, he would kill him and his wife and the law would protect him in defending his honor. However, he was standing on Indian soil and Christie wasn't a Muslim woman to be scared by his threats or his anger. Nevertheless, Sheikh Ahmed continued to aggressively force his way into the house. He was barred entry by

Christie's new husband, to whom the old man was certainly no match. Bobby was a big, tough guy and would have squashed him like a bug. Sheikh Ahmed shouted at Christie,

"Who is this man and why have you allowed him to enter my house in my absence?"

"This is my husband, Bobby, and this is my house and it's in my name."

Sheikh Faiz bin Ahmed could not believe his ears when he heard his beloved Christie say she had married another man and claimed that he no longer had a right to enter the residence. A woman would never say something like that to a man in a Muslim country and expect to survive. Her husband would strangle her to death or cut her into pieces and her blood would be upon her head for the law would clearly be on his side in this matter. He would not be condemned or prosecuted and he would be hailed in his society as a hero, receiving praise and glory for his bravery. If there was ever a need for an honor-killing, this was it. But Sheikh Ahmed could do nothing to exact justice that day. When he refused to leave, Christie called the police and he was escorted off the property in an undignified manner, one befitting an unwanted guest and trespasser. After that, the angry old man sought help from some foreign students studying at Bombay University who had come from various Arab countries. The Arab students collectively advised him to forget about this Christian woman and return to his country. Moreover, they told him that if he tried to harm his ex-wife or her new husband he would land in jail and rot in an Indian prison.

Sheikh Ahmed did not listen to the advice of the foreign students. He was determined to seek revenge and right this wrong. He took with him one Sudanese student and sought the advice and aid of a lawyer who was also an Indian Muslim. The lawyer knew only too well that the secular Indian laws could not force a woman to stay with a man she did not want to live with and had already divorced. His client could not receive recompense for all the money he spent during his marriage or for the two homes he had bought for his ex-wife and her family. Both houses were registered in Christie's name and that was that. Despite that, the greedy Indian lawyer accepted the case and promised to fight it in court with due diligence. He told Sheikh Ahmed the case might take a long time before the court would come to rule in his favor. In India, if the client happened to be a rich foreigner, the lawyer might conspire with the judge and ask him to keep prolonging the case for years. During this long period of waiting for the final ruling, the lawyer and the judge would drain the wealthy client making him a little less richer, or to the point where he would spend no more to pursue the case.

While the court proceedings were going on, someone advised Sheikh Ahmed to go and seek the help of one of the greatest politicians in Bombay. The person that Sheikh Ahmed was told to go to was a famous politician and gangster. He was the leader of the anti-Muslim political party known as Sev Sena (i.e. Army of Shivaji). Shivaji was an ancient Indian warrior who stopped the advance of Muslim invaders in Bombay. He defeated them and routed them out of Maharashtra state. The name of the political leader was Bal Thackeray. Thackeray was responsible for the destruction of the Babri Mosque in Ayodhya city. He stirred up the religious sentiments of the Hindus by convincing them that the Muslims built their mosque in the birthplace of the Hindu god, Rama.

Historically speaking, Thackeray was right. Two hundred years before, during their invasion of India, Muslims destroyed the temple of the Hindu god, Rama, and built in its place a Mosque. Muslims are known for converting non-Muslim places of worships such as churches, synagogues, temples into mosques. In his book, "Hindu Temples—What Happened to Them," Sita Ram Goel included a list of 2000 mosques built on Hindu temples. According to the Belgian historian, Konreraad Elst, "The Muslim conquests, down to the 16th century were, for the Hindus, a pure struggle of life and death. Entire cities were burnt down and the population massacred, with hundreds of thousands killed in every campaign, and similar numbers deported as slaves. Every new invader made (often literally) built his own hills made of Hindus skulls. As a contribution to research on the quantity of the Islamic crimes against humanity, we may mention that the Indian (subcontinent) population decreased by 80 million between the year

1000 (conquest of Afghanistan) and 1525 (end of Delhi Sultanate). The American historian, Will Durant, states, "The Islamic conquest of India is probably the bloodiest story in history. It is a discouraging tale, for its evident moral is that civilization is a precious good, whose delicate complex of order and freedom, culture and peace, can at any moment be overthrown by barbarians invading from without, or multiplying within."

Thackeray told his Hindu followers to travel to Ayodhya and destroy the Muslim Mosque and rebuild the temple of their god, Rama. As consequence, on December 6, 1992, the ancient Babri Masjid was razed to the ground. It was the first ever mosque to be demolished by Hindus. In retaliation, the Muslims planted bombs in thirteen important government buildings and hotels in Bombay city. The bombs were loaded in cars and parked near the Stock Exchange building, Air India building, Taj Mahal Hotel, Sea Rock Hotel. Those, among others, were targeted. Most of these buildings were skyscrapers and had many floors, offices, stores, and other rooms. All the cars exploded at the same time and killed many innocent people. It was a Friday afternoon when this cowardly terrorist attack took place. Those who planned the attacks chose Friday afternoon because most Muslims would, at that time, be at their mosques conducting the compulsory Public Prayer. The Muslim terrorists did not want any Muslims to be caught in the buildings and killed.

After the terrorist attack, a lot of fighting ensued between the Hindus and the Muslims. Due to the fighting, the city was placed under a strict curfew. During the rioting, Hindus and Muslims slaughtered each other like wild animals. Some people were burned alive. A man was identified as a Hindu or a Muslim through the checking of his private parts. If he happened to be circumcised, then he was a Muslim and he would be burned by Hindus; and if he happened to be uncircumcised, then he was a Hindu and he would be burned by Muslims. In case of the female, her dress would identify her. Therefore, the woman would not be stripped fully naked to see whether she was genitally mutilated because the Indian Muslims do not practice female genital mutilation.

The person who advised Sheikh Ahmed to go to Bal Thackeray to help him was either stupid, ignorant, hated him or simply wanted to add to his troubles. Luckily, before he approached the political gangster, Thackeray, the old man went to his Sudanese friend and requested he accompany him on his visit to the great political leader. The Sudanese student told him never to go to that anti-Muslim leader from the Hindu Sev Sena political party. He narrated the story to him of what this man did to the Muslims' Mosque in Ayodhya City, and the consequences that followed, and what his political party stands for. Therefore, following the advice of his Sudanese friend, Sheikh Ahmed decided against this idea of approaching Mr. Bal Thackeray and returned to his country, a very sad man with a broken heart. The loss of money and property did not trouble him as much as the loss of his adored and beloved young wife.

For two years, every three to four months Sheikh Ahmed was called by his lawyer to come to India to attend hearings concerning his grievances against the divorce and loss of his wife and estate. After two years, the case still had not been resolved and Sheikh Ahmed became exhausted with all the court proceedings. He realized his dispute with Christie was nothing more than a never-ending battle. He was fed up with all the trials and arguments and told his lawyer to forget about continuing the case and to withdraw the lawsuit. By the time Sheikh Ahmed finally gave up his fight and accepted defeat, his ex-wife had delivered her second child. She had a baby boy and a baby girl when he saw her for the last time at Bandara court. Christie had become one of the richest women in the city of Bombay. After she left her Saudi husband and married her Indian boyfriend, she started many businesses and became very successful in her ventures, adding to her wealth.

CHAPTER 3

MUHAMMAD TOURS AND TRAVELS

The day the Muslim woman approached him and requested a visa to work in an Arab country, Sheikh Ahmed's hope and pride were instantly resurrected and restored. He felt as if his Allah was again offering him love on a silver platter, recompense for all that he had lost and endured. Rayhana was a million times more beautiful than Christie. Above all, she wasn't *an infidel* like his former wife, the Christian. One strange thing, although Islam condemns Christians and Jews and labels them *infidels, brothers of apes and pigs,* Muslim men are still permitted to marry their women. I think the founder of Islam created a major bungle. Why would he condemn a people as infidels and unclean, liken them to monkeys and pigs and even rats yet allow his followers to marry their daughters? I just don't get it. I guess Muhammad could not resist the feminine attraction of his fourteen-year-old Christian maidservant, Maria bint Sham'un the Copt and his Jewish female slave, Rayhana bint Zayd. Which probably explains why he created the license to legalize his dalliances with his young maidens?

Maria was an Egyptian Coptic Christian girl who wasn't even Muhammad's captive slave. The Qur'an allows Muslim men to have sex with their female captives without marrying them (Surat Al-Nisāa 4: 3). There is no verse in the Qur'an that permits sex with maidservants. This minor exclusion didn't seem to be any great difficulty for Muhammad, or prevent him from sleeping with his maidservant out of his marriage bonds. (Following the example of Muhammad, some modern Muslim religious clerics issued fatwas justifying having sex with maidservants from Indonesia, Pakistan, India, etc). Again, Maria the Coptic wasn't a female captive of the prophet of Islam. She was gifted to him and became his maidservant. She would do work for all of his eleven wives. Every day she was sent to a different house to help each one of his wives with their household chores. The narrators of the biography of Muhammad stated that one day, Maria was working in the house of the prophet's wife, Hafsa. Then, the prophet suddenly told Hafsa to go and see her father because he might be sick. Although Hafsa did not want to go to her father's house, the prophet was very persistent. When she arrived at her father's house and found him well, she quickly returned to her house. I guess Hafsa knew something fishy was going on and realized the prophet had tricked her. She arrived at her house just in time to discover what the prophet was up to.

Upon her return, Hafsa caught the prophet having sexual intercourse with Maria in her room and on her bed. She became angry and shouted: "*O Prophet of God, in my house, on my bed, and in my night!*" Afraid of the anger of his other wives, and especially of his most beloved Aisha, the prophet apologized and promised Hafsa that he would never touch Maria again if she would keep the matter quiet. His words were to no avail. Hafsa was fuming and the matter reached the ears of Aisha. When his beloved Aisha confronted him, and most probably reproached him for his improper act with the maidservant, the prophet claimed to have received a revelation from heaven that justified and legalized his action with Maria. *"O Prophet! Why holdest thou to be forbidden that which Allah has made lawful to thee? Thou seekest to please thy consorts but Allah is Oft-Forgiving, Most Merciful"* (Surah Al-Taharim 66: 1). When Aisha heard the above justification, she said to him, *"Why should I see your god in a haste to satisfy your whims?"*

Sheikh Ahmed decided to exercise some wisdom and act cautiously for he had learned some valuable lessons. His former mistakes cost him dearly and deprived him of the love of his life. He even remembered what the prophet said, "*The Muslim believer shouldn't be bitten twice from the same hole*". That means he should not allow the same snake to bite him twice. Therefore, following the example set by his prophet, the Sheikh decided this time to play his cards well. His calculated mind reasoned that he should not rush things and not be too generous, too quick, or make great promises. Moreover, this time he would take his new beloved with him to the land where women are deprived of all their rights, imprisoned in homes, and treated like children and domesticated animals. In his country, a woman would never dream of disobeying him or kicking him out of his house, or dare bring a man into the home to sleep with and have fun with. The Qur'an compels a man to beat a disobedient wife (Surat Al-Nisāa 4: 34), but here in the land of the infidels, the law prefers the rights of women and allows a wife to rule over her husband.

Consequently, Sheikh Ahmed told the Sudanese interpreter to tell Rayhana Khan that because she was a good Muslim girl, who refused to sell her body for thousands of rupees, he was going to fulfill her desire and grant her wish. He was going to make preparation for her to receive, free of all charges, a work visa as a maidservant, and her air fare to the kingdom of Saudi Arabia. He also conveyed to her that she would be working in his own house, be treated with all respect, and would be paid well. He had the interpreter inform his newly beloved that he was already a married man and had four wives. She would be working in the house of his fourth wife. His other three wives already had their own maidservants from Indonesia, Egypt, and Pakistan. All three maidservants were good Muslim girls and well-behaved. Therefore, to start work in his employ, he required from her the same obedience and good conduct, that she be in full compliance with all that was required of her, and that she continued her commitment to her religious duties.

She should pray regularly, five times in the day, and wear the Islamic niqab 24/7 (i.e. twenty-four hours a day and seven days a week). He told her that in Saudi Arabia a woman is not allowed to reveal her face in front of a man who is neither her husband nor her father. He quoted for her a hadith of the prophet to support this restriction imposed upon every Muslim woman by the Qur'an. "Ibn Tayimiyyah said, Women used to roam about without Cloaks (Jilbaabs) and men used to see their faces and hands, but when the verse stating 'O Prophet! Tell your wives and your daughters and the women of the believers to draw their cloaks over themselves.' (Surah Al-Ahzaab, verse no. 59) was revealed, then this was prohibited and women were ordered to wear the Jilbaab. Then Ibn Tayimiyyah goes on to say "The word Jilbaab means a sheet which Ibn Mas'ud explained as a cloak covering the entire body including the head, face, and hands. Therefore, it is not permissible for the women to reveal the face and hands in public" (Ibn Taymiyyah's book on fatwaas p, 110 Vol, 2 also in the book Hijaab p. 15).

This law is also based on the hadith of the prophet, which says, *'The woman is a'warah. When she goes outside (the house), the devil takes charge of her"* (Tirmizi, Volume II, p. 65). This hadith says that whenever any woman goes out of her house she becomes possessed by the Devil. Being a tool of Satan, she is extremely dangerous and detrimental to society. The welfare and benefit of society is best served as long as she stays in the home under lock and key. She must be kept imprisoned inside the home to protect the city streets and rural areas, or men might succumb to this temptation and epitome of evil. They would fall victim to the sin of adultery, pornography, and fornication. If she has to go out for any emergency, the Shari'a law requires that her entire body be covered, for even her voice is considered by the Shari'a to be *a'warah, or a vagina,* and therefore she should not speak at all.

There is no definition so widely used among Muslims for defining the woman than '*the woman is a'warah.*' The term "a'warah" is defined in the Encyclopedia of Islam as 'the external genitals, especially of the female' (Haqq & Newton 1996: 5). So to put it simply, 'every woman is a walking, talking vagina.' Every part of her body is considered a vagina. This restriction was imposed on women's movements within society because the prophet Muhammad once saw a young woman on the street and became so aroused by her that the only way to deal with his frustration and excitement was to rush quickly to his wife, Zainab bint Jahsh, and get the relief he needed for his predicament. *"Jabir reported that Allah's Messenger (may peace be upon him) saw a woman, and so he came to his wife, Zainab, as she was tanning leather and had sexual intercourse with her. He then went to his Companions and told them: The woman advances and retires in the shape of a devil, so when one of you sees a woman, he should come to his wife, for that will repel what he feels in his heart"* (Sahih Muslim, Book 8, hadith Number 3240). However, this hadith offers no solution for a Muslim man who sees a woman and has no wife! Should he run to a goat or just jump on any female and rape her. The virtue of temperance or self-control seemed not to exist in the life of Muhammad at all. When he saw a woman in the street, he ran to his wife Zainab and had sexual intercourse with her and when he saw his 14-year-old maidservant, Maria the Copt, he just jumped over her although she wasn't his wife and he had many harem at the time. Even a six-year-old child was not spared.

Additionally, Rayhana Khan was warned that flouting this law could result in her being arrested, flogged, and deported back to her country. She might even be mistaken by the Saudi police for a prostitute and stoned to death. Sheikh Ahmed told Rayhana about a recent case of a Filipino woman who was caught talking to a man who was neither her husband nor her father or brother and arrested as a prostitute. On the following Friday she was stoned to death by the faithful after their Public Prayer. Even inside his house, Rayhana should not talk to any of his sons. She should keep herself at a distance from any male in his house. Sheikh Ahmed said that in his country people believed in the saying, "keep the egg away from the stone and the female away from the male." These restrictions on women, and many other do's and don'ts, were pronounced by Sheikh Ahmed through the Sudanese interpreter while the three acquaintances sat by the seashore of the Arabian Sea at Bombay.

Afterwards, Sheikh Ahmed requested that *his newly found beloved and most treasured woman* come to the office of the recruitment agency the following day so that travel preparations could be completed for her journey to the Kingdom of Saudi Arabia. This time Sheikh Ahmed decided to be out of the picture until everything was processed and his beloved ready to be sent to him in his country. He phoned the recruitment office and told them to make all necessary arrangements for his maidservant. Rayhana had no passport and had no clue what the word "passport" meant. From her employment with several rich families, she thought all an Indian woman would need was a visa to go to one of the rich Muslim countries in the Gulf. She believed that as soon as a visa was obtained, all she had to do was say good bye to her family, and fly immediately to her new promised land. Being naive and unsophisticated in worldly matters, she thought the visa would allow her to board a plane and travel overseas. She did not know a person had to purchase a ticket and book a flight on an airplane. She did not know that to get a work visa in Saudi Arabia or other Gulf country she had to pay the recruitment office three lakhs rupees (i.e. 300,000 rupees). Then, her ticket and airfare would be an additional sum of 50,000 rupees. On top of that, the agency charged a fee to expedite the process of obtaining a passport since the normal waiting period for such a document was between six to twelve months.

The agency office's modus operandi would be to bribe the passport officials to expedite the issuance of a new passport in only three weeks. In order to get a passport in that short period of time the agency had to bribe at least a hundred employees at the Passport Facility. Otherwise, getting a passport in an overpopulated city like Bombay with nineteen million citizens might take close to a year. Sometimes, a passport is stolen from the mail and sold on the black market for all manner of illegal purposes. Innocent people were charged in murder cases and thrown behind bars, and some hanged to death for murders that they had not committed. Sometimes, the postman would purposely hide the passport and not deliver it over to the legal owner until he got a share in this extortion. Imagine a city of nineteen million inhabitants with only one single Passport Office. For applicants to get a chance to reach the window to submit applications, they would have to arrive as early as 4:00 o'clock a.m., if they wanted to reach the window before sunset, and that was if they were fortunate. While standing endlessly in queue, they had to endure the blazing heat of the sun during the summer or the heavy monsoon rain during the rainy season. Sometimes, if a passport office employee saw a young pretty girl coming all alone to apply for her passport she should not expect to get her passport except in exchange for a sexual favor. A sexual favor might not work alone in itself, unless it accompanied a financial payment as well. Sexual harassment is such a common thing; it is not easy for a female to escape becoming a victim. They are easy game for those that prey upon fragile, defenseless females.

These sexually frustrated men are like flies everywhere. They love crowded places. In fact, there is no public place in Bombay that is not crowded. Many of these lustful predators would not ever dream of getting married due to their utter poverty, homelessness and wandering. Being without a home is not unusual in Bombay and many of the poor live in the railway stations. The most famous place for homeless people was the Victoria Terminal, or VT station, as it was commonly known. It was the largest railway station in Bombay and was named after the British Queen Victoria. However, the Sev Sena political party, headed by Bal Thackeray, changed its name when the party won the election. It was renamed Shivaji Terminal. Nonetheless, people still called it the VT station. Although the slum dwellings were better habitats than the railway track shacks, poor people still set up residence at the sides of the tracks. What they lived in could not be called homes by any standard. Mostly beggars and sexually frustrated men lived in those shacks, "homes" made out of discarded boxes and rags that could hold no more than one or two people. The dwellers of the shacks had no public washrooms and were forced to urinate and defecate at the railway tracks. With no bathroom, they could not take a bath, and had to wait for the rain to rinse them off.

Sexually frustrated males hunt females wherever they can find them. A sexually frustrated man loves being in an overcrowded bus or local train. Shielded by the utter mass of people and the anonymity it affords, they lean and caress any female within reach. It is uncommon for a beggar to purchase a bus or train ticket, since money is obviously an issue. He is what is termed a non-ticket passenger; one who jumps inside any crowded bus or local train and is disregarded by the conductor when he is found to be without a ticket. However, other passengers, judged by the conductor as being more than capable of buying a ticket, are arrested and charged ten times the fare of the bus or train.

This has taken us too far from Rayhana and her desire to go to the kingdom of Saudi Arabia, so we shall now return to her problem of obtaining a passport in the overpopulated cosmopolitan city of Bombay, and the uncountable hassles involved. As we mentioned, Rayhana was naive and knew very little about the difficult procedures involved for traveling overseas. Some Indians sell their homes and property in order to meet the costs involved in traveling to a Gulf country, or for immigrating to Canada or Australia. Rayhana needed at least four lakhs (i.e. 400,000 Indian rupees) to meet the cost for her work visa to Saudi Arabia. The day she met Sheikh Ahmed in front of the Taj Mahal Hotel, she had on her person her savings of four hundred rupees, which she naively thought could buy her a visa to travel to a rich Arab country to work as a maidservant. As the first interpreter (who cheated Sheikh Ahmed and then ran away) had told her, four hundred rupees would not even pay for a taxi to Bombay Sahara International Airport. Nevertheless, her persistence that day landed her a wealthy Saudi business tycoon, a man who was so struck by her marvelous beauty and youthful appearance that his mission was to get her to his country of Saudi Arabia, no matter the means. He agreed to cover all her travel expenses from India to the Kingdom of Saudi Arabia—her visa, ticket, and passport. Sheikh Ahmed told the travel agency not to charge Rayhana a single rupee. Before he flew back to his country, the old man handed over the work visa for Rayhana to the recruitment agency and purchased her airfare. Then, he promised to reimburse the office for any other costs incurred in processing Rayhana's travel accommodations. He asked the travel agency to hasten the process and fly her over to him as soon as possible.

Everyone in the travel agency office was astonished when they heard the unbelievable news that a wealthy Saudi man was not only going to cover all the costs of a work visa for an Indian maidservant, but was also prepared to purchase her airline ticket. No one in the office had ever heard of such an incredible offer, which made them suspicious that there must be a more guarded reason that they weren't made aware of. The wealthy Saudi man had told no one why he was being so generous to this one Indian woman. Millions of Indian women wanted to go to the rich Arab countries and work but they could not afford to buy visas or cover the other costs associated all the arrangements. This was a perplexing matter indeed, and a great mystery to everyone in the office who wished they could solve it.

In the travel agency office there were nine employees; six of them were young girls, two were men, and one was a male Sudanese interpreter. The Sudanese interpreter was the same foreign student who had tried to help Sheikh Ahmed during the dispute he'd had with his Christian wife, Christie. Since that time, they had developed a kind of symbiotic relationship and it was the Sheikh who got him a job as a translator in the agency. Usually Indians would not employ foreign students because it was forbidden by law to employ any foreigner in India, a restriction that was implemented due to the alarmingly high rate of unemployment. Nonetheless, because Sheikh Ahmed brought hundreds of visas to the recruitment office every few months, the owner took the risk and secretly employed the Sudanese student.

The owner of the agency was a Muslim man and all his employees were Muslims, too. The six female employees were pretty, young girls. The owner of the business refused to hire young girls except on the promise that they paid him sexual favors. He was a wicked man who remained indifferent to the plight of any young woman that stepped into his office to ask for a job or a visa. He cared not that he stripped them of their dignity when he sexually harassed them, and cared even less when he fired them on the spot for objecting to his sexual advances. For those whose lives depended on earning a living to care for their families, they were forced to surrender to his abuse of authority in exchange for job security. I must add that, even in the Bollywood film industry, some directors will not give a beautiful, young girl a leading role in his movie unless she agrees to sleep with him first; and if she wants to continue working for him, it is required that she continues to entertain him. Unless she quickly rises to stardom, at which point she will likely discontinue the sexual relationship, she must accept that she will be at the director's beck and call, ready to service him as his sexual needs arise. That being said, employing attractive, young girls became a common feature in Bombay, a trait that seemingly drew more customers, especially Arabs.

A girl or woman in India would not be able to prove she had been sexually harassed unless she was working in a government job. In the private sector, it would be very difficult to prove harassment. If a young woman or lady called the police to complain about her boss, the boss would bribe the police to keep his mouth shut. The police inspectors themselves would not spare the girl who brought them this kind of complaint. In fact, the police in India are more dangerous to young women than their abusive employers.

In the travel agency, two young men worked with the six pretty, young girls. One of them was named Jamaal and the other Javed. The Sudanese interpreter was known as Babikir. He was nicknamed by his Sudanese friends, *Babikir Al-A'awar* because he was a one-eyed man. The owner of the business was named Muhammad. The names of the six female employees are not relevant at this point because they do not all play a significant role in the case of Rayhana Khan. Those who do their names will be revealed later on.

When Rayhana showed up at the travel agency the following day, all three male workers were overtaken by her beauty and each fell madly in love with her. The six female employees understood immediately why the wealthy Saudi business tycoon wanted to cover all the expenses for Rayhana's hasty trip to his country. The owner, Muhammad, was a very proud and arrogant man who had never stood to greet any Indian visitor to his office. He stood and shook hands with Arab clients, but he never stood to greet an Indian. Normally, he would place both feet atop his desk and if the Prime Minister of India walked in, he would remain unmoved. He would never stand to greet an Indian…except for today, the day that Rayhana Khan walked into his office.

She was the first Indian visitor that weakened his self-righteous, conceited attitude. She, without a word of greeting, compelled him to his feet and commanded respect. Not only did he rise from his seat and shake her hand, he offered her a chair to sit down. Rarely did he invite visitors to sit in his office. He much preferred them to stand and assume the place of an inferior. Any conversations would take place within this arrangement. It did not matter how long the transaction took, he never offered anyone a chair to sit down. None of his nine employees had ever occupied a seat in his office. His office door was always closed and whenever an employee wanted him to sign any papers, they had to phone him and ask for permission to enter his office. When permission was granted the employee had to knock on the door to his office and wait for him to invite them in. Then, he/she had to walk in, close the door behind them, and sometimes, the employee might find him talking on the phone. In that case, he/she had to remain standing and be quiet until Mr. Muhammad finished his phone conversion. He had two phones on his wide desk and one cell phone. Very often, if he were talking on one phone another call would come in on the other phone. He would put the first call on hold and switch to the second phone and then the cell phone would start ringing and he would switch to the cell phone. In that way, the employee could remain standing for hours. Today was different. Rayhana Khan took a seat in his office and sat down. Only then did he return to his own seat. He was not a man known to be generous with his smiles, but he smiled gleefully at Rayhana.

Mr. Muhammad Khan was a married man and in his late fifties. He had a wife and five children. Yet he slept with hundreds of other women and girls outside his marriage. Outwardly, he appeared to be very religious man, but inside he was a very wicked and corrupt man. He had a very long beard and sometimes he carried an Islamic rosary in his hand. He always kept a big copy of the Qur'an in his table. His outward religiousness easily fooled his Arab clients but not his employees or close friends and family. Everyone around him knew that he was a notorious womanizer and pedophile. He was also associated with several Muslim gangs in Bombay. In India, every businessman needed some kind of protection from the outlawed gangsters known as the Gondas.

It was very common in Bombay for the Gondas to send anonymous letters to rich people and demand ransom money. If no money was handed over, they would shoot them, or kidnap one of their children, or sometimes their wives. If you lived in India, every now and then you would read an article in the Times of India, or other local newspapers, that so-and-so had been shot and killed in front of his office or his home because he refused to pay the ransom money. So, in order for rich people and businessmen to protect themselves from the Gondas, they either had to be affiliated with an existing gang and buy protection from them, or became Gondas and establish their own gang. The police are hopeless in this regard. Of all the gangs, Muslim gangs are the most dangerous in Bombay. The most notorious Gonda who was infamously known as the No. One Enemy of India was a Muslim by the name of Dawood Ibrahim. He controlled almost all the gangs and drug activities in Bombay and no one challenged his turf. He did not live in India but directed his operations from his safe haven in Dubai, where he practically ruled the entire city of Bombay. The Bombay crime branch of CID had repeatedly tried, without success, to have him arrested and deported to India but the police of Dubai refused to do so. The government of Dubai said that as long as Dawood Ibrahim wasn't involved in any criminal activity in their country he would not be arrested or made to leave the country.

Being a Gonda and a notorious womanizer, Muhammad Khan was awe-struck by Rayhana's extreme beauty. He concluded Sheikh Ahmed had already slept with Rayhana and that was why he had promised to provide her with a free visa, airfare and to cover all the costs of her travel. Muhammad did not believe in a "free lunch" and no young woman had ever stepped in his office alone without him trying his luck. As a matter of habit, he slid into character and asked Rayhana, "*How come the old man has given you everything for free*?" He had expected two responses from her. She would either be straightforward and tell the truth or smile demurely and refuse to answer. However, Rayhana did not respond as he expected. She narrated to him what had happened between her and the Saudi man. Muhammad did not believe a word she said and told her straight to her face, *"Why are you hiding the truth from me? Is it because you are a married Muslim woman and you do not want to admit that you have slept with a man that isn't your husband?"*

(Muhammad had already come to know through his employee, the Sudanese boy, that Rayhana was a married woman. After her conversation with her benefactor, the Sudanese boy invited Rayhana to travel with him in a taxi to the local train station. He told her that he lived in a hostel just behind Churchgate station, the station she was going to, and he met her there the following day to escort her to the travel office where he worked. He also became interested in Rayhana from the moment he saw her from her initial meeting with the Saudi. During that short period, the Sudanese boy asked Rayhana hundred of questions and came to know many things about her).

Rayhana told Muhammad simply that she had never slept with a man except her husband and she would never sleep with any man in the future who wasn't her husband. Rayhana spoke the truth in this regard. Although she was sexually harassed by her male employers, she never allowed anyone to have sex with her. Something about the way she spoke convinced Muhammad that she was not lying. He was such a shrewd person that no one could pull a fast one on him. He knew all the tricks of the trade, and deeply understood the intricacies of deception because he was a very accomplished deceiver himself. He was like a police officer in the West who would keep staring directly into your eyes while you were speaking and would know immediately whether you are lying or speaking the truth. Sometimes, just by reading a person's body language and the inflection in their voices, the officer would know what the person was going to say even before they said it. Although, Muhammad understood that Rayhana had not slept with the old Saudi guy, he could easily guess why the old man wanted her to come and work in his house in Saudi Arabia. Therefore, he felt his second duty as a Muslim man was to warn *his sister in faith* of the great risk involved for a beautiful young lady to travel all alone at such a young age, to a male dominated society, to work in the home of a rich old man. Rayhana thanked him for his advice and told him that she could take care of herself. The third question that he felt it was his duty to ask since he knew she was a married woman, *"How come your Muslim husband agreed to allow you to travel all alone to a foreign country?"* He knew that a Muslim man would not usually allow his young wife to go overseas by herself because Islam did not allow a woman to travel without her husband, or a male Muhram (Muhram was any close male relative a woman could not marry such as her father, brother, or an adult son. However, if the woman was married, then she was allowed to travel with her husband). He even quoted her the hadith of the prophet Muhammad, which said, "*a woman does not travel except with a Muhram" (Sahih al-Bukhari and Sahih Muslim).*

Rayhana had never been to school and she knew very little about her Islamic faith. She told Muhammad that her husband had recently passed away and that she had become the only breadwinner to her big family. She had to take care of her six children, her elderly parents and also her late husband's aging parents. Muhammad was shocked when he learned that such a young and pretty woman had already given birth to six children. He asked whether she had informed her sponsor that she was a widow and had six children. When she said she had not he asked her what she was going to do with her children since she would receive only a single visa, as promised by her sponsor. Rayhana said that she was planning on taking her seven-year-old daughter with her since the slums were not safe for her, but that her parents and in-laws would keep her five sons. Muhammad understood Rayhana's concerns but told her that her Saudi sponsor had given his agency only a single work visa, which was meant for her alone, and with only the one visa, she wouldn't be allowed to take her seven-year-old daughter with her. Rayhana told him that if her daughter could not go with her then she would not go to Saudi Arabia either. He tried to convince her to leave her daughter and travel alone because it was a golden opportunity. Rayhana insisted that without her daughter she wasn't going anywhere.

At first, Muhammad was inclined to put her in her place and tell her to "just forget it and go back from where you came from" but suddenly he remembered that he had no right to make such a decision. Instead, he decided to phone his client, Sheikh Ahmed, to let him decide on the matter. He picked up his phone and dialed the number of Sheikh Ahmed while Rayhana sat in front of him. He told her sponsor of Rayhana's marital status and the situation with her daughter. Sheikh Ahmed immediately agreed that Rayhana should bring her daughter with her. Muhammad was shocked at the old man's response. He sounded as though he was overjoyed to know that Rayhana had a seven-year-old daughter and wanted to bring her as well. Sheikh Ahmed told Muhammad that he would be sending the appropriate visa for her daughter immediately and he should expect to receive it in less than forty-eight hours. Muhammad told Rayhana the good news and an unreserved smile appeared on her lovely face, making her ever more sexually desirable and attractive in the tormented heart of Muhammad. It made him want her even more than before. The fact that she had lost her husband recently convinced him that if he didn't rush things he might sleep with her before her wealthy sponsor took possession of her. With that wicked thought in mind, he stretched out his hand and took a hold of her hand, and congratulated her. Now that his client had given the green light for Rayhana's daughter to travel to Saudi Arabia with her mother, Muhammad found he could not keep Rayhana in his office any longer. He called his employee Jamaal and told him to begin working on Rayhana's travel accommodations.

CHAPTER 4

JAMAAL

Jamaal Khan was the employee to whom Muhammad Khan gave Rayhana's paperwork for processing. His first assignment was to get passports for Rayhana and her daughter. Jamaal was a young, handsome Indian man and single, at that. He was also Muslim. He was elated to be chosen out of the three male employees and given the responsibility of processing the travel documents for the young, beautiful Rayhana. He knew from the Sudanese employee that Rayhana was married. Rayhana had told the Sudanese she was married but she did not tell him that her husband had died. So Jamaal, like the other eight employees, did not know the entire situation of her marriage status. Although Jamaal liked her, he did not like the idea of a Muslim woman leaving her husband and traveling to a male-dominated country like Saudi Arabia. He was brought up with the knowledge that it was unsafe for a young woman in Saudi Arabia once the Arabs discovered that she was all alone. His experience in dealing with Arab clients in Colaba convinced him that Arab men viewed women as nothing more than meat. In Jamaal's opinion, Arab men are crazy for women. They loved big-breasted women with large bodies and large backsides, and see her as nothing more than a good hearty meal. They just want to eat her.

Jamaal was not alone in this belief. There was a well-known Muslim Imam and Mufti in Australia that shared the same opinion. The Imam, Sheik Taj Din al-Hilali, the nation's most senior Muslim cleric, in his public sermon which he delivered before five thousand worshipers in Sydney on the occasion of the Eid festival, said that women are just meat, and men have no more obligation to exercise when they see a woman than a stray cat that finds meat left out in the street. The Imam was speaking about the increasing social phenomena where more and more young Australian women were getting raped regularly by Lebanese and other Muslim immigrants in the city of Sydney, Australia. He blamed the victims rather than the rapists. According to him, the Australian women readily walk the streets without covering their bodies and without wearing niqabs. The Muslim men see them as exposed meat and that's why they are raped. In order to justify this theory, he gave the example of a starving cat that finds a morsel of meat in the garbage or on the streets and ravishes it. For him, the cat is not to blame because the person should not have left raw meat out on the street. So this person is to blame for leaving fresh meat out on the street. He concludes that the rapist should not be blamed but that the victim who leaves her body uncovered is at fault. What an evil, atrocious thing for a religious leader to say. He should be locked up for life for his wicked teachings, or kicked out and deported back to the Muslim country where he came from. This mentally twisted Imam learned his lessons from his prophet who could not control himself when he saw a woman walking on the street of Medina without a niqab on her. The two choices for the Imam and his prophet were either to rape the woman or run to a wife and remove the lust on her body. The third choice was to force each and every female walking on the street to cover herself from head to toe and that itself was not enough but sending her husband or a Muhram along with her to prevent her from tempting or jumping on someone.

Jamaal's main worry was that if Rayhana traveled without her husband or father to Saudi Arabia she would be raped by her Kafeel (sponsor). Jamaal Khan did not wait for long before he began to discuss these pent up, serious issues with Rayhana. He talked with her about these things while they were traveling together in a taxi to the Worli Passport Office. Rayhana informed him that her husband passed away recently and her father was too old to accompany her on such a long trip. Besides that, her father was the only one among her four old relatives that could take care of her five sons while she was away. This made Jamaal feel both happy and sad. He was glad to know that Rayhana was a single mother. He concluded that his conscience would not trouble him if he fell in love with her. Before her news of her husband's death, Jamaal had decided not to push his feelings to the extent of falling in love with her. He was an unmarried man but it would never be his intention to take a woman from her husband and elope with her. Now that he knew that her husband had died, he decided to release the reins of his heart and fall headlong in love with her. Unbeknownst to him, Rayhana's feelings were mutual.

Jamaal Khan was a very handsome young man and he could easily make a girl fall in love with him. He was sweet, kind and mild-spoken with a very pleasant personality. He was very honest in his dealings with people, unlike his vicious and arrogant boss. Humble and down-to-earth, he spoke from his heart. He treated others like he wanted to be treated and he wished for the best for everyone he met. When he helped people, he did not expect anything in return. Rayhana liked him from the very moment she met him. She enjoyed his company and she felt as if she had known him all her life.

In one hour, Jamal had told her almost everything there was to know about himself and he asked her hundred questions in return. Jamaal discovered that Rayhana was a sincere, unsophisticated and a deeply moral woman. Whatever he wanted to know about her she told him. The one-hour drive from Colaba to Worli was nothing compared to the typical two-hour commute to work by local express train the rest of the Bombay was subject to. At the passport office, Rayhana discovered that she was not allowed to submit an application for her daughter because her daughter was not with her. She would also need her daughter's photos to apply for a separate passport for her. Jamaal took Rayhana to a nearby studio to have her passport photo taken. He explained that she would have to bring her daughter to the travel office the following day to have her daughter's photos taken for her passport application. After visiting the passport office, Jamaal took Rayhana for lunch at a beautiful restaurant and afterwards they walked to an ice-cream shop and had dessert. It was the first time Rayhana had eaten food in a restaurant and the first time she had ever tasted ice cream. She was pleasantly thrilled by the generosity of Jamaal who spent time with her and paid for her lunch with money from his own pocket. Jamaal dropped Rayhana off at the Dadar local train station. He did not leave until Rayhana was safely inside the train, which was jam-packed, and headed back toward her slum area. Jamaal felt as if his heart was inside the train with her. Rayhana, although childlike in many ways, knew she had stolen someone's heart and she was quietly confident in her womanly abilities.

Rayhana had not experienced love with a man before. Her late husband did not love her and neither had she loved him. Her husband married her through the customary Indian *arranged marriage*. The majority of Indians hated "*love affairs*" because it might result in an "*inter-caste marriage.*" Most parents didn't allow their sons and daughters to enter into a "*love marriage.*" All parents in India reserve the right to choose their children's life-partners. Within the religious communities, Muslims did not like their daughters marrying Hindu boys and Hindus did not like their sons and daughters marrying non-Hindus; Christians did not like to marry Hindus or Muslims and Buddhists did not like mixed-marriages between Hindus and Muslims. Hindus themselves did not like inter-caste marriages, etc. To avoid these intermarriage alliances, parents would simply choose and do away with an uncomfortable social scandal. However, in big cities like Bombay, Calcutta, Madras, and New Delhi where there are many foreigners and international media influence, many young people rebel against the traditional "arranged marriage system." In high schools and universities, boys and girls mingled during their school sessions and some would fall in love with their classmates from different religious backgrounds and/or castes.

Love affairs are socially and religiously unacceptable and often led to terrible consequences. Many Muslim girls were killed by their parents the moment it was apparent that they were with child, a result of a liaison with their Hindu boyfriends; Christian girls eloped to other cities with their Muslim lovers and lived together without the benefit of marriage; Hindu girls took their own lives by committing suicide when their parents did not allow them to marry their lovers from other castes. Before the Indian government changed the marriage laws, there was no other recourse for young lovers. To stop such crimes against young innocent lovers, the government of India introduced "court marriages" as an alternative to the traditional religious marriage ceremony.

Court marriage is open to any couple who want to get married regardless of their religious affiliation. They could wed without the express permission of their parents or religious authorities. However, court marriage did not completely solve the long-held views of parents holding steadfast to family traditions and religious customs. Parents, all too often, would discover where their daughter was living with her *unrecognized husband* and kill them both. Sometimes, no matter where the couples went or where they lived, they still carried with them the stigma of this taboo disobeying their god(s) and parents. A curse and disgrace to the sanctity of the holy sacrament of marriage, they were viewed as being devoid of all moral fabric and compass.

In the case of Rayhana and Jamaal there would be no problem if they decided to get married because both of them were Sunni Muslims. As a point of interest, Sunni and Shiite Muslims do not form marriage bonds because they hate each other to the point of death. To date, hundreds of Shiite Muslims in Iraq are killed within their mosque walls by Sunni suicide bombers. Likewise, Shiite Muslims, in return, will plant bombs in the crowded market areas of Sunni Muslims and take the lives of thousands of innocent women and children. To this very day, of all the religions of the world, the followers of Islam continue to kill each other without remorse. The hatred and violence between Sunni Muslims (85% of Muslims in the world) and the Shiite Muslims (15% of Muslims in the world) goes back to the first few years after the death of Muhammad. Aisha, the child-bride and the beloved wife of Muhammad, and Ali Ibn Abi Talib, the cousin and son-in-law, of Muhammad hated each other. Their armies fought one another and in one single day 14,000 Muslims were killed by their fellow Muslims in the famous Battle of the Camel. The camel refers to *the camel* that Aisha rode astride when she led her troops to fight Ali's army. After the slaughter of Ali's son, Hussein, and his family by the first Umayyad caliph, Muawiyah, the followers of Ali were known as Shiite of Ali (or faction of Ali) and separated themselves in a sect known as the Shiite sect. The Shiites rejected the next three caliphs who succeeded Muhammad-Abu Bakr, Omar, and Othman—and reckoned them as infidels. They considered Aisha, the beloved wife of Muhammad, a whore and an apostate and condemned to hellfire. Aisha was known for exposing the Prophet Muhammad's secret sexual life. In her hadiths she spoke openly about how he used to do sex with her when she was a child and even while she was menstruating, which is a Muslim taboo. For that reason, Shiites hate her and consider her a betrayer and a notorious whore. If a Sunni Muslim girl named Aisha happened to fall into the hands of the Shiites, she is liable to be raped and then slaughtered. Likewise, if a taxi driver in Iraq happened to have the name Abu Bakr, Omar, or Othman and entered a Shiite area in Bagdad he would be burned alive by Shiites. The Sunni Muslims don't mind returning the evil in an even greater magnitude toward the Shiite Muslims anywhere within their arena, and the cycle of violence continues even today.

The following day, Rayhana Khan brought her cute, seven-year-old daughter, Iffat, along with her. Before Rayhana and her daughter arrived at the office, the other eight employees noticed something different about Jamaal's behavior and the way he was dressed. It was as if he had won the lottery, or something extraordinary had happened in his life and turned this mild-mannered Clark Kent into Superman overnight. He was changed from an ordinary hardworking and struggling young Indian boy to the happiest man in the world. His clothes were spiffy and he was joyfully chatting and joking around with everyone in the office. But there was nothing in that travel agency to make anyone happy. The wages were miniscule, the boss was best friends with the devil, and the workload was beyond anyone's capacity—not to mention the sexual harassment endured by the female employees in order to continue working in this "sex for hire" hellhole. There was nothing to be happy about, so the puzzled employees questioned Jamaal's unwarranted happiness in what amounted to a legalized system of slave labor.

For an unknown reason, females in India seem to be smarter than the males. In fact, India is the only country in the world where the women appear to have the upper hand and dominate the men. Some people believed that the late female Prime Minister of India, Indira Gandhi, who ruled the country for fifteen years, changed the social order in which women gained an advantage, or control in many aspects. Whether this theory is true or not isn't our concern, but it becomes obvious to every visitor to India that women rule their husbands and take the lead in most family affairs, as well as work side-by-side with the men.

The six female employees of the travel agency deduced that Jamaal had fallen in love with Rayhana and they whispered this notion among each another. Their suspicions were confirmed when they saw Rayhana walk into the office with her little daughter and saw Jamaal's jubilant reaction. In India, only Hindus bowed to each other in greeting, a tradition leftover from the dreadful caste system. The person of the lower caste had to bow to the person of the higher caste. Shaking hands or touching was not allowed because the person of the lower caste would defile the person of the higher caste if a mere touch was involved. Only greeting through bowing was permitted and the Hindu woman would never shake hands with a man. Instead, she would clasp her hands together and bring them in front of her face and say, "Namaste." However, Indian Muslims, Buddhists, Sikhs, and Christians never bow to anyone.

Even so, on this day, Jamaal exposed the true affections of his heart when he stood up and bowed to Rayhana as she walked into the office. He ran from his desk and shook her hand and then picked up her lovely daughter into his arms and gave her a gentle kiss on the cheek. While he carried her daughter, he brought a chair and placed it in front of his desk and requested Rayhana to sit down to conduct business. Jamaal then called the peon and asked him to bring some cold drinks for his important female visitor and her little daughter. Of course, from Jamaal's extraordinary attention, it was evident he was infatuated with his female visitor. A blind man could see the immense love growing in his heart minute by precious minute. At first, Rayhana's disposition did not readily reveal her emotions. She was good at hiding how she felt for she had lived for so long with a husband that she didn't love. For this reason, the girls concluded this love affair was a one-sided love on Jamaal's part and he was acting like a love-struck fool. The male employees took a different position. They knew from experience that the inner workings of a woman's heart held deep secrets that weren't always easy to detect. This determination was for the future to reveal.

Before Jamaal called a cab for the trip to the Worli passport office, he asked his very important client many questions as they enjoyed their refreshments. He could have asked her these things during the one-hour drive in the taxi. However, just to show off, Jamaal asked Rayhana to tell him what her date of birth was, the place of her birth, her height and weight, color of her eyes and hair, and many more unnecessary questions. One agitated female employee whispered to another female employee and said: *"He should also ask her to tell him the color of her underwear."* Jamaal was a very respectful man and did not mention private matters or unspeakable things. Surprisingly, he did not ask Rayhana to tell him anything about her daughter. Everyone in the office knew he had already applied for Rayhana's passport and that day he was supposed to apply for her daughter's passport. One female employee, out of jealousy, confronted Jamaal with why he had not asked anything about the daughter, which had everyone baffled. Being exposed, Jamaal smiled and said to her,

"But she is the mother and I need to know everything about her before I ask her about her daughter".

The female employee responded:

"Did she not tell you yesterday about the color of her eyes and hair? And by the way why do you want to know the color of her dress, and shoes? Do they ask those personal questions in the passport office?"

Jamaal was duly embarrassed in front of his colleagues and did not answer this question. Instead, he suggested to Rayhana that it was time to leave for the passport office. He took her daughter by the hand and led the way out of the office. When Rayhana left, the female employees felt relieved, but the two male employees felt disheartened. The male employees wanted her to stay as long as possible so they could stare at her beautiful face and daydream of what could be. After Rayhana and Jamaal left, the office turned into a rumor mill. Everyone gossiped and created his/her own story about the goings on between Jamaal and Rayhana. Jamaal was accused of being foolish and stupid for falling in love with a married woman. What was more, they were aware that her wealthy sponsor had offered Rayhana a free visa, free airfare and provisions for her daughter as well. The girls knew from experience that nothing comes for free in this world, especially from the world they lived in. They convinced themselves collectively that Rayhana had to have given up something in return. Therefore, one of them asked openly,

"How can a young man like Jamaal foolishly fall in love with a married woman who cheats on her husband and is prepared to sleep with any man that's ready to buy her at a high price?"

This question was posed by the girl who felt envious of the attention Rayhana was receiving, and had sought to embarrass Jamaal by initiating an inquisition concerning the way he was conducting his job.

"She is a bad woman, no doubt about it," responded another girl.

"How can you be so sure that she is a bad woman when you haven't known her for more than two days?" asked the Sudanese boy.

"I know a bad woman by looking at her eyes. This woman, from the time she walked into the office, did not take her eyes off Jamaal's face, not for one second. I am sure that she enticed Jamaal as she enticed that stupid Arab for a job and a free ride."

"Hello, Tahriah," shouted a girl by the name of Rukhsana, *"You believe Jamaal's version of the free visa and ticket story? Personally, I don't believe that the old Arab is stupid enough to give an Indian maidservant a visa and a ticket if she did not entertain him in his hotel room and promise to be his mistress when she arrives in his country"*.

"No doubt about it," responded Tahirah.

What Rukhsana and Tahirah had said about the old Arab guy was half true, but what they said about Jamaal was absolutely true. The old

Saudi guy did not present Rayhana with those things for free, for he wanted her to come to his country and she, in turn, would become his mistress or concubine, or the chattel which *the right hand possesses,* as the Qur'an so clearly dictates. He believed his money had bought him the beautiful young Indian woman. He concluded that Rayhana had already become his property and now it was just a matter of time. He expected the travel agency to process her papers shortly and ship her airmail by special delivery to him in his country so that he could start enjoying her as his mistress…or rather, his female slave.

In this short holding period, a critical incident took place in Rayhana's life. Rukhsana had correctly observed that Rayhana could not keep her eyes off Jamaal. She kept observing him from her station. She didn't seem to notice what others were saying. She did not even look at the other two young men who kept staring at her constantly. Rayhana was not a complicated person to understand. Although she kept her emotions deep inside, she was too naive to hide her love forever. As mentioned, she had never fallen in love with a man before, neither had she felt loved by any man, even her own father. It was a very sad and wretched life growing up living with her poor parents. For her to remember these heartbreaking details might spoil the seeds of love that had just sprouted in Rayhana's heart, making her smile inwardly for the first time in her life. Before she met Jamaal, many rich men in the houses she had worked in wanted to have her, but none of them were willing to descend to her level and fall in love with her, or ask her to marry him. She was fortunate that none of her employers thus far had attempted to rape her. Rich men in Bombay do not ordinarily want to be involved in a crime such as rape, especially when the victim is a slum woman. Although a rich man definitely could buy his freedom by bribing the police, the victim's lawyer, the judge, and all parties involved, his name and reputation would be 'dragged through the mud' once the media got wind of the scandal. For this reason, a rich man, or a man of a high caste, would think twice about raping a poor woman or girl from a low caste for fear of destroying his reputation and good standing in society. He would not want his family dishonored or smeared because of his reckless behavior. Now, he wouldn't mind soliciting a woman for sex to buy her body but he would not force her to have sex with him. This self-imposed guideline is not because he fears the god(s) or the law but his name, social status and religious positioning is far more important to him than the former.

The first man who ever loved Rayhana from the depths of his heart and with all his being was Jamaal Khan. Likewise, Rayhana Khan did not love any of her rich male employers and did not allow any of them to have sex with her no matter how much money they offered her. (By the way, 75% of the 150 million Muslim Indians have the family name of "Khan" and the remaining 25% are the "Sheikhs." So, it wasn't a mere coincidence that Rayhana's father, husband, and lover had the same last name "Khan"). The wily old Saudi could not purchase Rayhana's sexual favors for nine and a half thousand rupees. If Rayhana worked for two and a half years, she would not be able to save nine and a half thousand rupees. In all her hard work in those rich families' houses, she was able to save four hundred rupees and she thought that was enough money to get her a visa to take her to a rich Arab country.

Once again, after applying for the daughter's passport and bribing the requisite hundred-and-one passport officials so that the two passports could be issued in three weeks time, Jamaal took his beloved and her daughter to a nice restaurant and fed them a delicious meal. This time, instead of spending an hour in the restaurant like the previous day the lovers spent three and a half hours together. In India, if you were a lover, or did not have any work to do and wanted to sit in a restaurant for six hours you would be allowed to do so as long as you keep ordering different items from the menu.

After consuming the delicious food, Jamaal ordered the dessert, then the sweet dish, then the ice cream, then the cold drink, then the tea, and lastly, the coffee. Incidentally, dessert and sweet dishes are not the same thing for Indians. Every state in India has its different kind of sweet dish. Jamaal's love wasn't anything like his office colleagues had concluded. This was no one-sided affair. He could see the love in

Rayhana's beautiful eyes and could hear it in every word she spoke to him. He read it in her smiling lips and felt it in her joyful laughter. In the third world, the girl wasn't expected to tell the boy, *"I love you,"* nor should she respond affirmatively when her lover says, *"I love you and I am ready to die for you."* Her silence was her consent. Jamaal knew that if he did not confess his love for her that very day, he might not see her again until the day the two passports and accompanying visas arrived at the travel agency. Until that day, it was conceivable that his unpredictable boss might fire him, or he might fall ill or be hit by a car and admitted to the hospital. Jamaal asked himself "*why I should take a risk?"* He did not know where Rayhana lived. She told him that she was living in a slum in Dharavi but there are more than five million slums in that dense overpopulated place. (Dharavi is the second largest slum area in the entire world. The largest, apparently, is in Mexico City).

For Jamaal to find his beloved in that jam-packed slum area would be like searching for an ant in the Amazon. People in Dharavi area were stuffed together like eggs. They had no addresses and none of them known how to read and write or expect to receive mail. Jamaal's boss told him that when he filled out Rayhana and her daughter's applications, he should use his own address. At that time, Jamaal lived in a chawl with an address. Moreover, he studied until grade twelve. When the two passports of Rayhana and her daughter were issued, they were supposed to be mailed to Jamaal's address. However, since many employees in the passport office had already been bribed, the two passports would possibly go directly to the travel agency. So, Rayhana and her daughter were supposed to come after twenty-one days to collect their passports, visas, tickets, and some US dollars. They would then head to the Bombay International Airport the very same day. Mr. Muhammad himself would be waiting for them at the airport to see them off. He would not pick them up in his expensive car and take them to the airport. Rayhana and her daughter would be given the taxi fare so they could travel by themselves. Their flight was already booked at 9:45 pm on the same day they were supposed to receive their passports.

Jamaal knew all details of Rayhana's trip. He also struggled with the knowledge that she was going away on a two-year work visa. If he wouldn't reveal his love to her that day and ask her to meet him before her trip then he might not see her for two years. What guarantee would he have that after two years, Rayhana was going to wait for him or remember him. Therefore, that day Jamaal decided to reveal his love to his beloved and if she responded affirmatively then both of them could make plans for their future and decide when they should get married to each other.

Jamaal and Rayhana's case was worse than that of Christie and her boyfriend, Bobby. Jamaal had more than ten mouths to feed in his chawl. He lost his father and his mother wasn't working due to some kind of chronic illness. She had last stage terminal cancer and was expected to pass on at any time. Jamaal had many younger brothers and sisters for who he was the sole provider. He needed to wait for a quite long time before his brothers and sisters could finish their grade ten and become employable. Two of his brothers were working in coffee shops on Sundays. (In third world, public schools and government offices were open six days in the week. Even private sector employees and workers had to work Saturdays). Jamaal's three sisters used to do some cleaning and washing works for rich families after their school hours. However, their mother stopped them, one after another, when each one began to menstruate. When the three sisters reached puberty and their mother stopped them going to rich families' houses, the burden on Jamaal was tripled. The mother was scared that one of her daughters might get impregnated by her male employer. In India, a pregnant unmarried girl has already dug her own grave and, in the process, destroyed her family name. She is no longer marriageable and the odds are that her brothers or father would send her off in an honor killing. In any case, until his three sisters were safely married off, Jamaal had care for them.

Jamaal Khan did not like the idea that Rayhana Khan was going to the kingdom of Saudi Arabia because he knew what she might face over there. However, since she had six children and four old people in her slum to look after, he felt he would be selfish to tell her not to go. Circumstances of poor people sometimes might force them to compromise in important issues in their lives. We had already seen the case of Christie who married the old Saudi because she wanted to fulfill her life's dream of living with her boyfriend Bobby. Jamaal likewise found himself in a similar situation. If Rayhana agreed to marry him after two years then she might open the door for him to join her in that rich Arab country too.

After weighing all the pros and cons, Jamaal began to reveal his feelings to Rayhana. He found it difficult to put his confession in crude, direct sentences like, *"I love you. Do you love me?"* He had only just met her the other day and she might say, *"No."* Therefore, he decided to help her to take the initiative and ask him a question that would make it easier for him to reveal his love in more acceptable manner. He asked her many personal questions but he discovered that she was romantically very dull and lacked the ability to indulge in small talk. She did not know how to speak the language of love. For example, he asked her what her favorite color, singer, movie, and film actor and actresses. She had never been to a movie theatre or seen any movie. She said she had no favorite color, song, singer, or movie. So, she could not answer any of those questions in an engaging manner. Therefore, he stopped pursuing that strategy and downshifted into simpler ideas by complimenting her. *"I like your hair, eyes, smile, laughter, height, shoes, dress, and figure."* He did not go beyond the outer appearances. He stayed away from asking questions that were too revealing or intimate. Nevertheless, all those questions and praises did not lead her to ask him, *"Why do you want to know everything about me or why do you compliment me so much?"* He thought if she asked him any of those questions then he would tell her plainly, *"Because I love you."*

When none of his tactics worked out, Jamaal decided to go deeper and told her *"I like your body."* No signs of a positive response. *"You look hot in your lovely dress."* She had no clue what this sentence stands for. He was tempted to tell her, *"You have sexy body"*. However, his sentence somehow changed to, *"I like your lips and breasts."* At this stage, Rayhana showed some signs of a positive response. She became shy and turned her face downward. Then, Jamaal took hold of her both hands and began to caress them. She did not pull her hands away or stop him. The feeling of her hands generated great pleasure in him. He had never had that kind of strong desire and pleasure before. His right hand released her left hand and moved slowly to hear cheek. He began to feel her smooth and delicate cheek. He could hear that she was breathing a bit louder than before.

Rayhana had never been so lovingly touched before. She had never been kissed either. Her late husband had no idea that the man should kiss and fondle his wife before making love to her. He just used to fall on her body like an animal jumping over the body of its mate. That day for the first time, Rayhana enjoyed touch of a man. She did not know what she should do and just let Jamaal's hands continuing to caress her hands and feel her cheek. However, when Jamaal's hand moved from her cheek and began to feel her lips, she responded. Her legs beneath the table spread and she became ready for love. She closed her eyes, opened her legs, and waited. At that moment, she was ready to give Jamaal whatever he desired of her. She was fully carried away by the touches of her lover and forgot where she was. Instead, she heard his voice saying to her, *"I love you."* No man ever told her before… *"I love you."* Rayhana did not know what to say in response. She just remained silent. Her silence was considered by Jamaal as a confirmation of her love for him. If it wasn't for the fact that they were out in public, seated in a restaurant, and the daughter was with them, he would have kissed her lips and she would not have minded at all.

Before saying his goodbyes, Jamaal asked his beloved to meet him again. Rayhana agreed to meet him but she didn't know where to come and meet him. She asked him another silly question, which exposed her social awkwardness. Should she see him at the travel agency and what was the reason of their next meeting. Jamaal knew if she come to meet him in the office his wicked boss would fire him and he might go further than that and rape Rayhana. Considering the risks, he warned her in no uncertain terms not to step foot into the office again until the passports arrived in three weeks. Then, he explained to her in simple and straightforward words that he loved her so much and for that reason, he wanted to meet her again and again until the time of her departure. He told her that it was customary for Bombay lovers to meet and be intimate by the beaches. Then, and only then, the inexperienced Rayhana come to the realization that as lovers, they were to meet and enjoy each other's company.

There are places in Bombay that would not look out of place in Western countries. Among the most beautiful were Colaba, Churchgate, Nariman Point, and Cuffe Parade. Of course, there are other wonderful areas in that cosmopolitan city but the beauties of those places are blemished by the ubiquitous slums and chawls that encircled them. However, the above-mentioned areas were bereft of the usual deluge of poverty-stricken homes. In other Indian cities, people would tell you that just because you had seen Bombay don't say that you had seen India. Some Indians hate Bombay because they believe that it does not portray the Indian people and their culture correctly.

In Bombay, everything was allowed and practiced openly. Lovers sit by the beaches of those wonderful areas and hug and kiss each other with impunity and the police would protect their right to privacy and intimacy. There were three red light areas and each area had thousands of prostitutes. Call girls were everywhere. Drugs were sold in the streets like groceries in stores. Every restaurant was allowed to sell alcohol.

Colaba was known as *the Colaba of the Arabs*. Every hotel was full of Arabs and their attendant call girls. Arabs customarily pick up six to eight street girls for their evening pleasure. Of course, no normal man would handle such a large number of girls but the Arab man would use each girl for a different duty. One girl for massaging his body, one for serving his drinks, one for lighting his cigarettes, one for killing the bugs in his hair, one for serving his food, and one or two for sex. In India, the Arabs revived the wild lives of the notorious caliphs of the Abbasid dynasty who used to have thousands of female slaves in their palaces for entertainment.

Jamaal asked Rayhana to meet him the following day in front of the travel agency office at six o'clock in the evening. He knew that the office would close by five and each employee would leave immediately after that. Even his evil boss would leave as soon as his office was closed. In order to be on the safe side, Jamaal decided that a grace period of an extra hour would take care of the possibility of a colleague staying back a few minutes to finish their workload. He did not want anyone to see Rayhana or see him with her. He knew what was going to happen to him if his wicked boss came to know that he was having an affair with her and he was meeting her secretly after work hours. Rayhana was a naive girl and he felt that it was wiser to err on the side of caution. He told her to keep their relationship discreet in the event that she might bump into any of his colleagues. In addition, he asked her not to bring her daughter or any of her family members with her.

Rayhana had no idea what Jamaal had planned for their next meeting. She did not know that Jamaal wanted to hug and kiss her and have a nice time with her. She wasn't expecting that Jamaal planned to marry her after her return to India in two years. She had no future plans, content only to delve in the immediate future. She simply liked him and was happy to hear his words of endearment. She did not understand what he meant by the phrase, *"I love you and I want to meet you again."* Although, she had already fallen in love with Jamaal, she did not understand the meaning of the phrase *"I love you."*

Things went perfectly and the two lovers met near the office. Taking a taxi to Churchgate, they picked a wonderful spot by the beach at Marine Drive. If you did not arrive in time with your date, chances are all spots would be taken. By 7 p.m., the place would be packed with lovers. The whole area from the Malabar Hills to the Air India Building and the Oberoi Towers was called the Queen Necklace. It was called so because it resembled a half circle like a necklace. It was such a large area that one needed an hour of driving to cover it from one end to the other. The cool breeze generated by the waves of the Arabian Sea made it the location of choice for lovers in India.

Bombay was built around an ocean that some people called Arabian Sea and some called the Persian Sea. It is the northwest part of the Indian Ocean between Arabia and western India. Everywhere you would go in Bombay, you would discover the whole city is essentially one huge beachfront property. In fact, it should be called a Gulf rather than a Sea. In Arabic, it is correctly called the Arabian Gulf and not the Arabian Sea.

By the shore of the beautiful Queen Necklace and while surrounded by young lovers, Rayhana Khan, for the first time in her miserable life, was hugged by a lover and experienced her first kiss on the lips. Before that day, she had never known what a kiss was, or that lovers were to hold each other and enjoy each other so dearly. Tears sprang from her eyes when she remembered her miserable past life with her late husband and coursed down her face at the realization that in a few days she was going to leave her lover and travel to an unknown destination. It wouldn't be a separation of one day, or one month, but two long years. Would Jamaal wait for her that long? Would he remain single until her return? Would he even think of marrying a second hand wife?

In the third world, a girl loses her value and worth as soon as she is married, divorced or a widow, no matter what her situation. As if the woman was a car that registered and re-sold, she would be considered 'pre-owned'. Every man around her would like to have sex with her but no one would want to marry her. And if she found someone to marry her that person would be an old man, or an ugly man, or poor, someone who was mentally retarded, or half mad, or handicapped. Since she had already been married and lost her virginity to another man, she was expected to compromise and marry someone like the above-mentioned defective males of her society. In Hinduism, the widow was supposed to be burned alive with the corpse of her dead husband. If the widow refused to practice *Sati* with her dead husband then she had to remain unmarried for the rest of her life. She would be kept in a small room in the basement and she would not be allowed to wear shoes or put on colored dress or any makeup. Hindu people believed that their day would be spoiled or cursed if they happened to see the face of a widow. She would become a curse and unwanted person.

Before that first kiss, Rayhana had not thought of getting married again. However, after her lover took her to the Marine Drive seashore and kissed her on the lips, she wished that she could be with him forever. It was as if Jamaal had read her thoughts, and he blurted out to her that he wanted to marry her and spend all his life with her. Rayhana was overjoyed when she heard her thoughts coming out of her lover's mouth instead of hers. She did not respond and Jamaal understood that she agreed. If Jamaal had asked her at that moment to forget about her trip and to get married tomorrow she would have agreed, for sure. Unfortunately, Jamaal's family's responsibility and circumstances would not permit him to make such a commitment. Rayhana was very disappointed when he told her that he would wait for her until she returned in two years. "*Two years,*" said Rayhana softly. *"Yes, Rayhana, after two years. I would love to marry you right now but my family's responsibility and your family's condition would not allow us to get married now. We must sacrifice our love for a couple of years and live separately for the sake of our dear ones."* After hearing his words, Rayhana could not able to hide her tears any more. She began to weep. Her new happiness was over-shadowed by the pain inside her soul.

CHAPTER 5

LIVING IN A BLISS

For twenty-one days, Jamaal did not leave any place untouched in all of beautiful downtown Bombay for his beloved to explore. He did not spend a single day without beholding her loveliness. In order to meet the love of her life each and every day, Rayhana rearranged her work schedule. Whereas she used to work for the rich families from six o'clock in the morning until eight o'clock in the evening, after she met and fell in love with Jamaal, Rayhana cut her working hours from fourteen hours to ten hours a day. She used to work seven days a week more than eight hours a day and she never received any overtime pay. She had no day off from work or rest day. Even during official public holidays, she went to work. The work in the homes of those families never ceased. She had to sweep the floors, wash clothes, cook meals, massage women, take care of their babies, and do hundreds of other household chores.

Rayhana was not afraid she would lose her job even when some of her employers threatened they would fire her if she did not come to work every day. For Jamaal she would do anything including forfeiting those extra rupees she earned working like a slave from sun up to sun down and not being paid overtime. After all, she knew that in a few days she was going to be in a rich Arab country where money could be found literally everywhere on the street. Yes, Rayhana wasn't exaggerating when she thought that money could be collected off the streets of the *Promise Land.* Many simple-minded people in third-world countries like Rayhana believed that in Arab countries *Petrodollars (money)* could be found scattered all over the streets.

Someone on the Al-Jazeera TV network said in an interview that the Arabs at the time of the prophet Muhammad conquered the world by the Sword but today they were conquering it through Petrodollars.

Rayhana's new work schedule gave her some space to pursue and enjoy her new-found love interest. She changed her work schedule from six o'clock in the morning until eight o'clock in the evening to six o'clock in the morning to four o'clock in the afternoon. As soon as she finished with the last house, she would rush immediately to the bus stop and travel to the local train station nearby. She would then take the train to Churchgate where Jamaal would be waiting for her near his work place. As soon as they met, their romantics began. He would embrace her in his arms and start kissing her in the taxicab on the ride to their desired place.

It was okay to hug and kiss in the backseat of a taxicab but sex was not allowed. However, some overly anxious lovers and men picking up street women or girls often go further than kissing and hugging. They manipulate their hands to do things a decent man like Jamaal would never do to his beloved in a public place. In fact, Jamaal had not asked Rayhana to make love to him this way for he wasn't intending to take advantage of her love before they wed after *seven hundred and thirty days*. He was determined to abide by their initial agreement. Nonetheless, on a few occasions while he was kissing her by the seashore he was carried away by her charm and strong femininity. He touched her in very sensitive areas, which might be counted as lovemaking in progress but not fully consummated sex. In order to prevent our imagination from running wild and assuming things happened between the lovers which did not occur, it is sufficient to say he just touched her breasts and the area around her waist but his hands did not descend lower than that. A few times, his hand ventured below her shoulders and breasts and slipped beneath her upper dress and felt her smooth, delicate body. Rayhana would not have stopped him if he had gone further in arousing her every sensation. In fact, if Jamaal had suggested they rent a room for one hour and have sex she wouldn't have objected. During those three weeks, she had fully surrendered her mind, body and soul to him. (In Bombay, there were small hotels and motels that rented rooms for an hour or a couple of hours for couples wanting to have sexual activities. Most of those rooms were made of wood and they were as small as washrooms. These kinds of acts were illegal of course and sometimes the police would crack down on prostitutes and their clientele. Many times foreigners were arrested along with their call girls and street women. Those detained among the many foreigners were the usual suspects; namely Arabs).

For Rayhana Khan those twenty-one days were the most wonderful days of her life. During those blissful days, she enjoyed her lover in every way possible physically, mentally, and above all emotionally. She saw things and visited places that she had never seen before. She never would have known such a life was possible if she had never met Jamaal Khan and fell in love with him. For the first time in her life, she experienced watching a movie in a theater sitting by her lover. When she said she liked the movie, Jamaal took her to see other motion pictures at the Eros and Regal cinemas. He also took her to tourist places such as *Elephanta Caves Island, Hanging Gardens, Malbar Hills, Chowpatty Beach, Juhu Beach, Prince Charles Museum, Essel World, Haji Ali's Mosque, Gateway of India, etc.* They even visited beautiful areas where foreign consulates and banks were located in *Cuffe Parade* and *Nairman Point*. During those twenty-one days, not a single day passed without the lovers visiting *the Queen Necklace* where their love was sealed with their first kiss. This first kiss was not alone but gave birth to many more hidden and explosive passions of love.

To describe in detail all the wonderful days Rayhana enjoyed with her object of desire, one would need to speak volumes and write a fairly good-sized book. You see the destiny of poor people was not in their own hands. Their uncontrollable circumstances would decide for them where to go, when to go, and how to go. Their circumstances also determined what they would eat, when they would eat, and how they ate. Many had no fixed mealtime and they had to eat food whenever and wherever they could find it. If their luck ran out and they did not work for several days, they would starve to death and die like stray dogs on the streets. If you happened to see one of the two movies *Slum Dog Millionaire* or *Salaam Bombay,* you would have an idea of what I am trying to say. In India the destiny of a poor person would be decided by someone richer or greater than them or as Indians say: by the '*Operwalla*.' Indians refer to this term as meaning the One in Heaven or God. An Indian professor once said to her students, *"Even God would not solve the problem of poverty in India"*. The Indian professor was a sage and it would not be appropriate to disagree with her being a wise person if you could not present a logical refutation or practical solution for what she had wisely spoken.

Anyway, after three weeks Rayhana and Jamaal's circumstances forced them to come down from that heavenly cloud and face reality. Jamaal could not forget the day his most treasured and beloved whom he had romanced for so many days came to collect her papers and say 'good bye my love and see you after two years.' Rayhana could not keep her eyes from shedding tears in front of the other employees when she knew that she was not going to see her Jamaal for very long time. The boss himself came out of his office and handed over to Rayhana in front of his employees two passports, visas, tickets, and five hundred rupees. He also gave her a closed envelope containing currency in US dollars. He did not tell her how much was inside the envelope but told her not to open it until she reached the airport.

At the last moment, the boss made a slight change in Rayhana and her daughter's itinerary. Previously, he had decided he was going to meet her and her daughter at the airport, pay for their taxi fare to the airport, and give them the envelope with funds for their trip. However, Mr. Muhammad told Rayhana in front of his employees that he had some urgent work needing his attention and he could not go to the airport to see her off on their flight. He said further, instead of him the Sudanese boy, Babikir Al-A'war, would meet them at the airport and help her and her daughter check their bags and continue on to board the plane.

Why did he choose Babikir and not Jamaal? At the moment, we don't have an answer to that question. Muhammad was not the kind of man to be questioned. Once he made a decision, it wasn't his nature to change it. Nevertheless, the employees knew why their boss had changed his mind and decided not to go to the airport. Just before Rayhana arrived at the office, a rich Indian lady from Bangalore called the office and informed one of the girls that she was coming to Bombay and asked her to tell her boss to meet her at eight o'clock in her luxurious suite at the Oberoi Hotel. Every employee knew that Muhammad was having a secret affair with this rich businesswoman. Besides, what kind of business would a woman have to do with a man in a hotel room? If they were conducting business, it could be done in the hotel restaurant, lobby, or even in the travel agency. Anyway, the boss had made his decision and it was final. The Sudanese employee would see Rayhana off at the airport and not Jamaal.

As soon as Rayhana and her daughter collected their travel documents and left the office, Muhammad returned to his office and locked the door behind him. Then, he picked up his phone and dialed the number of Sheikh Faiz bin Ahmed and informed him that everything had been processed and the Indian maidservant and her seven-year-old daughter were on their way to the airport. He told him how much his office had spent on preparing all the necessary paperwork for Rayhana and her child. Of course, being greedy, he doubled the amount actually spent processing the documents.

The Saudi told Mr. Muhammad that he would send his secretary immediately to the bank and transfer the exact amount to his account. After that, Muhammad gave the Saudi client the name of the air carrier and the flight number of the plane that was going to bring him his pretty young maidservant to the Kingdom of Saudi Arabia. When Sheikh Ahmed received all the details about his last chance at love, he felt overjoyed and thanked his Allah and Mr. Muhammad. He promised to do more business with him and bigger and better deals sending him hundreds of visas at reduced prices.

This sizeable windfall Muhammad received for processing Rayhana and her daughter's paperwork and the promises of continued business transactions filled the heart of the greedy boss with indescribable joy. Moreover, the arrival of his rich Indian mistress from Bangalore city and the wonderful time he was going to spend with her in the most beautiful and expensive hotel in town added to his merriment. A few hours later that day the boss called the bank and inquired if the amount Sheikh Ahmed had promised was deposited to his account. His bank confirmed the arrival of the money from an account in Saudi Arabia. Being elated and overwhelmed with joy, Mr. Muhammad went the extra mile and gave all his employees half a day off from work, which was on a Friday. The employees were wishing their boss had given them Saturday off as well so they could have two and a half days off from work. Unfortunately, time is money and the greedy boss was not that generous in time or money. Therefore, he told all the employees to come back to work the following day.

CHAPTER 6

AT JEDDAH AIRPORT

On Saturday morning, Mr. Muhammad arrived at his office with a hangover. The night before while enjoying his mistress in her suite at the Oberoi hotel, he drank so much liquor the effects did not wear off even after he spent most of the morning trying to recuperate in his office. The wonderful time he spent with his mistress in her opulent room and his sudden gold rush of wealth the day before along with greater potential business dealings were totally spoiled by alcohol. And what further added to his really bad mood was that four of his employees did not show up for work. Two of his female employees had called in sick and the third absentee was the Sudanese boy, Babikir Al-A'war. He had a bad habit of coming in late to work and Muhammad could not fire him because he employed him upon the recommendation of his Saudi client. The fourth employee who did not show up for work or call to report the reason of his absence was Jamaal Khan.

The angry boss swore by the name of Allah to divorce his wife if Jamaal Khan did not call and report the reason for his absence by lunchtime or he would fire him. This meant he was going to either divorce his wife or fire Jamaal but not both. The five employees present heard the boss when he shouted this proclamation and concluded that Jamaal Khan's days at the travel agency were close to an end. After making that irrevocable decision the wicked boss entered his office and slammed the door shut behind him. The employees were afraid he would come out of his office at any moment and fire all of them without hesitation. When he did not come back out of his office, they thought their Most Gracious, Most Beneficent Allah had mercy upon them and saved them from the wrath of a madman.

But later, just a few minutes before the lunch break the five employees heard their boss shouting in his office as if he was fighting with the Great Satan himself. Everyone began to wonder what was going on in his office. One of the girls suggested that someone should go and find out what had happened. The other employees silenced her and told her if she was so interested in finding out what was going on, then she should go find out for herself and get fired. While he was still shouting, Mr. Muhammad burst open the door of his office and stormed out as if he was being chased by a pack of wolves or either the office had caught fire. The five employees immediately stood on their feet and waited for their demise. Then, he shouted at the top of his lungs:

"Where is that f...g Sudanese slave...?"

They had never seen him so angry before or use such vulgar, filthy language. They began to shake and tremble as if they had seen a demon or their worst nightmare had come true. It was like a scary movie where monsters attack from outer space or the dead come alive and take possession of your soul. It was Rukhsana who even dared to answer him and at the same time ask what had happened.

"That f...g street woman did not board the plane last night and her plane arrived at Jeddah airport without her". This was the last news on earth the five employees would have expected to hear.

"Rayhana Khan did not fly to Saudi Arabia?" asked Rukhsana softly, speaking rather to herself than to her boss. Her mind constantly working immediately came up with an explanation but she was scared to share it with her outraged boss. She was afraid he might hold her responsible for not coming forth earlier and revealing something was going on between Rayhana and Jamaal. The love affair between the two was just speculation in the beginning but was confirmed when Babikir Al-A'war swore by Allah that he saw with his both eyes Jamaal and Rayhana sitting by the seashore off Marine Drive. (He had only one Seeing Eye but he loved to say his both eyes see). The Sudanese said further he even saw with his own eyes Jamaal kissing

Rayhana on her lips. All the other employees believed the Sudanese because he was staying at the international student hostel located behind Churchgate.

Babikir Al-A'war whispered this juicy bit of gossip to one of the girls in the travel agency with whom he had a crush, but she didn't care for him at all because he was a Black boy. Although, she was the least attractive of the girls, she would not fall in love or marry a Black boy if she had to remain unmarried the rest of her life. Just to avoid being distracted by this side issue...to put it in a nutshell, *Indians are some of the most racist people on the face of the earth when it comes to a person's skin color and matrimony.* If you were a Black foreigner, Indians would treat you kindly, but if you fell in love with their daughter and wanted to marry her, you would be out of your mind. They would never permit it. No matter how rich you were and no matter how much you offer as dowry for their daughter's hand in marriage, they would never agree. They would rather live and eat dirt the rest of their lives than agree for their daughter to marry a Black man. Black South Indians encounter great obstacles and face untold difficulties stemming from discrimination and prejudices in Indian society.

We might examine this topic later on so we can give a fuller explanation why Indians are such racially biased people. If someone happened to be reading this account and he or she was from the South of India, I'm sure they are well acquainted with this painful and ugly side of Indian life. Men and women being Malayali or Tamil from the southern states of India are often targets of racial bias from their fellow countrymen. Even dark skinned Indian girls from the South would not be quick to marry a Black man. Such a marriage would be a rarity indeed, but occasionally there are exceptions. When these socially unacceptable unions take place in which a Black man marries an Indian girl, the couple will find it extremely difficult even to walk down the street together. If any Indian saw an Indian girl walking in a public place with a Black foreign student, he would mistake her for a prostitute.

A friend of mine married a black Malayali Indian girl and he could not be with her in public without people accusing her to her face of being a prostitute. One day, an old Indian man stopped my friend's wife and asked her, *"My daughter, have you not found any man to marry in India that is why you went for this Black man?"* My friend and his wife eventually applied for refugee status due to their continually having to deal with such humiliating public confrontations and ridicule in their own homeland. Their applications were accepted on humanitarian grounds and they were sent for resettlement in a Western country.

Although Babikir saw Jamaal and Rayhana sitting by the seashore and swore by Allah he caught them red-handed kissing and romancing endlessly, the story did not reach the ears of his boss. He reported these things to his love interest and shall we say the love interest *who did not love* him. The girls in the office kept whispering these things among themselves but did not ask Jamaal about it. However, when the matter reached its boiling point, the enraged boss demanded an explanation or he would fire them all. One of the girls decided to throw Jamal under the bus. It was Rukhsana again who spoke up and suggested the boss contact Babikir and Jamaal and find out why they did not show up or call in to work and report the reason for their absence. Mr. Muhammad had told Babikir Al-A'war to go to the airport to see Rayhana and her daughter off but he wanted to know why Rukhsana mentioned Jamaal Khan. What did Jamaal's absence have to do with anything? Being hard-pressed to provide answers, Rukhsana began spilling the beans about the relationship between Jamaal and Rayhana having a secret love affair.

The information increased the wrath of the already incensed man. He shouted at Rukhsana and scolded the others for not informing him about this unacceptable affair going on between one of his workers and a customer. He told them that Jamaal Khan was for sure going to be fired for committing this serious indiscretion and conflict of interest. However, he did not see how such an affair could possibly prevent this poor slum woman from traveling to a rich Arab country. He was a man of calculations and his business intuitions would calculate the benefits he could reap from having a relationship with any woman. Therefore, his money-minded perspective on life reckoned that anyone in the place of Jamaal would never stop his girlfriend from going to a rich country and profiting from such an opportunity. Later he would expect her to help him get his foot in the door and follow afterward. Moreover, he understood that Rayhana would not be that foolish a woman to throw away free visas and tickets to Saudi Arabia for a life of living in dirt and having an affair with a poor boy living in the chawls. At the most, she might have sex with him and kiss him goodbye, but then forget all about him when she reached her *Promise Land*.

Muhammad Khan told his employees for the time being forget about the affair of Rayhana and Jamaal. He said he wanted to know what happened to that *f...g Black Sudanese slave*. He wanted to know whether Babikir had gone to the airport or not. Therefore, he ordered two of his female employees to go to the international student hostel and bring to him Babikir Al-A'war. He told them strictly that if they returned without him they would be fired. Even if he was dead and buried, they had better dig him up and bring back his body from the grave. The two who were selected for this task were the girl whom Babikir loved and whom *didn't love him* and Rukhsana. Those two girls were not selected at random. They were chosen for a specific reason. The boss, Muhammad, had picked up the fact that the ugliest girl in his office was the love interest of Babikir but she in return did not love him. Since it was a one-sided love and the girl was extremely unpleasant to look at, the boss didn't see any reason to bother worrying about half-hearted inclinations. So he decided to send her for this task of finding the boy who loved her even though she didn't love him. Rukhsana was chosen because she was the boldest of the employees and the smartest.

When the two envoys reached the international hostel, they did not find the Sudanese boy in his grave *as his evil boss had said* but they found him lying on his sickbed. Rukhsana and the other girl informed Babikir the boss wanted him to come to the office right away. They told him emphatically he had to come with them immediately for a bad situation had arose in the office and he was the prime suspect. They did not speculate about the nature of the problem because they had been informed by the boss not to do so. (By the way, I have not mentioned the name of the girl that Babikir *loved, whom did not love him...* until now! All this time, I purposely avoided mentioning her name because it did not suit her. Her name was "Jamilah" which means "beautiful girl". However, this girl, Jamilah, was far from beautiful. She was not only ugly but she was very hateful and self-serving. She was employed in that travel agency because her mother was the sister of Mrs. Khan. If it wasn't for the family relationship, Mr. Muhammad Khan would not allow her to sweep the street in front of his travel agency. Jamilah knew Babikir loved her and he often gave her many costly gifts, such as flower bouquets and fancy chocolates. She would use him often to buy her food and other high-priced items. Yet, she did not tell him, '*I don't love you*', or '*please stop buying me these expensive gifts*'. Whenever, she wanted something to eat or buy something costly she always asked Babikir to get it for her. She knew that Babikir would not take money from her and whatever she wanted, he would purchase for her out of his own pocket. In this way, she used him to fulfill her selfish desires. She always spoke bad about him behind his back and boasted that she was making a fool out of him. At any rate, if someone was stupid enough that he could not distinguish between a girl who loved him from a girl that was using him for his money, nothing can possibly be done for someone blind as a bat).

The two girls resurrected the bedridden Sudanese boy out of his grave…I mean sickbed, and forced him to come with them and face the Devil's advocate. It was true that Babikir Al-A'war was very sick. He was coughing with severe cold and fever. Nevertheless, in India health issues were not considered a good reason for a worker or an employee not to come to work. The Sudanese boy was dragged hook, line and sinker back to the work place while his angry boss screamed directly in his face. Although, he could not at first discern the meaning of the words his noisy boss was shouting at him, he immediately jumped backward fearing that he might be strangled to death by this tyrant. Only after shouting the same words over and over again did Babikir get the sense of what this lunatic was yelling.

His enraged boss demanded an immediate answer as what he had done with Rayhana Khan and her daughter at the airport. Before we reveal just how the Sudanese boy responded, let us first state some very important facts concerning the matters of this case. First of all, Babikir truly went to the international airport to see the maidservant and her daughter off but for some reason he did not see them. He thought he either arrived too late or Rayhana and her daughter did not see him and went directly inside the departure hall. Secondly, he tried to enter inside the departure hall but he was prevented by airport security. After the Bombay bomb blasts that devastated the entire city and killed thousands of people, the airport authority stopped allowing non-passengers from entering the departure hall. Thirdly, as we have already mentioned, Babikir had one blind eye and he had a vision problem in his seeing eye. During the night, he would not recognize his own mother and father if they happened to pass in front of him. Fourth, it was raining heavily when he reached the airport. Like many non-travelers visiting the airport that day, he stood in the wind and rain for three hours until he fell sick. For three hours, it rained cats and dogs like a broken water pipe in the clouds. His clothes were soaking wet as if he had jumped inside a swimming pool fully clothed. His socks were soggy like a sponge and his shoes were squeaking every time he took a step. Finally, he learned from someone standing nearby him that the plane heading for Jeddah, Saudi Arabia had taken off and he then concluded that his mission was successfully accomplished. Out of mere duty, he waved his hand to the flying aircraft and felt pleased by doing so. Then, he returned to his hostel. When he removed his wet clothes and shoes and fell asleep, it was four o'clock the following morning. Naturally, we would not expect him to rise and shine and be ready for work after having less than 5 hours of sleep. He would have to be at work by nine o'clock the next morning. If he made it to work, he would surely be damned tired and unable to concentrate if not sick from standing outside for hours in the damp air.

After truthfully and precisely stating the facts about Babikir's airport saga, let us hear what Babikir provided as an answer in his defense. Babikir's boss was furious and shouting indistinguishably and spitting in his face and he just wasn't making any sense. Babikir perceived something bad had happened to Rayhana and her daughter at the airport and the boss was holding him responsible. The angry boss frustrated at Babikir's lack of response and becoming exhausted from his continuous ranting and late stage hangover, managed to catch a breath. He shouted at Babikir again, *"What did you do with Rayhana and her daughter at the airport!?!"* Babikir now understood what the fire-breathing dragon was spewing out of his mouth. A few possibilities popped into Babikir's mind although he was not able to think clearly due to his sudden bout of sickness. Despite the throbbing pain in his head, he came up with the possibility that perhaps Rayhana and her daughter had missed their flight. The second possibility was maybe there was a mix up with the luggage; and the third, Rayhana may have accused him of quarreling with her and due to that, she lost her luggage or missed her flight. He quickly rejected this last silly thought because he did not meet her at the airport, so how could Rayhana possibly accuse him of quarreling with her. Fearing that he might be fired if he told the truth, Babikir quickly came up with a fake story and narrated it to his boss and colleagues. The story was simple and straight to the point. He said truthfully that he went to the airport but did not meet Rayhana and her daughter face to face. He could not meet them because he wasn't allowed by the airport security to enter into the departure hall. Here is where the bogus story began. He claimed that he saw Rayhana and her daughter through the glass partition at the airport while they were standing in line at the checkpoint. Of course, if Rayhana and her daughter had stood one meter in front of him he would not have been able to identify them with one half-blind Seeing Eye. Then, he added something extra to make his story more convincing. He said he waved his hand to them while he was standing outside the departure hall but Rayhana did not wave back because she was busy talking to a lady who was standing in front of her in the line. Babikir then finished the story by saying in an emotional tone of voice, *"Her cute little daughter saw me though and waved to me through the glass"*. This story seemed to satisfy the infuriated boss and the other employees and they were convinced he had fulfilled his assignment responsibly.

Muhammad Khan was a person drowning in shallow waters willing to hold onto anything to save his life and the life of his business. His mind started working like clockwork once he heard Babikir's *convincingly phony story*. He concluded Rayhana and her daughter had boarded the wrong plane. He knew it was common due to overcrowding at the Bombay international airport that sometimes passengers were sent to the wrong gate and boarded the wrong plane. He recollected a case of an African boy who bought a ticket from his agency and was flying back to his country of Kenya. At the airport however, he was sent by mistake to the wrong gate and flew to Paris instead. Therefore, the flight crew of Air India had to take care of him for five days until they could fly him back to Bombay. During those five days, the boy flew with Air India from city to city throughout Europe and they provided lodging for him at five star hotels. Finally, the boy was put on the right plane and sent to his correct destination in Nairobi. Therefore, Muhammad thought Rayhana and her daughter were most probably flying in Air India somewhere in Europe or Africa or either enjoying delicious meals in a restaurant of a five star hotel somewhere in America or Australia.

As soon as this fairy tale was hatched, Muhammad's face grew less tense and became less distorted. However, the boss still had a serious problem on his hands. He returned to his office and took Babikir with him as an eyewitness to the still developing story, which he decided to convey on the phone to Sheikh Faiz bin Ahmed. He picked up his phone and dialed the number of his client in Saudi Arabia and narrated to him this account that Babikir had just recounted to him. He added some lies to it to make it more persuasive. He claimed fallaciously that he contacted the international airport authorities and investigated the matter of the maidservant and her daughter. From a reliable source at the airport, he came to find out that Rayhana Khan and her daughter Iffat Khan had boarded a plane by mistake and were flown to Mauritius. From Port Louis, the course of the Air India plane would fly to a few African cities such as Cape Town, Lagos, Nairobi, and Abidjan. Then it would return to Bombay. It might take five to seven days before Rayhana and her daughter would be back in their homeland. Continuing the lie, Muhammad said, *"I am trying with the help of some very high officials at the Bombay international airport to get hold of the captain of that plane and request him transfer the misplaced Indian passengers in another plane heading to Jeddah".* Moreover, the boss made Babikir to speak to the Saudi man in Arabic and pass on his half-true and half-false story. In this way, Sheikh Ahmed got suckered into these two fake narratives of Babikir and Muhammad and decided to wait a few extra days for his maidservant and her daughter to arrive.

On the third day, Sheikh Faiz bin Ahmed received a call from Jeddah International Airport. The airport authority informed him that a woman by the name of Rayhana Khan had arrived from Bombay, India and she was looking for him. The airport authority did not mention the woman was traveling as a maidservant on a work visa or had a little daughter with her. Sheikh Ahmed did not ask or waste time asking unnecessary questions. He flew from his office to the airport as fast as he could to receive his darling maidservant in his arms and bring her to his house so he could enjoy her. His soul had sank in deep despair from sadness and frustration for three days without word of where she was and now suddenly he found himself like an eagle soaring high above the clouds. At last, his beautiful picture of perfection had come to him on a silver platter with gold trimmings. He recalled the suffering and humiliation he went through when that *"infidel bitch"* cheated on him. She kicked him out of his villa in Ban Stand and brought that *"filthy dog"* into his house and held his hand right in front of him. At last he was being rectified by Allah blessing him with "*The most beautiful woman in the world".* He had never seen such a beautiful Indian woman in all his life and she was coming to live with him in his mansion in Jeddah. In his country, no mortal man would ever dare touch his highly esteemed possession and survive for even a second. She was his and his alone.

Sheikh Ahmed decided to sleep with his maidservant as soon as he brought her to her new abode. A wicked thought then entered his disgusting mind but he decided not to act on it so quickly. He remembered Rayhana was bringing her seven-year-old daughter with her and his conscience troubled him a little. He remembered his prophet married a six-year-old girl and then his conscience didn't trouble him so much. He told himself that maybe he should not be in such a big hurry to touch the little girl so soon. He should wait until she reached the legal age under Islamic law. The Islamic law called Shari'a law allows a Muslim man to have sexual intercourse with a female at a very young age. The law sets the legal age for a female to be ready for sex as nine years old.

With evil thoughts rummaging through his mind, Sheikh Ahmed reached the airport. He began searching for Rayhana and her daughter. He searched everywhere at the spacious arrival area. He climbed stairs and escalators from floor to floor and ran in all different directions but he could not find the object of his desire. Finally, he approached an office and gave the names of his Indian maidservant and her daughter. The person who checked the names was able to verify the name Rayhana Khan in the system but the computer showed she arrived alone. Sheikh Ahmed was puzzled when he learned his maidservant arrived without her daughter Iffat Khan. However, his joyful heart dismissed this puzzling dilemma and he requested the office person announce Rayhana Khan's name over the intercom system to direct his beloved to the office where her *Kafeel* was waiting for her. The person who confirmed the arrival of the maidservant spoke into the microphone and the maidservant heard her name echoing throughout the huge airport. She came holding her passport and small luggage bag in her hand. Her bag she brought with her from India was as small as a school backpack. The maidservant located the office and showed her passport and visa to the person at the front desk who had broadcast her name. Sheikh Ahmed did not recognize her when she walked inside the office. When the airport employee said to him,

"Here is your maidservant Rayhana Khan", Sheikh Ahmed could not believe his eyes…His heart almost stopped. He had never seen such an ugly woman before in all his life. She was short, black, skinny, and looked like a man. Her eyes were huge like the size of golf balls and looked like they were about to pop out of their sockets. Half her teeth appeared to be missing even though her mouth was closed. Her nose was small and pointed like a bird's beak. She was unbelievably ugly…

CHAPTER 7

THE WICKED BOSS

Sheikh Faiz bin Ahmed concluded he had been double-crossed and cheated by Muhammad Khan. He took out his cell phone and dialed the number of the travel agency the same day the South Indian woman arrived at Jeddah International Airport and claimed to be his maidservant, Rayhana Khan. When the phone of Muhammad rang, he happened to be lecturing the two girls who supposedly fell sick purposely on the previous Saturday. Although the two girls brought doctor excuses, he refused to believe them and accused them of forging the medical documents. One of the two girls was crying and begging him to believe her. The other girl was weeping and waiting for the first girl to finish pleading her case so that she could also beg for mercy. Added to this dire climate was the absence of Jamaal Khan. For the second day, he had not called in or reported the reason for his being absent from work. His not showing up for this second day increased the merciless rage of the unforgiving boss. He had also quarreled with his wife at home after she accused him of having an affair with one of the girls in his office. The wife's accusation was based on practical evidence. For two weeks, he did not sleep with his wife even though she begged him to take her to bed and make love to her. Every day he pretended to be so damned tired and too tired for sex. On top of all this, he could not figure out what had happened to the real Rayhana Khan and her daughter.

Mr. Muhammad Khan took out his cell phone and looked at the number that was calling him. He recognized the number to be that of Sheikh Ahmed and ignored the call. Then he heard the phone on his desk ringing. He told the Sudanese boy to go inside his office and answer his phone on the desk. He never trusted or allowed anyone to enter his office when he wasn't there except the Sudanese boy, Babikir. Mr. Muhammad had spent a few years living in Saudi Arabia where he made some money and returned to India and invested in his own travel and recruitment business. During those years, he theorized that the most honest people in the Muslim and Arab world were the Sudanese. For that reason, he always trusted his Sudanese employee more than his Indian employees. That is why he sent Babikir to the airport in his place when his Bangelorean mistress suddenly showed up unexpected.

The wicked boss enjoyed lecturing and torturing his employees especially the female ones. He always looked for a justifiable cause to intimidate a female employee so that he could use it to blackmail her sexually. When a girl was put in that situation, she had either one of two choices—She could either voluntarily leave her job or entertain him inside his office. He was such an unscrupulous man he wouldn't hesitate to have sex with his female employees inside his office. One of the two girls he was lecturing was a new girl and she was very beautiful. From the day she started working at the travel agency, he kept searching for a way to manipulate her into having an illicit sexual relationship with him. This day she found herself in a most despairing situation and begging him to forgive her absence and not let her go. Her name was Bulbolah (Cuckoo bird). She was twenty-one years old and unmarried. She had a slim and medium stature with brown eyes and hair black as coal. The degenerate boss liked her from the very first day she came and applied for a job at his office. Here was his chance to take advantage of her since she failed to show up for work on Saturday, he was doing his best to frighten her into submission and ultimately leave her no choice but to please him sexually or lose her job.

So while Muhammad was standing like the Pharaoh of ancient Egypt and shouting at his two female employees and scaring the hell out of them, Babikir entered his office and answered the phone that was ringing on his boss' desk. Suddenly the voice of the Sudanese boy began to scream in a high pitch higher than the ear deafening voice of his boss. No employee had ever raised their voice aloud in the office like this before. As if someone had suddenly switched on one of these new rap beats and turned the DVD player to maximum volume, the screaming voice of Babikir forced the disturbed boss to stop harassing the petrified young females and listen to what was going on inside his office. This was the second time in less than three days his amusement had been interrupted. Unfortunately, the Sudanese boy was shouting in Arabic and no one could understand what he was saying. Although the boss had lived a few years in Saudi Arabia, he could not make out the Arabic to understand what was being said by his employee or with whom he was speaking. His first reaction was to run to his office and snatch the phone from Babikir and choke him for daring to shout in his office and worse; scream at one of his most valuable Arab clients. Before he could turn his thoughts into actions, Babikir sprang like rocket fire out of Muhammad's office and broke the incredible news in front of everyone. Shall I say it was startling to say the least—So startling everyone stared at him in a maze. For a few seconds you could hear a pin drop. Babikir didn't know why they were not reacting, so he started squealing and squeaking all over again.

The Sudanese boy said that Sheikh Faiz bin Ahmed had called and said that an ugly Indian woman arrived at Jeddah International Airport and claimed to be his maidservant, Rayhana Khan. The woman had all the official documents of Rayhana Khan, which were issued by Muhammad Tours and Travels. Accordingly, Sheikh Ahmed was accusing Muhammad Khan of cheating him by sending a woman he had never seen before or chosen to be his maidservant. Muhammad could not believe what he was hearing and did not believe a single word Babikir was saying. He ran into his office and picked up the phone to speak to Sheikh Ahmed and inquired as to what had happened. Sheikh Ahmed began shouting at the top of his lungs into the ears of Muhammad every vile and disgusting word you can imagine. Surprisingly, although Sheikh Ahmed could barely say hello in Hindu, he did not leave one word unspoken of every single vulgar and degrading word he knew in Hindu and Arabic.

Muhammad could not believe his ears. This angry Arab was making accusations against him, shouting derogatory and reviling insult after insult, calling him every filthy and disgusting name known to man. No one had ever risen to any level to speak down to Muhammad in any way or use such colorful and descriptive adjectives. He had never had someone rival him in his obnoxiousness. It was absolutely incredible! He thought for a moment maybe this was not Sheikh Ahmed screaming obscenities at him but someone had mistakenly dialed the wrong number. If by chance this actually was Sheikh Ahmed and he happened to be standing in front of this extremely outrageous "sand n…", he would not hesitate to kill him. He even imagined he killed the old goat by grabbing a knife and stabbing him to death. And if he happened to have a gun he would not hesitate for one second to empty all its bullets in his brain. Sheikh Ahmed continued shouting at Muhammad for what seemed like forever until all of a sudden…he lost his voice…apparently due to a heart attack caused by his uncontrollable rage…or he could have had a contusion of the brain or burst a blood vessel. Whatever the case, the phone went dead silent for several seconds. Muhammad waited a few more seconds and when he no longer heard this raving mad asshole of a man, he quickly disconnected the line. Once he put down the receiver, he could still hear Sheikh Ahmed's voice loud as two claps of thunder in an outpour of vulgarity and disrespect. Those words were forever etched inside his mind and nothing could ever erase them.

Muhammad was a very proud man and that day his pride was shaken to the core. His pride could not shield him from the anger of Sheikh Ahmed's barrage of insults. The old Saudi not only insulted him and seriously injured his pride, but his insults reached Muhammad's dead mother in her grave and his wife in her house. Even the honor of his sisters was not left untouched by the humiliation he endured from this wrathful Arab calling him in Hindi *"mother chute and bahan chute"* (i.e. your mother's vagina and your sister's pussy). [During his many visits to India, the old Saudi learned nothing useful and polite from the

Hindi language except filthy expressions]. Those were fighting words and the ugliest insults an Indian could ever say to someone. A man would be inclined to extreme rage upon hearing such indecent things and feel the need to retaliate in word or deed. Only street people used that kind of filthy, vulgar language. After sinking in the devastating news and trying to overcome the unbelievable ignominy, Muhammad stormed out of his office as a mad lioness chasing away anyone that comes near her cubs. The first one he attacked in retaliation for his seriously damaged pride was the Sudanese boy. He called him every word he knew that would hurt him and even spit in his face many times. He scolded him for lying to him and then threw him out of his office and told him never to come back again. After that, he turned to his remaining seven employees and shouted at them for no specific reason. He shouted and shouted until he began to cough violently. His coughing was so severe it forced him to stop shouting and instead he started banging his hand on the table of one of the girls that happened to be near him. His glasses fell off his face and tears ran out the corner of his eyes. One girl ran and brought him a glass of water and handed it to him. After he gulped down the glass of water, his coughing stopped and his hand stopped beating the table. From there, a few minutes of quietness ensued from a day of never ending chaos.

The employees had never seen their boss this way before. They expected the next time he was able to open his contemptible mouth he would fire them all. All seven employees were standing and trembling in fear like slaves standing before their taskmaster. At that crucial moment, one employee dared to open her mouth and speak in his direction. The other employees thought she had just secured a death sentence for herself or for a certainty about to lose her job. I'm sure you can guess who that employee was...Yes, that employee was Rukhsana. With her voice trembling, she said:

"Sir, I think I know what happened to the maidservant".

Instead of telling her to "Shut up!" or saying "You're fired, get out of here!", Muhammad barely able to speak said to her in a hoarse tone of voice,

"Tell me what do you think happened to Rayhana and her daughter!?!"

"Sir I believe that Jamaal Khan convinced Rayhana not to go to Saudi Arabia and promised to marry her. And because she is in love with him she agreed and then he perhaps took her ticket and visa and sold them to another travel agency. That travel agency sold the ticket and visa of Rayhana Khan to another Indian woman. And that woman..."

"You are absolutely and perfectly right Rukhsana" shouted the boss with the thick husky voice of an ogre. *"Right now I want all of you to go to Jamaal's chawl and find out what he's up to. If you see that woman in his house just give me a call and I know what I am going to do to him for double crossing me and stabbing me in the back."*

The seven employees began to prepare themselves for this spontaneous mission. All six girls gathered their handbags and emerged from behind their desks. The last man standing or young man was the first one to reach the door and emerge from it. The girls followed behind him one by one in succession as if they were students lining up for lunchtime in the school cafeteria. However, before the last employee could step beyond the door frame, the conniving weasel with his voice crackling in spots changed his mind and shouted,

"Wa...it a mi...nute!"

The long line of female employees came to an immediate halt. Clearing his throat so he could be clearly heard;

"Jamilah must stay and answer the phones and finish some work here so it doesn't pile up".

Since Jamilah was the ugliest girl, no one doubted the boss' intention. Jamilah came out of the queue and walked back to her desk and sat down in her chair. The other girls felt free to go. However, the boss changed his mind again and this time asked his favorite employee to stay behind too. He pretended to be requesting a favor of her rather than ordering her.

"Bul…bo…lah" said the boss, in an endearing fashion and his vocal chords nearly intact, *"Can you also stay behind dear and help your sister Jamilah with the workload and help her answer the phones?"*

Jamilah wasn't Bulbolah's sister. The scheming son of Satan was religiously imposing a relationship between the two girls in order to hide his evil intentions. When his favorite female employee had returned to her desk and sat down, his demeanor changed and the wickedness of his mind switched back to normal mode. He shouted to the other employees and ordered them to go search until the ends of the earth, *"that son of a bitch, Jamaal Khan and that slum prostitute, Rayhana Khan. When I get my hands on them I will skin them alive and burn their bodies on a stake high enough to light up all of downtown Bombay."*

When the five couriers went about carrying out their fact-finding mission, they carried with them the heavy weight of death upon their consciences. The boss then returned to his office. He sat on down on his oversized armchair and pressed the bell to call in the peon. The peon wasn't allowed to sit inside any of the two offices. He had to sit outside on a small stool. His duties were to respond whenever he heard someone ring the bell and do whatever he was told to do by the others. He also served as a guard and janitor cleaning the office. He had to come every day at eight o'clock in the morning and clean both the front office of the employees and the office of the boss. He was a watchman, a janitor, and a peon doing the work of three people but only getting paid for the job of one.

That day, when the peon came in Muhammad gave him three hundred rupees and instructed him go buy him a bottle of Black Level whiskey. Black Level was a finer brand of Indian whiskey. There was a popular form of liquor in India called *daro*. Daro was a cheap kind of bootleg liquor usually made in the chawls and slums and sold for very little. It was illegal to make daro but some people in the chawls and slums take the risk. The bottle or container of this acid-like liquor had no label so no one knew the exact percentage of alcohol in it. From its effects one could guess at least an alcohol content of 70-80%. With an alcohol volume that high, a person consuming even a small quantity of daro would lose his senses and behave like someone mad.

Persons under the affects of daro you can find sleeping on the streets, near garbage bins, or just about anywhere. If you took off their clothes or ripped the skin off their flesh, they would not wake them up. It would be just as if they had been put under general anesthesia to undergo a serious operation. Drunkards love to test their daro before they purchase it. There were two methods of testing daro. The first method is when the buyer asks for a half glass of daro from the seller and then he would throw the daro over his head. If one drop fell on his head, he wouldn't buy it. It is said the good daro is expected to vibrate immediately as soon as it had been flung into empty air. In the second method, the drunkard lights a match and exposes the quantity of daro to a small flame. If the daro shoots out like rocket fire when lit then the daro passes the test with positive results and he would purchase it.

Muhammad was a drunkard but he did not drink daro. He was like other affluent Indians who believed that *daro* was for poor and uncultured people. He had never drank alcohol inside his office but today was different from any other day at the office. Harboring the humiliating insults of Sheikh Ahmed ringing in his ears and the misadventures of Jamaal Khan and the so-called *"slum prostitute,"* he needed a drink to calm his nerves and this self-help remedy would allow him the ability to begin repairing his injured pride. Besides that, he had an evil design developing in his corrupt mind and only when he was drunk could he begin this carefully thought-out evil. Therefore, when the peon brought him the bottle of Black Level liquor, he swiftly emptied one third of it in his gut. Most of the drunkards in India like to drink their alcohol pure without mixing it. They believe that undiluted alcohol would give them a faster kick than a mixed one. When the sharer with demons emptied half the bottle of Black Level down his throat, his eyes became redder than red-hot chili peppers. He looked as though someone had punched him in the face or he had been in a fight with Satan the Devil and lost. Then, he came out of his office and pretended to be sorry for firing the Sudanese boy. The alcohol had given him a false sense of remorse and his mood changed from ugly to kind and courteous. Politely he requested Jamilah go to the International Student Hostel and ask Babikir to come back to work. He even told her to apologize for him and say just how sorry he was. When Jamilah took her purse and came out from behind her desk, Bulbolah stood up and said to her boss, *"Sir, can I go with her?"*

"Why?" Muhammad shouted at Bulbolah, which caused her to jump backwards.

"Are you a little girl afraid someone is going to come and steal you?"

"I don't mean that sir. I just thought you might allow me to go with Jamilah".

"And who is going to answer the phone calls if both of you go?"

In fact, Bulbolah was afraid to be left alone with this grotesque monster. She had heard from the other girls that he was a womanizer and cheating on his wife. He frightened her so by the alarming tone in his voice, she felt she had no choice but to sit back down in her chair and stay behind. Although, Jamilah knew why Bulbolah wanted to come with her, she did nothing to intervene and rescue the panic-stricken girl. The ugliness in her didn't show any sign of sympathy and couldn't care less about leaving Bulbolah alone to be taken advantage of by a drunken lush.

In the third world, there were three kinds of public institutions more dangerous to the public than the 10 Most Wanted Fugitives In The World. They were teachers, employers and the police. As a matter of fact, if a suspect fell into the hands of the police he would be beaten up and tortured to the point of death. In India, very often suspects were killed during interrogations. If the suspect happened to be female she would be raped by the male officer who took her in for interrogation. Most of the school teachers especially in male-dominated Arab countries sodomize their young students. Some of them confidently boast about their evil acts among their just as wicked friends. They like small school boys who have yet to reach the age of puberty because they believe at that age the body of the male child is soft and supple like that of a female. Teachers were the least paid of all government employees. Most of them cannot afford to marry a woman and for this reason, they go about satisfying their sexually frustrated desires by sodomizing their pupils. In strictly segregated social settings, there exists a huge gap between males and females. Most of the schools in Arab and Muslim countries have no coeducation facilities where males and females study together in the same classrooms. This segregation of the sexes and other economic factors increase the resulting homosexual tendencies, which lead to young males being raped by their schoolteachers and older boys. Other operators of this moral decay are employers and business owners. They specialize in taking advantage of their lofty positions to harass those under their control. Ninety percent of public servants and employers abuse those in their employ. This abuse of power as we are about to see is worse in the private sector than in the public sector.

Muhammad had his own private business. Hence, he had no superior authority to give an accounting to or any chain of command whereby his employees could make or file a grievance or complaint. Therefore, after Jamilah had left, Muhammad returned to his office and drank some more from his bottle of Black Level whiskey. Then, he pressed the button of his peon bell and called him to come in again. When the peon came in, he told him not to allow anyone to enter into his office and if anyone asked him the reason he should tell them the boss was in a private meeting with an important Arab client. He also told him not to allow any of his employees to come in if they returned sooner than expected until he heard directly from him. As soon as the peon left Muhammad picked up the phone receiver and dialed the number of Bulbolah and ordered her to come to his office at once.

Bulbolah's heart started to pound so hard she thought she was going to die. The first thought that came to her mind was to take her handbag and run for dear life. It was crystal clear to her when the ugly one left, her deceitful boss was up to no good. She recognized his wicked intentions from the start. She knew that he wasn't the kind of boss who would fire an employee and so quickly feel regret afterward, let alone apologize and ask him to come back. This was just an excuse to get rid of Jamilah so that he could be alone with her. This was a very pivotal moment for Bulbolah and a very trying situation. She was having great difficulty trying to help provide for the needs of her family and had a huge obligation to shelter. She knew that if she ran away today, she would have to run away tomorrow. She would always find herself running everywhere she went. There would always be a reprehensible jerk with an unfair advantage over her. She would either have to compromise her dignity or run away and keep what belonged to her. She remembered how her mother was firmly against her decision to go out of the house at her young age and work in a place full of males. She disobeyed her mother because her brothers and sisters were considerably younger than her and could not work without leaving school. Her father died and the entire burden fell on her mother alone. Her mother was working like a machine in hundreds of houses for a very long time and still could not make enough money to feed all her children and send them to school. When her mother could no longer make enough money to educate them all by herself, her last resort was to remove her sons and daughters from school and send them to work.

At that time, Bulbolah had completed grade nine and she knew how to read and write. She asked her mother to allow her brothers and sisters to continue their education and she volunteered to work with her so they could have extra income to meet the family's needs. The mother accepted her daughter's suggestion and began to take her with her to work in rich people's houses. At that time, the mother had no fear for her daughter's welfare because she was with her everywhere she worked. However, when the greatest enemy of poor people attacked the mother and rendered her defenseless, the family became impoverished without a penny to live in. While the mother was lying sick in a government hospital, Bulbolah and her brothers and sisters had nothing to eat.

At first, the sick mother told her three little sons to either go find some kind of work to do and bring money home to feed their sisters or stand on the streets and beg. Bulbolah knew jobs were few and far in-between and if her little brothers left school for a life scrounging on the streets, they would become prey for the Gondas to recruit them in their gangs. Whenever children fell victim to the streets, gang members would blind their eyes with hot oil or cut both their legs or hands and use them to beg for money and take what they collect. If children were fortunate enough to escape this type of initiation, they would become part of a gang of juvenile delinquents on the path to becoming career criminals.

After the mother became seriously ill and could no longer work, Bulbolah decided to take on the entire responsibility of caring for the family herself. Her mother told her not to go to work in the homes of rich people because at her young age she might get raped. Bulbolah listened to the advice of her mother and stopped going to the houses where she used to go work with her mother. She told her mother she would find a job in a respectable place where no one would harm her. When she found a job working at the travel agency her mother wasn't happy when she learned her daughter was going to be working in an office with men. Bulbolah told her mother that she wasn't the only girl in the office but there were five other girls working in the office as well. The mother still wasn't satisfied with this explanation but because of the family's circumstances she was resigned to accept her daughter's decision. Bulbolah's was making ten times what she and her mother used to make while they were working like slaves in rich people's houses. She was able to feed her family and pay for her mother's treatment. She also purchased nice clothes for her brothers and sisters and sent them to school. However, that day when her devilish boss called her to come to his office she found herself standing on a crossroads. She had either to run away and protect her honor or stay and give in to what he wanted and continue to work and feed her family. Bulbolah chose to sacrifice her honor for the sake of her family…

Babikir Al-A'war was another unfortunate employee. He had a really tough time before he came to work for the travel agency. His cousin's brother had sponsored his education a little over a year by sending Babikir money every month for him to study in India. The cousin used to work in the rich gulf country of Kuwait. After Saddam Hussein's troops invaded that Arab country, the cousin like many foreigners ran for their lives and returned to Sudan. He left behind everything he had earned during his years of employment in the country. After he lost his job and returned to his homeland, he was no longer able to send money to his cousin anymore. He wrote a letter to Babikir and told him to forget about continuing his education in India and return to Sudan. Babikir had already finished one year and had two years left before he could graduate and earn a university degree in Business Administration.

Babikir knew it would be a disgrace to his people for him to return to Sudan without a university degree. At least with a degree in English medium he could find a good job in one of the rich gulf countries and make a good fortune. After his cousin's brother lost his job and returned to Sudan, Babikir found himself at a loss as to what to do. He discussed his problem with his Sudanese friends. Some of his friends advised him to return to Sudan and some told him to continue his studies and he may be able to rely upon whatever little help he could get from other Sudanese students. Babikir followed the latter advice and began to depend on others to feed him and pay for his tuition fees. However, he soon discovered it wasn't a pleasant experience to depend on the charity of others. He had no place of his own and he had no control over what he would eat or the ability to wash and wear suitable clothing. He found himself to be a heavy burden to the other students. Sometimes some of the Sudanese students rebuked him for not caring for his own financial needs and always asking for food.

It just so happened at that time, Sheikh Ahmed was having a problem with his first wife, Christie, who had cheated on him and stole his money, kicked him out of the house and married her boyfriend instead. After he had been kicked out of his house at Bandara Ban Stand, the old Saudi came to the international student hostel and asked the Arabic speaking students to help him. All the Arab students collectively advised him to forget about his ex-wife and his stolen property and money and return to his country. However, the only one who stood by his side and helped him was Babikir. He told him the best way to fight the case was to hire an attorney to petition the court and ask for the judge to reverse the decision. He even went with him to his court hearings and translated the proceedings for him. At this fork in the road, a kind of mutual friendship between Babikir and Sheikh Ahmed commenced. Babikir anticipated that the Saudi might not get a positive result but he convinced him to try anyway. Sheikh Ahmed came to know about Babikir's problem and hence helped him to get a job with his client, Muhammad Khan. In fact, Sheikh Ahmed and Mr. Khan knew each other since the time Muhammad used to work for Ahmed as a chauffeur in the Kingdom of Saudi Arabia.

For twelve months, Babikir worked as a translator and clerk at Muhammad Tours and Travels. He was now able to pay for his tuition fees, hostel, and he was able to eat whatever he wanted to eat and dress the way he wanted to look. Not surprisingly, when he was caught lying about the missing maidservant and was fired by his atrocious boss his troubles started all over again. He still had one more year to study in India before he could graduate from Bombay University. On the day, Muhammad humiliated him in front of all the employees it was too much for him to bear. After being insulted, spat upon and kicked out of the office, Babikir felt like a complete failure. He went and sat on the seashore all alone by himself. He wept so much and wondered why life for him had to be so hard. He did not want to go back to begging his Sudanese friends for food or to help him with his tuition and expenses, but he also wanted to continue his education and return to his country as an educated man. What troubled his heart most of all was he would not be able to see his Indian girlfriend *whom he loved but she did not love him.* Jamilah deliberately had led him on to believe she loved him too. He being confused and misguided asked himself many times, *"She never says she loves me and if she doesn't love me why does she keep accepting my gifts and other things?"* Because he had only one eye and because of the color of his skin, Babikir knew inside he would not be able to get a good looking Indian girlfriend. The artificial affection he felt by buying her love gave him some measure of emotional satisfaction to at least hope he could one day marry her. And so, he continued to show her how much he loved her by buying her things. Whenever he bought her food or costly gifts, Jamilah flattered him with flowery talk and grinned a big crocodile smile. After he was called a *f...g, lying n…and son of a bitch* and kicked out of the office, he concluded that he had lost his most beloved along with his source of income and dignity. He felt ashamed in front of her and the other employees and felt as though his life had come to an end. He even contemplated suicide but the fear of dying a miserable death and landing in hellfire prevented him from taking his own life. Although, Babikir wasn't a religious boy still he was strongly believing in the Qur'an and his prophet Muhammad. He had a girlfriend and drinks alcohol with his Sudanese friends and very often goes to Farris Road to buy sex from hookers. His religious status like all Muslim men, whatever evils they do still they believe that somehow they are going to end up in paradise and enjoy the virgins.

As her boss had instructed her, Jamilah went to the international student hostel and asked the whereabouts of Babikir. His Sudanese friends told her that Babikir had gone to work. Jamilah told his friends Babikir had gotten fired from his job but the boss changed his mind and wanted him to come back. His friends told her he had not returned to his room at the hostel. Jamilah left the hostel and decided to return to the office and inform her boss she was unable to locate him. When she reached the bus stop, she sighted someone that looked like Babikir sitting across the street on the seashore. She crossed the street to see if it was indeed him and it was. She tapped him on the shoulder and called him by his name. Shocked and overwhelmed by the vision standing before him, Babikir thought he was dreaming and his heart could not believe what he was seeing. This was the biggest surprise of his life. He thanked Allah for this blessing and his deep sadness turned into tears of joy when standing right in front of him his dearly loved Jamilah. Jamilah did not tell him immediately why she came looking for him. She never failed to use an opportunity to take advantage of him and she was hungry and wanted something to eat. Therefore, the ugly, selfish girl requested Babikir take her to a local restaurant because she had something very important to tell him. Babikir became overjoyed and thought his Jamilah had at last decided to reveal her love for him. Therefore, he took her to the Fairy Restaurant and ordered her whatever she wanted to eat. Her deceiving heart did not tell him the good news until he filled her stomach with food, sweet dish, ice cream, tea, and coffee.

Jamilah had taken the bus to the international hostel but she lied to Babikir and told him she had taken a taxi. She said she did not like to travel by bus or train because male passengers harassed her. Accordingly, to protect her from being sexually harassed, Babikir flagged down a taxi and traveled with his ugly girlfriend back to their work place. When they arrived, the peon prevented them from entering the office and told them the boss was in a very important private meeting with one of his Arab clients. Jamilah did not believe the peon and asked him whether Bulbolah had gone home or if she was still inside the office? When the peon informed Jamilah that Bulbolah was still inside the office, it didn't take much for her to figure out what was going on inside between Bulbolah and her boss. Being the ugliest girl in the office, Jamilah silently amassed deep resentment and envy for the new girl because she was the most beautiful. She always looked for whatever might tarnish a person's reputation and especially Bulbolah's. The green-eyed monster disobeyed the boss' directive and forced her way inside the office. The peon did not feel he could put his hands on a woman so he did not stop her. He rubbed his head and hoped he wouldn't get fired. It was not Jamilah's intention to catch Bulbolah in the act of having sex with the boss, but if she could eavesdrop and actually hear the act in progress this would make her story more convincing to the other girls. However, when she entered the office she found Bulbolah sitting at her desk weeping with her face in her hands. Jamilah seemed to derive some sort of gratification in knowing the new girl was now a sex slave.

The other five employees took five hours to accomplish their mission. It took them two hours to travel from Colaba to Locanwalla Chawls. It took them another one hour to find Jamaal's chawl. Upon questioning Jamaal's sisters, they were informed that their brother, Jamaal, went to the international airport on Friday evening and had not returned back since then. They said further their brother informed them his boss asked him to go to the airport and help a woman who was traveling to Saudi Arabia along with her little daughter. When Rukhsana told the sisters their brother had not been to work for two days they began to cry. Rukhsana felt vindicated by this new information confirming her story of events. She concluded Jamaal had ran off with the maidservant to another city and forsaken his family. Without asking anything further, the five employees left the family of Jamaal Khan and traveled back to Colaba having fulfilled this most important business operation.

Carrying the findings of their investigation, the burden of Jamaal's life was a little less burdensome than before. Since he could not be found, his life was no longer in their hands. When they arrived, they were surprised to find Babikir sitting inside the office with the two girls. They had to ignore their curiosity concerning Babikir being back at work and concentrate on the case at hand. They had to relay the news of their mission, which was much more important. Rukhsana picked up her phone and dialed the number of her boss. She was eager to convey the bad news to her boss as proof positive her story about Jamaal Khan and Rayhana Khan was indeed true. However, her boss did not respond to his phone. She waited for some time and tried again but without any result. Then, she called his cell phone. When the boss did not respond to his cell phone either, Rukhsana began knocking on the door to his office. She could not hold the information inside her for it was boiling up like steam inside a teakettle. She wanted to get rid of this fire burning inside her before it exploded and drove her insane. Rukhsana was interested in Jamaal but he always ignored her. Jamaal was the most handsome guy in the office. Rukhsana felt crushed when Jamaal repeatedly avoided her efforts for a relationship. When that slum woman, Rayhana Khan, came and stole Jamaal's heart, Rukhsana's anger knew no limits. She had waited for a time like this to avenge her rejection and broken heart.

Rukhsana knocked and knocked on the door of her boss many times to no avail. She thought maybe she should go in and see what the problem was. She consulted with the other employees. Some warned her about the danger of venturing inside the boss' office without his permission. Nonetheless, Tahirah supported her decision to go in and promised to go with her. Rukhsana went back to the boss' office and started to turn the knob on his door. She gently pushed on the door and it began to sway open creaking on its hinges. She cautiously walked inside her boss' office and Tahirah was a snail's pace right behind her. They could not believe their eyes! The boss was sleeping on top of a table in his office and half-naked. He was lying there like he was dead without his shirt, trousers, and shoes. He was only in his underwear. There was a strong odor of alcohol that made it apparent the reason behind this strange and debauched behavior. He had never drunk before in the office. He had never slept before inside his office. He had never removed his clothing to such an extent and this was by far a new level of unholiness.

Rukhsana and Tahirah could not believe their eyes and were totally dumbfounded by this despicable view of vulgarity. They went and summoned all the other employees to come quickly and showed them the state of raunchiness their boss was lying in. The eight employees then decided to conduct a group meeting and discuss what they should do about this. Should they leave him sleeping in the office and just go home or should they try to wake him up? The majority of the group supported the decision to try and wake him up. Rukhsana shook him lightly at first to rouse him but this did not work. The others joined in shaking him more aggressively but he continued in deep slumber. For a moment they believed no one could possibly sleep that soundly unless maybe he was dead. They rapidly dismissed this notion as an improbability since he was snoring so loudly they thought he was in hell being tortured for his sins. Jamilah suggested that they should throw a bucket of cold water on him or slap him in the face. The other employees completely rejected these propositions for fear he might wake up and fire all of them. Finally, when there was nothing else left they could do to awaken him, the employees left him to hibernate overnight in his hideousness. It was more than one hour after closing hours when they came to a meeting of minds and determined each one of them should leave and go to their separate homes and maybe in the morning this will have all been a bad dream.

Muhammad slept throughout the night. He did not awaken out of his alcoholic induced coma until his employees came back to work the following day and woke him up. His consumption of good whiskey seemed to have caused him a blackout of several hours. He did not know whether it was day or night until Rukhsana told him the day and time. His office reeked of a foul odor and he was smelled like he had been lying in the sewer. He also complained about a terrible headache. He commanded the employees leave his office at once and then he struggled to redress himself. He came out of his office to breathe some fresh air and sat with the employees. Rukhsana began to narrate to him their mission to Lokhanwalla Chawls and disclose their findings about Jamaal and Rayhana Khan. Propelled by this new information, this set the boss off on another round of temper tantrums fueled by the thumping in his head and the rottenness in his bones. He retreated like a wounded animal and returned to his office. He then picked up the phone and made three important phone calls. The first call he made was to the main newspaper outlet in Bombay. He asked the newspaper to publish a case of rape and robbery committed in his office by one of his employees, a boy by the name of Jamaal Khan. He said this employee had stolen three lakhs rupees from his office and raped one of his female employees, a girl by the name of Bulbolah Sheikh, and stole her jewelry. He claimed further that Jamaal Khan had stolen visas, tickets, and passports of one of his female clients. The client was supposed to fly to Saudi Arabia but her documents were stolen by Jamaal Khan.

Then, Muhammad Khan promised to pay ten thousand rupees as a reward to the person that provided information leading to the whereabouts of Jamaal Khan to him personally or to the nearest police station. After requesting this service announcement be made public, the despicable canine called the police and reported the same alleged case of rape and robbery in which he implicated the same employee. To make the complaint valid, as a good citizen of the community, he was willing to assure a bounty of ten thousand rupees to anyone that could provide information in locating this criminal wherever he may be found. Lastly, Muhammad called a notorious Muslim Gonda who usually did his dirty work and promised to pay him fifteen thousand rupees if he would find Jamaal Khan and bring him to his office in fetters and chains.

After making these most essential calls, the piranha came out of his office and ordered his eight employees to go clean up the mess in his office made from his previous day of gluttony. After that, he called the peon and ordered him to bring to him a kettle of black coffee. When the peon brought him his coffee, his head was still rumbling inside and stars were circling in front of his eyes. He gulped down half the kettle like it was just what the doctor ordered. He then sat in the chair next to Bulbolah's desk and raised his legs and placed them up with one leg on top of the other, then closed his eyes to relax. After about five minutes, he felt some relief from his hangover and satisfaction the wheels of revenge had been set in motion.

Muhammad was sitting all alone while his eight employees were working like house servants cleaning his office. His eyes were shut and his legs were resting on the table of his recent sex victim, Bulbolah Sheikh, when suddenly he felt someone grab his left leg and jerk it violently. His whole body was sent flying through the air and he landed about five feet away from the chair he was sitting in. His head hit the hardwood floor with enough impact to split his skull in half. When his big head hit the solid wood floor it created a loud bang as if someone had pushed him from a ten-story building and he landed below onto a concrete asphalt road. The rest of his fat body landed on the floor like a dump truck emptying a two-ton load of garbage. He screamed bloody murder and thought someone was trying to kill him. A terrible pain shot up the back of his spine like a jolt of electricity. The agony was unbearable. It took him a couple of seconds to overcome the shock of his body being turned upside down like a roller coaster. Extremely incensed, he decided whoever did this to him he was going to kill them. He forced his old rustic body to stand up and scramble to his feet. Turning around to assault his attacker, he had both fists ready for a fight. His assailant however was more than prepared for a counter-attack. Muhammad stopped his fist mid-way when he saw pointing in his face a black revolver.

"Police inspector, Guru Aurobindo Shankaracharya," said the aggressor waving his police identification card in his left hand while holding his revolver in his right hand.

"Mr. Muhammad Khan, You're under arrest!"

CHAPTER 8

THE TERRORIST PLOT

The sin of rich people was pride and the sin of poor people was envy. If something good happened to you, although a person could be your relative or claiming to be a friend, your good fortune would make them very unhappy and if evil befell you, it would bring them great comfort. This kind of evil-heartedness can be found among the rich and the poor alike. However, poor people are more subject to be this way due to their poverty and ill-fortune. People living like animals in the slums of Bombay, India for sure suffer this type of covetousness and jealousy. Only a miracle or an extraordinary determination could possibly free a person from such a wretched life. We saw how Rayhana's lot in life was transformed from the grave she lived in with her husband to the happiest days of her life spent with her lover, Jamaal Khan, in the city streets and sandy beaches of Bombay.

Rayhana came alive and vibrant during the days of her awakening. She was fully immersed in an ocean of ecstasy, happiness and the delights of womanhood. She blossomed like a rose and the sun smiled upon her every minute of the day even though she was living and working in drudgery. Everyone around her and in the slums noticed a sudden change manifesting itself in the way she walked and in the way she talked and the very aura of just being around her. Her inner joy made her smile and talk to everybody. She began to love life. Before, she was hopeless and unhappy dealing with the sacrificial/suicidal death of her husband and carrying the heavy burden of ten mouths to feed. A new life knocked on the door of her slum after her trip to Colaba. After her encounter with the old Saudi, her life began to change dramatically every second and every minute. Her poor, miserable neighbors noticeably felt jealous of her. Some of the women tried to find out the secrets of her happiness but they did not go further in their curiosity. If only they could get a glimpse into her world or spy out her every move. That would surely give them something to talk about but Rayhana did not reveal to them the secrets of her ever-developing brand-new life.

One woman who was also a Muslim like Rayhana could not tolerate seeing her dressing up nice everyday and leaving her slum early in the morning and returning late at night. She suspected her neighbor was having an affair. In her scandalous mind, a Muslim widow having an affair and sleeping around and not being married was the biggest sin in the world. This Muslim woman was not about to let a woman like that get away with sin and not suffer the consequences. She had to help Allah and find some supporting evidence to condemn her soul to hell and make sure it was forever. Rayhana was now a marked woman and a target of vicious rumors. Once this evil rumor was concocted, she would suffer the judgment of the self-righteous, tainted minds of her neighbors and peers. Yes, the moral majority of slum dwellers were going to make sure Muslims act like Muslims should.

For three days, Rayhana was being followed by the self-appointed religious police and holy woman of Allah. This faithful Muslim woman followed Rayhana to several of the houses she was working in. While following her, the Muslim woman did not see her stopping on the way to meet or talk to any men. She concluded Rayhana was having a secret affair with one of the rich men living in the houses where she worked. She could not follow her inside each house of course, nevertheless, she decided to spread her unsubstantiated suspicions to anyone she could find that would listen to her. Then, she added a few more lies to her story to make it more believable and swore by Allah she saw Rayhana walking side by side holding the hand of a rich man. She asked Allah to curse her with blindness if she was telling a lie. Despite putting herself under a curse of blindness, she continued her lies saying she followed behind them down a lane as they turned off onto a narrow road. Then, she saw with her eyes the man hugging Rayhana from behind and rubbing against her backside. Rayhana did not stop him when he opened her blouse and grabbed both her breasts with his hands and started squeezing them. While engaged in this shameful, lustful act, they were thrusting against each other and Rayhana was forced to the ground while her lover fell on top of her. Then the woman swore by Allah, may all of her children die and rot in hell, that she stood and watched them do it by some trees like wild animals.

This salacious dribble of juicy gossip spread like wildfire in every nook and cranny of the slums. Rayhana knew nothing about the evil rumors spreading about her and continued her wonderful life with her real man. If her jealous neighbor knew about her cuddling and carrying on with Jamaal Khan, she would have had a real picture of what really was going on. The Muslim woman wouldn't hesitate to pay a small fortune to have someone take their photos so they could be hung on the rags of every slum. These rumors however, did not affect Rayhana at all. They had no affect upon her until the day she was to fly to the Kingdom of Saudi Arabia. This was the day her real troubles started.

Rayhana knew about the envious nature of her neighbors and she also believed in the evil-eye. (The evil-eye is the belief that some people can bestow a curse on victims by the malevolent gaze of their magical eye. It is a look that is believed by many cultures to be able to cause injury or bad luck for the person at whom it is directed for reasons of envy or dislike). For this reason, Rayhana did not tell anyone she was going to the rich country of Saudi Arabia. She did not even tell her own parents or in-laws. Just a day before her scheduled trip she went to a Muslim man, she knew who had a teashop. She made arrangements with him to care for her family. She told him that she was flying to Saudi Arabia along with her daughter. Then, she said she would be sending money to her children and parents through him and she promised to pay him some commission for his services.

The Muslim man accepted this responsibility and agreed to see after her family. He was surprised though how a poor widow could afford visas, tickets, and passports. This man became interested in Rayhana after her husband died. He even sent someone to propose marriage to her. Rayhana rejected his proposal because he was a married man and his wife was her neighbor and supposedly her friend. This woman was the one who spread the vicious rumors about Rayhana and told everyone she was having an affair with a rich man and having sex with him out in the open like a bitch being chased by a pack of slum dogs.

The husband of this Muslim woman was a somewhat knowledgeable man as compared to other men in the slums. Although he had accepted Rayhana's proposal, he wanted to know how she got such a huge sum of money to buy visas, tickets, and passports. He directly told her to her face he did not believe a poor slum woman like her could possibly make that much money to afford such an expensive trip while working as a maidservant in India. Rayhana simply told him the truth but he did not believe her. At first, he thought she was selling her body as a prostitute. However, he knew a prostitute would need to sleep with hundreds of men every day for at least ten years to make that much money to cover the costs for traveling outside the country. He had some idea of how much prostitutes charged a customer for occasionally a working girl would come to his teashop to offer her services. Whenever a prostitute showed up, he hired her to sleep with him inside the teashop. So, he seriously doubted the possibility Rayhana was able to pay for visas, tickets, and passports with money she charged for selling her body.

These questions puzzled the teashop owner so much that finally he shared this fascinating riddle with his wife. His wife had already spread rumors about Rayhana that were not true and this goody bag of perplexity added to her resentment and twisted thoughts. When the woman's husband told her about the unbelievable chance of the Muslim widow traveling to the rich Arab country of Saudi Arabia with her daughter, the woman's hate and envy reached an all-time high. She wished she could burn down Rayhana's slum with her and her daughter in it to prevent them from leaving to go someplace better like a rich Arab country. The woman used to boast that her husband was alive and had a big teashop. She looked down upon Rayhana because *"She killed her husband."* and was a maidservant working like a slave in rich people's houses. In India, if a woman's husband died while she was still living, people around her especially her in-laws and neighbors would say, *"She killed her husband."* Hindus go further in their accusations. They burn the widowed woman alive along with the corpse of her dead husband. The evil practice of Sati was considered a religious obligation. If the widow refused to practice Sati she would be treated as a curse by her late husband's family. Her head would be shaved and she would be prevented from wearing shoes and colored clothing. She would be kept in a small room in the basement. Bald-headed and shoeless widow, people would not look upon her to see her face. For them to see her face was a bad omen.

To examine more closely the bitterness of Rayhana's neighbor, the Muslim woman's jealousy did not allow her to sleep the whole night. She stayed awake all night thinking about how to stop her neighbor from traveling to Saudi Arabia. Her treacherous plotting reached the point where she felt as if she was going to burst open. What troubled her the most was the fact that Rayhana Khan was not going to just any rich Arab country but she was going to the *Muslim Holy Land* where *The House of Allah* was. Millions of Muslims longed to visit the *Holy Cities of Mecca and Medina* and perform the Hajj ritual but for many their financial situation would not allow them to fulfill this life-long dream. Only the very rich Muslims in India could travel to the *Holy Cities* and visit *the House of Allah.*

The suspicious woman just as her husband, wanted to know how her neighbor obtained such a large amount of cash. She didn't think anything foolish like her husband who thought Rayhana was selling her body to men. After brain storming throughout the night the jealous woman concluded Rayhana Khan had stolen the money from the rich people she was working for. When her evil mind settled upon this supposition, she conjured up exactly what she would do to stop this immoral woman from traveling to *the Holy Land and House of Allah.*

Allah would bless her with paradise from preventing this slum dog trash from defiling the Holy Ground Prophet Muhammad walked on. So as soon as her husband left their middle-class slum and went to his teashop, the evil witch put on her burqa and concealed her face and headed to the nearest police station. She told them she wanted to report a crime that had come to her attention. She claimed it was her duty as a good citizen to help stop crime in her neighborhood. She told the police inspector-in-charge that her neighbor had possibly murdered one of the wealthy men she worked for as a maidservant and stolen his money. At first, the police inspector did not take her complaint seriously because she was from the slums and he knew slum women to be backbiters and notorious gossipers. However, when she told him that the neighbor was flying that day to Saudi Arabia along with her seven-year-old daughter, he took the matter seriously and decided to investigate it. He knew if a slum woman had to work twenty-four hours a day, seven days a week, she would not be able to afford to buy an airplane ticket to fly her from Bombay to Poona City.

The police went to the slum of Rayhana's family and raided it. Rayhana however, happened to be away. At that time, she had gone to the travel agency to collect the two passports, visas, tickets, the Indian rupees and US dollars. The police inspector returned to the station but kept two constables in front of her slum. He instructed them that as soon as the suspect returned to her slum they should apprehend her and bring her to him in ropes. In India, the police's hand and the suspect's hand would be tied together with thick long rope.

I myself would prefer to fall into the hands of the Taliban or Al-Qaeda terrorists than to fall in the hands of the police in India. When a suspect reached the detention area, the police would apply what they called *third degree interrogation methods.* Water boarding or any other kind of harsh interrogation methods utilized in the *Guantanamo Bay Detention Center* was nothing compared to the third degree torture techniques of the Indian police. If the suspect happened to be a young lady, the least that would happen to her is she would be raped by at least three different police officers. Those who interrogate the suspects were called extortionists because they extract information by force. If you had not committed a crime and were accused falsely, you would be forced to admit you committed the crime.

A friend of mine was held as a suspect in a drug case and was beaten, tortured, and forced to confess his involvement even though he was not guilty of a single thing. After three years of rotting inside Bombay's local jails and Poona's Central Prison, he was acquitted after finally being declared not guilty. He wasn't compensated at all nor did he receive an apology from the police, judge or prosecutor. The entire court system was a sham. It's a wonder he was ever set free at all. He lost three years of his life in a dangerous bottomless pit inside those filthy dungeons. He was not able to finish his studies at the University for his body was worn and battered from being beaten day and night by the notorious Indian criminal element known as the Gondas who hated and despised foreigners.

For three weeks, Rayhana Khan ascended upon high. Her life had turned over a new leaf. While searching for a better life for herself and her family, she found her benefactor, Sheikh Ahmed and captured the love of her life, Jamaal Khan. Whether due to the evil-eye or the envy of a jealous woman, her happiness was snatched from her the very same day she was to fly with her daughter to the Kingdom of Saudi Arabia (KSA). When she returned to her slum, she saw a huge gathering of *"Slummiers."* At first, Rayhana thought one of her elders had died inside her slum and so she quickened her steps dragging little Iffat by the hand. When her daughter complained she picked her up and carried her in her arms and rushed to her slum.

Upon arriving, the two constables standing outside arrested her and bound her hands with rope. They did not allow her to enter her slum. She tried to find out why they were tying her up but they just ignored her questions and continued to bind her with rope and hold her in custody. Her daughter began to cry out when she saw her mother being tied up. Her other children came out of their slum and tried to surround their mother but the constables kicked and pushed them away. Her parents and in-laws were helpless and unable to come to her rescue because of their old age. She heard the women who pretended to be her friends and good neighbors laughing and calling her in Hindi, *"Thief! Prostitute!"* In her evil frame of mind, the Muslim woman and Holy Woman of Allah who had reported her to the police shouted: *"You are a shame and a disgrace to all of us Muslims!"* Some bad boys with nothing else to do cried out, "*Teri maa ki chute, teri bahan ki chute, chutiya,...sala.*"

Rayhana wasn't arrested alone; her little daughter was also taken into custody. When she reached the police station, she was beaten nearly to the point of death. The police seized her passports, visas, tickets, her Indian rupees and American dollars. She was forced to admit to more than ten crimes of which she had not committed. One charge she falsely admitted to was being involved in a prostitution ring and servicing Arabs nationals. She was also accused of stealing money from the household of the rich families where she was employed. The police did not believe her story that she met an old elderly man from Saudi Arabia or that he had offered her a job as a maidservant in his country. They did not believe he freely provided her with visas, tickets, rupees and foreign currency and paid for the processing of her and daughter's passports without anything in return. What complicated the matter as well was that her passport id listed the address of a chawl. Rayhana told the police the travel agency that processed her papers entered that address on her application because she did not have an address. The police knew that slum people did not have addresses but they still refused to accept her explanation for using another address. The address led the police to a second suspect.

The day that Rayhana Khan collected her travel papers was the saddest day of Jamaal Khan's life. He could not hide his tears when his loved one collected her papers and walked out of the office. He ran to the washroom and cried like a newborn baby. The pain building up inside him was too much to bear. He had begun to miss her even before she returned to pick up her documents. He knew it would be extremely hard for him to be without her for two long years. Jamaal wanted to go to the airport but he was afraid that his boss might see him. When his boss changed his mind and decided to send the Sudanese boy instead, Jamaal saw an opportunity to see his beloved one last time from afar and wave his last good bye to her. He returned to his house and rested until eight o'clock in the evening. Then, he dressed up and told his sister he was going to the international airport because his boss asked him to help a client traveling to Saudi Arabia along with her seven-year-old daughter.

Jamaal did not go more than a few meters away from his chawl before three policemen stopped him. It was either a coincidence or a bad omen when the policemen asked him about the chawl of Jamaal Khan. He did not suspect anything and was honest and told them he was the one they were looking for. The policemen immediately grabbed his hands and tied him up. When he tried to inquire about the reason for his arrest, one of the policemen hit him repeatedly on his back and shoulders with a big stick until he fell down to the ground. The same policeman forced him to his feet and told him if he asked any further questions they would beat him unconscious to make him shut up and drag his dead body to the morgue.

Stunned, he decided to keep quiet as directed and went with the three policemen to the city transport vehicle. Jamaal knew that Bombay police would not hesitate for a second to kill a suspect for resisting arrest. He was ordered to sit down on the floor inside the police van. He was not allowed to occupy a seat. When the vehicle sped up his body began to bounce like a rubber ball hitting against the metal seats, with his head and body banging against everything. His hands were tied behind him, which made it impossible for him to brace himself. It was in this bruised and battered state that Jamaal was taken to lock-up missing the last goodbye to his beloved. Tears fell like a waterfall down his face when he visualized his beloved Rayhana walking down the departure hall at the airport with her little daughter knowing he would not see them until after seven hundred and thirty days if ever again.

Jamaal did not know the reason for his arrest until he reached the police lockup. It was police Inspector Guru Aurobindo Shankaracharya who applied the brutal third degree interrogation method and extracted the same story he had received from the slum woman. Jamaal admitted he filled out the applications for Rayhana and her daughter and gave them his chawl's address because they did not have an address living in the slum. Then, he told the police how Rayhana got the visas, tickets and currency. The police Inspector refused to believe a single word Jamaal said. He could not wrap his mind around the fact that a wealthy Arab business tycoon would spend lakhs of rupees on a slum woman and her daughter because he wanted her to come and work as a maidservant in his mansion in the Kingdom of Saudi Arabia. What made the story of Rayhana so impossible for police Inspector Guru Aurobindo Shankaracharya to believe was that he was a Hindu that absolutely despised Muslims and wanted to believe the worst about them. He once told his Hindu friends that he hated Muslims with a passion and detested the "Muslim dogs and alley cats." Hence, he was intensely interested in the case of Rayhana Khan and Jamaal Khan because they were both Muslims. He was especially enthusiastic when Jamaal dragged another cat into the fray and volunteered the name of another Muslim—his boss, Muhammad Khan.

The police Inspector, Guru Aurobindo Shankaracharya believed that all Indian Muslims were enemies of the Hindus and a threat to the country of India. He even believed that peace-loving, law abiding Indian Muslims like Jamaal Khan and Rayhana Khan were terrorists and enemies of the Hindus. Whenever, he would see a Muslim man dressed up in that Pakistani Pajama-like dress and having long beard with a Muslim hat on top and walking down the street he would view him as if he was a ticking time bomb. It was granted to him commission from the gods of India to root out this Muslim scrum of the earth; each and every one, and he made it his mission and personal vendetta to rid his countrymen of these cockroaches. Whenever a Muslim fell into his grasp, he would try to pin a terrorist plot on him or accuse him of being an agent of the Pakistan's I.S.I. (Inter-Services Intelligence). If he could not establish sufficient evidence against a Muslim suspect, he would try to involve him in a drug conspiracy. In India, being charged with murder is preferable to being accused of plotting a terrorist attack or involvement in a drug crime.

Accordingly, when Jamaal Khan mentioned his Muslim boss, Muhammad Khan the police Inspector Shankaracharya tried for two days to establish a terrorist plot before arresting the new suspect. His suspicion was increased when Jamaal gave him the same name of the

Saudi businessman mentioned by the first suspect, Rayhana Khan. Then, the Police Inspector G. A. Shankaracharya wrote a detailed report and sent it to the Home Ministry in New Delhi. In his report, he accused a wealthy Saudi of conspiring with some Muslim Indians to carry out a terrorist attack in Bombay. The Saudi man supplied visas and tickets to a female Muslim suicide bomber to blow up an Air India plane on its way to Saudi Arabia. The Arab man probably was a member of Al-Qaeda of the Arabian Peninsula Branch operating from Yemen.

Police Inspector G. A. Shankaracharya stole the visas, tickets, passports, and money of the so-called female suicide bomber the same day that she was arrested. The following day, he contacted another travel agency and sold them Rayhana's passport, visa, and ticket and her daughter's documents as well. The travel agency removed the photo of Rayhana and replaced it with a photo of a Malayali woman originally from South India. This woman flew to the Kingdom of Saudi Arabia arriving on the third day of Rayhana's original departure date claiming to be Sheikh Ahmed's maidservant. While waiting for a response from the Home Minister, the police Inspector Shankaracharya put a tail on the new suspect, Muhammad Khan by enlisting some plain-clothes police officers to follow him and gather information about his daily activities.

The spies followed the unsuspecting and clueless weasel when he left his office to meet his Indian Mistress at their rendezvous, the Oberoi Hotel. From the hotel management the police inquired about the name of the woman, where she was from and what relationship there was between her and Muhammad Khan. The information about the woman made the terrorist case a bit complicated. The woman was a Hindu named Gita Parkash Desia, a businesswoman from Bangalore city, married with a husband and four children. She was a regular guess at the hotel visiting many times with her husband, Mr. Desia, along with their children. The hotel management also informed the undercover officers that the woman had come alone several times and met with the Muslim man, Muhammad Khan, in her room. The nature of the business being conducted between the Hindu woman and the Muslim man was unknown.

The undercover officers followed the suspect from the hotel to his house in Juhu. Although the officers cased out the area in front of the suspect's home for several hours, they did not gather any additional information about him from his friends or neighbors and they had no way of knowing what transpired between him and his wife while he was inside the residence. That night the wife of Muhammad quarreled with him throughout the night and accused him of having an affair with one of his female employees. She suspected that was the reason he was no longer interested in having sex with her anymore and for a long time. After a few hours when there was no period of activity and the suspect remained at this location, the undercover operatives concluded he would not leave again until the next morning.

On the following day, the secret agents came early at dawn, watched, and waited until Muhammad emerged from his family residence. They followed him from place to place to monitor his terrorist activities until he reached his base of operation. They had not come equipped with surveillance cameras or a monitored installation inside the stakeout location. If they had, they would have captured a drunk inside his office raping a defenseless and terrified young woman. Unfortunately, while the wicked, deplorable wild beast was raping and violating his young female employee, Bulbolah Sheikh, Thing One and Thing Two were stupidly unaware of what was happening right under their noses. They kept to their stations standing guard outside as if they were Muhammad Khan's personal security force and look-outs while he carried out his own undercover dirty work.

The police Inspector Shankaracharya received the okay from the Home Ministry on Tuesday morning to go ahead and investigate the terrorist plot of the Muslim female suicide bomber. As soon as he got the green light, he rushed out to detain the last of the Indian conspirators. He was the one who toppled Muhammad off his throne, grabbed him by his left leg, and turned him upside down. When Muhammad found himself on the other end of a surprise attack, he got up and attempted to ward off his attacker with his fist aimed right for the attacker's face. If he had reached his mark, he would have been dead and gone by now. The revolver pointed at his head convinced him to concede defeat, which probably saved his life.

His eight employees ran into the other part of the office where they heard all the commotion going on. They all entered about the time to see their boss' hands suspended halfway above his head. They were all shocked when they saw the police inspector pointing a gun right at him. Then they witnessed the incorrigibly wicked man being bound with his hands tied behind his back with thick rope and yanked out of the office like a dangerous criminal. It was unbelievable to see for the very first time the pride and arrogance of Muhammad disappear into thin air and he became as small as a mouse in the mouth of a maned young lion. Bulbolah wished deep down in her soul the insolent violator and evil transgressor would be taken directly to the gallows and hung by his genitals. She prayed Allah would leave his soul in hell to burn for all eternity.

Although Police Inspector G. A. Shankaracharya did not fulfill this explicit wish of Bulbolah, if she were to see what had actually been done to him that day inside the lockup, she would have seen what was inflicted upon him was worst than a hanging. Muhammad was stripped of all his clothes and left with only his skimpy playboy underwear barely covering his private parts. Then, they tied his legs with a long rope and hung him upside down. His big stomach was about to burst open and spill its contents. His baldhead was just off the concrete floor. He was hanging like an animal ready to be slaughtered. Then the police Inspector brought a long stick and began to hammer him with it relentlessly leaving huge red welts. Blows rained on his head, stomach, back, legs, hands, buttocks, hips, neck, shoulders, etc. No place on his body was left untouched by the extractor of information.

The police Inspector Shankaracharya enjoyed nothing more than beating a Muslim that was suspected of a terrorist plot. Muhammad private parts were not spared from the rod. If he were to survive such a thorough beating, rest assured he would never have sex with his wife or any other female again. He screamed so much from the excruciating pain he lost his voice all over again which was already overworked from screaming at his employees the previous day. When Inspector Shankaracharya felt tired of beating the Muslim terrorist suspect, he threw hot water on him. Nearly beaten out of his mind and flung around like a rag doll, he was burned and bleeding profusely. The retribution from God was so great that all Muhammad was thinking of was that his little tryst with his female employee, Bulbolah Sheikh, was maybe not so good an idea since it was evident she has reported him to the police for rape or either Sheikh Faiz bin Ahmed had telephoned the police inspector and bribed the police to arrest him concerning his missing maidservant. He never suspected he was being accused of terrorism. Not able to comprehend why or for what reason he was being tortured to death, he got the shock of his life when then the police inspector began to interrogate him about his involvement in an alleged terrorist plot. The formal charges were committing terrorist threats and treason against the country and nation of India. Now hearing for the first time the actual charges being brought against him, Muhammad knew his days were numbered…

CHAPTER 9

THE SUICIDAL FEMALE BOMBER

Sheikh Faiz bin Ahmed decided to do everything he could to find out what happened to his expensive treasure that had cost him dearly. He was one hundred percent certain that Rayhana Khan wanted to come to Saudi Arabia since that was why she refused his money and asked him for a visa. He concluded that lying Jinni Son of Iblis, Mahound had stolen Rayhana's visas and tickets and sold them to the ugly woman that claimed to be his beloved maidservant. (In Islam, jinn are genies that turn into black dogs and snakes and Iblis is Satan the Devil. Jinn are males and females and can fall in love and marry Muslim men and women and have children with them. Some of jinn in the Qur'an embraced Islam, Surat Al-Jinn 72: 1-6). Muhammad Khan worked with Sheikh Ahmed for many years in Jeddah as his private chauffeur. Sheikh Ahmed knew Muhammad was a greedy and selfish man. He was the kind of man who would sell his wife to another man if he offered him the right price.

Therefore, Sheikh Ahmed decided to go and find Rayhana himself and bring her back with him to Saudi Arabia. He knew the Sudanese boy, Babikir, was more honest than Muhammad. He could use him to find out where his beloved was being kept from him. This time he did not want to be involved with any travel agency. He wanted Babikir to handle all the paperwork and future processing of Rayhana and her daughter's documents. As for the ugly woman, he took her directly from the airport to the prison and accused her of stealing and falsifying documents and impersonating the maidservant he had hired; an accusation if proved true in the local Shari'a Court of Law, the Malayali woman would be returned to her country minus one hand.

Sheikh Ahmed flew back to Bombay the following day after he handed the imposter over to house of detention. He did not inform anyone he was coming, deciding to make a surprise visit to Muhammad Tours and Travels. This time, he would not seek the help of the law to get his money back. This time he would follow through in taking matters into his own hands. He would hire a person of the Indian Gondas to avenge what Muhammad had done in switching his beautiful maidservant and sending him an ugly woman. He would obtain the services of the Gondas as a last resort if the greedy man refused to reimburse him all the money he spent out for Rayhana and her daughter's travel arrangements. From the Bombay International Airport, he took a taxi directly to Colaba. He booked a room in the Taj Mahal Hotel and stored his luggage away at once.

It was lunchtime when the Old Saudi reached Muhammad Tours and Travels. When he arrived, Mr. Muhammad had already been arrested and taken into custody. He found all the employees alone in the office. When he asked about the whereabouts of their boss, none of them was ready to risk his/her job and tell him what had happened earlier to their boss. Rukhsana appointed herself in charge of the office but had not moved into her arrested boss' office. She lied to Sheikh Ahmed and told him her boss wasn't feeling well (which was actually the truth) and for that reason he took the day off. Sheikh Ahmed did not believe Rukhsana and asked her to telephone him at his home or call him on his cell phone. Rukhsana told him she was under strict orders not to disturb him unless an emergency occurred like in the case of a death. Sheikh Ahmed tried to pick up the phone off the desk and call himself but she stopped him and reiterated no one should try to contact him either by phone or messenger. Her actions confirmed his suspicions that Muhammad was hiding from him.

Sheikh Ahmed left the travel agency determined to carry out his plan to hire thugs to pummel Muhammad to a pulp like yesterday's garbage. He did not know where or how to find Gondas, so he decided to seek the help of the Sudanese boy. He returned to his hotel and waited until evening. He knew that Babikir would return to his hostel as soon as he got off from work at the travel agency. He did not want anyone from the travel agency to know he was recruiting the Sudanese boy after hours for shady purposes. At seven o'clock in the evening, Sheikh Ahmed took a cab, went to the international student hostel, and asked about his Sudanese friend.

For one year, Babikir Al-A'war was acting as a double agent or spy. He spied on his boss and passed along a smorgasbord of information about him to Sheikh Ahmed and he also supplied some personal information about the Old Saudi to his boss. For example, he told his boss about Sheikh Ahmed's Christian wife, Christie, who cheated on him and stole his money and property. He told him about how she kicked Sheikh Ahmed out of his house and then married her Christian boyfriend. Likewise, Babikir told Sheikh Ahmed about his boss' adulterous affair with the married Hindu woman and how he sexually harassed his female employees.

Since the information that Babikir passed back and forth from the Old Saudi to his boss and from Muhammad to Ahmed was mere gossip, none of the two parties was affected by it. That particular day, Sheikh Ahmed took Babikir to a beautiful restaurant, treated him to an excellent meal, and then asked him about the case of Rayhana and why Muhammad was avoiding him. Babikir was scared he might lose his job if he disclosed information his boss would not like revealed. Remembering how a small lie caused his boss to call him a *f...g N...* and kick him out of the office, Babikir decided he'd better create a full proof story half truth half lie better than the last one he told. This new invention would be an even greater creation and harder to verify; and so the story began:

Mr. Muhammad had truly processed the paperwork of the maidservant and her daughter and Babikir was a witness to Rayhana picking up the visas, passports, tickets, and money. Mr. Muhammad was supposed to meet them at the airport and see them off; however, he did not go because his girlfriend or mistress from Bangalore showed up unexpectedly and requested he meet with her which he then changed his plans about going to the airport. (Babikir told the truth up unto this point but now here is where the lies began). Muhammad sent Jamaal Khan in his place instead. (At this stage, the Sudanese boy threw in a rumor mill of saucy tidbits). Babikir told Sheikh Ahmed something was conveyed to him from his Indian girlfriend, Jamilah, of which he wasn't sure whether what he heard was true or not.

Whether fact or rumor, Babikir claimed during the processing of Rayhana's documents, she developed a strong attachment to one of the male employees in the office; a handsome boy by the name of Jamaal Khan. Jamilah, his Indian girlfriend swore by Allah that she saw the two of them sitting by the seashore hugging and kissing. The Sudanese boy did not want to tell Sheikh Ahmed he was the one who had actually witnessed Jamaal and Rayhana kissing and hugging on the beach. He did not tell him he was the one who reported these things to his girlfriend, Jamilah, and that she was the one who passed the information onto the others. Now here Babikir was going to drop a bombshell, but he decided to be careful and put it in a way that his Saudi friend would not get a heart attack and have to be rushed to the hospital. That would cause Babikir to end up having to pay the bill for the expensive meal they had just eaten together. He told Sheikh Ahmed that the girls in the office were spreading false rumors that Jamaal and Rayhana ran away together to another city. Adding another lie of his own imagination, he said Jamaal and Rayhana quite possible had gotten married and settled down somewhere in India. When Babikir finished his half-truth, half-false story, Sheikh Ahmed's heart stopped for a few seconds. He stared at Babikir as though he was seeing an apparition and his body became cold and his hands began to shake. When he tried to speak his voice failed him. He was all choked up from being half sad and half angry. His emotions betrayed him and he could not control the tears dripping down into the palm of his hands having lost another opportunity at love.

Babikir was astonished when he saw the old man weeping. He did not know how much Sheikh Ahmed really cared for Rayhana. He wondered what he should do as he felt the old man grab hold of his hand and pull him close. Then, Sheikh Ahmed said to him in a very angry voice,

"This time I have decided not to seek the help of the law to get my woman back. I know the right people who can bring Rayhana to me in less than a week. Babikir I want you to help me to find my woman. I want you to show me where I can find the Gondas."

"Gondas!" shouted Babikir while trying to free his hand from the firm grip of the old man.

"Yes Babikir," said Sheikh Ahmed, *"Only the Gondas can do this kind of work. The police are corrupt and the law is helpless. You know how I was humiliated when I lost my home and my property to Christie, the Christian woman I took as a wife. She took advantage of me when everything I had to give I gave to her gladly. What did the law do for me? While I was fighting in the court for over a year to get due process from the law, she was getting fucked day and night by that uncircumcised-infidel-dog, Bobby."*

"But Gondas are dangerous criminals. They kill people!" cried Babikir.

"They don't kill those who are paying them, do they? I am not going to ask them to kill anyone. I just want them to get my woman back to me. If they kill anyone who tries to deter them from bringing my woman to me, I don't care. I just want my Rayhana found and unharmed and safely brought to me."

Babikir Al-A'war now regretted feeding the old man lies. He wished in his heart instead of one blind eye, his tongue had been cut too. However, it was too late. He decided to try and convince Sheikh Ahmed to forget about the Gondas. No matter how much Babikir tried, he couldn't convince the angry man to leave this idea alone. Finally, he gave up and decided to help him find some Gondas to aid him in his dirty work.

Babikir happened to know some Gondas in Vakola. He had come to know about them when a Sudanese student got into some trouble with them. The Sudanese student used to tease his landlady and once he touched her body in an improper way when she came to collect the rent from him. The Indian woman got so angry that she paid some Gondas to beat him up. The Gondas approached the Sudanese student and tricked him by telling him his brother in Saudi Arabia had sent him some money and clothes.

The Sudanese student believed the Gondas and went with them where they told him someone was waiting to deliver the items to him. They lured him away from the main roads and beat him severely. They left him for dead on the side of a dusty dirty lane. A Good Samaritan who happened to pass through the lone pathway rushed the boy to the hospital. The case was reported to the police but the police did nothing about it. The problem Sudanese students encountered living in that area was that once the Gondas beat you up, you became marked as a never-ending target. Wherever you go, they would come after you until sooner or later you were dead. Some Gondas would consider all your friends and family members enemies too. They were like the Somalians in that once they began to fight with you then they would fight with you forever. The virtue of forgiveness did not exist in their hearts. So to avoid any further blood-shed, the Sudanese students decided to take the student that had been beaten up and meet with the Gondas. They apologized begging for forgiveness on their knees and paid them some ransom money to forget the whole thing. The Gondas accepted the money and the apology and the problem ended there. The beginning of a beneficial relationship between the students and the Gondas was the result. Babikir happened to be among those students who went and sought forgiveness from the Gondas. After that whenever any Sudanese student had trouble with anyone, his Sudanese friends would go to the Gondas gang of thugs and pay them a sum of money and ask them to get rid of the problem. Whether the problem had to do with the law or a woman or with the Devil himself, the Gondas was sure to settle the score.

Babikir was at a loss as to what to do when he saw the Old Saudi in tears and getting angrier by the minute. He felt obligated because his lies were the key that started the wheels in motion and now he was in the driver's seat headed down the path of no return. He would be the main operator of this dangerous vehicle once he decided to assist the revenger of broken hearts. Babikir remembered the *Vakola Gondas*. He told Sheikh Ahmed he knew some Gondas and took him to them. The Saudi man was prepared to pay the Gondas whatever they asked for if they could get him his woman back. He told them to find Muhammad Khan and hammer the shi…out of him until he paid back the money he stole. Sheikh Ahmed's rage demanded that all the employees of Muhammad Tours and Travels except Babikir be beaten at will. In order to save his ugly girlfriend from being beaten and raped by the ruthless Gondas, Babikir convinced his Saudi friend to take all the employees off the hit list except the real culprit, Jamaal Khan, who was suspected of stealing the maidservant and running away with her.

It seemed that everyone in Bombay wanted to do harm to Jamaal Khan. Before he went to jail, Muhammad hired some cold-blooded Gondas and told them to find Jamaal Khan and give him a good beating and deliver him directly to him bound hands and feet. He also sent Jamaal's photo to the most popular newspaper outlet in Bombay and requested he be publicised as a wanted thief and rapist. On the following day, everyone in Bombay cut out the article in the newspaper and carried it around with them everywhere they went hoping to find the most wanted criminal in all of India and get the reward of ten thousand rupees. Muhammad also derived a long list of crimes Jamaal was alleged to have committed and lodged a complaint with the police. This set up a citywide search and an all points bulletin by every police precinct.

Sheikh Faiz bin Ahmed through the help of his Sudanese friend approached the Vakola Gondas and paid them in advance ten thousand rupees. He promised to give them another fifteen thousand rupees after they found Jamaal and beat him up and snatched the maidservant. The relentless man told the Gondas he could care less if Jamaal got killed during the recovery process.

While the whole city of Bombay was searching for Jamaal Khan, he lie half-dead already in police custody. Ironically, it was the safest place for him for the time being. If it came to the knowledge of the Gondas he was in jail they would either use their contacts inside to kill him or send someone on the outside to murder him. Obviously, for the Gondas, the best place to catch and kill someone was in prison.

The Gondas were the most dangerous people in India. They were not just gangsters or criminals. Their membership included a combination of corrupt cops and the residue of gangs and thieves who got their start robbing passengers on trains and buses, trucks and farmland. Indira Gandhi was able to break up this crime syndicate to some extent when she called on the military to occupy the trains to protect innocent citizens. The soldiers were armed to the teeth and prepared to do battle with the highwaymen. They were decimated and those who survived the all out warfare sought refuge in the cities, becoming today's Gondas. They modified their tactics and adopted some police methods. Therefore, Gondas like the police would help get back stolen items or find people that had run away like a wife or a daughter or offer protection from someone who wanted to kill you. Even if you were indicted on serious criminal charges, the Gondas could ignite fear in the hearts of judges, lawyers and prosecutors or bribe them to get you out of jail without a conviction.

Gondas specialized in killing police. When the number of the slain police officers reached the highest on record, the government of India adopted new laws to protect police from being completely wiped out. The new law was called *encounter*. That law allowed the police to shoot and kill the Gondas whenever they met them face to face. Although, that law reduced the number of slain police officers, it created another serious problem, which resulted in the killing of many innocent citizens. The police misused the law of encounter and abused their authority. Many innocent citizens were accused falsely and killed by police as Gondas. Whenever, someone wanted to get rid of a person he could bribe the police to say they were part of Gondas and kill them in an encounter. The police would kill the person and plant a knife or gun on them or a sword or axe and falsely claim they were Gondas.

The whole city of Bombay was in search of Jamaal Khan for the bounties that had been placed on his head by Muhammad Khan and Sheikh Ahmed. Rayhana Khan too was a wanted person but her photo wasn't published in the newspaper. Wherever she was to be found, she was to be captured and taken away from her kidnapper and handed over to her ransomer and the highest bidder, Sheikh Ahmed. While the nation-wide hunt was on for the two lovers, they were dying inside a Bombay prison from the torture pangs inflicted upon them by their extortioners.

Luckily, police inspector, Shankaracharya, by chance came across the daily newspaper and was dumbfounded when he read Mr. Muhammad Khan was offering a huge reward to anyone who would direct the police to the hiding place of his employee, Jamaal Khan, who had stolen lakhs of rupees from him and raped and robbed one of his female employees, a girl by the name of Bulbolah Sheikh. This news refuted his theory of a terrorist plot and threw a wrench in what was a solved case. He was determined to get to the bottom of this quagmire before he totally discarded this terrorist strategy. Therefore, he found and interviewed the victim, Bulbolah Sheikh. If Jamaal Khan had truly raped Bulbolah and robbed her of costly jewelry, then he would not be a terrorist. If Jamaal did not rape and rob the female employee, then he was a terrorist. These were the two premises of his new theory. For him, Jamaal Khan was either a rapist or a terrorist but in no way was he an innocent person. When the long arm of the law and religious fanaticism are combined together into one mind, it became the worst of both worlds and a deadly combination.

Bulbolah Sheikh became frightened when the police approached her and asked her whether she had been raped and robbed by someone from the travel agency. The police told her they had some information regarding her rape and robbery but did not mention the name of the alleged rapist and robber. Bulbolah was afraid to talk or reveal what had happened to her because she knew that if she would say she had been raped by someone then the police would take her into custody for further questioning. She heard that any girl voicing any sort of dispute or complaint or involved in some sort of misdeed, the police would take her in for questioning and she would be raped by many cops inside the lock-up. She would also put her job in jeopardy and her family in serious trouble. Therefore, she thought the best thing to do was to leave her Allah to avenge the injustice done to her and punish her rapist. By then all the other girls in the office had heard that Bulbolah had stayed alone in the office with the boss and had sex with him. There was a strong reason to believe the incident occurred but when the police came and took Bulbolah aside and questioned her, the girls knew why their boss had gotten arrested and hauled away. They concluded Bulbolah filed a complaint with the police and accused the boss of raping her. But they were puzzled with one question; why would Bulbolah keep coming to work every day after she complained of the boss raping her and then sending him to jail?

The answer to this question was quite clear and the answer to the police inspector's questions was just as crystal clear. After Bulbolah denied the information reported in the newspapers, the inspector's assumptions of a terrorist plot solved the mystery of the fake rape and robbery. He concluded this cock-and-bull story was created by none other than the diabolical genius of a home-grown terrorist, Muhammad. When Muhammad came to know the police had foiled the terrorist plot and arrested Rayhana Khan and his employee, Jamaal Khan, he orchestrated this bogus rape and robbery story in order to refute the confessions of his accomplices to relieve himself of any involvement. As soon as the police inspector Shankaracharya connected all the dots and crossed all his t's in these carefully conceived deliberations, he decided to announce these new developments to the public and involve the media. The next day the photos of Muhammad Khan, Rayhana Khan, and Jamaal Khan were in the front page of every newspaper in Bombay city. This sensational news story included many other details connecting the suspects with other international and notorious terrorist groups such as Al-Qaeda, Lashkar-e-Taiba, the Taliban and even Pakistan's I.S.I. (Inter-Services Intelligence) was hinted at as being involved in the female suicide bomb plot that was targeting an air India flight.

Rukhsana was the one who read the morning newspaper first and showed the disturbing news to the other employees. None of the eight employees believed these trumped-up charges. All of them knew Jamaal Khan was a peace-loving and law-abiding young man.

Although he was a Muslim, he wasn't very religious. He smoked cigarettes and had a girlfriend, he hugged and kissed openly in public. In the same way, Rayhana Khan was a Muslim woman living in the slums but wasn't all that religious either. She had no problem being hugged and kissed out in public and if she had the chance she wouldn't hesitate to make out with her lover. She had never dressed up in a burqa or a hijab. You couldn't tell by the way she dressed if she was a Muslim, Hindu or Christian. She put on whatever she liked. One day she came to the travel agency in a Panjabi dress and on another day, she would be wearing a sari. Likewise, the boss made himself out to be a devout Muslim and yet he was a notorious womanizer. He harassed all his female employees in one way or another. He also had a Hindu mistress, another man's wife, with which he convoluted with her on many occasions in her room at the Oberoi hotel. He was a cheater and a thief always overcharging his customers, and he deceived his Arab clients. He was too busy cheating people to be bothered with spiritual matters and he certainly could not be bothered with religious lunatics like Lashkar-e-Taiba, Taliban and Al-Qaeda. No one could ever convince his employees that he loved his religion enough to blow up an airplane. They thought why would he want someone to blow up an airplane. He would not blow himself up even for 72 virgins in heaven when he had more virgins than he could handle right here on earth. His sex drive was greater than the fires of hell. Therefore, all eight employees concluded there had to be a gross misunderstanding or someone just wanted to pin a terrorist conspiracy on innocent Muslims.

The breaking news directed the Vakola's Gondas to the hiding place of Jamaal Khan and his girlfriend. The Gondas approached Sheikh Ahmed and pretended that they had after much searching unearthed the hiding place of the lovers. They found out from inside sources that the woman, Rayhana Khan, and her lover were being kept under police protection because of what appeared to be initially a false news report and everyone in India was seeking a reward for their capture. Since both of them were in special police custody, there was nothing they could do to get them out. They then demanded the rest of their money.

Because of his past experience, the old Saudi was clever to the wiles of crooks and knew the Gondas were trying to swindle him out of his money. He told them to get Rayhana out of the jail first and help him smuggle her to Saudi Arabia and then he would give them the rest of their money. The Gondas then confessed that the news circulating about Rayhana Khan and Jamaal Khan is that they were accused of terrorism. They said even the Prime Minister of India could not remove a person out of prison that was involved in a terrorist plot. Sheikh Ahmed was still unwilling to pay them. The Gondas then threatened to kill him instead. Following the wise advice of his Sudanese friend, Sheikh Ahmed chose to save his life and paid them the remainder of the money he had promised which was fifteen thousand rupees in cash and thus ended his dealings with them.

As soon as the Gondas left, Babikir pulled Sheikh Ahmed aside and showed him the newspaper that carried the photo of his beloved Rayhana and the article concerning her involvement in a terrorist plot. What troubled the old Saudi wasn't that his beloved was in jail undergoing unpleasant conditions but what scared the hell out of him the most was that his name was mentioned in the terrorist plot as clear as day. He was mentioned as a foreign terrorist who was a member of Al-Qaeda who supplied visas, tickets, money, and other needed materials and explosives to the female suicide bomber, Rayhana Khan. It also revealed in the article that he was the one who paid over a million rupees to the Muhammad Tours and Travels and convinced its owner and another male employee to process the travel papers of the young female suicide bomber.

When he read these details and false charges against him, Sheikh Faiz bin Ahmed wished that the earth would have opened up and swallowed him whole and then regurgitated him back in his homeland of Saudi Arabia where he would be protected by his countrymen. At that critical moment he hated Rayhana and hated the very day he met her in Colaba. He also cursed Muhammad and cursed every Muslim Indian he ever knew in his whole life. He asked Babikir, *"How could those accursed Muslim beggars and uncircumcised Hindu idolaters ever dare to involve me in such a dangerous crime?"*

After he had overcome his anger, shock and disbelief, Sheikh Ahmed began to solicit his Sudanese friend and lean upon him even more than before. He asked him how could he escape out of this dangerous trap that had been set for him by the schemes of criminals and the Indian police. Babikir told him the only way possible out of this was to approach the police and tell them that he was innocent and had nothing to do with the plot. That was the last thing the petrified old Saudi was prepared to do. He knew that to go to these corrupt lawmen and plead not guilty would be setting himself up for endless torture only to be falsely accused and hanged as a terrorist. When Babikir understood that the frightened old man wasn't willing to go to the police he advised him to make his escape out of India through the Pakistani border.

Sheikh Ahmed left the hotel without checking out and rented a car. He told Babikir that he would give him fifty thousand rupees if he would accompany him on his trip from Bombay to the Pakistani border and help him reach his destination safely. Babikir told him he could not risk going on such a dangerous trip and put himself in jeopardy unless he gave him one million rupees. *"I just can't take such a high-risk trip like that with someone like you who is wanted all over India."* This decision of Babikir terminated the beneficial friendship between the once good friends. When Babikir rejected the offer and left, Sheikh Ahmed found a Muslim Indian and bribed him. He convinced the man to help him to rent a car and be his chauffeur because he said, *"I want to tour your magnificent country of India."* He said that his final destination would be Kashmir. (Kashmir is known as Paradise on Earth but it is now the most dangerous place on earth. It is the disputed region between India and Pakistan).

Sheikh Faiz bin Ahmed's escape to Pakistan was carefully thought out but he would have been better to do as Babikir suggested and contacted the police to explain his dilemma and throw himself on the mercy of the court. Before he could make a clean getaway out of the city, it did not take long for him to be arrested by Bombay police. On the same day, he planned to flee, Bombay investigations became aware through airport authorities that he had arrived recently from the Kingdom of Saudi Arabia. A further investigation revealed that he was booked at the Taj Mahal hotel. While police inspector Shankaracharya and his men raided his room at the hotel, the Sheikh was with the Sudanese boy in a restaurant somewhere in Colaba. The police kept undercover police officers stationed at the hotel and maintained a citywide vigil for this threat to the security of India. The hotel also supplied the police with a copy of his passport, which contained his photo. The photo and the passport information were displayed throughout the city on bill boards and shown on all local TV channels. Even the radio stations announced the warrant for his arrest. The same person who leased him the car turned him into police. It did not take the police more than a couple of hours to find the rental car and Sheikh Ahmed was arrested along with his Indian driver and thrown in a prison cell, beaten up and tortured.

CHAPTER 10

THE TRIAL

To be arrested in India for whatever crime no matter whether you did it or not, whether you committed an iniquity or had broken the law, whether you were falsely accused or caught in the act, you were guilty until proven innocent. The result of the initial interrogation would be the same. Through their harsh third degree interrogation method, the police would force you to admit to the charges of which you were suspected. They would make you sign your confession and then the prosecutor would establish a case against you in court. Once again, if you paid your lawyer well he could then bribe the judge handling your case and whether you were guilty of a crime or innocent you would be acquitted. From the time you were arrested until the final adjudication of the court could take years. You would be stuck in jail for years, beaten up every so often, and ruffed up by other criminals and Gondas.

To escape imprisonment and beatings, you would need to bail yourself out and buy your freedom until trial. If you were rich enough, you could pay the huge amount of bail and save yourself a whole lot of trouble. If you were a foreigner and paid your bail, you would be forced to surrender your passport and attend every hearing required by the court. If you were Indian, you had to be present at all scheduled hearings and you could not travel out of the country. Hearings would take place every three to four months as a formality. The clerk would call out your name and when you hear your name you would just need to hold up your right hand and shout "present" or "here" and stand up for the court to see you. Then, the judge would more than likely give you a disinterested glance and announce yet another day for the next hearing. After that, you would be free to go only to present yourself in court again after other three or four months. Then you would have to do the same thing over again for the next assigned hearing date and leave again. This procedure would continue for three to five years. If you asked a lawyer or a policeman why it took so long for your case to get to trial, they would just give you a reserved smile and tell you that suspects arrested three to four years before you were still waiting for their day in court.

Rayhana, Jamaal, Muhammad and Sheikh Ahmed were all subjected to harsh interrogation methods to admit their involvement in a terrorist plot to place a female suicide bomber on an Indian airline flight on domestic soil. These confessions became facts in court. Rayhana and Jamaal were not financially able to hire lawyers to defend them in court. Nevertheless, they were more than lucky to have rich suspects accused along with them pertaining to the same case. If Sheikh Ahmed and Muhammad Khan were proven innocent, then Jamaal Khan and Rayhana Khan would automatically be acquitted. Therefore, the same lawyers who were defending the two rich suspects were also the de facto defenders for Rayhana and Jamaal.

Never before in the history of the India's justice system had a court case been brought to such a rapid conclusion as this one. The case of the female suicide bomber was tried and concluded in just a few short months. There were many reasons that led the Bombay courts to push the case to the top of the waiting list and render a judgment in six months. The first reason was that the Kingdom of Saudi Arabia exercised immense influence over the trial and there were rumors that the richest Arab country paid the Indian government off and/or threatened to kick out all India's diplomats and close down the Indian Embassy and Consulate if the case wasn't resolved in favor of the accused and soon. Rumors also had it that the Saudi government would rule to deport all the thousands of Indians who were working in Saudi Arabia. The second reason was that the lawyers of the wealthy suspects paid a considerable size of money and bribed the Judge of the High Court and the jury. In addition, the high-priced lawyers for the four suspects presented a good line of defense that no one could refute.

Rayhana Khan was a slum woman and uneducated. She could not possibly be involved in such a sophisticated plot to blow up an airplane. Moreover, she was taking her seven-year-old daughter with her on the same plane and leaving her five sons alone with her parents and in-laws who could not work or provide for them. Also, if she wanted to kill herself so she could kill others, why did she want to kill her young daughter too?

Jamaal Khan wasn't a religious boy and had never been to a mosque his whole life. He smoked daily and drank alcohol occasionally and the lawyers presented evidence obtained from the stores of non-Muslims such as Hindus and Sikhs where he often purchased cigarettes and liquor.

The lawyers also provided proof of an ongoing love affair between Jamaal and Rayhana. The lawyers provided eye-witness testimony of the lovers kissing and embracing on the beachfront, in the restaurants and movie theaters. This scandalous affair between a widowed Muslim woman and a Muslim boy strengthened the arguments that neither of the two were committed Muslims.

Muhammad Khan likewise was proven to have been engaged in an adulterous affair with his female lover. Testimony supplied by the management of the Oberoi hotel verified the illicit relationship between him and the married Hindu woman and he drank so much at times, he had to be helped back to his hotel room. He was also a chain smoker and was asked on several occasions to step outside and smoke because of the many complaints from restaurant guests. The lawyers presented thousands of unpaid bills and receipts from hundreds of hotels, restaurants, liquor stores, and nightclubs. This was strong evidence supporting the fact that he lived a wild, debauched lifestyle far from the lifestyle mandated by Islam.

Sheikh Faiz bin Ahmed was also proven to be an irreligious person and a playboy. Some of the hotel staff testified to this fact and the lawyers brought forth their testimonies in open court. All the official papers that were found with Rayhana Khan indicated that she was supposed to fly to the Kingdom of Saudi Arabia on a maidservant visa. The other three suspects verified this fact by their testimonies in court as well as employees of the passport office. Rayhana Khan's papers were processed legally and she did not obtain those papers through any illegal means. They were truly gifted to her by the wealthy business tycoon, Sheikh Ahmed.

The strongest evidence that led the court to drop the terrorist charges and acquit all the four suspects was the return of Sheikh Ahmed to India. If he was the mastermind behind a terrorist plot, financier and supplier of bomb making materials, why did he return to India after his alleged accomplices were arrested? Added to that, the Indian police could not find the explosive device that the female suspect was supposed to have used to blow up the plane.

Six months in Bombay jail was the most painful experience Rayhana had ever been through her entire life. During all the years of suffering while her husband was alive and after his death, she did not suffer as much as she suffered in jail. She was beaten, tortured, and denied basic human necessities. She was abused by the police and treated like a traitor by the female staff and other prisoners. The jailers beat her, insulted her, and sometimes spit in her face. They accused her of trying to blow up the Air India plane and kill innocent people. No one believed her when she pleaded her innocence. It was nothing short of a miracle she survived for six months in that treacherous environment among dangerous criminals and hostile tormentors.

What troubled Rayhana especially during her incarceration and made her spend sleepless nights and unbearable days was worrying about her children and her elderly parents. How were they going to survive without someone to help care for them? Who was going to be the breadwinner and where would they get food to eat? She had left what little money she had with her parents and she was planning on the day she got arrested to give them whatever money she had. Unfortunately, the police helped themselves to the money she received from her benefactor. She thought there was just a little misunderstanding and that she would be allowed to go home as soon as that little misunderstanding was cleared up. She never expected that she was going to be jailed for such a long period of time. Moreover, what disturbed her conscience most of all was the fear that her little daughter might be raped at night by some of those lawless slum boys. She knew her elders would not be able to stop those boys if they broke in at night and attempted to rape her little daughter. She also knew that her slum neighbors would not come to the rescue of her precious child if she screamed for help. The slum dwellers were scared to death of Gondas. None of them would put their life at risk by coming between the Gondas and their intended victims.

After her release, Rayhana went directly to her slum. She found some of her little children had become beggars. Three of her relatives had died. She lost her father, father-in-law, and mother-in-law. Only her old mother was still alive. Her mother told her that she was the one who sent her sons to the streets to beg in order to feed the family. The mother refused to allow Rayhana's daughter to go to the streets for the fear of being raped at that young age by good-for-nothing men. (On the day of their arrest, the police returned the daughter to her slum as soon as she was questioned and told them she was going with her mother on a trip to help her work in some people's houses and pick up some money on the street).

Rayhana wept day and night for her family while she was in jail. She had no one to send them any messages to tell them what was going on. She learned from her tormentors that Jamaal Khan had been arrested too on the same day she was apprehended. Before her arrest, Rayhana was a simple-minded person with a pure heart. She hated no one. More than her unjust arrest and the terrible cruelty she underwent, she began to hate with every bone in her body those responsible for the injustice that had been done to her and her dear ones. She wept bitterly thinking about the suffering and hardship her children and elders were having to endure without her. She wept twice as much when she learned the person who gave her the happiest days of her life was also accused falsely and thrown inside a filthy jail and knew he was being tortured just as much as she was.

Rayhana never forgot her trip to Saudi Arabia. After her release, she took her mother, went back to the police station, and requested the return of her visas, tickets, passports, and money. The police inspector who had arrested her became belligerent and shouted he was going to arrest her and her mother if she didn't leave and it would be better for her for him never to see her face again. Rayhana no longer had an attorney to represent her or make a formal complaint to get back what was rightfully hers. There was no one to fight for her rights against an unlawful and unforgiving system of wickedness. When the unscrupulous man of the law didn't return her travel papers, she concluded that her chance to go to the rich country of the Arabs had gone forever. Being left with no hope, Rayhana returned to the rich people's homes and began to work for them again slaving for hours. Some of the families refused to give her work again because of her involvement in an alleged terrorist plot.

During her long hours of working Rayhana always remembered her lover, Jamaal. She wondered whether he would be willing to accept her again after all the trouble he had endured because of her. She thought his only sin was loving her and because of this he was arrested and jailed for helping her in her desire for a better life. She also did not expect the travel agency that had prepared her paperwork to ever be interested in helping her again. The old rich Saudi who so freely gave her the visas and tickets to paradise would not be interested in having her as a maidservant any longer. She believed she had caused so much trouble for him he would not ever wish to see India again or the ground she walked on. She saw him whenever there was a hearing in court along with the other two Indian suspects.

Many weeks passed after Rayhana Khan was released from jail and allowed to return to her slum. Every day she got up at five o'clock in the morning, went to work in the homes of the rich and she did not return to her slum until nine o'clock in the evening. She had stopped her children from going to the local train stations and begging. Her daughter Iffat once again became the babysitter of her little brothers, cooked their food, and washed their rags. That same old sad cycle of her former life was repeating itself day in and day out.

One day Rayhana returned at nine o'clock in the evening and found a visitor waiting for her inside her slum. He was the last person on earth she thought she would ever see again. She did not know his name. She did not know how to speak his language and she had no idea what language he was speaking. It was the Sudanese boy, Babikir Al-A'war. How did he know where she lived? How did he in his tall height and stature manage to walk through those narrow lanes and ghastly slums? Rayhana was afraid to shake his hand when he offered his hand to her. She kept her distance away from him and continued to stare at him. She did not expect him to speak her language either. However, her curiosity was tripled when she heard him speaking to her in broken Hindi. With much difficulty, she grasped some of what he was saying. She could understand the words visas, tickets, and Saudi Arabia. She even heard him mention the word passport. Nonetheless, Rayhana didn't trust him thinking he was trying to get her alone and rape her. The color of his skin and African features made her distrust him all the more.

Babikir repeated each sentence he spoke ten times before Rayhana could understand what he was saying. What she understood was that Babikir wanted to give her the same papers she used to have and help her go to Saudi Arabia. Although she was afraid of him, she realized he was the only person who had come to look for her and offer her help. Neither her lover Jamaal Khan nor the owner of the travel agency had come to look for her and offer her another chance at anything. She was afraid to be alone with this man she barely knew but after much hesitation Rayhana agreed to meet the Sudanese boy on the following day at the bus stop that was not far from her slum. Babikir told her to meet him at ten o'clock in the morning and not to bring anyone with her. Rayhana refused and told him she could not come alone and insisted she had to bring her little daughter with her. Babikir unwillingly accepted her condition and left.

That particular night everybody in the tight-knit slum community manufactured up their usual run of back alley gossip. The black Negro boy came to ask Rayhana for sex. With the help of the Muslim and Most Holy Woman of Allah, everyone's opinion of Rayhana evolved around her having sex on the street like dogs. Now this Black African man showing up at her slum confirmed their opinions once again. (Many Indians think Africans are very dangerous men and are notorious sex fiends. Therefore, any Indian girl seen walking with a Black man in India is considered a prostitute). Well, let us not dwell for now in trying to analyze and refute these erroneous and racially biased preconceptions but let us continue with the plans of Rayhana and Babikir to meet the next day.

When Rayhana met Babikir, he took her to a restaurant and talked with her for a long time being repetitive in his long rehearsed Hindi. With quite some difficulty he tried to communicate to her that the same old Saudi who had provided her before with tickets and visas to Saudi Arabia was still interested in giving her work as a maidservant in his country. Babikir told her that the old Saudi wanted to know whether she was still interested in coming to his country. Before answering, Rayhana asked Babikir to tell her where the old man was. Babikir told her the old Saudi after his release had returned to his country. However, a week ago he phoned him in his hostel and requested he find her and tell her his offer still stands and the job was still hers if she wanted it. Babikir told Rayhana it took him a full week to find her slum. Rayhana then gladly accepted the offer on the same condition she had made previously that she would need her daughter to come with her also to Saudi Arabia. Babikir promised he would advise her sponsor about her condition.

That day the kind Sudanese boy did not allow the poor slum woman and her daughter to go until they agreed to have a meal with him at the restaurant. Then, he asked Rayhana to meet him again in a week at the same restaurant at the same time. He said he was going to contact her benefactor and inform him about her consent and condition and at the end of one week, he would let her know his reply.

Before we go any further, two important things need to be mentioned right away. Babikir was kicked out of the travel agency by Muhammad Khan wife who took over the business while her husband was in jail. It was her husband who asked her to fire Babikir. What is more, the number of the employees was reduced to five. Muhammad wife also fired two girls without giving them any reason for their being fired. The other employees could plainly see why his wife fired Bulbolah Sheikh and Tabasum Sirajudeen. They were very beautiful and stiff competition for her husband's sexual pleasures. Although, Mrs. Khan pretended to run the office and be the boss, the main person running the business was Rukhsana Rehman. After his release from jail, Jamaal Khan wanted to return to his work at Muhammad Tours and Travels but under order of Muhammad Khan, his wife refused to hire him again. He was fired and was not entitled to receive any severance pay or benefits.

Next, we need to mention quickly; after the trial was over Sheikh Faiz bin Ahmed returned to his country and swore by his Allah that his feet would never again touch the soil of the land of the accursed Hindu idolaters. He began to hate Hindus with a passion because the police inspector who tortured him during his interrogation was a Hindu. He recognized his religious affiliation by his sir name, *Shankaracharya.* He knew that *Shankar* was one of the Hindu gods. Although he hated Hindus, Hindustan, and all Indians, Sheikh Ahmed never forget about Rayhana and he was determined to get her by all means even if it cost him his life. He had no one to trust in India expect his old friend, Babikir Al-A'war. After he came out of the hospital, he phoned his friend and apologized to him for the misunderstanding that terminated their long friendship. (By the way, as soon as he returned to his homeland, Sheikh Ahmed went directly to the hospital. He was exhausted from the long trial and was being treated off and on from the brutal treatment he received in jail and hundreds of ailments and infections he contracted while there).

Babikir suffered a lot after he was fired from his job. His struggles started all over again and he was having a very difficult time. Again, he was dependant upon his Sudanese friends to help him out and they were not happy about his never-ending penniless condition. After his ever mercurial friend called him and apologized for all the misunderstandings, some hope shone in his life once more. Sheikh Ahmed promised to send to him some money on a regular basis if he managed to find Rayhana and get her papers processed over again so she could come work for him. The Old Saudi swore by Allah he would send him fifteen thousand rupees to start. He said to Babikir, the much needed Indian maidservant was worth the money and expense and he requested her services as quickly as possible. He would take care of everything and all the costs of reprocessing of her papers and documents. This time he said to Babikir, he did not want any "filthy" Indian to process her papers. He specifically mentioned them each by their names, namely; Muhammad Khan and Jamaal Khan. He told Babikir neither of them should know of these new arrangements for Rayhana to fly to the Kingdom of Tartarus.

After some days had passed, Babikir was able to locate Rayhana Khan and he called Sheikh Ahmed and presented him with the good news. To be extolled for his efforts and make Sheikh Ahmed feel overly indebted to him, Bakikir recounted for him all the trouble he went through to locate his maidservant. He mentioned how he had to use Gondas to help him in locating her slum. As a matter of fact, Babikir would never have found Rayhana Khan if he did not get the assistance of an Indian because of his poor Hindi language skills and his ethnicity. He sought the help of a lawman to locate the slum of Rayhana. He bribed a Muslim police constable and asked him to direct him to the place of the Muslim woman who was falsely accused of the recent terrorist plot. His angle was that he was a foreign reporter from a Muslim country and wanted to conduct an interview for a cover story in a news article. He said further to receive sympathy from the Muslim constable that the mission of the article was to show to the outside world how infidels in the idolatrous Hindu nation of India wrongly accused an innocent peace-loving and law-abiding poor Muslim woman.

The Muslim constable being moved by his love of Allah's chosen people believed Babikir and promised to help him in finding Rayhana Khan. After one week of searching, the constable found out where Rayhana was living and took Babikir to her slum. Babikir thanked him, gave him some money, and asked him to leave. The reason being, he did not want Rayhana and her family to see him coming to their slum with a policeman. Sheikh Ahmed praised Babikir over and over that he almost started crying. He then told him he would be sending the work visa and ticket for Rayhana. Babikir mentioned the condition of Rayhana before she would travel to work as his maidservant. The Old Saudi immediately agreed and said, *"Bringing her daughter with her will be an additional blessing from Allah."* Babikir did not suspect any ulterior motives on the part of his Saudi friend when in his dirty mind he praised his Allah for the daughter that would become heaven for him and hell for her.

CHAPTER 11

IN SEARCH FOR THE LOVER

Through the Western Union establishment, Sheikh Ahmed sent fifteen thousand rupees to Babikir and asked him to give ten thousand to Rayhana and keep the rest of the money for himself for his trouble in finding her. After one week, Babikir met Rayhana again in the same restaurant in which they sat and talked before. He informed her that her Saudi sponsor agreed to send her a new work visa and tickets for her and her daughter. He also told her that her sponsor had sent money so that she could use it to get new passports. He explained to her that Sheikh Ahmed informed him that Rayhana's previous passport was stolen by the police at the time of her arrest and was sold to another Indian woman. That woman came to Jeddah and claimed to be Rayhana Khan. She was arrested by Jeddah police and confessed how she came to be in possession of Rayhana's passport, work visa and ticket. The passport was rendered as an invalid document because of forgery. For this reason, Rayhana needed to get her passport reissued in the correct identity. Regarding her daughter's passport, Babikir advised Rayhana not to go to the police to try to retrieve her daughter's passport because the police might either arrest her again or try to blackmail her.

After that, Babikir took the ten thousand rupees out of his pocket and gave her the money. Rayhana had never seen such a large sum of money before. The highest amount of money she ever had saved her whole life amounted to about four hundred rupees. Therefore, she was simply flabbergasted and elated at the same time! She thanked Babikir more than she thanked her Saudi sponsor as if Babikir was the one who personally supplied her this huge sum of cash. She told him she needed someone to go with her to Worli passport office. Before Babikir could respond, she said she would go to the travel agency and ask Jamaal Khan to take her to the passport office.

"Never make that mistake again," shouted Babikir, *"Your sponsor told me to tell you not to go to Muhammad Tours and Travels ever again. Besides, Jamaal Khan no longer works for them. He was fired by Muhammad wife. As for me, I too, no longer work there."*

Rayhana felt very grieved in her heart when she was told her lover no longer worked at the travel agency. Babikir further stated to her that her sponsor requested he help her take care of all the necessary paperwork and this entire responsibility was now in his hands. Therefore, he asked her to meet him the following day at the same restaurant so that he could take her to the passport office. Rayhana wasn't happy about the new arrangement, however, she had no choice in the matter and hence she agreed to meet her new assistant. The Sudanese boy once again insisted that the Indian slum woman share a meal with him before she left. He also ordered some takeout sandwiches and told her to take them to her daughter and sons. Babikir learned about Rayhana's other children from his surprise visit to her small slum.

Before she returned to her slum, Rayhana went to a small market and bought clothes, cookies and candies for her children. She also bought some clothes for her mother. It was for the first time in her life that she was able to buy new clothes for her family. Before, she used to bring her children hand-me-down clothing from whatever her employers no longer wanted. Many times the clothing would either be too large or too small for her children but poor can't be choosy. Nevertheless, on this day, thanks to her sponsor, she picked the exact size for each of her sons. She bought a couple of lovely dresses for her daughter too. Because of the hefty endowment she received through Babikir, she went and phoned her employers and asked for an indefinite leave of absence. Some of her employers threatened to fire her if she did not show up for work. She did not care and hung up on them. She returned to her slum and fed her children with the sandwiches that Babikir had bought for them. Then, she showed them the beautiful new dresses she had purchased for them. Finally, she opened the boxes of candies and cookies and her children jumped for joy and said, *"Mommy, you're the best mommy in the whole world!"* While her children were still consuming their sweets, Rayhana lied to her mother and daughter and told them that she was going back to work. She did not tell her mother or daughter about the money she received from her sponsor. She just took off and promised to return late evening.

Rayhana longed to reconnect with her lover and enjoy the same wonderful times they had spent together in downtown Bombay. She did not believe Jamaal had been fired from his workplace and decided to find out for herself. She was longing for those endearing hugs and affectionate kisses. For all that she endured over the last seven months, what she suffered even more was the loss of her lover. She recognized he had suffered so much because of her and she wanted to apologize for his suffering a crime he didn't commit. This time was different and she would show her love by letting her money speak for itself.

When Rayhana reached Colaba it was 3:15 p.m. She had no watch. She asked someone for the time. She remembered Jamaal telling her he got off from work at 5 p.m. By her calculations, she had about an hour and forty-five minutes to wait for him to appear. After that, she would be able to catch sight of her lover walking out of his office and heading home. She wanted to surprise him. Rayhana thought the Negro boy had lied to her on purpose. She suspected the old Saudi learned of her affair with Jamaal and wanted to separate them. Somehow, it never occurred to ask herself why the Negro boy did not want her to meet Jamaal or why the old Saudi wanted to separate them.

Rayhana waited eagerly across the street, behind the shadow of a Neem tree (Azadirachta or Margosa tree). She did not want anyone from the office to see her. She was planning to follow her lover until there was a fair distance between them and the office before she approached him. The minutes felt like hours and her heart became anxious for him so much so that she started to walk back and forth across the street, pausing every so often to glance at the door to the office. Every time she looked, she saw the peon sitting on a wooden stool with a blank stare looking at the people and cars passing by. His head swayed back and forth in semi circles. Rayhana was tempted to go and ask him to go inside and ask for Jamaal to come out but she had a nagging feeling that this might jeopardize his situation with his boss.

At long last Rayhana saw the employees of the travel agency begin to file out one after the other. She recognized most of them except for two new girls. She did not see Jamaal among the employees, and the one man who appeared at the doorway was someone else. Rayhana's heart began to beat when she saw the girls and the one boy come out of the office and quickly merge into the busy rush hour crowd. She waited for her Jamaal to come out but he never did. After a few minutes, she saw the owner of the travel agency come out. He stood and talked to his peon before he walked away. Rayhana was very much disheartened and her heart began to beat inside her so much she thought it would surely jump out of her chest. At this moment in time, she could feel she lost her love forever. This was the only place she knew to look for him and that was at his workplace. When they met over seven months ago, he had told her to send him letters to his work address. He had never taken her to his chawl.

Rayhana's tears fell like the floodgates of heaven when she realized she had lost her love forever. She had no other means of contacting him. While her tears flowed like a river down her cheeks, an idea flashed into her mind. She left the shadow of the Neem tree and crossed the street and went directly up to the peon. He had just finished closing all doors and was about to leave. She approached him and asked him about the young man that used to work there by the name of Jamaal Khan. The peon recognized her from many months ago and from the trial. He answered in wry, *"He is not working here anymore."*

Rayhana asked him to tell her the name and address of his new work place. The peon looked at her and said angrily, *"How do I know where his new work place is?"*

Rayhana: *"When did Jamaal stop coming to work?"*

Peon: *"He stopped coming when he got fired."*

Rayhana: *"Why did he get fired?"*

Peon: *"I heard the girls saying he was fired because he went to jail."*

Rayhana got angry and said to the peon, *"Even the boss went to jail for the same reason."*

The peon looked at Rayhana for some time before he turned and walked away. Standing there alone Rayhana felt as if she was cast onto a deserted island to live the rest of her life all alone. She knew no one else was going to fill the aching hole in her heart the way Jamaal had. She had missed his love so much during the time of her incarceration. When she was acquitted of all charges and set free from her imprisonment, the needs of her children was what held her distracted from her own immediate desires. Inside, she was always waiting for the day she could reunite with him and resume what a love interrupted. She now had enough money to care for some of the needs of her family so she worried a little less. Now, love set aside came knocking on the door of her heart and she could not ignore the urge to open the door and welcome it with all her very being. But her lover wasn't there and she had no way of finding where he was, where he was living or where he was working. How could she find one single person among nineteen million others?

Rayhana's feet felt like the concrete she was walking on and she strolled aimlessly as her tears obscured her vision. She stumbled and bumped into a few people and they told her to watch out where she was going. She almost fell off the pavement when a woman caught her just in time by the shoulders and stopped her from falling off the curb. The woman asked if she was alright and told her to try and be careful where she was walking. If she had fallen, she would have been trampled by thousands of people leaving their work who were rushing to catch the local train to return to their homes. It took Rayhana two hours to return to her neighborhood of slums. Her heart was heavy with sadness feeling she had lost the love of her life. In a few weeks after her papers were reissued, she was going to fly to the rich country of the Arabs and with her work visa, she would be gone for two long years. That night, Rayhana could not sleep and remained awake all night mourning the loss of her lover.

The following day, early in the morning Rayhana forced her body out of bed and got dressed. She went to the restaurant where the Negro boy asked her to meet him. When Babikir saw her coming towards him, he thought that she had lost one of her children and had been crying throughout the night. Something drastic seemed to happened overnight. She was no longer smiling as the day before and she was not the same simple, innocent, and beautiful woman he had come to know. She looked very sad or deeply ill as if she was going to die anytime. Babikir welcomed her and tried to find out what had happened but she remained quiet. She was not in the mood to talk about anything. Babikir decided not to press her further for fear she might burst out in tears any moment. He just asked her to come with him to the passport office. She stood up and followed him silently as though he was leading her to a funeral procession.

At the passport office, Babikir claimed that Rayhana was one of his clients and he wanted to get her passport reissued. He knew all about the procedures from his previous employment working in a travel agency. Before they reached the passport office, he convinced Rayhana to say that her passport and her daughter's passport were stolen while they were on their way to the airport. Usually, when someone claimed that their passports had been stolen, they had to bring a letter from the police showing that they filed a complaint. However, this procedure was not required for Rayhana and her daughter because Babikir inserted in each application five hundred rupees. In this special instance, the legal requirement was waived. The person who accepted the application looked at Rayhana in a familiar way but could not place her face from all the hundreds of applicants they see every day. They were told it would take three months to process the applications. Those three months were reduced to three weeks when Babikir took out of his pocket a couple thousand rupees and slipped them beneath the two applications. After that, he tried to reduce the time to a week but the clerk said that wasn't possible. The Old Saudi told the Sudanese boy whatever amount he would spend on the paperwork of his maidservant and her daughter he would reimburse him.

Babikir and Rayhana were about to leave the office but the passport clerk asked Rayhana, *"Have you changed your address or is it the same as before*?"

Rayhana looked at the Sudanese boy and said, *"I have no address."*

The clerk raised a brow with a serious look and asked, "*How did you get a passport without an address?"*

Rayhana answered, *"I live in a slum. We don't have addresses in the slums."*

The clerk replied, *"Then, how did you get a passport before? No passport can be issued without an address."*

Babikir tried to stop any further inquiry about her address. He was afraid Rayhana and her daughter might not get their passports reissued if they could not show how she obtained the passports in the first place. He knew Sheikh Ahmed might kill him if his maidservant was prevented from coming to him for something so small as an address. Therefore, he said softly,

"Sir, last time most likely her passports were issued listing the address of the travel agency. Can you check her previous applications?"

It took the passport officer twenty minutes to find the old applications of Rayhana and her daughter. Then, he came and shouted at Rayhana,

"Why did you say you didn't have an address? Here is the address you wrote last time. It is an address in Andheri Lokhandwalla Chawls."

When he mentioned this address, Rayhana lit up like a Christmas tree. Suddenly a switch ignited a fire in her dying heart, the light of love illuminated her eyes, and she became the way she once was. Her wounded heart was now joyful at the possibility that she had found her lost love. Allah was opening doors for her where once they had been closed. She shouted joyfully,

"Oh my, I forgot that I gave the address of my uncle who lives in Andheri."

The clerk said, *"Then this is your address?"*

Rayhana: *"Yes sir, it is my permanent address."*

Before, the passport officer asked her anything further and spoil the happiness within her, Rayhana requested he write down the address of her uncle, [*Jamaal Khan*] on a piece of paper so that she could tell him when to expect her two passports from the Passport Office. The passport officer jotted down the address of her lover and gave it to her. If it wasn't for the people standing all around her, Rayhana would have kissed the paper and held it dearly against her bosom before she hid it just inside her bra. She had no handbag or purse and kept her valuables in her bra. She could not hide her happiness and flashed the Sudanese boy a gigantic smile and a wink with her beautiful dark eyes. She also bit her lower lip and released it slowly. Babikir was caught off guard and extremely surprised by her sudden change in mood and her flirtatious gestures. He thought all of a sudden Rayhana had fallen in love with him and realized just how much she really needed him. Finally, she was appreciating him for the man that he was and was expressing her strong emotional awakening towards him with her beautiful eyes and sexy lips.

They then walked outside the passport office where the two were supposed to say goodbye to each other but first discuss what day they were to meet again after three weeks had passed and after the two passports had arrived in the mail. However, Rayhana just walked away almost flying on air without thanking Babikir or saying goodbye to him. Babikir was annoyed by her rude behavior towards him and lack of manners. He immediately jumped to the conclusion she was prejudice against him because of the color of his skin and he felt very angry after all he had done to help her even bribing the clerk with his own share of money he received from Sheikh Ahmed. His dignity was dashed to pieces and his injured pride impelled him to stop her before she proceeded any further.

"Why are you running off like this without even saying thank you or good bye to me? Do you think I am your servant that I have to do your work whether I like it or not?"

"I am so sorry dear brother. I did not mean to hurt your feelings but I am in a great hurry to get back to the children. I am very sorry

that I walked away without thanking you or saying good bye to you. Please forgive me brother. I am so very thankful to you for all you have done to help me. You are a very good boy. Lakh lakh shukria."

"Well, that is okay. Anyway, we must meet again to do your booking for the flight to Saudi Arabia. I can book your flight before you get your passports. If you want me to do that, I need to see you in a couple of days. Will you be able to meet me two days after today in the same restaurant and at the same time?"

"Yes of course I can. I will meet you there after two days."

Rayhana waited for Babikir to speak further but when she saw him turn his face in the opposite direction and began to walk away, she felt free to find the love she was missing. She would not stop him even if he wanted to kiss her in a crowded place. She believed she belonged to him and he had the right to do whatever he wanted with her. With a joyful heart and great expectations, Rayhana flew to Andheri and ended up at the Lokhandwalla Chawls area where the street of her lover was listed on her paper.

Lokhandwalla Complex was the most beautiful and the most expensive shopping center in Bombay. Only Bollywood film stars and very wealthy Indians could afford to shop there. Nonetheless, chawls and slums in every place surrounded the grand metropolis except the downtown area. Jamaal Khan's address indicated that his small chawl was buried somewhere behind those beautiful buildings of the Lokhandwalla Complex. Rayhana asked many people for directions to the place on her piece of paper as she made her way through the crowded chawls. Finally, her legs took her to the chawl of her lover. It took her one and a half hours traveling by bus, local train, and rickshaw until she reached the chawl of her lover. Before she received the ten thousand rupees from her sponsor, Rayhana very rarely sat in a rickshaw. A rickshaw was something between a taxi and an animal transport. There were two kinds of rickshaws in India; a motor-rickshaw and a cycle-rickshaw. A motor rickshaw was a motorbike converted into a small taxi. A cycle-rickshaw is a tricycle or bicycle configured and used for transportation. In China, there was something worse than that which was called a human-rickshaw. It was a human reduced to an animal and used by rich people to carry them around from one place to another; a form of abuse and slavery

The cheerful Rayhana was excited and overjoyed despite her tiredness and fatigue. Her long sleek legs finally reached the doorsteps of her lover. Jamaal had already informed her that he had three sisters and six brothers besides his sick mother. Rayhana expected that one of his three sisters or six brothers would open the door and greet her and she would ask them to call her lover. She knocked on the chawl door and waited. While she was waiting she was surrounded by six stray dogs and fifteen children. The children were very dirty and smelled of urine, waste, and smelled worst than the animals surrounding her in their filthy rags and emaciated bodies. They looked as if they had been playing in dried up mud and swimming in the gutter, then let out to roam the streets. It was a wonder they were still alive or not deathly sick. Rayhana heard the door of the chawl slowly open. A woman stood in the doorway. She did not look sick. She was short and behind her stood a man who was a little taller than her. The woman stretched out her right hand and shook it three or four times, a sign understood in India as *"What do you want?"* The woman's mouth was full of Indian *paan*. Her mouth was so full of stuff she could not talk. Rayhana asked politely, *"I am looking for Jamaal."* The woman spit out the *paan* in her mouth, which looked like vomit or a soiled diaper. Some of it landed on Rayhana's shoe, which made her shoe red with spit. One famous Egyptian journalist visited India and when he saw how the Indians were chewing and spitting Indian Paan everywhere without caring about where it landed he described them as, *"The people who menstruate through their mouths."*

"Who is Jamaal?" shouted the woman after she was able to open her mouth and talk.

"My friend Jamaal Khan gave me this address and told me to come and meet his sisters and his mother."

"There is no one by the name of Jamaal Khan that lives here in this chawl. We are Hindus and there are no Muslims living here", said the woman. However, the man behind her came out and said to Rayhana,

"Do you mean the Muslim family that used to live here?"

Before, Rayhana responded to his question he continued,

"The Khan Family sold to us their chawl last year and moved to some slum area. We don't know their new place."

Rayhana listened intently as those words launched forth out of his mouth as if they were sharp poisonous arrows shot right through her heart. Each word one after the other struck and pierced deep within and clung to the very bottom of her liver and kidneys. Tears came to her eyes and she wanted to cry and scream at him but somehow she concealed her pain and restrained herself out in public. She lowered her face to hide her tears and turned her head and walked away followed by stray dogs and children…

CHAPTER 12

THE TRAGEDY OF JAMAAL'S FAMILY

None of the four Muslims detained in the pseudo terrorist plot paid more dearly or had their lives devastated more than Jamaal Khan. His mother was in a government hospital dying of cancer when he was arrested. She was in the last stages when her son wound up in prison charged with terrorism. Five days later, she breathed her last breath. Jamaal had nine siblings. All his siblings were younger than he was. His father died a few years ago and he was the only breadwinner. His three sisters used to work in rich people's houses but when they reached the age of puberty their mother stopped them from working.

Jamaal Khan was the first-born followed by his three sisters and then his six brothers. Poor people in India did not use condoms or any type of birth control. What added to the population explosion in India is the majority of destitute Indians had nothing else to do for enjoyment or pleasure except having sex. Indira Gandhi's son, "Sanjay Gandhi came up with a plan to stem the rapid population growth. He promised to pay a few thousand rupees to any Indian male who would agree to receive an injection to have himself permanently sterilized. His plan however was misused by government officials and police officers forcibly performing vasectomies in order to meet quotas and in some cases, sterilizing women as well. Officially, men with two children or more had to submit to sterilization, but many young unmarried men, political opponents, the ignorant, and poor men were also believed to have been sterilized. Therefore, the program was stopped because of its many abuses, total failure and lack of accountability from its erroneous administration by officials" (Wikipedia).

After Jamaal Khan was arrested, his three sisters were forced to go work in the rich people's houses to help provide for their younger brothers. They were young themselves being thirteen, fourteen, and fifteen years old. The fourteen-year-old sister was impregnated by someone in one of the houses she worked in. It was illegal in India to impregnate a female at that age but Jamaal's sisters were ignorant of their rights. The thirteen-year-old sister fell in love with a teenager boy living near her chawl and she too got pregnant by him. When the fifteen years old sister discovered that her two sisters were pregnant, she beat them up and scolded them severely until the two sisters ran away. What made them run away was that the fifteen-year-old sister threatened that she was going to go to Jamaal in prison and inform him about their pregnancies.

India like any other third world country, honor-killing was a common practice especially among Muslim families. The two small sisters expected that their brother would either manage to get out of jail and kill them for the sake of the family's honor or send someone to kill them. The sisters knew their names and their reputations among their chawl neighbors would be ruined. No one was going to respect them anymore and no family would allow their son to marry a girl who had gotten pregnant outside of marriage. They also realized they were now considered whores and that other boys would hunt them down and force them to have sex whenever they ventured out in public.

After they ran away, the two sisters went to Grand Road and joined the thousands of other prostitutes on Farris Road. The fifteen-year-old sister did not know what to do after her sisters ran away. She went to her brother in jail and informed him what had happened to their sisters. Jamaal wept bitterly when he learned about his two younger sisters becoming pregnant and running away. He blamed his sister for beating them up and scaring them off. He blamed her for allowing them to go and work in people's houses. In order to avoid any further disaster to the family, Jamaal told his fifteen-year-old sister to stop going to the rich people's houses. The sister told Jamaal that they would starve to death if she stopped working. They had no money after he went to jail. Jamaal was the only wage earner and provider for his family. This is why he had to wait before he could marry Rayhana and be with her. He sacrificed his love and did not present an obstacle for her going to Saudi Arabia so she could also provide for her own family. After she returned at the expiration of her two-year work visa, he would marry her and perhaps join her in Saudi Arabia.

Jamaal was aware of the problems that were going to face his family from the day he was arrested and thrown behind bars, but he could do nothing. He placed his trust in Allah to work a miracle and provide for his family while he was away. Yet, there was no savior, only catastrophe and devastation. His two sisters had run away being victims of an immoral world and a wicked society. He felt he had to do something even though he was locked behind concrete walls and steel bars. He told his fifteen-year-old sister to contact his workplace and ask for a loan. His sister phoned the travel agency and talked to Mrs. Muhammad Khan who was now in charge of the business after her husband was also arrested and taken into custody. Mrs. Muhammad refused to extend any credit to the poor family of her husband's former employee. She told Jamaal's sister that business had fallen off and the office had a huge loan to pay off. Then, Jamaal told his sister to talk to the employees of the travel agency and ask them for a donation or a soft loan until he was released from jail. None of the employees was willing to donate or loan any money to Jamaal's family. Finally, when there were no other options available and everywhere they turned doors were shut in their faces, Jamaal gave his sister permission to sell their chawl and move to a slum area and buy a small slum.

Still being a minor the fifteen-year-old sister sold the chawl but was seriously cheated by the woman who bought the house. The buyer of their chawl was a Hindu woman. She paid ten times less than what she promised to pay. She cheated Jamaal's sister and made her sign papers written in English. The fifteen-year-old girl understood nothing of what she signed. When she discovered that, the Hindu woman had cheated her she was scared to go to the police and complain for fear of being raped by the cops. She knew that at her young age the policemen would take advantage of her and possibly rape her. Therefore, she accepted the little amount that the buyer gave her and moved with her six little brothers to a very small slum.

In the over-crowded slum, all the males harassed Jamal's young sister. She lived behind the shadow of her two pregnant sisters who ran away and became prostitutes on Farris Road. The uncultured, backward males and slum people hovered over her day and night like evil spirits dwelling in a haunted house. Every man wanted to have sex with her. She would quarrel with them and scream for help whenever some boys came and tried to break in her slum and rape her at night.

Jamaal's sister followed the advice of her brother and stopped going to the rich people's houses. The little money that remained after she bought the slum did not last more than a couple of months. When the family ran out of food, she was forced to send her little brothers to the streets to beg. She managed to get a small job for one of her brothers. It was an unpaid job. He was working in a small coffee shop and the shopkeeper gave him only food to eat for cleaning the shop. He refused to give him money. One of the five small brothers who were begging on the streets got hit by a car and died. It was a hit and run accident and no one was able to get the license plate number of the car. The brother who was working in the coffee shop disappeared one day. No one knew whether he was kidnapped by Gondas or joined them willingly.

Jamaal's sister was afraid to go out looking for her brother to see what had happened to him. She was scared to go to the police too. She went to her brother in prison and told him what had happened to their two small brothers. Jamaal wept bitterly and began to bang his head on the wall of the visiting room until blood ran down and covered his face. His sister began to cry and begged and begged him to stop hurting himself. When Jamaal continued to hit his head on the concrete wall two jailers came and dragged him away by force. Another jailer shouted at the sister and chased her away. From that day on, the sister stopped visiting her brother in jail.

When Jamaal came out of jail after six months he found his family was in deplorable condition and totally ruined. Some of his brothers were begging on the streets and two of his sisters had run away from home and had become prostitutes. Two of his brothers ran away and joined the Gondas and his mother died of cancer. One of his brothers was killed in hit and run car accident. Whatever had happened to his family he knew he couldn't change it. He just wanted to take care of his sister and remaining brothers. He went back to his workplace but Muhammad Khan refused to see him and ordered the peon to throw him out if he didn't leave immediately. Jamaal tried to talk to Muhammad again by going to his house and begging him for his job back in front of his wife and sons and daughters. The begrudging boss reminded Jamaal of his affair with the Muslim woman, Rayhana Khan. He said to him,

"You took advantage of the trust I had put in you and had an affair with the maidservant of one of my Arab clients. You stabbed me in the back and made my business client, Sheikh Ahmed, insult and humiliate me in front of my employees. What if you had gotten that woman pregnant and we had sent her pregnant to her sponsor?"

Then, Muhammad reminded Jamaal that when he applied for work with him he signed a contract for employment that specified he would adhere to certain standards and principles. According to those stipulations, no employee was allowed to have an interoffice romance or intimate relations with another employee. No employee was allowed to take advantage of his position and have an affair or inappropriate relationship with a client or customer. Muhammad said to Jamaal by having an affair with the maidservant of his most important Arab client, the business had suffered major losses. Muhammad Tours and Travels had received much bad publicity from his trial and arrest and he suffered the mistrust of the air industry to do business with his office anymore. He claimed that because of his indiscretion, the wealthy Saudi, Sheikh Faiz bin Ahmed, had broken his partnership with Muhammad Tours and Travels. After lecturing him for a long time, Muhammad threw Jamaal out of his house.

Nevertheless, Jamaal Khan did not give up and kept phoning Muhammad wife and begging her to convince her husband to take him back. Jamaal told the wife what had happened to his family while he was in prison. Although, she was a hardhearted woman and no less wicked than her husband, Mrs. Khan was fed up with Jamaal's continuous begging and pleading and agreed to ask her husband to give him another chance. However, she told him strictly never ever to repeat what he did before, namely; having an affair with a woman at work or a customer and never ever do anything like that again behind her husband's back.

Jamaal swore he would abide by the rules and regulations of the job. When Mrs. Khan promised Jamaal she would speak to her husband about getting his job back, Muhammad Khan happened to be on a five-day business trip to New Delhi. She told Jamaal to come back to the office after a week's time. Her husband would be back by that time and she said she would convince him to rehire him. In fact, her husband was in Bangalore enjoying another man's wife. He lied to her and told her that he was going to New Delhi to meet an important Arab client. Jamaal believed the promise of Mrs. Khan and waited those seven days.

After Jamaal was released from prison, he spent five weeks working various jobs. During those five weeks, he worked hard doing manual labor or whatever he could find to provide food for his sister and three brothers. The money he made was so little compared to what he used to make working in the travel agency. For that reason, he wanted to get his job back by all means. He wanted to send his sister and brothers back to school. He also wanted to buy another chawl and provide a better place to live for his family. He knew the slums were not safe for his teenager sister especially when she started back to school. The slum area was full of jobless loafers, perpetual drunks, and dangerous Gondas. While he was away working during the day, he was always afraid his young sister might be raped by useless, lawless scum. When Mrs. Khan promised she would speak to her husband about getting his job back, he had a glimmer of hope that perhaps they could rise above their hopelessness. Every waking moment and in his sleep, Jamaal was counting the minutes and seconds for his boss to return from his business trip, so he could go back to work.

Muhammad Khan had the bad habit of using his employees to spy on one another and report things back to him. He even used his peon to spy on his employees. Unbeknownst to Jamaal, his troubles were mounting and this time through the person who loved him completely. While Jamaal was waiting for Muhammad to return to Bombay and take him back, Rayhana Khan came to spy out the travel agency looking for him and after everyone had left, she approached the peon. The peon knew that Jamaal had been fired so he didn't know why he had showed up at the travel agency. This was strange too that this young Indian woman he had an affair with, also showed up looking for him. As part of his spying duties, the peon felt it was necessary to report the visit of the young Indian woman to his boss when he returned from his business trip. Another bump lay in the road ahead, which added to Jamaal's troubles. While the wicked one was in Bangalore enjoying his time with another man's wife thanks to a steady supply of Viagra, another serious problem developed which was attributed to Jamaal.

Muhammad recruitment business suffered a considerable loss after Sheikh Ahmed stopped his business dealings with his office. Before the pseudo terrorist plot, the old Saudi sent hundreds of work visas to the recruitment agency. Muhammad would sell the visas to Indians ten times the actual amount of the visas. This highly profitable business venture with Sheikh Ahmed was the crux of the success for Muhammad Tours and Travels. When the partnership was severed, Muhammad business suffered major losses. He struggled to make ends meet. He tried hard to get new Arab clients but none would commit to working with him. When nothing worked in his favor, he came up with a plan to force Sheikh Ahmed to have to deal with him only. He wanted to block the Saudi's ability to do business in Bombay so that he would come and beg him to accept his visas again. He did not want any other agency to profit from his business. To that end, he was prepared to use intimidation and threats against any travel agency that the old Saudi might be tempted to conduct transactions with.

In order to carry out his plan Muhammad kept spies everywhere. He even contacted some employees at the passport office and the

Sahara International Airport. He knew that the Old Saudi was perversely infatuated with the slum woman. Therefore, he anticipated that he might use another travel agency to find Rayhana Khan and fly her over to him. For this reason, he gave his spies at the passport office and the international airport the names of Rayhana Khan and her daughter. He wanted to know which agency the Old Saudi might be using to process the papers of the slum woman and her daughter. He was planning to use the Gondas to stop the agency from dealing with his ex-client.

The first reported matter of espionage came from the passport office. While Muhammad was away in Bangalore someone from among his spies at the passport office called his office and left a message. The informant mentioned that Rayhana Khan had come along with one of the employees of Muhammad and applied for reissuance of her passport and her daughter's passport. The informant did not mention the name of the employee that accompanied Rayhana Khan.

As soon as Muhammad returned from his trip, his wife talked to him and requested he take Jamaal Khan back as an employee. Somehow, she convinced him to take him back on a religious and humanitarian basis. She narrated to him the many tragedies that had struck his family and all that had happened to the Muslim brothers and sisters of Jamaal while their brother was in prison. Muhammad agreed to give Jamaal another chance. He told his wife that if Jamaal Khan tried to do anything else behind his back, he would not only fire him, but he would send him to prison forever.

When Muhammad arrived at his office the following day, his peon informed him about the young Indian woman who came and asked about Jamaal Khan. At first, Muhammad did not take the information seriously because his peon did not tell him which woman came to inquire about Jamaal. However, as soon as he entered his office, checked his answering machine, and heard the report of his operative from the passport office he quickly connected the dots. He called his peon in and asked him to describe to him the woman who asked him about Jamaal Khan. The peon described the woman and added he saw her before when she used to come with her daughter to the travel agency for her travel papers. He told his boss he remembered that Jamaal used to go with the woman to help her do some work.

When the peon gave the description of the slum woman, Muhammad almost exploded from the rage bubbling inside him. He concluded that somehow Jamaal Khan was still in contact with Rayhana Khan. His thought was that Jamaal was helping her to get her passport reissued. He knew Jamaal had access to all the information concerning Sheikh Ahmed while he was working for him at the travel agency. He figured Rayhana met Jamaal and got the phone number of Sheikh Ahmed from him. Then, she talked to the old Saudi and somehow managed to convince him to reissue new visas and tickets for her. When Sheikh Ahmed agreed to resend the visas and tickets, she asked her boyfriend to reprocess her paperwork. He quickly jumped to the conclusion that Jamaal Khan was the employee that was with Rayhana at the passport office and applied for the reissuing of the passports for Rayhana and her daughter.

Muhammad picked up his phone, called the police, and reported a serious crime had taken place in his travel agency. He told the police that he had already reported the crime long before but nothing was done to the culprit. Due to some legal issues he was involved in, he got distracted from following up to make sure justice was done. After he was released from prison, he decided to pursue the crime that had been committed by one of his male employees against one of his female employees. The next day when poor, pitiful Jamaal Khan came to see about getting his job back, he found the police waiting for him at the travel agency. He was arrested, tied up, and taken into custody for the very serious charges of rape and robbery.

When Jamaal was informed about the charges against him, he strongly denied them. No matter how much he was beaten and tortured by the police, he refused to admit the false allegations. The future of his sister and his brothers were in his hands and for these very strong reasons he preferred to be beaten to death than to admit to false charges and endanger their lives. The determination of Jamaal not to admit to the charges led the police to investigate the complaint further. The first person the police tried to get hold of and question was the female employee that allegedly had been raped and robbed by Jamaal. Unfortunately, when the police found the slum where Bulbolah Sheikh used to live while she was working at the travel agency they did not find her. The police found out through her family that she died a couple of months ago. The family refused to reveal the cause of her death. The police questioned the neighbors and were told the cause of her death was that she had committed suicide. The police went to the hospital where her body was taken after she committed suicide. The medical report confirmed her suicidal death. The report mentioned that Bulbolah was pregnant at the time she took her life. On the basis of the medical report the police concluded that Bulbolah Sheikh was impregnated by her rapist, Jamaal Khan. The Bombay police had *found* enough evidence to condemn Jamaal Khan for rape. At trial, Muhammad Khan placed his right hand on his holy Qur'an and swore under oath that Jamaal Khan stole money from his office and from Bulbolah Sheikh and she tearfully confessed to him Jamaal raped her when the other employees were out for lunch. Spoken like a pathetic liar and monster deceiver, he truly felt the need to testify and bring justice to this young girl that could no longer speak for herself and may her soul rest in peace. Due to the seriousness of the crime and the money paid by the wicked man, Muhammad Khan, the case was pushed to the top of the waiting list and concluded in short time. As the events unfolded in court, Jamaal Khan was tried, convicted, and sentenced to fifteen years hard labor.

CHAPTER 13

NAFISA KHAN

Jamaal's sister contacted the travel agency after her brother did not return home for five days. She still had the work phone number her brother had given her while he was in prison. Muhammad Khan was the one who happened to answer the main line. She asked about her brother and Muhammad told her that her brother had been arrested by the Bombay police and taken into custody. He did not tell her the exact charges. He then lied and told her Jamaal had some money owed to him that the travel agency was supposed to pay him. The iniquitous man already knew from his wife that Jamaal had only one sister left and his other two sisters had run away from home after they became pregnant. (Jamaal sorrowfully related the tragedy of his family, which occurred while he was in jail). Muhammad's wife also told him Jamaal's sister was only fifteen and a half years old. The evil workings of his mind devised a wonderfully wicked plan. Evil was his middle name. When the young girl called and inquired about her missing brother, he told her to come and collect the money that was owed to her brother for the wages he had earned.

When Jamaal's sister came, the wicked and cunning gave her two thousand rupees and offered her a job. The sister wasn't qualified to work at his business but he just couldn't help himself. It was like shooting fish in a barrel and fresh meat was hard to turn away. His befouled conscience would have her succumb to his lustful desire with the help of a steady supply of Viagra. (Due to the beatings he received in jail, he had trouble maintaining an erection and therefore he was never without his favorite medication). He knew that the sister was underage and hence he wasn't supposed to hire her. At that time, Jamaal's sister was fifteen years and six months. He convinced her to lie to the other employees about her age. In India, a girl was allowed to work at the age of sixteen, however, there was no specific minimum age limit for boys.

Jamaal's sister was called Nafisa Khan. She was so happy to get a job in a place where no one would sexually harass her. The presence of other female employees in the office reassured her that she was in a safe working environment. Just as her boss had advised her, Nafisa did not tell anyone in the office that she was Jamaal's sister and she lied about her age and told the other employees she just turned sixteen. Nafisa was scared to go to the jail and meet her brother for fear the police would find out she was working under the legal age requirement. After she began to work in the office, one day her boss called her into his office and showed her a newspaper that mentioned the charges against her brother. Nafisa cried tremendously when she learned her brother was accused of several serious crimes including rape, robbery and impregnating a girl. She began to despise her brother when she learned the girl had killed herself when she discovered that she was pregnant by her rapist, Jamaal Khan. Therefore, Nafisa vowed that she would never visit her brother in prison again.

The counterfeit man of Allah followed the same evil tactics that he used with his other female employees. He allowed Nafisa to work for him for a few weeks without harassing or approaching her in any inappropriate way. During this period, Nafisa loved her job because she was making good money. When he saw that she loved her job and the money, he decided now was a good time to carry out the evilness of his mind. One day Nafisa fell sick and did not come to work. When she came in the following day, she brought with her a doctor's excuse. However, the merciless tyrant began shouting at her and accused her of lying. Then, he commanded her inside his office, locked the door, and began to ask her very embarrassing questions.

"Now tell me Nafisa," said the wicked boss, *"were you truly sick or did you just decide to take the day off and go meet your boyfriend?"*

"I don't have a boyfriend sir," replied Nafisa.

"How come, you don't have a boyfriend at your age?" asked the boss.

"I have younger brothers to look after and I am not interested in having a relationship with a boy at my age."

"Amazing," said the wicked boss pretending to be impressed. *"Every girl in Bombay at your age would definitely have a boyfriend. I fell in love with my wife when she was sixteen years old and married her when she was eighteen. However, during those two years until we married, we enjoyed each other so much in very loving and intimate ways."*

Nafisa did not like the story the boss was relaying to her. She thought he wasn't supposed to tell her stuff like that.

"By the way, can I ask you a personal question?"

Before Nafisa gave her permission, the unconscionable diseased loathsome python kept pressing his agenda and asked her a very embarrassing question.

"Was the reason of your sickness something to do with your period?"

Nafisa remained silent and refused to respond to that improper question. However, when her wicked boss repeated his question she answered it in one word,

"No."

"By the way, when was the last time you got your period?"

This time Nafisa refused to answer his question even though he repeated it three times. To show his concern for her well-being he came over to her and she felt the hand of the snake slide over hers. She immediately pulled her hand away from his and said to him angrily,

"Please don't touch me again."

Nafisa knew what her boss was up to. He didn't care about the reason she was sick the previous day. She stood up without his permission and walked over to the office door; unlocked it and then walked out of his office. The wicked boss picked up his phone and dialed the number to her phone. Nafisa picked up the phone and when she heard it was her boss she slammed the receiver down and disconnected the line. After a few minutes, the peon came and told her that the boss was asking her to come to his office. Nafisa found it difficult to tell the peon she wasn't coming in the presence of the other employees. Therefore, she stood up and returned to his office. The crocodile put before her two choices. She could either entertain him sexually or loose her job. Nafisa without a second thought turned around and left his office; she went back to her desk, grabbed her handbag and walked immediately out the front door to the office.

Nafisa Khan was a very smart and strong-willed girl. During her few weeks working in the travel agency, she saved most of her money. She did not behave like the other female employees who wasted their money buying pretty clothes and going out with their boyfriends. When her brother landed in jail the first time, her family suffered greatly which led to her having to allow one of her sisters to work outside the home. Rich wicked people took advantage of her younger sister and raped her. She was also forced to send her brothers to the streets to beg for a few rupees to feed the family. After her brother landed in jail the second time and she was fortunate to get a job with his former employer, she decided to work hard and save money for a rainy day or for unforeseen expenses.

After she walked away from that very trying situation, Nafisa spent one month searching for another job. She could not get the same kind of job working in a travel agency, but she found a job as a salesgirl in a big mall and continued to lie about her age. In her new job, she made less than what she used to make in the travel agency. Nonetheless, the money she was making was enough to feed her and her three brothers. She continued to work while her three brothers were going to school.

Nafisa Khan decided to remain single and unmarried until her three brothers would finish school and begin to work. She did not bother falling in love with any boy. She sacrificed her life and falling in love for the sake of her brothers. She shared the same sacrificial spirit of her brother, Jamaal. Everything Nafisa did for her family was selfless except for one terrible mistake on her part. She believed the lie of her boss, Muhammad Khan over love and trust for her brother who had always cared for the family as best he could. When she read in the newspaper this girl was raped and impregnated by Jamaal Khan and then killed herself, she thought the worst about her brother and vowed never to speak to him again.

CHAPTER 14

AT VAKOLA COLONY

If Rayhana knew that her visit to the travel agency would have cost her lover his freedom, she never would have gone. If she knew that applying for passports would have sent her lover to jail as a vicious criminal, she never would have applied for them. If she had foreseen that, her desire to travel to the rich country of the Arabs would lead the Bombay court to sentence her lover to fifteen years she never would have wished to travel out of her country for even a second. And if she knew what was awaiting her and her daughter in that rich Arab country where *the House of Allah* was, Rayhana never would have desired to go there at all. After Rayhana received the heartbreaking news from the residents of her lover's former chawl, she returned to her slum and grieved for her lost love for what seems like hours and days.

When Rayhana met Babikir after two days at the restaurant, he told her some good news. Her Saudi sponsor had sent the two visas and tickets to his address and soon the passport office would mail her passports to her address. The word address reminded Rayhana that her passports would go to the wrong address and reach the wrong people. She expected the Hindu family that bought the chawl of her lover's family might destroy the two passports if they saw they were addressed to Muslim people. Therefore, she told Babikir that her uncle died and his wife had sold the chawl and moved to a slum area. Babikir got mad with her when she told him this news and she did not take it upon herself to go to the passport office and give a valid address. Rayhana told him that she did not have any other address because she was living in a slum that had no address. Babikir lived long time in India but he had never heard in all his life that a citizen of a country could be without an address. In his country, even farm animals have addresses.

Anyway, after overcoming the shock, Babikir gave Rayhana his address and told her to go and give it to the passport office before they sent her passports to the wrong address. Rayhana requested Babikir go with her to the passport office but he apologized and said he could not go with her this time because he had to study for his exams. He said to her he would not be able to go anywhere for one week because final exams were coming up. He told her she could go alone to the passport office and speak to the same clerk that he had bribed and pay him one thousand rupees to change her address. Rayhana would rather wait for one year to get her passport and the passport for her daughter than give someone one thousand rupees. With one thousand rupees, she could feed her children for six months. In India, some poor people could survive for many years on *Dahl and Rice (lentils and rice)*. Dahl and rice are the daily staple diet for the majority of the population of the Indian subcontinent.

From the day the Sudanese boy had given Rayhana the share of currency her benefactor had so liberally furnished, she had not spent more than one hundred rupees out of the ten thousand rupees she received. She was so grateful and thought there must be so much money lying on the streets of Saudi Arabia this was just a drop in the bucket. Soon, she would be able to swoop up all the money off the streets of Saudi Arabia and all her worries for her family would disappear. Since she had never received such a huge amount of money, all at one time she was careful to safeguard it and spend it wisely. She went to the toilet of the restaurant and removed her clothes. Then, she tore a long piece of cloth from her dress and made something like a belt. She tied up the notes of currency and wrapped the belt of money around her privates as if it was an adult diaper. Then, she put on her underwear and the rest of her clothes and came out. For two days, she did not change her underwear or remove her clothes except when she needed to answer the call of nature. She was afraid someone could see right through her and sense she had a secret vault wrapped around her private parts and kill her for thousands of rupees. Rayhana was also scared to go to the bank because the management of the bank might accuse her of stealing the ten thousand rupees from someone and call the police to arrest her. Besides that, she had no address to give to the bank. She had never saved more than four hundred rupees from all her hard work slaving for the rich. By the way, the cheapest labor rate in the world was in India. There was nothing called minimum wage in that country where the majority of its citizens were living under the poverty level.

When Rayhana got tired of hiding her treasure under her clothes, she decided to create her own personal bank. On the third day night, while her mother, children, and all her slum neighbors were sleeping she woke up and like a thief in the night, she took a knife and dug a hole in one corner of her slum. Then, she removed her money belt and carefully buried it in the hole. To hide the trace of the hole she dug she placed the jar of water on top of it. Whenever she needed some money, she would get up in the middle of the night, remove the cistern of water, open her underground bank, and take out what she needed. Then, like a cat that must burry its feces, Rayhana carefully hid her underground treasure.

When she went to change her address at the passport office, Rayhana had only one hundred rupees on her person. When the passport office clerk started creating problems for her by asking unnecessary questions, she gave him fifty rupees and her address was changed instantly while she was still standing in front of him. Satisfied at what money can buy, she then left the passport office to go back to her slum. She did not have to buy a train ticket because she was a slum dweller and by order of the government, they are exempt from having to pay bus fare and thus can ride free. In fact, Rayhana did not purchase a local train ticket even during her three weeks of courtship with her missing lover Jamaal Khan. She always rode in the crowded ladies' compartment and traveled wherever she wanted to go. Thank God, women in Bombay were allowed two separate compartments. If a young beautiful woman like Rayhana dared to enter a men's compartment on the local trains she would be touched by hundreds of men and raped in broad daylight in front of everyone.

Women in Bombay frequently suffered from sexual harassment also while traveling the local bus routes because there were no sections designated just for them. In some other cities of India, local transportation often provided reserved seating for the benefit of women travelers. It was better for women to commute by trains for although they were allowed to travel in any of the ten compartments of the men's section, no man was allowed to enter into any of the two ladies' compartments. On the other hand, there were human beings in Bombay who were neither male nor female. They were called No. 6. They were also neither gay nor lesbian. These unisex citizens were allowed to travel in ladies' compartments because they posed no threat to women passengers. They lived by begging because no one would give them a job. If they came and asked you for money and you refused to give them anything, they would curse you to your face. Many people believed that their curses would come to pass. If you gave them money they would bless you.

The second visit of Rayhana Khan to the passport office was reported to Muhammad Khan by one of his informants. The information revealed Rayhana Khan had changed her home address. He even supplied the new address. When he carefully transcribed the new address, Muhammad was surprised. It wasn't a chawl address but an apartment in Vakola. At first, he thought that Sheikh Ahmed had moved Rayhana from her slum area in Dharavi to an apartment in Vakola. He decided to send someone to find out who was living at the residence.

Muhammad sent his peon and told him to go and ask the neighbors about the person who was staying at that address. When the peon came back, he brought with him information that was mystifying indeed. The boss could not get a clear picture in his head. The spy related that there were five foreign students living in the apartment. The information did not reveal their names, nationalities, college attendance or field of study. It also could not be ascertained as to what their daily activities were. Therefore, Muhammad contacted some Muslim Gondas and asked them to provide him with more detailed information about the foreign students who were living in the apartment. The Gondas brought to him the names, nationalities, and the colleges of the five foreign students. The revenger and conjurer of evil immediately demystified the mind-boggling mystery and suddenly everything began to make sense to him. Sheikh Ahmed was definitely still in the picture and was using the Sudanese boy to process the papers for Rayhana and her daughter. His evil mind steadily working schemed out a devious plan to stop this collaboration dead in its tracks. He thought of three ways to stop Rayhana Khan from traveling to Saudi Arabia and punish the Sudanese boy who was helping her. He thought of creating a problem for her at the passport office by accusing Babikir of some illegal activity thereby sending him to jail and blocking Rayhana's exit at the international airport.

The apartment Babikir was living in was rented by four Sudanese students. The four Sudanese students and fellow countrymen allowed him to stay with them on a humanitarian basis. Babikir hadn't been able to share in paying the rent for the apartment so he was being allowed to stay on charitable grounds. After his boss' wife kicked him out of the office, he became destitute. Babikir was another extravagant employee and he wasn't wise like Nafisa Khan. Whatever money he earned while working at the travel agency he spent on his *selfish and not at all beautiful* girlfriend. Therefore, shortly after he lost his job he began to depend on his Sudanese friends again.

All five Sudanese students had girlfriends. One of them had a Kenyan girlfriend, one an Ethiopian girlfriend, one a Palestinian girlfriend, one a Southern Sudanese girlfriend, and one an Indian girlfriend *who did not love him*. The last girlfriend was Jamilah Malik. By the way, Jamilah did not cut ties with Babikir after he was fired from the travel office. For some time she avoided Babikir whenever she saw him. However, one day he stopped her and told her something, which led her to agree to meet him again. She met him the following day after work and agreed to what was a last-ditch effort at a proposal from a foolhardy love sick puppy. Babikir told her that after six months he was going to Saudi Arabia to work as a translator for the wealthy business tycoon, Sheikh Ahmed. He showed her a letter that he received from his future sponsor proving the offer was genuine. It was one of the deals the old Saudi made with Babikir when he asked him to find his beloved woman at all cost and get her back to where she belonged and that was with him.

When Babikir told Jamilah he was going to work in the rich Arab country of Saudi Arabia with a wealthy business tycoon, being self-centered, Jamilah agreed to marry him, albeit with some conditions—Babikir had to get over there first, then return after one year and marry her. The crazed Sudanese was ecstatic when his *Layla* finally agreed to marry him! This type of beneficial union was common in India. Many foreign students married Indian girls in a kind of *"How can I benefit and how can my family benefit kind of marriage?"* There was a case of a Sudanese boy who was in love with an Indian girl. Her family at first rejected his proposal for their daughter's hand in marriage because for them he was a Black Negro. However, after they became aware of his refugee status and resettlement to Vancouver landing him an immigrant visa, they agreed to the marriage. Nevertheless, behind his back, they convinced their daughter to marry him with a condition attached. The Sudanese boy did not know the secret agreement between his girlfriend and her parents until he married her and took her to Canada. After three months, the girl walked out of his apartment, found a job, and rented an apartment. Then, she began to process the immigration papers for her parents. This was a problem that the Canadian immigration authorities could not find an answer to. In another case, an Indian wife walked away from her Sudanese husband at the airport and went directly to her Indian lover's apartment. She used her husband as a means to reach her boyfriend in Canada.

Sheikh Ahmed sent Babikir two visas and tickets for Rayhana and for her daughter to travel with her along with a letter of employment. He also sent fifteen thousand rupees and five hundred US dollars. He ordered Babikir to help Rayhana get her travel papers, give her ten thousand rupees, and the American dollars, and keep the remaining five thousand rupees for himself. Before he met Rayhana to give her share, he sought out his girlfriend and asked her for a date because he had some very important good news to share with her. The following day, after he filled her stomach up with food, sweet dishes, and whatever else she desired to eat, he revealed to her the good news and showed her the promise letter. Then he asked her to marry him. Jamilah's selfish ambitions quickly weighed the "Pros and Cons" and agreed to marry him if certain conditions were met.

It was on a Saturday evening when Babikir received the promise of Jamilah Malik's hand in marriage. After that, he went to meet Rayhana and handed her the money sent to her from Sheikh Ahmed, along with the visas and tickets for her trip. Babikir was afraid that someone in the apartment where he was staying might steal these important documents and money from his bag. His roommates were having a party and many foreign boys and girls were invited. His friends were celebrating the end of their exams, which concluded on Friday. Every one of them had invited his girlfriend and his girlfriend's girlfriends. Each girlfriend would bring her boyfriend and there would be a wild and loud gathering of young people losing control of themselves. Essentially, it was fear of getting drunk and loosing all the important travel papers and documents that drove Babikir to ultimately decide to give them to Rayhana with her share of the money. Then, he promised her that as soon as the two passports reached his apartment he would come and hand them over to her. He added that her sponsor had already booked her flight and he told her the date and time of her flight. Giving Rayhana possession of her paperwork relieved Babikir of responsibility in this regard and left him free to enjoy the party with his friends. The only person at the party who would be without a girlfriend was he. Babikir mentioned the party to Jamilah and that he would like her to come but she told him she wasn't that kind of girl. So, he apologized and promised never again to ask her to come to the apartment where he was staying because she was not his wife yet. After Jamilah refused the invitation to the end of exams party, Babikir went to the liquor store, bought one bottle of rum, and headed back to the apartment for some fun.

That night nineteen girlfriends and boyfriends gathered at the Vakola apartment and jubilantly celebrated one less semester to worry about. The party continued until 2:30 am in the wee hours of the morning and it might have continued until daybreak if the Indian neighbors had not called the police and reported the loud noise caused by the wild orgy of the African students. (Most Indians believe that Africans are savages who still live in the bush and sleep like monkeys on trees). The Indian police barged in and kicked out all the guests, bringing some measure of peace to the apartment complex. No one was arrested because two bottles of whiskey and two thousand rupees were offered as ransom to release the transgressors of calm and quiet. The bribe paved the way for the police to allow four of the girlfriends to stay with their Sudanese boyfriends and send the other five couples on their way. The next morning Babikir was so tired and exhausted from all the goings on of the festive occasion that he slept like Rip Van Winkle. He would have slept until the following night if the Kalina police had not shown up at his door.

Babikir woke up with a yelp when he felt someone jerk him out of bed by his left leg. When he opened his eyes and saw a policeman hovering over him, he thought he was having a nightmare. The police grabbed him by the upper arm and forced him to stand on his feet. Without saying anything to him, the Indian policeman lead Babikir by his night shirt to the living room. Babikir was shocked when he saw more than ten members of the Kalina police department inside the apartment. All of his four roommates and their four girlfriends had been forced out of their beds and brought into the living room. Babikir asked his Sudanese friends in Arabic why the police had come back. None of them had a clue why their apartment was being raided once again by the cops. One of the cops shouted at Babikir and told him to be quiet. While the nine foreign students were sitting in the living room surrounded by six fully armed cops, the other police inspectors went inside their bedrooms and began to search their bags and cupboards. After every bag and cupboard was ransacked, the Bombay narcotic officer claimed to have found what he was looking for. Then, they informed the nine foreign students that they were under arrest for smuggling and selling drugs.

In India, it would better to be arrested under the charge of first-degree murder or a terrorist plot than to be charged with smuggling drugs. The Indians believed that the murderer would kill one person and the terrorist would blow up a few thousand people, but the drug dealer would kill millions and cause widespread devastation to all of society. Even more, in Bombay the common misconception was that each and every African student that came to India smuggled or distributed drugs. While this is by no means correct, the facts show a predisposition for this type of infringement. One would not be exaggerating if one claimed that most every Nigerian student in India was in some way or another involved in some clandestine operation. Almost every week a Nigerian student was caught at the Bombay Sahara International Airport with drugs in their luggage. Sometimes, Nigerian students were caught with drugs inside their body cavities. When the Bombay narcotic division decided to get tough on drug traffickers, the Nigerian students came up with new tactics to evade capture and detection. The drug mules would encapsulate the drugs and swallow them. The capsules would remain intact for a few hours before their digestive system would dissolve the capsules. IN the event that the capsules were not removed within the specific timeframe, the person would drop dead. It didn't take long for the police to catch on and soon scanners were brought in to detect drugs hidden in cavities and in people's stomachs. Having said that, one could say with confidence it wasn't true that every African student was involved in drug trafficking. Regardless, many Indians believed that every black person came to India not for studying but for drug trafficking.

In Bombay if someone hated a foreign student and wanted to destroy his life he would find a way to hide drugs in his bag or apartment and then he would make an anonymous phone call to the police and report him being involved in some kind of drug activity. Another way some Indians would harm foreign students was through false medical reports. In the city of Aurangabad, a Sudanese student fell in love with the daughter of the police commissioner. When the father came to know of the affair, he broke up their relationship in a very cruel way. (By the way, most Indian Universities will administer a mandatory AIDS test for all foreign students at least once. If the test results proved positive, the foreign student would be deported). When the police commissioner found out about the love affair between his daughter and the Black student from Sudan, the commissioner had him arrested and then re-tested for AIDS. He then bribed a doctor at the civilian hospital to produce a positive result. The Sudanese student was blacklisted and deported back to his country.

After raiding the foreign students' apartment, the Bombay narcotic police force found drugs in Babikir Al-A'war's bag. (A word of truth must be said here. During my fourteen years of living in India, I never heard of a Sudanese student taking drugs or dealing drugs or being arrested for a drug offense. I lived three years in Nagpur, one year in Ahmadabad, and ten years in Bombay but I never saw or heard of a Sudanese student being involved in drugs activities). The apartment where Babikir was staying with his four Sudanese friends was in one of the tallest four buildings in Vakola. Each building was at least ten stories high. This part of town was called Vakola Colony and surrounded by high fencing. There was only one way to get in and one way to get out and that was through the main fenced gate. During the day the community was always protected by a watchman sitting in a small booth with a big long stick. There was another guard during the night watch. Each guard would cover a twelve-hour shift. There was a third guard whose duty was to make rounds during the night and keep hitting the pavement with his baton. It was imperative that he strike the asphalt making a *tat tat tat* sound.

The colony was well guarded during the night by the watchman who sat by the main gate and by the guard who circled the fence during the 3rd watch echoing his location with his billystick. When I arrived, new in India, I was puzzled by the night guard who kept up this meticulous ritual all night long, keeping me from a restful sleep. The following day I asked my Indian friend Vishwas the reason for this continuous disturbance throughout the night. He told me that burglars identify the strikes of a stick as a guard on his rounds awake and alert, as opposed to sleeping in a corner of the building. The residents would hear the sound of the stick and know the night guard was awake and vigilant and hence they could sleep securely during the night. Night guard tapping was a phenomenon in every city and town in India. Another strange thing about the night guards is that they would always be from the Nagaland state. I asked my friend Vishwas, *"Why are the night guards always from Nagaland state?"* He said because no one could keep watch throughout the night or stay awake going in circles and striking the ground except a man from Nagaland. I could not refute my friend because I couldn't do the job even if they gave me a thousand rupees for each night. (Nagaland people are citizens of India but don't look like Indians. They resemble Chinese and Japanese in features and height).

The Vakola's colony had two guards during the day too. The first guard was the watchman whose duty was to sit for twelve hours in his booth at the gate and make sure no stranger entered the compound unless express permission was given by the relevant apartment owner. The second guard was called the liftman. In India, the elevator was called a lift. If you say elevator in Bombay most of the people would not understand what you were talking about. The liftman's duty was to sit inside the elevator from 8 am to 10 pm. If anyone came between 10 pm-8 am, he/she, no matter how old, had to use the stairs to get to his/her apartment even if it was on the 14th floor. The liftman had a lunch break and a dinner break. If someone came during the lunch or dinner breaks, they had to use the stairs at these times too. The liftman had a key and it was his duty to lock the elevator during his breaks and while he was off duty. His most important duty was to keep an eye on who came in and who went out. If someone managed to jump over the tall fencing or fool the watchman and made his way to the elevator, the liftman would not allow him to go any further. He would not be able to use the stairs either unless he was a resident of the colony and had a key to unlock the door to the stairway. The liftman had a stool inside the elevator and it was his duty to sit there all the time on the stool and watch with his eyes wide open all the residents and visitors going in and out. His duty was also to protect married women and young girls from being harassed and/or attacked in the lift.

Since Vakola's colony was relatively well guarded by night and day, how did the drugs end up in Babikir's bag? There were several possibilities; either one of the ten visitors who was invited to the party somehow entered Babikir's room and put the contraband there to implicate him or someone entered the apartment when no one was there and put the drugs in Babikir's bag. The four Sudanese flat mates were exempt from suspicion because they were all arrested at the same time along with their girlfriends. Only someone above the law would attempt to do something like that or a person lacking adequate mental capacity would be so stupid as to do such a crazy thing. It would be highly unlikely that all five friends were persuaded to leave the party at 2:30 am by the cops leaving room for the drugs to be placed in Babikir's bag. Another possibility is the only reasonable assumption left to explore. If someone broke into the apartment in their absence, Babikir and his other four roommates would have found out about the break-in and they would have reported it to the police or complained to the secretary of the colony. Every year the residents of each colony would get together, select a secretary from among them, and pay him a salary. If anyone had a complaint about his neighbors or any problem in his apartment, he would make a complaint to the secretary. The only other possibility was that someone either had stolen the key from one of the five roommates or had a spare. All the spare keys were kept with the secretary.

It was breaking and disturbing news when the midday newspapers in Bombay published the arrest of the five Sudanese students and their girlfriends at Santa Cruz, Vakola Colony. It was the first time that Sudanese students were arrested on drug charges. All one thousand nine hundred Sudanese students at Bombay University went to the colony and tried to find out how this could have happened. None of them believed the charges. The huge gathering of the students in front of the colony led the secretary to call the police and disperse them. At the police station, the five Sudanese students and their four foreign girlfriends were battered and tortured. The *so-called confessions* were compelled by force right out of their bleeding mouths.

Narcotic police interrogators were crueler than other police divisions. Whatever they wanted you to admit, they would force you to admit it and then record your confession and use it against you in court. Among the nine foreign suspects, Babikir's face was almost unrecognizable after the relentless beatings. Not even his mother or his father would have recognized him. They broke all his front teeth and blinded his seeing eye. The area around his good eye was swollen shut and disappeared in its socket. Every single inch on his bare-naked body had received heavy blows with an iron rod. He was beaten to the point where he could no longer cry out and could only muster a feeble groan, struggling to breathe through his broken nose. His jaw was dislocated. Some of his ribs were broken. Some of his fingernails were plucked out. In the third world, there were no people more evil than the police. People would say, "If your finger becomes a policeman cut it off." I believe all those heartless police officers will burn in hell for all eternity.

CHAPTER 15

AT THE AIRPORT

Rayhana Khan waited for Babikir in the same restaurant he had told her to meet him every Saturday. Their usual routine every Saturday was for him to update her on the developments of her case. Rayhana spent nearly four hours waiting for him, mechanically ordering items from the menu until her stomach protested. She knew that if she stopped ordering the waiters would kick her out. However, after four hours she concluded that Babikir had either forgotten about their meeting or else he was too ill to keep his appointment. She did not have any other way to contact him or reach him by phone. She returned to her slum and waited the next day. Her main worry was about the tickets and visas that he had given her. He told her he would meet her on the following Saturday and get them back from her. Then he would give them back to her on the day of her flight. Rayhana was very careful to keep her important travel documents safe. She fastened them inside her pocket all day and when she fell asleep at night she put them under her blanket and slept on them. Slum people and chawl dwellers don't use beds. They simply put a blanket or mattress on the floor and sleep on it. Rayhana was scared her important papers might get destroyed if she deposited them in her underground bank where she kept her thousands of rupees. Her savings grew when Babikir gave her ten thousand rupees more. With so much money, Rayhana stopped feeding her children *Dahl and rice.* She bought a chicken and cooked it for them. Before she became rich among slum dwellers, necessity forced her and her children to endure vegetarian diets although they were not Hindus.

Rayhana waited for seven days before she went to the same restaurant again and waited for Babikir. After three and a half hours of waiting and ordering food, tea, and coffee, she got up and went back to her slum. This time she felt very sad. She thought perhaps the Negro boy had died or something had happened to him. She remembered Babikir had told her that her sponsor had booked her flight and he gave her the departure date. Rayhana simply convinced herself that maybe she had misunderstood what Babikir told her when he gave her the tickets and visas. Maybe he wanted her to go to the airport on that day and meet him there and then he would get her and her daughter onto the plane and send them to the rich Arab country of Saudi Arabia.

There were only two days left for her scheduled departure date when Rayhana came to this conclusion. Therefore, she went to the market and bought nice dresses for her daughter and for herself. After two days, she revealed her hidden treasure to her mother and told her to use the money to feed her grandchildren and herself. She even gave the five hundred American dollars to her mother. She took only five hundred rupees with her. Then, she took her daughter and headed to the airport. She carried a small piece of hand luggage. She did not know where the airport was located. She did not want to take a taxi for she was afraid that the driver might kidnap and rape her. She had heard stories from some slum women about how young women were kidnapped and raped by their taxi drivers. Therefore, she decided to take the local bus to the airport. Rayhana had never been to an airport before. She went to the bus station and asked someone to tell her which bus would take her to the airport. She did not mention which airport she was going to. The person she asked looked at her and at her bag and concluded that she was going to the domestic airport. Therefore, he told her which bus would take her there. She took the bus and went to the Santa Cruz Domestic Airport.

When Rayhana reached the Domestic Airport along with her daughter, she sat on a bench and told her daughter to sit on her lap because the bench was crowded with people. One curious Indian woman of wealthy descent asked her why was she at the airport.

Rayhana told her that she came to take a trip on the airplane. The woman was surprised and then asked her which city in India she was traveling to? The Indian woman asked her this question because she could not believe that a slum woman like Rayhana could possibly afford to buy an airplane ticket.

Rayhana said to the rich woman that she was flying to Saudi Arabia. The rich woman burst out laughing when she heard the name of the country the slum woman said she was going to. Then, she said to her still laughing, *"You need to have visas and tickets to go to a country like Saudi Arabia and you would need at least five hundred thousand rupees to buy the visas and tickets for you and your daughter."* Rayhana smiled at the rich Indian woman who was questioning her and looking down upon her because of her appearance. She then opened her small bag, took out the tickets and visas, and showed them to the rich woman. The woman's eyes widened with her mouth agape when she saw the travel documents. She took five minutes examining them to determine if they were genuine. Then, she asked Rayhana how did she come about getting her visas and tickets. Rayhana told her truthfully that an old Arab man had gifted them to her. The woman did not believe Rayhana, however she told her that she was in the wrong airport. Then she told her she had to take a taxi and go to the Sahara International Airport, which was in Andheri.

Rayhana trusted the words of the rich Indian woman, took her daughter, and left the airport. Again, once she got outside she did not take a taxi but asked a man to tell her which bus would take her to the International Airport. The man was surprised when she asked him this. He too couldn't believe a woman like Rayhana had any business at an International Airport. She did not look like a passenger or a person who would travel abroad. In spite of what he thought, he didn't think it was his business to question her any further. He told her the name of the bus that goes from the Domestic Airport to the International Airport and then he turned around and walked away. Rayhana and her daughter waited for the bus for more than half an hour before it came and she asked the bus driver if this were the bus that goes to the international airport. He also had a hard time understanding why a slum woman would be going to the International Airport, but he said yes and she and her daughter climbed in.

Rayhana did not know the time of her flight. She was illiterate and hence could not read the time on their tickets. She and her daughter also did not have their passports. Nevertheless, she convinced herself that the Negro boy would be waiting at the airport for her with their two passports. When they reached the Sahara International Airport, Rayhana began to look for the Black boy everywhere. She did not remember his name or where he came from. All this time, Rayhana was under the impression that Babikir was an Indian like herself. Some people in India if you were to ask them where is New York or London in which country, they would tell you New York is in Bombay and London is in New Delhi. Rayhana had no clue where Babikir came from. She knew he was different from other Indians because he was Black and had hair like raisins. Moreover, everywhere she went with him she heard other Indians calling him *Negro*. She thought that Negro was an honorable title. In order to show respect for this very important and honorable person, on the day when he handed her, her first allotment of ten thousand rupees, she said to him, *"Shukria Negrogi"* (i.e. Thank You the Great Negro).

Anyway, Rayhana and her daughter kept walking from place to place inside the huge airport searching for their great Negro. They walked and walked and searched and searched until fatigue overtook them and they sat down to rest. At the place where they rested, there happened to be a Black woman who looked like their great Negro. Rayhana saw that the woman was a Black woman and thought that she was either Babikir's wife or sister. Therefore, she began to talk to her. The Black woman did not understand what the Indian woman was saying to her because she did not speak Hindi. However, she spoke to an old Indian man sitting nearby in English and requested he help translate for her. The old man talked to Rayhana in Hindi and then he told the Black woman in English that she was looking for a Black boy who looked like your husband or your brother. The Black woman laughed and said that she wasn't married nor did she have a brother in India. She then added that she was from South Africa and flying en route to Johannesburg. She told the old man to ask Rayhana which country was she flying to along with her cute daughter. When the old man translated for Rayhana what the Black woman has asked, she took out her tickets and visas and showed them to the Black woman.

The South African woman looked at the tickets and shouted loudly, *"Oh my God! They only have half an hour before takeoff."* Then, she stood up, grabbed Rayhana by the hand, and pulled her up to her feet. Rayhana got scared and was stunned when the Black woman took her by the hand and pulled her to get up. She looked at the old man for explanation. The man told her to go with her. He further explained that she had to hurry up because there were only a few minutes left before her plane would be taking off. Calm returned to Rayhana after the old Indian man reassured her it was ok to go with the woman and she then turned to pick up her daughter.

The South African woman did not let go of Rayhana's hand and kept leading the way though the airport. When they reached the end of the long departure hall, they found four security men guarding the entrance to the departure corridor. The South African woman spoke to the security men in English. She showed her passport and ticket. Then, she took the visas and tickets from Rayhana's hands and showed them to one of the security men. The man waved his hand and allowed them to enter. The woman then rushed Rayhana and her daughter through the corridor. When they reached the crowded departure room, there were twelve checkpoints and twelve lines of passengers waiting impatiently. The woman kept pulling Rayhana right past all the lines of people standing and waiting. When they got beyond the last line, the woman found an airhostess and asked her which of the checkpoints was processing the papers of passengers going to the Kingdom of Saudi Arabia. The airhostess told her that she was one of the crew of the Saudi Arabian aircraft.

The airhostess then asked the Black woman whether she was flying on this particular flight. The South African woman did not answer and grabbed Rayhana's tickets and visas from out her hand and showed them to the airhostess. The airhostess told her she had been looking for these two passengers because it was the final call and the doors were about to be closed in a few minutes. Then she asked Rayhana in English about her boarding cards. The South African woman interceded and told her they had not gotten their boarding cards yet. Without saying a word further, the airhostess took Rayhana's hand and rushed her and her daughter to the nearest checkpoint. The airhostess then spoke to an Indian clerk in English and explained to him that there was less than ten minutes left for boarding the aircraft.

The Indian man took the tickets and visas from the airhostess and glanced quickly at them. He checked the computer and verified the booking of Rayhana Khan and her daughter, Iffat Khan, for the flight to Saudi Arabia. After that, he took out two boarding cards and quickly filled them out and gave them to the airhostess. Some of the passengers who were standing in line for a long time voiced their displeasure and objections to the Arab airhostess and the airport official who had allowed others to jump ahead of them. The airhostess ignored their complaints and started jogging towards Gate 15 with Rayhana and her daughter in tow. As they made their way to the Gate, the South African woman smiled and waved good bye to them. Rayhana did not bother to look back and thank the woman. However, her seven-year-old daughter turned around and waved her little hand back at the Black woman who had helped them. The South African woman was very pleased to know that she had done a good deed to help an inexperienced passenger just in time to avoid missing her flight. However, neither the kind South African woman nor the hasty Arab airhostess would be happy if they knew they had just broken the law and sent two passengers out of the country without their passports…

Muhammad Khan, the devil's advocate, had done all he could to ensure Rayhana Khan and her daughter would not be flying out of the country. He bribed his informant at the passport office and ordered him not to send the two passports to Babikir's address but instead he was to send them to his office. The informant complied with his request and the two passports were sent to Muhammad Tours and Travels. As soon as the passports reached his hands, the self-anointed overlord of Gehenna incinerated them with fire. He knew that burning the two passports would not in itself enough to stop Sheikh Ahmed in his tracks and prevent his beloved Indian woman from being delivered into his hands. Rayhana could still complain about her missing passports and get new ones reissued. He remembered that Sheikh Ahmed had told him that an Indian woman arrived at the Jeddah International Airport and claimed to be Rayhana Khan. On that basis, his *travel agency* made a complaint to the airport that two of its clients' passports were stolen from his business. He then bribed one of his operatives at the Sahara International Airport to blacklist the passports of Rayhana and her daughter and if any female passengers showed up with passports issued in these names; Rayhana Khan and Iffat Khan, they should be arrested immediately.

The devious scoundrel still wasn't satisfied with the two obstacles he had created to block Rayhana and her daughter from flying to Saudi Arabia. He wanted to do something to secure his evil scheme. He expected that Sheikh Ahmed had sent the visas and tickets to Babikir to give to Rayhana. So, he decided to steal the visas and tickets from the Sudanese boy and then fix him with a serious crime. He already had gotten the address of the apartment where Babikir was staying. He contacted a notorious Gonda at Vakola and hired him to his dirty work. He told the Gonda to enter the apartment of Babikir and remove the visas and tickets issued to Rayhana Khan and her daughter, Iffat Khan. In place of the visas and tickets, drugs were to be planted inside Babikir's bag. The masterfully wicked man hated nothing more than catching one of his employees or former employees doing something behind his back or refusing to obey his commands. For that reason, he sent Jamaal Khan to jail. Likewise, he became furious when he found out that the Sudanese boy who used to work for him was conspiring with his former business partner and sworn enemy, Sheikh Ahmed, to process the papers of his Indian maidservant.

In India when a Gonda marked you as a target and put your name on his hit-list, no mortal being on the face of the earth could remove you from peril. Even the police could not protect you. The only way to escape this helpless situation was to kill the Gonda before he killed you. However, killing the Devil and his demons might be easier than killing a Gonda and his gangsters. When the Gonda in Vakola accepted the assignment of Muhammad Khan, he did one thing to give himself unimpeded access to Babikir's apartment. He made an anonymous phone call to the secretary of the building and told him he would kidnap and kill his son and rape his wife and then shoot him if he refused to hand over the key to the apartment of the five Negro foreigners who were staying in his building. The secretary knew that when a Gonda made a threat to someone's life, it was sure to pass. The words of a Gonda were more predictable than any soothsayer or foreteller of events and had more force and effect than all the gods of India. So, in order to protect his life and his family, the secretary agreed to hand over the spare key without question. The Gonda told him he would send three of his boys to get the key from him. He also told him that both the watchman and the liftman were not to stand in the way when his goons entered the complex to get the spare key or when they needed access to the apartment of the five Negroes. The secretary in fear and trembling promised that he would comply with the demands and conditions set forth by the Gonda. The secretary assumed that the Gonda wanted to send his gangsters to rob the apartment.

While Babikir and his four friends were taking their final exams, the three thugs arrived at the apartment building, got the spare key from the secretary, and entered the apartment of the five Negro students. They did a thorough search in every room and identified Babikir's bag through his photo ID card. They were not able to find the visas and tickets; however, they did put the drugs inside Babikir's bag. They made sure to leave everything as it was before they left the apartment. After that, they locked the apartment and returned the spare key to the secretary and left. The secretary was surprised when he saw the three gangsters come out of the apartment empty-handed. He was sufficiently frightened and held his tongue not questioning what they had done inside the apartment.

It was the hideous Muhammad Khan himself, who placed the anonymous phone call to the Bombay narcotic police and reported that there was drug activity taking place inside a certain apartment located at Vakola Colony. He refused to reveal his identity to the police, but gave them the building and apartment number in question and made sure to mention to the police there were African Negroes involved. The police could not trace the call because he made the call from a public phone. As expected, the Bombay police raided the apartment of the five Sudanese students and arrested them along with their four girlfriends. The next day when the wicked boss read the Midday Newspaper, he laughed until he fell out of his chair. Then, he went to his employees and showed them what the Negro boy who used to work for him had done.

As soon as the police took all nine students away, the neighbors knocked down the door of their apartment and stole everything. They did not leave the furniture or anything and took even the tables and chairs. They also took the food out of the refrigerator. The apartment was left empty as if its tenants had vacated and moved to another place. Shortly after the robbery, the secretary brought in three jobless slum women and paid each one of them twenty rupees to clean up the apartment. Then, he called a carpenter and asked him to fix the battered and damaged door. After that, he rented the apartment to some foreign Arab students from Jordan and Palestine.

CHAPTER 16

THE FEMALE TERRORIST

For inexperienced passengers like Rayhana Khan and her daughter, the airplane wasn't much fun at all. Whatever she had heard from the gossipmongers in the slums about plane crashes, hijackings and mid-air explosions all came to mind when she boarded the Saudi plane. Her heart began to increase its rhythm the moment the airhostess practically dragged her and her daughter inside the plane and showed them to their seats. The same airhostess who had gotten them their boarding cards and fastened their seat belts, smiled at them, and left. In haste, no one had bothered to ask them for their passports. When they entered the boarding ramp with the Arab airhostess, another member of the flying crew checked their boarding cards and waved them in.

If Rayhana happened to be a female suicide bomber as the police inspector, G. A. Shankaracharya, had previously alleged, she could have blown up the airplane and sent all the crew and passengers flying directly to the heavens. No one at the Sahara International Airport checked her small handbag or scanned her body to see whether she had any weapon or a belt fastened with explosives around her waist. It was fairly common at the Bombay International Airport for passengers to check their bags and get their boarding passes and then disappear. Those same passengers would go back to the city and commit murders. The paid killers would later use their boarding passes as alibis to prove that they were out of the country when the crimes were committed.

Thank God, Rayhana Khan was neither a female suicide bomber nor a paid killer. When the plane took off, she began to shake from her head down to her feet. She was holding onto her seat with one hand and her daughter with the other. She was thinking that they might fall out the plane any moment or the plane would fall out of the sky and they would crash on the ground or drown in the Arabian Sea. Her tears were streaming like a fountain, but her silence did not hide her fear. Those fearsome moments soon passed as the plane began to fly horizontally and Rayhana began to think that they had reached their destination. She whispered in the ear of her daughter and told her that they had reached the rich country of the Arabs. This idea was incorrect for one of the attendants approached her row of seats and asked her in broken Hindi whether she was a vegetarian or a non-vegetarian. Rayhana did not understand the question of the pretty young woman. The airhostess checked her boarding pass and saw her name was Rayhana Khan. From her name, she knew that Rayhana was a Muslim woman and hence she concluded that she was a non-vegetarian. Then she asked her whether she would prefer chicken, beef, or lamb. Rayhana being inexperienced thought she was sitting in an expensive restaurant and the food would be beyond her budget of five hundred rupees. She shook her head indicating that she did not want to eat. The airhostess pointed to her little daughter indicating she should have something to eat.

When Rayhana rejected the offer for her daughter to have a meal, the airhostess then understood that perhaps the poor Indian woman felt she had to pay for the food. She used an interpreter and told her that the food was already paid for with her tickets. As soon as Rayhana heard that the food was free, she changed her mind and said she wanted to eat something as well. She ordered lamb biryani for herself and chicken biryani for her little daughter. Biryani is the most delicious Pakistani/Indian food. It originated in Persia (Iran) and it was brought to the Indian Subcontinent by Iranian travelers and merchants. It is prepared out of tender morsels of chicken meat simmered in a creamy spicy blend of rice, saffron, onion, garlic, ginger, turmeric, cumin, tomatoes, ghee, cloves, cardamom, cinnamon, and mint leaves. It seemed that the person who created this tasty dish used every edible herb and spice in the world to produce this biryani recipe. Biryani is not a daily dish but reserved for very special occasions such as weddings, parties, and holidays. It is also cooked during religious festivals like Ramadan, Eid, Diwali, Christmas, *et cetera.*

Rayhana and her daughter had not often made use of a knife and fork except when they were eating in the public restaurants. They forgot they were in public and starting eating the delicious biryani dish as if they were at home in the slum with their hands and licked and sucked their fingers. During her three-week honeymoon with Jamaal, Rayhana noticed that after every meal they ate in the restaurant, her lover put some money on the table for the waiter. Trying to be generous and gracious for the nourishing and tasty free meal, Rayhana took out a note of five rupees from her handbag and placed it on the tray for the airhostess to have as a tip. When the airhostess came to collect the empty trays, she laughed and returned the money to Rayhana. While she was handing the rupees back she whispered to Rayhana and thanked her for her generosity. She then explained to her that the plane wasn't a restaurant and they didn't accept tips from the passengers.

After all the food trays were removed, some of the passengers removed their seatbelts and began to move around in the plane. Some of them were going to the restroom and some were just stretching their legs. Rayhana thought that the plane had reached the rich land of the Arabs. Therefore, she asked one airhostess to unfasten her seatbelt and her daughter's seatbelt. As soon as they were freed from their seats, Rayhana grabbed the hand of her daughter and began to walk her towards the front passenger exit door to the plane. When they reached the door, she caught hold of the handle and was about to pull the door open. An airhostess saw her at the right moment and pulled her hand from the door handle.

"What are you doing Madam!?!" The airhostess screamed at Rayhana.

"We are going out."

"Go back to your seats and don't move until we tell you the plane has landed in Jeddah airport."

The angry airhostess held Rayhana's hand and took her back to her seat. She fastened her and her daughter into their seatbelts. Then she informed the rest of the flight crew what had happened. After that, she came back to Rayhana followed by another airhostess. The second airhostesses told Rayhana never to move again from her seat and if she or her daughter wanted to use the restroom, she should press the button above her and a flight attendant would come and take her to the restroom. The airhostess then requested that the passengers sitting around and near Rayhana not help her unfasten her seatbelt and if she managed to unfasten her seatbelt by herself, they should notify someone immediately from the flight crew. Therefore, the inexperienced passengers were grounded and imprisoned in their seats until another problem occurred.

Before the plane was to land at Jeddah International Airport, the airhostesses distributed forms to the passengers and asked them to fill them out. By filling out the forms, the passengers would avoid unnecessary delays at the airport upon their arrival. The forms were in Hindi, Arabic, and English. Rayhana had never been to school in her life and hence the writing on the forms appeared to her to be like ants crawling together and all bunched up. She turned to the passenger who was sitting next to her and asked him to help her fill out the forms. The man was an Indian. He agreed to help the illiterate Indian woman. He began to ask her the questions on the form and then he started to fill in the specific information in the appropriate boxes and lines.

'What is your *First name: Rayhana, Last name: Khan, Coming from: Bombay, Going to: Jeddah, Purpose of visit: maidservant visa, Address: I have no address.'* The gentleman laughed when Rayhana said she had no address. Then, he asked her where she used to live before she flew from Bombay. She told him she was from Dharavi slum area. The man put as address: *Dharavi slum area, Bombay. Passport number: I have no passport!* The man was shocked when Rayhana said she had no passport. He asked her that question three times before he told her to give him her papers so he could find her passport. He was going to show her what her passport looked like. Rayhana gave him the tickets, visas, and boarding cards. The man told her that none of the papers she had given him was a passport. Then, he took out his Indian passport, showed it to her, and demanded that she should show him the same official document. Rayhana told him that their passports with the Negro boy. The gentleman asked her to look inside her handbag again. Rayhana knew she had no passports in her handbag. She handed her entire handbag to him. The man went through Rayhana's small handbag and slowly pulled out one Panjabi dress, underwear, and one sari of Rayhana, and one dress for her daughter. Then, he searched the empty handbag painstakingly as if he was hunting for gold. Finally, the gentleman was convinced that the slum woman and her daughter somehow entered the plane without their passports.

Out of compassion, the gentleman waved his hand to an airhostess and called her to come over and whispered to her that the Indian woman who was sitting next to him along with her daughter had no passports. The airhostess could not believe him. She talked to Rayhana to verify the claim of the gentleman. Rayhana gave her the same vague answer, *"Our passports with the Negro boy."* The airhostess happened to be the same one who shouted at her and stopped her from opening the door to the plane. Therefore, she doubted Rayhana's credibility and thought there was something suspicious about her behavior. She returned to the other crew members and informed them about the suspicious behavior of the Indian woman. One of the flight crew drew the conclusion that the Indian woman might be a terrorist, which scared the hell out of the others. Her conclusion was immediately seconded by another frightened airhostess. The belief that Rayhana was a female terrorist was supported and approved by all the members of the flight crew. Even the pilot and co-pilot agreed this woman must be a terrorist.

The conclusion was accepted because it was based on several observations. First of all the air hostess argued that she could not believe someone could pass through all that tight security and check points at the Sahara International Airport without a passport. Secondly, no passenger was dumb enough to try to open the cabin door of a plane while flying in midair as this Indian woman had done. Thirdly, the Indian woman did not pass through the legal route that each passenger had to go through before she could enter the plane. Therefore, the Indian woman had been smuggled inside the plane by a well-planned and executed terrorist plot.

When the flight crew collectively came to believe Rayhana Khan was a female terrorist, they informed the air Marshall. The air Marshall took the matter seriously. He was an Arab man from the KSA. He was fully armed from head to toe. He told the plane crew to try not to alarm the suspected woman. The passengers also should not be informed so as not to cause a panic. The Marshall went over to Rayhana and unfastened her seatbelt and asked her to come with him. Rayhana refused to come with him without her daughter. She told him to unfasten the seatbelt of her daughter and then both would come with him. The Marshall unwillingly agreed and freed Iffat from her seatbelt too. Then, he asked the two of them to follow him. When they reached the restroom, he told Rayhana to enter inside. This time, Rayhana obeyed his order without demanding her daughter come with her. After that, the Marshall called one of the air hostesses and told her to tell Rayhana to remove all her clothes including her underwear.

Rayhana refused to remove her clothes when the airhostess told her to do so. The Marshall told Rayhana that if she did not remove her clothing he would come in and remove them for her. Rayhana was scared that the angry man might forcefully remove her clothes and tear them, so she removed her Panjabi dress. She felt timid and afraid standing there only in her bra and underwear in front of a man. The Marshall wasn't satisfied with her removing her outer dress. He insisted next that Rayhana remove her bra and underwear. Rayhana began to cry. She begged the Marshall and asked him not to uncover her nakedness. Nonetheless, the Marshall refused to change his mind and while she stood crying, he shouted at her again and again to remove her bra and underwear.

By this time, all of the passengers became aware of the Indian woman suspected of being a suicide bomber and that she might blow up the plane at any moment. Some women and children began to cry. The male passengers were shaking with fear and looking at the lavatory where the female terrorist was expected to carry out her terrorist attack. Some religious passengers began to pray for their unavoidable death. The Marshall kept insisting Rayhana completely undress herself while she continued to refuse to obey his orders.

When the suspected female terrorist continued to refuse to remove the rest of her clothing, the Marshall took one step inside the restroom, screamed at the top of his lungs shouting *"Take off your underwear and bra!"* Rayhana concluded the angry man was going to rape her. She began to cry out loud and begged him not to come inside. She promised she was going to remove the rest of her clothing. Then, trembling and shaking Rayhana unwillingly removed her bra and underwear, covering her private parts with her hands

The Marshall asked her to put her hands on top of her head and turn around. Rayhana obeyed the order and placed her hands on her head. She had never expected that one day she would stand before a man who wasn't her husband fully naked. Her tears were falling like water down her face and her body was shaking from head to toe. The Marshall had a metal detector in his left hand and on his right hand, he was holding a gun and pointing it in her face. Then, he moved one step inside the restroom and began to check the naked body of the suspected female terrorist. His metal detector moved from Rayhana's breasts and passed by her stomach and legs until it reached her feet. Then, he told her to turn around and face the opposite direction. His metal detector moved from Rayhana's shoulders, passed her waist, and stopped for a few seconds on her large backside. The Marshall had in mind the case of the Nigerian male terrorist, Omar Al-Farooq, who had concealed plastic explosives in his underwear. After satisfied that the suspected Indian woman had nothing inserted inside her private parts the Marshall asked her to hand to him all her clothes. Rayhana was sweating as if she was inside a sauna. She bent her knees while she was still facing the opposite direction and picked up her scattered clothes piece after piece. She was scared to turn her face toward the angry man. She thought if she made any move without his permission, he would shoot her naked body with all the bullets in the gun.

The Marshall examined the clothes of Rayhana carefully before he returned them to her. Then, he ordered her to put on her dress. After she dressed herself, the Marshall asked her to stay inside the restroom until he returned. He then locked her inside. The Marshall was not satisfied with what he did to the mother and then thoroughly checked her daughter. Iffat began to cry when she heard her mother crying inside the restroom. She thought they wanted to kill her mother. She wasn't allowed to enter when they forced her mother to go inside the restroom. Rayhana was so humiliated having had her privacy terribly violated. She was forced to undress herself and expose her nakedness. She was a victim of a misunderstanding.

After checking her daughter, the Marshall went to the seats of the suspected female terrorist and began to search her bag for the hidden bomb and inside and around her seats. Finally, after all the humiliation, embarrassment, and mortification she endured, the Marshall declared that Rayhana Khan and her daughter were not terrorists. Rayhana was released from her imprisonment in the restroom and allowed to return to her seat along with her daughter. Then, and only then did the flight crew began to question Rayhana about her passport and her daughter's passport. Once again, Rayhana said their passports were with the Black Negro boy. All the members of the flight crew did not understand Rayhana except one. It was the airhostess who brought her and her daughter inside the plane. She was able to figure out what Rayhana meant by the Negro boy.

She narrated to the flight crew where she met the suspected female terrorist and her daughter and who brought them to her. Then, she laughed until she held her stomach. When she managed somehow to speak through her laughter, she said that the Indian woman and her daughter mistook the Black woman who brought them to the checkout for a Negro boy because she had hair like a boy and a face like a man. Then, the airhostess concluded her great observation by saying, *"Most probably the Black woman forgot to hand over the passports to them because they were in such a great hurry.*" This brilliant disclosure of the airhostess solved the mysterious disappearance of Rayhana and her daughter's passports. Therefore, the flight crew felt relieved and no longer had the problem of a female terrorist on the plane. Shortly after that, the Saudi plane landed at the Jeddah International Airport.

CHAPTER 17

ZARINE SHEIKH

Sheikh Faiz bin Ahmed tried many times to contact his Sudanese pimp but to no avail. His many calls and letters to him went unanswered. After some time, the old Saudi concluded that Babikir Al-A'war had stolen the tickets and visas and sold them. He already suspected the Sudanese wasn't on the level with him from the start. He doubted the money he sent to his beloved had ever reached her or that Babikir had ever made contact with her. In Bombay, you could sell anything even your own identity or bodily organs. Some poor Indians sold their kidneys to hoax doctors for illegal kidney transplants for treating sick rich Arabs. Sometimes foreign students also sold their passports and other identification due to financial difficulties. The photo on the passport would then be changed to that of the purchaser and used to go to whatever country he wished to go to. Among the foreign students at Bombay University, the Nigerian students were known for their drugs trafficking and the Somali students were widely renowned in the art of counterfeit and forgery. Whatever you wanted from paper money to bank drafts, the Somalis were masters in their profession.

I did not mean to be harsh in insinuating the Sudanese boy was a pimp for the wealthy old Saudi. Babikir Al-A'war knew exactly why Sheikh Ahmed was interested in Rayhana Khan. So excuse me if my opinion of him is less than stellar. By helping him to get her into his country for basically pennies on a dollar (or paisas on a rupee), and the promise he would secure a job in the future, Babikir put himself in a position of a Sudanese pimp in the modern day slave trade of the Arabs. A decent person would not help someone who wanted a woman for his own sexual pleasure, knowing she was being deceived with the offer of a maidservant visa. Rayhana was under the impression the old Saudi offered her free visas and tickets as a gift because she was a Muslim like him. Instead, her life and the life of her daughter were sold and traded between broker and dealer.

The typical Arab changes maidservants annually as if they were turning in a trade for a new car or putting away summer clothes to prepare for the winter. If in the first year he chose a maidservant from Sir Lanka, the second year he would choose one from the Philippines, the third year one from Indonesia, and the fourth from Pakistan, the fifth from India, etc., etc., etc. As soon as the maidservant reached his house, he would either rape her or buy her body with a few riyals or dinars. The maidservant would work like a slave during the day and at night, her Kafeel (owner or master) would use her for his sexual pleasure and for his entertainment. Sometimes, the same maidservant might be shared by the father and his adult sons. A Pakistani policeman in a gulf country was beaten to death by an angry Arab mob because he was quoted in a newspaper saying that the Pakistani girls who were working as maidservants were sex slaves to the Arabs. ("As recently as the 1950s, Saudi Arabia's slave population was estimated at 450,000—approximately 20% of the population." Saudi Arabia continues down to this very day to enslave people of all nations while their government and the governments of the world turn the other way for profit).

Sheikh Ahmed decided never to give up on love. He thought that it was a big mistake enlisting the help of a *Sudanese slave*. In order to avenge this matter and punish the Sudanese boy he had to return back to his old partner in crime if he ever wanted to find his beloved Rayhana. Muhammad Khan, his former chauffeur, would be his savior and last resort. Besides, he was unable to find any travel agency willing to purchase his visas. After much thought and nagging suspicions of Babikir double-crossing him and stealing Rayhana's visas, tickets, and money, Sheikh Ahmed contacted his former Indian consort and apologized to him. Then, he told him how the Sudanese boy had cheated him and stole his Indian maidservant's money, visas, and tickets. In order to hide his attempts to maneuver his own outcome and failing, he claimed that Babikir was the one who had phoned him and told him he could find Rayhana Khan and process her travel papers.

Muhammad Khan promised to find Rayhana and reprocess her papers and get her on her way to her rightful benefactor as soon as possible. He swore by Allah he would seek revenge for this miscarriage of justice and the Black Negro would be hauled away to jail and never again see the light of day. Sheikh Ahmed thanked his former car driver immensely over and over again before he hung up the phone. Muhammad Khan was so happy he thought he had died and gone to heaven and enjoying the seventy-two virgins. His wealthy Saudi client was returning to him, which made him see dollar signs and rupees in his near future.

The first big business deal between the evil characters took place shortly after that and involved a huge recruitment of nurses to the Kingdom of Saudi Arabia. The Saudi Ministry of Health decided to change its methods in acquiring medical staff or nurses in particular. In the past, the Ministry used to solicit foreign nurses from Western countries such as USA, UK, Canada, and Australia. However, the Western nurses demanded far more wages than the doctors who came from the poor Arab countries like Egypt, Lebanon, Jordan, and Sudan. The white nurses knew their rights and constantly came up with new demands wanting access to the same facilities and accommodations as doctors and demanding extra holidays and pay, less work load, etc., etc., etc.

Therefore, the Ministry of Heath stopped recruiting nurses from the West and began to bring Arab nurses from the above-mentioned poor Arab countries. However, experience proved that the Arab nurses were not very qualified or hardworking. Many patients complained that the Arab nurses were mean and treated them with disrespect and sometimes abused them. Accordingly, when it became impractical to employ nurses from the Western countries as well as the Arab countries, the Ministry of Health decided to hire nurses from India. The pilot study showed that the Indian nurses were qualified, caring and hardworking, and very cheap to employ. In India, the nurses had to be female. No man was allowed to work as a nurse. Indians believed that the nurse had to be loving, caring, patient, pleasing, good-looking, and very kind. According to them, all those virtues combined together could only be found in a female.

Sheikh Ahmed got the contract from the Saudi Ministry of Health. According to the contract, he had to hire five hundred and fifty qualified and experienced Indian nurses. The Ministry would send its own employees along with the contractor to interview the candidates. Sheikh Ahmed got the contract about the time he resumed his business with Muhammad Tours and Travels. Therefore, the wealthy old Saudi assigned the contract to his former car driver. Besides the contract, Muhammad Khan was assigned the task of finding and processing Rayhana's travel papers. As a matter of fact, Sheikh Ahmed gave Muhammad Khan three important assignments; find his most beloved maidservant, make preparation for the recruitment of 550 nursing candidates, and provide a young beautiful Indian damsel for entertainment at his hotel.

Muhammad Khan was another procurer for the wealthy old Saudi. In the past, he sent two of his female employees to entertain him in his room at the five star hotel, the Taj Mahal. Sheikh Ahmed wasn't pleased by the two female employees. The first female employee sent to sleep with the rich Arab was Rukhsana. Sheikh Ahmed did not like Rukhsana. She had a good-looking face but a very skinny body. As an Arab man, a large backside and a big body were very essential requirements in a female. Rukhsana was lacking in these feminine qualities. The second female employee sent to the Arab man was Tahirah. Sheikh Ahmed wasn't pleased with Tahirah either. She had the requisite large rear end and buxom body but was lacking in the face department. Therefore, the next time Sheikh Ahmed gave exact specifications as to what a proper female should possess in order to satisfy him. He said to Muhammad, his services as a pimp were deficient considering the money he had paid him. He wanted a female employee who had Rukhsana's face and Tahirah's body.

Sheikh Ahmed could easily find a girl among Colaba's hundreds of call girls and prostitutes who would have been a hundred times more beautiful than the female employees of Muhammad Khan. However, he was interested in the female employees for three reasons. The first reason he did not like a prostitute because she wasn't safe without the use of a condom. He hated condoms. The second reason he did not like having sex with an ordinary girl who had already been used and shared by hundreds of men. (He liked a virgin or one who was close to 'showroom status'). The third reason was the female employee would come for sex because her circumstances forced her to sleep with her boss and entertain his Arab clients. The Saudi man loved to have sex with a girl who resisted him. It was an acquired tasted, developed over a long period of time with his former Pakistani, Filipino and Indonesian maidservants.

When the old Saudi man demanded that his next female entertainer possess the face of Rukhsana and the body of Tahirah, Muhammad decided to employ a new girl to meet those requirements. He advertised in the local paper and paid for a spot on the public information station the need for a clerk with specific qualities and qualifications. He did not entirely list all the requirements but encouraged all interested applicants to come in person and find out what the *travel agency* wanted in the new female employee. He stated a generous salary that was two times more than what he was paying his other female employees. When his female employees saw the advertisement on the local TV station, radio and in the newspapers, they objected and demanded a raise in salary. He rejected their demands and told each girl if she wanted a raise in pay then she could quit her job, go to another *travel agency* and seek higher pay. Not one of the girls quit her job or dared to open her mouth again.

Nevertheless, one of his employees decided to take advantage of the new offer. He was the only employee who did not object to the high salary that was offered to the new candidate because he was a male. By then the *travel agency* had only one male employee remaining. The other two male employees were falsely accused and thrown behind bars.

The only remaining male employee was Javed Sheikh. When Javed came to know that his workplace was offering a job with a higher salary, he informed his sister and encouraged her to come and apply in person. His sister was nineteen years old. Her name was Zarine Sheikh. She was a very beautiful girl. When Zarine presented herself for the job, she got hired on the spot. Muhammad employed Javed's sister because she met the specified requirements of the old Saudi exceedingly. The pimp picked up his phone and called his Saudi client. He told him that he found a girl for him who was extremely beautiful and a virgin too. Yes, the girl was extremely beautiful but how did the slimy worm know that she was a virgin. Muhammad Khan was a Muslim and he knew a Muslim man's mentality when it came to women. Virginity was a very important asset to an Arab man. That is why their prophet promised them that each one of them was going to get seventy-two beautiful female virgins in paradise. According to the prophet Muhammad, the virgins of paradise were going to remain virgins forever. How could a virgin remain a virgin forever after deflowering? Let's see how the prophet of Islam solved that riddle. *"The prophet was asked: 'Do we have sex in paradise? He answered: 'Yes, by him who holds my soul in his hand and it will be done* ***dahman, dahman*** *(that is the intercourse done with such shove and disturbance).* ***And when it is finished she will return pure and virgin again****" (Haqq & Newton 1996: 17, emphasis is mine).* According to this hadith, Allah would either stitch up the virgin's vagina after each time she was penetrated by a male's penis or he would recreate a new hymen and insert it in her privates.

The number of those perpetual virgins of paradise differed from one hadith to another. In one hadith, the prophet Muhammad said they are seventy-two and in another hadith the number was increased into the thousands.

"The Messenger of Allah said, upon him blessings and peace: '...he shall be coupled with seventy-two spouses from the wide-eyed maidens of Paradise'" (Reported by Ahmad and al-Tirmizi).

"The Messenger of Allah said, upon him blessings and peace: 'Every man from the People of Paradise shall be married off to four

thousand virgins, eight thousand slave-girls, and one hundred wide-eyed maidens of Paradise. They shall all meet him within every seven days. They shall say with their exquisite voices no creature has ever heard the like before: 'We are the everlasting women, we never grow old, we are the refined women, we never grow sour, we are the ever-pleased women, we never anger, we are the sedentary ones, we never travel away, blessings to him who is for us and we are for him!'" (Abu al-Shaykh in al-`Azama and al-Bayhaqi in al-Ba`th wal-Nushur).

Fulfilling his other job assignment, Muhammad Khan booked interviews for the nurse positions at a local Muslim schoolhouse and received more than one thousand five hundred applicants. He would have received more than five thousand applications in one-week's time if he had not locked the doors preventing other interested candidates from entering. He also had to put a notice on the door of his *travel agency*, which said, in big red letters; NO MORE APPLICATIONS WILL BE ACCEPTED.

Under the direction of the interview committee, Muhammad Khan was advised to gather as many possible applications so that the committee could select the most qualified nurses. However, when he got over 1,500 applicants the interview committee advised him to stop accepting applications. The interview committee consisted of eleven qualified doctors from the King Fahd Royal Hospital at Riyadh city. Each member was supposed to interview seventy-five nurses and select fifty. Nonetheless, the huge number of applications would require every member interview one hundred and fifty candidates, choose only fifty and send hundreds of others away.

Two days prior to the interview, a small problem cropped up at the travel agency. It had to do with the newly employed girl. Javed and his sister Zarine hid their relationship from everyone in the recruitment agency including their boss. Javed pretended not to know Zarine before and Zarine never told anyone that Javed was her brother. Therefore, everyone thought it was a mere coincidence that the two of them had the same last name. Khan and Sheikh were very common last names among Indian and Pakistani Muslims. The problem had nothing to do with the concealed relationship between the new female employee and the only remaining male employee. The main cause of the problem was envy and jealousy.

When the *travel agency* advertised the new position for a salary of fifteen thousand rupees per month, every girl in the office wanted to get it. All the female employees desired to have the new position because each one of them was being paid seven thousand rupees and the new job would make her earn more than double her current salary. Besides that, most of them had ample work experience with Muhammad Tours and Travels. Nevertheless, Muhammad refused to promote them to the new position and sent away many more girls who came to apply for the job. When Zarine Sheikh was hired for this highly paid position, the other girls in the office hated her and were mean to her from day one. Javed did not like the way his sister was being treated by the other girls but he could do nothing to make it better. Whenever his sister was called by the boss to come into his office he heard the nasty remarks the other girls were saying about her. One day Rukhsana took the lead in nastiness and said Zarine was employed because of her looks and because she agreed to f…k the boss. Rukhsana was a bold, tenacious young woman and when she got mad, she used very vulgar street language.

The girls said if it wasn't for Zarine's figure and good looks she wouldn't have qualified to even be a peon at the *travel agency*. The girls were right. Zarine did not know how to write one full sentence correctly in English or in Hindi. She completed her twelfth grade education in intermediate Urdu language. She didn't know how to type or use a computer. She just sat like any other visitor in the office. The other girls did all the work and she stared at them hustling about while she did absolutely nothing. However, every now and then she got called into the boss' office and spent a long time with him. Every time she went into her boss' office, the girls began to whisper and gossip in front of her brother.

Javed decided to put an end to all this gossip. When he and his sister returned home, he told her to complain to the boss about all the murmuring that was going on. He told her what kind of things they were saying about her behind her back. He said to her openly the implied accusations being directed against her. The other girls were accusing her of having an affair with the boss and having sex with him inside his office. On the following day, Zarine reported the matter to her boss. The no nonsense boss, Muhammad Khan, decided he had to immediately put an end to this interoffice muttering between females and called a special meeting to deal with the matter. He began to lecture his female employees as follows:

"First of all there is nothing going on between Zarine and me. Moreover, I have not employed her but she had been employed by one of my Arab clients. Her position is called 'Foreign Academic Assistant Educator."

The girls had never heard of a position like that before. It's highly unlikely that even the boss himself knew exactly what the wordy job title meant.

"She is required to be with my Arab client whenever he comes to Bombay for his business. She is his personal secretary. Her duty is to educate him in the Indian culture. She has to assist him in how to interact and deal with Indians wherever he goes."

Rukhsana was the first one to catch a hole in his job description for the new position. She rose up to challenge him. *"Sir,"* shouted Rukhsana, *"in which language is she going to educate and assist her Arab employer?"*

The boss got very angry when Rukhsana interrupted him. *"How dare you to cut me off while I am talking and who are you to question me as if I am your employee?"*

"I am sorry sir, but this girl knows nothing. She can't speak English or Arabic. She just sits and stares at us all day while she does absolutely nothing at all. I can speak..."

"Shut up Rukhsana" shouted the boss. *"If you ever dare tell me how to do my job again, I will personally throw you out of here with my foot up your ass."* His voice was like rolling thunder and Rukhsana startled slowly sat back down at her desk.

Rukhsana's big mouth did not help her case one little bit. After the angry boss threatened to kick her out of the office, he returned to his personal office, called in the Foreign Academic Assistant Educator, and began to tell her what her main duties were.

"Listen Zarine, I know those girls hate you and are desiring to have your position. If I were in their position, I would feel the same way too. However, as I have said, I have employed you to work with one of my foreign clients, an Arab man. He is a good man but he wants a young, beautiful girl like you to be his secretary. I have lied to the other girls and you don't need to do anything for him except..."

The boss paused and looked at Zarine's face to see if she was annoyed in anyway by what he was saying to her. When he saw her face remain undisturbed, he was encouraged to reveal the most important duty of that peculiar job position.

"Except be with him in his hotel room and wherever he goes you must accompany him."

The boss moonlighting as a pimp paused again and glanced directly into Zarine's face. She still had the same solemn look.

"Will you be able to do that?"

"Yes sir" said Zarine with full confidence.

"That is why I chose you for the job. Okay since you are a very understanding girl, I would like to tell you a little more about your duty. See Zarine, it is natural that a young and very beautiful girl like you when she is alone with a man in his hotel room that he might like just to touch her hand or her hair. Remember, I have told you he is a good man. He is already married and has four wives."

The pimp grooming his victim paused again and checked the facial expression of his *Foreign Academic Assistant Educator.* She did not seem to be disturbed in appearance.

"Maybe, but I am not sure of what else he might require you to do, but maybe he might just want to give you a fatherly kiss or a hug."

The calculating deceitful manipulator paused once more but this time looked away from Zarine worried that she might start to object. However, her lack of concern or objection assured him she was still accepting of her job duties. Out of envy, he decided to cause a roadblock and reserve one duty for himself.

"Never allow him to have sex with you. If he gives you one million dollars don't ever allow him to sleep with you."

"Okay sir."

The "okay sir" sounded like Zarine might agree to have sex if she was tempted with the right price and that troubled the heart of the wicked boss. He wanted to reserve the beautiful girl for himself. After he went to jail and his wife fired his favorite female employee, Bulbolah Sheikh, he had not gotten any new especially pretty female employee to fill the gap that the absence of Bulbolah Sheikh created.

"Well Zarine, that is about all I can tell you about your duties. You will start work as soon as your foreign boss arrives in Bombay two days from today."

"But sir" said Zarine softly. She spoke as if she was scared the other girls might overhear her and that's why she spoke in a whisper. Muhammad waited to hear Zarine voice her objection to her new assignment but she remained with the same disposition when she whispered, "but sir". He said, *"But what?"*

"But sir, do I need to tell my family I am going to sleep with my foreign boss in his hotel room when he comes in two days?"

The wicked boss felt like getting up from his chair and slapping Zarine in her face with all the force he could muster.

"Who said you are going to sleep with him in his hotel room. You will work for him the same hours and same time you are working for me. If he asks you to stay with him one minute after hours say no."

"Okay sir."

Muhammad Khan did not like her nonchalant and careless attitude. He couldn't believe that a girl could be so unconcerned and couldn't care less.

"Now go back to your desk and don't tell those envious girls anything what I have told you."

"Okay sir."

After her last "okay sir," Zarine got up and walked out of her boss' office just as she went in. After all, it was just another day at the office and she resumed sitting and doing nothing all day. As soon as she left, the befuddled boss began to regret he had told Sheikh Ahmed about her. He hated the fact that he had selected her for the job especially after she asked him whether she should tell her family that her job required she sleep with her foreign superior in his hotel room. If he had known she was that easy and eager to jump into bed, he would have kept her for himself.

Zarine went back to her desk as though nothing wrong had been said to her. She wasn't offended in any way by what her boss had propositioned. She wasn't saddened, scared, insulted, humiliated or anything like that. Even so, Zarine Sheikh wasn't as easygoing and carefree as she pretended to be in front of her boss. She understood what her boss was suggesting and what he wanted her to do for his foreign client. She knew that with her twelfth grade intermediate certificate in Urdu, she couldn't get an office job anywhere in Bombay. She understood her beauty got her hired in what was a very difficult-to-get overpaid position. Who in Bombay would give a twelfth grade girl who primarily spoke Urdu, a salary of fifteen thousand rupees per month? It's understandable her circumstances would force her to compromise and accept certain conditions for employment to keep her job.

Zarine Sheikh was in love with a Muslim boy who was seven years older than her. Her lover was semi-jobless for more than five years. He was a tenth grade dropout. His limited Urdu education would not qualify him to even work as a peon in an office. For five years, he worked blue-collar jobs like carrying bags for passengers at the railway station, carrying heavy loads of cement bags on his head and climbing up a ladder ten, fifteen stories, hand pulling carts loaded with various goods, *et cetera*. During those five years, he worked from hand to mouth. He saved nothing. He proposed to Zarine three times and every time her father rejected his proposal and kicked him out of the house.

Zarine loved her boyfriend to the point of no return. He was her *Amitabh Bachan*. He was very handsome and Zarine saw him as a film hero. When his proposal was rejected for the third consecutive time by her father, Zarine lost hope of marrying her dream man. The moment she landed her golden fifteen-thousand rupee once in a lifetime opportunity, her hope was revived and she decided to hold onto her job with her hands and the back of her teeth. Why should she bother about her honor if an old man wanted to kiss on her cheek or hug her for a few minutes? Even if he demanded more than that, she would tolerate it until she could find a way to be with her lover. She believed her new job could help her get a visa to a rich Arab country and then she could take her dream man with her and live happily ever after. Every Indian wants to go to one of the OAPEC countries (the Organization of Arab Petroleum Exporting Countries) or immigrate to a Western country. Some people sold their houses in order to purchase visas to an OAPEC country or paid huge lump sums of cash to travel agencies to obtain immigration visas to the United States of America, Australia, or Canada.

Zarine did not tell anyone about her new duties given to her by her supervisor. When she got home after work, she did not tell her brother or anyone a word of what her boss had said was to be her official duties. Her pimp had made it clear she was to keep her mouth shut. While Zarine was waiting for her foreign boss to arrive, Muhammad Khan sent some of his most trustworthy of friends, the Gondas, to search for Rayhana Khan in the biggest slum area in Asia and second largest slum area in the world. It took the Gondas six days to locate the hiding place of the slum woman. Rayhana's sons and mother were found inside the slum but she and her daughter weren't there. According to the mother, Rayhana and her daughter flew to the Arab country where there was *the Holy House of Allah*. The Gondas took some pictures with the mother and her grandchildren as evidence that they had succeeded in their mission of finding the slum of Rayhana Khan.

Although, the photos were presented as proof to Muhammad Khan along with this incredible report, he still did not believe his messengers. He asked himself repeatedly how Rayhana and her daughter could possibly fly to the Kingdom of Saudi Arabia without their passports. He was certain of the fact he was the one who had received their passports and burned them to ashes. He also remembered that Rayhana's previous passport was stolen by the police and sold to that Malayali woman who went to Saudi Arabia and claimed to be Rayhana Khan. In order to clear his doubts, he picked up his phone and called the Worli passport office and inquired about how many passports were issued to Rayhana Khan. His spy checked the computer and gave him all the details concerning the separate dates and addresses that were used in the processing of both passports for Rayhana and for her daughter. The spy assured him that Rayhana Khan had not come to reapply again for new passports.

At first, Muhammad thought that the Gondas had cheated him by taking some pictures of some slum children and their grandmother and presenting these as evidence to him just to get their money. If that was the case, he reasoned that he had better use more capable Gondas for this mission. They would be better suited to find Rayhana and at the same time, he would have reason to get his money back from the incompetent Gondas. However, before he would carry out this new plan, he decided to check with the Sahara International Airport. He picked up his phone and called the airport and spoke to one of his spies there. When the spy checked the computer, he confirmed the claim of the low-level Gondas. The computer showed that two Indian passengers by the names of Rayhana Khan and Iffat Khan had flown by a Saudi jumbo jet to Jeddah International Airport. Muhammad Khan asked the spy to find out what kind of travel documents the passengers used to fly out of the country. The spy told him a passenger must have a valid passport, visa, and ticket to travel or board a flight out of the country. The computer showed nothing to indicate that the two passengers did not have the necessary travel documents. Instead of thanking him, the angry, ungrateful, dumb-founded galoot shouted at the spy because he had failed to block Rayhana and her daughter's exit out of the country. The spy refused to give an explanation or apologize to Muhammad Khan and instead abruptly hung up the phone.

CHAPTER 18

THE VIRGIN

Sheikh Ahmed and the eleven medical doctors arrived in Bombay a day prior to the interviews. The doctors were booked into the Oberoi hotel while Sheikh Ahmed was booked in the Taj Mahal hotel. Muhammad Khan made the accommodations under the direction of his Saudi client. Sheikh Ahmed did not want the Saudi doctors to know what he was planning to do in his hotel room with the beautiful nineteen-year-old virgin that his call-girl service had found and reserved for him. As soon as he checked in at the Taj Mahal hotel, Sheikh Ahmed took a taxi to the Muhammad Travel Agency. He was eager to consult with his pimp and view his beautiful virgin. He also wanted to know what Muhammad Khan had done to the *Black slave boy* who had cheated him.

(By the way, Muslim Arabs named the Christian Nubian Cushitic tribes "Sudaneen" meaning black slaves or people with black faces because they resisted their invasion and occupation of the Christian Kingdom of Kush. For over a thousand years, the Muslim Mujahedeen could not defeat the Nubians and spread their religion in that religion. When finally defeated them they forced them to accept Islam and enslaved them through unfair treaty to pay them the Jizya as 360 slaves each year. Therefore, the names Sudan and Sudanese are insult and racially loaded terms rather than praise for the people of the ancient Kingdom of Kush. The Egyptian Muslim scholar, Sayyid Al-Qimni recently proposed that the Committee of Fatwa of the Al-Azhar Al-Sharif should elect delegates and send them to Sudan to apologize to the people of that land for bestowing on them such depredating and derogatory names. According to him, Sudanese should no more be treated with disdain because they have embraced Islam and applied the Shari'a laws).

On his arrival, Muhammad Khan called in Zarine and introduced her to her foreign boss. The foreign boss was well pleased by the beautiful virgin. He paid her price in cash in front of his Indian pimp. However, the nineteen-year-old girl appeared to him modest as compared to his gorgeous, beautiful, sensuous and womanly Rayhana Khan. Therefore, as soon as Zarine took her price and left the office, Sheikh Ahmed inquired about his missing maidservant and whether the black slave received his punishment. The pimp told Sheikh Ahmed that he had indeed found the Negro boy and sent him to prison forever. Sheikh Ahmed felt a great sigh of relief and appreciated the good work that his client had done in punishing his deceiver. Regarding Rayhana and her daughter, Muhammad Khan decided to be half-truthful. He told Sheikh Ahmed according to his spy at the Worli Passport Office, the new passports for the maidservant and her daughter were mailed to the Sudanese slave's residence and apparently he sold the passports to another travel agency. That was a lie of course for he had burned them. The truth of the matter Muhammad Khan was happy to report to Sheikh Ahmed is the incredible news he received from his Gondas and spy at the international airport. Rayhana and her daughter somehow managed to board the flight to Saudi Arabia anyhow without their passports. However, he did not tell him that he had received their passports and destroyed them.

Sheikh Ahmed refused to believe that Rayhana and her daughter had reached Saudi Arabia without their passports until Muhammad Khan swore by Allah to divorce his wife if what he said wasn't the absolute truth. Halfway believing this too good to be true story, Sheikh Ahmed thanked his Asian nation pimp and told him to send his *Foreign Academic Assistant Educator* as soon as possible to his hotel room at the Taj Mahal hotel. This was so he could begin *work on her*.

Before Sheikh Ahmed had arrived in Bombay and come into his office and then left, Muhammad Khan was planning to send the young beautiful virgin to him. However, when he called Zarine in and she came and stood in front of him and he examined her up and down, he changed his mind. Muhammad had already told Zarine to agree to everything except sex with Sheikh Ahmed. Zarine gave her word and promised her concerned boss that she wouldn't sleep with the old Arab. But from the moment she came and stood before him, his wicked heart began to doubt her resolve. He had come to know her as a happy-go-lucky, carefree girl. She might agree to have sex with the wealthy old Arab if he tempted her with more money. She had already received fifteen thousand rupees from the Old Saudi. Nevertheless, Muhammad decided to keep his promise and send the virgin to the hotel room but he also decided to make sure that Sheikh Ahmed would not touch her. Before he executed his plan, he explained it fully to Zarine and told her not to disappoint him. Zarine gave her word and swore by her Allah that she would do everything he told her to do.

It was one of the most exciting times in the life of Sheikh Ahmed. His mind was occupied with the problem of where his beloved maidservant was at this point in time and his penis was thinking about the young virgin who was supposed to come entertain him at any moment. However, the arrival of Rayhana and her daughter in Jeddah without their passports occupied most of his mind. While he was thinking about them, something suddenly entered his thoughts. Although Muhammad Khan was a genius in doing evil and cheating people, that day he made a huge mistake that would soon expose him for who he really was. Sheikh Ahmed discovered that mistake by himself as soon as he reached the hotel. He was about to see just how fragile his new realigned partnership really was. He asked himself, *"If Babikir had cheated him and stolen the two tickets and visas and sold them to anther travel agency then how did Rayhana and her daughter reach Jeddah?"* The information that Muhammad Khan obtained from the Sahara International Airport revealed that Rayhana and her daughter had flown to Jeddah with all their necessary documents. Then, Muhammad Khan contradicted himself and said they did not have their passports but they had their tickets and visas. That means Babikir didn't lie to him and didn't steal the visas and tickets.

The logical conclusion was that the Sudanese boy had truly found Rayhana and given her the visas and tickets. Sheikh Ahmed expected that Rayhana and her daughter would be held up at the Jeddah airport. He anticipated that the airport personnel would contact his office from the Jeddah airport because he was their sponsor. Sheikh Ahmed realized his next step would be to arrange travel accommodations from the airport for his beloved and her precious child. The airport might not allow him to take his Indian maidservant and her daughter home without their passports. If he failed to convince the airport officials to allow them to enter the city or produce their passports, Rayhana and her daughter might be arrested, tried, and deported back to India. Therefore, his main concern was to get passports for them before they would be sent back to their country.

Sheikh Ahmed's mind became so preoccupied about how to get his beloved through Jeddah International Airport that he totally forgot about the fresh beautiful virgin that would soon be lying naked in his bed; until the doorbell rang. He got up from his bed and opened the door. The beautiful Zarine was standing in front of him. He wanted to hold her voluptuous body in his arms but stopped when he saw another girl standing behind her. At first, he thought the other girl was a housekeeper in the hotel who had come to do his room. However, he slowly realized that he had seen the girl before that very day in the travel agency. She was the ugliest Indian girl he ever seen in all his life. She came forward and introduced herself to him as *"Jamilah Malik."* When she said her name was "Beautiful" he hated her even more.

Sheikh Ahmed did not allow the two girls to enter his hotel room but kept them waiting by the door and he went back into his room and called the travel agency. He asked Muhammad Khan the reason for sending the ugly girl along with his beautiful virgin. The pimp told the old man that Zarine Sheikh refused to go to meet an Arab man all alone by herself in a hotel room. He further told him that although he threatened to fire her she said she would rather choose to quit her job than to go meet a man alone in a hotel room and stay with him by herself. For that reason, the panderer of flesh said he was compelled to send another girl with her.

The pimp, however, put some hope in the heart of the old Saudi by telling him to try to fool Jamilah by sending her somewhere to buy food and drink or when she goes to the washroom lock her up inside or any trick like that. With a few suggested tricks up his sleeve, Sheikh Ahmed returned to his two female guests and welcomed them in. Despite three hours of trick or treat, nothing worked. It was as if the two girls were joined together at the hip or stuck together with glue. Neither of them would stay behind with the old man whenever the other was sent out of the room to buy food or do an errand like make the bed or look for the best Arab speaking channels on TV. They both went to the washroom together four times. Whenever one of them would say I am going to pee, the other would say I need to pee too.

When all the best tricks did not work, Sheikh Ahmed decided to use alcohol. He wanted to liquor them up so he could rape the virgin. Jamilah said she never drank alcohol in her life and she would never ever touch the forbidden drink. Zarine admitted she had drunk alcohol before but only with her boyfriend. She said she made a vow with her lover that she would never ever drink alcohol with anyone else except him. When Zarine mentioned "boyfriend" and the fact that she drank, it led the Arab to suspect that the Indian pimp had deceived him about her virginity. Finally, the Saudi got fed up with the two girls and kicked them out of his room so fast it made their heads spin. It didn't matter though if they were kicked out, for this was the most extravagant day they had ever had. The two girls enjoyed the most delicious and expensive foods and drank all kinds of sweet drinks and juices. That's why they went to the washroom four times together.

Sheikh Ahmed knew that Muhammad Khan had fooled him. He concluded that Zarine didn't want to come alone to his hotel room and imposed certain conditions as to why she needed someone to come with her, but he figured his former car driver gave in to her request for he wanted to save the beautiful young teenager all for himself. He also knew that Muhammad Khan was behind the arrest of the Sudanese boy. Muhammad openly admitted that he sent Babikir to jail. Since Babikir delivered the visas and tickets to Rayhana why did his former boss get him in trouble with the law? Sheikh Ahmed picked up his cell phone and put this question to his business associate. Muhammad Khan said to him that he had followed his order and did what he wanted him to do. He punished the Sudanese slave by framing him with a serious crime. Sheikh Ahmed then regretted he had ever asked the former car driver to punish the Sudanese boy.

After he talked to Muhammad Khan, Sheikh Ahmed visited the international student hostel and inquired about his best friend. Some Sudanese students narrated to him in tears how some evil people hid drugs in Babikir's bag and he was charged with the most dreaded crime in all of India. They told him further that Babikir would be tried and most probably after three years, he would be convicted and sentenced for life. Sheikh Ahmed thought that because of him the Sudanese boy's life was completely destroyed. Nonetheless, he did not linger on the great evil that had been done to Babikir through his instigation. His main concern was to visit Babikir in jail and find out why Rayhana and her daughter did not get their passports and why he sent them to Saudi Arabia without the proper paperwork.

Babikir saw some hope when his wealthy Saudi friend came and visited him in prison. He requested him appoint a lawyer to represent him and fight his case. He swore by Allah and his prophet Muhammad that he was innocent of the drug charges *as the wolf was innocent of the blood of Yusuf (biblical Joseph)*. (Joseph was the son of

Jacob whose brothers threw him into a pit to be rid of him and claimed that an evil beast had devoured him). Sheikh Ahmed made an empty promise to Babikir with no intention of keeping it. He decided never again to waste a single rupee on another Indian lawyer. He learned a good lesson from his experience with his ex-wife, Christie; the Christian girl who stole his money and kicked him off his property. Why would he spend another rupee on useless lawyers when the law allowed his wife to replace him with her much younger Indian lover?

In speaking to his friend, Sheikh Ahmed learned that Babikir had found Rayhana and delivered the money he sent to her and the two visas, and two tickets. The Sudanese boy informed Sheikh Ahmed that he never told Rayhana to travel out of India without her passports. He said the two passports were supposed to come to his address but he got arrested before they arrived. Then, he gave his Vakola Colony apartment's address to Sheikh Ahmed and told him to go there and find out from the secretary of the Colony whether the passports had arrived in the mail.

Sheikh Ahmed's main concern was to get those two passports in order to rescue his beloved woman and her daughter from being prosecuted and deported back to their country. Therefore, from Arthur Road Jail he traveled to Vakola Colony and met with the secretary. The Colony secretary was glad to meet a wealthy Saudi business tycoon. He gave him all the details about the activities of the young Sudanese men who used to live in the Colony prior to their arrest. Sheikh Ahmed wasn't interested in those details but in order to win the trust of the secretary he listened to him. When he asked him about the two passports, the secretary said he did not know anything about any passports. He did inform him however, that the apartment had new tenants who moved in shortly after the Sudanese students were arrested. The new tenants were foreign students from Jordan and Palestine. Sheikh Ahmed requested the secretary introduce him to the Arab students.

When the old Saudi met the Arab students, they told him that they had not seen any Indian passport in their mailbox. Sheikh Ahmed requested one of the Arab students go with him to the passport office to investigate the matter of the missing passports. The Arab student agreed to help and the Old Saudi paid him for his time. They proceeded the same day to the Worli Passport Office and made good time. The persistent old geezer paid a heavy bribe to get information about the two passports of his beloved Rayhana and her daughter. The bribe was successful and revealed the exact cause of the mysterious disappearance of the two passports. The two passports were reissued and sent to the office of Muhammad Tours and Travels through a speed post. Therefore, the search for the two missing passports began and ended with the wicked, Muhammad Khan. Sheikh Ahmed instantly saw that in retaliation for the humiliation and breaking up of his partnership with his former car driver, he had stolen the two passports and destroyed them. He not only destroyed the passports alone, but he destroyed the life of Babikir Al-A'war and caused Rayhana and her daughter to travel to the city of Jeddah, Saudi Arabia without their passports. Finally, they just like the Sudanese boy would land in jail.

Sheikh Ahmed decided it was time for a real payback. Muhammad Khan would feel the full force and effect of Sheikh Ahmed's wrath when he executed the ultimate punishment and revenge upon his former car driver. Before he carried out his revenge, he paid twenty thousand rupees as bribe to the most senior passport officer and demanded the two passports of Rayhana and her daughter be reissued and handed over to him at once. The passport officer pulled out the two files and took out the photos of Rayhana and her daughter and made new passports and handed them to Sheikh Ahmed the same day. After that, Sheikh Ahmed went to the eleven medical doctors at the Oberoi hotel and told them the interview was called off because there was a great fraud committed by the travel agency that he had entrusted with the contract. He told them clearly that it was brought to him from very reliable sources that many of the candidates were not qualified nurses. Some of them were still studying at the nursing schools and some of them had never been to any nursing school. Worse than that, some of them received forged medical certificates obtained through bribes stating five to ten years of work experience at a hospital when in actuality they had none. The travel agency accepted their applications because they were being paid huge bribes and kickbacks.

The eleven doctors were shocked and outraged when they heard that these fraudulent practices had occurred at a trusted recruitment agency. Sheikh Ahmed promised them that he was going to find a reputable travel agency and transfer the contract to this new Indian agency. The doctors thanked Sheikh Ahmed for his honesty and for his sincere efforts in unearthing this crime at just the right time. On the advice of Sheikh Ahmed, the eleven doctors changed their booking and flew back the same night to Jeddah along with their Saudi contractor. In the plane, Sheikh Ahmed told the medical team that he had contacted a reliable recruitment agency in New Delhi and arranged for interviews in the near future for the desired number of highly qualified and well-experienced Indian nurses.

Muhammad Khan spent every single rupee he had in the bank to prepare for all the arrangements for this special event and major business transaction. He was supposed to get a lot of money from the selected five hundred and fifty nurses. Each nurse was supposed to pay him three lakhs rupees if she was selected (i.e. 300,000 x 550 = 165,000,000 Indian rupees). Muhammad Khan had already paid for the hotel accommodations of the twelve Saudi men who came to conduct the interviews and he had also paid the Muslim school that he rented for the scheduled gathering to take place on Sunday. He hired many security personnel and off-duty police officers. Therefore, he spent every single rupee he had in the bank for preparing for this life-time opportunity and huge business dealing. It had never happened before in the history of Bombay that a travel agency conducted such a huge recruitment of Indian labor to any Arab country. For that reason, all the newspaper outlets advertised this upcoming event and the television stations aired news of a big recruitment of Indian nurses to the Kingdom of Saudi Arabia.

On Sunday morning, Muhammad Khan and all his staff arrived at the Muslim school two hours before the interview time. Even his wife and his children came to help out for this great event in the history of his travel agency. He also called many of his friends and relatives and invited them to come witness the outstanding event. He promised to pay all the volunteers for their hard work. He even promised to provide their breakfast, lunch, and dinner. He was supposed to feed all his staff, security men, and policemen. He hired all the teachers of the Muslim school including the principal. He selected some students from tenth, eleventh and twelfth grade and promised to pay them well and provide them three square meals. The interview was supposed to begin at ten o'clock in the morning right up to six o'clock in the evening.

CHAPTER 19

"THE BLACK SUNDAY"

From six o'clock on Sunday morning the nurses began to gather outside the fenced schoolyard. By eight o'clock, every candidate had arrived. All one thousand five hundred nurses had come for their interviews and not one of them was missing. Each nurse came with at least three relatives and two friends for emotional support. In India, young people were very weak emotionally due to various reasons. Many students committed suicide because they failed their twelfth grade exams or could not obtain high enough test scores to enable them to get admission into a medical or engineering college. It was also a very common practice for lovers to kill themselves because they were forsook by their beloved ones, and girls took their lives because their parents forced them into arranged marriages. Others committed suicide for failing to get visas to OAPEC countries or their applications were rejected for immigration to a Western country such as Canada, America, and Australia.

On this most important day, the nurses brought with them their parents and friends for encouragement and emotional support in case they were rejected. Some of them came from out of town as far away as the cities of Poona, Aurangabad, Nagpur, Baroda, Seurat, Ahmadabad, Nasik, and Kolhapur. The out-of-town nurses and their parents stayed close by in local hotels and motels. They spent a lot of money for travel expenses and hotel accommodations in Bombay. Every nurse knew that she was facing a cutthroat environment and the competition would be stiff. Out of one thousand five hundred candidates, only five hundred and fifty nurses would be selected, leaving almost a thousand hopes dashed. None of the candidates knew exactly what the interviewers were going to ask, nor on what basis she would be judged. Almost all the nurses had more than five years experience working in the best hospitals in their individual cities. All of them graduated from the best nursing schools. All of them looked pretty and very pleasing to look at.

In India people believed that, airhostesses and nurses must look pretty and very appealing to the passengers and the patients. So on this day of opportunity, every nurse was worried that she might be rejected because other nurses might look more beautiful than her. There was a general belief in India that Arab men loved girls with big bodies and beautiful faces. Of course, that belief had a huge amount of truthfulness to it; truth based on thousands of years of interaction between the people of the Arabian Peninsula and the people of the Indian Subcontinent. Unfortunately, most of the Indian girls were extremely beautiful but very few of them had big bodies. In fact, Indian men did not like girls with big bodies. They were very much influenced by the criteria of the film industry of Bollywood, which was copied from the criteria of Hollywood. For example, the superstar Aishwarya Rai was called the Queen of Bollywood, and she was the highest paid film actress in India. She was also a former Miss World. An Arab man might reject Aishwarya Rai because she had a small backside and no meat on her bones. For this particular day, it was not unusual for some crazy nurses to go to extremes and put on extra clothes to look bigger than they were and some stuck extra padding inside their underwear and bra to increase the size of their buttocks and breasts.

On this special sunny morning, Muhammad Khan felt he was more important than the superstar Amitabh Bachan and his wife thought she was greater than Hema Malini. Muhammad Khan was running around everywhere talking to everyone as though he was a senior delegate of the United Nations. You could see him talking to one nurse here, and then suddenly he would disappear, reappear, and talk to another nurse there. He checked every security person and every police officer. He was carrying a microphone in his left hand and a huge log journal in his right hand. Every now and then, he would stop running and announce the interviewing committee would be arriving soon. The nurses were divided into ten groups. Every group formed a long line of nurses standing and waiting patiently. Each queue contained one hundred and fifty nurses. Their families and friends were not allowed to step inside the forbidden area of the school ground. The schoolyard was treated as if it was Muslim holy ground. Only the pilgrims, security, necessary attendees and helpers were permitted to enter heaven's gate to gain access to the committee from Paradise and the Promised Land of Petro dollars.

Another qualification to enter heaven's paradise was that all candidates had to be either Muslim or Christian since Hindus were barred from entering the Kingdom of Saudi Arabia. Hindus and the followers of other religions used to work in Saudi Arabia but they were not allowed to come within 40 kilometres of the official city of Mecca-Medina, which was known as Ard Al-Hijaz (i.e. The Land of Pilgrimage). In January 19, 1997, there was startling news from Riyadh, the capital of Saudi Arabia, which said that the Saudi Arabian government would from that point on deny entry of all Hindus into Saudi Arabia. Following that royal decree, all Hindu employees and workers were expelled from the Kingdom of Saudi Arabia. Some Hindus chose to convert to Islam and kept their jobs rather than return to their country. Christians were exempted from the ban because of the need for adequate armed forces and American armaments.

Up until 10:00 o'clock midday, Muhammad Khan was not worried about the fact that the Saudi medical team had not arrived. He was absolutely sure that they would arrive at their stations in due time. The interviewers were supposed to arrive at 9.00/9.30 a.m., but from about 10:00 a.m., every second and every minute that passed caused Muhammad Khan to become more and more impatient. When the clock struck 10:30 a.m., the nurses began to check their watches and ask each other about when the interviews would start. Each one was told that the interviews would begin at 10:00 a.m. sharp.

By 10:45 a.m., Muhammad became restless waiting for the team to arrive and his heart began to beat in his chest with a great thumping.

He became paranoid knowing everyone was looking at him and everywhere he walked. He kept looking at the gate and then at his watch. His heart started to beat louder and louder. He was expecting to see the taxis of the interview team showing up any moment. When all watches showed the time as 11:00 a.m., the nurses began to voice their concerns so much, so that he began to shake and tremble. They had been standing on their feet under the blazing sun for more than two hours and waiting in line even longer. Muhammad Khan came up with so many lies you would have thought it was April Fool's Day. He created more and more excuses to silence the rising tide of discontent among the nurses. His long working experience with the Saudis taught him that they were very arrogant and hot-tempered people. Because they were Arabs and the prophet of Islam was an Arab, and because they were living in the holy land of Muslims, the Saudi people considered themselves to be the most holy and righteous human beings on the whole planet. They looked down upon everyone else residing on the surface of the earth. They even counted themselves to be superior to other Arabs and Muslims. For this reason, Muhammad Khan felt it might be construed as an insult to telephone the hotel and find out why they were late. If he did, he was sure to find himself on the other end of a barrage of insults for ordering Holy People of Allah to be at his beck and call.

Starting at 12:00 p.m. noon, the nurses broke up standing in queue and confronted Muhammad Khan and his staff and his family. They began to shout at them. Muhammad Khan's body was shaking and sweating from head to feet and he feared the angry nurses might assault him and his family members and staff. He grabbed a big chair and sat it in front of him for protection. He ordered his family and staff to move to the raised platform. Then, he announced through his megaphone that he was going to phone the interview team and find out why they had not arrived. After this his announcement, there was dead silence. The momentary silence allowed him to climb the platform where everyone could see him in the open auditorium. He took his cell phone out of his pocket. Every eye was on him. Then, he dialed the number to the front desk of the Oberoi Hotel and requested the girl who responded transfer his call to one of the ten rooms of the Saudi medical team. When the girl told him that the Saudi medical team had checked out the previous evening, he felt as if the school's ceiling had collapsed and fallen on his head. His ears became deaf and numb. He tried to speak but his voice failed him. For a few seconds his heart stopped beating and he could feel the blood rush from his face down to his feet and he lost all five of his senses. When his lifeless body somehow intermittently came back to life, he began to shake and murmur unintelligibly.

Some of the nurses screaming and screeching demanded an explanation for his silliness. He could not answer them; his mouth paralyzed and his body in shock. His left hand dropped the microphone and he waved to the objecting nurses to silence them. Greatly disturbed inside his mind, he thought maybe the arrogant Arabs had more than likely quarrelled with the hotel staff for some silly reason and then they checked out or moved to the Taj Mahal Hotel where his valuable client, Sheikh Ahmed, was staying. Muhammad Khan had already told his valuable client there was no need for him to come before lunchtime. That remembrance brought some steadiness to his shaking hands and hence enabled him to dial the number to the front desk of the Taj Mahal Hotel.

This time, Mr. Khan decided to complain and inform his valuable client about the irresponsible and unacceptable behaviour of the Saudi medical team. Therefore, with some determination and little confidence, he asked the girl who responded to his call to transfer his call to room no. 907. The girl purposely made her feminine voice sound more sensual and thanked him for calling. She then transferred his call to room no 907. Instead of hearing the loud and arrogant voice of Sheikh Ahmed, Mr. Khan heard a very sweet and soft voice of a foreign girl. From her fluent English, he knew that she was not an Indian girl. At first, he thought that the dirty old Saudi had picked up one of the pretty European drug addicts from one of the cheap motels in Colaba and brought her to spend the night with him in his deluxe hotel room at the Taj Mahal. His suspicion was confirmed when he remembered the case of the virgin, Zarine Sheikh, and how he succeeded in stopping him from deflowering her.

The following conversion took place in a loud voice, magnified by the microphone that Mr. Khan was holding in his other hand, which all the nurses could hear. However, the attentive nurses could only hear his end of the phone conversion and were quick to fill in the blanks.

"Hello, madam. May I speak with his Excellency Sheikh Faiz bin Ahmed?"

"Sheek what?" responded the woman.

"Sheikh Ahmed of Saudi Arabia."

"I am not in the Sahara Desert of Saudi Arabia. I am in the Taj Mahal, Bombay, India."

"I haven't asked you where you are. Can you pass the phone to Sheikh Ahmed?"

"My name is Diana Peterson."

"I haven't asked you to tell me your name. Just hand over the phone to your man."

The rudeness of his words annoyed the white woman, which led her to respond in kind. She switched to a lower level of language.

"F…k you" shouted the white woman and then she hung up the phone.

Muhammad did not give up. He called the front desk again and requested that his call be transferred to room no. 907. The same woman answered the phone and said, *"Hello?"*

Muhammad ignored the foul language she used before and he continued to be polite.

"Madam, I want to speak to my Saudi client Sheikh..."

"You are a mother f...ing Indian. You just want to f...k me. F...k you. Stop teasing my ass."

Mr. Khan had never been spoken to by a woman in such a filthy manner before and hence he could not control his temper.

"I said I want to speak to the Arab man who picked you up from the streets of Colaba and f...ked your ass all the night."

"F...k you, you ignorant bastard. I will complain to the front desk about you stupid ass..."

"Shut up bitch. Do you know who the hell you are speaking to!?!"

"F...k you, and f...k every mother f...ing Indian in this stinking rag infested country. Come see me at the Taj Mahal hotel and I will f...k you up, you ugly Indian dog. How dare you to call me a 'bitch.'"

"You are a cocksuc...ing whore you filthy slut shi...ass bitch, you f...ing dicksuc...ing drug addict prostitute..."

The white woman disconnected the line. She could not match Muhammad Khan's street level language. Even though the white woman had called it quits and hung up the phone, the outraged man continued to echo insults and filthy language into the phone. He even shifted from the common English street language of thugs to nasty Indian slum and foul chawl talk.

"Mother chute, bahan chute. Teri maa ki chute, teri bahan ki chute, chutiya, sala..."

Either the nurses enjoyed hearing that distasteful phone conversation, or they were too scared to interrupt. That is why none of them spoke a word or tried to interrupt his tirade. Not even his wife, children, or staff tried to reprimand him for being disrespectful in public or try to calm him down.

Muhammad Khan changed his mind and decided to talk directly to the front desk and request someone go and knock on the door of room no. 907 and tell Sheikh Ahmed to call him immediately for a very urgent matter. However, this time the conversion did not last more than a few seconds. Muhammad gave the name of his valuable Saudi client and his room number. Then, he requested the front desk girl send someone to knock on his door. The girl checked her computer and then politely told him that the guest in question checked out last night and flew back to the Kingdom of Saudi Arabia. On hearing her words, Muhammad Khan fell off the platform and in front of the five nurses standing directly in front of him. He blacked out and was totally unconscious. When he opened his eyes again, he found himself in the hospital. His body was wrapped in white linen from head to toenail.

He could not move a limb. Every inch of his body had been bruised or badly injured. His two legs and hands were broken. He had lost all his teeth. His chin was dislocated and he was in excruciating pain despite all the painkillers running through his IV. If he miraculously managed to survive, he would never ever walk again.

Between the time Muhammad Khan fell off the platform and from the time he was revived at the hospital, he was conscious of nothing at all. From the time he closed his eyes and lost consciousness and the time he opened his eyes again, twelve hours had elapsed. During the twelve hours he was unconscious, misfortune and chaos reigned inside the Sacred House of Allah and outside on Hallowed Ground. When he fell off the platform, everyone started screaming. The place became wild and disorderly and his wife ran down to try and help him. Hundreds of nurses were pushing and shoving and tripping over each other. Muhammad Khan was treaded underfoot by scores of nurses scurrying everywhere like ants. Nurses ran over each other and trampled on the bodies of the nurses who had fallen down.

Mrs. Muhammad Khan feared that her husband might be crushed to death under the feet of the throngs of nurses. She used her cell phone and called the police. However, before the police could arrive, she also got knocked down while trying to see about her husband. She was crushed by the stampede of nurses. Some of the sharper nurses realized they had been scammed and this was nothing more than a scheme to defraud them of money by the recruitment agency. The news spread like wildfire that there was no Saudi medical team and no visas. This caused many nurses throughout the school to faint and fall out. Many nurses were hurt, bruised and battered. Almost five hundred nurses were admitted to nearby hospitals for some very serious injuries. Other nurses in an un-nurse-like behavior along with their boyfriends picked up stones and threw them at Muhammad Khan's staff. Rukhsana, Tahirah, Jamilah, Zarine, Javed, the peon, and the other new employees, Muhammad Khan's wife and children, and many volunteers and helpers were also seriously injured. No one escaped being pummeled by stones. Angry nurses entered the classrooms and broke all the tables, chairs, benches, windows, doors, and set papers on fire.

After two hours, the police came and dispersed the nurses and their families and friends with teargas. Yet, the turmoil did not end at the taboo ground of Allah. Havoc ensued all over the city when the news spread about what had happened at the Holy House of Allah. Some other nurses enlisted the aid of their boyfriends, sending them to Muhammad Khan's Tours and Travels, where the boyfriends set both offices on fire and burned them down to the ground. It was a complete loss and total ruin of the business of the Messenger of Lucifer. When the police arrived, they could not find anyone to make an arrest for the setting of the fires. That day came to be known as *the Black Sunday* after *the Black Friday* in which Muslim terrorists caused 13-planted bombs to explode in thirteen public places in Bombay and killed and injured thousands of innocent Indians…

BOOK II

IN THE HOLY LAND

CHAPTER 1

THE MISSING LAYLA

Sheikh Ahmed began his obsessive search for his beloved and her daughter at the Jeddah International Airport. When the airport officer checked his computer, he did not find any record of a Rayhana Khan or Iffat Khan arriving from the country of India. Sheikh Ahmed checked with three other airport offices before he came to terms he had lost love again. The first thought that arose in his head was that his former car driver had fooled him once again. He thought that Muhammad had failed to locate Rayhana and her daughter and then to hide his inadequacies, he came up with this unbelievable story that Rayhana and her daughter traveled from Bombay to Jeddah without their passports. He concluded Muhammad Khan fabricated the whole story because he feared that he might break up his partnership with him again. He remembered Babikir told him he had found Rayhana and gave her the tickets, visas, and money he had sent to her, but he did not say she actually made it to the airport to make her flight to Saudi Arabia. He also recalled at the Worli passport office he was informed that the two passports were reissued and mailed to the office of Muhammad Tours and Travels instead of Babikir's address.

When Sheikh Ahmed reached this resolve, he then regretted his hasty decision to punish his Indian client so quickly. He knew he could not go back to Bombay so soon to search for his beloved again for he was afraid that if he returned to India so soon, Muhammad Khan might hire Gondas to attack him in retaliation for his public humiliation. He also knew that Muhammad Khan had spies everywhere and he would know the minute he arrived at the Sahara International Airport.

Rayhana and her daughter's arrival was not entered into the computer system at the Jeddah International Airport because they were considered illegal aliens. Therefore, their arrival was considered to be an illegal entry and a criminal offense. The case was transferred to the airport security and passed onto the police division. Sheikh Ahmed would have known that if he had checked with the airport security. The desperate lover had lost all hope and thought he would never find or see his Layla again. He sat down on one of the airport benches and sorrowfully took Rayhana's passport from out of his suitcase and peered at her photo when tears began to stream down his cheeks. Her innocent face and marvelous beauty troubled his heart and made him feel like screaming out in pain to release all the heartache accumulating inside him. Staring at the photo of his beloved Layla, his heart bled and tears watered his long beard. He blamed all his troubles on the wicked ex-chauffeur and he began working out two possible scenarios in his mind; how to find his missing Layla and how to give Muhammad Khan a double dose of revenge.

While the distraught lover was sitting at the airport and trying to find a way to locate his missing Layla, his cell phone began to ring. He removed the phone from his pocket and looked at the number. He did not recognize the phone number calling him and so he didn't bother to answer it. The cell phone continued to ring and he waited to see whether or not the caller was going to leave a message. He suddenly heard a harsh voice saying,

"This is Jeddah Airport Police. This message is for Sheikh Faiz bin Ahmed. It is regarding your Indian maidservant Rayhana Khan and her daughter Iffat Khan. Your maidservant arrived in Jeddah along with her seven-year-old daughter without their passports. They were arrested by law enforcement authority and transferred to the Jeddah Detention for Women. For further information please contact the Jeddah Police Authority."

Sheikh Ahmed had never kissed his cell phone before that day. He felt as if his Allah saw his bleeding heart and had mercy upon him. Allah had sent an angel to guide his path to the most exquisite object of his desire. He immediately jumped on his feet as if he were an eighteen-year-old soccer player. First, he decided to go confirm the message he had received with the airport police. However, in a second thought, he dismissed that idea and decided to go directly to the Jeddah Jail and affect the release of his beloved Rayhana and her little daughter. Sheikh Ahmed said to himself, *"Why should I waste my time going to the airport police authority? I have already received the good news from them and I should go directly and get my poor beloved Rayhana out of jail with her little girl."*

Sheikh Ahmed married many Saudi women but he did not love any of them. The very first time he had ever fallen in love, it was a one-sided love affair. His former wife, Christie, an Indian Christian, was the first woman he had ever fallen madly in love with. His second love was Rayhana Khan, an Indian Muslim woman, and it was also a one-sided love affair. His present first three Saudi wives were old, and their children had already given him grandchildren. His fourth Saudi wife, however, was forty-two years old. According to Arab criteria, the woman was considered too old for sex once she was thirty years of age. The most desirable marriage age for a female was somewhere between nine years old to thirteen years of age. In big cities, the age would range between fourteen to nineteen years. Arabs believed that when a woman reached twenty years old, as she continued to grow her body would become rigid and less flexible day by day.

Virginity is very important, very essential, very crucial, and imperative for marrying a female in the Arab world. A female whose virginity had been lost or stolen would either be killed on the wedding night or sent back to her parents. In some Arab tribes, the bridegroom or his mother would wrap his/her finger with a white handkerchief and insert it into the vagina of the bride. If the bride were a virgin, the finger and handkerchief would come out stained red with blood because the hymen would bleed when it was broken. If the bride were already deflowered, the handkerchief would come out wet by the moisture of the vagina. In that case, the bride did not pass the virginity test.

In some backward Muslim countries, the virginity test might be done before marriage whenever the girl exhibited suspicious behavior or conduct or if there was a rumor the girl was in love with a boy. A girl in this case would be subjected to a virginity test! Her mother, aunt, or other close relatives or friends, neighbors or reliable old women, would secretly conduct the test. It was a local test in which the girl would be stripped of all her clothes. When she became fully naked, she would be asked to immerse her body in a tub filled with water. The water had to cover her body up to her waist. Then, she would be asked to cease from any movement and hold her breath. Her examiners would examine the surface of the water to see if there were any bubbles. When the expert examiners were fully satisfied there was not a single bubble to arise or be seen on the surface of the water, the girl would pass the virginity test.

The virginity qualifiers believed that the deflowered vagina would suck in some water and that would cause bubbles to come up. I have no clue whether that was the correct way to test the virginity of a female. There was a test even more silly and primitive than that. Some people believed the virginity test could be carried out without the knowledge of the intended test taker. This kind of test was common among men. According to this test, it was proof positive if a girl was either a virgin or not through her footprints on the sand. If her footprints showed full marks of her feet on the sand, then she was not a virgin. If her footprints revealed half marks of her feet on the sand, then she was a virgin. The danger to these kinds of primitive ideas and idiotic myths and old wives' tales is that many innocent girls might not find men to marry them; or worse than that, they might get slain by a relative in an honor killing. The girl might also lose her virginity through some sickness or heavy bleeding due to menstruation or some girls might break their hymens accidentally while they were masturbating.

Masturbation wasn't forbidden in Islam. There is not a single verse in the Qur'an or a hadith of the prophet Muhammad that forbade masturbation. There was a fatwa issued by a Muslim scholar who encouraged Muslim women to masturbate when they had a strong desire for sex but had no husbands to satisfy them. According to the fatwa, if a Muslim woman felt a great need or desire for sex and she had no husband, then she could take *akranbij* leather shaped like a penis and insert it inside her vagina and rub it until she got satisfied. The greatest Muslim scholar, Ibn Qayyim writes, *"If a woman does not have a husband, and her lust becomes strong, then some of our scholars say, 'It is permissible for the woman to take an akranbij, which is a piece of leather worked until it becomes shaped like a penis, and insert it in herself. She may also use a cucumber.'"*

If some religious followers in India were accused of worshipping the private parts of males, some Arab men should also be accused of worshipping a woman's virginity. A woman's vagina to the Arabs is like the cross to Christians. In fact, the Black Stone, which Muslim pilgrims touch and kiss during their Hajj ritual, is a leftover tradition from ancient pagan idol worship of the female's private parts. The ancient Arabs used to worship the woman's vagina and hence the Black Stone was shaped like a female's private part. In those days, the Hajj was called *Hak* (rubbing of the body). Pagan women used to rub their bodies on the Ka'bah and apply menstrual blood on the Black Stone to increase their fertility. The pagan men and women would perform the ritual while they were bare-naked. Women used to perform the Hajj during the night and men during the day. Today Muslims perform the same ritual without wearing underwear.

Islam incorporated the pagan rituals of the *Hak* with slight variations. The *Hak* was a kind of temple prostitution. Women offered themselves to men as part of their pagan idol worship, which consisted of many male gods and female goddesses. The Black Stone was considered the cornerstone of temple worship revolving around female prostitution. Although Islam removed the idols from the pagan temple, one idol remained. The Black Stone was the only idol spared and the *Hak* was reborn as the Hajj. Pagan *Hak* worshippers were now born again Muslim reverts, and worshippers of the one moon-god, Allah. However, the pagan rites and rituals, and immoral practices between men and women continued and remained the same.

An Egyptian scholar said that the Black Stone was in the shape of a woman's vagina because in those days, the pagans worshiped the private parts of the female. That is why women used to apply the blood of their menstruation on the vagina-shaped Black Stone.

Today, a Muslim female might not be able to reach the stone due to the crowd, but she was required to point her right hand towards it from afar. The Muslim man had to kiss the Black Stone at least once during his seven circles around the Ka'bah. The kissing of the Black Stone had no spiritual significance but Muslim men do it because the prophet Muhammad used to kiss it whenever he performed his Hajj. The second caliph, Omar Ibn Al-Khattab, said while he was kissing the Black Stone, *"I know you are just stone and can do no good or bad to me, but I am kissing you because I saw the messenger of Allah kissing you."* Omar may not have known why the prophet Muhammad had kissed the stone but for the pagans, kissing the Black Stone was a form of worshiping the woman's vagina. Muslim men today are continuing this pagan rite in worshiping this organ of the female body. Until today, Muslim men go around the Black Stone and kiss it while they are semi-naked.

Hajj is the most horrifying and immoral experience a Muslim woman could ever have in her life. A Muslim woman who performed the Hajj with her husband and sister made the following comments on her visit to the holy place of Muslims: Zeena says, "*What I saw in Masjid-Ul-Haram was the worst sight of all...* [Masjid-Ul-Haram is the Sacred Mosque. It is the largest mosque in the world. Located in the city of Mecca, it surrounds the Ka'aba, the place that Muslims worldwide turn towards while performing daily prayers and is Islam's holiest place] *I saw almost a million people squished in that small place, sleeping on the floor, on the steps and even in bathrooms. Eating their foods in bathrooms...that itself was gross. There was no place to perform hajj peacefully. There was not even enough place to breath fresh air...there was a sea of human beings...public bathrooms and toilets were full of feces and urine and on top of that people were sleeping in those places, eating food and exposing their small kids to those extremely noxious and contaminating environmental conditions where there was nothing, but, human filth and stink. Everyone was coughing and was sick, so many people were having food poisoning including myself."* (Hajj, My Broken Dream, by Zeena Zeena).

Zeena continued to say, "*During Tawaf (when we have to take 7 circles around Kabbah) I saw men squishing and squeezing other people without caring for anyone...I was shocked to see their aggressive behavior...everyone wanted to go in to that place and be done with 7 circles, so many people died because of stampede and I saw them dying, and other people jumping on their dead bodies without any feeling...while I was doing my circles, all of a sudden I saw few groups of Black Nigerian and Somalian men and also Iranian men jump inside pushing others including women...it was such a chaotic gathering that I was shocked and speechless...all I was experiencing and observing was people pushing and pulling physically the weaker and letting them die and then running over their dead bodies...a point came when these groups came closer to me, I felt my whole body was being squeezed forcefully from both sides...and I felt as if I am dying any time and I didn't feel that I could breath...till I gathered my whole strength and screamed," STOP IT, YOU ANIMALS, ENOUGH IS ENOUGH, WHAT USE OF THIS HAJJ, IF, YOU HAVE NO FEELINGS FOR YOUR FELLOW HUMANS? All of a sudden I felt some kind hand pull me out of this psychotic crowd...and that was my own sister, who rescued me out...thank God, it was the end of my last circle...I was pale, shivering, nauseous and dizzy. All my dreams about performing Hajj were shattered by now. All I saw was extreme selfishness, filth, extreme cruelty, aggression and psychotic behavior. Where was the main essence of Hajj? Where was Humanity? Where were humans? Majority of people were not humans, yes, they were acting like some jungle beasts which are struggling for survival*" (Ibid).

Zeena summarized her horrifying experiences by saying, "*It is a violation of Human Rights to allow 3 million people including young children to gather together in the name of religion called Hajj subject to dying, being looted, plundered, wounded, being exposed to different diseases, sleeping with feces and urine, women being exposed to strangers in an unethical way, being used in the name of religion, being discriminated racially and based of gender, being divided as rich and poor, being hijacked by Saudi thugs, being cheated by Hajj Mafia (Hajj companies), being tormented by fellow humans"* (Ibid).

Returning now to our main topic of the importance of a woman's virginity, some Muslims in France began to pay huge amounts of money to doctors in an attempt to return their wives to a virginal state. A Muslim man in Paris was prepared to pay a French doctor five thousand dollars in order to "restore" his wife's virginity. He enjoyed repeating the process of deflowering his wife. By doing so, he presupposed that this might be a substitute for polygamy, which the French law wouldn't allow him to practice in France. Sheikh Ahmed seemed to have discovered that there was something more lovable and enjoyable in a woman than her vagina and virginity. On his many visits to India, his attitude toward women improved somewhat. He discovered that there was nothing better than a woman giving herself to a man to please him. Even if it were a one-sided love, the love of a good woman would give a man the happiest days of his life. In this way, his first experience at love with his Indian wife, Christie, made his life so wonderful, he came to love life to the fullest measure. Before that, he was such a materialistic and selfish man. He used to use women for sexual satisfaction but had never loved them nor had been loved by them. After his first love experience, he discovered a great secret, which had been hidden from all the men of his country.

He eventually came to realize that a man could not possibly or practically love more than one woman at a time. So, he discovered that polygamy was a kind of abuse to women and a torture for the man. Having two, three or four women at the same time would mean countless troubles for the man and his life would be a living hell. Rival wives would fight to be the alpha female and this would go on day and night and cause much misery for the male. He would wish he was in hell wearing a pair of gasoline underwear. Instead, he had to live with these demons possessed women in real life and wish for death in the afterlife as an escape from the turmoil and conflict in his own house. Many Muslim men believe that the woman's mind is always haunted by the devils. The prophet of Islam said, *"The woman comes in the form of Satan and goes in the form of Satan"* (Sahih Muslim).

Alas, whereas his first love story was a one-sided love affair and ended in a train wreck, nonetheless, the joy and happiness Sheikh Ahmed had felt during that short-lived love affair would never be forgotten. He cherished and treasured it in his heart for a very long time. He longed for a similar experience no matter how it would turn out. Then, his luck brought him another much beloved Indian woman. As Mahatma Gandhi once said, everyone is a lover and looking for a beloved.

The old Saudi man fell in love with the slum woman at first sight. If he loved Christie a thousand times over, he loved Rayhana one million times more. From the time she met him at the Gate of India, the fires of love were rekindled in his heart. He believed that she had reawakened in him the power of love. When he was in school, he read about the love of a woman in thousands of poems in classic Arabic literature without experiencing it. No people had written more beautifully or wonderfully about the love of a man and a woman than in the poems of the ancient Arabs. However, once Islam was founded, it forbade any relationship whatsoever between men and women before marriage. The restrictions Islam placed on the woman resulted in untold evils and despicable punishments to women known as honor killings. Before Islam, the Arabs delighted in the love, romance and beauty of the woman. They wrote *the Renowned Seven Poems* known as *Mu'allaqat*. These were very sweet and deliberate writings of love. The poetic writings were so loved and revered by the Arabs of pre-Islamic period, they began to hang these popular poems on the Holy Ka'aba at Mecca, which is known today as the House of Allah. Islam outlawed love and destroyed that golden period of Arabian poetry reflecting the intimacies between a man and a woman.

Sheikh Ahmed read thousands of poems and writings of ancient Arab lovers and poets and memorized them by heart. However, love did not make sense to him until he began to go out of his man-dominated society and see beautiful young women walking all alone on the streets of Bombay with their faces and hair exposed. He even saw young girls walking in short pants with half of their bodies nude and visibly exposed. He also visited the paradise city of Goa and saw the beautiful young Indian women in their bikinis lying on the golden sand of the warm sunny beaches. From afar, he could make out whether a woman or girl had a nice body or a beautiful face or not.

In his country, women were wrapped up head to foot in a clothing called a abaya/burqa and nothing could be seen of her except her black cocoon. In fact, the women were like a watermelon you would buy at the supermarket. One could not know whether she was beautiful or had a nice body until he purchased her first and then opened her up. She is like a box of chocolates. You never know what you're going to get. Some you like and some are absolutely awful. The most beautiful creation of God is covered from head to toe in a black coffin. The style of dress being the niqab or the burqa, however the curtains in a funeral parlor are much more pleasant to look at. The Queen of God's creation is now a phantom of evil. A ghost in the minds of men; she should neither be seen nor heard.

Sheikh Ahmed arrived at the Jeddah jail with the two passports in his hand as if they were won in the green card lottery and issued by the United States of America. He came with the attitude of *"Receive and Release."* He expected that he would show the two passports and receive his beloved woman and her daughter. After all, he had a million plans running through his crooked mind. When the police told him that there were no detainees by those names, he felt as if someone threw a bucket of cold water on him. He argued with the police and insisted that they were mistaken until they threatened to throw him behind bars if he didn't leave.

Totally pissed off, the enraged lover left the Jeddah jail, headed directly back to the airport and demanded an explanation and accurate information about his beloved maidservant and her daughter. The airport police confirmed the information he received on his phone. However, they said they had no idea where the two police officers had taken his Indian maidservant and her daughter. They also refused to reveal their names or the number of the police car that was used to transfer the two Indian detainees. This last bit of information brought Sheikh Ahmed to his knees and his renewed and short-lived hopes to a dead end.

He was back to square one. Once again, the old Saudi managed to crawl back upon his feet and dragged himself back to the same bench he had sat upon before he received the phone message from the airport police. While he sat, this time he was not trying to figure out how to punish his bitter enemy, Muhammad Khan, but rather, how to find his beloved Rayhana and her daughter. Suddenly, a great dread came over him and his heart was filled with gloom. He started to murmur to no one in particular. More than fear, sheer terror paralyzed both his body and mind and made him speak twisted things. Every single hair on his body stood up. In fact, he had no hair on his bald head but he was a very hairy man. His whole body was full of hair as if he was a wolf in sheep's covering. Pale, reddish hair covered his hands, feet, chest, back, and his neck in front and from behind, not including his mustache and long beard. Fear, dread, and terror pained his heart and physically impaired his ability to function when he began to visualize the body of his beloved lying in the desert underneath the unforgiving heat of the sun.

Sheikh Ahmed feared that the two Saudi police officers saw the marvelous beauty and sexually appealing body of Rayhana and decided to rape her. They then killed her to cover over their crime and dumped her body in the desert. He imagined that by now, the hot gusty sand winds had already buried her body and he would never see her again. He concluded they had also raped her daughter and killed her too. Sheikh Ahmed knew that Saudi men could not be trusted with a beautiful woman, especially if she had her face, hands, and legs open to the public. He knew in his country, a man would not spare a female if he found her all-alone, even in an elevator. Therefore, he concluded that the two Saudi police officers took advantage of his beautiful Indian maidservant and hence, instead of taking her to prison, they took her for their own pleasure. They took her out of the city, raped her and her little daughter and murdered them leaving their dead bodies to rot in the desert. The old Saudi had never cried so much in all his life. He had not cried this much even the day his wife Christie threw him out of his house. He began to sob uncontrollably putting his face in the palm of his hands trying to hide his tears. Instead, his tears exposed his weakness and the deep sorrow rent in his heart.

The fear of Sheikh Ahmed is based upon practical evidence. Hundreds of maidservants from Asian countries who come alone to work in this male-dominated society get raped every year. It is a society where the woman is considered to be meat and imprisoned in the house and never allowed to come out. And if she is allowed to step out of the house, she had to have a male for protection or she will be raped. Female foreigners who come from free societies are always the victims of this unholy Arab empire of rapists and pedophiles. In a Western country such as Australia, a Muslim Imam justified the rape of white girls by Muslim Lebanese men. I have quoted this before, but allow me to refer to it once again. I believe this is the right place to put it. The Australian Islamic Imam and Mufti Sheik Taj Din al-Hilali, the nation's most senior Muslim cleric, said in his public sermon, which he delivered before five thousand Muslim worshippers in Sydney on the occasion of the Eid festival, that **women** are just **meat**, and **men** have no more obligation to exercise restraint when they **see women** than a cat does when **meat** is left out in the open. The Imam was speaking about the increasing social phenomena of young Australian women getting raped regularly by Lebanese and other Muslim immigrants in Sydney, Australia. He blamed the victims rather than the rapists. According to him, the Australian non-Muslim women (i.e. female infidels) go out in public around town on the streets with exposed bodies without wearing hijabs/niqabs/burqas, and the Muslim men see them as exposed meat, and that is why they rape them. To justify his theory, he gave an example in the case of a cat when it finds meat on the street eats it up. For him, the cat could not be blamed, but the person who dropped the meat on the street is the one that should be blamed. Therefore, he concluded his talk by saying the rapist should not be blamed at all, but the woman or girl who leaves her body uncovered is wholly to blame. What an evil man he is to teach these things as a religious leader and instructor of the masses. He ought to be locked up for life for encouraging men to commit crimes against women and commit evil deeds against his fellowmen and society. Even the five thousand Muslims who listened to his sermon and did not object should be kicked out of Australia and all the West and all free democratic societies. They should not be allowed to flourish amidst productive, thriving nations, lands, and peoples, but returned to their own ever increasing closed sick-minded oppressive governments. They should go back to their own countries and lands where the women are treated like meat, covered from head to foot in oppression and imprisoned in the home like criminals.

The most dangerous places for women on earth are in Muslim countries. In the West, a young woman can live by herself in a building full of men, and it will be unlikely that anyone will knock on her door or break in to rape her. In a Muslim country, it is not permitted for a single woman to live alone. No property owner is allowed by law to give an apartment for rent to an unmarried woman. Even in a hotel, the law will not allow a single woman, whatever her age, to check in if she has no husband, father, brother, or an adult son with her. They have to produce official government documents to prove their relationship before they will be allowed to stay together in a hotel.

If a couple wanted to stay in a hotel, they had to produce their marriage certificate. A father had to show official documentation to prove that the woman who came with him was his daughter. In 1983, my sister and I were denied a room in a hotel at Cairo. We had our passports, but they refused to accept them as proof because my sister and I had different fathers. When all hotels refused to allow us to check in, we were fortunate to be able to stay with a Sudanese family in their apartment. In Saudi Arabia, a woman would be raped inside an elevator if she dared leave her apartment to visit her neighbor.

CHAPTER 2

THE FIRST DAY IN THE HOLY LAND

When Rayhana Khan arrived in the King Abdul Aziz International Airport, she removed her shoes and told her daughter to remove her shoes too because they were standing in a holy ground. Then Rayhana knelt down on her knees and kissed the sacred sand with her lips. She took some dust in her hands, sprinkled it on her daughter's head, and blessed her. After that, she took some more dust and rubbed it on her head and face, and blessed herself. Then she hugged her daughter and said to her, *"We have reached the holy land of 'Sayyidina Rasulullah Sallallahu A'layhi Wasallam.' Here lies the Holy House of Allah and the Shrine of Muhammad, our blessed prophet, (PBUH)."*

Rayhana was not a religious woman but that day she felt as if she was on a pilgrimage to the most holy of holies. She thought that she and her daughter had fulfilled the dream of every Muslim in the world by visiting the city of the prophet Muhammad and circling seven times around *the Old House of Allah*. Rayhana expected that as soon as she entered the holy city she would see the holy men and women of Allah filling the streets in pilgrim garb and money would be scattered on the streets like garbage filled the streets of Bombay. Everything around her looked so beautiful and clean. She could not believe her eyes when she looked everywhere without seeing one piece of garbage or one destitute child.

Rayhana could not see cigarette butts beneath her feet or walls of spit lined with red stains of tobacco *Paan*. Rayhana's eyes could not spot one single beggar. In Bombay, beggars could be found everywhere. They were as numerous as flies hovering over garbage containers or mosquitoes in gutters and swamps. While they were walking inside the arrival area Rayhana felt as if she was walking on a street of glass shining like the sun. She could see the reflection of her image in the glassy white marble from which the floor was made. While she was walking, her head was turning in all directions. She wanted to see everything because she had never before seen such an amazing sight.

Rayhana's innocent heart was overflowing with joy. Her joy suddenly was clouded with sorrow when she remembered the only man that she had ever loved. She wished that her lover was walking right beside her and holding her hand. The memory of Jamaal Khan turned her face to her little daughter who was walking by her side and looking very happy. She bent down and gave her daughter a kiss on her check and whispered in her ear, *"Allah has blessed the people of his holy city because they are good and worship him only."*

Rayhana made a quick contrast between the misery and poverty of the people of India and the happiness and richness of the people of the holy city that she had come to abide for the next two years. The contrast led her to believe that Allah cursed the people of India because they were evil idol worshipers and the people of the holy city were blessed by Allah because they were good and worshipped the only true God. She also thought that she and her family were living in utter poverty and misery in that filthy and hellish slum because they were not following or worshipping their Allah properly.

When she came to that realization, Rayhana decided as soon as she reached the house of her sponsor she would begin to pray five times a day and she would never allow any man to touch her body if he wasn't her husband. She even asked her Allah to forgive her for allowing her lover to touch her body and kiss her lips. She blamed herself for doing great "haram" by allowing Jamaal who wasn't her lawful husband to touch areas of her body and fondle her breasts. While she was still walking on that glassy passage, Rayhana repented for her terrible sins that she committed with her lover and made a vow to her Allah that she would never ever repeat that haram again. She asked her Allah to grant her great success while she was living in his holy city and after two years unite her in a lawful marriage relationship with her Muslim lover, Jamaal Khan.

Unfortunately, things did not go well with Rayhana and her daughter upon arriving at the first airport security checkpoint. When they were asked by the airport security to show their passports they said they did not have them. The security official repeated his question ten times, thinking the dumb Indian woman did not understand what he was saying. He was talking to Rayhana through an Indian interpreter. Each time Rayhana gave him the same answer and each time he did not believe her. He refused to believe that two passengers could possibly fly from India to Saudi Arabia without passports. Finally, he became fed up and contacted the flight crew of the Saudi plane that brought Rayhana and her daughter from Bombay. He was shocked when he discovered that the two Indian passengers had entered the plane without their passports. Since the aircraft was a Saudi plane, this was considered by him to be a terrible infraction. He informed his senior officer and asked him what to do with the two Indian passengers who had arrived in the country without passports. Without asking why or how the passengers arrived without their passports, the senior officer gave the order for the two passengers to be returned as soon as possible on the next flight back to India. Now the two questions before the Saudi airport official were which plane should take them back and who was going to pay for their return tickets? Both passengers arrived with one-way tickets.

First, the airport police contacted the Saudi airlines and informed them of the two Indian passengers and requested they fly them back in the first Saudi flight going back to Bombay. The Saudi airlines agreed to take the passengers back to India but since the passengers were ordered to be deported by the Saudi senior airport official, they requested the Saudi government pay for their return tickets. When airport security contacted the proper office in the Saudi government administration and informed them about the demand of the Saudi airline, the office refused to pay for the tickets of the two Indian passengers. The government office then advised the airport personnel to refer the case of the two Indians to the Indian airline representatives at the Jeddah International Airport. The Indian airline representative rejected the request of airport officials and made it very clear that they were not going to spend a single dollar on the transfer of illegal Indians who were to be deported to India. Then, the airport official contacted the Indian airline office. The office rejected the request and argued that it wasn't the Indian airline's responsibility to pay for deportation of illegal Indian immigrants or unlawful visitors from India. Finally, the case of the two illegal Indian aliens reached the Indian Consulate at Jeddah. The Consulate said it would neither issue passports nor pay for the deportation of the two Indians who smuggled themselves aboard an aircraft from a foreign country without official documentation.

When every concerned party refused to shoulder the responsibility of deporting the two illegal Indian immigrants, the police placed Rayhana and her daughter under arrest and arranged for their transfer to the Jeddah's Women Central Jail. While these phone conversations were taking place, Rayhana and her daughter were placed in a small police lockup at the airport. They spent many hours in that small lockup. They had no knowledge of what was going on regarding the discussions for their transfer back to India. They received free meals and felt grateful to enjoy such delicious Arab food.

On the evening of the day of their arrival, two Saudi policemen came and took them out of the airport lockup. They handcuffed Rayhana's hands but left her daughter's hands free. Only when she was handcuffed did Rayhana understand that she was in trouble. She asked the two police officers why they were arresting her but she did not get an answer because none of them could understand Hindi. The two Saudi policemen could only speak Arabic. Then Rayhana tried to show them their visas but they just ignored her papers and took them inside their police car and drove away.

While the police car was building up speed and traveling through the busy streets of Jeddah, Rayhana was looking at the people who were walking on the pavement. The first sight that caught her attention was the two kinds of human creatures that were walking along the streets. She recognized the men from their white clothes and their long beards. During the three weeks of her honeymoon in downtown Bombay, she saw many of Colaba's foreign visitors were dressed up in that fashion. She even recollected that her kind Saudi *sponsor* wore the same strange clothing. The long jolbab that each man wore appeared to her to be like a woman's nightgown. She could see the men's private parts through the slightly transparent clothing. The other kind of human creatures she saw were women. If human society wasn't made up of men and women she wouldn't have known that those fully concealed creatures were human beings. Each woman was fully covered from head to foot by a black burqa. For Rayhana, those women looked like ghosts. She was worried that her sponsor might force her to put that black bag over her head. She was scared that if he made her wrap up like that, she might not be able to breathe and die a slow death. Rayhana ignored the human beings and began to take in the view of the beautiful tall buildings. She was surprised when she did not see any shacks, slums, chawls, or any other type of poverty-stricken habitats. Once again, she reminded herself that Allah had blessed the people of his holy city because they were so righteous and worshipped him from their hearts.

After a long drive, Rayhana could no longer see human beings or buildings. She could not see any tree or mountain. Wherever she looked, she saw the empty sands of the desert wasteland. Rayhana thought that if she were in the hands of the Bombay police in India in such a deserted and empty place they would rape and kill her. She remembered how the Indian police had beaten and abused her in jail. She thanked her Allah that she was arrested by Muslim police officers. She thought that she and her daughter were safe in the hands of these most righteous city policemen who feared the Most High, Allah. When her eyes could not find anything else to see, Rayhana began to doze off and finally she fell asleep. While she was sleeping inside the police car, she began to snore. She was so tired and exhausted from her long trip from Bombay to the holy city, and the long time she spent in that small police lockup. Her daughter had fallen asleep as soon as the police car left the airport and entered the city.

Rayhana's sleep was interrupted when a rough hand shook her head and woke her up. She found one of the two policemen sitting so close to her. She was very scared when she discovered that a man was sitting so close to her until his body was touching hers. She tried to move away from him but she couldn't because she was hemmed in by the car door and his body. She spoke to him in Hindi and told him to move away from her. The policeman did not pay any attention to what she was saying and began to touch her body. She began to tremble and her body was stunned by fright. It took her a few seconds to overcome her fear and shock.

The Saudi policeman moved his hand from Rayhana's shoulder and took hold of one of her breasts. Rayhana decided to act fast and push him away. However, she could not use her hands because they were handcuffed behind her back. The policeman caught her by the chin and forcefully began to kiss her on the lips. Rayhana struggled violently to release her lips from his mouth. She managed to free her mouth for a few seconds before he overpowered her again. She butted him with her forehead and even bit his lips. The policeman released her lips and began to squeeze her breasts and his other hand slid down quickly to her private parts. Then he tried to pull down her Salwar. Rayhana did everything she could to prevent him from undressing her.

While she was struggling to free herself from the policeman who was trying to rape her, Rayhana suddenly heard her daughter began to cry and call to her mother for help. Rayhana turned her face and looked out of the car. She could not believe her eyes when she saw the second policeman was holding her daughter's hand and trying to make her touch his penis. He was half-naked. His trousers and underwear were rolled down. He was standing out of the car with his penis standing fully exposed and erect before her seven-year-old daughter. The policeman managed to make the little girl to hold his penis. Then, he tried to make Iffat insert his penis in her mouth and suck it for him. At first Rayhana thought she was still asleep and having a nightmare. The never ending groping of her assailant and her daughter's screams bellowing hauntingly in her ears made her senses believe that what she was seeing was more than real. When her senses realized the impact of what she was seeing, Rayhana became furious and began to use her feet to kick violently at the policeman who was molesting her inside the car. The shock of seeing a grown man trying to rape her little daughter was more than she could bear and she fought with all her might to try and save her.

The policeman meanwhile was trying to subdue Rayhana in every way he could. He hit her in the face several times and tried to close her mouth with his hands but he couldn't. Every part of her body was moving and pushing him away from her. If her hands weren't handcuffed behind her back she would have strangled him to death and rescued her child. When he could see she was going to be hard to control, he shouted at his colleague and informed him that the Indian woman might kill him if he did not let go of her daughter. He knew that when the Indian woman heard her daughter crying and saw what his colleague was trying to do to her little girl, she became extremely angry and aggressive and difficult to control. Nevertheless, the other policeman did not respond to the words of his colleague and continued with his evil act upon the child. He began to hug the little child and rub his penis on her body while trying to kiss her mouth. Rayhana began to scream and cry out loudly and showered the evil policeman with all bad words she knew. The policeman ignored her outpouring of insults, which he didn't understand anyway.

Rayhana knew she could not stop these evil men from raping her and abusing her daughter. She decided to give up her resistance and allow the men to rape her alone and spare her child. She used her body language to signal to the policeman who was trying to rape her to ask his friend to stop touching her daughter and come inside the car and do whatever he wanted to her. The policeman understood her body language and got out of the car and caught hold of his colleague and told him what the Indian woman wanted and agreed for them to do. The evil man was not willing to release the small child until his colleague pulled the child from him by force.

The evil policeman was angry as a wild beast whose easy prey was just snatched away from him. His game was over and he could no longer play this wicked vile act he was enjoying so much. Therefore, he ran like a leopard in leaps and bounds to the car in his hunt for another victim. He caught hold of one of Rayhana's legs and pulled her out of the car. When Rayhana was out of the car, he stripped off his remaining clothes. He then straddled Rayhana's body as she surrendered like a lamp to the slaughter and he began to rape her. The other policeman joined him and the two evil men began having sex with Rayhana both at the same time. One raped her from the front and other sodomized her from behind.

It was as if these Arab men had never touched a woman before. One of them was fully naked and other was half-naked. While they were raping her, they were biting and hitting her viciously and violently, as if they were ferocious hungry desert beasts found a stray deer. They looked like one was a striped hyena and the other a spotted hyena devouring the flesh of a helpless prey. Rayhana screaming while trying to silence her pain endured their violent and sadistic rampage motivated by love for her child. She knew that if she resisted or tried to stop them they would leave her and go for her defenseless child. Little Iffat saw everything from the moment the two evil men of the holy city of Allah, stripped her mother naked and ripped off her clothes. She saw when they began raping her as she stood by herself crying and begging the men to stop and leave her mother alone. She screamed and begged on her knees, "Pleaaase stop! Pleaaase stop! Pleaaase stop! Leave my mother alone, you're hurting her!" She did everything she could to ask them to stop, but they continued. She watched with eyes clouded in tears, and yet her pleadings went unanswered. There was nothing she could do to help her mother.

CHAPTER 3

THE BEDOUIN FAMILY

The two Saudi police officers violently raped Rayhana Khan until she lost consciousness and hovered between life and death. The wicked Arab men were not satisfied in leaving her unconscious body undisturbed, but they continued to rape her lifeless body. Each one of them raped her three times and sodomized her. Finally, they got into their vehicle and drove away leaving her for dead. They neither bothered to put her clothes back on or cover her naked body. They did not care about her crying child. They expected both mother and daughter would eventually die in the hot desert and their bodies would be buried by the shifting winds of sand.

After they left, little Iffat went over to her mother and covered her mother's private parts with the dress that was ripped from her body. She tried to awaken her thinking she was asleep. She shook her mother's body vigorously and called to her to please wake up, but her mother did not respond. Iffat remembered that her father had killed himself so she had some idea about death. She began to think the police officers had killed her mother while they were beating her and doing those terrible things to her. She had seen everything they had done to her mother but she did not understand what they were doing or why they were removing all her clothes or what her mother had done to make them angry with her. After they left, she believed her mother was dead and she stood up and began to wail loudly with a strong outcry. The place was a desolate area located far away from the city. It was on a deserted road where cars very rarely passed by. It was evening and the sun was setting. It started to get dark and Iffat became terribly frightened. She had no idea of what to do and she was afraid to leave her dead mother to go in search of help.

Iffat sat beside her mother where she cried and cried until she lost her voice. Finally, she fell asleep upon her mother's body. It started to turn cold within a couple of hours after the sun went down. The chill shook Rayhana from out of her long deadened state of unconsciousness. She forced herself awake. She was in horrific pain radiating_from every part of her body. She then remembered what had happened to her and she moved quietly so as not to wake up her daughter. She moved her daughter's head slowly from her lap and strained to get up on her knees. She tried to stand but she could not. She discovered she was naked except for the single piece of clothing draped across her. She dragged her sore and aching body across the sand and began to collect her clothing piece by piece.

Her movements woke up Iffat. Rayhana told her daughter to close her eyes until she could put her dress back on. Her daughter obeyed her and closed her eyes. It took Rayhana more than half an hour to put on her clothes. Then, she told her daughter to open her eyes. Iffat ran to her mother and hugged her. She felt so relieved when she saw that her mother had come back to life. Rayhana knew that Iffat had seen everything those evil men had done to her. She remembered hearing Iffat's tender voice screaming and crying for her while those vicious animals tore her apart and ripped off her clothes. While they were stripping her naked in front of her child, she felt as if they were skinning her alive. They had removed her handcuffs and stripped every piece of clothing from her body. She could not resist or try to protect her honor. She was afraid if she resisted, they would go for her little daughter instead. She was thus paralyzed by the thought of these ruthless men raping and attacking her daughter. At this moment, if it were not for her daughter, Rayhana would have killed herself. (It is a tradition in India that when a woman got raped she would kill herself. She would choose to die rather than live with a defiled body).

Iffat's loving touches and hugs gave Rayhana strength and she asked her daughter to help her stand up. Iffat tried to pull her mother up by her hands with all the strength she had but she wasn't able to help her mother get up. Therefore, Rayhana decided to crawl on her knees and move away from the place where she had been raped in front of her little daughter. She felt her body had been ruined and made unclean by the wicked and ungodly men in that place and it was now unholy ground. She hoped that if they moved away from the spot maybe her daughter would soon forget and not remember what had happened.

Rayhana's crawled away very slowly and every now and then she became exhausted to the point where she had to stop and rest. The pain she felt exerting herself was more than she could bear. When she felt she was far enough away she asked her daughter to sit upon her lap. She ached terribly from the wounds and injuries she received to her body and the pain was beyond anything she had ever experienced. Some of her wounds were bleeding and she tried to hide them from her daughter. She tried to hide her pain and the emotional trauma hoping if she pretended nothing was wrong, her daughter would soon forget everything that had happened. With all that she had endured and survived, she worried most about her daughter's welfare and how could she get her to a safe place. Rayhana worried even more when she realized in a place like this they could be bitten by snakes or scorpions if they didn't freeze to death in the cold desert air.

While in and out of a haze, Rayhana thought that she was living through an awful nightmare. She couldn't wrap her mind around what had happened to her on her first day in the holy city where the tomb of her Prophet Muhammad and the House of Allah stood. It was the last thing she would have ever imagined could happen in the most divine and sacred place on earth. (Rayhana's little knowledge of Islam made her believe that Jeddah was Mecca City whereupon reigned the House of Allah and Medina City, where the tomb of her prophet Muhammad was laid to rest. In fact, from Jeddah to Mecca it will take you around 1 1/2 hours to drive the distance of 80 km. It is the most crowded road in the world. Over three million pilgrims travel on that single highway. However, some crazy Arabs would drive 120 km an hour and make it in 1/2 hours-time).

If Rayhana had had any knowledge or warning that this terrible thing was going to happen to her, she would have never come. Of course, for that matter, no mother in the world would ever dream of her young child witnessing such a brutal act. Whatever she allowed or suffered at the hands of wicked men it was because she wanted to save her little girl from being raped and violated by these dangerous criminals posing as public servants.

Rayhana's mind was occupied with many thoughts bubbling up like hot, molten lava inside a volcano. She wanted to cry but she suppressed her tears and did not allow them to disclose the deep pain and anguish she was feeling inside. It was best not to fall apart in front of her daughter and so she hid her fears, worries and all the devastation she felt. She hated herself for bringing her daughter with her and exposing her to such evil. Only the devil could do this to a human being and not care about raping a mother in front of her small child. If only she had foreknowledge that the devil was alive and well inside the Kingdom of Saudi Arabia.

Rayhana could not believe a human being could become like a beast. How could a human being lust after a seven-year-old child? How could a man behave in such a beastly manner? What troubled Rayhana more was the fact that these police officers were Muslims like her. While she was living in her slum surrounded by thousands of Hindu men, none of them had attacked or assaulted her inside her unprotected slum. She had never been accosted by anyone and no one had attempted to rape her while she was returning all alone at night through those dark and narrow lanes. Her Hindu neighbors were bowing down and worshipping their idols day and night, whereas the two Muslim men who raped her were supposedly kneeling down and worshipping her Allah five times a day.

Rayhana began to feel dizzy and her eyes began to flutter uncontrollably. She knew that she might collapse and faint any moment. She wanted to tell her daughter to leave her and continue walking with the hope that she might find someone to rescue her. She did not want her daughter to see her dying in such a lonesome place. She figured she was going to die anyway. When she could not crawl anymore, Rayhana shared her thoughts about what she wanted her daughter to do. She told her to continue walking and not look back. Iffat was scared and refused to leave her mother and walk all alone in the dark and lonely dead of night. Rayhana felt her child's anxiety and fear and did not insist that she leave her anymore. She did, however, gently tell her that if she fell asleep, she might never wake up again. She reminded her of how her father had fallen asleep and had not returned to them. She then told her plainly that she was going to die, and when that happened she should leave her and go away.

Shortly after speaking these words to her daughter, Rayhana stopped crawling, and her body fell silently into the sand and became motionless. Her daughter thought that her mother had died and would never wake up again. Iffat was afraid to walk alone in what was a strange, dark and frightening place. She just sat near her mother's body and began to weep all over again. She was so afraid and started to shake trembling from the chill of the brisk night winds. Her fear prevented her from falling asleep and she remained awake throughout the night. When the light of dawn ascended, her eyes became heavy with sleep and she could not stay awake any longer. She held onto the body of her mother and went to sleep on top of her. However, the hot sun and the moving sands of the desert woke her up before too long. She became very thirsty and hungry. Her thirst and hunger forced her to get up and move away from the lifeless body of her mother. She kept walking and every now and then, she stopped and looked back at her mother's still body. The road that she was walking on was rough and full of holes. Whenever one of her little feet stepped into a hole, she would fall down. She fell many times on the dusty barren road. Wherever her eyes looked, she could see nothing except the empty stretched landscape of the Sahara Desert of the Rub' al Khali (The Empty Quarter is the largest sand deserts area in the world). Anyone got stranded in that awful place he would never find his way out until he would die of thirst and hunger.

Nevertheless, the little Iffat did not walk more than an hour before her eyes spotted a small tent. She had never seen a tent before. She instinctively walked in the direction of the tent. She left the road and began to walk on the sand. She began to walk with much difficulty for the sand slowed down each step she made. Sometimes, her small feet sank into the sand up to her knees. Fortunately, she did not get stuck in what was like quicksand. When she got closer to the tent, she could hear sounds of animals and voices of human beings. Before she reached the tent, Iffat saw someone come out and begin to walk toward her. When she saw him, she became very frightened. She had never seen a person like this before. His clothes were different from any clothes she had ever seen in her life. In one hand, he was carrying a stick, and in the other hand, he was carrying a whip.

Iffat thought that the man was coming to beat her. She turned around and began to run away. The man ran toward her and overtook her. She began to scream loudly when the man grabbed her and picked her up. She was screaming and looking at his face. She began to beg him in Hindi not to beat her. The man smiled and talked to her in Arabic. He could see the little girl was speaking another language. He understood the reason for her fear and threw down the stick and the whip. Iffat felt less afraid when the man threw down the stick and the whip.

The Arab man carried Iffat back to his tent. When he brought her inside his tent, Iffat found she was in the presence of other children like herself and a woman like her mother. The woman gave her water and some food. After she ate the food and drank the water, the woman gave her milk to drink. The milk somehow reminded Iffat of seeing her mother nursing her little baby brother.

She tried to tell the man and his wife that her mother was lying dead outside. When they did not understand her, she caught the hand of the woman and began to pull her out of the tent. The man understood what Iffat wanted and told his wife to go with her. The woman got up and walked outside the tent with Iffat. The man came outside too and followed them. Iffat took them back to the road and pointed in the direction where her mother was either dead or buried alive in the hot desert sand. She continued to pull the woman by the hand and walk her toward the place where she left her mother. It took them less than an hour to reach the area. When they arrived, they found Rayhana lying in the sand. Half of her body was already buried by the moving winds of sand.

The man had never seen the face, hands, legs, or body of a grown woman so openly spread and exposed before him, with the exception of his wife. He was so struck by the marvelous beauty and the physical attractiveness of Rayhana's body despite her obvious wounds and bruises. His wife however, had different feelings when she saw Rayhana's body. She thought she was already dead. Nevertheless, she bent down and put her ear upon the chest of the woman. Then, she told her husband that the woman was still alive. At first, she did not want her husband to touch the body of a woman who wasn't his wife. Therefore, she tried to pick Rayhana up to carry her but the dead weight of her unconscious body made it impossible. She told her husband to carry her instead. The man immediately bent over the body of Rayhana and pulled her up. His wife helped him to put Rayhana's body upon his shoulder. Rayhana's body slowed the man down and his wife came from behind, took Rayhana's legs, and put each leg on each one of her shoulders.

The man felt a little relief when his wife helped him but he was shaking from head to toe. He had never touched a woman, other than his wife; nor had any woman's body ever come so close to his, except for his wife's. He felt a strong desire for sexual intercourse. If the little girl wasn't with them, he might have had sex with his wife out in the open. He remembered that his prophet Muhammad saw a woman walking on the street and got tempted by her. He ran to his wife Zainab bint Jahsh as she was tanning leather. He ignored what she was doing and promptly had sex with her. Then, he went back to his companions and said, *"When the woman comes toward you, it is Satan who is approaching you. When one of you see a woman and feel attracted to her, he should hurry to his wife. With her, it would be the same as with the other one."*

Therefore, the feeling of the body of Rayhana on his shoulders and hands drove the man extremely crazy. He waited impatiently until they reached their place. As soon as they laid down the half-dead woman, he pulled his wife out and took her to where they kept their livestock. Out in the open, he jumped on the body of his wife. His wife understood what the problem was and hence she did not resist or object to her husband pouncing on her driven mad with lust. She had never felt the full aggressiveness and force of her husband's passionate rage or the powerfulness of his desire to such a magnitude. This time she enjoyed sex with him so much because for the first time in her life, she experienced an orgasm. Relieved of his lust, the man managed to tell his wife to go back to the tent and take care of the strange woman. He feared going back to the tent and seeing the beautiful woman in her exposed condition again.

The people who rescued Rayhana and her daughter were Arab Bedouins living in vast Saudi Arabian desert. Although they were in the 21st century, they still lived as they did in the 7th century. They had no knowledge that they were living in a country that had geographical and political boundaries. They were nomadic and moved freely from place to place in the desert.

The Bedouin woman used water to revive Rayhana. She kept sprinkling drops of water on her face until Rayhana opened her eyes. She could not see anything, but her mouth moved. The Bedouin woman began to pour some milk onto her dry lips and mouth. The Bedouins believe that if someone is dehydrated from exposure to the desert sun, water is not the best thing to administer. They believe that milk is preferable in this instance.

Rayhana's revival and recovery was very slow. For twenty-four hours, she could not fully open her eyes or eat anything. Every few hours, the Bedouin woman kept alternating milk and water slowly into her mouth. She used Dettol liquid to treat her bleeding wounds and cuts. She changed her bloodstained clothes and dressed her in one of her black abayas/niqabs. Rayhana did not get any proper medical treatment. Therefore, her recovery was slow and took a long time. During her treatment, the man never came inside the tent. He ate and slept outside. His wife brought him food and water. At night, she came and slept with him.

The Bedouin family was part of a big tribe of Bedouins who lived in tents. They are nomadic people. They move from place to place according to the seasons of the year. The Bedouins have always lived in the desert. Once or twice a year, the men go to a nearby suburb and purchase commodities for their families. The Bedouins' animals supply them with whatever food is needed. These families have many animals. They have dogs, cats, chickens, cows, goats, sheep, donkeys, and camels. They keep dogs for guarding the family and for protecting their other animals. They keep cows for supplying milk. The goats and sheep are used for two purposes: to sell some of them once or twice a year to earn income, and to slaughter a goat or a sheep each month to feed the family. The chickens are used for producing eggs to eat. The family will also slaughter the chickens to eat. The donkeys and camels are used for transportation. However, the donkeys are used for traveling short distances, like going to a nearby suburb. The nomadic Arabs use the camels for traveling long distances. The camel and the donkey are for the Bedouins like cars and trains to the modern world for they are used as transportation to move from one place to another or to a faraway place.

The camel is a very important and valuable animal for desert people because it provides transportation, food, and milk. The Arabs call the camel *the Desert Ship*. In fact, the Arab Bedouins love to drink the milk of the camel. It is the only milk they can drink without boiling. They also drink camel urine when they fall sick. The prophet Muhammad ordered his followers to drink camel milk and urine whenever they fall sick. A visitor to a Bedouin family might think at first that the only animal the family keeps devoid of any benefit is the cat. However, he would soon discover that of all the animals, the cats are the most useful. They are kept for warding off rats, snakes, scorpions, and lizards.

For one month, Rayhana and her daughter were allowed to stay with the family. They treated them as if they were their own family members. Iffat was treated as if she was a daughter born into the family. The Bedouin man did not harass Rayhana in any way. He always kept himself at a far distance from her. His wife was the same age as Rayhana. They had three daughters and one son. Their children were all younger than Iffat but as soon as the new girl came into their family, they began to like her and play with her. Iffat, in a surprisingly short time, was able to pick up some Arabic.

Although she was living among good people, Rayhana constantly thought of her five sons. She also thought a lot about her mother. She knew that she had left her sons and her mother enough money to live on for a long time. How would her mother feed her sons after all the money was gone? Would she send her grandchildren into the streets to beg for money and food? And what would happen to her children if her mother died? For these reasons, Rayhana knew that one day she would have to leave the Bedouin family. She would either have to find some work to earn money to send back home or she would have to return to India to work again in the homes of the wealthy people in order to feed her family. It took her one month to come to that agonizing conclusion.

CHAPTER 4

THE TRIP

One of the major problems for Rayhana's was where she would go to find some work and just how would she go about getting to this work. She feared the police might arrest them again because they had no official papers. Their papers, money, and clothes were left in that vehicle of death that brought them from the airport to the desert. Shortly after pondering this dilemma, a solution presented itself with the appearance of the Bedouin man who happened to be saddling up his donkey for a trip. He was going to the nearest suburb to sell one of his sheep and to buy some commodities for his family. His preparations didn't go unnoticed by Rayhana and she motioned for him to take her with him on the donkey. She initially thought about leaving her daughter with the Bedouin family to venture out to find work or a solution to her problem. The Bedouin woman, however, objected and stood in between her husband and Rayhana flatly refusing to allow her husband to travel alone with a strange woman for endless hours. Additionally, another huge difficulty presented itself. As custom mandated, Rayhana could not travel alone with him for she was not his wife, sister, or daughter. His wife was acutely aware of her husband's behavior once he had set his eyes upon Rayhana's unconscious body and carried her through the desert to their tent. She fully expected that he would either convince Rayhana to sleep with him or force himself upon her should she refuse his advances. The hadith of the Prophet Muhammad came to mind: *"A man must never be alone with a woman unless there is someone who is a Muhram with them" (Agreed upon in Sahih Al-Bukhari and Sahih Muslim). He also said, "A man must never be alone with a woman, for verily the Satan is their third." (At-Tirmizi and Ahmad). This hadith narrated slightly different as, "When a man and a woman are isolated in the presence of each. Satan is bound to be their third companion."*

Rayhana yielded to his wife's uneasiness with the situation and chose to take her daughter with her. Even so, the Bedouin woman was still not in favor of Rayhana accompanying her husband. The wife asked her husband to leave Rayhana with her and to travel alone. The Bedouin man insisted she should come along to find her family. When his wife continued to strongly object, he used his stick to chastise her. Rayhana felt guilty witnessing this sudden flogging. The kind woman who had taken care of her and her daughter for the past month was now being punished because of the presence of an uninvited visitor. Rayhana's conscience greatly disturbed her and she could not go against the wishes of her most loving caregiver. Having practiced various forms of communication while staying with the Bedouins, Rayhana used gesturing and signing in an attempt to resolve the matter and the guilty feeling she felt inside. She took hold of the woman's hand and beckoned the children to come along with them. It was in this way that she convinced the Bedouin man to bring his wife and children along with them. The Bedouin man seemed to understand but looked unhappy with the additional company.

The Bedouin customarily traveled to the suburbs on his donkey. On this particular trip, he changed his mind and decided to take his camel. He wanted to show off his abilities to care for an extended family and growing harem of women. The rest of his entourage were given donkeys to mount. The first donkey bore the Bedouin's wife and two of their children. Rayhana and her daughter shared their beast with one of his daughters. This was Rayhana's first time riding a donkey. She had a nagging fear that the donkey might throw them off. The gentle beast soon placated her fear as it began to clop along dutifully behind the camel and the other donkey. Rayhana was preoccupied with thoughts of her unknown future but gradually gave in to the newness of travel by donkey. Her delight increased at the sound of the Bedouin singing in his native tongue. Not understanding the language, she somehow supposed that he was happy and singing to his camel. In those unfamiliar surroundings, Rayhana remembered her lover and longed for his company and warm embraces. She wished he was sitting with her on the donkey and singing romantic love songs to her as she enjoyed the slow stride of the small caravan.

Whereas it takes only an hour by car to travel the same distance, the trip took six hours by slow moving beasts of burden. It did not help that the little children would every now and then ask to answer the call of nature. As is the custom, a child urinates and defecates by the roadside. Lacking water or the option of toilet paper, the Bedouin children use stones to clean up. The Bedouin himself stopped his camel three times to relieve himself. Both Rayhana and the Bedouin's wife made a stop, and like the children, they used smooth stones to clean themselves. In fact, using stones is a recommended practice in the religion of Islam. The prophet Muhammad himself endorsed using three smooth stones for cleaning should there be no water. After cleaning, a Muslim is expected to utter the following prayer of thanksgiving to Allah, *"Praise be to Allah who relieved me from my pain and filth."*

Muslims will proudly tell you that prophet Muhammad teaches them everything about defecation and every matter conducting daily life. From the time of awakening, until one retires at night, the prophet Muhammad provides the commandments of Allah for the faithful. There are even rules and regulations regarding a woman's menstrual cycle. Rules also dictate how a Muslim man should initiate sex with his wife. An Egyptian Muslim scholar quoting the prophet Muhammad, once said that on the wedding night, the bridegroom is permitted to remove all the clothing of his new bride with the exception of her underwear. He added that it is unlawful for the man at any time or under any circumstances to touch or remove his wife's underwear. This right belongs to the woman. The prophet Muhammad also said, *"when anyone goes to the lavatory, he/she should not touch his/her penis/vagina nor clean his/her private parts with his/her right hand"* (Sahih al-Bukhari). Islam commands Muslims to use their left hands for this purpose. This hand, however, is not used for eating.

As it goes, the right hand is for the mouth and the left hand is for the privates. This is why the Muslim's daily life is like a drill. Muslims from Burkina Faso to Jakarta behave the same way because of these compulsory and strict daily rules and regulations. The way they walk, talk, pray, dress up, and treat their children and women are dictated to them by the Shari'a laws. A Muslim is a robot created out of a programmed bundle of laws.

The travelers broke their journey to eat, and in this, the legacy of the prophet loomed once more. The prophet charged Muslims to eat and drink together from the same plate and cup. Following this, it is recommended that a person must suck and lick his fingers after eating. This might sound unhygienic, but Muslims obey this because their prophet dictates it. As the six-hour journey drew to a close, the beasts of burden arrived at a suburb on the outskirts of Jeddah. After some shopping, the Bedouins bid Rayhana and her daughter farewell and wished them success. Rayhana shed tears while hugging the Bedouin woman and kissing her children good bye. She offered her hand to the Bedouin man to say goodbye, but he refused it. He muttered something in Arabic, of which Rayhana understood only one word. As a Muslim, she was intimately acquainted with the word "*haram*", which means forbidden. Not shaking hands with women is based on the words of Prophet Muhammad, *"I do not shake the hands of women"* (Al-Nasaei, Al-Tirmizi, and Ibn Majah). Moreover, Aisha said, *"By Allah, the hand of the Messenger of Allah never touched another woman (other than his wives). He used to take their pledges verbally only*" (Sahih Al-Bukhari and Sahih Muslim).

As the Bedouins mounted up and rode away, Rayhana became emotional and troubled with the uncertainty of what lay ahead. She was tempted to take her daughter; go back to the Bedouins, and live with them. It was only for the well-being of her family in India that forced her to restrain her rising panic and stay behind. She stood still for a long time while gazing at the loving family fading into the distance disappearing from her life and that of her daughter. They had been so kind and caring to them. But now that she was alone here with her daughter, one thought repeatedly troubled her. She wondered if the people in this holy city would be anything like the Bedouin family. Long after the Bedouin family vanished from sight, she pondered her options. They had no money. They had no home. They had no proof of identity. They had become nothing. What were they going to eat and where were they going to sleep? They had no protection. Anyone could take advantage of them or harm them.

As it was, while Rayhana was standing and looking at the people walking by, two men were watching her very carefully. One wanted to take advantage of her and the other intended to do her harm. The former was an Indian, and the latter, a Saudi. The Indian man was a pimp from Hyderabad. Prior to getting his Saudi Arabian visa, he was part of "a marriage agency company" catering to Indian and Arab Muslims wanting to connect. Hyderabad was the only city in India that had marriage agencies. The main business of these "marriage agencies", however, was the procurement of young female children for Arab pedophiles. The Saudi, a correctional police officer, was watching Rayhana. He suspected her of being a "Christian prostitute" from the Philippines, Indonesia, Malaysia, or India. He was reasonably sure that she was Christian because Muslim prostitutes prefer the holy cities of Mecca and Medina. This is where big money can be made. A woman without a husband or a male Muhram is considered a prostitute waiting for someone to pick her up in his car. Being a prostitute in Saudi Arabia is the most dangerous job in the world. If a prostitute is caught red-handed, she is to be stoned to death the following Friday. If the correctional officer finds a woman walking, standing all alone, or talking to a man other than her husband, father, or brother he will arrest her as a prostitute. Countries that criminalize prostitution all have prescribed penalties for prostitutes, pimps, enablers, and sometimes, for the customers. A Muslim country, however, often requires the prostitute to be executed.

The Indian was trying to discreetly draw Rayhana's attention so that he could make a deal with her. He had many wealthy Saudi customers for just such a transaction. He stood in a corner waving to her but Rayhana did not see him. He even whistled to her but she was preoccupied, miles away in thought. In another dark corner, the

Saudi correctional police hid and passed the time. He was just waiting for a man to come and talk to the woman or pick her up in his car. He could then have her stoned to death on the following Friday. He noticed the woman's little daughter with her but it did nothing to sway his conviction she was a prostitute because he knew full well that prostitutes often use children as a cover for criminal mischief. When no one approached Rayhana, he decided to punish her for a lesser crime. In Saudi Arabia, a woman is not allowed to be in public alone. She must be accompanied by her husband or a Muhram, defined as a man that is unlawful for her to wed such as her father, brother, or an adult son. A cousin is not a Muhram, because in Islam a woman is allowed to marry her cousin or close kin. A Muhram is also neither a father-in-law nor a brother-in-law as the prophet Muhammad has decreed that in-laws are like death to the wife. Rayhana, being alone on the street according to Shari'a law, should be flogged.

Still rooted by indecision, Rayhana felt a sharp crippling blow that paralyzed her and sent her to her knees. Iffat screamed at the sight of her mother's assailant bearing a staff as long as she was tall. As he lifted his staff once again and brought it down on the crumpled form of her mother, Iffat turned and fled. Her escape was blocked by the Indian man. Iffat was screaming, *"Let me go, let me go, he's hurting my mother!"* The Indian spoke to her in Urdu. Speaking urgently, he explained that he could save her and her mother "from THAT man." All she had to do was say that he was her father. Iffat, not knowing any better, agreed. The man rushed towards the correctional officer with Iffat in his arms, animatedly announcing in Arabic that the woman was his wife and the little girl, his daughter.

Rayhana lay crumpled on the pavement weeping. She did not know why the Arab was beating her. The officer did not wear a uniform. She could be forgiven for thinking he was psychotic, but she wasn't too far off. He was an Arabic Mutaw'a by definition; one whose duty is to tame wild animals. Here was a man whose place in society was to domesticate 'wild women'. This particular designation comes about because of the relative status of the Muslim woman in Muslim societies. The degradation of women to the level of animals is enshrined in the misogynistic teachings of the prophet Muhammad. Amongst is the following, which says:

"When one of you prays without a sutrah, a dog, an ass, a pig, a Jew, a Majian, and a woman annuls his prayer" (Sunan Abu Dawud, 2704). In his Farewell speech the prophet Muhammad said, *"Treat women well, for they are* ***domestic animals*** *with you and do not possess anything for themselves"* (Al-Tabari Vol. 9. Page no. 1754). "*Narrated Amr Ibn al-Ahwas al-Jushami, the Prophet said in his farewell address on the eve of his Last Pilgrimage, after he had glorified and praised Allah, he cautioned his followers: 'Listen! Treat women kindly; they are like* ***prisoners*** *in your hands"* (Al-Tirmizi #276).

Rayhana was so enraged at the sight of the Indian carrying her daughter that she forgot about the Arab. Still weeping she demanded of him,

"Why didn't you call the police and have him arrested? He beat me for no good reason."

"You must be new here in this country. That man is a correctional police officer. He would have arrested you and you would have been stoned to death if I had not come at the right time and rescued you from his hand."

"I haven't done anything wrong. I was just standing here with my daughter. He came behind me and just started beating me. He did not even talk to me or ask me to go."

"It is his duty to beat any woman he finds standing or walking without her husband, father, or brother. I lied to him and told him that you are my wife that is why he left you alone. Otherwise, he would have arrested you. By the way, where is your husband and where do you live?"

"I have no husband. I have no place of my own. My daughter and I are strangers in this city. Some policemen beat us and robbed us of our traveling papers."

Rayhana began weeping again and the Indian knelt down and comforted her. He promised to help her by inviting her to his home and extending an offer for accommodations, with them both being Indians and all.

CHAPTER 5

ASLAM ALI KHAN

Aslam Ali Khan was the jack of all sex trades and master of all marriage ceremonies. He was prepared to do anything to make money. He was an Indian Muslim from Hyderabad, India and operated a small marriage agency. While in India, apart from his main business of selling young Muslim girls to old Arab men, he would steal babies from hospitals and sell them to Gondas (Indian gangsters). He specialized in marrying simple village girls. Unbeknownst to the victims and their families, these mock weddings supplied more than thirty village girls only for them to be brought to the city and sold to a pimp. Eventually the law caught up with him while he was stealing a baby from a local hospital in Hyderabad. The police 'interrogated' him and was soon able to extract enough of an admission of guilt. He was tried, convicted, and sentenced to ten years of hard labor. Ten months later, he escaped and fled across the border into Pakistan. There he bought a Pakistani passport and made his way into the Kingdom of Saudi Arabia.

In Jeddah, he found employment as a taxi driver. Old habits die hard, and soon he began procuring prostitutes for his Arab customers. Sometimes, he used married women who were interested in making a little extra money on the side. He dealt with women from all over the world. His business was not limited to prostitutes; he also supplied men for sexually frustrated Saudi women that were neglected by their polygamous husbands. In Jeddah, he was drawn to provide for the particular Saudi quirkiness of having sex with small boys. Having a high percentage of homosexuals within the Kingdom of Saudi Arabia, Aslam began connecting Saudi homosexuals with interested parties.

Aslam Ali Khan was neither gay nor impotent. He just fancied money for sex of any kind. Oddly asexual, he made his living in a land with very odd sexual mores, where bestiality is common and tolerated. This phenomenon among the Arab Muslim nations involve ordinary stock animals such as goats, sheep, and donkeys. Occasionally, a chicken will do.

Aslam Khan led Rayhana Khan and Iffat Khan to his apartment. After hearing her story, he offered to marry her. Rayhana rejected his proposal. Then, he explained to her that she could not stay in his apartment if she was not his wife. The neighbors would call the police and both of them would go to jail. Rayhana remained unmoved. Finally, he convinced her to marry him on paper. Rayhana fell for this well worn trap and agreed to marry him in principle. A Pakistani Imam was then summoned to conduct their marriage contract. For Aslam Ali Khan, this was a well traveled route. In his previous career, he acted as matchmaker in front of the Hyderabad marriage court. In the event a Muslim girl fell in love with a Hindu boy, and her parents objected, it was Aslam's job to arrange the marriage in civil court. He would provide the two witnesses, the wedding gown, the lawyer and judge, paid with a hefty bribe of course and then a bona fide court marriage certificate was issued.

Once Rayhana was married to him, Aslam invited one of his rich Arab customers to his apartment to show her off. The man was struck in awe at the vision of her loveliness. She had far surpassed his definition of a beautiful woman. Becoming overeager in his longings for her, he requested time alone with Rayhana. He promised to pay whatever Aslam would ask for her. Aslam pretended to be grieved at heart reminding the Saudi that this girl was now his wife. He added that she had just arrived from India and he showed him their new marriage certificate. The Saudi offered to double his offer if Aslam would "get down from his wife" and give her to him "to climb on her." This saying goes back to an ancient wife swapping custom between Arab men. The prophet Muhammad forbade this custom at the time a great

Arab chieftain asked him to get down from his beloved wife, Aisha, so that he could mount over her. (Muslim Mujahedeen throughout the Islamic history praised themselves for climbing over the women of their enemies). However, Muhammad did not forbid the switching of female slaves. In fact, sex with female slaves, without marrying them, is permitted in Islam to this very day (Surat 4: 3). Moreover, he allowed his followers to rape the women of their enemies even if they are married and their husbands are alive.

"Abu Sa'id al-Khudri said: The Apostle of Allah (may peace be upon him) sent a military expedition to Awtas on the occasion of the battle of Hunain. They met their enemy and fought with them. They defeated them and took them captives. Some of the Companions of the Apostle of Allah (may peace be upon him) were reluctant to have intercourse with the female captives in the presence of their husbands who were unbelievers. So Allah, the Exalted, sent down the Qur'anic verse: "And all married women (are forbidden) unto you save those (captives) whom your right hands possess" (Sunnan Abu Dawud 2150).

"Muhairiz said: I entered the mosque and saw Abu Sa'id al-Khudri. I sat with him and asked about withdrawing the penis (while having intercourse). Abu Sa'id said: We went out with the Apostle of Allah (may peace be upon him) on the expedition to Banu al-Mustaliq, and took some Arab women captive, and we desired the women, for we were suffering from the absence of our wives, and we wanted ransom; so we intended to withdraw the penis (while having intercourse with the slave-women). But we asked ourselves: Can we draw the penis when the Apostle of Allah (may peace be upon him) is among us before asking him about it? So we asked him about it. He said: It does not matter if you do not" (Sunan Abu Dawud 2167).

Aslam Ali Khan agreed and accepted the deal. He was fully aware that Rayhana was neither his wife nor a prostitute. Expecting her to resist and scream bloody murder and attract the attention of the neighbors, or even the police, Aslam decided to take another route. He would sell her to the Saudi as a maidservant. That being the case, both buyer and seller would be in the clear. Aslam reasoned with the

Saudi mentioning that as long as his wife was staying with him, he would be tempted to climb on her or sell her to his other customers.

"If you want to have her all to yourself, then you should take her to your house as a maidservant."

The Saudi man broke into a broad smile at the brilliant idea that immediately would reduce Rayhana to an unpaid maidservant and sex slave. The price Aslam demanded was more than he had ever charged anyone. Writing down his client's address, he promised to bring Rayhana and her daughter to him the following day. The Saudi man wrote a check in Aslam Khan's name for exactly half of the agreed upon amount, and promised to pay the balance upon delivery.

As soon as the Saudi left, Aslam approached Rayhana and told her that he had found a very good job for her. He then said that the Arab who came to their apartment was his friend and a very wealthy one at that who just happened to be looking for a good Muslim woman to work in his house as a maidservant. Leaving out all of the other details, he painted a lovely picture of how she was going to work for him in his house and how well she was going to be paid. Rayhana was ecstatic. She thanked Aslam repeatedly and called on Allah to bless him abundantly. He quieted her down and told her that she would live in his friend's house with her daughter, but would still remain his wife on paper. As such, she would be able to return home anytime. However, in the back of his mind, he was already planning his next move to another apartment.

The Saudi, Sheikh Hamza bin Khalid, was older than Rayhana's father. The Sheikh had already married and divorced several women. He was compulsively driven by his hunger for women but soon became tired of them. As a compulsive sex addict, he treated them like meat. This Saudi, however, liked his meat fresh. Each newcomer would hear him say, *"I love your body so much and I feel like eating one of your breasts."* Sheikh Hamza looked like the kind of man that might actually eat human flesh had one of his women actually cut off one of her breasts and cooked it for him. None of his sex victims escaped being bitten all over her body while having sex with him. He was that kind of sexually deviant cannibal.

Sheikh Hamza bin Khalid's infatuation for Rayhana ran deeper than the oceans. He had never liked any woman as much as he liked Rayhana, nor had he ever paid such a large sum of money for a woman before. This time the Sheikh was planning for once to keep a woman wholly to himself for good. He wanted her to be his "Habibti" and he would be her only "Habibi". When he first feasted his eyes upon Rayhana Khan, he thought she was a great Indian film actress. From the time he paid the required deposit for her, he waited impatiently for his perpetual virgin of paradise to come to his house and satisfy his lustful desires. Of course, Rayhana did not see a single coin from this closed-door transaction.

As any good business owner, Aslam Ali Khan wanted to impress Sheikh Hamza bin Khalid. He sacrificed a few riyals, which is the basic monetary unit of the Saudians. He took Rayhana to a beauty salon to prepare her for her new role. He convinced her that she would find more favor in the eyes of her employer and his wife if she had a beauty makeover. Rayhana had never been to a beauty parlor before. She accepted the suggestion and went along with him; her daughter tagging behind them. At the beauty salon, Aslam offered to take Iffat for a walk in the city. Rayhana did not trust any man with her little girl. She apologized to Aslam and firmly told him that she would keep her daughter with her.

A Filipino woman ran the beauty parlor. All the staff were Filipino women too. According to the rules of the salon, no man was allowed to enter inside. Each and every man that brought his wife would be told to leave and return in two hours. Aslam Ali Khan, like all others was expected to comply. He introduced Rayhana as his new wife, just in from Bombay. He proved his matrimonial relation by showing their marriage certificate. From the service brochure, he selected the special preparations from the bride package.

The Filipinos marveled at the stunning beauty that had earlier been hidden by her niqab. Rayhana remained enshrouded in her under dress, as was customary. All three beauticians set to work upon her hair, face and body with the eagle-eyed salon owner observing them from out the corner of her eye. The shrewd salon owner was in the routine of collecting all money due up front before any work commenced and Aslam paid her in full. Reading her magazines and newspapers, she kept a close eye on her workers. She was a very strict woman. She had after all, come all the way from the Philippines to make money. That was why she adamantly refused to have a second child despite her husband's pleading. Children cost money, and that was that.

The salon owner was quick to notice Rayhana's beauty but lost interest quickly, only to be immersed once again in her newspapers. She was acutely aware that her own eyes were tiny and her insecurities were not made better while looking at Rayhana, whose eyes were large, attractive and alluring. Small as her eyes were, they were quick and observant with a penchant for fine details. A corner of her eye swept across a photo of a woman in the newspaper. Her other eye stopped and decided to join its sister. The size of the reward offered for information about the lady in the picture galvanized her into action. Jumping out of her chair, she slid over to Rayhana and scanned her face with the intensity of a mongoose sizing up a cobra. She could not find a single iota of difference between the photo of the woman in the newspaper and the Indian woman that was sitting in her salon. She remained silent and returned to her chair. Picking up the phone, she dialed the number mentioned in the advertisement and counted the seconds nervously, full of anticipation. This day, she lost all interest in watching her workers and reading her newspapers.

A half hour crept along, punctuated by the arrival of an old man running into the salon. With the exception of this particular man, the Filipino salon owner had NEVER allowed any man to step inside her salon. It was a taboo and hallowed ground that only totem animals were allowed in. However, that particular male was allowed to enter the holy ground and claim his female. She did not allow him *to take his dead, resurrected, lost and now found maidservant,* until he wrote a check to her as was promised in the newspaper. The Filipino woman broke all her divine rules that day. First, she allowed a man to enter the taboo area of her salon where young females could be seen without niqabs on, where their faces were revealed, open shoulders, exposed breasts, and exposed thighs and buttocks. Second, she allowed the

Saudi man to take a woman out of the salon, which he did not bring to the salon. This was probably the most iron clad rule of the salon; only the person accompanying the woman and paying her fees is permitted to pick her up. Even her husband, father, or brother would not be allowed to lay claim to her if he was not the person who brought her there. Thirdly, without asking for proof of his identity or relationship to Rayhana, the Filipino woman allowed the old man to take *his lost and found maidservant* after he wrote out a check and handed it to her. After examining the check and its amount very carefully, the happy Filipino business woman gave in to Sheikh Faiz bin Ahmed's insistent demand for his maidservant and her daughter.

After about thirty minutes, Aslam Ali Khan was due to return for his new wife and deliver her to her high bidder. Needless to say, upon his arrival, he was told that the Indian woman and her daughter were taken away by their Kafeel. Aslam became extremely belligerent and started threatening to wreck the salon. His anger was dissipated once the salon owner picked up the phone and threatened to call the Jeddah police on him. Quickly remembering his not so clean background and criminal history, and the more than likely risk of getting his head chopped off, Aslam's countenance changed and he begged the Filipino salon owner to forgive him for the intrusion. There was no need for her to call the police for he would leave quietly. Ever the shrewd one, he managed to convince her to part with the business card of his wife's sponsor, which included his phone number and address. Despite the phone being firmly in its cradle, and the threat of beheading diminished, Aslam Ali Khan began to worry about his life. He had to devise a plan to escape from the Kingdom of Saudi Arabia in order to save his life from Sheikh Hamza bin Khalid. He could either return to Sheikh Hamza bin Khalid a refund of his purchase price or either he could run for his life. He chose to run for his life.

CHAPTER 6

MRS. CHAM CHUM CHI

Sheikh Faiz bin Ahmed was a man accustomed to getting his way in life. He had tried every possible means to get possession of the most beloved woman he had ever loved. He had gone to every police station in the city of Jeddah and showed the passports of his maidservant and her daughter to report them missing. He lodged an official complaint against the two unknown police officers who allegedly had kidnapped his maidservant and her child. He put advertisements in all the newspapers concerning the kidnapping of the two abducted females; the mother and the child. He promised a huge reward for anyone who could provide information about the two missing newcomers, lost in the land of no return.

After a short time when no one had phoned him or had come forward and inquired about the reward, Sheikh Ahmed doubled the bounty. He paid the most popular newspaper in Jeddah to advertise and publish the photo of his maidservant every Friday. He chose Friday because it was the only official public holiday in Saudi Arabia. He anticipated that everyone would be home on this day and read their newspapers. For more than one month, the phone remained silent. The Sheikh was in great desperation. Day and night, he constantly lamented over her mysterious disappearance and he could not forget the woman he had paid for handsomely. Many a time, he instructed his Pakistani driver to take him to the desert where he could search for her. He searched all around the city for any clue that might lead him to her whereabouts and the whereabouts of her daughter. It was all for naught and nothing came of his desperate search.

One particular Friday afternoon, he was on his way to the public prayer when his cell phone began ringing while he was sitting in the backseat of his brand new Mercedes. As it is in other OAPEC countries, it would be downright shameful if his relatives or friends caught sight of him driving his own car. Men of his stature and wealth are obligated to have a chauffeur. Sheikh Ahmed's chauffeur was a Pakistani. Strangely enough, it is rumored that most of the children of OAPEC countries were probably fathered by Indian or either Pakistani chauffeurs employed by their wealthy employers. In the face of sexually repressed polygamous wives, a personal chauffeur is inevitability practical.

When his cell phone began to ring, Sheikh Ahmed took the phone out of his pocket and looked at the number. The caller's ID displayed "The Filipino Beautiful Women's Salon." At first, he thought it was a wrong number and hence decided to ignore it. However, his sixth sense reminded him of his weekly Friday ad. Biting back negative thoughts, he responded to the call, only to be greeted by the voice of a Filipino woman with a funny Arabic accent.

"Ths Mrs. Cham Chum Chi, owner of Filipino Butifl Womn Salun. I callin regardin you advateasmen bout you missin maid, Rih a naa Khn. She sitting here righ now in salun. Come immeedly and bring reward money and you get her."

The astute, Mrs. Chi, did not give Sheikh Ahmed a chance to interrupt her monologue. She mechanically rattled off her address and hung up. Glancing up from his phone, the love sick Sheikh pronounced a new destination to his chauffeur forgetting about his obligatory Friday prayer. He urged his driver to speed to the location immediately and ignore all traffic signals and speed limits. The driver was concerned they would attract the attention of police surveillance vehicles but Sheikh Ahmed shouted *"You work for me, not the police! If you want your next paycheck do as I say or go back to being nothing!"*

"Don't stop the car until we arrive at the salon! I'll take care of the police!" The address recited by Mrs. Chi lay on the outskirts of Jeddah. Under normal conditions, it would take an hour's drive;

however, with his belligerent employer barking at him like a love sick puppy dog, the Pakistani chauffeur closed the distance in a mere half hour. The car racing at the speed of light arrived at Mrs. Chi's place of business in record time, but not before it was captured by the flash of at least four highway cameras.

When the crazy Qays reached the salon, the three Filipino beauty consultants had already finished the face, hair, and body of the lovely Layla and they began to work on her nails. Rayhana soaked in the ambiance of attention being lavished upon her. She enjoyed being Queen for a Day in this luxurious salon. She was dimly aware of her beauty, but that day she could not believe the glorious sight of the beautiful woman staring at her from across the huge mirror reflecting an image greater than all the goddesses of India. She thought her Allah had given her more beauty than all these valueless goddesses because he had chosen her to be Muslim. Her miserable life and present troubles never gave her the possibility to really see herself. With her lot in life, she was always worried about something. Now with the promise of a new job, a free and safe shelter just around the corner; she succumbed to the seductive atmosphere of the salon, relaxed a little while she enjoyed her salon treatments and new confidence in her beauty and appearance.

As usual, whenever a ray of hope shone in her saddened heart, Rayhana always remembered her lover. Once again, Jamaal suddenly appears in a vision standing before her. He sees her exquisite beauty and cannot resist taking her into his arms. She closes her eyes and surrenders to her lover melting into the safety of his loving embrace, the lusciousness of his lips, and the tenderness of his touch. Her imagination took her away from all the torture, rape, humiliation and violence she had lived through for she knew what real love was and it was this love she kept safe inside her heart and mind. This dreamy state was suddenly interrupted by a firm abrasive grasp shaking her right arm. Opening her eyes, she was startled by the sight of an old man speaking to her in Arabic. Her moment with Jamaal was cut short. A gamut of emotions overcame Rayhana as she struggled to recognize the elderly man standing before her. Her heart rate spiked remembering the brutal beating of the correctional officer. She assumed that the police had come to arrest her again. By now, she learned that in this "No Woman Land" everything is possible. A woman can be taken away from her husband and raped for breaking some stupid Shari'a law such as there is nothing with them to prove their relationship to each other. A vulnerable woman like Rayhana without a male guardian for those Arabs is just like an open vagina that any man can jump over her. A police can arrest and flog her or kidnap and rape her or do whatever he wants with her. Anyhow, peering into his happy face and hearing him call out to her repeatedly, her feelings of panic evaporated. It dawned upon Rayhana that his face was familiar to her. With her memory failing her, it came as an absolute shock to her when the old Arab showed her an Indian passport with her photo. Another passport carrying the photo of her daughter followed. She recognized the two passports as the ones she had received from the travel agency, which had been taken away from her by the Bombay police officers.

Rayhana did not recognize her sponsor until he mentioned the words Taj Mahal and Colaba. She immediately recognized Sheikh Faiz bin Ahmed and recalled that he was the one who had met her at the Gate of India in front of the Taj Mahal hotel at Bombay. This was the man who had promised to give her a work visa to the rich Arab country. Her suspicion turned to joy when she realized that the old Arab had somehow brought their passports from India and had come to rescue them. The happiness reflected in Rayhana's beautiful face filled the heart of the old man with indescribable joy. He did not even bother to ask her where she had been or how she had come to be in the salon. She appeared to him as a bride prepared for her bridegroom. Without further ado, and with much haste, he forked over the reward, grabbed Rayhana by her hand, and took her out of the beauty salon as a bridegroom escorting his beautiful bride from her father's house to his home to consummate the marriage. Little Iffat followed behind her mother like a little bridesmaid.

The reunited pair made an odd couple comparing Rayhana Khan's twenty-seven years and five days to Sheikh Ahmed's sixty-nine years, eleven months and twenty-five days. Rayhana was betrothed to her late husband at the age of nineteen. His idea of family planning was to give her a daughter and five sons in just six years of marriage. Had he not taken his own life, Rayhana might have had ten children. Some Indian families have been known to have twenty-five children. There was an old Muslim Indian man living in the city of Bombay who was featured on the front page of a popular newspaper celebrating his eightieth birthday with the birth of his seventy-fifth child. Of course, not all of them were from one woman. He was a notorious polygamist. (Although India is a secular country, it still allows Muslims to practice polygamy. Nevertheless, polygamy in India is still illegal for Hindus, Sikhs, Christians, Buddhists, and followers of other religions). The current saying then was if this notorious polygamist were to sit near an Indian girl in a bus, she would become pregnant. Indian women can be very fertile, much like Chinese women. In 2020, the Indian population is expected to reach one billion. China of course has already hit a record number of one billion people.

Rayhana spoke to her sponsor in Hindi but he understood nothing of what she was saying. Although he visited India many times, Sheikh Ahmed was not a linguist, and neither had he picked up any Hindi except for two words—yes and no (Jihaan and Nahi) aside from his very fluent pronunciation of obscenities. It came as no surprise his entire conversation with Rayhana consisted of her name in the affirmative.

"Rayhana, Jihaan, Jihaan, Jihaan."

The old Saudi had only let go of Rayhana's hand once up unto that time—to pay the crafty Mrs. Chi, who was holding onto Rayhana's other hand. With a wide smile on his face, he had rummaged through his suitcase, retrieved his checkbook and made out a check. He handed the check over to the empress of beauty salons bowing low to this eagle eye that had found his missing diamond amidst a land of desert sand and walking coffins. After much grandiosity, he then reattached himself to Rayhana.

Mrs. Chi skimmed over the check for errors. Satisfied with the amount and the signature on the check, she released Rayhana's other hand and gladly accepted the old man's business card with a smile.

With such a huge amount in the palm of her hand, the Filipino woman had completely forgotten about the man posing as Rayhana's husband. Rayhana herself had also completely forgotten about Aslam Khan and her new employer. By the time, it came to her mind, the glimmering Mercedes was halfway to its destination.

While in the vehicle with her rescuer, Rayhana Khan was emotionally engrossed in narrating her tragic experience in the holy city. Noticing the chauffeur was Pakistani, she began speaking to him in Urdu and using him as her interpreter. When Rayhana remembered Aslam, she told the chauffeur to turn the car around and return to the salon. She said that she wanted to thank him and apologize for not going to the house of his Arab friend who wanted to hire her as a maidservant. The Pakistani related this suggestion to his boss. Sheikh Ahmed suspected something fishy about this Aslam and his Saudi friend. This story about her becoming a maidservant to someone else did not sit well with him. His suspicion was peaked when he realized that the Indian man had taken Rayhana to the beauty salon to have her prepped before handing her over to this new employer. Firm in his decision not to turn back, Sheikh Ahmed told his chauffeur to explain to Rayhana that the Filipino woman had been instructed to hand his business card over to Aslam Khan.

CHAPTER 7

MRS. AHMED

Rayhana Khan narrated her story without fear or favor, neither adding nor omitting anything that she could remember of her ordeal. She related her kidnapping, her beatings and her rape at the hands of the two Saudi police officers. She described how her daughter had found the kind Bedouin family that saved both of them and invited them to live with them in their home. Finally, she spoke of the *Good Samaritan*, Aslam Ali Khan, a kind and caring Muslim man who had saved them from the streets and more beatings and imprisonment. She neglected to mention the marriage of convenience. When she was done, Sheikh Ahmed thanked Allah for using this kind Bedouin family and the good Indian man in helping his maidservant and her little daughter.

While the chauffeur was racing toward home, Sheikh Ahmed remembered his Friday obligatory prayer. A glance at his watch revealed only fifteen minutes to prayer time. He decided he should go pray. He wanted to go the house of Allah and thank him for finally bringing his beloved woman to him. (Muslims consider every mosque in the world to be the house of Allah. Muhammad claimed that Allah has given him the entire earth planet as MOSQUE. Following this promise, Muslims want to build mosques everywhere even over the graves of their victims). Once again, Sheikh Ahmed set off a new round of orders to his chauffeur, reminding him to make haste. As the car pulled up to the entrance of the mosque, he got out and instructed his chauffeur to take Rayhana and her daughter to the house of his fourth wife. Sheikh Ahmed would not dare to take Rayhana and her daughter with him to the mosque because that is strictly forbidden. Prophet Muhammad discouraged women from attending the mosque. He is recorded to have said: *"The best places of prayer for women are the innermost apartments of their houses"* (Report by Imam Ahmed and Abu Dawod). Moreover, he forbade the woman from being muezzin (the caller for prayer) and Imam (the leader in prayer), *"A woman may not lead a man in Prayer, nor may a Bedouin lead a believer of the Muhajirun or a corrupt person lead a committed Muslim in Prayer"* (Sunan Ibn Majah #1134). Nonetheless, a Muslim female professor in US who was believed to be a self-ordained "Imamah" went in record when she led a group of 100 Muslims—men and women—in prayer in the USA. When all mosques in America refused to allow her conduct her prayer, she was led to conduct it in an Anglican Church. Muslim leaders from all over the world condemned her action. Woman is not allowed to lead men in prayer or be a leader because Prophet Muhammad believed that the woman is deficient in religion (religiously unclean due to her menses) and deficient in intellect (mentally defective) (Sahih al-Bukhari, hadith No. 301 and 856).

Sheikh Ahmed had four houses and four wives. In each house, he had children, servants, animals, and two washrooms and one wife. (It is imperative that each Muslim's house must have two separate washrooms; Men—Women). All four of his wives were older than Rayhana. The fourth wife and the youngest was a forty-two year old divorcee. He had married her, the only divorcee in his harem, because she was the daughter of a very wealthy Saudi.

When they arrived at Sheikh Ahmed's house, the chauffeur came around quickly and opened the door for Rayhana. He then stretched out his arms to Iffat, she reached up, and he carried her out of the car. This act of kindness was not lost as Rayhana observed how he was carrying her daughter. From the time they met, Rayhana liked his friendly nature. The only thing that marred her impression of him was a remark he made after the Sheikh had exited the car. He commented Sheikh Ahmed loved her so much he couldn't think straight, and if she was smart, she could make more money than she could count.

His remark disturbed Rayhana and she was quick to respond that she was not interested in making money in that way. She also reminded him that Sheikh Ahmed was old enough to be her grandfather. After Rayhana's sharp remarks, the Pakistani decided he had better keep his opinions to himself. A seed of suspicion however was now planted in Rayhana's mind, and she thought there had to be a reason the old Saudi must have gone to such great lengths to hire her and maybe it was more than her good looks and because she was Muslim. Upon reaching the house of wife number four, she consciously dismissed what her mind was slow to acknowledge.

Their arrival at the front gate was greeted by a very dark skinned night guard wielding the muzzle of a machine gun and a large dog. The guard appeared to Rayhana as if he had colored his face and hands with black paint. She mistook the guard for a Bhoot "scary ghost" and the dog for a lion. Rayhana and her daughter began to tremble when they saw the guard and the large dog. The chauffeur saw the fear in their eyes and told the guard to take his dog aside. The guard held his dog back until the chauffeur took Rayhana and her daughter inside the house. As soon as they stepped inside the compound, Rayhana saw a woman standing halfway between the gate and the house. She was tall and slender and her face was somewhat contorted. With her arms on her hips, she looked as though she was ready to put up a fight. The chauffeur approached the woman and greeted her politely in Arabic,

"Good afternoon Mrs. Ahmed." The angry woman remained silent.

"Madam, this is your new maidservant, Rayhana Khan and this is her daughter Iffat."

Rayhana noticed the woman's face had an angry look. She started to feel like she wasn't going to have an easy time working there in the house of her sponsor's wife. She was going to have to deal with a lion masquerading as a dog, a ghost-like guard, and a woman mean as a cobra.

"Where have you come from?" Mrs. Ahmed asked angrily. Immediately, the chauffeur resumed his translator role, giving Rayhana her first conversation with the woman of the house.

"India."

"What kind of work have you come to do here?"

"Anything you want me to do, I will do for you madam."

Mrs. Ahmed already had been informed by her husband about the new maidservant. Sheikh Ahmed called her while they were on their way back from the beauty salon and informed her about the new maidservant.

"Follow me," said Mrs. Ahmed.

Rayhana and her daughter followed the woman while the Pakistani driver remained stationary. The woman stopped, turned her back, and shouted at the chauffeur to come with them. Following a few steps behind the tall Arab woman, Rayhana began to admire the beauty of the large house. As they passed through the opulent rooms, Rayhana hoped that she and her daughter might be given one of those rooms to stay in.

They continued to walk until they reached the last room. Entering the room, Rayhana recognized the room to be the kitchen. Mrs. Ahmed took her station in the middle of the kitchen and placed her hands on her hips. She pivoted around to face Rayhana and began listing her instructions when she discovered something about Rayhana, which had escaped her earlier.

"Where were you before you came here?" shouted the woman angrily.

"I was in the beauty salon," answered Rayhana frankly.

"So, he took you to the beauty salon before you came here?"

Before Rayhana could respond, Mrs. Ahmed shot off a new round of questions.

"Where is your luggage? Where is your daughter's bag?"

"We have no bags and we have no clothes madam."

"How did you travel all the way from India to Saudi Arabia without clothing or luggage?"

Rayhana remained silent and the chauffeur decided it would be best to keep silent.

"So, my husband met you on the street and decided to hire you as a maidservant. He then took you to the beauty salon before sending you here."

"Madam, your husband met me in Bombay. He asked me to come to his country and work as his maidservant. Some bad men stole my bag and belongings when my daughter and I arrived in the city."

"Well, I will talk to my husband and find out more about you when he gets home. Right now, I want to give you your cleaning instructions. First of all, you must know that I am a very strict woman. I hate dirtiness and filthiness and I detest immoral behavior."

Mrs. Ahmed paused and surveyed Rayhana from top to bottom. She raised her voice even louder with no attempt to disguise her hot temper. Her voice resounded against the walls and it was as though she was crying inside,

"First, you must know there are males living in the household. I have two sons and my husband. One son is sixteen years old and the other is fourteen years old. They are good children and are doing well in their studies. If I perceive any immoral behavior on your part, I will beat you and wipe your face on the ground. I know you are not an ugly woman and you might try to use your beauty to entice the good men in my house. I didn't like your face from the moment I laid eyes on you. If any man in this house smiles at you, you are not to smile back. If he calls you to come to his room do not enter. Keep yourself at a distance from them. I will never tolerate any kind of love affair between any one of the noble men in this house and a lowly servant. If I happen to leave the house for any reason, don't be surprised if I lock you up in your room and keep you confined."

"Okay, madam."

"Now, we will go over the rules and your duties in this house."

Mrs. Ahmed eased herself into a chair and crossed her legs at the knees. The briefing began. She did not tell Rayhana or her daughter to sit. Even the chauffeur was standing on his feet while translating the conversion between the noble Saudi woman and her new maidservant.

"Rule No. 1. You have to be in the kitchen from six o'clock in the morning until nine o'clock at night.

Rule No. 2. You are not allowed to sit on any chair, stool, or couch during working hours. You are also to neither watch TV nor listen to the radio during working hours.

Rule No. 3. You have to cook and prepare the breakfast, lunch, and dinner, wash the clothes, bed sheets, pillow covers, and the tablecloths. You will clean all of the dishes and other utensils, sweep and mop the rooms and hallways, water the plants, iron the clothes, and do whatever else I require."

After she finished telling her new maidservant the rules and regulations, "the noble Arab woman" went to every room in her mansion and gathered all the clothes, bed sheets, mattress and pillow covers, table cloths, etc., and then ordered Rayhana to commence her work. When Rayhana entered the women's washroom and saw the huge pile of clothes and linens, she reasoned within herself that if she worked continuously without letup, she would not be able to finish half of the laundry even in a week's time. When she used to work in the homes of the rich families in India, no family had ever asked her to wash such a large heap of clothes and linens at one time. In most Indian homes in Bombay, the rich people had washing machines that made it easy for Rayhana to wash their clothes and linens. However, Mrs. Ahmed had no washing machine. There were only two oversized sinks and she expected her new maidservant to use her bare hands to wash the entire stockpile of dirty clothes and laundry. When Rayhana protested, the noble woman threatened to kick her out of the house at once and never allow her to set her foot back in again.

Rayhana brought her daughter inside the washroom with her and asked her to sit nearby as she reluctantly began washing the mounds and mounds of soiled laundry. She washed nonstop for three hours. Then through her interpreter, Mrs. Ahmed came and ordered her to the kitchen to start preparing dinner for the family. Rayhana felt a great weight lifted off her shoulders. She got up immediately and headed towards the kitchen followed by her little Iffat. When she reached the kitchen, she noticed a big tray with many dishes and plates. In every step of the dinner preparation Mrs. Ahmed was screaming at Rayhana. Twenty minutes were wasted in rebuking, correcting, and shoving Rayhana for her many errors and mistakes. Then, the noble woman told Rayhana to wait for five minutes and bring the dinner tray to the dining hall. Mrs. Ahmed felt it was below her dignity to be seen by her husband and two sons walking with a lower than dirt maidservant.

Waiting for her five minutes to pass, Rayhana tried to straighten the kitchen. The three hours in the washroom had left her with a bad pain in her back. Hunched over, she carried the heavy tray to the dining hall. The weight of the tray aggravated her back and caused her to bend forward in posture. Her position was particularly appealing to the males of the household. If she approached them, they would be able to see her two healthy breasts clearly through the opening of her dress. If she turned toward them, they could see her dress accentuating her hips and buttocks from the wetness of washing clothes and dishes. It was the maidservant's good fortune that all these revealing temptations escaped the attention of this very strict Muslim woman or she would have been beaten mercilessly.

While waiting for their meal in the dining hall, Sheikh Ahmed, his noble wife, and their two teenage sons were seated at the table. The children sat side by side, facing their parents.

"How is your new maidservant coming along?" asked Sheikh Ahmed.

"I am not happy to have her here in this house," Mrs. Ahmed replied.

"What is wrong with her? She is young and strong. Surely she is going to be a great help to you."

"I am not worried about her strength or her age. I don't like her face."

"What did you say mama!?!" shouted the sixteen-year-old son, *"Have you brought an ugly face into the house again!?!"*

"Papa, please tell me you didn't get another maidservant that looks like a monkey! I am still getting nightmares just thinking about that last ugly maidservant you brought to work here. I do not believe that that ugly girl is gone," said the fourteen-year-old.

"Where are you getting them from? The zoo? The first one looked like a chimpanzee, the second like a dog, the third like a monkey, and this one I am sure will look like a gorilla," said the older son.

"Why don't you just get a girl with a normal human face?" said the youngest son.

"Why do you always bring maidservants from Africa? Can you just once time get an Arab maidservant or someone from a country like Lebanon or Egypt?"

"Hisham and Husam!" shouted the noble woman, *"I am your mother and I know what's best for you. I chose the previous maidservants but this time your father has chosen a maidservant and I don't like her face because it doesn't qualify her to be a maidservant."*

Before the sons could pry their mother further with questions, the new maidservant entered the dining hall. They first saw the big tray, followed by a face that obviously impressed them. Their eyes were fixated on each step she made and they were staring at her face and breasts. By the time the new maidservant made it to the table, the young boys were on their feet. Hisham, the first to recover his composure, rushed behind her to pull up a chair, gesturing for her to sit. He sneaked a glance at her backside and felt an electric rush of excitement run up his spine. By the time he noticed the wet dress clinging to her buttocks, he was sporting an erection. His brother reached out to relieve her of the huge food tray and repeated the gesture for the maidservant to sit down. The maidservant understood this kind consideration and gladly sat in the chair. Hoping to gain favors with the new maidservant, the brother then proceeded to pile a plate full of food and offer it to her. The mother became fed up and could not stand it anymore. She went from irritated to furious.

"Get up you stupid girl!" screamed Mrs. Ahmed, *"You are here to serve us and not to be served by us! Have I not told you that your place is in the kitchen? How dare you sit here at this table?"*

Rayhana had not understood one single word but jumped out of her chair as if she had heard the hissing and rattling of a rattlesnake beneath her seat. She didn't need to know Arabic to interpret her mistress meant business and she instantly flew headlong into the kitchen.

"Have I not told you, Sheikh Ahmed, that this girl is not suitable as a maidservant!? You can see with your own eyes the effect of her

face on your sons! If you want to destroy their good manners, then let her stay here!"

"Mastoora" said Mr. Ahmed, *"this woman is a poor Muslim Indian. She met me in Bombay and begged me to help her to come to Saudi Arabia and work as a maidservant in my house. She is widowed and has no one except her little daughter."*

"Then, don't blame me if she corrupts your sons!"

"Mama, how can she corrupt us? She looks so innocent," said Hisham.

"Yes, Hisham is right. She looks like an angel," said Husam.

"How do you know what an angel looks like? Have you seen an angel before?" asked the mother.

"No, mama, but today I think I have."

"See, they've started calling her an angel, and tomorrow they will be calling her darling."

"They are just teasing you my wife. I know they are good boys and they know their limits."

"Mama, we will treat her as our sister."

"You are a good boy, son," said Sheikh Ahmed to Husam.

"I will hold you entirely responsible if anything wrong happens in this house because of this woman."

"I am certain that nothing bad will happen. To be beautiful is not a crime."

The last words of Sheikh Ahmed caused his wife to get up from the table without eating her dinner. She then went into the kitchen. There she found the new maidservant sitting with her daughter eating a meal. In a short time, Rayhana had developed a petrifying fear of this noble Muslim woman. Whenever she saw her or heard the voice of the cobra woman, she felt the evil of demons and jinn trying to possess her soul. The hairs of her body would bristle up and she would shake uncontrollably inside.

Mrs. Ahmed screamed at her maidservant in Arabic. Rayhana did not understand but she dashed up and ran to the women's washroom leaving her daughter in the kitchen. She resumed washing the stacks of laundry and after about an hour, the cobra woman came and grabbed her by her hand and dragged her back to the kitchen. She pointed at the dirty dishes. Rayhana understood and began cleaning them. After she finished cleaning the dishes, the cobra returned, grabbed her by the wrist and took her back to the washroom. In stone silence, Rayhana spent many hours again washing in the washroom until the flesh of her hands were white and numb. Her daughter fell asleep nearby.

It was 10:30 pm when Rayhana finished washing and left the washroom. With another crick in her back, she carried her sleeping daughter but she was not able to stand up straight. Her back was completely bent over. Her feet felt as though the arches had completely fallen flat and her head was dizzy. Her stomach was empty and she felt nauseous. She wasn't able to stand without supporting herself against the wall. The weight of her daughter made it almost impossible to walk. Nevertheless, the cobra woman appeared like a haint out of nowhere and confronted her just outside the washroom. She took hold of her hand and began to drag her toward a storeroom. Rayhana then understood that the storeroom was to be her room. Without saying good night or uttering a word, the noble Muslim woman locked the door of the small storeroom where there was no way out. She left Rayhana and her daughter bedded down in the comfort of home to face a horrible night with rats, cockroaches, lizards, and mosquitoes.

Rayhana could feel the movement of the venomous viper fading away into the distance. Looking around her new dwelling, she noticed broken furniture, old toys and some unidentifiable equipment. It was very small and had a foul odor. On top of it was a dimly lit light. The rats and mosquitoes were making enough noise to awaken dead persons in their graves. Rayhana wasn't bothered about the mosquitoes because her slum was full of mosquitoes, but she had a morbid fear of rats. She believed that rats eat human flesh if they were hungry enough. There was one small single bed. She laid her sleeping daughter onto the bed and sat beside her to keep watch. She found a knob and switched off the dim light. The small room had no windows. Therefore, as soon as she switched off the light, the room became as dark as a tomb. With her fear of rats magnifying, she put her legs upon the bed. From sheer fright, she dared not let her legs down. Despite fatigue, she fought to stay awake but lost the battle quickly, falling asleep beside her daughter as if she had been drugged.

CHAPTER 8

IN THE TUB

In this third world country, rich people treat the poor worse than they treat slaves. The rich are free to do as they please. A murder of the household help is easily solved with a bribe to set things straight. If a rape occurred, a little money would more than solve the problem. Everyone is up for sale, including medical doctors. You can abuse the poor for a price and it would be as though nothing ever happened. Not only was there corruption and fraud in the justice and financial institutions, but religion was an added protection further empowering the rich. Whether compensating authorities to get away with a crime or rewarding a victim to keep their mouth shut, it is a perfect system operating behind a closed society. You can even buy the Wizard of Oz behind the iron curtain.

In the Kingdom of Saudi Arabia, most of the unfortunates sentenced to stoning every Friday are women. According to their law, it is easy to prove adultery in the case of a woman, but not so much for the man. A pregnant woman is by no stretch of the imagination, the result of a sexual liaison since birth control pills and condoms are illegal. It is assumed an unmarried woman has committed adultery once pregnant for whatever reason, which explains the gender bias. Moreover, there was another method for proving adultery on the part of a woman. If a woman was accused or suspected of adultery or immorality, the court would issue something called "Form No. 8." The accused would be sent to the hospital and her vagina would be examined by a female doctor. The doctor's job then is to ascertain if the accused is a virgin. An unmarried girl who has lost her virginity is deemed to have committed the crime of adultery or some sort of premarital sex. If she happened to be married, then the doctor would take a swab to test for semen. This second method should not be confused with a DNA test. None of the third world countries is obligated to conduct DNA tests.

Those in first world countries have trouble understanding this because they have largely closed the huge gap between the rich and poor. Religion does not dictate state law in every aspect. Opposition to religious norms is not criminalized. No one gets stoned for adultery. No one loses a hand for theft. No one gets hanged or beheaded for changing his/her religion. In the OAPEC countries, most of the citizens are very rich. The poor comprise migrant workers who leave their impoverished homes to work for rich Arabs. Their Arab masters/employers take advantage of their situation, which gives them virtual *carte blanche.* Rayhana was one such person, treated by the rich as subhuman and untouchable, yet not a slave. A dog in the house of her Arab employer was better fed and got better treatment than the people in the slums of India, Rayhana's country. The storeroom she was allowed to sleep in was much bigger than the shanty that her family members were living in.

Rayhana began her second day in the kitchen and the noble woman forced her to go from room to room and from passage to passage sweeping, mopping, dusting, organizing furniture and a whole host of other petty chores. At that time, there were no men in the house. The two sons were at school and Sheikh Ahmed went to one of the homes of his other three wives, as did his chauffeur. The second day saw Rayhana's daughter become an unpaid maidservant. The cobra-woman gave Iffat some work to do too. Rayhana, simple and naive, did not know her rights and allowed her daughter to become an unpaid child-servant.

Before Rayhana had come to work in the house of the noble rich family, Sheikh Ahmed used to spend one day at each wife's home. According to the Shari'a law, a polygamist is supposed to treat his wives equally. If he had sex with his first wife one day, he is obligated to sleep with his second wife on the second day and so on. After that, he would come to the first wife and the cycle would repeat itself.

The prophet Muhammad was more than accomplished with his women than just about any Muslim man alive then or now. He had nine wives and two female slaves. He used to sleep with each and every one of his nine wives daily. His biography says that he would have sexual intercourse with all of his nine wives in a single hour. Imagine a man having sex with nine women in sixty minutes—a wife every six minutes. The hadiths record that he would have sexual intercourse with his nine wives washing only once. I do not think this is something to be proud of, and washing up after each session would probably leave the wives with less than four minutes apiece. However, Muslim Imams consider it an honor and are proud to relate this story of their prophet having sex with nine women in one hour and only one washing. If you would ask them how could an upright normal human being have sex with nine females in one-hour's time or do something that even a sex maniac or an animal could not do, they would tell you that their prophet was unlike any other normal human being, but he was given by Allah, the power of forty men. This might answer the question of normality but I do not think it would even begin to touch on the question of morality. Even the great King Solomon with more than 1000 wives could not accomplish this feat. According to the ancient Mosaic law, he could only sleep with one wife and after washing remain unclean until evening.

The second day for Rayhana was much better than the first. She did not need to spend as many hours in the washroom washing clothes. Her duties that day were cleaning and preparing food. She had not prepared a whole meal unsupervised because she had not yet learned how to cook Arabic food. After two uneventful days under the Sheikh's roof, something terrible befell Rayhana on the third day. Rayhana went to the washroom to take a bath as the cobra woman had ordered her. Rayhana was under the impression that she was not allowed to take a bath in the washrooms of the noble family. She picked up that notion from her experience keeping houses for the rich Indians she used to work for in India. Indians will never allow their menservants or maidservants to use their toilets. If their servants felt the need to go, then it was off to the nearest public washroom. In

Bombay, most of the public washrooms are in the local train station. There are also public washrooms in the crowded chawls and slums. There is nothing in the entire world filthier than the public washrooms in India.

Since her arrival, Rayhana and her daughter did not use the washroom except for the most dire emergencies. On her third day, the noble woman discovered that her maidservant had not washed her body or her clothes since her arrival. This discovery prompted the dragging of Rayhana from the kitchen to the bathroom. Gestures were made in the direction of the faucet and the tub. She made Rayhana take off her outer dress and she threw it in the sink and turned water over it. She tugged and pulled at her under dress to instruct her to wash it as well. Signing her intent, she made it known to Rayhana that she was to spend at least 2 hours washing off the accumulated filth on her body and washing her clothes and underwear. That done, she was to wait inside the washroom until her clothes dried before coming out in clean, dry clothes and she pointed to the curtain rod above the tub. Then she pointed to the daughter who had followed them into the washroom and said she was to repeat the process for her also.

As soon as the cobra went out of the washroom, Rayhana told Iffat to wait in the kitchen until she finished her bath. As soon as Iffat left, Rayhana removed all of her clothes and stood bare-naked. When she stripped off all her clothes, she walked toward the mirror and looked at her image. She began to turn around and look at her reflection in the mirror. She felt pleased at the full figure standing before her and the shapeliness of her naked body. Rayhana had never seen a full-sized mirror before. For the first time, she could see her entire body and she liked it. She felt shy and covered her face with her hands. Then, she remembered her bath. She walked toward the tub and looked at it. She had never seen a tub except in an Indian movie she had watched with the love of her life, Jamaal Khan, at a movie theater. In the movie, she saw the heroine taking a bath in a tub and that gave her some idea of what she was supposed to do while she was bathing herself.

Rayhana stepped carefully inside the tub and turned on the facet. The warm water began to fill the tub. While the water was running, she started to check all the perfumes and makeup bottles on the shelves. She opened each bottle and smelled its scent. Each one she liked, she would spray some of it on her body. After that, she picked up something that looked like soap powder and emptied half of it on the water. She shook the water with her hands until it looked like it was covered with white bubbles and cotton balls. Then, slowly she immersed herself in the warm water. She felt a wonderful sensation. She became as happy as a child. Then, she began to imitate what she saw the heroine doing in the movie. She stretched her legs and lifted them up, and brought them down again. She lifted her legs up again and opened them. She separated her legs as wide as she could. She enjoyed the slight pain she felt in the area around her privates. She did this exercise many times until she couldn't do it anymore. Then, she began to play with her hands and breasts. She held her two breasts with both her hands and jingled them and fondled them.

Rayhana became really naughty and stood up. With soap suds covering parts of her body, she went to the mirror and began to dance and tease her image. She even boxed her image in the mirror. She turned around and began to dance with her backside facing the mirror. She enjoyed playing with herself so much. She returned to the tub and immersed her body in the warm water again. This time, she began to paddle the water with her legs as if she was swimming. She learned that from the Indian movie too. Then, she began to throw the soap suds up into the air.

After playing inside the tub for a long time, Rayhana remembered she had to wash her clothes. She came out of the tub and went to the sink with the smaller mirror. She filled the sink with water and began to wash her clothes piece by piece. She first washed her top dress and then her under dress. After that, she took her bra and washed it. Lastly, she washed her red underwear. She hanged them on the curtain rod above the tub. She knew that she had to wait inside the washroom until her clothes were dry. Once again, she began to dance and repeat her naughtiness all over again. This time, she stimulated her body beyond her ability to control it. Relishing the rare moment of privacy, she sat on the edge of the empty tub and masturbated. Rayhana spent what seemed like a long time inside the washroom until the cobra woman knocked on the door and shouted at her. She quickly put on her clothes and rushed out of the washroom. Her clothes were sticking to her body because they were only half-dry. As a punishment for her unnecessary delay, the noble woman did not allow her to wash the clothes of her little daughter or give her a bath.

CHAPTER 9

MAKSORA AND SABIR

Rayhana would not have removed her clothes, stood bare naked, spread her legs wide open and exposed her private parts, danced naked, fondled her breasts, washed her bra and red underwear while she was standing fully naked, or inserted her fingers into her vagina and masturbated, if she knew that everything she did would be filmed on tape. Husam and Hisham had bought a surveillance camera, installed it inside their mother's washroom, and waited for their gorgeous maidservant to take a bath. While Rayhana was playing in the nude and exploring every inch of herself, the two sons were sitting in another room watching her and masturbating too.

The two brothers showed the tape to their friends at school. They then downloaded it onto the internet under the title "An Indian Film Actress Taking A Bath." Husam and Hisham did not simply stop at secretly photographing their new maidservant bare-naked; when they saw her prancing around in the nude enticing and exciting them, they decided to go even further and get her. They knew their mother locked her up in the storeroom every night, so they stole the key from their parents' bedroom and went to the local hardware store and made a duplicate copy. They then returned the key back to their parents' bedroom without them ever noticing it was missing.

The Pakistani driver returned after five days and Mrs. Ahmed called him to the kitchen and told him to translate for her. She then supplemented her rules and list of chores for the Indian maidservant. Whatever she could not impart to Rayhana during his absence, she more than made up for. She insulted and humiliated her in front of the chauffeur telling him to not leave one word out that she was saying. She told him to tell Rayhana that she was a dirty filthy animal and behaved as if she came straight from out the jungle. Rayhana cried as the chauffeur translated all the revilement, insults and derogatory remarks from the cobra mistress. The noble woman felt pleased at the great distress she was able to inflict and now that her goal was accomplished, Mrs. Ahmed dismissed the Pakistani driver. She remained for some time with Rayhana in the kitchen and forced her to do as many unnecessary chores as possible. The noble woman then abruptly marched out of the kitchen and left without telling Rayhana what to do next.

Rayhana knew that if the evil woman came back and found her sitting with her daughter in the kitchen doing nothing she would shout at her. Therefore, she decided to go to the other rooms and start cleaning them. She just wanted to be busy doing something. She had already swept and mopped all the rooms, passages, and hallways. She told her daughter to sit and wait for her in the kitchen. It was one of the new rules she learned that day through the translator that her daughter was not to follow her from place to place all over the house. When the mother wasn't working in the kitchen, the daughter had to sit either in the storeroom or in the kitchen. The cobra woman never showed any compassion toward the little Iffat either. She detested her the same way she hated her mother. She did not give her any of her sons' old toys to play with or buy her any dolls. She did not promise or suggest she go to school to get an education like her privileged sons. She even forced her to do menial tasks. When her mother left, Iffat sat on the floor of the kitchen, folded her legs, and began to look blankly at the empty walls. With nothing to do to amuse herself, she hugged her legs and rocked back and forth waiting for her mother to return.

Rayhana began her stretch down one of the long hallways. She thought that there was no one else in the house except Mrs. Ahmed. She expected that Mrs. Ahmed would be in her bedroom. She decided to clean every room except the room of the mother lion. She knew that if she dared step inside the cobra lioness' bedroom without her permission and oversight she would be scolded and beaten. The cobra had already told her never to step foot inside her bedroom without her permission or when she wasn't there. However, she gave her permission to enter all the other rooms in the house. She expressly told her to keep herself away from the rooms of her sons when they were at home.

Rayhana spent a short time cleaning the hallway and then she began with the other rooms. She began with Hisham's room first. When Rayhana stepped inside Hisham's room, she remembered how the two juveniles had come to the storage room at night and showed her a video of her nude inside the washroom and her naughty behavior while she was alone. Then, they began to touch her body. Rayhana understood what they wanted from her. She was scared that the two brothers might show the video to their mother and father if she would not allow them to touch her. She thought that if she refused to give them what they wanted, she would lose her job and be sent to the streets along with her little daughter. She did not know the way to Aslam's apartment. She had no money to purchase tickets to return to her country. She was totally at the mercy of her employers. She regretted what she had done in the washroom. Therefore, against her wishes, she allowed them to abuse her body.

In Bombay, no one had ever tried to blackmail her. She remembered that some rich Indian men tried to buy her body with money but she always refused their money and their advances. She threatened them with going to the police if they dared touch her. She even walked away from some jobs when the harassment became unbearable. Outside of this house, there was nowhere to go. She was petrified of the Saudi police. The last thing she wanted was a repeat of her encounter with the police and the horrible experience of being raped and nearly beaten to death. Once she succumbed to the two brothers, they figured their manipulation had worked as planned and decided Rayhana was now their sex slave. They even decided on their next visit to bring their video camera and shoot a film version of their sex with the beautiful maidservant and show their friends at school.

Rayhana did not like the situation she had put herself in but was powerless to do anything about it. She had hoped that the good man of the house, who had spent a lot of money on her and her daughter, might intervene and stop his wife from treating her so badly and prevent his sons from continuously blackmailing and raping her. She had not seen her sponsor since the day he had brought her to his house. She was surprised when the chauffeur returned without her sponsor. She held her tongue deciding not ask him where his employer was. Deeply engrossed in a thousand thoughts, she finished cleaning up Hisham's room and made off for Husam's. She pushed the door open without knocking and strode in, knowing that the two boys would be at school for several hours. She froze upon entering. She felt as if her heart stopped and her mouth opened up in disbelief. For a few seconds, with her mouth agape, her eyes bulged as she took in the scene of the Pakistani chauffeur atop the noble Arab woman. Both of them were buck naked on top of each other in Husam's bed. She averted her eyes in another direction and was met with a porn movie splashing across a 54-inch LCD TV screen. Rooted to the floor, she could neither advance nor retreat. Mrs. Ahmed saw her first. She fired off a few Arabic words to her lover, which had the effect of making the chauffeur jump off her and stand about face. Rayhana closed her eyes when she saw his male organ like a big stick shooting up in front of him.

Rayhana expected two things to happen to her now; either the Pakistani would run towards her, catch her by the neck and strangle her to death; or the cobra woman would shout at her and kick her along with her daughter out of the house. As she gradually opened up her tightly squeezed eyes, nothing could have prepared her for the pleading faces of the two adulterers begging her for mercy. In the awkward silence that followed, with no violence, direct or implied, she counted her good fortune, turned on her heels and fled for her life. She ran to the kitchen and sat near her daughter. Hugging her, she waited to see what was in store for them both. Shortly thereafter, the personal driver of Sheikh Ahmed came into the kitchen. Clothed, he looked very different. For the first time, Rayhana came to know his name—"Sabir Ibrahim Shah." Everyone in the family called him *Rafeeq* and she thought it was his real name. (Every Indian calls every Arab man in the world Rafeeq and every Arab calls every Indian man in the world Rafeeq. We will not let this stupidity distract us from the serious issue at hand, which is the adulterous and scandalous affair between Mrs. Ahmed and her husband's chauffeur. The only thing we can mention in passing is that Rafeeq in Arabic means a companion in a journey).

Sabir Ibrahim Shah looked stunned. When he mentioned his full name, Rayhana could hardly hear him. Then, he sat on the floor and faced the wall. He could not look Rayhana in the face. He told her he did what she had seen because he had no choice. If he refused to do that, he would lose his job. Rayhana did not say a single word. She just kept looking at him. She was still scared that he might attack her or kill her. Then he told her that most of the Arabs were doing the same thing with their servants. If the servants refused to comply, they would be dismissed. Occasionally they would be falsely accused of something and then suffer a lifetime of pain and imprisonment, beheading or stoning.

Rayhana began to weep. Her heart broke when she realized the price of refusing sex could cost a person their life in this country of Jinn. Amidst her sobs, the ignoble woman quietly walked in, looking totally different in her some decent dress. Rayhana had a flashback from the horrible way she appeared without her clothes. She was skinny and tall. She had nothing by way of face or body to attract a man, which explains why she had a porn movie playing to arouse her chauffeur. It was under these circumstances that Rayhana walked in on them.

Sheikh Ahmed had simply married the ignoble woman because her father was a very wealthy Saudi tycoon. Marrying her was an investment that figured well for business deals. Her name was Mastoora, meaning *a woman who protects her honor and that of her family.* That day, however, she might as well have changed her name to *Sharmoota*, which means adulteress or prostitute. Rayhana vividly remembered her first day lecture when Mastoora drilled into her that she hated immoral relations between the servants and members of the most noble family. Hence, we are now more than adequately acquainted with the problem of the rich in third world countries. They claim to be the most righteous and most holy people of God and they look down on the rest of the world and view the poor as immoral, uncouth and ill-mannered.

Anyway, Mastoora opened her mouth but she spoke softly in whispers. Her loud, harsh voice and her rudeness had disappeared. She asked Sabir delicately if he had spoken to Rayhana or not and the amount of money she had asked for in order to keep her silence. Sabir had spoken to Rayhana but never broached the topic. Not daring to tell Mrs. Ahmed the words he had spoken to her, he turned again to speak to Rayhana, telling her of Mrs. Ahmed's offer. Sabir's words took Rayhana by surprise, so she just stared at him and glanced at the ignoble woman hiding behind him. Of course, Rayhana had no clue that Mrs. Ahmed would be stoned to death in Saudi Arabia for such a transgression.

Seeing Rayhana was keeping silent, Sabir made up her mind for her and told Maksora that the maidservant had agreed to keep her lips sealed and would gratefully accept whatever money she was offered. (I renamed Mrs. Ahmed, Maksora because of her pitiful condition. She was a lioness and strutted around like the most moral woman on the face of the earth and suddenly she was totally broken with her pride in pieces. Maksora in Arabic means a broken person). With trembling hands, Mrs. Ahmed took her checkbook from her pocket and quickly wrote out a check and put it in Rayhana's hand. Rayhana looked at the paper that the ignoble woman gave her without knowing what it represented. Sabir explained to her in Urdu that Mrs. Ahmed had given her a check and he could take her to the bank and open an account for her. Mrs. Ahmed decided to sweeten the deal, telling her secret lover to take Rayhana Khan and her daughter, Iffat, to the nearest bank and open an account for her and assist her in making the deposit. After that, she told him to take them to the Super Mall and let them buy whatever clothes they wanted and whatever dolls Iffat wanted. He could then have the bills brought to her for reimbursement and she would gladly pay for everything.

CHAPTER 10

SHE SAID QABOOL

After opening an account at the bank and depositing her first check, Rayhana and her daughter went with the chauffeur to the Super Mall to purchase clothes and dolls. Rayhana chose four beautiful dresses for her daughter and three lovely dresses for herself. She selected three pairs of shoes for her daughter, two for herself, plus some underwear for both. She also chose some beautiful Barbie dolls for her daughter. Iffat had never seen a doll before; she was all together joyful when her mother bought them for her. To top off the day, they were escorted to an Indian restaurant, digging into delicious mutton curry and chicken Tandoori.

While they were going from place to place, the chauffeur kept talking to Rayhana about one certain subject. He was trying to convince her to accept his advice and be a secret mistress or kept-wife for Sheikh Ahmed. He said to her in that way she could make more money and secure the future of her daughter. He tried to reason with her that she would be able to buy a house in Bombay with the money she saved and return to India. No matter how much he tried to tempt her with money and future prosperity, Sabir could not convince her to accept his advice. Rayhana firmly stood her ground and simply told him that she would not like to be in a secret affair with a married man who was as old as her grandfather.

Eventually Sabir stumbled upon a concrete reason to make her reconsider. Rayhana had confided in him about Sheikh Ahmed's two sons. She could not keep inside herself how the boys had secretly recorded her naked in their mother's washroom and how they used it to blackmail her. She told him of how they threatened to show the video saying, "show mommie, show mommie" over and over in her native tongue. Sabir was shocked into silence. When he overcame the shock, he advised her to talk to their father. He reasoned that failing to do so would allow the boys to continue in their ways and blackmail her forever. Rayhana rejected this advice for she did not want their father to know what she did in the women's washroom and what his sons had done to her. She did not want Sheikh Ahmed to watch that disgraceful video of her masturbating in the washroom. She thought that the old Saudi man might take advantage of the video and blackmail her too. She did not enjoy the idea that the father might show the video to his wife and it would be even more humiliating for her. However, Sabir repeatedly reminded her that she would be blackmailed and raped every night by the two sons if she did not complain to their father.

When nothing else he said convinced Rayhana, Sabir explained that she would eventually get pregnant, by one of the two boys, which would end up being a death sentence for her. He narrated to her the sad and alarming story of a Pakistani maidservant who was impregnated by a Saudi boy and was sentenced by the Shari'a court to death. Although the maidservant was impregnated by the son of her sponsor, the Saudi family insisted that she was impregnated by someone else. The maidservant was jailed until she delivered her baby inside the prison. Finally, she was stoned to death on a Friday afternoon. This story served its purpose. Rayhana became horrified at the idea she could be stoned to death and her daughter and family would be left alone without her to help provide for them. Sabir told her how she could escape this sad and tragic end. According to his carefully thought out advice, if Rayhana agreed to be the mistress of Sheikh Ahmed and if she happened to be pregnant, Sheikh Ahmed would either send her to India to deliver the baby or bribe a Pakistani or an Egyptian doctor to abort the baby. Sabir knew that Pakistani and Egyptian doctors who worked in the OAPEC countries were known for conducting secret abortions. Although, abortion was illegal in those countries, for the sake of money, quite a few Pakistani and Egyptian doctors were more than willing to take the risk. They charged dearly in their quest to profit from the illegal impregnation of lowly maidservants.

Rayhana gave rise to fear when she remembered that she had missed her period. She concluded that she had already become pregnant. She figured that one of the two police officers who had raped her had gotten her pregnant. Who was going to believe her if she said she had been raped? That was tantamount to admitting adultery. Sheikh Ahmed might think the Indian man who kept her in his apartment for the one week before he came and took her from the beauty salon had impregnated her. She even remembered that she had married Aslam Ali Khan on paper. Her sponsor might have him arrested and the police might find their marriage certificate in his apartment. How could she convince the court that she just married him on paper in order to stay with him for protection? And if she claimed he was her lawful husband and he was the one who impregnated her then the court would ask her why did she forsake her husband and go with another man without her husband's knowledge and permission. Finding herself in a dilemma, she then realized she had only two options. She could either follow the advice of Sabir and become Sheikh Ahmed's kept-wife safeguarded by him OR face the consequences of her pregnancy. Once again, Rayhana was faced with choosing the lesser of two evils.

Since Rayhana traveled without her husband or father to Saudi Arabia, she became *the right hands possess* to her *Kafeel*. The word Kafeel in Arabic should not be translated as a sponsor as many people often mistakenly do. The Kafeel in its essence means "master" or "owner." It is a leftover term from the system of slavery that was practiced in Saudi Arabia for thousands of years and still being practiced today behind the closed walls of their society. (Until today, Slavery System in Islam is taught in Al-Azhar Al-Sharif University. It is also included in all curriculums of schools, institutes, universities in Muslim countries as well as Muslim schools in Western countries. No Muslim scholar or religious authority can dare to remove it from the Islamic educational system because it is in the Qur'an and the prophet Muhammad endorsed and practiced it). The relationship between the

Kafeel and the Makfool is nothing other than a relationship between the "master" and "slave."

The Kafeel had many rights granted by the law toward his Makfool. He had the right to kick his Makfool out of the country any time he wished. He could send his Makfool to jail and if he/she were arrested by the police for any reason no one could get him/her out of jail except their Kafeel. If the Kafeel beat his Makfool, he would not be sent to prison and if he killed his Makfool, he might receive a very light sentence. Although, the law did not say it openly, the Kafeel had the right to sleep with his female Makfoolah. There are many recent fatwas issued by high religious authorities equating the maidservants to *the right hands possess*. The maidservant is considered to be the *right hands possess* of her Kafeel. The Qur'an allows the Muslim man to sleep with whatever number of female slaves who are deemed, "what your right hands possess". Surat al-Nissa 3: 4 reads: "*marry of the women who seem good to you, two or three or four and if ye fear that ye cannot do justice (to so many) then one or what your right hands possess.*"

We need to write a large article to help explain the above verse, however, in a nutshell, this verse allows a Muslim man to have four wives and hundreds of female slaves, as many as he chooses. Abd Alrahman Ibn A'ouf, one of the preeminent companions of the prophet Muhammad, had ninety female slaves and he slept with them all without marrying them. Some Muslim clerics issued fatwas allowing the Kafeels to sleep with their maidservants. Many Indonesian, Filipino, Egyptian, Somali, Indian, and Pakistani maidservants working in Saudi Arabia and Gulf countries complained that their employers had raped them but all had their lawsuits summarily rejected.

Yet, another fatwa issued recently by a prominent Muslim scholar which encouraged unmarried female employees at workplace to breastfeed their male colleagues because it is unlawful for Muslim man and Muslim woman to be together if they are not married or closely related to each other. The fatwa says, "*Women who come into regular contact with men who aren't related to them should give them their breast milk so they will be considered relatives. Fatwa applied to men who live in the same house or come into contact with women on a regular basis, except for drivers,"* Fatwa by Sheikh Al-Obeikan, Advisor, Royal Court and Consultant, Ministry of Justice, Saudi Arabia. According to this fatwa, for Rayhana Khan to work as a maidservant in her Kafeel's house, she has to breastfeed Sheikh Faiz bin Ahmed. However, the fatwa exempted the Pakistani chauffeur because he is the family driver. So, Mrs. Ahmed need not to breastfeed Sabir Ibrahim Shah because he is her driver. Another option, Sheikh Ahmed has to treat Rayhana Khan as his right hands possess and sleeps with her any time if he chooses to do so.

After the scandalous marriage of the prophet Muhammad with Zainab bint Jahash, the wife of his adopted son, Zayd Ibn Muhammad, the Qur'an forbade adoption. The cancellation of adoption created a problem for those families who already had adopted sons and daughters. One woman approached the prophet and asked his advice regarding a domestic problem she was experiencing at home because of the new teaching of the Qur'an (Surat al-Ahzab 33: 5). Let us see how the prophet solved that problem.

"Aisha reports that Sahla bint Suhayl came to the Messenger of Allah (Allah bless him and give him peace) and said: "O Messenger of Allah! I see on the face of Abu Hudhayfa [her husband] (signs of dislike) on the entering of Salim [their adopted son], who is an ally, (into our house). The Messenger of Allah (Allah bless him and give him peace) said: "Suckle him." She said: "How can I suckle him as he is a grown-up man? The Messenger of Allah (Allah bless him and give him peace) smiled and said: "I already know that he is a young man" (Sahih Muslim, hadith no. 1453). In another hadith, *"She returned and said: "I have suckled him and what (was there) in the heart of Abu Hudhayfa has disappeared"* (Sahih Muslim).

Before we go further and see what was the consequence of that bizarre teaching one would like to ask how a young woman can breastfeed a grown up man? Can you imagine a woman opening her breast and allowing a young man to suckle her nipple? Believe it or not, some wives of the prophet Muhammad applied that teaching in their daily lives after his death. Aisha and Hafsa, wives of the prophet, would not allow any man to enter to them if he would not be breastfed first by their sisters and nieces.

"Aisha took that as a precedent for whatever men she wanted to be able to come to see her. She ordered her sister, Umm Kulthum and the daughters of her brother to suckle to whichever men she wanted to be able to come in to see her" (Muwatta Malik, hadith no. 31).

"Yahya related to me from Malik from Nafi that Safiya bint Abi Ubayd told him that Hafsa, umm al-muminin, sent Asim ibn Abdullah ibn Sad to her sister Fatima bint Umar ibn al-Khattab for her to suckle him ten times so that he could come in to see her. She did it, so he used to come in to see her" (Muwatta Malik: book 30, no. 30.1.8).

Such an immoral teaching led recently an Egyptian Muslim Sheikh to issue fatwa permitting, Muslim women to follow the recommendation of the prophet Muhammad and breastfeed their male colleagues at workplace. Dr. Izzat Attya who is the head of the department of Hadith in Al-Azhar University, which is the most prestigious and oldest Islamic Institute of learning in the world, issued a fatwa. The fatwa declared that, it is legitimate for a working Muslim woman to breastfeed her male colleague to avoid the sin of "khulwa" (staying with a stranger in one room). Similar fatwas had been issued in the past by many sheikhs in many Middle-Eastern countries, but this is the first time it came from a highly qualified academic Sheikh of Al-Azhar University.

Dr. Izzat Attya justified his fatwa by referring to authentic hadiths of the prophet Muhammad that permitted a Muslim woman to breastfeed her adopted son to make him her son through breastfeeding. In order to justify his scandalous marriage with his daughter-in-law, Prophet Muhammad forbade the noble social institution of adoption and deprived millions of orphaned or illegitimate Muslim children from being adopted by other families. Without this option of adoption thousands of Muslim girls every year either killed themselves for fear of bringing disgrace to their families or got killed in honor killings by their families when they get impregnated out of the marriage bond. For instance, in Khartoum, Sudan every year hundreds of Muslim girls are impregnated through the so-called *alzawaj alo'urfi* and then delivered their babies and threw them in the garbage containers to be eaten up by stray dogs. Alzawaj alo'urfi is a kind of an Islamic marriage, which is socially unrecognized and unaccepted by Sudanese Muslim families. It is like the Shiite Mutta marriage (i.e. enjoyment marriage) where the boy and the girl marry themselves to each other without the knowledge of their families and without Mazoon, witnesses, and any official document. Sometimes people rescue those misfortunate babies before they die. Many times those unwanted babies lost some of their limps such as a hand or leg, which had been eaten up by stray dogs. The alarming increase in the number of those cast away babies forced the Islamic government of Sudan to open the Dar Al-Maigoma Center to take care of those unwanted babies. However, no one is allowed to adopt one of those children and give them his name because adoption is illegal in Islam.

In any case, the moment Rayhana agreed to his suggestion, the Pakistani chauffeur picked up his cell phone and dialed the number of his employer to break the news. Sheikh Ahmed was the one who told Sabir to convince Rayhana about his secret proposal. He promised to give him a hefty reward if he succeeded in convincing his Layla to marry him secretly and become a beloved mistress and his kept-wife. The word "kept-wife" brings us to explain again, why Sheikh Ahmed did not legally marry Rayhana. Of course, he would if he could, but the law in Saudi Arabia forbade marriage to non-Saudi women, even if the woman was a Muslim and an Arab. For that reason, Sheikh Ahmed was left with the only workable option of making Rayhana his "kept-wife." The need to own and possess is implied in the word, "wife". Even though it wouldn't be a real marital relationship, it would suffice for the crazy old man. Sheikh Ahmed could have easily raped Rayhana as soon as she came under his control and under his roof. After all she is counted his right hands possess. Nonetheless, he decided not to resort to coercion regarding this sensitive matter, but decided to use his money to buy her heart as he did before with his first Indian wife, Christie. Sheikh Ahmed could have married Rayhana and put her in a palace in India but his bitter experience with Christie and Bobby taught him a lesson that he would never ever forget for the rest of his life. He did not want to fall into the same hole again.

After Rayhana said "Qabool" a really naughty and crazy idea crept into the mind of the old man and he jumped on it. At the time of conducting the marriage contract, any Muslim girl in India would be asked by the religious Mazoon to say 'Qabool' which means she agreed to marry her husband-to-be. This is only in India because it is a secular country and the law requires the girl's consent. In most of the other Muslim countries, the Mazoon would not even meet the girl or see her. Her father was the one who was supposed to meet her prospective husband and the Mazoon and the father was the one who had to say Qabool. Whether the girl agreed to the marriage or not, that wasn't the Mazoon's business. For the Mazoon to conduct a lawful marriage and issue the marriage certificate, he needed the signatures of the father, the future husband, and the witnesses. Most marriages in Muslim countries were conducted in the mosques as if the marriage was between the future husband and the father-in-law. I think Muslims should be given credit for being the first people on earth to come up with the idea of gay marriage. According to the Islamic Shari'a law, "a woman is utterly incompetent to enter into a marriage contract herself or for anyone else even though her guardian could authorize her to do so. A father can contract the marriage of his virgin daughter without asking her consent whatever her age" (Verma 1988: 24).

When Rayhana said Qabool to be a kept-wife, Sheikh Ahmed all of a sudden changed his mind and decided to marry her properly. However, he wanted to marry her in a very strange way. No human being had ever thought or dreamed of what he was planning to do. If his plan worked, he would be the first to conceive the idea. *He wanted to hire a man for Rayhana to marry.* It made sense to him as the hired husband would be a husband on paper but she would be all his and his alone. She and her *paper-husband* would live in his house, but no one would touch her except him. In fact, in Islam there is something very close to this crazy plan of his. There is a hired-husband in the Shari'a law known as *the Muhalil*. The only outstanding difference between Sheikh Ahmed's paper-husband and the Shari'a Law husband (*Muhalil)* was that sex is forbidden for the paper-husband and in the latter instance, allowed once.

Some Muslim men who divorced their wives three times and wanted to have them back would not like their ex's and soon-to-be-wives fornicating with other men. To play around with this Muhalil's business, they would arrange for their wife's safe return by getting their wives married to Muhalils on paper for a day and have them divorced the next day. Alas, the prophet Muhammad said otherwise. In the book of "Asbab al-Nuzul" (p. 46), the Suyuti stated that a woman came to the prophet Muhammad and told him, *"Abdul-Rahman (the Muhalil whom she wed after she was divorced three times) has divorced me without having any sexual intercourse with me. May I go back to my ex-husband?' Muhammad said to her, 'No, that is not permissible until Abdul-Rahman has sex with you first, then you may go back to Rafa'a."* The same case was narrated differently by the beloved wife of the prophet Muhammad. *"Aisha said, the woman of Rafa'a al-Qarzi came to the prophet Muhammad and told him: 'Abdul-Rahman has divorced me and I was with him like a piece of his cloth (without having any sexual intercourse with me), the prophet told her you cannot go back to your husband until you taste his honey and Abdul-Rahman tastes your honey"* (Sahih al-Bukhari). In other words, sexual intercourse should be done at least once between the wife of Rafa'a and her Muhalil, Abdul Rahman. The Muhalil's penis should enter in the wife's vagina and ejaculation must take place therein. Unless that prerequisite condition is fully fulfilled, the Muhalil will not legalize the wife for her ex-husband to reclaim her back.

Sheikh Ahmed now had to convince his Pakistani chauffeur to marry Rayhana on his behalf, but never ever have sexual intercourse with her. He smiled at his brilliant logic. He did not want Rayhana returning to her country. According to the Islamic Shari'a Law, a married woman cannot travel to any place without her husband or a Muhram. This restriction was directly from the mouth of the prophet Muhammad; "a woman does not travel except with a Muhram" (Sahih al-Bukhari and Sahih Muslim), which is usually a father, brother, grown up son. Thus, the wife is literally tied to her husband or Muhram wherever she goes. Should Rayhana and her paper-husband decide to double cross their employer and flee together to India, Sheikh Ahmed knew that the Indian Consulate in Jeddah would never issue a visa to a Pakistani man. It would be easier for a Pakistani terrorist to get a tourist visa to the USA than get permission to visit India for one day or even one hour. The Indian government was thorough in blacklisting almost every single Pakistani male alive. Secondly, Sheikh Ahmed, like most men in the third world, abhorred the use of condoms. So, he expected that his kept-wife might get pregnant from their first encounter. If so, he would just take her to a Pakistani doctor, bribe in hand, and have the baby aborted. This would however, expose his sundry indiscretions unnecessarily to all. His way, he reasoned, if a baby should result from the union, the baby would be considered by his family members and Shari'a law the child of the paper-husband. Thirdly, Sheikh Ahmed wanted to give his Saudi wife peace of mind. He knew from day one, his wife had became restless and worried about the moral integrity of the male members of her family, him included. She had voiced her concern to him and in this way, she could take comfort in the knowledge that Rayhana was safely married to their Pakistani chauffeur. Ironically, if he only knew what was going on between his *righteous wife* and his *faithful Pakistani chauffeur* he would not have bothered with her peace of mind. Lastly, Sheikh Ahmed wanted to protect his beloved woman from his teenage sons. He knew that, as long as she was single and sleeping all alone in her room, his sons would be tempted to approach her at night and rape her. His eyes did not lie when he witnessed the boys' first sighting of her.

Sheikh Ahmed seemed to have thought of every possible loophole except one. What about the paper-husband? How could he trust a young man like Sabir to sleep chastely with his beloved? Both were young and close to each other in age. They spoke the same language and shared the same culture. He mused, perhaps Rayhana would prefer to have sex with a younger man four decades his junior. In fact, when Rayhana said Qabool there were only six days remaining before the old Saudi man would celebrate his seventieth birthday. Sabir had no wife in Saudi Arabia or in Pakistan. Therefore, such a beautiful and young woman like Rayhana sleeping by his side every night would be the perfect temptation. It was akin to leaving fresh meat near a hungry dog expecting the meat to remain intact and untouched.

A meticulous predator like Sheikh Ahmed would not make such a grave error. It was, in fact, the first loophole he thought of and so he planned on just how to cover it. Here, he openly exposed his evil and selfish nature. Here also, the old religious practices of the Muslim Caliphs, the Kings of the Umayyad and Abbasid dynasties, and the Muslim Sultans of the Ottoman Empire were resurrected. Sheikh Ahmed justifiably decided to act as a Muslim caliph/sultan and turn his Pakistani chauffeur into a eunuch. However, he knew that Sabir would rather die than became a castrated man. Therefore, he decided to castrate him without his knowledge. In his selfish obsession for Rayhana, the lives of many were destroyed that crossed the path of the noble, Sheikh Ahmed. Jamaal Khan went to jail and was eventually sentenced to fifteen years in prison, the Sudanese foreign student, Babikir Al-A'war was suffering in an Indian jail waiting for trial, which might land him in prison forever, and the devil's advocate, Muhammad Khan and his business were ruined completely.

CHAPTER 11

THE EVIL GENIUS

That day, when Rayhana returned to the house of the noble family, there were some noticeable changes. She was informed by Mrs. Ahmed that her quarters had been moved from the small storeroom to a big room near the kitchen. She had been given the key to her new room. Mrs. Ahmed told her that if she needed to go to the washroom or her daughter at night she could open her door whenever it was convenient. This important human need was ignored before and during those five days, if Rayhana or her daughter wanted to go to the washroom, they were unable because they were locked up like dangerous wild animals. If a fire broke out, they would have been burned alive inside that dungeon with no windows.

As icing on the cake, Rayhana was told by *the suddenly kind and generous woman* that her daughter Iffat was going to be sent to an all girls' school. She would not need to worry about transportation because the girl's bus would come every day and take her daughter to school and bring her back. In addition to that, Iffat would not need to work anymore. She had to tend to her studies and in her playtime, she needed to get some exercise and play with her dolls.

In most Muslim countries, co-ed schools are unheard off. No mingling of boys or girls, even at the grade school level. However, in some Muslim countries like Sudan and Egypt, Christians could attend private schools where boys and girls studied together. It was only after Sudan implemented Shari'a law that those schools were shut down by the Ministry of Education and the Ministry of Religious Affairs. Recently, the Kingdom of Saudi Arabia witnessed the opening of the first All Females University. Everyone is female in that University—professors, students, clerks, guards, sellers of food and books, etc. If they could, I am certain they would have made the books and food feminine too. Muslims have serious problem with "THE WOMAN". From childhood they separate her from the male, destroy her private parts through female genital mutilation, conceal her body through burqa, imprison her in the house, she goes out of her father's house to her husband's house or her grave, deprive her of the right to fall in love or choose her life partner, abuse her through child marriage, force her to share her husband with other rival wives, etc. In the Kingdom of Saudi Arabia, women are not allowed to drive cars. Only men are allowed to drive vehicles and the driver of the girls' bus had to be a male seventy years of age or older. If the girls' bus broke down or was involved in an accident, the traffic police would close down all streets leading to the location. If any male dared defy the police and ventured into the cordoned off area, he would be killed. The police would then phone the Ministry of Education and report the matter. The Ministry of Education would send another girls' bus with another old male driver. This might take hours. Nevertheless, the girls are to sit inside the bus and await the second bus to arrive. Then and only then, where the girls told to quickly board the new bus. The girls were covered from head to foot with black niqabs, which wrap their bodies like onions. Even if you were to use long-range binoculars, you would not be able to see a finger or a toe of any one of them.

Only until all the creatures were transferred in full secrecy from the first bus to the second bus and the second bus had left the restricted area, would the police open up the street to traffic again. I am not trying to belittle the Muslim women of this country by calling them creatures. In the Kingdom of Saudi Arabia, the holy land of Muslims, no one refers to the woman by her name or gender. For example, no one would call a girl by her name like *Fatima* or by her gender. A woman or girl is not called *She* or a *Female*. Every girl and every woman was called *"Al-Makhloqah"* which literally means *The Creature*. It is in this spirit of things that you will find the windows of every Girl School Bus adorned with black drapes. So, if the bus happened to pass you by, do not ever dream of catching a glimpse of what's inside. Even if one of the naughty girls happened to defy restrictions of total separation and privacy and rolled back one of the curtains or pulled them down, you would not be able to see anything except a spook covered from head to foot in a black coffin and a mysterious spirit of thick gloom.

On the fifth day, Rayhana's sponsor sent his proposal to her through his Pakistani pimp Sabir Ibrahim Shah. Out of fear for her life and due to her strong belief that she was pregnant, Rayhana consented to become the secret mistress to a man who was forty-three years older than her. She was petrified when she saw the old Saudi again. She was afraid he might jump on her at any moment and rape her because she was, for all wants and purposes, his.

Not in the know, the odd behavior of the family puzzled Rayhana. Every one she met in that house turned out to be abnormal and amoral. She was troubled by the unnatural behavior of the two sons who managed to enter the women's washroom and videotape her naked. She was under the impression that the two sons somehow entered the women's washroom, hid themselves, and shot the video. She was also baffled by the sexual intercourse she witnessed between Mrs. Ahmed and the Pakistani chauffeur. She was puzzled as to why the wife of the old man wasn't satisfied with her husband. Why did she need a servant for sex? Lastly, Rayhana was really confused by Sheikh Ahmed's desire for her. Why was he not content with his four wives? She had already learned through Sabir Shah that Sheikh Ahmed had four wives and everyday he visited one each night of the week to perform his husbandly duties. Therefore, Rayhana asked herself, why did the old Saudi want or need a maidservant for sex? She was puzzled by the sexual prowess and strength of such a man. How could he manage to have sex every night with a different woman and still want another one? Did he bring her all the way from India to his country for sex? While Rayhana was wrapping her extremely naive and unsophisticated mind around these things and trying to understand what it all meant, the Pakistani chauffeur approached her in the kitchen and told her something that confused her even more.

The report from Sheikh Ahmed suggested that she and he get married on paper. As she listened to his explanation, it made no sense to her whatsoever. She vividly remembered that Aslam Ali Khan convinced her to marry him on paper out of fear his neighbors would report him. So it was doubling perplexing to her, that now she was to be married to the chauffeur of her sponsor, on paper.

Sabir Shah told Rayhana Khan that Sheikh Ahmed had to deal with his wife's insisting he kick out the new maidservant because she might corrupt her sons. The chauffeur revealed her sponsor knew full well that his wife's rantings were justified on the grounds the new Indian maidservant was young and beautiful and possessed a very irresistible body. For that reason, her sponsor thought that if the maidservant agreed to marry the chauffeur on paper, his wife would have peace of mind. The wife would then be satisfied knowing that her sons would understand the maidservant was now married with a husband to protect her and therefore they would not come near her. Rayhana did not like the idea at first, but when she heard that the chauffeur would protect her from the two evil sons, she changed her mind and once again said Qabool.

Sheikh Ahmed used to spend only one day with his fourth wife, but for reasons known only to himself, he decided to spend three days with wife number four. When wife number four asked him about why he was spending more days at her residence, his reply was that he was not feeling well and needed to take some rest until he recovered. The ignoble woman did not like that her husband was spending all this time at her house. She knew it didn't matter really how many days he stayed at the residence because he wasn't going to touch her anyway. Try as she might, she could not remember the last time her husband actually had sex with her. It had been years. For that reason, she went for the handsome, young Pakistani, Sabir Shah, to satisfy her needs. She was twelve years older than her secret lover and twenty-eight years younger than her husband. When the two servants agreed to marry, Sabir Ibrahim Shah was thirty years old and Rayhana Khan was twenty-seven years old.

That day, Sheikh Ahmed sent his Pakistani chauffeur to request the presence of his Indian maidservant to have her come into the living room. Rayhana left the kitchen and walked into the living room. The old Saudi told the chauffeur in front of his wife to take the new maidservant to the Super Mall and have her purchase a total of seven dresses; four for Rayhana and three for Iffat. They should also purchase inner garments and three pairs of shoes each. The kind sponsor ordered that when little Iffat returned from school, she should have at least three beautiful new Barbie dolls in her room.

When Sheikh Ahmed extended his wonderful generosity towards his maidservant and her little daughter, his noble wife was sitting near him in the living room. The ignoble wife was careful not to let it be known the fact that she had already bought clothes and dolls for the maidservant and her daughter. Therefore, she kept silent and offered no objections. What troubled her heart more was seeing her secret lover going out with the young and beautiful maidservant. She was afraid they might get along a little too well.

It would seem Sheikh Ahmed had immediate plans for the young maidservant and the chauffeur. He had already phoned many places and made many preparations for the pseudo marriage between Rayhana and Sabir. He had told Sabir some of the details of his scheme but hid many other details from him. He decided to keep the marriage of his two young servants a surprise from his wife and their two sons. Rayhana had technically given her Qabool the previous day, but Sheikh Ahmed decided not to rush things and be prudent. He could have crept into the room of his beloved for she had already agreed to surrender herself to him, but he controlled his lustful inclinations and decided to wait until everything was done properly. He knew it was only a matter of a few short hours before his Layla was going to be his and his alone. He would then have her to possess forever. He had to admit that he had never enjoyed such a dreamy, peaceful, good night sleep in all his life until after his Layla had come to his abode and said to him, Qabool.

Following the orders of his master, the chauffeur took Rayhana first to a private clinic. It was owned and run by a corrupt medical

Pakistani doctor. Sheikh Ahmed had told Sabir that he met Rayhana by chance while she was roaming the streets of Colaba in Bombay. Therefore, he was scared Rayhana might be a prostitute and carrying some dangerous sexually transmitted disease such as aids. Therefore, before he would sleep with her he wanted to make sure that she was not carrying any infectious disease. Accordingly, before conducting the paper marriage, Sabir was to take Rayhana to the Pakistani doctor for a thorough medical checkup. On the other hand, the story he told Rayhana was that the law in Saudi Arabia requires every couple to go through a medical checkup before they were to get married. In the interests of keeping that facade, Sheikh Ahmed told his chauffeur to undergo a checkup too. In that way, Rayhana would not be suspicious of his intentions.

Of course, that was just what the old Saudi told his Pakistani driver. The Pakistani doctor had received a totally different set of instructions as far as the chauffeur was concerned. First, he knew very well that Rayhana wasn't a prostitute. She refused to give him her body even though he offered to pay her thousands of rupees. Secondly, he told the corrupt Pakistani doctor to put Sabir to sleep and castrate him. Thirdly, regarding his Indian maidservant, he strictly warned him not to expose her nakedness or even touch her body. He demanded one of his female nurses check Rayhana for any possible disease. If need be, the nurse should treat her ailments, if any.

When the soon-to-be married couple arrived at the clinic, the Pakistani doctor kept up the charade and promptly sedated the Pakistani chauffeur. He then castrated him under a general anesthesia. When Sabir gained consciousness, he felt a dull ache in his privates, never suspecting what had transpired. Rayhana underwent a full body checkup and blood work, performed by a female nurse. All tests were negative. After her check up, Rayhana had to wait a long time for the chauffeur to rejoin her. She felt a great relief when Sabir finally appeared, but was curious why his checkup took so much longer than hers. Having no knowledge or reason to question the procedures at the clinic, she did not bother to find out the reason for the delay from him or the clinic.

Immediately after the clinic appointment, the two servants went to the appointed Pakistani religious Mazoon and asked him to conduct their marriage. As soon as she laid eyes on the Mazoon, Rayhana recognized his face. He was the very same man who came to the apartment of Aslam Ali Khan and conducted her pseudo marriage. The Mazoon did not fail to recognize Rayhana, but minding his own business, he did not say anything to her. He photographed them with his little camera and then conducted their marriage contract. After receiving his fees, he issued their marriage certificate and handed it over to the two newlyweds. Rayhana, in yielding to the complicated situation, kept mum.

After the civil ceremony, the couple was free to leave the Mazoon's place of business and Sabir took his on-paper-bride to the Super Mall. Sheikh Ahmed had already phoned a boutique and placed his order for a beautiful wedding gown for his kept-wife and a dashing suit for his Pakistani pimp. The eccentric lover wanted to see his Layla in her wedding gown so that he could enjoy his first wedding night with her. His dream was at last coming true. He had already lost her twice before. The first time he lost her was when she was jailed for many months in a Bombay prison cell and the second time when he thought that she had been raped and murdered and her body dumped somewhere in the sands of the Saudi Arabian desert. However, after his Allah had resurrected her from the desert plains and given her to him on a silver platter at the Beautiful Filipino Women's Salon, the old Saudi had a conviction that no power on earth could snatch her from his hands again. In his mind, she had come into his house, agreed to be his kept-wife, and therefore, destined for him and him alone. The crazy Qays even concluded that not even his Allah could separate him from his Layla again.

Sheikh Ahmed had no trouble with his conscience because he knew his prophet slept with his maidservant, Maria the Coptic, without marrying her. We will not get diverted by this trivial unethical behavior of Muhammad and crack our mind in explaining in details why he went for a maidservant although he had nine harem at the time. In short, Maria the Coptic was not counted by Muslim scholars as one of the wives of the prophet or "Mothers of the faithful" because she remained a Christian and slave until she died. Muhammad never married her. She bore him a son, Ibrahim, who died in infancy. The prophet's desire for Maria was described in a dramatic way by the books of the Sira (biography of Muhammad).

Maria was a maidservant in Muhammad's house and used to help his wives in their daily chores. Every day she was sent to work in the house of one of his nine wives. Hafsa, one of the prophet's wives, caught him in the very act of committing adultery with Maria in her room and shouted angrily, *"O Prophet of God, in my house, on my bed, and in my night!'*. According to the Qur'an, Muhammad was supposed to be stoned to death for committing adultery with a woman who was not his wife while he was a married man. Nonetheless, that law somehow was waived in his case. Afraid of the anger of his other wives, and especially of his most beloved Aisha, the prophet promised his wife Hafsa that he would never touch his maidservant Maria again if she would keep the matter secret. Nevertheless, Hafsa spoke out, and the matter reached the ears of Aisha. When his beloved Aisha confronted him, Muhammad claimed to have received a revelation from heaven that corrected him and justified his adulterous act with his maidservant. *"O Prophet! Why holdest thou to be forbidden that which Allah has made lawful to thee? Thou seekest to please thy consorts but Allah is Oft-Forgiving, Most Merciful" (Surat Al-Taharim 66: 1).* When Aisha heard the above justification she said to him, *"Why should I see your Lord in a haste to satisfy your whims?"*

Let us keep aside the traditional *Playboy Magazine* that contains the adventures of Muhammad with his harem and maidservants and focus on the modern Playboy. Sheikh Ahmed had given his chauffeur a secret password. He told him not to bring his maidservant/kept-wife in her wedding gown to the house until first contacting him on his cell phone and the correct passwords were exchanged. The paper-bridegroom was supposed to pick up the phone and say "Layla" and as a response, Sheikh Ahmed would return with "Qays". This would signal that the coast was clear and they were to enter the dining room without asking for permission. Without the password, they were supposed to stay and wait outside the dining room until Sheikh Ahmed phoned them back. The Sheikh's strange behavior did not escape Mrs. Ahmed's observation. She had no idea what the evil genius had for her in store. Although he claimed to be ill, he looked well and happy. He was cracking jokes and showing so much affection towards her. He even came in the kitchen and helped her while she was cooking lunch. When the lunch was prepared, he was the one who carried the tray into the dining room. While the joyful old man was sitting at the dining table surrounded by his wife and two sons, his cell phone began to ring. He took his cell phone out of his pocket and glanced at the caller ID. He raised his voice and shouted a greeting. Then, he shouted even louder and said "Qays." After that, he cut off the phone and replaced it in his pocket. His wife and sons did not know what to make of this brief exchange. His son Hisham asked him,

"Who is Qays?"

"My beloved sons and my dear wife, today I have a great surprise for you. I am sure it is going to make each one of you very happy."

Before, his beloved sons and dear wife were able to demand an explanation about this great surprise, the door of the dining room was thrust open and the incredible surprise walked in. The two sons already considered Rayhana gorgeous, but clad in her wedding gown, they thought a virgin of paradise had descended from heaven and appeared in human form before their very eyes. They stood up, mouths agape without uttering a single word. Mrs. Ahmed had a totally different set of emotions boiling inside her, when she saw the newly wedded couple. She felt the urge to pick up the knife from the dining room table and run Rayhana through for having the audacity to marry her secret lover. Every passing second did nothing to quell the rising flame ripping her heart into pieces. If anyone had touched her at that critical moment, she would have exploded for sure. As fate would have it, it was the hand of her husband who touched her at that very instant. What followed was the loudest, angriest filth anyone had ever heard coming out of her mouth. Her husband did not reprimand her physically. Instead, he requested the newly married couple occupy two chairs near her and have lunch with the noble family. Before, she could do or say anything, the two servants sat down and occupied their seats. Rayhana sat beside her, carefully arranging her beautiful wedding gown around her when it touched the woman of the house. That was the feather that broke the camel's back. She used both her hands to push Rayhana and her gown far away from her and the shove made the new bride plop down on the floor right next to her chair. Then, with the fury that followed, she opened her mouth wide open and shouted, *"How dare you come sit with us, you stupid Indian slave!"*

Rayhana shot up on her feet and fled for her life. Sabir stood up and began to tremble from head to toe.

"You stupid Pakistani Qolam how dare you marry that stupid Indian servant without asking my permission!"

"I gave them permission to get married Mastoora!" shouted Sheikh Ahmed.

"She has come here to serve us, not to get married and have a honeymoon!"

"She is our servant and not our slave! We cannot decide for her when she can marry or to whom!"

"Okay, go and book her a room in a five star hotel and let her enjoy her honeymoon there! I don't want to see her any more in this house!"

"Mastoora... calm down. Remember I am the one who brought her to work for you. I could have sent her to any of the other three wives, but you said you needed a maidservant."

"I don't want her! I will do all the housework by myself! Send her wherever you want to send her. I don't care! Except she's not staying here! "

"No! You cannot order me! Rayhana is going to stay with her husband Sabir and work in this house!"

"Yes mother let her stay. She is a very good housekeeper and very nice lady. We like the way she cleaned our rooms better than those other maidservants. She does very good work here and we're very happy with her," said Hisham.

"Yes, Rayhana is our beloved sister and we love her so much. She shouldn't go to any other house," said Husam.

Feeling the walls closing in on her, Mrs. Ahmed got up from her chair and marched straight toward her bedroom, the sound of slamming doors followed. Immediately Sheikh Ahmed stood up and asked his chauffeur to follow him to the kitchen. When he entered the kitchen, he found Rayhana sitting in a corner, crying. He sat beside her and embraced her dearly. It felt so good for he had never touched his Layla so tenderly before. If it wasn't for his two sons who came running in behind the chauffeur, he would have kissed her on her lips and more than likely consummated his marriage right there on the kitchen floor.

CHAPTER 12

ON THE FIRST WEDDING NIGHT

Sheikh Ahmed waited impatiently for the sun to go down so that he could spend his *first wedding night* with his *kept-wife*. His beloved Layla gave her Qabool and his convoluted plan of getting her married to his chauffeur worked perfectly, furious wife aside. He phoned the Pakistani doctor and confirmed that Sabir Ibrahim Shah was rendered totally sexually impotent. After hugging his Layla for the first time in the kitchen, he helped her to stand. Then, in front of his sons and playing his role to the hilt, he led Rayhana by the hand to her room. His sons and his chauffeur followed them silently. The two sons were very much touched by the fatherly affection their father showered upon their beloved maidservant. If not for his sons shadowing them, Qays would have carried his Layla in his arms to their wedding suite and begun enjoying her.

Reaching the room, Sheikh Ahmed sat Rayhana on her bed. He insisted that she lie down on the bed and rest. The bride followed his request and lie on the bed motionless and in shock. While the lovely bride was laid out on the queen-sized bed in her beautiful wedding gown, Sheikh Ahmed whispered in her ear. He promised that his wife would not bother her anymore. Seeing her lying there aroused the crazy old man to a heightened passion and desire such as he had never felt before. Ever the strategist, he knew that it was just a matter of time until his life's dream would come true. Just before leaving, he gave Iffat a sweet fatherly kiss on her forehead. All this time, Iffat was sitting in the bedroom playing with her beautiful new Barbie Dolls. She returned from school an hour before her mother came back. Mrs.

Ahmed, not knowing what was about to transpire, had fed her well and told her to go play with her dolls in her room.

After that Sheikh Ahmed along with his sons and the paper-husband left Rayhana's room and went and sat in the living room. They talked to each other in whispers. They did not want to risk provoking the angry lioness. The measure of her fury led them to believe she might just spring out of her bedroom at any moment and attack them or run to the maidservant's room and kill her. Hisham and Husam peppered their father with questions. How did you find Rayhana? Why did you suggest they marry? In general, they were happy about the marriage. They knew that Rafeeq didn't always sleep in their house. He had to follow their father from house to house and stayed with him wherever he went. So, it was clear to them that they could still blackmail the chauffeur's wife for sex. The biggest problem they faced was that they did not have the key to Rayhana's new room. They were already planning to steal the key and make a copy. The events did nothing to change their interest in the maidservant—sex, videotapes, and showing off in school.

Sheikh Ahmed waited many hours for his wife to come out of their bedroom and talk to him. He regretted that he had challenged her. He knew that if she left the house and returned to her father's house he would be in some serious trouble. Half of his business came from her wealthy father. Therefore, to avoid any problems, Sheikh Ahmed shrewdly decided to compromise. He decided to accept her decision and send Rayhana and her daughter to the house of his third wife. However, the marriage between the chauffeur and the maidservant would remain valid. He would not agree to force Sabir to divorce Rayhana. When his wife did not come out until the evening, he took it upon himself to go to her bedroom and try talking to her. Before he went to his bedroom, he sent Sabir to Rayhana's room and promised to join them late night.

Mastoora was lying on her back when her husband came in. Her eyes were wide open, staring at the ceiling. When she heard him entering the bedroom she averted her eyes and fixated on him. Her eyes were the gateway to hell. He sat beside her and tried to touch her.

She pushed his hand away and stood up. Then, she marched out of the bedroom, headed to the living room and sat down. Her sons had already gone to their rooms and the chauffeur was nowhere to be found. She became more outraged when she visualized her secret-lover and sex-satisfier having sex in her house with that *dirty Indian slave*. Thoughts of stabbing Rayhana still clouded her mind. Her husband came and sat in front of her, trying to engage her in conversation. Once again, she ignored him and remained silent. Through her silence, he apologized and promised to send Rayhana and her daughter to his third wife's house. Her face revealed to him that his apology and compromise had done nothing but make her even more furious. Nothing could quench the boiling anger in her heart and the flaming fire in her eyes save sending her rival to the grave or to jail.

Sheikh Ahmed sat more than two hours in front of his wife and tried patiently to get his wife to talk, but he could not make any headway nor pacify her. She seemed to have gotten stuck in a sullen and sulky mood. Finally, he decided it was best to leave her to cool off by herself and talk to her tomorrow. He got up from the couch and went to his bedroom. He changed his clothes and put on his nightdress. He had wanted to rest for some time, tired by the exertion of the day's activities. He fully expected his wife to return to bed once she got sleepy. Tired of trying to appease her, he was resigned to stay put and he began to imagine the great enjoyment and pleasure awaiting him on his first wedding night. He was determined not to close his eyes. He was afraid that due to his advanced age, he might fall asleep and miss the splendor of his first wedding night with his latest wife. He enjoyed imaging how he would approach his beloved. He asked himself, what should he do first to her. Should he take her in his arms and hug her for a long time or should he start kissing her immediately on her lips. Should he remove her clothes piece by piece or ask her to undress herself. And when she became ready to consummate the union, which position should he assume. Should he do it doggy style or classical style? He knew that in his advanced age he would not be able to do anything too strenuous. He told himself that he should just ask his beloved to climb on top of him and do it her way. The crazy old man was so lost in his fantasies that his mouth was ajar with a trickle of drool running down the side of his face.

Suddenly, the old man stopped his daydreaming and looked at his watch. He began to worry about his first wedding night. He checked his watch intermittently. Each passing second made his heart beat faster. His wife was not back. Worried that things were not going according to plan, he jumped out of bed, cracked the door open and peered at her. She was sitting exactly as he had left her, stationary, like an alabaster statue. He now regretted trying to talk to her in the bedroom. If he had anticipated that she would come out and sit in the living room, he would not have tried to placate her. Now she was sitting like a night watchman, and there was no way he could go to his kept-wife's room without passing directly into her line of fire. From where she was sitting, she had an eagle's eye view of the maidservant's room. The old man now had a serious problem. He went to his bed, sat for some time, returned to the door and peeped out again. His wife was still sitting motionless in exactly the same spot. He felt like doing something rash like taking a knife and scaring her. Divorce her and send her home to her father TONIGHT! However sanity returning, he calmed himself down and fidgeted, waiting impatiently for his wife to tire and come to bed. Checking again, his wife was still in the same position, looking blankly at the wall. However, a thought flashed in front of his restless mind and gave him a glimmer of hope. It looked like his wife had fallen asleep sitting upright. He made his way as quietly as he could and slowly as possible into the living room. Looking into her eyes, he saw anger shooting like a lightning bolt of thunder and he was struck dead to his soul. He tried to reason with his wife and convince her once again to come to bed. She just ignored him and continued to look at the wall. Begging her one last time and not getting any response at all, he gave up, made his way back to the bedroom and fell asleep at 4:30 am.

The following morning, Sheikh Ahmed's sleep was disturbed by the last person he expected to see. His wife pulled him up out of bed, her face radiant and happy. She could not hide her joy. She was laughing hysterically to the point where she could not talk. Sheikh

Ahmed thought that he was dreaming the unattainable dream. His mind informed him that the woman who woke him up while she was bubbly, giggling, and laughing could not possibly be his wife. Even if heaven rained down gold and silver, his angry wife would not suddenly change overnight. She shook him over and over again and laughed hysterically. By now, he was fully awake and convinced that this was indeed no dream. He had no choice but to accept the unavoidable fact that this cheery and jovial woman was none other than his wife. To him, it looked as though she had lost her senses due to emotional trauma. His first reaction was to slap her. Some people believe a powerful slap is the remedy for sudden madness. So, Sheikh Ahmed lifted his right hand as far as possible and struck his wife on her cheek. Mrs. Ahmed shocked back to normal reverted back to being the angry cobra woman and shouted at her husband,

"Go and slap the Indian prostitute that you have brought to me from the streets. Go and see who have come to take her away."

Sheikh Ahmed was so troubled when he heard the tone of her challenge. It frightened him to hear her say, *go and see who have come to take her away*. He asked her in fear and trembling,

"Who have come to take Rayhana away?"

"The Jeddah policemen have come and arrested her. They are waiting to talk to you before they take her away."

If his wife had brought a knife and severed his heart, Sheikh Ahmed would not have felt so much pain. His body became so hot it was as if someone had set it on fire. He began to murmur unintelligibly. He tried to stand but his feet failed him. His wife helped him stand with much difficulty and assisted him until she managed to bring him out. The sight of four policemen standing in the living room greeted his eyes. *He saw his beloved Layla in chains, kneeling on her knees on the floor.* Instead of asking them why Rayhana was arrested his eyes were begging the policemen to have mercy on him and release his kept-wife. One of them spoke to him in a harsh voice and said,

"This woman is a professional prostitute. She goes around the city cheating men, getting them to marry her and eventually she robs them of their money and runs away. In less than ten days, she deceived

two men and married them. Here are copies of her two marriage certificates. One marriage certificate is with an Indian man by the name of Aslam Ali Khan and the second marriage certificate with a Pakistani man by the name of Sabir Ibrahim Shah."

Sheikh Ahmed could not take the impact and shock of what he had heard and fell on the couch and fainted.

CHAPTER 13

THE SECRET LOVER

Rayhana Khan was arrested with the most serious crime ever committed in the Kingdom of Saudi Arabia. No one had ever committed this crime in this manner before except for an adulterous Sudanese woman. The Sudanese woman was married and had a husband in Sudan and also got married to another man in Saudi Arabia without divorcing her first husband. When her case came to the attention of the Saudi authorities, she was arrested, tried, convicted, and stoned to death, on a Friday of course. The evidence against Rayhana was overwhelming. The police had found out that she got married to an Indian and then a Pakistani, a few days later. Marital law in the Kingdom of Saudi Arabia stipulates that any foreign couple getting married should have a copy of their marriage certificate sent to the Ministry of Religious Affairs. Likewise, any married couple getting divorced are required to do the same. In the case of Rayhana, there was no proof of a divorce from her first husband. Even if a divorce certificate would be produced later the Shari'a law would not allow a divorcee to remarry until she waited three months and ten days.

Rayhana's crime became more serious after the Jeddah police sent her for the pregnancy test. The result of the test showed that she was six weeks pregnant. It means that she was impregnated by a third man. She had to produce proof of her marriage with the man who impregnated her and further prove that he had divorced her before she married the other two men. When she failed to produce the needed documents, the Jeddah Police concluded that she was indeed a professional prostitute whose business was cheating men out of their money while sleeping with them under the cover of marriage.

When Sheikh Ahmed came to senses and regained consciousness, he heard the charges against Rayhana. He knew that his beloved was going away forever never to return to him again. He understood that she was going to be stoned to death for these serious crimes. His happiness and joy overnight were turned into the deepest gloom and sorrow. He had spent a lot of money and had done many things to get his beloved woman but it was just not meant to be. Everything was in vain. He could not enjoy his Layla even once. He cried in front of his family members. His sadness and tears now exposed his true feelings. For the first time, his wife and children understood how deeply he loved the maidservant.

On the other side, Mrs. Ahmed was openly rejoicing and celebrating her victory. She thanked her Allah a million times for seeing her tears and hearing the cries of her deeply pained and wounded heart and avenging this great wrong done to her. When she saw her secret lover beside the young and beautiful Indian maidservant, she thought she had lost him forever. But suddenly, her Allah had snatched him from the arms of the enemy slave and by the grace of Allah, returned him to her. Once again, the Pakistani chauffeur was to be her lover and hers alone. As she had wept silently throughout the night, she now rejoiced and celebrated all the daylong in the preconceived thought that she was going to rejoice forever and ever.

Rayhana's serious crime filled all the newspapers and the media in Jeddah and spread all over the entire Kingdom of Saudi Arabia, even to the OAPEC countries. In a short time, even the international TV channels like the Arabic BBC in London, UK and the Aljazeera TV in Doha, Qatar covered the case. The Jeddah police was able to lay hands on Aslam Ali Khan and interrogate him. Aslam was found hiding in the city of Riyadh. After his failure to hand over his wife to his wealthy Saudi client, Aslam ran away from Jeddah and was hiding in the city of Riyadh. The Pakistani friend that provided him shelter revealed his whereabouts to the police. The media spotlight led Aslam's Pakistani friend to become an informant. He had read about the sensational case and knew the friend he was sheltering was no doubt involved in one of the most serious crimes ever committed in the Kingdom of Saudi Arabia. When Aslam was taken into custody, his friend called the local newspapers and told them he was the good citizen who revealed the hiding place of the first husband of the adulterous Indian woman. His fifteen minutes of fame was realized when media men came and knocked on his door for his statement.

According to Aslam's confessions, he admitted that he married Rayhana Khan legally, according to the Sunna of Allah and his Messenger. She stayed with him in his apartment in Jeddah for one week. He slept with her many times during those seven days. He said further that he did not divorce her. One particular morning, he took her to a Filipino Beauty Salon and when he returned after two hours he found out she had run away with another man. She did not even bother to leave a note. He searched for her everywhere, but could not find her. She went to his apartment in his absence and stole all his savings and disappeared from his life. He was now totally broke after she robbed him of all his money.

Aslam was detained for twenty-four hours and released. The police did not find him guilty of any crime. Likewise, the police took into custody the second husband and interrogated him. Sabir also confessed that he had married Rayhana Khan in good faith. He did not know that she had another husband. She did not tell him that she had a previous husband who did not divorce her. He just saw her in the house of his sponsor and liked her. Then, he asked her to marry him and she agreed immediately. He also claimed that he married her and consummated the marriage the very same day. Sabir was released the following day too,

The police was able to gather more incriminating evidence against Rayhana. The airport police reported that Rayhana and her daughter smuggled themselves inside the country without passports. Somehow, she managed to run away from the police and enter the city. For almost two months, she lived in the Kingdom as an illegal alien. The accumulated charges led the police to take her sponsor into custody for questioning. Sheikh Ahmed denied his knowledge that his Indian maidservant and her daughter had arrived in the country without their passports. He claimed falsely that his Indian client in Bombay phoned him and informed him about the arrival of his maidservant and her daughter. When his maidservant and her daughter came to his house they had their Indian passports. He even handed over the two passports to the Jeddah police. He showed copies of the visas that he sent to his client in India.

Jeddah police could find no reason to detain Sheikh Ahmed and so let him go. For the crazy lover, it appeared that his great love had suddenly turned into a mere lusting after a young beautiful woman who was as young as his granddaughter. When his beloved woman was charged with one of the most serious crimes ever committed in the Kingdom of Saudi Arabia, he washed his hands of her and had already begun to think of finding another young Indian woman to purchase.

The only one that was happy at the Indian maidservant's fate, of course, was Mrs. Ahmed. She rejoiced and celebrated, shouting joyfully from the rooftop. She waited eagerly for her husband to go to his other wives so that she could rebuke her secret-lover and reclaim her place in the heart of her sex satisfier. Sheikh Ahmed began to hate his fourth wife for her continuously reminding him that he had brought a prostitute home. So he left her, if anything, just to get some peace of mind. His heart was filled with a mixture of anger and sadness toward Rayhana. Mrs. Ahmed demanded that her husband either send the daughter of "the Indian prostitute" to her country or to the jail where her mother was waiting for her execution. When he refused to carry out her demands, she asked him to take her to live with one of his other three wives. Sheikh Ahmed did not know what to do with little Iffat. Staying with wife number four was not an option. He decided to take her to live in the house of one of his other wives until he could hand her over to the Indian Consulate for her to be deported to Bombay.

As soon as her husband took the daughter of the maidservant and left, Mrs. Ahmed brought her candles and invited her lover to the house. The excuse to her husband was that she needed him to take her to the supermarket. In Saudi Arabia, a correctional officer would not arrest a woman who was found in a car with the chauffeur of her husband. The police might demand some proof that the driver of the car was actually the chauffeur for the family. Anyway, the happy woman spent more than an hour in the washroom. She applied *henna* on her hands and legs as if she was a bride prepared for her bridegroom. She cleaned her body and removed every strand of hair from her legs, arms and hands. She even shaved clean the hair covering her private area and underarms. To top it off, she painted her nails and brushed her hair. She applied lipstick on her thin lips and put Kohl on her eyelashes and eyebrows. (Kohl eyeliner is an eye cosmetic, which mostly used by Muslim women but some Muslim men used it too because the Prophet Muhammad used to apply on a regular basis Kohl in his eyes). The happy woman did everything she could to make herself look Rayhana's age. She emptied almost half a spray container of costly Indian perfume on her clothes and body. She also put Musk on her underarms and some private parts. (Once again, Musk is aromatic substances use as perfume by Muslim women but some Muslim men apply Musk on their bodies because the Messenger of Allah used to apply Musk on his body too. In fact, the prophet of Allah said he loved two things, Perfume and Women. Oh my Goodness, I forgot to mention that although *henna* mainly used by women some Muslim men apply it on their bodies because the prophet Muhammad used to apply henna too).

When her secret lover showed up, Mrs. Ahmed gave him a long lecture in the living room. She made him swear by Allah that he would never repeat what he did to her again. She demanded that he should place his right hand on the holy Qur'an and promise allegiance of everlasting fidelity. After forcing him to repent in tears and took the oath of allegiance, she brought him to her holy chamber. Mrs. Ahmed for the first time, decided to allow her lover to enter her bedroom. Before that day, she believed whatever a Muslim woman did, she should do away from her husband's bed. She heard that the Muslim woman who cheated on her husband in their marital bed would have the angels of Allah cursing her night and day. Her lot in this life and the life to come would be same like the disobedient wife who refused to allow her husband sleep with her. The angels of Allah would curse her until the morning. However, that particular day, her victory made her ignore this commandment: *'Thou shall not fornicate in thy marriage bed',* and so she took her lover to the bed of her husband. She was looking to maximize her self-indulgence and this risky move made her feel like this would give her the greatest amount of pleasure.

Sabir was shocked when he saw they were going to be spending time in the master bedroom with beautiful candles and the sweet smell of perfume circulating in the air. He saw the biggest bed he had ever seen, the likes of which he had never seen before. There was a blue movie playing on the big screen just above the bed. Mrs. Ahmed asked her secret lover to remove her dress. While Sabir was removing her clothing, he was looking at the beautiful white girl who having sex with a young white guy. Mrs. Ahmed decided today to go the extra mile. She decided to imitate everything the young white girl was doing to her sex partner. She ordered her lover to remove his clothes and be like her. Mrs. Ahmed did many things differently this day. She was so overjoyed that she found herself singing vulgar Arabic song she learned from some Egyptian porn movies where the words go as, "n…kni wa aftah k…si," "n…kni fee k…si almu'asil," "dakhil z…bk wa ashrot t…zi" (f…k me and open up my virgin pussy, f…k me up in my juicy pussy, and stick your d…k and f…k up my ass).

She began to mirror the white girl on the screen. For the first time, she used her mouth on her Pakistani but things seemed not to work the way it did on the LCD screen. Her lover's genital organ was not responding to her tender manipulations. She tried and tried to stimulate him, but it was as if her secret lover could not feel her hands or mouth. She told him to keep his eyes glued on the screen. She knew that if he looked at her fully naked body, he would lose interest. Being practical, she was aware she was very skinny and ugly, with a face resembling a man rather than a woman. She had a nose as big as a spade. Sabir followed her express orders and kept staring intently at the goings on on the screen. He liked and enjoyed what he was watching on the big screen, but his sexual organ remained cold and soft as if it did not belong to his body.

Mrs. Ahmed thought the Pakistani man was no longer interested in her and that his heart was stolen by that Indian prostitute, killing all his desire for her. She reflected that while she was sitting in the living room silently weeping with her heart bleeding inside her chest; her secret lover was sleeping with the Indian slave. She stopped what she was doing and began to question him. He denied her accusations. He swore by Allah that he had not touched Rayhana. When he said he did not have sex with the Indian maidservant, she slapped his face. She absolutely refused to believe that he just slept by her side in bed and that they had done absolutely nothing. She demanded an explanation for his lack of response. When he could not give any acceptable reason, she hit him in the chest and shook him by the shoulders and then began to cry. He begged her to allow him to go, but she refused. She kept beating and punching him. She even grabbed him by his shoulders and bit him, which caused him to scream out in pain. Mrs. Ahmed would have killed her secret lover if he had not managed to push her away at the right time. When she fell on the floor, he picked up his clothes and ran out the room. Mrs. Ahmed did not run after him. She remained on the floor and sat sideways beating her body and pulling out her thin graying hair like a raging lunatic.

When she overcame her rage, Mrs. Ahmed swallowed her pride, went to the black guard, and forced him to sleep with her. Before that day, she used to look at him as a dirty, filthy black slave. She used to call him Khaal and Zonji (The Black Negro). Her children called him on his face Abedana (our slave). Arabs consider every black person their slave. Moreover, they believe that *the black man will remain slave even if he becomes the richest man in the world as the dog will remain dog even if it stops barking*. Nevertheless, that day, Mastoora considered her black slave her right hands possess and slept with him.

CHAPTER 14

LOVERS IN THE HOLY LAND

Abu Islam was a Pakistani man living in Saudi Arabia for ten years and working as a medical doctor in a hospital in Jeddah City. He was a widower who lost his wife many years ago. He had only one son from his late wife. His son also died in a car accident along with his mother. His late son was named Islam and that is where the doctor obtained his precious nickname, Abu Islam. His real name was Muhammad Ali but everybody knew him as Abu Islam (i.e. Father of Islam). For many years, after the death of his wife and son, Abu Islam remained single. Recently, however, his parents made him marry his cousin, Sakina Ahmed. It wasn't a love marriage but an arranged marriage. There was a twenty-year age difference between Sakina and her cousin, Abu Islam.

Sakina was a University graduate. She got a B.A degree in sociology from University of Karachi, Pakistan. She was in love with a young man that was her neighbor. Her lover was also a graduate student with a degree in Engineering from the same University. They were in a serious relationship and wanted to get married. For some reason, Sakina's parents objected and married her off to her cousin, Abu Islam, in order to put an end to what they called *shameful love affair*. Abu Islam of course never knew anything about the love affair between the neighbor and his new bride. He spent only one week in Pakistan with his new bride. As soon as he returned to the Kingdom of Saudi Arabia, Abu Islam began the process of bringing his new bride to live with him. After her arrival in Jeddah City, Sakina resumed her affair with her long distance lover, secretly communicating with him by phone and sometimes writing letters to him. She told her lover not to write back or telephone her. She would phone him whenever there was an opportunity for her to do so. Since her husband was always busy at work, Sakina found ample time and space to communicate with her true love and dream of what could be.

Nevertheless, the separated lovers weren't satisfied communicating just through writings and talking on the phone. They felt the need to be near each other and express their love for each through other means. In order to work toward this goal, the lovers made a secret plan. Accordingly, this plan called for Sakina's lover to apply for a job in Saudi Arabia and then come and live near his beloved. The lover followed the plan and applied for a work visa to Saudi Arabia. As soon as he obtained the visa, he traveled from Karachi city to Jeddah city.

Yasin Sheikh, Sakina's lover, refused to accept the fact that, love affairs had no place in Muslim society, and he was determined to pursue his beloved wherever she went. He had studied engineering at Karachi University, and after his graduation, he became a very successful engineer. When he arrived in Jeddah, he stayed briefly with his Pakistani friend. Shortly afterward, he moved from his friend's apartment and rented an apartment in a building occupied mostly by Pakistani tenants. Yasin did not move to this apartment complex because he loved his people but because his beloved was living there with her husband. As it turns out, everything worked out perfectly for the lovers and they were able to live and be close to each other. Not only that, whenever Sakina's husband went to work, she called her lover on the phone and asked him to come over to her apartment. Meeting for the first time after a long and painful separation, the lovers did not deny their passions and expressions of love and all the feelings they had for each other. Whenever they met, they kissed, hugged, and had sexual intercourse. Before Sakina was married to her cousin, the lovers had never had sex. In those days, they believed sex before marriage is haram and a disgrace. They were hoping sooner or later they would get married to each other with the blessings of their families.

What Sakina and Yasin were doing would not remain hidden forever in a closed and strict Muslim society like Saudi Arabia. Their Pakistani neighbors had eyes to see and ears to hear. Many times, some curious Pakistani neighbors spotted Yasin entering the apartment of Dr. Abu Islam in his absence. According to the Islamic Shari'a Law, the Muslim wife was not supposed to allow any man to enter her house in her husband's absence even if that man happened to be her father-in-law or brother-in-law. She could only allow her own father or brother to enter her house if her husband wasn't there. Some of the neighbors being moved by what they saw as an unholy alliance made it their business to contact Dr. Abu Islam by phone and disclosed to him what was happening behind his back. Some of them even wrote anonymous letters and sent them to Dr. Abu Islam to his address at the hospital.

Although Dr. Abu Islam by then had lived with his wife for over a year, he never suspected that she was having an affair with another man or that she would do something like that behind his back. Therefore, the news of his wife cheating on him made him feel the ultimate betrayal especially when he had succumbed to his parents' wishes and had married her. He wanted to punish her for her unfaithfulness but decided to verify the rumors first. If she really was dishonoring him in this fashion and defiling their marriage bed, he would catch her and her secret lover red-handed and thus he would have the right to divorce her, sending her back to Pakistan. Dr. Abu Islam never thought of killing his wife or sending her to the Shari'a court to be stoned to death for cheating on him. He did not want a guilty conscience of having caused the death of his own wife or exposing their families unnecessarily to bad publicity and a bad reputation. After all, she was his close relative.

However, before Dr. Abu Islam could carry out his plan to punish his unfaithful wife, his self-righteous neighbors took it upon themselves and did what they thought was their duty as good Muslims to do. They thought that perhaps Dr. Abu Islam either did not believe the information he received through the various means of communication, or either he believed the news and was too busy to do anything about it. Accordingly, the news of the Pakistani wife who was cheating on her husband by sleeping with her boyfriend reached Saudi police headquarters. The Jeddah police carefully planned a surprise raid being given the exact day and hour of the criminal indiscretion. Upon arriving at the apartment of Dr. Abu Islam, they broke down the door and rushed inside. Unfortunately, when the cops entered the apartment, the lovers happened to be in bed making love to each other. They were arrested bare naked and taken into custody.

After their arrest and harsh interrogation, both lovers admitted their secret affair and adulterous relationship. During her interrogation, Sakina was not only beaten up by the male police officers, but she was also gang raped by them. A few days later, the lovers were tried and convicted by the Jeddah Shari'a court. Yasin was sentenced to receive a hundred lashes because he committed adultery while he wasn't married. Sakina was sentenced to be stoned to death because she committed adultery with another man while she was married and having a husband. Yasin received his hundred lashes with a whip and went back to work the following day. The flogging he received to his back was less painful than a massage. The person who flogged Yasin, held a copy of the Qur'an in his right underarm between his right shoulder and his chest and he was not supposed to drop the holy book while he was carrying out the flogging.

Nevertheless, the case of Sakina's punishment was different and carried out by over a hundred men. Around 12:45 pm on the following Friday afternoon the public ground was crowded by men dressed in white cloths and all of them had long beards. Shortly, after the gathering of the faithful, the condemned Pakistani girl was brought to the area in a well-guarded police escort. She was handcuffed and her legs chained together. She was dressed up in a black niqab that covered her entire body. When they dragged her out of the truck, she was resisting and screaming for help. She was begging the police to spare her life. In her sobs, she promised she would never ever repeat that sin again. However, her tears and pleadings fell in deaf ears. None of them seemed to heed her pleas and cries for help. A couple of police officers dragged her like an animal until they brought her to the middle of the ground. There was already a hole dug for her burial. The police forcibly dumped her body inside the hole kicking and screaming and she twisted her ankle upon impact. Then, some men came and buried her up to her neck. Only her neck and head were visible while the rest of her body was completely buried in the ground. After that, her face was uncovered so that everyone could see her. She was expected to see her executioners. It was 48 degrees Celsius plus when poor Sakina was buried up to her neck in hot sand. The heat of the sun and the hot sand scorched her body causing second-degree burns to her flesh and she was screaming louder and louder. Underneath the black coffin-like niqab, she was sweating and burning like steam boiling inside a teakettle. It would have been more tolerable to put her in a furnace than to bury her in hot sand. They did not have to stone her to death, for being left just one hour in the hot dry ground, she would have been cooked alive instead.

When her head was uncovered, her face was shining with the reflection of the blazing sun. Sakina was a very beautiful Pakistani girl. She had a very fair complexion as if she was the daughter of a white woman and a Pakistani man. She had very long black hair. Through her beautiful face, one could see a very frightened young woman. She continued to scream and call for help. She even called the names of her Allah and Prophet and begged them to rescue her from this cruel and painful death. Neither Allah came out of his House to rescue her from the holy city of Mecca nor was her prophet resurrected from his grave in Medina to come and save her.

Instead, an old man came forward, shouted Allah Akbar, and cast the first three stones at her head. He came so close to Sakina, she had no way of dodging him or moving her head out of the way. One stone missed her and the other two hit her on the side of her face and the upper part of her forehead. Her face and head began to bleed. Sakina felt a terrible pain shoot right through her head like electric shock waves inside her brain. She began to scream louder and plead even more for them to have mercy upon her. Then, the old man retreated to his place in the line of men who formed a half circle around the victim. As soon as the old man reached his place at the opposite end of the line, the other men began to cast their stones at Sakina. The stones hit her from all different directions and blood gushed out from her face and head like a waterfall. Sakina's head jerked each time she was hit and she tried desperately to move her head in different directions to avoid the stones. Her screaming could no longer be heard due to the men shouting in unison: "Allah Akbar, Allah Akbar…" Sakina felt as if a construction worker was pounding her face with plywood and driving a hammer and nails into her skull. Blood was running out of her nose and mouth and she was trying desperately to breathe through her mouth. When she opened her mouth to breathe, the stones pierced her lips and inside her mouth nearly breaking all her teeth. Her teeth fell out of her mouth and her long hair became meted with blood; her skull was smashed by the crushing rocks and her brains oozed out of her head. No normal human being could witness such a cruel punishment and remain sane except a demon-possessed person…

Sakina's head stopped moving and fell backward; a sign her neck had been broken by the heavy stones. Although her head became lifeless, the cruel men continued to throw stones at the victim until she was covered in a heap of stones. After Sakina's head was fully covered with stones, the police authority announced over the loud speakers to cease all stoning. Then, a group of cops came with a shovel and removed the stones from off the victim. When all the stones were removed, Sakina's face was brutally marred and completely disfigured. Blood still ran from her body. Her body was dug out of the ground and dragged like a dead animal and hauled away as trash…

CHAPTER 15

THE DOUBLE PUNISHMENT

Rayhana's life was turned into a nightmare after her arrest. She was worried about the future of her daughter. She was also worried about what would happen to her mother and children in Bombay if the Shari'a court in Jeddah sentenced her to be stoned to death. The police had already told her that she was going to be tried and stoned to death. Even her prison inmates predicted her end. As soon as she arrived at the Jeddah Women's Jail, Rayhana met a Pakistani girl by the name of Sakina Abu Islam who was arrested before her under the similar charge of having sexual relations with a man while she was married to another. Rayhana became acquaintance with Sakina and in a few days, a kind of friendship developed between the two suspects. After two weeks, the Pakistani girl disappeared. When Rayhana asked about her friend Sakina, she was told that she had been stoned to death on a Friday afternoon.

As soon as Rayhana heard about Sakina's cruel death, she cried until she lost her voice. Ever since then, she began to have nightmares and wake up in the middle of the night sweating profusely. She always dreamed about the young Pakistani girl. Many times Sakina came to Rayhana while she was asleep and begged her to stop the Saudi police from stoning her to death. Sometimes, she hallucinated during the day and saw the poor young woman standing in her cell begging her for help. The continuous visions and dreams led Rayhana to believe that her cell was haunted by the soul of this young woman. She begged the guards to transfer her to another cell where she could be with other inmates, but her requests were rejected.

Rayhana's double marriage was discovered merely by chance, by an employee of the Ministry of Religious Affairs. That employee happened to be an Indian Muslim. The beautiful face of Rayhana reminded him of his favorite Indian film heroine, Pariyanka Chopra. Pariyanka was a Bollywood superstar and former Miss World. Before he came to Saudi Arabia, he used to watch every movie made by Pariyanka. He almost worshipped the very ground she walked on. However, after he came to Saudi Arabia he could not see her movies anymore because there was not a single movie theater in that 7th century country. So, when he saw the first marriage certificate of Rayhana Khan, her photo stuck in his mind. Every day he sneaked a glance at her file and stared at this gorgeous beauty. When Rayhana got married the second time and her marriage certificate reached the Ministry of Religious Affairs, he was shocked when he saw the same face and the same name of the newly married Indian girl. He checked the previous file and found everything to be the same except the names and photos of the two bridegrooms. He showed his discovery to other employees. Everyone confirmed his discovery that the same girl had married two different men, in less than two weeks.

The first thing the employees of the Ministry did was to contact the Pakistani Mazoon and inquire if Rayhana had showed him a divorce certificate from the first husband. The Mazoon confirmed that she did not produce any divorce certificate. As a rule, a divorced woman could not get remarried unless she showed proof of her divorce from a previous husband. Moreover, the Qur'an states that a divorcee has to wait three months and ten days before she marries another man. However, such a requirement was not applicable in the case of the man because the Shari'a allows him to marry four women.

It didn't help her case, either, that when the police raided the house of Sheikh Ahmed, Rayhana was inside her bedroom with her new husband. Her new husband swore he had no knowledge that she had a previous husband or if they had divorced. Even Rayhana condemned herself, when she said that her former marriage and her present marriage were just on paper. She further stated that neither of the two men had slept with her. She also admitted that her first pseudo husband had not divorced her. The policemen, who interrogated her, told her that even a child would not believe such a story. They could not see how it was possible for a young beautiful girl like her to stay with two men all alone without either of them having sex with her.

Another rule for women accused of adultery is before they appear in court they are required to take a mandatory pregnancy test. So after her interrogation, Rayhana was sent for a pregnancy test. The result of the test came back positive. This was the final nail in her coffin that sealed her fate and added to her list of infringements. It appeared that she was six weeks pregnant. The first question the police asked her whether she had a third husband. She condemned herself again when she confessed that her Indian husband died two years before. When the police interrogated her about who impregnated her, she said she had been raped by two Saudi policemen, two months ago, on the day of her arrival in Jeddah. However, once again she condemned herself when she said that she did not lodge a complaint against her alleged rapists. The policemen wasn't about to buy that story either; they assumed and then concluded that she was a professional prostitute who made her way around the city on a sleeping spree under the cover of marriage.

Rayhana appeared before the Shari'a court in Jeddah after about a month from the day she was arrested. Looking at all the evidence against her, the judge delivered her over to the jailer to be stoned to death. However, the sentence would be postponed until after she delivered her child and nursed it for two years. So she received a double punishment. While it was a temporary reprieve, for her it meant a three-year jail sentence and then to be stoned to death. The judge quoted the following story to back up his decision,

"A woman came to the prophet Muhammad and, 'said that she had become pregnant as a result of fornication. He (the Holy Prophet) said: Is it you (who has done that)? She said: Yes. He (the Holy Prophet) said to her: (You will not be punished) until you deliver what is there in your womb. One of the Ansar became responsible for her until she was delivered (of the child). He (that Ansari) came to Allah's Apostle (may peace be upon him) and said the woman of Ghamid has given

birth to a child. He (the Holy Prophet) said: In that case, we shall not stone her and so leave her infant with none to suckle him. One of the Ansar got up and said: Allah's Apostle, let the responsibility of his suckling be upon me. She was then stoned to death." (Sahih Muslim, *book 17, hadith no. 4206).*

Accordingly, Rayhana was sentenced to three years in prison, and she was to be stoned to death, after completion of her jail term. It was a double punishment. Imagine a woman being told that she was going to be killed after serving three years in jail. How is any woman in such a situation to sleep at night? That was the mental condition of Rayhana after she heard her sentence. During the day, she was thinking about her death, and every night, she dreamed she was being stoned. In addition to that, her conscience was torturing her endlessly about the fate of her daughter in Jeddah and the future of her children and mother in Bombay. She cried day and night. Whenever, she thought about her daughter, she blamed herself for taking her from her home in India and bringing her to this rich Arab country, lured by the promise of money. She regretted she had ever come to this accursed land of the Arabs. Nothing of what she had heard about the Holy Land of Allah and the land of petro dollars came to be. From day one, she and her daughter had seen nothing but torture and abuse. She was brutally raped in front of her little girl and she was reduced to being an indentured slave, by the evil cobra woman. In her country, she had experienced none of these evils. Rayhana wished that she could go back in time and turn around from entering inside that wretched plane, which took her and her daughter from their free and safe country and brought them to the Land of the Great Satan. She remembered that her abuse began inside that damn plane of the Arabs, when she was accused falsely of being a female suicide bomber. She was humiliated and stripped naked by an evil Arab man. If a human being could exhaust all the tears that could be shed, Rayhana would not have been left with one tear to cry.

Rayhana was worried that the evil sons of her Kafeel might rape her daughter, in her absence. She was also scared that the evil cobra woman of her sponsor might force her daughter to do all the work required of a maidservant by this vile snake of a woman. Rayhana thought of every possible evil that might happen to her daughter, except what her wicked sponsor had decided to do to her seven-year-old daughter. He couldn't care less, her sponsor did not bother to bring her daughter to see her in prison. As soon as she was safely out of the picture, he began to plan how to abuse and rape her little girl. Of course, his conscience was soothed by the evil example of his prophet Muhammad. Because of his child-bride, Aisha, thousands of female children get raped every day in Muslim countries due to the example set by an alleged prophet of God. No Muslim would dare challenge what Muhammad did to a nine-year-old plaything as an act of child-abuse or child-rape for fear of losing his/her life.

BOOK III

THE CHILD BRIDE

CHAPTER 1

BARBIE DOLLS

Mrs. Ahmed allowed Iffat to stay in her house for one week before finally she forced her husband to take her away. She hated her with a passion. Whenever she saw her, she saw the face of her mother. Iffat was not only an exact copy of her mother, but she looked as if her mother had cloned her, without a father. She had the same beautiful eyes, same golden color, same hair, and same mole on the middle of her left cheek. If Iffat stood among a thousand young Indian women, no one would confuse her with any of them, except her mother. The only difference between her mother and Iffat was their age and the size of their bodies. Her mother was a bit heavier and had a larger backside. Iffat might develop a more voluptuous body over time, much like her mother's once she started to develop into a woman. The situation of her resemblance to her mother created a very serious problem for her.

Sheikh Ahmed looked at Iffat as a heavy burden. At first, he did not know what to do with her for a certain. She had no address of her own in India. The old Saudi man knew that Iffat used to live with her mother in a slum. He knew that the address on her passport was the address of the Sudanese student, who was awaiting trial in Bombay. She had no father whom he knew of at this point in time. He did not know any of her relatives. Even if he decided to send her back to India, where should he send her and to whom? If he wanted to keep her, how long should he keep her in his house? Which one of his wives would agree to raise up a child that wasn't her own? Moreover, the scandal of her mother would be a stigma, which would follow her wherever she went for the rest of her life or wherever he would take her.

At first, Sheikh Ahmed decided to keep Iffat in the house of his first wife, until he could talk to the Indian Consulate and convince them to take her away. He thought that the Indian government might find a wealthy Indian family to adopt her. Those thoughts and worries were going on in the mind of Sheikh Ahmed on the day he was transferring the little Iffat from his fourth wife's house to the house of wife number one. His Pakistani chauffeur was driving him in his Mercedes while Iffat was sitting near him on the backseat. She was playing with her Barbie dolls. When the old man saw the small child so involved playing with her beautiful Barbie dolls, he gazed at how innocent she was. She seemed unfazed by the disappearance of her mother. His wicked wife repeatedly told Iffat in his presence that her mother went to jail because she was a prostitute and a thief, but Iffat did not understand Arabic. He had taken the trouble to tell Iffat through his chauffeur, that her mother had gone to a place far away, and he told her that she might not come back for a long time. He deliberately left out that she would be stoned to death after sentencing by the Shari'a court. He figured that little Iffat would come to know about this terrible tragedy once she was older.

The lovely dolls lying in Iffat's lap and in her hands reminded Sheikh Ahmed of a story he read about his prophet Muhammad. He remembered that the beloved wife of the prophet Muhammad, Aisha bint Abu Bakr used to play with dolls at the time he married her. Even Aisha admitted that the prophet married her when she was six years old and she still played with dolls. Before we see where Sheikh Ahmed's mind was going to take him with this idea, we should confirm his claim that his prophet married a female child of six years old who used to play with dolls at the time of their marriage.

"Narrated Aisha, I used to play with the dolls in the presence of the Prophet, and my girl friends also used to play with me. When Allah's Apostle used to enter they used to hide themselves, but the Prophet would call them to join and play with me" (Sahih Al-Bukhari Volume

8, Book 73, hadith No. 151). This hadith is explained in Fateh-al-Bari, *(The playing with the dolls and similar images is forbidden, but it was allowed for Aisha at that time, as she was a little girl, not yet reached the age of puberty) (Fateh-al-Bari page 143, Vol.13).*

"The prophet wrote the (marriage contract) with Aisha while she was six years old and consummated his marriage with her while she was nine years old and she remained with him for nine years" (i.e., till his death)" *(Sahih al-Bukhari, book 62, hadith No. 89).*

"'A'isha (Allah be pleased with her) reported: Allah's Apostle (may peace be upon him) married me when I was six years old, and I was admitted to his house when I was nine years old" (Sahih Muslim Book 8, hadith No. 3310).

"'A'isha (Allah be pleased with her) reported that Allah's Apostle (may peace be upon him) married her when she was seven years old, and she was taken to his house as a bride when she was nine, and her dolls were with her; and when he (the Holy Prophet) died she was eighteen years old" (Sahih Muslim Book 008, hadith No. 3311).

Notice that Sahih Muslim mentioned in one hadith that Aisha was a seven-year-old child and in the next hadith she was six-year-old. However, both Sahih Al-Bukhari and Sahih Muslim agreed upon her age (9 years) when the marriage was consummated and both mentioned that she used to play with dolls at the time of her marriage. Well, Sheikh Ahmed was right and his memory was vivid with regards to the age and the childish behavior of the beloved child bride of his prophet. The prophet Muhammad married Aisha when she was six years old and began to have sex with her when she was nine years old and while she was still playing with her dolls. The dolls of Iffat and the dolls of Aisha suddenly solved the problem of Sheikh Ahmed. At this junction, a devilish idea leaped into his evil mind, and he decided to carry it out in real life. He asked himself, *"Why should I not follow the example of my gracious prophet and marry the little Iffat?"*

Iffat was seven years and eleven months old when Sheikh Ahmed decided to marry her. He knew that legally he would not be able to marry her for two reasons. First of all, he already had four wives and the Shari'a would not allow him to marry a fifth wife unless one of his wives died. Secondly, the Saudi law would not allow him to marry a foreigner. However, his scheming mind quickly found a way around that particular obstacle. He would divorce one of his four wives and, in so doing, his Shari'a law would allow him to marry a new wife. The Islamic law places the right to divorce entirely in the hands of the man and does not require him to give any reason for divorcing his wife. He can just say "I divorce you" and the divorce will take place. No Mazoon, no Shari'a court, no witnesses, and no divorce certificate are required. Moreover, the man is not like the divorced woman that he needs to wait for three months and ten days before remarrying another woman. He can divorce one wife today and marry another one tomorrow. Al-Hassan the grandson of the prophet Muhammad used to divorce four wives in one go and marry another set of four women in the same day. He was a marriage addict. He married two hundred wives plus his uncountable number of right hands possess or female slaves. The prophet Muhammad praised him for his ability to marry such unbelievable number of women. The King of Saudi Arabia have married forty-three wives and has one hundred and five children.

Regarding the Saudi restriction around foreign brides, Sheikh Ahmed knew that it was just a man made law. Shari'a law never forbade marriage to a foreign woman or child. He had already married a Christian girl in India, who wasn't a Saudi and consummated his marriage with her. Regarding which wife he should divorce, two immediately popped up into his mind. He should either divorce the one he had just taken Iffat away from, or the one he was taking Iffat to. The fourth wife was ugly, skinny, always complaining and hard to please. The third wife was obese, ugly, and evil like him. The second wife was old and decrepit. His first wife was old and dying of cancer. Twirling the idea in his head Sheikh Ahmed dismissed the idea of divorcing Mastoora for fear of losing her father's favor. He then, understandably decided to divorce Khadija, wife number one, so that he could upgrade. After coming to that conclusion, Sheikh Ahmed began to justify this decision in his head. He thought that Rayhana Khan had just used him to come to Saudi Arabia to be with her Indian lover. He reasoned that she lied about being raped and rescued by a Bedouin family. She might have just allowed the two policemen to have sex with her and then she asked them to drop her off at her Indian lover's apartment. If he wasn't her lover, why did she agree to marry him? When he convinced her to marry his chauffeur, why did she not mention that she had already gotten married to another man? Why didn't her first husband phone him or come to demand his wife back? What husband would keep quiet and do nothing if another man came and took away his wife from a beauty salon? Therefore, Sheikh Ahmed concluded that Rayhana was either truly a professional prostitute or a big cheat, who used him to come to Saudi Arabia to be with her Indian boyfriend. (By the way, in Saudi Arabia and other Gulf countries many foreign workers from countries like India, Pakistan, and Indonesia are not allowed to bring their wives and children due to their low incomes). Satisfied with his logic, the old man now felt justified in forsaking the love he felt for Rayhana and leaving her to face her demise. This justification left him free to marry her daughter.

In the back of his mind, Sheikh Ahmed remembered that he had already been cheated by two Indian women; Christie and Rayhana. There would not be a third. His mind was now made up about marrying Iffat, but a few obstacles still stood in the way. How could he marry her and where should he keep her? He knew Shari'a law would allow him to marry a seven-year-old girl, but Saudi law forbade marrying foreigners. Even if he married her secretly, where would he keep her?

At first, the old Saudi thought of marrying Iffat and keeping her in another Muslim country. However, which country should he choose? A number of Muslim countries popped up immediately in his mind; Somalia, Sudan, Eritrea, Djibouti, Gambia, Comoros, Niger, Egypt, Libya, Algeria, Morocco, Mauritania, Yemen, Jordan, Syria, Palestine, Kuwait, Bahrain, Qatar, Oman, Dubai, Abu Dhabi,

Indonesia, Bangladesh, Iraq, Iran, Pakistan, Afghanistan, Azerbaijan, Uzbekistan, Kyrgyzstan, and Burkina Faso. (In fact, there are fifty-five Muslim countries, but these are the only ones that popped into his mind). All of these countries are Dar Al-Islam and allowed child-marriages. He decided to write the name of each country on a piece of paper and fold it up and then ask Iffat to pick a piece of paper and whatever she drew from the lot would be her country. However, on second thought, he dismissed that idea. If he sent his soon-to-be child-bride out of the country, he was afraid that when she grew up she might find a boyfriend and run away with him. He recollected the mistake he had made by marrying Christie, only to have her cheat on him in *HIS* house with her Indian boyfriend. She then abruptly dumped him for the infidel dog, Bobby. Before he could come to a conclusion, the car reached the house of wife number one.

CHAPTER 2

THIGHING OF FEMALE CHILDREN

There is an evil practice among the Arabs called "Mufakhazat Alzigaar," loosely translated as the *thighing of children*. There is no proper English translation for this practice, simply because it is not a Western norm. The thigh is the part in humans between the hip and the knee. The nearest evil practice to thighing in English would probably be child-molesting. However, thighing is infinitely more evil than child-molesting. It is done by an adult man to a female child, with the sanction of religion. Now let us see how it is practiced on a female child and who began this evil practice. According to an official Fatwa issued in Saudi Arabia, the prophet Muhammad began to practice thighing his child-bride, Aisha when she was six years old until she reached nine years of age (Fatwa No. 31409). The hadith, which was quoted earlier, mentioned the prophet Muhammad started performing literal sex with Aisha ONLY when she reached the age of nine (Sahih al-Bukhari, book 62, hadith No. 89). Therefore, Muslim scholars collectively agree, by virtue of divine example, a child becomes an adult, available for sexual intercourse as soon as she reaches the age of nine. Likewise, the Shari'a allows any of the faithful to marry a six-year-old child.

According to the fatwa, the prophet Muhammad could not have sex with his fiancée, Aisha when she was six due to her small size and age. However, the fatwa said that at age six, he would put his penis between her thighs and massage it gently because he did not want to harm her. Imagine a man of fifty-one removing the clothes of a six-year-old girl and slipping his erect penis between her thighs, rubbing her until he ejaculated and his semen ran down her thighs. To this day, this is considered a benevolent act on the part of the adult male "not wanting to harm her." What harm could be inflicted upon a young girl mentally and emotionally if not a grown man showing her his penis and stripping her of her clothes and rubbing his male organ between her legs? Of course the twisted mind that does such an evil to a female child, would not hesitate to ejaculate on her body. And if this sexually perverted evil frame of mind committed such an act upon a child, the pedophile would not stop at ejaculating on her. His evil desire would go further and rape the child before she was a mature adult. This is exactly what Muhammad did to Aisha when she was yet a child of nine. Before she reached puberty, he began to have sex with her. Let us see what the fatwa said about the prophet of Islam and his child-bride, Aisha.

"Praise be to Allah and peace be upon the one after whom there is no [further] prophet. After the permanent committee for the scientific research and fatwas (religious decrees) reviewed the question presented to the grand Mufti Abu Abdullah Muhammad Al-Shamari, the question forwarded to the committee by the grand scholar of the committee with reference number 1809 issued on 3/8/1421(Islamic calendar). The inquirer asked the following:

'It has become wide spread these days, and especially during weddings, the habit of mufakhathat of the children (mufakhathat literally translated means "placing between the thighs of children" which means placing the male erected penis between the thighs of a child). What is the opinion of scholars knowing full well that the prophet, the peace and prayers of Allah be upon him, also practiced the "thighing" of Aisha—the mother of believers—may Allah be pleased with her?'

After the committee studied the issue, they gave the following reply: 'It has not been the practice of the Muslims throughout the centuries to resort to this unlawful practice that has come to our countries from pornographic movies that the kofar (infidels) and enemies of Islam send. As for the Prophet, peace and prayers of Allah be upon him, thighing his fiancée Aisha. She was six years of age and he could not have intercourse with her due to her small age. That is why the prophet peace and prayers of Allah be upon him placed his penis between her thighs and massaged it lightly, as the apostle of Allah had control of his penis not like other believers'" (Fatwa No. 31409).

Thighing of children is practiced in many Arab and Muslim countries, notably in Saudi Arabia, Yemen, Iran, and the Gulf countries. These countries are notoriously known for this evil practice. There are many more such evil practices like *altamatu'a bil almufakhaza* (pleasure from sexual contact with her thighs), *altamatu'a bil almuka'aba* (pleasure from sexual contact with her breasts), *altamatu'a bil alsagirah* (pleasure from sexual contact with a baby girl), *altamatu'a bil alradi'ah*, (pleasure from sexual contact with a suckling female infant), (Reported by Baharini Women's Rights Activist, Ghada Jamshir). These are all different styles practiced on the female child by placing the male erected penis in different parts of the child's body for getting sexual pleasure.

The Islamic Shari'a authorizes a grown up man to marry even one-year-old female baby. It is very common to see a man of seventy or eighty years of age marrying a child of eight or ten. Recently, an eighty-year-old Saudi man married a ten-year-old girl. On the wedding night, the child's privates hemorrhaged so badly, that they had to take her to the hospital. Another recent case was of a Yemeni man, who raped his child-bride, until she died. These are just a handful of the thousands of rapes **of female children** that take place each year legalized by marriage.

Sheikh Ahmed intended to marry the child of the Indian maidservant and practice thighing on her until she reached the age of nine. At the time, Iffat was almost eight. She was seven years and eleven months. She did not even know what sex was. When she saw her mother stripped naked by the two policemen she thought they were killing her. When the Saudi policeman took her out of the car, showed her his male parts, and tried to force her to hold it in her hand and put it in her mouth, she did not have an inkling about what he was trying to do to her. What she did know was that it was wrong to show your private parts in public, and she resisted his attempts to force her to fellate him. As it turns out, the sacrifice of a mother offering herself up to the two policemen prevented Iffat's from being raped. Alas, now with her mother unjustly incarcerated and sentenced to death, Iffat lost her one and only guardian, with no one to protect her from life's evil.

Upon reaching the house of his first wife, Sheikh Ahmed changed his mind. He told his wife he was going to send the daughter of his Indian maidservant to her family in India, after a few days. His first wife agreed to keep Iffat in her house. He did not tell his wife that he was planning to divorce her and marry the little girl in her place. Sheikh Ahmed's wife was bedridden, suffering from the last stages of cancer. She could die at any moment, but her selfish husband could not wait for her to die. He had remarried her after divorcing her to marry his Indian wife, Christie. After Christie divorced him, kicked him out of his house at Bombay, brought her Christian boyfriend and married him, Sheikh Ahmed remarried his first wife, Khadija just to show off that he was a kind husband. However, now circumstances were different and, for all wants and purposes, he was willing to send Khadija to the grave as a divorcee. Death for Muslim women generally means going to hell. Prophet Muhammad said that the majority of Muslim women would end up in hell. The Muslim man, in abject contrast is promised seventy-two virgins in paradise, but the Muslim woman can look forward to burning in hell for all eternity.

Sheikh Ahmed's never-ending evil worked out a new plan to marry his child-bride, Iffat following the unrighteousness of his prophet of Allah. He figured that he should send her to Eritrea. He had learned from some Eritreans in Saudi Arabia that Eritrea was well-known for child-marriages. Most Eritreans traditionally give their female children in marriage as soon as they have reached seven, eight, or nine years of age. Sheikh Ahmed knew that Islam forbade adoption, so he could not try to adopt Iffat and then pretend she was his daughter. He also anticipated that one day, someone from the media or the Indian government might ask him the whereabouts of the daughter of his condemned Indian maidservant. Therefore, he planned to send Iffat to Eritrea via India. If he was asked about the child of his Indian maidservant, he could say that he had sent her to her relatives in Bombay.

The old Saudi feared taking Iffat himself because he expected his former car driver, Muhammad Khan, might find out about his arrival in Bombay and send Gondas to kill him. To avoid retribution, he decided it would be safer to send his Pakistani chauffeur to travel with little Iffat. This plan didn't work out too well, as Sabir's application for a visa at the Indian Consulate in Jeddah was promptly rejected on the grounds that he was a Pakistani. To get around that particular obstacle, Sheikh Ahmed booked the trip of his soon-to-be child-bride and his Pakistani chauffeur on a Saudi flight to Eritrea through India and the Philippines. The route taken by the Saudi plane would be Bombay-Manila-Asmara. In the end, the old man believed his plan would exclude him from any culpability and absolve him of any blame if anyone starting asking questions. He began rehearsing his story about how he sent her to her family in Bombay through his Pakistani chauffeur. And if he was asked where his Pakistani chauffeur was, he would simply say that his chauffeur decided to stay in India and make his way to Pakistan. Sheikh Ahmed already planned to keep Iffat in Asmara and keep his castrated Pakistani chauffeur, as her guardian angel. He had no intention of allowing Iffat a chance of falling in love with another man and running away with him. He was going to keep the young damsel in distress in her own Barbie doll castle. Only her Ken would not be there to protect her and she would be well guarded by Sabir, the Pakistani pimp.

To make his story more plausible, Sheikh Ahmed convinced his Pakistani chauffeur to pretend to be Iffat's uncle. When they both applied for visas to Eritrea, Sabir Ibrahim Shah claimed that Iffat Khan was the daughter of his sister Rayhana Khan who was married to a Muslim man from Bombay by the name of Khan. However, before they approached the Eritrean Consulate in Jeddah, Sheikh Ahmed told Iffat another story. He told her that he was going to send her with Sabir to her mother in India. To that end, she was supposed to say that Sabir was her mother's brother.

The plan of the evil old man worked out perfectly, and his child-bride began her trip to Eritrea. He flew to Asmara the very same day Iffat and Sabir started their long trip to Eritrea via India and the Philippines. On a direct flight, he reached the destination before them, and he booked two rooms in a five star hotel; one for Iffat and her uncle and one for himself. He suspected that if he touched the little child in the hotel she might scream out and get him into big trouble with the police, especially since she was not his wife yet. So, he decided to wait until he could conduct the marriage ceremony and then move her to a place in the city. He was planning to buy a house in Asmara and keep his child-bride as his new wife and sex slave.

CHAPTER 3

WOMEN IN MUSLIM SOCIETIES

The most dangerous place for women in the world is the Kingdom of Saudi Arabia. The first couple of months Rayhana spent in Jeddah, showed us just how dangerous it is for a woman to be without protection in a jungle full of sexual deviants. Recently, a fifteen-year-old Moroccan girl, who went with her parents on the holy pilgrimage, was brutally raped by three Saudi men. After raping her in the terrace of a hotel, they threw her body from the fifteenth floor. She died for her want of getting a better view of the holy city from the terrace on the top floor. Her Moroccan parents had no idea of the violent mentality of Saudi men, and so they allowed their daughter to go alone. After all, it was *just* within the hotel. They mistakenly thought that they were still in Morocco. They were like Rayhana under the erroneous belief that people of the holy city of Mecca were righteous and fearing their Allah. Therefore, the fifteen-year-old Moroccan girl like Rayhana was a victim of ignorance. Nothing in their lives had prepared them for the abusive nature of Saudi Arabian men. In that society, if a woman put one leg outside her door with her other leg still inside the doorway, she would be raped. For that reason, Saudis do not like to live in a building that has many apartments in it. The Saudi government built many buildings with very beautiful and spacious apartments. The government extended a generous invitation and asked the Bedouins to leave their desert villages and tents and come and live comfortably in the city by occupying these luxurious apartments. The Bedouins refused simply because they feared their neighbors might come in their absence and rape their daughters and wives. It was also common for women to be raped in elevators and public women's washrooms. Many Saudi men and even foreign workers would not allow their women to go to public washrooms for fear of being attacked and raped by men disguising themselves under burqas. Majority of men simply don't trust their women. They are brought up with the belief that the women like wild beasts that can get easily carried away by their uncontrollable lusts wherever they get little freedom.

Saudi men like many other Muslim men all over the world have sexually corrupt minds because of the misogynistic teachings of their Prophet Muhammad. The greatest Muslim scholar and theologian, Abu Hamid Al-Ghazali, in his well-renowned book, "The Revival of the Religious Sciences" said, *"be careful of women for their guile is immense and their mischief is noxious; they are immoral and mean spirited...It is a fact that all the trials, misfortunes, and woes which befall men come from women.*" (3.2). A Muslim man would not trust even his father and brother with his wife. This is because the prophet Muhammad said that the in-laws were in imminent danger from the wife and she was a death sentence for them. Muhammad himself could not control his lust when he saw his daughter-in-law, Zainab bint Jahsh, in her tent while she was half-nude. She was the wife of Muhammad's adopted son, Zayd Ibn Muhammad, and therefore, in the eyes of the Arabs, as good as his own daughter-in-law. Muhammad went to her house when her husband was away, saw her in a state of semi-nudeness, and was aroused. According to the Sira (the prophet biography), Allah sent a wind, which lifted up the curtain of the tent and Muhammad saw Zainab lying on her bed half-naked. Zainab is described by the Sira as fair, beautiful, and has sensual body. Then, the Sira goes to tell us that Muhammad desired Zainab and Zainab desired Muhammad too. In order to get her from her husband Muhammad fabricated verses in the Qur'an and claimed that Allah had given her to him in marriage (Qur'an 33:36-40). According to the Sira, she was the only wife of the Prophet that had been married without Wali (guardian), her Mazoon was Allah, and the witness for the marriage was the angel Gabriel.

Simply put, no man should trust his wife. This stems from yet another Islamic tradition. The prophet Muhammad said, *"Four things can never be trusted, the Money, Sultan, Time, and Woman even if you have lived with her for a very long time"* (Quoted in Al-Qimni, *Rab Al-Zaman [The Lord of This Time],* "Women In Religious Heritage and Legends" 1996: 220). I know a case of a Muslim Arab man who married a Muslim Indian girl in Bombay. They lived in a rented apartment in the same building that I was living in at that time. Many families lived in the building. Whenever he went out, he locked the door with a huge padlock and she remained locked up in the apartment until he returned. Some of his friends had advised him that if he was afraid of someone raping his wife in his absence, he should just ask her to lock the door from inside the apartment. He simply replied, "I lock her up because I don't trust men around her, and I don't trust her either."

In order to understand the misogynistic mind of the Muslim man and the low position that Islam has placed on woman, we need to refer again to the above-quoted book. The Egyptian Muslim liberal thinker, Sayyid Al-Qimni, held the Islamic heritage responsible for degrading Muslim woman (Al-Qimni *Rab Al-Zaman [The Lord of This Time],* 1996: 219). According to him, the Islamic religious heritage made the Muslim woman believe "she has been created from a bent rib, deficient in religion and intellect, her testimony equals half of a man's, her inheritance is half of a man's, she cannot divorce" (Ibid: 220). The Muslim woman believes herself to be a Satan and therefore she cannot control her sexual desires (Ibid: 221). According to the Islamic heritage "woman succumbs to her lust and not intellect, she has a natural tendency to cheat on her husband, because she was one of the four that could not be trusted, 'money, Sultan, time, and woman…" (Ibid: 220). Woman had been created for the comfort and enjoyment of her husband. In that way, the religious heritage made the Muslim woman "to believe herself to be a mere **vagina** and hence she became horma (taboo) and haram (forbidden)" (Ibid: 221, emphasis in the original). Therefore, "if she kept her faith and her vagina and gave enjoyment to her husband/master, she would enter heaven" (Ibid:

220). A Woman's faith "could not be perfected except by her complete obedience and submission to her husband and such obedience would secure her a place in heaven as a prostitute among the many harems of the man" (Ibid: 221). This gloomy picture that Al-Qimni depicted for the Muslim woman irritated many Muslim female professors and ulama or "scholars" of Al-Azhar University who believed that Islam had honored the woman and put her in the best place. Al-Qimni was condemned as a kafir or "unbeliever" by the female professors and doctors of Al-Azhar Al-Sharif University because he exposed in his book, *Al-Fashoon wa Al-Watan, (Fascists and the Nation),* the low status in which Islam put the woman—that she was inferior to man in every respect and made for his sexual pleasure. The main reason for their protest was that Al-Qimni "made a mistake by demanding rights for women, which Islam gave to men only" (Ibid: 177).

THE MISOGYNISTIC TEACHINGS

Wife-beating: "The Qur'an states "...Righteous women are therefore obedient. And those you fear may be rebellious (nushuz) admonish them; banish them to their couches, and **beat them**..." (Qur'an al-Nisa 4: 34).

"Narrated Umar ibn al-Khattab: "The Prophet said: A man will not be asked as to why he beat his wife" (Sunan Abu Dawud, book 11, hadith no. 2142).

Female Genital Mutilation or Cutting: Although female genital mutilation is not mentioned in the Qur'an but this evil practice is based on authentic hadiths came directly from the prophet of Islam.

1. "Umm Atiyya al-Ansarite narrated that a woman used to circumcise in Medina, and the prophet said to her, 'Do not overdo it, because this makes woman more favourable and it is more agreeable for the husband" (Sahih al-Bukhari, Libas 63, 64, Isti'dsan 51; Muslim, quoted in Tahara 49, Shaltut, Khitan al-untha, in Liwa' al-Islam, 1951: 55).

2. "Aisha narrated another authentic hadith that the prophet Muhammad said: When a man sits between the four parts (arms and legs of his wife) and the two circumcised parts meet, then ablution is obligatory" (Sahih Muslim, hadith no. 349). By the two circumcised parts the prophet Muhammad meant the circumcised penis of the man and the circumcised vagina of the woman.
3. "The prophet Muhammad said, Circumcision is a sunna for men and a preservation of honour for women" (Hadith of Abu al-Malik and Abu Dawud).

Female Child-Marriage: "The prophet wrote the (marriage contract) with Aisha while she was six years old and consummated his marriage with her while she was nine years old and she remained with him for nine years (i.e., till his death)" (Sahih al-Bukhari, book 62, hadith no. 89).

The Qur'an said, "Such of your women as have passed the age of monthly courses, for them the prescribed period, if ye have any doubts, is three months, and for those who have no courses (it is the same): for those who carry (life within their wombs), their period is until they deliver their burdens: and for those who fear Allah, He will make their path easy" (Qur'an Surah Al-Talaq 65: 4).

Polygamy: Qur'anic authority, "...marry of the women who seem good to you, two or three or four and if ye fear that ye cannot do justice (to so many) then one (only) or (the captives) that your right hands possess" (Qur'an Surah al-Nissa 4: 3).

Burqas/Niqabs: "Ibn Tayimiyyah said, Women used to roam about without Cloaks (Jilbaabs) and men used to see their faces and hands, but when the verse stating 'O Prophet! Tell your wives and your daughters and the women of the believers to draw their cloaks over themselves.' (Surah Al-Ahzaab, verse no. 59) was revealed, then this was prohibited and women were ordered to wear the Jilbaab. Then Ibn Tayimiyyah goes on to say "The word Jilbaab means a sheet which Ibn Mas'ud explained as a cloak covering the entire body including the head, face, and hands. Therefore, it is not permissible for the women to reveal the face and hands in public" (Ibn Taymiyyah's book on fatwaas p, 110 Vol, 2 also in the book Hijaab p. 15).

Woman's Witness half of a Man: "The Qur'an states, 'And call in to witness two witnesses, men; or if the two be not men, then one man and two women, such witness as you approve of, that if one woman errs the other will remind her" (Qur'an al-Baqarah 2: 282).

Woman is Deficient in Religion and Intellect: "Allah's apostle once said to a group of women; "I have not seen anyone more deficient in intelligence and religion than you. A cautious, sensible man can be led astray by some of you." The women asked: "O Allah's Apostle, what is deficient in our intelligence and religion?" He said: "Is not the evidence of two women equal to the witness of one man?" They replied in the affirmative. He said: "This is the deficiency of your intelligence."…"Isn't it true that a woman can neither pray nor fast during her menses?" The women replied in the affirmative. He said: 'This is the deficiency in your religion" (Sahih al-Bukhari, hadith No. 301 and 856). "The prophet Muhammad said "the woman is like a rib; if you try to straighten her, she will break. So, if you want to get benefit from her, do so while she still has some crookedness" (Sahih al-Bukhari, Volume VII, Hadith no. 113).

"The prophet Muhammad said, "the woman is like a rib; if you try to straighten her, she will break. So, if you want to get benefit from her, do so while she still has some crookedness" (Sahih al-Bukhari, Volume VII, Hadith no. 113).

"The prophet Muhammad said, 'Women are ungrateful to their husbands and are ungrateful for the favors and the good (charitable) deeds done to them. If you have always been good (benevolent) to one of them and then she sees something in you (not of her liking), she will say, 'I have never received any good from you" (al-Bukhari Volume I, hadith no. 28).

"Allah's apostle said, "When a woman comes, she comes in the form of Satan and when she goes, she goes in the form of Satan" (Sahih Muslim, hadith no. 3240).

"The prophet said: "I have not left any calamity after me more detrimental to men than women" (al-Bukhari and Muslim agreed upon this hadith, Sahih al-Bukhari, Volume VII, hadith no. 33).

"The prophet Muhammad, 'O women! Give alms, as I have seen that the majority of the dwellers of Hell-fire were you (women)" (al-Bukhari, Volume 1, Hadith no. 301).

"The prophet said, "Men are already destroyed when they obey women."

"Again" he said, "Women are ungrateful; therefore, can't trust them" (Sunan Abu Dawod).

"Woman is 'AWARAH: Tirmizi reported that the prophet said, 'The woman is 'awrah. When she goes outside (the house), the devil takes charge of her' (Tirmizi, Volume II, p. 65). This hadith says that whenever the woman goes out of her house she is possessed by demons. So she is dangerous to society and hence she should be confined inside her house. There is no definition so widely used and accepted among Muslims for defining the woman than 'Woman is A'warah.' The term A'warah is defined in the Encyclopaedia of Islam as 'the external genitals, especially of the female' (Haqq & Newton 1996: 5). The word is derived from the noun 'nakedness or nudity.' So to put it in a simple meaning 'woman is bare-naked.'

"The prophet said, 'There are three (persons) whose prayer will not be accepted, nor their virtues be taken above: The runaway slave until he returns back to his master, the woman with whom her husband is dissatisfied, and the drunk until he becomes sober (Mishkat al-Masabih, book I, hadith no. 74).

"The prophet of Allah said, 'When a man calls his wife to satisfy his desire, let her come to him though she is occupied at the oven" (Mishkat al-Masabih, book I, hadith no. 61).

"The prophet said, 'Had I ordered anybody to prostrate before anyone, I would have ordered women to prostrate before their husbands on account of men's rights over the women ordained by Allah' (Mishkat al-Masabih, hadith no.70). (Abu Dawood, Ahmad, Tirmizi, Ibn Majah, and Ibn Hibban).

"The Qur'an states '...Righteous women are therefore obedient. And those you fear may be rebellious (nushuz) admonish them; banish them to their couches, and **beat them**...' (Qur'an al-Nisa 4: 34). This verse of the Qur'an gives the husband the right to beat his wife if she disobeys him. Although the verse doesn't give the reason for beating except the fear of disobedience, the Shari'a law singles out five reasons. Beating of the wife is allowed by the Shari'a for five reasons:

1. When she does not wear fineries though wanted by the husband.
2. When she is called for sexual intercourse and she refuses without any lawful excuse.
3. When she is ordered to take a bath [to clean herself] from impurities for prayer and she refuses.
4. When she goes out of her house without permission of her husband.
5. **When she allows a man inside her house in the absence of her husband.**

"Aisha the beloved wife of the prophet Muhammad admitted that one day the prophet got angry with her and struck her on her chest until it caused pain. "He struck me on the chest, which caused me pain, and then said: 'Did you think that Allah and His Apostle would deal unjustly?' (Sahih Muslim, book 4, hadith no. 2127).

Types of Marriage in Islam: There are four types of marriages in Islam:

1. Monogamous Marriage: A lawful relationship between one man and one woman.
2. Polygamous Marriage: A lawful relationship between one man and more than one woman, not to exceed four wives at a time.

3. Muta'a or Enjoyment Marriage: A temporary lawful relationship between a man and a woman. The relationship could be one hour, two hours, three days, a month, etc. The enjoyment marriage doesn't require a Wali, a judge or witnesses. The man has to say to the woman 'I marry you myself' and she has to say to him 'I marry you myself.' This kind of marriage differs from the ordinary marriage because it does not aim at a continuous married life, but the enjoyment in a lawful way. It has been permitted by the prophet, but abolished by the second caliph, Omar Ibn al-Khattab. The Shiite sect argues that because this kind of marriage is permitted by the Qur'an (Surat al-Nisa 4: 24), the caliph Omar has no legal right to abolish it. According to the Shari'a law, no one has the right to abrogate any verse from the Qur'an after the death of the prophet. However, Muta'a marriage is unlawful in Sunni Islam, but practiced until today by the Shiite Muslims. In Iran, it is estimated that over 70% of temporary wives become prostitutes (Woodsmall 1983: 119).
4. Al-Misyar Marriage: Al-Misyar marriage institution in Islam, allows for a lesser form of relationship between man and woman than normal marriage. Al-Misyar is an official relationship between man and woman, but does neither require that the two live together, nor that the man is economically responsible for his wife. Al-Misyar allows the man to have a normal wife in an addition to his wives. The misyar wife is expected to live with her parents, and her husband can visit her according to a predetermined schedule. Al-Misyar marriage has been practiced in Saudi Arabia and Egypt for years. The Egyptian Sunni Imam Shaykh Muhammad Sayyed Tantawi and the Mufti of Egypt officially legalized it in February 1999, and has also been defending the arrangement of misyar. Marriage is defined as 'a permanent, immediate, and unconditional civil contract (which is not contingent) between two persons of opposite sex for mutual enjoyment and procreation of children' (Verma 1988: 56). As we shall see soon this definition doesn't

apply to the concept of marriage in Islam. The two concerned persons who sign the marriage contract in Muslim countries are not the husband and wife. According to Shafi' and Maliki Shari'a schools, 'a woman is utterly incompetent to enter into a marriage contract either herself or for another even though her guardian should authorize her to do so. A father can contract the marriage of his virgin daughter without asking her consent whatever her age' (Verma 1988: 24).

5. Child Marriage: Islam authorizes and legalizes the marriage of female children and underage girls (Surat Al-Talaq 65: 4).
6. Islam allows Muslim men to marry Christian and Jewish women without forcing them to change their religions. However, it strictly forbidden for Muslim women to marry men from other religions.
7. Islam allows Muslim men to practice sex with their female slaves without marrying them. Some Muslim clerics extended this licence and included today's maidservants working in Arab countries. Most probably, the sanction is based on the case of prophet Muhammad and his maidservant, Maria the Coptic.

No Minimum Age for Marriage:

This is because the prophet Muhammad had married Aisha at the age of six and slept with her when she was nine years old. The Qur'an allows the girl to get married before she reaches the age of having her menstruation. Qur'an states, "Such of your women as have passed the age of monthly courses, for them the prescribed period, if ye have any doubts, is three months, and for those who have no courses (it is the same): for those who carry (life within their wombs), their period is until they deliver their burdens: and for those who fear Allah, He will make their path easy (Qur'an Surat Al-Talaq 65: 4). The commentator Ibn Kathir explains this verse as follows; there are three kinds of women, those who are grown old and their periods ceased and those small girls who do not yet have their periods. The old women and the underage girls who have not yet menstruated if they get married and divorced they have to stay three months before they are allowed to get married again. The third type of women is those who still have their periods or are pregnant. Those women have to stay three months and ten days before they remarry.

CHAPTER 4

THIGHING OF THE CHILD BRIDE

Sheikh Faiz bin Ahmed bought a house in Asmara and transferred Iffat Khan and "her uncle" to the home. Then, he found an Eritrean Mazoon and asked him to bring two witnesses to his house to conduct the marriage ceremony with his young Indian fiancée. Islamic law would not require Iffat to sign her marriage contract. According to the Shari'a law, "A woman is utterly incompetent to enter into a marriage contract either herself or for another even though her guardian should authorize her to do so. A father can contract the marriage of his virgin daughter without asking her consent whatever her age" (Verma 1988: 24). Since Iffat Khan was a virgin, her consent was not required. When her mother was contracted in marriage to Sabir, the Islamic law required her consent because she wasn't a virgin. In some Muslim countries, a Muslim widow or divorcee would not be forced into another marriage without her consent.

When the Eritrean Mazoon arrived, with his two witnesses, Sheikh Ahmed and Sabir signed the marriage contract. As her uncle, Sabir was considered the guardian of Iffat Khan. Muhammad said no marriage without wali (guardian), and two male witnesses. The prophet said further that if a woman gets married without her guardian's consent she is a prostitute. Somehow, Muhammad exempted himself from this law when he married Zainab bint Jahsh and Safiya bint Huaya. In case of Zainab, he claimed that Allah became her wali and married her to him and Safiya had no one left to be her guardian because Muhammad had already killed her father, husband, brother, and all her Jewish relatives. The Prophet Muhammad (peace and blessings of Allah be upon him) said: *"Any woman who marries without the permission of her wali, her marriage is invalid, her marriage is invalid, her marriage is invalid"* (Reported by al-Tirmizi, 1021 and others; it is an authentic hadith). According to the Shari'a the woman is not acceptable as a wali or a witness in a marriage contract, nor can a mother be a wali or a witness for her own daughter to marry. The Prophet (saws) said, *"A woman may not give another woman in marriage, nor may a woman give herself in marriage"* (Ibn Majah, al-Bayhaqi and others—verified to be authentic by al-Albaani). The Prophet (peace and blessings of Allah be upon him) also said, *"No woman may conduct the marriage contract of another woman, and no woman can conduct the marriage contract on behalf of her own self, because the zaaniyah (fornicatress, adulteress) is the one who arranges things on her own behalf"* (Reported by Ibn Majah, 1782). Therefore, in case of his marriage to Safiya, Muhammad either broke the law and he married to a prostitute or somehow considered himself above the law. If the girl's father was deceased, then it would fall to her brother, grandfather, or uncle to be the signatory. If she had no father, brother, grandfather, uncle, or any male relative then the judge of the Shari'a court shall sign her marriage contract. In other words, by way of the Shari'a, a widow would have her nine-year-old son become her guardian and he would sign any contracts in her behalf. If he could not write, his thumbprint will suffice. Shari'a law also allows a boy to get married when he reaches the age of nine. There is, however, no minimum age for a girl. A father, then, is allowed to contract his one year old daughter in marriage if he so desired.

When Iffat Khan was contracted in marriage to the seventy-year-old husband, she was seven years old, almost eight. She had no idea what marriage was. She was not even informed that she was to become the wife of Sheikh Ahmed. The Eritrean Mazoon made up the marriage contract, issued the certificate, received his fees and left. As soon as the Mazoon and the two witnesses left, the *EVIL* old man decided to imitate the example of his prophet Muhammad. He took his child-bride to his bedroom and asked his Pakistani pimp to translate his first words to his child-bride. Through his interpreter, he told Iffat that she had become his wife. Iffat did not understand what he meant by "wife." Then, he told her that he was not going to harm her. He told her that he was going to give her beautiful gifts if she agreed to remove her clothes and show him her underwear. Iffat refused. He added that he would give her beautiful Barbie dolls and golden ornaments. Then, he opened a cupboard and showed her some lovely dolls, golden necklace, and bangles.

The child liked the beautiful dolls and ornaments. She took them from his hands. While she was playing with the dolls and putting on her ornaments the evil old man began to touch her body and lustfully feel her up. Then, he began to remove her dress. Iffat did not resist. She was scared that if she did not allow him to remove her clothes, he would take away the beautiful dolls and ornaments that he had given her. When he stripped her of her outer dress and left her in her underwear, the old man ordered his pimp to go out and lock the bedroom from the outside.

The evil Saudi was prepared; he had various kinds of chocolates, candies, and cookies. He also purchased lovely dolls, ornaments, dresses and shoes. He bought some games too. He filled the cupboard with every kind of attractive gift tempting to a small child like Iffat. Then, he began to coerce her with more tempting gifts. After she allowed him to remove her dress, he asked her to sit on his lap. When she refused to obey him, he showed her more dolls and chocolates. When she wanted to take them from his hands, he held them back. He used his arms to motion for her to come sit on his lap or he would not give them to her. Iffat obeyed him and sat on his lap. When he began to feel her body, kiss her and touch her privates, Iffat got scared and tried to run away from him. Of course, he restrained her and promised to give her more gifts. Then, he opened his garment and showed her his privates.

Iffat refused to look at his private parts, closed her eyes, and began to cry. He let go of her and he allowed her to get up from his lap. He stood up, went to the child-sized cupboard, and opened all the drawers and doors. Then, he showed her many more dolls, ornaments, candies, and cookies. He waved his hand and invited her to come and select whatever she would like. Tempted by the gifts, Iffat went to the cupboard and began to grab whatever she liked. While she was bending over selecting all the fascinating and colorful gifts she had never seen before and would like to have, he came up from behind and began to "thigh" her. Iffat did not understand what he was doing to her, so she just continued to explore the cupboard.

That day the seven-year-old girl saw things she should not have seen at her age, and she was sexually abused the way no child should ever be. Only pedophiles would contemplate schemes that culminate in the ruination of a young girl's childhood. Little by little, the evil old man blackmailed Iffat until he had accomplished his first "thighing" of the innocent child and ejaculated all over her backside and down her thighs. Then, he allowed her to take her collection and go to the washroom and wash herself and then play with her dolls. Sheikh Ahmed felt no guilt. His conscience was clear because he knew his prophet Muhammad used to do the same thing to his six-year-old child-bride, Aisha bint Abu Bakr.

CHAPTER 5

CHILD-RAPE

The reader might wonder why I felt the need to narrate the details of what the Saudi did to Rayhana's little girl. I wanted the reader to know and feel the pain, that any underage girl who gets raped by a Muslim man would experience, while his evil act is condoned, even encouraged by the example of the prophet Muhammad *vide* the Qur'an in Surat 65 verse 4. To this end, in the previous chapter, I showed how the old Saudi accomplished this with a child who had no carnal knowledge, and did not react, as there was 'no pain' in thighing.

Iffat Khan was still a child and obviously not developed enough, neither physiologically or psychologically for sex with an adult, much less, one who was not inclined to be gentle. For her, it was simply a horrifying nightmare and unbearable torture. When the evil old man began to rape her, she felt like someone was inserting a knife in her private parts, a deep wound tearing her up inside while she screamed. Thighing was painless, and her young intuition already told her something was amiss. But a child's resolve will crumble when coerced day after day, occasion after occasion. He tried to get her to fellate him, failing which, he resorted to harsher methods. He made her starve for many hours, and he refused to give her water.

He locked her up in a small room, and he denied her basic human needs. For more than twenty-four hours, he imprisoned her in a room, with no lights and windows. She was not allowed the use of a washroom and had to use the same room as a toilet. Up against, what must be for a small child, insurmountable odds and pressure, she agreed to do anything he willed. When she allowed him to use her hand to masturbate him, he gave her food, cold drinks, and some pretty gifts. Every evil deviation that came into his dirty mind, he used it to satisfy his lust. What he did to her for seven months did not only harm her physically, but it destroyed the child within. He replaced the innocence of a child with ugliness and shame that she would have to carry with her for the rest of her life.

Sex with the old Saudi was exceedingly painful for Iffat. She fought and struggled, but with uncaring, harsh, and brutal methods, he forced himself on her. Sheikh Ahmed, like many evil men, enjoy inflicting pain on his female victims during sex. Some Muslims believe that the Jihad of the woman should be on the bed of her husband. The good Muslim wife was the one who is supposed to feel the pain during sexual intercourse and the noise and sound of distress allows her husband to validate his manhood and strong sexual ability. That is why Muslims in France pay huge sums to French doctors to have their wives made virgins again. A Muslim man in France was prepared to pay a French doctor five thousand dollars in order to re-virginize his wife. He enjoyed having her re-virginized and deflowered over and over again.

The act of penetrating a woman's hymen causes bleeding and pain, for some more than others, especially the very young. Evil and perverted is the mind of a husband who enjoys causing pain to his wife and seeing the blood running out of her vagina? Muslim men get these twisted ideas directly from the teachings of Islam about the virgins of paradise. The Qur'an and hadiths simply state that the virgins of paradise remain virgins after intercourse.

"The prophet was asked: 'Do we have sex in paradise? He answered: 'Yes, by him who holds my soul in his hand and it will be done ***dahman, dahman*** *(that is the intercourse done with such shove and disturbance).* ***And when it is finished she will return pure and virgin again*** *" (Haqq & Newton 1996: 17).* According to this hadith, either Allah would stitch up the virgin's vagina immediately after she was devirginized by insertion of the male's penis or he would recreate a new hymen and insert it in her privates.

In fact, in Islam the woman is nothing but a "vagina." The prophet Muhammad said, *"The woman is A'warah. When she goes outside (the house), the devil takes charge of her"* (Tirmizi, Volume II, p. 65). According to this hadith, whenever the woman goes out of her house she is possessed by demons. So, she is dangerous to society, and hence she should be imprisoned inside her house. There is no definition so widely used and accepted among Muslims for defining the woman than, *"The Woman is A'warah."* The term A'warah is defined in the Encyclopedia of Islam as "The external genitals, especially of the female" (Haqq & Newton 1996: 5). So, to put it bluntly, 'a woman, from head to toe, is a big vagina.' Sex occupied the mind of the prophet Muhammad throughout the twenty-five years of preaching his new cult. As if, 72 virgins were not enough, every Muslim man is entitled to 100 young boys that the Qur'an described as diamond-sparkling boys (Surat 52: 24). The Qur'an describes the beautiful young boys as not getting a headache or bleeding. Some Muslim scholars hide the fact that the Qur'an has promised these 100 beautiful boys for sex. They argue that, the purpose of the boys in paradise is to serve the faithful. However, if the beautiful boys are to *serve* the faithful (Muslims) only, why then does the Qur'an say that they would neither bleed nor have headaches? It is very clear that the Qur'an meant the young beautiful boys would not bleed during sex because there is no hymen to tear.

Sheikh Ahmed did not live for seven months in Eritrea. He kept his Pakistani Qolam as guard, to keep his child-bride imprisoned in his Asmara house. (Qolam means a male-slave and Khadim means a female-slave. No wonder the maidservant is called Khadamiah). African and Asian Muslims show high respect for their Arab masters/employers and look at them as superior to them as if those Arabs are Brahmas and they are Untouchables in a Hindu society. The Arabs are revered and exalted because the Prophet of Islam was an Arab. This stupidity led some Black Africans like Sudanese, Somalians, and Mauritanians to claim that they are Arabs too. The Pakistani chauffeur was such a faithful and obedient slave to his Arab master. He was prepared to do anything to please him. The old Saudi would spend a few days every month with his imprisoned child-bride and then return to his country. He hired three Eritrean Khadamiat/maidservants for Iffat; one for cooking, one for cleaning, and one for washing. He also kept a guard at the gate of his big mansion. Whatever food she desired and whatever clothes she wanted was provided. She was decked in gold from head to toe.

It is not hard to imagine how little Iffat felt like a bird in a gilded cage. Since stepping foot inside the mansion, she had not been allowed to go outside the compound of the prison. It was a mansion but not a home; a palace of terror instead of a safe and loving environment. Many times, she begged Sabir to allow her to go outside and play in the grass with her dolls but he refused. She cried and begged the pedophile to take her to where her mother was, but he would sharply deny her request. He simply countered her pleas by telling her the Saudi police had taken her mother to a place very far away, because she had done something bad. He refused to tell her what her mother had done or when she was going to come back and get her. He did not like to talk about her mother, as much as he used to love her mother; he began to hate even hearing her name.

For several months, the evil Saudian thighed and molested his child-bride. When she reached the age of nine, he began to prepare her for vaginal sex. He intended to teach her about sex, or at least the part she had to play before he would start raping her. He brought porn movies and forced her to watch them with him. She didn't like them, but she agreed to after going through another round of his starvation and imprisonment techniques. He made her understand what he wanted to do with her, by example of the sex scenes in the pornographic movies. When he tried to rape her, she resisted and fought him off. He discovered that she had grown up and was much stronger than before. She was nine years old by then. So to get her into compliance, he simply broke her resistance by withholding all food and water. Crying and begging got her nowhere. He simply repeated his old line that if she didn't do exactly what he wanted, he would not give her any food or water. Iffat refused to yield to his requests and told him she wanted to die.

For two days, the small child went without food and water. She thought that she would starve to death and go to heaven to be with her father and mother. When her father committed suicide, Iffat was told by her mother and grandmother that her father died and went to heaven and was living in a better place. She believed that the same police officers who had beat her mother and did all those bad things to her, had come back, taken her away, and this time killed her for real. In her mind, it was simply better to die and go be with her parents, than continue living in the house of horrors with a nasty old bad man that made her do all those things she didn't like to do.

The old Saudi was furious and continually struck her face and flogged her with a big whip. When done with his revenge beatings, he would lock her up in the dark room again. A child like Iffat, or any other, is not capable of out-maneuvering the mind of a seasoned professional. He simply resumed his methods, and he eventually got exactly what he wanted.

On the third day, Iffat lost her strength and was no longer able to move around. Half conscious, the old man came in and removed her dress and underwear and began to rape her. She could not move a limb to stave him off. Sadly, her ability to feel pain was undiminished. The old man tried but could not penetrate her, because she was just too under-developed. Not giving up, he used his finger to widen her vagina. His finger felt like a sharp metal rod forcing itself inside her. She wanted to cry, but her dried up mouth and weak body could not scream out in pain. Only a steady flow of tears poured out of her eyes. Fingering a female child is very common in Arab countries.

The old Saudi man tried repeatedly to penetrate her, but he could not. He was very advanced in his years and had lost much of his vigor, but was determined to penetrate her by all means. He knew his fingers alone would not widen her vaginal canal, but he had brought along many sex toys. He changed his fingering method and began to use a plastic penis. His new method worked and he was able to insert half of the plastic penis inside the small girl's vagina. The blood ran out of her vagina and turned everything around it red. She felt as if he was using a sharp knife and sawing her in half. The pain was unbearable.

She lost her consciousness. He did not bother to find out whether she had lost consciousness or had died. His lust blinded him and he decided to penetrate her even if she was already a corpse. He mounted her seemingly lifeless body, and began to penetrate her. Finally, the wicked scum was able to insert half of his male organ in his victim's bleeding vagina and sawed away until he ejaculated. After that, he called his Pakistani Qolam and asked him to help him take his wife to the hospital.

It is a very common phenomenon in countries like Eritrea, Sudan, and Somalia for brides to be taken to the hospital on their first wedding night because of excessive bleeding. Hospitals considered such cases normal because of the widespread custom of female genital mutilation. If a new bride is wheeled into a hospital with an injury due to sexual intercourse with her husband, it is not considered rape nor is it considered a serious case. In Iffat's case, she was taken to the intensive care unit because she was dehydrated and starved. She was fed through her veins. She remained in a coma for three days before she came back to life. The hospital did not consider her case criminal in nature and treated her until she recovered. After five days, Iffat was transferred back to her former prison.

As soon as the hospital discharged Iffat and she was brought back to the mansion, the old man began to rape her again. This time, she felt the pain more than before. She felt more pain because she was fully conscious and the wounds in her privates were still not fully healed. She screamed at the top of her voice and resisted, but she was not able to stop him because her body was still weak and feeble. She felt terrible pain when his male organ began to press hard on the surface of her wounded vagina. This time, it felt like salt on an open wound. She bit his shoulder and scratched his face with her nails. She hit his back with her fists and kicked at his legs. Nothing she did could get him off her or prevent him from forcing his penis into her vagina.

As he began to penetrate her, she fainted. As before, the old Saudi did not bother to find out why she stopped resisting and screaming. He just continued to press on until he had fully inserted his penis inside her vagina. This time, he did more damage and after he ejaculated, blood pooled around her body. For the second time, he called his Pakistani pimp and asked him to treat the child-bride. This time, he decided not to take her to the hospital. He was afraid that she might be hospitalized again for a few days. He would not tolerate to wait until she got discharged. He wanted to enjoy raping her no matter what her health condition. He just told his pimp to clean up the blood around her vagina and to apply Dettol to stop the bleeding. The Pakistani Qolam followed the orders of his Arab master and began cleaning her up and applying the Dettol. After that, he used cold water to revive Iffat…

CHAPTER 6

SHAMA ABD AL-BARI AHMED

From the time, Rayhana Khan was arrested and sentenced to be stoned to death by the Shari'a court, and for more than two years and ten months in the Jeddah Jail, one could have written hundreds of books of her suffering and abuse and the horrible crimes that had been committed against her daughter in her absence. Rayhana lost half of her weight and beauty. She lost interest in everything. She concluded that even her daughter had believed the false charges and disowned her. She had no address to send letters to her children and mother in Bombay. She beheld hundreds of horrifying dreams and visions. For three years, she never ceased to see the visions of Sakina Abu Islam. That poor Pakistani girl, as if remained living with her inside her brain. She appeared to her every night in her dream and begged for mercy and help. Very often during the day, she saw her vision. Rayhana felt as if she were possessed by Sakina Abu Islam. Many times, Rayhana saw in her dream scary bearded men chasing her with stones and bricks trying to catch her and stone her to death. Whenever, she saw that nightmare she woke up in the middle of the night and began to scream on the top of her voice and call for rescue.

Sometimes, she saw visions of ghosts during the day attacking her in her cell. Those visions made her believe that she was living in a haunted cell. She became like a madwoman. Many times, the guards thought that she had lost her senses. She screamed and begged them to take her out of her cell and keep her in a place with other inmates. The guards ignored her requests and considered her insane. In fact, the guards and other inmates accused her of being possessed by ‘Afareet (In Islam ‘Afareet are evil jinns who are large, powerful and very crafty. Singular is Ifreet. See the Qur’an, Surat Al-Naml 27: 39). There were many episodes where, in exasperation and despair, Rayhana would bash her head against the wall until the guards would come and put her in chains. Anyone who had seen Rayhana Khan prior to her entering prison would not have believed that she was the same person.

Rayhana’s suffering was compounded by her pregnancy. Seven months from the day she was sentenced, she delivered a baby boy in prison. It was nothing short of a miracle that the baby survived in her womb after she had been hammered mercilessly by the Saudi police during her interrogation. She was tied up and flogged on her back and legs. She was slapped and spit upon, regularly. She was treated as a liar and dirty prostitute. They forced her to admit crimes she had not committed. They used a Pakistani translator who hated every Indian on the surface of the earth, even Indian Muslims. He added things she did not even say. He called her every filthy word he knew in Urdu. She tried to convince the Jeddah police that she was brutally raped by two Saudi police officers on the day she arrived in Saudi, but to no avail. The least evil that happened to Rayhana inside the interrogation lock-up she was raped by some Saudi policemen. Some Muslim policemen believed that a condemned Muslim woman might go to heaven if she did not get raped prior to her execution. Therefore, as soon as the Shari’a court passed the stoning sentence on her some evil policemen made it their religious obligation to ensure that the “filthy Indian prostitute” would not die and go to paradise to defile it.

For two years and ten months, not a single person came to visit Rayhana Khan in prison. It was as if she had fallen off the face of the earth and was exiled to another planet and no one even knew who she was or where she had come from. One day a Saudi Human Rights Activist came to her cell and talked to her through an Indian translator. When she narrated her story in tears, both the Saudi human rights activist and the translator wept. They believed every word she had told them; that she had for three years, waited for her execution even though she had not committed any crime. She had not indulged in consensual sex with anyone since her husband died. She told them that the two Saudi policemen raped her in exchange for the safety of her little girl. She told them that they raped and beat her so severely, she became unconscious and almost died. If it wasn't for her daughter and the kind Saudi Bedouins, she would have died and her body would have been buried amongst the moving sands of the desert.

After living a month in the tent of the kind Bedouins, she traveled with them to the city, homeless and without food. She was beaten mercilessly by a correctional police officer, but she was saved by a kind Indian man. The man told her that he would not allow her to live in his apartment unless she would agree to marry him on paper. She believed him and agreed. Finally, her Saudi sponsor somehow found her in a beauty salon and took her to his house. The Pakistani chauffeur of her sponsor also convinced her to marry him on paper but she would be the kept wife of her Saudi sponsor. Neither of these two men with whom she was married on paper had had sex with her. She said because of her fear of being pregnant she agreed to be the kept-wife of her Saudi sponsor but was arrested the next day. Rayhana concluded her narration by saying that *"I have never been a prostitute in all my life and I have never slept with any man except my husband who died when I was in India."* Moreover, Rayhana informed them that she also got raped by some Saudi policemen during her interrogation and shortly after her trial. Rayhana's story convinced the Saudi female human rights activist that she had conceived the baby she gave birth to while in jail, by one of the two Saudi police officers who had raped her on the day she arrived in Saudi Arabia. Touched, the human rights activist promised Rayhana that she would write her story and send it to the international human rights organizations and foreign feminist groups.

Rayhana begged the female human rights activist that interviewed her to search for her daughter and if she found her to convince her to come and visit her before she was stoned to death. She lamented that she did not know the address of the house where she left her daughter when she got arrested and thrown behind bars. She remembered only the name of her sponsor and the name of his Pakistani chauffeur.

However, the human rights activist was able to obtain from the prison officials the address and phone number of Rayhana's sponsor. When Rayhana was arrested, Sheikh Ahmed gave the police his business address. The human rights activist decided to go to his office and ask him about the daughter of his Indian maidservant who was in jail awaiting her execution. Before she visited his business, she phoned the office and asked for an appointment. His secretary duly informed her that Sheikh Ahmed was in Eritrea, and he would be back after a week

The human rights activist who interviewed Rayhana Khan was known as Shama Abd Al-Bari Ahmed. She was born to a Saudi father and an American mother. Her father studied in America. While he was doing his Masters in Medicine, he fell in love with one of his American classmates. Shama's parents did not marry, but lived as common law partners for a few years. As soon as her father completed his studies, he left America and returned to his country. He abandoned her mother and told her that he was going to his homeland and then he would come back to marry her. He told her that he would then, take her and their daughter to live with him in the Kingdom of Saudi Arabia. He never did come back or contact his girlfriend, nor did he inquire about his daughter. Shama was raised by her American mother. Her mother fell in love again with an Arab immigrant from Iraq. Her Iraqi boyfriend asked her to marry him and she agreed. Shama's stepfather escaped from Iraq while Saddam Hussein was in power. He came to the United Sates as a political refugee. However, after the fall of Saddam's regime and the occupation of Iraq, her stepfather convinced her mother to go with him to his country.

Shama did not go with her mother and stepfather to Iraq. She lived with her grandparents until she finished her Bachelor degree in Arts. She completed double majors in Justice and Human Rights and Religious Studies. While she was studying religion, Shama took some courses on Women in Islam. Through these courses, she learned about the misogynistic teachings of Muhammad about women. She decided to do her Master's degree in Religious Studies and specialize in the State of Women in Islam. She chose for her fieldwork, the Kingdom of Saudi Arabia, for two specific reasons. Firstly, women in Saudi Arabia are treated like chattel (personal property) and imprisoned in their houses as dangerous creatures. The second reason was simply, that Shama wanted to find her Saudi father. Although, she knew that her mother had bitter feelings toward her father because he had abandoned them a long time ago, Shama still longed to meet her father. She was a very small child when he abandoned them. She only knew him through photographs.

Shama had visited the Middle East several times during her studies in America, and she had spent most of her summer vacations with her mother in Iraq. She traveled to many Arab countries like Jordan, Lebanon, Syria, Egypt, Morocco, and Iraq. She was able to pick up the dialects of those countries and learned to speak Arabic. As part of her curriculum, Shama began to take Arabic language courses. In that way, she learned the Arabic language and was able to communicate well with Arab women. After completing her Masters in several courses of study, Shama decided to travel to Saudi Arabia and spend six months there and complete her fieldwork.

When she applied for a visa to the Kingdom of Saudi Arabia, Shama's application was rejected because she was a single woman and unmarried. She was so disappointed when she learned the reason for the rejection of her visa. Shama then convinced her American boyfriend to travel to Saudi Arabia with her. When they applied for their visas, the applications were rejected because they were living as common law partners and not legally married. Once again, Shama convinced her boyfriend to marry her. After that condition was met, Shama and her American husband flew to Jeddah and stayed in a small motel. In fact, Shama wanted to go to Mecca, but because she was a Roman Catholic Christian she was told by the Saudi Embassy she could not go to any of the holy cities.

Shama faced so many difficulties while she was trying to learn about the women in Saudi Arabia. Most of the Saudi women whom she tried to interview downright refused to talk to her. The husbands of some of the women threatened to call the police on her and some tried to harm her. Nevertheless, she was able to interview some maidservants who came from countries like Egypt, Lebanon, Somalia, Sudan, Indonesia, Pakistan, and India. After spending three months without gaining sufficient information and data, Shama discovered that the Jeddah Women's Prison was allowing foreign journalists and reporters to interview the female inmates. Therefore, she decided to go to the jail and look for some Saudi women to interview them. When she reached the women's jail, she was told that she could talk only with the condemned female prisoners. She was not allowed to meet or talk with any inmate who was awaiting trial. This made no sense to her but she was told that she might change the course of the trial by supplying information to the suspect.

In due course, Shama met a few Saudi women and interviewed them. Some of the interviewed women were waiting to be stoned for marital infidelities or faced beheading for crimes of murder. There were some unmarried women who were waiting to be flogged a hundred lashes for committing various forms of fornication and still others were in jail awaiting amputation of their hands for stealing. Some of the convicted women admitted their crimes, whereas others claimed to be innocent. Some said they had been raped and impregnated by their rapists, but they could not prove the identity of their rapists. One young Saudi woman said that she had been impregnated by her brother's friend who raped her in his house, when she went with her brother to visit his friend's sister. Although she witnessed the crime, which took place in the women's section of the friend's house, the friend's sister denied any knowledge when interrogated by the police. While she was getting raped her brother was sitting in the men's section clueless of what was going on in the women's section. Another Saudi girl said that she was raped by her own uncle in his house. Yet, another fourteen-year-old Saudi girl swore by Allah that she got raped by her own cousin. The last Saudi girl that Shama managed to interview claimed that she got raped inside public women's washrooms while her father and brother were waiting for her outside. Her rapist entered the women's washrooms dressed up in black woman's niqab. Shama knew that she could do nothing to stop these women from being cruelly punished by the Shari'a court. She came to know also, that Saudi Arabia would not allow DNA testing to verify or disprove any of the women's claims.

On her rounds, Shama came across Rayhana Khan and her baby boy. She discovered that Rayhana's crime was unique. It was the first time she had come across a woman being jailed for marrying two husbands at the same time. When Rayhana in tears, narrated her tragic story, Shama was extraordinarily touched by her situation. She was convinced Rayhana was innocent. However, she knew that she could do nothing to save her from execution. Nonetheless, she promised that she would find out what her sponsor had done with her daughter. She said further, that if her little girl was still with her sponsor, she would try to convince him to allow her to come and see her mother. When she returned to the motel, Shama shared the story of Rayhana with her husband. Her husband also was puzzled by the nature of the charges. How could a Muslim woman in such a strict society think of marrying two men in less than a couple of weeks? Therefore, both Shama and her husband doubted the charges. They believed that Rayhana was somehow manipulated by the two men. However, they knew that they could do nothing to help her.

In her mind, Shama knew the only thing she could do to help Rayhana was to fulfill her wish of seeing her daughter before she was stoned to death. So, she phoned Sheikh Ahmed's office and was told that she would be contacted upon his return from Asmara. Shama waited for two weeks, but did not receive any call from Sheikh Ahmed's office. She thought that the secretary forgot to inform his boss of her request for an appointment. Instead of telephoning his office again, she decided to visit the office in person to inquire about the daughter of Rayhana. She expected that if the sponsor was still away she might be able to get information about the daughter from the secretary, or they may provide her a phone number for his personal residence. Shama was also interested in meeting Sheikh Ahmed's wife and interviewing her. Rayhana had already told her how she was ill-treated by the wife of her sponsor.

Shama like any other woman in Saudi Arabia was not permitted to walk out of her home without her husband or male Muhram accompanying her. Like them, she was not allowed to walk on the streets with her face uncovered. When Shama and her husband arrived at the office, she found Sheikh Ahmed had returned from Eritrea. As soon as his secretary told him that a young white woman had come to see him, the evil man immediately began to think of sex. He shared that erroneous Arab belief that white women were free-spirited, and anyone could take them to bed. He told his secretary to send the white woman to him alone and **to** tell her husband to wait outside for her. Therefore, as soon as Shama walked inside his office he stood up and offered his hand to her. Then, in a very friendly and polite manner, he pulled up an armchair and offered for her to sit down.

"My name is Shama Thomson. However, my maiden name is Shama Abd Al-Bari Ahmed. I am an American, but my father is Saudi."

The evil Saudi had a son by the name of Abd Al-Bari Ahmed who studied medicine in the United States of America, but he failed to connect the dots because at this time he was thinking through his penis and not using his brain.

"I am glad to meet you Shama Thumbsun and whatever help you need I am under your service."

"In fact, I have come to inquire about the daughter of your maidservant Rayhana Khan..."

Shama, like most Westerners, tended to look people in the eye when talking to them. Understanding the cultural differences, she loved to see the effects of her words on the eyes and face of the person she was talking to. As soon as she mentioned *"the daughter of your maidservant Rayhana Khan,"* she saw Sheikh Ahmed's eyes react as if someone had just sprayed them with mace and his face appeared red and irritated. His smile disappeared, instantly, and in its place, an angry mood surfaced. She could see, clearly, that her words had disturbed him. His friendly manner was replaced by an angry and hostile attitude.

"Who are you and who gave you permission to come and ask me about my maidservant's daughter?"

"The mother of Iffat Khan requested me to inquire about her daughter. She sent me on this errand and asked me to tell you to

allow her daughter to come and visit her in jail before she is stoned to death."

"I don't want anything to do with that Indian prostitute!"

"I haven't asked you about your maidservant's crime. As a mother, Rayhana Khan has the right to see her child. Where is her daughter now?"

"I don't have her daughter with me."

"She said she had left her child in your house when she was arrested. Therefore, her mother left her daughter under your care and custody."

"I have sent her daughter a long time ago to her relatives in India."

"How could you send a seven-year-old child to India without the permission of her mother?"

"Who are you to question me on what I did three years ago?"

"I have told you that Rayhana Khan has given me permission to locate the whereabouts of her daughter. At least tell me how the little girl returned to India. No airlines would allow a seven-year-old girl to fly without an adult accompanying her."

"I had sent her to Bombay along with my Pakistani chauffeur."

"In that case I would like to meet your Pakistani chauffeur and talk to him."

"Why do you want to meet him and what do you want to ask him about?"

It was already clear to Shama that Sheikh Ahmed was lying to her. Her woman's intuition told her that the old Arab man was hiding the daughter somewhere and doing something evil to her. Therefore, she decided not to leave his office until she got something concrete about Iffat.

"Yes, I must meet him and find out about Rayhana's daughter."

"He left Saudi Arabia and returned to his country two years ago."

"Okay, I will need proof that he took Iffat Khan to Bombay."

"Which proof do you want? Are you a policewoman to interrogate me in such a manner?"

"Sir, I am not a policewoman. I am a human rights activist. I am inquiring about someone's child. As a mother, Rayhana Khan has

the right to know where her daughter is and to meet her before her execution. If you don't give me some proof I am going to go directly to the police."

In response to Shama's threat, Sheikh Ahmed touched the speaker on his phone and called in his secretary. He then told him to pull from out the old files, copies of the tickets belonging to Iffat Khan and Sabir Ibrahim Shah and show them to the white woman. He kept those copies on hand because he expected that someday someone might come knocking on his door asking him about Iffat. Shama followed the secretary and went out with him but came back in less than ten minutes.

"The copies of those tickets showed that Iffat and Sabir flew to Asmara via Bombay and Manila. The final destination on the tickets is Eritrea and not India."

"Yes, the final destination on the tickets is Eritrea, but Iffat's flight ended at Bombay while my chauffeur continued his trip to Asmara. The Indian Consulate rejected the application of my chauffeur for a visiting visa because he is a Pakistani."

"How did Iffat travel from Bombay international airport to her family's house and who came to receive her?"

"My Indian client Mr. Muhammad Khan came to the airport and received her and took her to her family's house."

Shama wanted to ask Sheikh Ahmed to give her the phone number of his Indian client in Bombay, but worried she might be going too far in her inquiry. Instead, she decided to go to Rayhana and give her the information she collected about her daughter. She figured the information about the whereabouts of Iffat Khan might very well be true. She then thanked Sheik Ahmed and left his office. The wicked old man did not believe the white woman was fully convinced of his story. He was worried that she might go to the police and somehow implicate him in the disappearance of the child. Therefore, he decided to take drastic measures to stop her before she was able to get him into some serious trouble with the police. As soon as Shama and her husband left his office, he rushed out and entered his vehicle. He asked his new Somali chauffeur to follow the taxi bearing the white couple. Then, he ordered his driver to run into the white woman and her husband the moment they got out of the taxi. He told him he was to hit the white woman in particular. The Somali driver was reluctant to follow the orders of his Kafeel/master, but when Sheikh Ahmed wrote him a check for a huge sum of money, gave it to him, and promised to testify in court in his behalf and swear the accident wasn't his fault, he agreed to hit the white woman.

When the taxi reached the motel, Shama came out first, but her husband remained inside the taxi to pay the cab fare. Then, he paid the taxi driver and got out. While he was emerging out of the taxi, he saw a Mercedes driving at full speed and hit his wife. Shama's body was flung into the air and landed onto the street. The loud impact of the car and human flesh was impossible to ignore and every person walking along the street stopped and looked. Shama's husband could not believe his eyes. When he saw what had befallen his wife, it was clear to him that the Mercedes targeted his wife and hit her with the intention to kill her. He took his pen and jotted down the number of the Mercedes and then ran to his wife. He saw blood everywhere. She was lying on her back, motionless, and the burqa came out of her head and her face and hair became visible. Her husband began to scream and call for help. He took out his cell phone and dialed 911. When he did not hear any dial tone, he remembered that he wasn't in his country. He tried to talk to the crowd in English, but no one understood him. He called for a taxi, but no driver was prepared to stop and take the body of his wife in his car. Everyone was scared to come near the body of the white woman. After a long wait, a police car came, followed by an ambulance. Unfortunately, Shama died before she ever reached the hospital...

CHAPTER 7

SENATOR THOMASON

Shama's husband was Joshua Thomason. His father was a Senator in the United States Congress. Joshua was against the idea of his girlfriend traveling to Saudi Arabia and doing her fieldwork in such a backward society and among barbaric men who looked at women like meat and treated them worst than dogs. It was his love for Shama that made him rearrange his life and agree to travel with her to the Kingdom of Saudi Arabia. At first, Shama wanted to go all by herself to Saudi Arabia to do her fieldwork and search for her father. When the Saudi Embassy rejected her visa because she had no husband or any close male relative to travel with her, Joshua felt inwardly relieved because now she wanted him to come along with her. He knew that his girlfriend would need a man to protect her from sexually perverted men who could see nothing in the woman except a vagina.

After their arrival in Saudi Arabia, Joshua felt as if they had landed in an open prison. Everything was different and life in the KSA was understandably boring for Shama and Joshua. There were no entertainment venues, no movie theaters, nightclubs, or sport bars. Whatever liquor they brought with them was seized at the Jeddah International Airport. Since their arrival, they were not able to find a place to buy even a can of beer. Whenever they went out for food, they found the restaurant inevitably divided into two sections; the men's and the women's section. The local women looked like roving phantoms in their huge black Abayas (cloaks). Women were not allowed to speak in public because the woman's voice was A'warah, which made Joshua and Shama distinctly uneasy. They were afraid that underneath one of those moving black shrouds, there might be a male terrorist just waiting for the chance to attack them simply because they were White people from America. Being Americans made them an easy target and vulnerable to being kidnapped by terrorists. Anyone would forgive Joshua for counting the days his wife would finish her fieldwork and they could return to a free and civilized society.

Joshua had a degree in law and specialized in international law. The brutal and cruel murder of his wife had just turned his life upside down. He had no one to support him in his hour of need or stand by his side through such a tragic event in his life. He wept bitterly when the hospital declared his wife dead. After overcoming the impact of her death, he made two phone calls. First, he called Shama's mother in Bagdad and broke the sad news to her. After that, he phoned his father and informed him about the murder of his wife and the reason behind her assassination. That day while they were returning from the office of Sheikh Ahmed, Shama narrated to Joshua what had happened between her and the sponsor of the maidservant who sent her to inquire about what happened to her then seven-year-old daughter. She even used her cell phone and recorded every word they spoke to each other. After hearing the conversion between his wife and the old Saudi businessman, which Shama translated to him, Joshua concluded that the Saudi was hiding the little girl somewhere and more than likely raping her under the pretense of marriage. Therefore, Joshua convinced Shama to take the case of the little girl to the police. Shama was planning to go to the police as soon as she had met with Rayhana again to tell her the information she had collected from her Saudi sponsor about her daughter.

Joshua's father told his son to leave Saudi Arabia as soon as possible and return to the United States. The father was worried that the same person who murdered his daughter-in-law might also try to kill his son. Joshua refused to listen to his father and decided to stay in Jeddah until the person who killed his wife was brought to justice. The first report that Joshua heard from the police regarding the car that hit and killed his wife was that the driver was a young Somalian by the name of Abd Al-Gadir Abrahim. He was arrested under the charges of drinking and driving and vehicular homicide. The report also showed that the car belonged to a Saudi businessman by the name of Sheikh Faiz bin Ahmed. The young Somali was the chauffeur of the wealthy businessman. Sheikh Ahmed was in the car when the accident took place. Joshua rejected this trumped up story because he had met the young Somali in the office of Sheikh Ahmed and spoke with him. The young man had approached Joshua while he was waiting for his wife and requested Joshua's help in emigrating to the United States of America. From his speech, Joshua knew that the Somali wasn't drunk.

Joshua went to the police and informed them that the story of the young man drinking and driving wasn't true. He said the story was made up and meant to cover up the crime committed against his wife by Sheikh Ahmed to keep her from exposing him to the police. Then, he told them about the case of the Indian maidservant and her daughter. The police rejected Joshua's claim as preposterous and told him to leave it for the courts to decide. Joshua insisted that his statement about the Somali driver should be included in the case. The police saw otherwise. When the police refused to include his statement, Joshua threatened to take the matter to a higher authority. Then, he told the Saudi police that his father was a Senator in the Congress of the United States of America and he would use the authority of his father and report the assassination of his wife to the King of Saudi Arabia.

By revealing that his father was a Congressman to the Saudi police, Joshua had inadvertently exposed his identity and put himself in grave danger. The Saudi policemen placed him under arrest for trying to use the position of his father to subvert their authority. The arrest of the son of an American Senator in Jeddah leaked to the media and spread all over the world. At first, the international media concentrated on the arrest of the son of an American Senator. He was arrested by the Jeddah police under the charge of interfering in the progress of an ongoing investigation and threatening the lawful authority of government officials. The international media was quick to express concern about the safety of a Senator's son inside a Saudi prison. It is a well-known fact that, the jails in Saudi Arabia are full of Al-Qaeda terrorists. Therefore, the son of an American Senator would not fare well at all in a Saudi prison. It also didn't help that Senator Thomason was one of the American congressmen who voted in the favor of the War on Terror in Afghanistan and Iraq.

With the arrest of the American Congressman's son, the White House mobilized the CIA, who in turn, contacted the highest law enforcement agency in the Kingdom of Saudi Arabia to demand the immediate release of the Senator's son. At first, the Saudi authorities refused to release him, but when King Abd Allah stepped in, Joshua Thomason was released and taken directly to the Jeddah international airport and sent off on the next flight.

Joshua Thomason reached the United States of America before the arrival of the body of his murdered wife. His deportation from Saudi Arabia was against his wishes. He was prepared to stay behind and fight and bring to justice those responsible for the death of his late wife. On his arrival in New York, given the circumstances of his incarceration, he was interviewed by many of the leading news desks. Working the media, he related the reason behind the assassination of his wife. Moreover, he also convinced his father to request the CIA to send a qualified team of investigators to probe the suspicious death of an American citizen on Saudi soil.

Shortly after Joshua's arrival, his wife's remains arrived in New York. Shama's mother flew in from Bagdad to attend the funeral of her daughter. When the burial was concluded, a team of seven CIA agents arrived in Jeddah and began their investigation into the murder of Senator Peter Thomason's daughter-in-law. The CIA team had already been briefed by Joshua and had a general idea as to what had happened. Their first move on Saudi soil was to force the Jeddah police to include Joshua's statement, particularly about the Somali chauffeur who had intentionally killed his wife. Joshua stated that he had met the Somali chauffeur and talked to him in the office of the suspect, Sheikh Ahmed, and received his personal card. Joshua gave the card of the Somali man to the CIA team. Joshua had the foresight to hand over the recorded conversation between his late wife and Sheikh Ahmed concerning the Indian maidservant's daughter.

That achieved, the CIA team tried to question the young Somali. The knee jerk reaction of the Jeddah police was to hinder the investigation and prevent any such meeting. When threatened to make this matter known to the royal family, they acquiesced, and allowed them to speak to the detained Somali. Under interrogation by the experienced team of investigators, the Somali changed his statement. He vindicated Joshua's allegation and admitted being sober when he hit the white woman. In an effort to escape culpability, he claimed that he was speeding when he lost control and hit the white woman. The investigative team remained unconvinced of his innocence. The team then informed him that his employer has already made a statement to the effect that he was drunk when he hit the woman. The Somali was shocked. It was clear to him that Sheikh Ahmed had double-crossed him and had no intentions to testify favorably in his behalf. He was under the impression that it was the Jeddah police who had nailed him with the charge of drinking and driving. He thought all the while, Sheikh Ahmed was supporting his claim that he lost control of the car and hit the woman accidentally. In fact, that was what his employer had rehearsed with him over and over again en route to commit their premeditated crime. Crushed, the Somali now saw that Sheikh Ahmed wanted to wash his hands of the matter and use him as a scapegoat. He understood that if he remained quiet and did not expose Sheikh Ahmed, he would either be beheaded or remain in jail indefinitely. The only option open to him was to tell the truth and implicate his employer. He reasoned that they both would be found liable for the crime and sentenced equally or either Sheikh Ahmed would be more culpable because he had masterminded the whole thing, and he himself would merely be an accessory to the crime. So, Abd Al-Gadir took the only option left to him and told the American team the truth, admitting that he had rammed into the woman with the intention of killing her, stating exactly why he had done so.

The CIA did not reveal this new information to the Jeddah police or the media, as investigations were still underway. They demanded to interrogate Sheikh Ahmed. Once they had established that Shama was murdered by Sheikh Ahmed, they needed a motive. Joshua's testimony gave them some idea of the circumstances around Shama's murder, but now they were eager to know who Rayhana Khan was and where the old man had hidden her daughter. Before meeting the old Saudi, they contacted Joshua Thomason and inquired as to where his late wife had met the mother of the missing Indian girl. Joshua told them that Shama met Rayhana Khan in the Jeddah Jail For Women and interviewed her regarding her stoning sentence. Then, he sent them a copy of the interview, which he found in the laptop of his late wife. Through the recorded interview, the CIA team was able to build a rudimentary profile around both Rayhana and her daughter. Their first suspicion was that Sheikh Ahmed accused his Indian maidservant of a false crime and had her sent to jail and sentenced to be stoned to death because he wanted to rape her little daughter. Like Shama and Joshua, the team surmised that Sheikh Ahmed was hiding the little girl somewhere so that he could rape her without raising suspicion. It stood to reason that Shama had stumbled onto his secret and the Saudi decided to kill her before she could expose him.

The CIA team expected that if they confronted Sheikh Ahmed outright about his crimes, he might kill the small child to get rid of the evidence. So they began a search for the little girl's location with a fine tooth comb. The cell phone recording of the conversation Joshua had given them of his wife's conversation with Sheikh Ahmed gave them their first lead. Analyzing the conversation, they suspected that he had fabricated a story about sending the daughter to her relatives in India. The team felt that the child was never sent to India, and made plans to confirm that theory. At this stage in their investigation, they requested an interview with the convicted maidservant of Sheikh Ahmed. This time the police did not try to stop them.

When the American team met Rayhana it was a month from the date of her execution. Rayhana narrated to them how on the first day of her arrival, she was detained at the airport and then handcuffed and taken to the desert and raped by the police officers. She spoke of her ordeal and that of her daughter when they were left alone to die and somehow they survived because of her god, Allah, and the good people that helped them. She told them about how she was falsely accused of being a professional prostitute, which led the Shari'a court to sentence her unjustly. Then, she begged the team to find her daughter and bring her to see her mother before she was put to death. Rayhana's tragic story touched a raw nerve with many of the CIA team members that caused some of them to tear up, even those who had never wept before. Her testimony convinced the seven-member team of her innocence. When the team related her sponsor's claim that he sent her daughter to her relatives in Bombay, Rayhana refused to believe it. She said that her daughter would not be able to find her way from the Bombay International Airport to her slum area. No one could get her daughter back to her slum except her. Rayhana said the Indian client of her sponsor did not know where she was living and he could not possibly find where her daughter used to live with her mother and brothers in the slum. Rayhana concluded her statement by saying that her Saudi sponsor lied about sending her daughter to India.

The CIA team members found themselves dealing with many more criminal offenses than the murder of the wife of the son of an American United States Senator. They understood that the only way to stop the Jeddah Court from stoning the innocent Indian woman was to expose her sponsor and find her daughter. As before, it was imperative that they not interrogate Sheikh Ahmed before locating the young child. His conversation with the late American woman gave them some clues about the place where the Saudi man might be hiding her. In the recording, the Sheikh was heard saying he had sent the daughter on a flight to Bombay. When Shama asked him for proof, he showed her copies of airline tickets issued for the daughter and his former Pakistani chauffeur. The tickets showed that the daughter and the chauffeur flew to India and the Philippines, but their final destination was Asmara and not Bombay. The team decided they would definitely have to check this discrepancy and find out if the little girl was hidden away in Eritrea.

The first logical stop for the American team was the Asmara International Airport. They made inquiries as to the arrival of the suspects, by the names of Sabir Ibrahim Shah and Iffat Khan, from Jeddah, Saudi Arabia. The airport authority confirmed the arrival of the two passengers in question. As soon as it was confirmed that Iffat Khan did indeed arrive in Eritrea, the CIA team contacted the Asmara police and reported the kidnapping of the young Indian girl by a Pakistani man. Within twenty-four hours, the Asmara police contacted the American team and informed them that the girl was found and the Pakistani man was arrested. When the police interrogated him, the Pakistani man claimed that he did not kidnap the girl, but he was employed by his Arab sponsor in Jeddah to bring her to him at Asmara. After their arrival in Eritrea, his sponsor married the young girl. The CIA team informed the Asmara police that the minor girl was kidnapped from her mother in Jeddah and sent to Eritrea. Therefore, the team demanded that the girl be sent to Jeddah as soon as possible. They asked the same for the Pakistani man.

After unearthing the entire plot of Sheikh Ahmed, the CIA members congratulated each other for their brilliant work and celebrated their clever discovery of the one of the most mysterious and convoluted crimes ever committed by a human being. Their joy and happiness was increased when they realized that the entire world would be captivated by this story and praise them for rescuing a woman from being stoned to death and freeing a female child from an old man who kidnapped, imprisoned, and raped her. The world would then appreciate their efforts in solving the mysterious circumstances surrounding the death of the daughter-in-law of Senator Peter Thomason. When everything became clear as the sun, the team handed over a copy of their investigation and demanded that Sheikh Faiz bin Ahmed be apprehended and charged with the crimes he committed against three innocent foreign women; Rayhana Khan, Iffat Khan, and Shama Thomason. As soon as the CIA team submitted their official report, Sheikh Ahmed was placed under arrest and charged with several serious crimes including murder. Shortly, after his arrest Iffat and Sabir were brought back to Jeddah. The CIA team members appeared on various international TV channels and disclosed the hideous crimes that a wealthy Saudi business tycoon committed against three innocent foreign women from India and America.

Nevertheless, the happy celebration of the CIA member team was short-lived. Sheikh Ahmed was detained and interrogated by the Jeddah police and released on bail after twenty-four hours. After questioning him about the alleged kidnapping and rape of the female child of his former Indian maidservant, the Jeddah police dropped this one serious charge against him. He was able to prove to the Saudi police that he legally married Iffat Khan and lawfully gave her enough time before he consummated his marriage with her. He admitted that **he thighed her up** for one year according to the blessed Sunna of the prophet Muhammad and had sexual intercourse with her when she completed the lawful age of nine years old in compliance with Shari'a law. He challenged the police to find out from his wife, Iffat Khan, if he had sex with her before she became a woman at the age of nine years old. He steadfastly denied he had ever bribed his former Somali chauffeur or convinced him to hit the American woman with his car. He claimed that the American CIA team had convinced his former chauffeur to alter his statement because they promised to release him from jail and send him to the USA.

When Iffat Khan arrived in Jeddah, she was eleven years old and pregnant. She had already been in the child marriage for three long years. The CIA team members were shocked when they came to know that Jeddah police had released Sheikh Ahmed and allowed him to take possession of his child-wife again. Their consciences troubled them tremendously when they learned that Iffat was pregnant with his child at just eleven years old. They also came to learn that the Jeddah police had dropped the charges of kidnapping and rape against the Sheikh.

The seven members of the CIA team stormed the police headquarters in Jeddah and demanded the kidnapper and rapist be rearrested and the release of his victim. If they were not from America, the Jeddah police would have arrested all seven members of the CIA team and had them beheaded or stoned the following Friday. The team reached the point of calling the Jeddah police "barbarians", "bastards", "animals", "criminals", "son of bitches", and openly the 'f' word. A female member from the team yelled at them threatening that if the Indian maidservant's child was not released from her Saudi kidnapper and rapist within twenty-four hours, the American army would move from Iraq and invade Saudi Arabia and blow up all the mentally retarded, sexually perverted, f...king diseased Arabs. No matter the threats or how many foul words they used, the CIA team could not change the decision of the Jeddah police. Finally, the American team decided to refer the case to the Royal Family. Prudently, they involved the Indian government too.

First, the CIA team wrote a huge report about the entire story of Rayhana Khan, Iffat Khan, and Shama Thomason. Then, they uploaded it onto the internet and circulated it all over the world. The case of Rayhana drew the attention and sympathy of millions of people. Her photo was circulated through emails and Facebook. The outside world demanded cessation of the stoning sentence against the Indian maidservant. The world demanded that Rayhana's daughter be released from her rapist. Secondly, the CIA team made a formal complaint to the Royal family. Thirdly, they referred the case of the young Indian girl to the Indian government. The royal family placed the stoning of Rayhana on hold and ordered the Jeddah police investigate the claim of the Indian maidservant regarding her claim that she had conceived her child through rape. The royals decreed that the court should retry her of the charges of marrying two husbands at the same time.

The Indian Consulate at Jeddah also stepped in and demanded the immediate release of the underage Indian girl who allegedly had been kidnapped, imprisoned, and raped by an old pervert. The Jeddah police rejected the demand of the Indian Consulate. Regardless, Iffat Khan was taken away from Sheikh Ahmed after the Royal family ordered she be released from his custody. The Royal family also ordered the Shari'a court to conduct a new hearing regarding the validity of Sheikh Ahmed's marriage to Iffat Khan and rule accordingly. On the streets of Saudi Arabia, the news that a young *child*-(wife) had been taken away from her *lawful husband*, created an uproar.

The Saudi Imams in the mosques openly preached against the Royal family in their sermons and condemned the Royals for allowing the Americans to interfere in the laws handed down to them by Allah and their prophet Muhammad (PBUH). They said that the marriage of the old Saudi and the Indian girl was lawful in every aspect and there was nothing in the marriage contract that was in conflict with Shari'a law. The condemning sermons of the Saudi clerics moved the hearts of the masses and created great havoc and restlessness around the country and all the Arab countries. When the Royal family felt pressured from the throngs of angry masses, they published an official royal decree and justified their decision concerning the marital status of the Saudi man and his Indian wife. According to the decree, Saudi men are not allowed, by Royal decree, to marry non-Saudi women. The royal decree appeased the angry crowds temporally. However, the masses were moved again when a great preeminent Egyptian scholar openly condemned the royal family for making laws contradicting the holy of holy, Islamic Shari'a law.

The preeminent leader was known as Sheikh Yusuf Al-Qaradawi. After condemning the royal family, Al-Qaradawi issued a fatwa (a religious council ruling). The fatwa declared that the young wife be returned to her lawful husband, Sheikh Faiz bin Ahmed, and taken to another Muslim country where the government wasn't hypocritical, but faithfully following the Shari'a of Allah and his Prophet Muhammad. He even suggested some Muslim countries by their names—Sudan, Somalia, Eritrea, and Pakistan. It has been alleged that this great religious leader is behind all the current ongoing revolutions in the Arab countries, which is known as the Arab Spring. He is using Aljazeera TV to instigate and move the masses in each Arab country to overthrow their current regimes. Al-Qaradawi today is one of the prominent leaders and pillars of the Muslim Brotherhood. He is working hard to fulfill the dream of the early founders of the Muslim Brotherhood, Hassan Al-Banna and Sayyid Qutb. These founders aggressively wanted to restore the traditional Islamic Caliphate to the

Muslim World and use Shari'a as the only form of governing Muslims. So far, his followers have succeeded in overthrowing secular regimes in Tunisia, Egypt, Libya, Somalia, and Sudan and creating Islamic rules. If his dream comes true, the Arab Spring will turn into a World Nightmare. Before we proceed further, I would like to take a short break and share some of my understanding of Islam and ask a few questions concerning the current issues on Islamic terrorism. I would do this in two separate sections. Consider them as bonus chapters that are helpful in grasping the main message of this book.

CHAPTER 8

WHAT IS ISLAM?

Let us begin with this important question, "What is Islam?" This question had been asked by many thinkers and historians and had been researched by many theologians and critics and most of them had given their answers according to their understanding of the religion of Muhammad. Pope Benedict XVI, on September 12, 2006, quoted the words of the Byzantine Emperor Manuel II, "Show me just what Muhammad brought that was new and there you will find things only evil and inhuman, such as his command to spread by the sword the faith he preached." John Quincy Adams, U. S. President, "The essence of Muhammad's doctrine was violence and lust: To exalt the brutal over the spiritual part of human nature." Alexis De Tocqville, French thinker and historian, "I studied the Qur'an a great deal…I came away from that study with the conviction that by and large there have been few religions in the world as deadly to men as that of Muhammad." Dr. Ambedkar, the father of Indian Constitution, "Islam is a false and dangerous way of living."

Swami Vivekananda, a contemporary Indian philosopher, "The more selfish a man, the more immoral he is. And also with that race which is bound down to itself has been the most cruel and the most wicked in the whole world. There has not been a religion that has clung to this dualism more than that founded by the Prophet of Arabia (Mohammed), and there has not been a religion (Islam) which has shed so much blood and been so cruel to other men. In the Koran there is the doctrine that a man, who does not believe these teachings, should be killed; it is mercy to kill him! And the surest way to get to heaven, where there are beautiful 'houries' and all sort of sense-enjoyments, is by killing these unbelievers. Think of the bloodshed there has been in consequence of such beliefs (Islam)!"

As contribution to this essential question, I would like to begin by saying that, Islam put in one word is "Muhammad." There is nothing called Moderate Islam vs. Radical Islam, the Islam of the Qur'an vs. the Islam of the Sunna/hadiths, the Sunni Islam vs. the Shiite Islam, Islam of the East vs. Islam of the West, etc. *Islam is Muhammad and Muhammad is Islam.* If anyone wants to become a Muslim, he must believe and bear witness that Muhammad is the Messenger of God. When a Muslim ceased to believe in Muhammad as the Messenger/Prophet of Allah, he is no more a Muslim. According to the Shari'a such a person became Kafir (an infidel), Murtad (an apostate), Halal Aldam (shedding of his blood is allowed by the Shari'a), or Istobiha Damihi (shedding of his blood is permissible for any Muslim). So Islam begins and ends with Muhammad. Indians correctly call this religion Mohammedanism and its followers Mohammedans. Even the Shari'a Law is called in the Indian Constitution, Court of Law, and universities and schools the Mohammedan Law.

Islam is not a religion in the sense people usually understanding religions such as Christianity, Judaism, Hinduism, and Buddhism. It is an amalgamation of two contradictory messages under one umbrella called Islam. Therefore, Islam has two contradictory messages, which effectively makes it two religions in one. You might have heard that a great many Western leaders and politicians state that Islam is essentially a religion of Peace but its gospel has been hijacked by various terrorist groups such as the al-Qaeda and Taliban to suit their terrorist agenda. I myself heard George Bush, Tony Blaire, Clinton, Obama and many more great leaders of the world trying to reassure the world that Islam is the religion of Peace. I am not entirely certain whether they are stating a fact or trying to convince themselves. Therefore, I would like to invite you to examine with me such a claim.

First, Islamic teachings about Muhammad exalt him to a position higher than God. Any careful researcher on Islam will conclude that Muslims worship Muhammad. Muslims believe that even God has to pray to Muhammad. Accordingly, whatever Muhammad did and taught is accepted as the divine benchmark for good Moral behavior and perfect teaching. For example, Muhammad slept with a nine-year-old girl and his followers consider that a good deed and imitate it. Muhammad ordered the killing of those who refused to accept him as the Messenger of Allah and convert to his religion and that is accepted as a divine order and hence every Muslim is ordered to kill the infidels if they reject the message of Muhammad. He prescribed the death penalty for those Muslims who dare to apostatize from his religion, and that closed the door of religious freedom of choice.

Muslims are strictly forbidden from questioning anything Muhammad did or taught. Any Muslim who dares to question the life or the teachings of Muhammad would be branded a *tatawala a'la alrsool*, which means, "exalted himself above the Messenger of Allah." Such a person is considered an apostate and his death is sanctioned, even encouraged to be carried out by any faithful Muslim including his family members. Every sin in Islam is pardonable except the sin against Muhammad. A Muslim can curse his religion, his god Allah, and doubt the teachings of the Qur'an. However, if he repents, his repentance will be accepted and he will not be punished. Nevertheless, if the Muslim curses or insults the prophet Muhammad his repentance will never be accepted and according to the Shari'a such an apostate has to be killed even if he is found holding on the coverings of the holy shrine, the Ka'aba (the house of Allah in Mecca). Just compare the reactions of Muslims to the Danish Cartoons of Muhammad with their reactions to the recent burning of a copy of their holy Qur'an.

Secondly, Islam has two contradictory messages—peaceful and violent. The peaceful message referred to the thirteen-year period when Muhammad lived in Mecca. He was then a fledgling leader with only a few followers and had yet to formulate his Shari'a laws, his Mujahedeen fighters, had yet not declared Jihad against infidels, had not given his fighters the right to kill infidels and possess their women and properties, and had not yet begun to invade other tribes and cities. Moreover, during that period he remained a monogamist with one single wife, Khadija. He had not yet begun his misogynistic teachings against women. The violent message referred to his last ten years that he lived in Medina. According to all Muslim scholars and the main four founders of the schools of Shari'a: Shafi`, Hanafi, Hanbali, and Maliki—the Medinian period had abrogated and cancelled all the peaceful approach and made Islam compulsory to all humanity. ("Merriam-Webster dictionary defines abrogate as: (1.) to abolish by authoritative action: NULL (2.) to treat as nonexistent. It lists abrogate's synonyms: abate, abolish, annul, cancel, disannul, dissolve, invalidate, negate, null, nullify, quash, repeal, rescind, roll back, strike down, vacate, void."). This duality of the teachings of Islam made it easy for Muslims to argue for both peaceful and violent approaches. The verses of the Qur'an are divided into the Meccan verses and Medinian verses. Those who wanted to show that Islam is a religion of peace and tolerance used the Meccan verses of the Qur'an to prove their point and deliberately suppress the Medinian verses and hadiths. While those who wanted to wage Jihad against the so-called enemies of Islam and oppress Muslim women, used in their sermons the Medinian verses and hadiths and turned a blind eye to the Meccan verses. This inevitably created confusion among non-Muslims and made it difficult for them to understand Islam.

The thirteen years that Muhammad spent in Mecca preaching his new message was a total failure. He failed miserably to form a new religion. He could not able to win more than a few followers and most of them were his immediate relatives, friends, and very few slaves. Muhammad was ridiculed and his message was rejected by the people of Mecca. The Meccans were able to see through his message. They understood that he was not a prophet of God because he failed to perform any miracles or prophecy any future events. Moreover, the stories of the Jewish prophets and the ancient Arab folklore he incorporated in his Qur'an were all known to the Arabs of Mecca. The stories of the Jewish prophets, which he claimed to have known them through direct revelation from God, were a mixture of true stories mentioned in the Jewish holy Scripture (i.e. The Old Testament) and the Jewish commentaries that included legends and fables (the Jewish Talmud). Moreover, Muhammad included in his Qur'an some

Christian legends such as the story of the Seven Sleepers (in the Qur'an the people of the cave) and the childhood of Jesus, which mentioned in some apocryphal books.

Muhammad exposed his ignorance and revealed his false claim when the Meccans sought the help of some Jews of Medina and tested his knowledge. They asked him to tell them what he knew about Alexander the Great (known to the Arabs and Jews as Dhul-Qarnayn), the Sleepers of Ephesus (the Seven Sleepers), and the nature of the spirit. He told them give me one day until I receive revelation from God through his angel Gabriel. Instead of one day, he took more than two weeks to answer those three questions. His answers are mentioned in the Qur'an (Surat Al-Kahf 18). Muhammad failed to tell the number of the Seven Sleepers and he added a dog to them that was not part of the story. Muhammad's answers were funny and revealed he was not sure of what he knew about those sleepers. He said some people said they were three, some said five and some said seven, but only Allah knows their number. Moreover, he said they slept for 309 years but only Allah knows how long they slept (Surat al Al-Kahf 18: 8-26). In fact, the story of the Seven Sleepers was a fable written by a Syrian Christian priest called Yakub/Jacob from Sarq (451-521 AD). This story made its way to Europe and became a fairy-tale. Washington Irving adapted it in his famous novel, Rip van Winkle (1819). Neither the Old Testament nor the New Testament ever mentioned such a story. However, the Syrian Christian fable said they were seven sleepers and they slept for two hundred years inside a cave. Muhammad made Alexander the Great a prophet of God who spoke directly with Allah (Surat Al-Kalf 18: 83-98). Later on Omar Ibn Khattab considered him an angel of Allah. Actually, Alexander the Great lived and died as a polytheist and he burned down the entire city of Ephesus because its inhabitants refused to allow him offer animals as sacrifice for his idols. According to the Qur'an Alexander the Great was able to reach the end of the world and saw the sun setting in a Muddy Hot Well. So according to the Allah of Muhammad the sun has a setting place at the end of the world in a muddy well. Finally regarding the last question Muhammad said only Allah knows the nature of the spirit (Surat al-'Isra' 17: 85).

When his three answers, which supposedly revealed by God through his angel Gabriel, were told by the Qur'an in Surat al-Kalf and Surat al-'Isra', Muhammad exposed his ignorance and false claim to be the prophet of God. His lies made the Meccans to ridicule him and flatly reject him as the prophet of God. When Muhammad failed to prove his claim through miracles, prophecies, or knowledge of history, he challenged the Meccans to produce some verses or one Surat as his Qur'an. Of course, such a challenge exposed him further. (Muslim scholars collectively agreed that Muhammad had never performed any miracle. For them his only Miracle is the Qur'an). Nevertheless, the Meccan leaders did not see any greatness or miraculous nature in the Qur'an. For them the Qur'an as a book lacked any claim to masterly work. It was a repetitive book, lacked honesty and historical authenticity, lacked chronological order, was full of contradictions, full of confusions, full of grammatical mistakes, full of legends and fables, and full of plagiarisms. (Many of its verses went missing after the death of Muhammad. Some Surahs got lost too). The author of the Qur'an confused many historical stories and events. Just to mention few, the well-known confusion of Mary the mother of Jesus with Mary the sister of Aaron and Moses and the daughter of Imram, the confusion of the minister Haman of the King of Persia Ahasuerus in the book of Esther in the Old Testament with the minister of Pharaoh king of Egypt at the time of Moses, and the confusion of the father of Abraham with his chief servant. The claim that at the time of Moses his brother Aaron was deceived by a Samaritan, who convinced him to make a Calf for the children of Israel to worship, falls apart when it was shown that the city of Samaria did not come into existence until hundreds of years later. How could there be a Samaritan man at the time of Moses and Aaron, when it is well known historical fact that the city of Samaria did not come into existence until hundreds of years later?

The Qur'an is a collection of verses spoken by Muhammad during his twenty-five years of preaching his new religion in Mecca and

Medina. However, the present Qur'an has no beginning or end. The verses of the Qur'an, which were spoken by Muhammad in various occasions, were scattered in the present Qur'an in a chaotic fashion. There is no way for the reader of the Qur'an to know which verse came before which verse and which Surat was supposedly revealed after which Surat. The verses and the Surahs/chapters are not arranged in a chronological order. The stories and events mentioned in the Qur'an without telling which event or story happened first or where the event took place. No chronological order, no geographical location, and no historical information. It is just like a story that its beginning put in its end and its end placed in its middle and its middle scattered all over the book. Sometimes it tells you about Moses and Pharaoh, then suddenly it jumps to the story of Adam and Eve, and shifts to Noah and the flood, then returns to Moses and Pharaoh, then Jesus performs a miracle when he was one day old, after that, it goes to David and Goliath, and suddenly you hear King Solomon was hearing an ant speaking to other ants or conversing with an Ifreet/Jinni, and then goes back to the story of Adam and how Iblis refused to bow down to him, then it picks up a story of an Arab prophet called Salih from the Arab folklore, then it tells you of Abraham and his son Ismail building the Black Ka'aba, the so-called House of Allah, then you hear of Muhammad's personal encounter with a group of the desert Jinns who heard his Qur'anic recitation and embraced Islam, and so on. Between those mumble jumble stories and fables, you find one law for flogging the adulterer hundred lashes, another verse allowing the man to marry four women and sleep with female slaves, cutting the hand of the thief, and one verse sanctioning an adult man to marry and sleep with a female child, etc. Even if the Qur'an were written by an illiterate old Arab woman she would have narrated it in a better fashion. No one could claim to have understood such a confused book without the help of the works of Muslim 'ulema/scholars like Ibn Kathir, al-Tabari, al-Qurotobi, Ibn Sa'ad, Ibn Hisham, al-Bihaqi, al-Halabi, al-Bukhari, Muslim, Abu Dawood, Ibn Majah, Malik, etc. Even each of those ulema would give you ten interpretations by ten companions of Muhammad with the attempt to explain one single verse. You will never know who among the ten companions got it right from Muhammad.

When Muhammad failed to convince the Meccans about his claim to be the prophet of God, he immigrated to Medina and there he changed his peaceful approach and dedicated a violent approach, which made Islam compulsory to everyone. He knew that he had not being supported by any divine power to perform miracles or utter prophecies to authenticate his claim to be the Messenger or prophet of God. The failed peaceful approach was set aside and the new message of violent approach was set on motion. Islam became compulsory and the only acceptable religion to Allah. If Muhammad did not declare Jihad against infidels, make Islam compulsory for everybody, allow his followers to possess the women and lands of the unbelievers, and come up with the law of apostasy we would not see a single Muslim today. The Sword and Violence are the two magical powers that made Islam to be recognized and remained until today.

Therefore, the so-called Moderate Islam, which is based on the verses of the Meccan period, was a total failure and not a religion at all. Only when Muhammad immigrated to Medina did Islam begin to take a shape of a new religion with rigid and strict religious laws later on formulated in the present Shari'a Law. At this stage, Islam divorced its claim to be a succession of Judaism and Christianity and Muhammad accused the followers of these two Abrahamic religions as corrupting their Holy Scriptures and hence deserved to be persecuted and killed. Muhammad began to borrow openly and freely from the religious practices and rituals of other pagan religions such as Hanafiya, Sabians and the religion of the Pagans of Mecca. He incorporated in his new religion the pagan rituals of the Hajj, the daily five prayers and fasting a full month each year of the Sabians, and the rigid doctrine of the Oneness of God that taught by the followers of Hanafiya. He even borrowed from Zoroastrianism the fancy teachings of the hurr virgins and beautiful boys and many more such fantasies about paradise. Neither the followers of Judaism nor the adherents of Christianity ever went to Mecca to perform the pagan ritual of Hajj, performed the five compulsory prayers in the day, fasted one month each year, or believed in the existence of virgins and rivers of wine and honey in paradise. All those are pagan religious rituals and practices and as such have nothing to do with the God of Abraham, Isaac, and Jacob.

When Muhammad was in Mecca with only a few followers; the verses of the Qur'an praised the Jews and Christians and accepted the Old Testament and the New Testament as heavenly Scriptures that had been revealed by God. According to the Egyptian scholar, Sayyid Al-Qimni, when Muhammad immigrated to Medina, "necessity and wisdom required that some verses of the Qur'an should go before the Muslims to praise the children of Israel and their Prophets, the admission that Allah has preferred them to other nations, that in their Torah there is guidance and light, and they should follow what it is written in their Torah" (Al-Islamiat: al-Qimni 2001: 588). However, this friendly atmosphere towards the Jews had changed for no other reason except that their alliance was no longer needed "after the victory of the Battle of the Great Badr in which Muslims possessed weapons and great wealth and strength" (Ibid: 589).

It is somewhat surprising that it was only after the battle of Badr, Muhammad suddenly made the determination that the Jews "had corrupted the original Torah and hence it became necessary to kill them for changing the verses of Allah" (Ibid). Therefore, the three existing Jewish tribes in Medina—Banu Qaynuqa, Banu Qurayza, and Banu Nadir—were systematically persecuted and dealt with immediately and swiftly. Banu Nadir and Banu Qaynuqa were falsely accused of trivial crimes and exiled out of Medina after seizing their properties and homes. The third tribe of Banu Qurizah was accused of treason and hence 900 of its men were beheaded in cold-blood in front of Muhammad while he was sitting and watching the horrific slaughter. Then, all their women, children, properties and homes were distributed among the Mujahedeen. In short, period not a single Jew was left in the Medina of the new Arab King-Prophet. According to al-Qimni, "The Prophet knew for sure that the existence of Jews with a heavenly book, a historical heritage, and series of prophecies that followed one after the other, means the existence of continuous denial of his prophet-hood, and inside his city and in the midst of his small state. Therefore, followed those quick steps of cleaning Yathrib [Medina]" from the Jews (Hurub Dawlat Al Rasul, Sayyid al-Qimni 2001: p. 367).

Even the Jews of Khaiber city were raided for no specific reason and kicked out of Arabia after confiscating all their properties and women and children. (At that time Khaiber was the third largest city after Mecca and Medina, and all its inhabitants were Jews. Muslims all over the Middle East are proud of the slaughter of the Jews of Khaiber and continue to chant until today, "Khaiber, Khaiber, Oh Jews, the Army of Muhammad will return soon." It was in Khaiber that Muhammad slaughtered the husband, father, brother, and the relatives of the Jewish girl, Safiya bint Huaya and raped her on the same day while she was crying for her dear ones whom her rapist and his terrorists had killed in front of her eyes. While this wicked man was raping the poor Jewish girl, his bodyguard Abu Auiob Al-Ansari was guarding his tent with a sword on his hands. In the following morning, Abu Auiob said to Muhammad, 'I scared that she might kill you because you have killed her father and husband and she is still Kafirah/infidel').

After accusing the Jews of corrupting their Holy Scripture and getting rid of all of them Muhammad turned to Christianity. There was hardly any Christian in Medina to be accused and killed. Nevertheless, Muhammad did more damage to Christianity than he did to Judaism. (I mean damage in the minds of Muslims and made them to hate Christians and their New Testament). Muhammad just accused the Jews of corrupting their Scripture without specifying where this corruption happened in the Old Testament. However, for Christianity he purposely attacked the main foundation or fundamentals of the Christian faith. He aimed his attacks at the pillars on which the main doctrines of the Christian faith were built. It has been said, Christianity stands and falls with the Divinity, Crucifixion, Death, and Resurrection of Jesus Christ. Muhammad spewed his venom and hatred on those essential Christian dogmas. He attacked the Holy Trinity. Then, he attacked the Divinity, Sonship, Crucifixion, Death, and Resurrection of Jesus Christ (Qur'an 4:171. 5:17). His Qur'an condemns Christians as infidels who deserve hellfire because they believe in these doctrines (Qur'an 5:70-75, 5:116-117). While he was in Mecca, Muhammad praised the Christians' Gospel and considered them the People of the Book (having heavenly Scripture). At that time the Qur'an said, there is Light and Guidance in the Torah of Moses and the Gospel of Jesus (Surat Al-Maaidah 5: 43-49). However, when he moved to Medina Muhammad changed his attitude towards Christians and began to accuse them of corrupting the Gospel of Jesus. Therefore, the Qur'an came up with the condemning verses, which abrogated his former assertion (Qur'an 5:70-75, 5:116-117). The Christians also suddenly corrupted the Gospel of Jesus. The People of the Book became Kafireen/infidels deserving to be killed by Muslims because they believed Jesus is the Son of God and God came on the flesh, God is the Holy Trinity the Father, the Son, and the Mother 'Mary' (Qur'an 4:171. 5:17). (Muhammad had no correct knowledge of the doctrine of the Trinity as The Father, the Son, the Holy Spirit. He obtained his knowledge of the Holy Trinity from an Arab Christian cult, which revered Mary).

The problem was not only the rejection and condemnation of the main Christian doctrines, but the accusation that he directed against the Christians. He claimed that the followers of Jesus corrupted the true message of Christ and created those "false" doctrines. He made Jesus to say that he had not taught those doctrines but his followers created them after he went to heaven (Surat Al-Maaidah 5: 116-117). This accusation might sound as just a matter of difference between Christians and Muslims. However, history proved and continues to prove that it has far-reaching fatal consequences for the followers of Jesus. It created hatred and enmity in the hearts of Muslims towards Christians and their Holy Scripture (The Bible). Muslims look at Christians as infidels, forgers and corrupters of the word of God, call them brothers of apes and pigs, deserve to be killed and their women, children, and properties are rightful possession granted by Allah to Muslims, having corrupted their heavenly Scripture, and on their way to hell. Moreover, they hate the Bible and consider it a corrupted and distorted book. Muslims all over the world believe that Christians have corrupted their Bible and continue to change and corrupt it every minute and every second. Muslim Imams, and religious leaders in the mosques, radios, TVs, schools, and colleges openly preach that "May Allah destroy the Jews and Christians, make their wives widows, their children orphans, and their women and properties booty for Muslims." They openly curse the Jews and Christians and call them brothers of apes and pigs. Everywhere Muslim Mujahedeen went, they destroyed Christian churches and converted some into mosques. They did not hesitate to slaughter Christian priests inside their churches. The Patriarch Sophronius of Jerusalem (634-638), who witnessed the spread of Islam in the Arabian Peninsula and the fall of Jerusalem with his own eyes, described the Muslim invaders as "godless barbarians" who "burnt churches, destroyed monasteries, profaned the Crosses, and blasphemed against Christ and the Church."

Christians are supposed to take the Qur'an to the court of law and accuse it of inciting hatred and defaming them. It calls them kofar, descendants of monkeys and pigs, forgers of the word of God, and instigates Muslims to hate and kill them. Moreover, the Qur'an is the only religious book that attacks the religions of others and calls for their destruction. Islam is the only religion that draws its legitimacy from condemning other religious books and their adherents. For Islam to be a true religion Jews and Christians have to be liars and followers of corrupted religious books and their religions are untrue. For Muhammad to be the Messenger of God, Jesus has to cease be divine and Son of God. For Muhammad to be the final prophet and the seal of all prophets, Jesus' crucifixion, death, and resurrection have to be null and the biggest lies of history. For the Qur'an to be the word of God the holy Bible has to be a corrupted word of God. In short, for Islam to be a true religion, Christianity and Judaism have to be false religions and their followers are infidels who are not worthy to live. Their places of worship are either to be destroyed or converted into mosques. Islam considered Christianity its bitterest enemy. If a Muslim becomes an atheist, communist, animist, secularist, Satanist, or even if he stops believing in the Qur'an as the word of Allah still he can live freely in Muslim country and among Muslims and no one will touch him or accuse him of apostasy. However, the day a Muslim embraces Christianity he can no more live in a Muslim country or lives freely among Muslims wherever they are. Everyone will consider him an apostate and he will be given three days to repent and return to the Islamic community. If he continues to follow Christianity, he will be killed and his body will be disposed off in inhumane ways.

Muhammad and his followers did every imaginable evil in order to destroy Christianity and the Church of Jesus Christ. Nevertheless, Christianity continued and it will continue forever to be the leading religion in the world. The Gospel of Jesus will continue to be preached all over the world. The Holy Bible will continue to be produced and distributed in millions. While I was doing my master degree in a University in Canada, I came across a Christian theologian who wanted the Roman Catholic Church to accept Muhammad as a Prophet of God!!?? Of course, the Vatican did not accept his demand. I just can get it why did he make such an acceptable and unholy demand. How can the Son of God and the lying Jinni, the son of Iblis have anything in common? If Satan could incarnate as a human being or if he could have a son, I believe that already took place in the desert of Arabia in 570 AD.

There is nothing called Moderate Islam vs. Radical Islam. There is only one Islam and there is one Shari'a. Islam as a religion is created out of the Medinian verses and hadiths. Almost everything Muhammad said and taught in Mecca was abrogated and set aside to give room to his new religion that he taught and dictated in Medina. In Medina, Muhammad was appointed the new leader of the two powerful Medinian tribes of Aws and Khazraj. All the people of Medina except the Jews were converted by their leaders to Islam. At this new period all the evils of Islam came to existence, Jihad (spreading the new faith by the sword and killing Infidels who refused to accept Muhammad as the Messenger of Allah), killing the apostates who deserted Islam, and all the misogynistic teachings against women were dictated at this period. At this ten years period in Medina every thinkable evil against the infidels are allowed such as attacking, raiding, invading, robbing, killing, stealing, confiscating, torturing, enslaving, raping and the like were authorized, legalized, and encouraged by the Qur'an and the hadiths of Muhammad. All the Meccan verses that preached peaceful approach and no compulsion in religion were abrogated by the new Medinian verses that dictated a violent approach and made Islam compulsory for everyone. One single verse of the Medinian Qur'an known as the Verse of the Sword (Al-Toba 9: 5) had abrogated and cancelled one hundred and twenty-four verses of the Meccan period. Islam became the only acceptable religion on the entire earth and anyone who dares to refuse this religion is to be killed and his property, cattle, women, and children to be distributed as war booty among the Mujahedeen.

What Muslim Scholars have said about the bloody and notorious Verse of the Sword?

"But when the forbidden months are past, then slay the Pagans wherever ye find them, and seize them, beleaguer them, and lie in wait for them in every stratagem (of war); but if they repent, and establish regular prayers and practice regular charity, then open the way for them: for Allah is Oft-forgiving, Most Merciful." (Al-Toba 9: 5).

The above verse is known among Muslim scholars as the Verse of the Sword and the Mother of all 'Abrogators' because it abrogated one hundred and twenty-four of the Meccan verses that spoke about a peaceful approach, no compulsion in religion, and granting freedom of faith to infidels. It is mentioned in the last Surat that was revealed in the Qur'an.

According to Ibn Al-Arabi, "everything in the Qur'an which speaks about forgiveness for infidels and avoiding killing them have been abrogated by the verse of the sword…this verse has abrogated a hundred and twenty-four verses" (Al-Islamiat: al-Qimni 2001: 584).

Ibn Kathir said in his commentary on Surat al-Toba 9: 5, "Al-Dahak said, this verse abrogated every treaty of peace between the prophet and unbelievers" (Ibid).

Ali Ibn Talha said, "Ibn Abass said about al-Toba 9: 5 that **Allah ordered the prophet to put the sword on everyone [who] refused to accept Islam**" (Ibid, emphasis is mine).

There is a Meccan verse you will hear in the tongue of every Muslim who wants to practice Taqiyya and deceive non-Muslims that Islam is the religion of peace and allows religious tolerance and grants freedom of choice, *"Let there be no compulsion in religion"* (Albaqrah 2: 256). Al-Nisabori said, "This verse has been abrogated by the Verse of the Sword" (Nasikh and Mansukh, al-Nisabori, pages, 96-97).

Commenting on some verses of the Qur'an (al-Baqarah 2: 191, 193, al-Nissa 4: 76, 89, 91, al-Touba 9: 5, 12, 14, 29, and al-Anfaal 8: 39), the Egyptian Muslim scholar, Khalil Abdul-Karim states, "These verses carry serious orders for the killing of tribes refusing to believe in the faith that is preached by Muhammad…And from the other side, there are hadiths issued by the Prophet that confirm this meaning very clearly by which we mean killing anyone who refuses Islam: *'I have been ordered by Allah to fight the people until they bear witness that there is no God except Allah and Muhammad is the Messenger of Allah, if they say it, they uphold from me their wealth and bloods' [Sahih al-Bukhari].* The meaning of noncompliance is that anyone who refuses to witness or utter the two Shihadah, [Islamic creed] there will be no protection for his wealth and blood. Accordingly killing the one who refuses to utter the two Shihadah (indicating his acceptance to Islam) is an obligation to every Muslim without exception…The message of Muhammad to all tribes is 'accept Islam and you will be safe'…Any tribe or an individual who refuses this offer would expose themselves/himself to physical annihilation and theirs/his wealth, women, children, and slave-girls will be taken by the Muslims" (Abdul-Karim 1999: 42-44).

Killing of the People of the Book (i.e. Jews and Christians) was not sanctioned when Muhammad was in Mecca. At that time, the Qur'an instructed Muhammad to argue and discuss matters with them in a friendly manner. Moreover, the Qur'an ordered Muhammad to acclaim the Jewish Scripture and the Christian Scripture as authentic revelations from God. However, in Medina fighting and killing the Jews and Christians who refused to acknowledge the Message of Muhammad became an obligation to every Muslims. Killing them became necessary because both refused to acknowledge the religion of Truth that preached by the last Messenger of Allah, Muhammad.

In Mecca, *"And dispute ye not with the People of the Book, except with means better (than mere disputation), unless it be with those of them who inflict wrong (and injury): but say, "We believe in the revelation which has come down to us and in that which came down to you" (Al-Ankabut 29: 46).*

Al-Nisabori said, "this verse is abrogated by '*Fight those who believe not in Allah nor the Last Day, nor hold that forbidden which hath been forbidden by Allah and His Messenger, nor acknowledge the religion of Truth, of the People of the Book (i.e. Christians and Jews), until they pay the Jizya with willing submission, and feel themselves subdued"* (Al-Tobah 9: 29), (Nasikh and Mansukh, al-Nisabori, p. 35). By the way, this verse is translated in a way to make it sounds less offensive to the English readers. The well-known translator, Yusif Ali is notoriously known for rending the verses of the Qur'an less offensive and less evil and cruel. The verse in Arabic never uses the phrase "willing submission" nor does it say, "feel themselves subdued". The verse says, "Muslims have to fight and kill the People of the Book because they rejected the religion of Truth that has been preached by Muhammad. Christians and Jews must either accept Islam or be killed. The third option for them must pay the Jizya on their knees and after they have been defeated and degraded. The third option is for a treaty which supposed to be made between a conqueror and a conquered". According to all commentators, this verse came to solve a financial problem, which arose after the Verse of the Sword ordered Muslims to kill the polytheists wherever they found. Nevertheless, the verse forbade the killing during the three forbidden or holy months. It was a pagan religious custom for the Arabs that during those three months they do not fight or kill anyone. Moreover, the Qur'an declared the polytheists as nijis (unclean or unholy) and banned them from entering the Ka'aba (the House of Allah). Some Muslims complained to Muhammad because their business at the House of Allah stopped when the polytheists were banned from performing the Hajj. To solve this financial problem the Qur'an commanded the Muslims to fight with the People of the Book and instead of killing them or forcing them to accept Islam, they should be given a third choice. If they refused to accept Islam, they have to pay the Jizya (blood money). In case, they refused to accept Islam or pay the Jizya then they have to be killed. Neither the Qur'an nor the Sunna specified how much the Jews and Christians have to pay to redeem themselves? It is left open for Muslims to decide how much to charge according to their needs. Moreover, the Jizya is not necessary always has to be paid as money. For example, when Muslim Mujahedeen invaded my country Sudan, destroyed the churches by the catapults, and slaughtered the priests who refused to surrender inside the altars, they forced the defeated Sudanese Christians to pay them every year 360 young slaves as Jizya.

Islamic atrocities and crimes against humanity are uncountable. Let me quote the words of two thinkers, one is a Muslim and the other a Hindu. Dr. Sayyid Al-Qimni, Cairo University lecturer on sociology of religion, "Terrorism is one of the important pillars of Islam and its means to victory" (Al-Qimni 1996: 192). "The Islamic troops attacked the tribes in the Arabian Peninsula and subjected them by the sword to the new Mohammedan State, after terrorizing them so that they have to join the Medinian alliance" (Al-Qimni 1996: 235). Al-Qimni gave many examples to show how Muhammad terrorized the Arabs and the Jewish tribes and subjected them by the sword to his new State. "The Arabs of Banu Salim that great tribe fled from their dwelling places as soon as they heard about the approaching Islamic troops. They left behind them their houses and cattle. The Muslims stayed three days in their houses and returned to Yathrib [Medina] with great booty" (Ibid).

Swami Vivekananda, a contemporary Indian philosopher, "Think of what…Mohammad did to the world, and think of the great evil that has been done through his fanaticism! Think of the millions massacred through his teachings, mothers bereft of their children, children made orphans, whole countries destroyed, millions upon millions of people killed."

"Their watchword is: There is one God, and Mohammad is his Prophet. Everything beyond that not only is bad, but must be destroyed forthwith: at a moment's notice, every man or woman who does not exactly believe in that must be killed; everything that does not belong to this worship must be immediately broken; every book that teaches anything else must be burnt. From the Pacific to the Atlantic, for five hundred years blood ran all over the world. That is Mohammedanism!" Vivekananda also said, "One religion may ordain something very hideous. For instance, the Mohammedan religion allows Mohammedans to kill all who are not of their religion. It is clearly stated in the Koran, 'Kill the infidels if they do not become Mohammedans.' They must be put to fire and sword. Now if we tell a Mohammedan that this is wrong, he will naturally ask, "How do you know that? How do you know it is not good? My book says it is."

The well renowned Qur'an commentator, Ibn Kathir commenting on Al-Tobah 9: 29, said, "It is permissible for Muslim Mujahedeen to fight and kill the people of the Book (i.e. Jews and Christians) if they refused to accept Islam or pay the Jizya (blood money)." According to him, Allah permitted the killing of Jews and Christians because they refused to accept their final Prophet, Messenger, Leader, and Master, Muhammad. Commenting on 'with willing submission, and feel themselves subdued' he said, "Christians and Jews living in Muslim lands must be persecuted, degraded, harassed, and treated as inferiors to Muslims, and second citizens." In addition, while Ibn Kathir was commenting on this verse he quoted the notorious Umarian Pact that the so-called Second rightly-guided Caliph Omar Ibn al-Kattab forced the Christians to sign a treaty in those lands his troops invaded and occupied. I am quoting only the first article of this unfair treaty. You can get the whole treaty in the Internet (27 articles or conditions). "We shall not build, in our cities or in our neighborhood, new monasteries, churches, convents, or monks' cells, nor shall we repair, by day or by night, such of them as fall in ruins or are situated in the quarters of the Muslims."

According to the historian Bat Ye'or Islam looks at a non-Muslim country such as America and its inhabitants as "The land of the non-believers, called the lands of war dar al-harb where infidels to be fought because they oppose the establishment of Islamic law in their lands. As enemies of Allah, they are accorded no rights: they, themselves and their property become fair game (mubah) for all Muslims. They can be taken as slaves, kidnapped for ransom, robbed, raped, maimed or killed with impunity. War is to be waged against them in order to Islamize their territory, which, according to the beliefs of Islam, must be conquered for Allah. If they resist, Islamic law provides for the deportation or massacre of the men and the enslavement of women and children."

From the same historian, we find that Christians and Jews living in a Muslim country are subjected to some discriminative rules that meant to dehumanize them.

Rules of the Dhimmi (Christian and Jew):

"Rules would be formulated to deny the dhimmi due process of the law. Discriminatory and restrictive dress and behavior codes would be enacted and severely enforced to reduce the dhimmi into a state of despair and poverty. Dehumanization of the dhimmi was not uncommon, and generally the rule. Various forms of physical abuse were common. Many times distinctive dress was specified to identify a dhimmi that he would be unable to either mix with a Muslim or even walk in a Muslim area of a city. Other rules specified such demeaning dress codes as not wearing shoes or sandals, not using certain colors, wearing stars on their clothing. Dhimmis were often prohibited from working in many occupations. Even rules were made as to how a dhimmi could ride a mule to distinguish him from a Muslim."

Penalties for breaking the rules:

"The non-observance of these rules would entail a severe beating. Often passing a Muslim on the wrong side would begin a beating that could leave a dhimmi mortally wounded. Since the dhimmis were denied the ability to testify against a Muslim, there was absolutely no recourse. If the local Muslim population became intolerant or jealous of the successes of the dhimmis, then a pogrom would ensue. Communities could find themselves evicted, women raped, exorbitant ransoms placed on them, children abducted and forced to convert, and in other cases mass murders of the dhimmi population was condoned."

Dr. Ambedkar, the father of Indian Constitution, "To Muslims, a Hindu and any non-Muslim is a kaffir. A kaffir (nonbeliever in Islam) is not worthy of respect. He is a low born and without status. That is why a country ruled by the kaffir (non-Muslim) is a 'Dar-ul-Harb' (i.e. the land of war) to a Muslim, which must be conquered, by any means for the Muslims and turned into 'Dar-ul-Islam' (i.e. land of Muslims alone). Given this, no further evidence seems necessary to prove that the Muslims will not obey a Hindu (or for that matter any non-Muslim) Government".

Accordingly, Islam has positioned itself to be the only acceptable religion to God and any other religion is false, corrupted, or abrogated by the message of Muhammad. Prophet Muhammad claimed that Allah ordered him to kill anyone who refused to accept him as the Messenger of Allah, and this he confirmed in one of his authentic hadiths: *"Allah's Apostle said: 'I have been ordered (by Allah) to fight against all people until they testify that none has the right to be worshipped but Allah and that Muhammad is the Messenger of Allah, and offer the prayers perfectly and give the obligatory charity, so if they perform that, then they save their lives and property from me except for Islamic laws and then their reckoning (accounts) will be done by Allah"* (Sahih AL-Bukhari).

The Shari'a laws were formed out of the Medinian verses and hadiths. In fact, not a single Shari'a law made out of a verse from the Meccan period. All the Shari'a laws were based on verses and hadiths that were related to the ten years that Muhammad spent in Medina. For this reason, today, we find the majority of Muslims are keen to implement the Shari'a whereas a few Muslims are reluctant to do so. In fact, Islam without the Shari'a is not a religion at all. That is exactly why many Muslim women do not mind living in a secular country and accepting Western secular laws that govern their daily life. That system gives them the rights sorely lacking in a Shari'a society—the freedom of choice and escape abuse and oppression by their Muslim men.

Anyone accepted this bloody religion or inherited it from his parents by birth cannot forsake it or otherwise he will be put to death. Accordingly, Muhammad became a ruthless dictator who killed and tortured anyone refused his message or dared to criticize him or leave his new cult. After the death of Muhammad, those evil and inhumane teachings became fixed and final and applicable to all times and places and no mortal human being can reform or modify them. They are believed to be divinely revealed to Muhammad no matter whether they are found in the Qur'an or the hadiths. The Qur'an strongly endorses the authenticity of the hadiths and leaves Muslim men and women with no preference between the two: *"Whenever Allah and the Apostle have decided a matter, it is not for a faithful man or woman to follow a course of their own choice"* (Q 33: 36). Moreover, the Qur'an says of Muhammad, *"he does not speak out of low desires. It is not but inspiration inspired"* (Q 53: 3-4). The only difference between the Qur'an and the Hadith is that whereas the former was revealed directly through the angel Gabriel with the very letters that are embodied by Allah, the latter was revealed without letters and words (Haqq & Newton 1996: 1). Many non-Muslims make the mistake of trying to understand Islam by reading the Qur'an alone. Muslims succeeded in deceiving large number of non-Muslims that the true teachings of Islam can be found only in the Qur'an. They argue that the Sunna or the hadiths of the prophet Muhammad are not always reliable sources of Islam because there are authentic and unauthentic hadiths. If you fall into that trap then you cannot establish any valid arguments against the teachings of Islam on terrorism and the abuse of women. 75% of the teachings of Islam, out of which the Shari'a laws are formed, come from the hadiths. Therefore, all Muslim scholars and theologians without a single exception collectively agreed upon that the two main sources of the Shari'a are the Qur'an and the Sunna which believed by all Muslims to be divinely revealed by Allah to his final Messenger Muhammad. No prophet after Muhammad and hence no Islamic authority can modify or change these fixed and rigid laws. Unless Muhammad himself would resurrect from his grave and change them, these Shari'a laws are going to remain and continue to be the sources of terror and abuse until the Second Coming of Christ. They are codified and encoded in today's Shari'a, which many Muslims have already brought with them to the West and began to use in their homes to abuse their women, to terrorize others, to use in courts of law, to convert the simple-minded, and to openly teach them in mosques, schools, and colleges. A Muslim cannot be a Muslim without the Shari'a. The Shari'a is the body of legal rulings that defines how a Muslim should behave in all circumstances wherever he/she lives.

CHAPTER 9

HE WHO HAS EARS TO HEAR, LET HIM HEAR

With the ebb of Multiculturalism and the alarming presence of the anti-freedom supporters in every city in the West, there are no more safe havens left. Unless the present laws in the West are modified or changed to address these phenomena, the whole world would soon devolve into a big Saudi Arabia or Afghanistan. The present Western laws are misused and abused by those who have religious laws that are contrary in spirit. Islam's so-called divinely revealed laws succinctly allow them to abuse all women and terrorize others. If their religious laws did little to protect them and grant them freedom while they were in their Muslim countries or origin, why would they want vernacular/ secular laws to grant them freedom to abuse and terrorize? Why do they want free license to build more mosques to preach Jihad against Infidels and recruit more terrorists?

In the same vein, why do they want to kill those who criticize their prophet or expose him for what he is? Why do they want the world to believe evil is good and unrighteousness is acceptable? Why do they term the rape of an underage girl as marriage? Why do they want the world to respect someone who practices child abuse/Aisha, rape/Safiya, adultery/Maria, incest/Zainab, torture/ Umm Qirfa, and who allows his followers to slaughter infidels, enslave their children, rob their properties, and rape their women? How can they justify crimes and atrocities committed by an aggressor, sinner, raider, murderer, torturer, adulterer, rapist, child abuser, imposter, terrorist, and instigator of evil? How is it that they want the world to follow a religion that justifies the killing of polytheists, infidels, and apostates? Why do they feel free to criticize other religions and kill those who criticize them? Why do they want to convert people to their religion and kill those who leave theirs? And why do they want to have Shari'a courts in Western countries and apply their religious laws, which are obviously incompatible with the Western values? Why do they want to build more mosques in the lands of the infidels and forbid Christians to build churches in Muslim countries?

How can they demand that secular courts allow a man to marry four women at the same time; a husband to beat his disobedient wife; a man's inheritance to be double that of his sister; the testimony of a man to be equal of two women and to set aside the testimony of a woman who witnesses the murder of her own child? They espouse a law that endorses female genital mutilation, allows female child-marriage, disallows any woman to divorce her husband, obtaining custody of her children, restricts the woman from appearing in public without her proper chaperone; adhere to the rigid female dress code of_hijabs/niqabs/burqas; demand that no woman is to step out alone without a male Muhram, honor killings, *et cetera*. A Shari'a codified in severe draconian laws, prescribes the amputation of hands and legs of thieves, flogging of those who drink alcohol, beheading of murderers, stoning of adulterers, hanging homosexuals in public places, among other atrocities. A religion that commands its followers to slaughter those who reject their faith and kill those who leave the order. Such cruel and barbaric practices and religious courts should not be allowed in any country.

No Muslim in the entire world will admit that Islam is the religion of violence, but none can deny that for most part, Islam's spread was at the point of a sword. Islam sword sanctioned invading, killing, robbing, raping, and enslaving the infidels' children; forcing people to accept Muhammad as a prophet on pain of death. Therefore, it is a waste of time and futile to debate those issues in TV or colleges with Muslim clerics or the so-called moderate Muslims. They will use their Taqiyya and deny everything and use abrogated verses of the Meccan Qur'an or change the topic and attack the Old Testament or criticize

Western life-style and equalizes secular life with Christianity. It is my humble advice to anyone reading these words never put yourself in such awkward situation with lying, hypocritical Muslims and their demagogues and those who support their lies *such as Islam is the religion of peace or there is Moderate Islam vs. Radical Islam* from the political correctness camp. Just go ahead, expose the evils of Islam, and do that in the media, schools and colleges, temples and synagogues, and churches. I know it is difficult to get chance to share your views about Islam in the Western media. The difference between the Western world and Muslim word, Muslim clerics have full access to the media and speak freely and openly condemning Jews and Christianity and calling them brothers of apes and pigs and denouncing the West and call for Jihads against infidels whereas in the Western media and schools this is completely forbidden and anyone dares to do it is labelled as "hater" and is liable for prosecution. Unless some brave people stand against political correctness and expose the evils of Islam, this epidemic and the Shari'a dominion will spread all over the West. Unless people learn the values of Christianity and turn to God, Islam will have advantage over the moral decay and lack of spirituality and convert many youth to its cult. Islam offers empty spirituality, superficial morals, fantasy of immoral promises of virgins and orgies, which based on hatred, violence, and blindly obeying demeaning laws. Secularism, atheism, and political correctness are giving Islam distinct advantages over the Western World. Only by turning back to the Gospel of the Prince of Peace and following His commandments of Love and righteous living, will we be able to refute and expose the Message of violence and oppression and hostility and hatred in the Qur'an, which embodied in the person of Muhammad.

While I am writing these words I received a message in my *facebook* from a friend, "*Dr. Ahmed, I do not know if you have time to address this, but if you do, I would appreciate it immensely.* New Bible Versions REMOVE 'Father' and 'Son Of God' Because It Offends Muslims (Wycliff Bible)". What a SHAME! First of all, let me say it straightforward, the Qur'an is from the antichrist and Muhammad's message is from the devil's to be sure. The Qur'an is from the antichrist because it denies and opposes the main tenets of Christianity. It denies the Holy Trinity, and strongly and openly rejects the Divinity, Sonship, Crucifixion, Death, and Resurrection of Jesus Christ (Qur'an 4:171 5:17). It condemns Christians as infidels who deserve hellfire because they believe in these doctrines (Qur'an 5:70-75, 5:116-117). Without these doctrines, the Gospel of Christ is empty and Christians have no message to preach to the world.

Fight lie with truth, hate with love, evil with good, fear with courage, and never ever hesitate to speak the truth and expose the evils of Islam. As we have seen in the previous chapter that the core message of Islam is pure evil and there is nothing good in it. Having said that, it is never my intention and you can tell by all my writings, to promote hatred, violence, or to incite anyone to kill any fellow human being. Muslims without exception are all victims of Islam. I pray for the freedom of all Muslims and especially Muslim female children and women who are the first victims to this cult, which they inherited from their families with no option but to blindly follow without ever realizing that it is the main cause of their abuse and misery. As Sri Aurobindo put it, "the only way of making the Mohammedans harmless is to make them loose their faith in their religion" and this can't be done through hatred and violence but through honest and direct confrontation and exposition of the evils that they are following. Muslims all over the world need to know that their religion is evil. By telling them "Islam is a religion of peace," you are doing harm to them and making mockery of the truth. We should neither appease them nor allow their demagogues to deceive us with such an untruth. Christ said, *"The thief [Satan] does not come except to steal, and to kill, and to destroy. I [Jesus] have come that they may have life and that they may have it more abundantly"* (John 10: 10). This is the best distinction between the mission of Jesus Christ on earth and the message of Muhammad to the world. Jesus also said, *"Then you will know the truth, and the truth will set you free"* (John 8: 32). Only speaking the truth can set Muslims free and save the world from the evil of Muhammad and his Qur'an.

You might not look at Islam as your enemy but Islam teaches its followers to treat you as their ENEMY and to kill you, *"I will cast terror into the hearts of those who disbelieve [non-Muslims/infidels]. Therefore strike off their heads and strike off every fingertip of them"* (Qur'an Surat Al-'Anfāl 8: 12). Islam commands its followers not to befriend you, not make you their leaders, or deal with you in anything. *"Let not the believers take disbelievers for their friends in preference to believers. Whoever does this has no connection with Allah unless you are guarding yourselves against them as a precaution. Allah bids you to beware of Himself. And to Allah is the journeying" (Surat Al-Imran 3: 28).* The preceding *verse* forewarns Muslims from *Muwalat Al-Kafireen* [no friendship or alliance with all infidels] and alerts them to the consequences of such an action, with one exception being in extreme necessity when one must avoid or protect oneself from the harm or injury inflicted upon by infidels by presenting an outer appearance that belies what one conceals inside. This is known as *Taqiyyah*, and it is only permitted under such circumstances. Today the so-called moderate Muslims and their demagogues are practicing Taqiyya openly, still there are those "infidels" of political correctness who want to force us to practice the same in order to please Muslims and Muslim countries. Although the abovementioned verse speaks about the infidels in general, the following verse specifies Jews and Christians and commands Muslims never to take them as friends. *"O you who believe! Do not take the Jews and the Christians for friends. They are friends of one another. And whoever of you takes them for friends is (one) of them. Surely Allah does not guide wrongdoing people" (Surat Al-Maaidah 5: 51).*

Only an ex-Muslim who has forsaken Islam can understand what it means to be an apostate from Islam. Muslims reserve their most vehement hate and terror for apostates. An apostate is the Muslim who left Dar Al-Islam (Land of Islam) and joined Dar Al-harb (Land of War or Infidels). In so doing, he commits treason and deserves to be cruelly killed and his body disposed off in inhumane ways. According to the Shari'a an apostate should be killed and his dead body should neither be buried in the Muslim graveyards nor in the Christian or

Jewish cemetery. The first caliph, Abu Bakr Al-Saddiq used to tell those whom he sent to fight the apostatized tribes: "Call them to re-embrace Islam; if they refuse, do not spare any one of them. **Burn them with fire, kill them with force, and take the women and children**" (Al-Tabari, Part 2, pp. 258, 272, emphasis is mine). The fourth caliph, Ali Ibn Abi Talib, used to kill the apostates and then order the burning of their corpses, "Some apostates were brought to Ali and **he burnt them**" (Sahih Al-Bukhari, part 9, hadith no. 59, emphasis is mine). "A man from the tribe of bani 'Ijl became a Christian. They brought him to 'Ali chained in irons. 'Ali talked to him for a long time. The man said to him, 'I know that Jesus is the Son of God.' Ali stood up and stepped on him. When the people saw that, they, too, stood up and stepped on him. Then 'Ali told them: 'Kill him.' They killed him. Then **'Ali ordered them to burn him**" (Ibn Hazm, part 11, p. 190, emphasis is mine). "Another Muslim apostatized and became a Christian. 'Ali ordered him to repent but he refused. 'Ali killed him and did not deliver his corpse to his family. They offered him a lot of money (to do so), but 'Ali refused and **burned the corpse**" (Ibn Hazm, part 11, p. 190, emphasis is mine).

The caliphs Abu Bakr and Ali followed the commandment of their prophet Muhammad who used to order his troops to kill and burn Christians and Jews. While Osama bin Zayd, commander of Muhammad`s army, was preparing his troops to commence the invasion of the Byzantine Empire and capture the lands of the Jews and Christians, the prophet Muhammad commanded him saying, "*Attack them in the darkness of the dawn and fall on them killing and* ***burn them with fire*** *and invade them and return with the booty" (Ibn Habib in al-Mahabir p 117, Ibn Kathir in al-Bedaiah wa al-Nihaiah p 139, 143, Ibn Said al-Nas in 'Auion al-Atharig p 145, al-Suhili in Rawd Alanif p 24, Ibn Hisham p 245, and al-Tabari in Tarikh al-Rusul wa al-Milook p 156, emphasis is mine).* To prove that the so-called rightly-guided caliphs, Abu Bakr and Ali did not invent such an evil and inhuman practice of burning infidels and apostates but they obeyed and followed in the footsteps of their prophet, I have mentioned a half dozen authentic Islamic references that included the above quote. Moreover, killing apostates is mentioned in the most authentic collections of Muhammad's hadiths—Sahih Al-Bukhari and Sahih Muslim.

Allah's Apostle said, "The blood of a Muslim who confesses that none has the right to be worshipped but Allah and that I am His Apostle, cannot be shed except in three cases: In Qisas for murder, a married person who commits illegal sexual intercourse, and the one who reverts from Islam (apostate) and leaves the Muslims" (Sahih Muslim, Vol. 9, book 83, hadith no. 17.). *The prophet Muhammad said, "Whoever changed his religion kill him" (Sahih al-Bukhari, hadith no. 6922).*

The law of apostasy also has been mentioned in other reliable collections of the prophet's hadiths such as,

"Kill those who change their religion," (Sunan Abu Dawud, hadith no. 4337). "*If someone changes his religion, then strike off his head,*" (Muawtta Malik, hadith no. 15). "*Whoever you see splitting away from the Islamic Jama'aha kill him,*" (Sunan al-Nasa'i, hadith no. 4025). "*Whoever changes his religion, then execute him*" (Sunan Ibn Majah, hadith no. 2535).

So far, I have been an apostate from Islam for over twenty years and I will not be exaggerating if I say there is not a single day passed without me receiving death threat from Muslims through the Internet chat rooms and *facebook*. My *facebook* account has been deleted five times, due to Muslims' group reporting all manner of imagined transgressions. Many times, I was banned from joining *paltalk* chat rooms by Muslim co-administrators. Until today, due to Muslims' complaining, I am banned from opening a chat room or joining any room as an administrator. For twenty-two years, I could not return to my country, Sudan due to the capital punishment of apostasy. From a reliable source, I came to know that my name is blacklisted at the Khartoum International Airport.

It didn't stop with Cyber Bullying, but Muslim harassment has reached my hometown. Recently, a member of the notorious terrorist group known as Muslim Brotherhood who lives a couple of blocks away from my apartment threatened to kill me more than ten times and the Western police did nothing to him. He is a well-known terrorist, went to jail four times, and the police confiscated two knives from him. I have recorded his life threats more than ten times and reported him to the police. In the recordings, he called me an apostate and accused me of defaming his religion and insulting his prophet. He even described how he is going to slaughter me with his knife. He mimicked the sound that would come out of my mouth while his knife is cutting my throat. He said, it would not take him more than three minutes to kill me. He mentioned me by name and mentioned his full name in those recordings. Then, he reminded me of the Dutch filmmaker Van Goph who was assassinated by a Muslim. (Van Gogh worked with Somali-born writer Ayaan Hirsi Ali to produce the film *Submission*, which was critical of the treatment of women in Islam. On November 2, 2004 he was assassinated by Mohammed Bouyeri, a Dutch-Moroccan Muslim).

This member of the Muslim Brotherhood believes that I am worse than the Dutch film director because of my books on the issues of women in Islam. The Western police went to his house and talked to him. Of course, he practiced his Taqiyya and denied it. He was not arrested or even detained for a single hour. The sergeant who is handling my case told me that his boss said to him the court would not accept life-threat recorded over the internet. Then, the sergeant said to me, if he meets me somewhere and threatens to kill me and I have witnesses or he comes to my apartment and tries to kill me then I should call on him 911. In other words, unless this jailbird and notorious terrorist carries out his life threat and kills me I have no sufficient evidence to accuse him of wanting to kill me!

Tracie Rolfe-Collins writes, "*This is absolutely crazy! This ex-Muslim is being relentlessly bullied, harassed and receiving death threats daily and unless he is ACTUALLY murdered the police are powerless to intervene????!!!! That's simply CRIMINAL!*"

Diana Stone's prayer, *"I pray a hedge of protection around you, your family, your home, and your surroundings, wherever you may be. The blood of Jesus is more powerful than the enemy, and I pray the blood of Jesus around you. The devil makes his plans and fills the world with threats and intimidation, but He who is in you is greater than he who is in the world."*

This kind of life-threat and intimidation is spreading all over the Western World and its perpetrators are openly carrying their placards and challenging the free societies with catch phrases like, "Bomb bomb USA, bomb bomb UK," "Nuke, Nuke Denmark," "We Will Invade Denmark and Take Their Wives As War Booty," "U.S.A. Osama bin Ladin on His Way," "Death To America," "Islam Will Dominate the World," "Islam is the Solution," "Shariah is the True Solution," "Freedom Go to Hell," "British Soldiers are Baby Killers, Rapists, and Burn in Hell," "Our Dead in Paradise, Your Dead in Hell," "Hang those who Insult the Prophet," et cetera. Every time and everywhere this kind of threat and intimidation happened, no one got arrested!!??

Europe is reliving the Dark Ages all over again. The Shari'a courts and the Inquisition Police of Political Correctness are everywhere in the heart of Western Civilization. No one is free to speak or write against their evil scheme. Anyone who dares to speak against them is crucified with the charge of "hate crime" by the goons of political correctness and risk being thrown behind bars or brutally murdered by their predators. Their leaders are given platforms to speak openly in the BBC, CNN, Fox News, Aljazeera, and proclaim their agendas of implementing their Shari'a and turning London into Londonstan and the White House into Black House after the model of their Black Ka'aba. Their dictators move freely, spreading their terror, and threatening to wipe out nations, and yet they are allowed to preach their evil in the United Nations' International Annual Meetings and Colombia University. Although the International Criminal Court has convicted some of them of war crimes, crimes against humanity, and genocide, still they fly from country to country without being detained or extradited to Hague. Their demagogues feed the world lies and convince the simple minded that there is a good religion known as moderate Islam and there is something evil called radical Islam. [H. L. Mencken, defines a **demagogue** as "one who will preach doctrines he knows to be untrue to men he knows to be idiots"]. No wonder they have many sympathizers in the Congress and a Leader after their kind presiding over the White House. From the White House, they are planning to move to Ground Zero and build their Cordoba Mosque on the graves of their victims and proclaim their official return and final victory over the pinnacle of Western World.

Their next movement is to demand the creation of their Shari'a courts in every city and every state. Then, there will be a law for Muslims and a different law for non-Muslims. Like India, it is legal for a Muslim man to have four wives and illegal for a Hindu man to marry more than one wife. A Muslim man can marry an underage girl and beat his disobedient wife because his so-called divinely revealed law allows him to do so (Qur'an 65: 4 & 4: 34), etc. According to one of their leaders, "Islam is not in America to be equal to any other faith, but to become dominant. The Quran should be the highest authority in America, and Islam the only accepted religion on earth" (Omar Ahmad, Chairman of Council on American-Islamic Relations (CAIR), in 1998). This means other religions such as Judaism, Christianity, Hinduism, and Buddhism, and their followers have no right to exist on earth. That is the message of Islam to the world, *convert to Islam or you have no right to live.*

In the Qur'an and the hadiths of Muhammad there is nothing called radical Islam and moderate Islam. Islam is one and its core message is pure evil. If you believe Islam is a religion of peace, you are either ignorant, hypocrite, or seduced by Political Correctness. Yes, it is true there are many peace-loving Muslims but they are so because they don't follow everything written in their Qur'an and practice everything mentioned in the hadiths of their prophet. There are also the law-abiding Muslims who practice Taqiyya while they are living in non-Muslim countries. And finally, there are the true Muslims who are sincerely following to the very letter the teachings of their religious texts and these are the so-called radical Muslims. The problem, how do I know the Muslim who is living behind my backyard is which one of the three? After all, Muhammad Atta and his terrorist gang were law-abiding Muslims until the morning of September 11, 2001.

Islam is the only religion in the world that its religious texts (Qur'an and hadiths), which are embodied in the Shari'a laws, are fixed and final and no Islamic authority can modify or reform them. After the death of Muhammad, no mortal being can change those laws. It is well-accepted doctrine that those laws are applicable to all times and places. To reform or modify those laws is to admit that Muhammad had committed terrible sins and hideous crimes and that the Qur'an is not applicable to all times and places and no Muslim can take such stand and remain Muslim or continue to live. Those who tried to reform or modify those fixed and rigid laws lost their lives such as Mahmoud Muhammad Taha and Faraj Foda.

Islamophobia is bogus and fear of terrorism is natural but necessary passion for defeating the evils of Islam. Why the terrorists are always from countries such as Afghanistan, Pakistan, Saudi Arabia, Yemen, Egypt, Somalia, Iran, Sudan, Indonesia, North African and Arabian countries? What is common among these countries? They are all Muslim countries. Why all those who carried out terrorist attacks or plotted to commit terrorist acts in Western countries were all Muslims. Why the so-called magnificent nineteen terrorists who carried out the cowardly attacks on September 11, were from Saudi Arabia, Egypt, UAE, and Lebanon? Why do we not see Hindus, Buddhists, Jews, Christians, Confuciusists, or even atheists carrying out suicide attacks on schools, churches, temples, restaurants, trains, planes, public buildings, *et cetera*? Why is it almost always a Muslim? Why are those who sanction honor killings on their daughters or wives always Muslims? Why is it only the Muslim who inflicts female genital mutilation and upholds child marriage? The answers to all these questions are found within the pages of the Qur'an and the books of the hadiths, which are believed to be divinely revealed and applicable to all times and places. And *"He who has ears to hear, let him hear"* (Mark 4: 9).

CHAPTER 10

THE TRIAL OF THE CHILD-BRIDE

The hearing to decide the validity of the marriage between Sheikh Ahmed and his child-wife was conducted shortly after Iffat was taken away from her husband. The Shari'a court wanted to render a decision on this sensitive issue before the wrath of the public became uncontrollable. The fatwa of Sheikh Yusuf al-Qaradawi had created serious problems for the Royal family and the judicial system in the Kingdom of Saudi Arabia. People openly protested and demanded the immediate release of the wife to the custody of her Saudi husband and the freedom to take her to any country and bed her like any good Muslim man. After issuing the fatwa, Iran invited the Saudi husband to bring his Indian wife to Tehran and live there. Sudan also promised to welcome the married couple on its soil.

The CIA team members were allowed to attend the trial with a translator. The trial was supposed to be conducted in Arabic. There are no lawyers in an Arabic Shari'a court. Islamic law would not permit any lawyer because in the day of Prophet Muhammad there were no lawyers. The court however, in the interest of justice, would allow the accused to call witnesses and produce evidence for his defense. These courts also used religious judges and assistant judges. In short, Sheikh Ahmed was allowed to present his case. Iffat was brought to the court too. She was kept in the women's jail until the court would decide on her status. She wasn't allowed to see or meet her mother while she was sojourning in the jail. It was widely predicted that should the court nullify her marriage to the old Saudi, she would be deported and handed over to the Indian Consulate to be shipped back to her home country. If, however, the court ruled in favor of Sheikh Ahmed, she would be returned to his custody. It was presumed that the court would then give him a week to make preparations to send her to another Muslim country.

"To the righteous judges and the honorable audience," began the old man and his story, *"when my Indian maidservant was arrested by the Jeddah police for practicing public deception and adultery I was left with two choices regarding her daughter; I should either send her back to her country to her relatives or keep her under my care until the Shari'a court would issue its ruling on her mother. I preferred to keep her in my house until the court decided on the charges against her mother. After the court condemned her mother and sentenced her to be stoned to death for marrying two men at the same time and being impregnated by a third,"* Sheikh Ahmed paused when he heard murmuring and the shuffling of feet in courtroom. Instead of continuing his sentence, he suddenly remembered the day he met her mother in India and decided to share his experience with the court and the audience. *"I did not know that her mother was a prostitute in Bombay and was cheating men and marrying them and stealing their money until the most highly exalted Allah exposed her and the Shari'a court convicted her."*

This was the way the old Saudi man falsified the story of his former Layla and told it to the court, *"I was performing my Friday public prayer in the renowned Muslim Mosque at Haji Ali in Bombay when someone approached me and talked to me about her mother. He was a Muslim Indian. He told me that there was a poor young Muslim woman who had lost her husband recently and had a small daughter. He said that she had no one to support her and her daughter. When she became a widow, she started to work in the houses of some rich Hindu families. However, because she was a young and beautiful Indian woman, the Hindu men harassed her sexually and some of them attempted to rape her. For that reason, she stopped going to their houses because she was a chaste and good Muslim woman. I asked him what I could do to help such a poor and helpless Muslim woman. He said to me you are the only person who can help solve her problems. I said to him only Allah can solve the problems of the poor people. However, if you want me to give her some money I am ready to do so. He said to me whatever you give her was going to finish one day. However, if you could help her to find some decent work to do, her problem would be solved forever. I said to him how could I give her a decent job when I am a foreigner in this country. Then, he said to me, take her with you to your country and make her your maidservant. Although at that time I had four wives and four maidservants, I agreed to help a widowed Muslim woman. I promised the Indian brother who brought her to me and shared with me her problem that as soon as I return to my country I will send two visas and two tickets to the widow and her daughter. I did not want to separate a seven-year-old daughter from her mother."*

Sheikh Ahmed took out of his suitcase the copies of the visas and tickets of Rayhana and her daughter and lifted them up and showed them to the judges and the court. Then, he continued his story, *"I swear by Allah and the divorce of all my wives that I had never given any Indian man or woman before or after a free visa and purchased his or her ticket except for this Indian maidservant and her daughter. And I challenge the court and any one present here to tell me about any Indian travel agency that issued free visas and tickets to any poor Indian family before or after as I did."* Sheikh Ahmed paused when he heard the audience began to clap their hands in appreciation of his generosity and kindness. Then, he continued to narrate his false story. *"I did that because I am a father and I am a Muslim. I did that because I did not want a young Muslim woman to bring up her daughter by selling her thighs to filthy Hindu infidels."*

The audience starting clapping their hands again and some of them jumped up and shouted three times; *"Allah Akabar!" "Allah Akabar!" "Allah Akabar!"* When the shouts of jubilation ceased, the old man continued his false story. "*When that young Indian Muslim widow came to Saudi Arabia, I decided to help her more than she expected. I understood that she was young and beautiful. At that time, I had two sons, a sixteen and fourteen-year-old, living with my fourth wife and me. I was afraid that my young, unmarried sons might be tempted by the beauty of the young Indian maidservant and do haram with her. Therefore, when she came to my house I convinced my Pakistani chauffeur to marry her. However, I did not want her to feel that I was forcing her to marry my driver. I shared with her what I had in my heart and she gladly agreed to marry my Pakistani driver."*

The old Saudi paused, expecting cheering from the audience, but he was disappointed when no one clapped at his well-rehearsed lie. He resumed his tale by saying, *"Whatever I had done for the mother of my Indian wife I did it with good intentions. I wanted to have a clear conscience. I did not want to stand before Allah on the Day of Judgment and tell him that I left a poor Muslim widow to starve in Bombay and sell her body to feed her daughter."* This time, members of the audience, rejuvenated, stood on their feet and shouted praises to their Allah and thanked the God sent, Sheikh Ahmed. As soon as the roar of the crowd died down, the old man put his right hand on his chest and lifted up his left hand and said loudly, *"As soon as my Indian maidservant had gotten married to my chauffeur, the exalted Allah exposed her. I did not know that she was a prostitute in Bombay and the man who brought her to me had cheated me. He might be the man who impregnated her. When the police found out that she had married two men in Jeddah at the same time, she was arrested. Imagine a single woman marrying two men at the same time and sleeping with them and she did that in less than ten days. I had never heard about such an abomination being done by a Muslim woman in all my life."*

Sheikh Ahmed paused when he heard the judges and the audience cursing the devil and asking Allah to protect their daughters, sisters, and wives from such an abomination. Sheikh Ahmed continued his presentation by saying, "*The police discovered that she had been impregnated by a third man before she married those two men. When I went to the police and I inquired about her, I was told that she is a professional prostitute who goes around the city and cheats men, marries them and steals their money."*

Sheikh Ahmed once again paused expecting some reaction from the court or the audience, but when no one uttered a word or moved a leg, he continued his fabricated story. *"I could not refute the police when they showed me the copies of her two marriage licenses and the result of the pregnancy test. It appeared that she had already been impregnated by someone before she left India. Either she had a husband and lied to me and said that he died or she slept with another man and became pregnant. Only Allah knows how she got pregnant. Anyway, I kept her daughter in my house and waited until the Shari'a court convicted her mother of those serious crimes of marrying two men at the same time and getting pregnant by a third man without a husband. The court sentenced her to be stoned to death. When I came to know that the mother was going to be punished according to our blessed Shari'a law and she wasn't coming back I was faced with the responsibility of her small daughter."*

"At first, I decided to adopt the little girl, but then I remembered that our gracious Qur'an forbids adoption. Therefore, I decided to send her back to India. I contacted the address that was mentioned on the daughter's passport and her mother's passport. I discovered that it was a fake address. The people who were living at that address were foreign students from Jordan and Palestine studying at the Bombay University. I talked to them personally on the phone and I learned that they had been living in that apartment for more than three years. Here are copies of the passports of my Indian wife and her mother and if anyone doubts my claim let him contact the address and prove me wrong. Nonetheless, I decided to send my Indian maidservant's daughter along with my Pakistani chauffeur to Bombay. I thought he might find her family in Bombay and hand her over to them. Unfortunately, the Indian Consulate rejected the application of my chauffeur for a visiting visa because he is a Pakistani. Indians think every Pakistani is a terrorist and their enemy. Here is a copy of my Pakistani chauffeur's passport and here is the rejection stamp of the Indian Consulate. The court can have this copy and verify my claim. Then, I talked to the employees of the Indian Consulate and begged them to help me to find the family of the small girl of my condemned

Indian maidservant. None of them was prepared to help me. After all doors were closed in my face, I decided to share the problem of the small Indian girl with my wives and children. I did not want to take an action that might create problems for the poor little girl and make my face condemned before my Allah and the people around me."

"One of my wives told me to keep the girl with her as her maidservant. I said to her first of all, the girl is too small to be employed as a maidservant. Secondly, I said to her, if I allow the girl to stay with you, how are you going to protect her from your growing sons. She has one son now seventeen and one nineteen years old. Of course, the small girl is going to grow up one day and she might tempt my two good sons and cause them to fall into the sin of zina. Therefore, I rejected the advice of my fourth wife. It was my first wife who gave me the right counsel. She said to me either tell one of your sons to marry the poor Indian girl or marry her yourself. I said to her how could one of my sons marry her when the Saudi law forbids a Saudi man to marry a foreigner. Then, she said to me marry her yourself and keep her in another country. At first, I rejected the advice. However, when I remembered that I travel often to some Muslim counties in Asia and Africa for business, I accepted the advice of my first wife. At that time, I had four wives and the Shari'a would not allow me to have a fifth one. I could just treat her as my right-hand-possessed and keep her as my jaria. However, I was scared people might accuse me of cohabiting with a young woman without marriage and blame me of not doing the right thing. I shared my problem with my four wives again. I did not want to divorce one of them to marry the small girl."

"My first wife who advised me to marry the small girl volunteered herself. At that time, she was too old and dying with cancer. By the way, although my wife was sick for two years and I was not able to sleep with her, I still kept her under my ropes. She said to me exactly what the blessed wife of our gracious prophet Muhammad, Sawda bint Zama'ah, had said to him concerning her age. Sawda donated her night to Aisha because she became too old and could not enjoy sex anymore. She gifted her night to the beloved and young child-bride of our prophet, Aisha bint Abi Bakr. Likewise, my first wife, Raqiya

bint Salih gifted her night and her marriage to the young Indian girl, Iffat Khan. I listened to her wise counsel and divorced her. After two days, my blessed wife died and went to her Lord." (The truth is that the first wife had a stroke of the brain and went into a coma when she heard her wicked husband divorced her again, and this time while she was on her deathbed. She did not come out of the coma and on the following day, she passed away).

Sheikh Ahmed waited for appreciation from the court, but no one seemed to have believed this last narration. *"After I received the right counsel from my first wife and divorced her, I began to work on the next step. I understood that the law of my country would not allow me to marry the small Indian girl, therefore I decided to follow the wise advice of my first wife. I knew that our blessed Shari'a did not forbid a Saudi man to marry non-Saudi woman. Therefore, I decided to take the poor and orphaned Indian girl to a Muslim country that allowed Muslim men and women to get married to each other regardless of their color, race, age and..."* ; Sheikh Ahmed was compelled to stop his lies for several minutes when the audience stood on their feet clapping their hands and praising the Prophet Muhammad and their Lord Allah. However, noticeably, the five religious judges were reserved in their applause, presumably because the old man hit a sensitive nerve regarding a law created by the Royal family. *"...Thank you kindly faithful brothers, ...and I came to know that countries like Pakistan, Afghanistan, Iran, Indonesia, Somalia, Sudan, and Eritrea will allow a Muslim man to marry a Muslim woman regardless of her age, race, and color."* The old man once again paused for adulation, but none was forthcoming. *"All these seven nations blessed among Muslim countries were applying the Shari'a of Allah and his gracious prophet to its fullest. Therefore..."*

This time, his words were interrupted by the clapping and commendations of the audience even though he did not expect it. Moreover, this time one of the five judges took a calculated risk and hit his table lightly with his hands. The old man felt that his words had achieved a good effect at least on one of the judges and that was a good sign. *"Therefore, I decided to take my soon-to-be bride to one of these*

Muslim countries and marry her. However, I did not want to be selfish and decide for my future-bride which country she should live in. For that reason, I wrote each country on a piece of paper and folded the papers and asked her to pick one. She picked up the piece of paper that had Eritrea written on it. I had never been to Eritrea before and I would have never gone there if she had not chosen that country herself. It wasn't because I did not want to visit my this Muslim country, but because of the language barrier. However, since I promised my Allah and my gracious prophet that whatever country my fiancée would choose I would take her there and marry her. I accepted her choice. I did not travel with her in the same plane because she wasn't my wife yet. I was determined not to stay with her in the same hotel room because that was against our beautiful Shari'a law. I decided to keep the commandment of our gracious prophet which said that, 'When a man and a woman are isolated in the presence of each. Satan is bound to be their third companion.' I booked her in one plane and I booked myself in a different plane. When we reached Asmara I..."

For the first time, since the old man began to tell his bogus story, one of the judges was forced to interrupt him and demand something of an explanation. *"How was it that an eight years old child was allowed by the airlines to travel alone? As far as my knowledge is concerned, no airline would allow a minor to travel alone from one country to another without an adult accompanying her."* Sheikh Ahmed knew about this technical issue, but he thought no one would notice it. He did not want to contradict his own rule of law and that of his prophet in allowing a man to travel with a girl when she wasn't his wife. Moreover, he did not want to introduce his Pakistani pimp at this stage of his made-up story. However, the clever judge put him on the hot seat and he had to give an explanation before his fake story would be accepted. *"Thank you my blessed judge for reminding me of something very important which I forgot to mention. As you all know that our blessed Shari'a would not permit a virgin woman to marry a man without a wali (i.e. guardian)."*

The judge who asked the question and the other four judges felt they were exposed when the old man reminded them of a very important question that they failed to ask from the beginning. *"I have forgotten to mention that I needed a wali in order to lawfully marry the virgin girl."* One of the judges thought to ask him, *"how did you know she was a virgin before marrying her?"* However, he ignored his thought when he remembered that the girl in question was only seven or eight years old at that time.

"Since the Indian girl had no relative to be her wali I decided to appoint her a righteous Muslim man to be her wali. I would not go to the prison and ask the permission of her mother because our blessed Shari'a said, 'A woman is utterly incompetent to enter into a marriage contract either herself or for another even though her guardian should authorize her to do so. A father can contract the marriage of his virgin daughter without asking her consent whatever her age (Verma 1988: 24)'. Moreover, I did not know of any male relative for the little girl so that I could ask his permission before I would contract her for marriage. I was about to drop the idea of marrying her when I discovered that I could not lawfully marry her without a male relative. I was in a dilemma. If I had to marry her without a wali, my marriage contract to her might be rendered invalid and I would be committing adultery with her. If I did not marry her, I would expose her and expose my sons to the danger of committing fornication. While I was mediating over my dilemma my faithful Pakistani chauffeur came forward and hit his chest with his right hand and said proudly, 'I will be her wali and I will give her to you in marriage'."

The old man stopped his fake narration and looked around. The faces of the audience and the judges gave him thumbs down on that detail of the story. No one in the court applauded this bright idea of his Pakistani chauffeur to become the young girl's wali. It wasn't because what he had said was something that didn't deserve praise, but because they hated Pakistani Muslims. If he had said, my fellow *Arab brother and chauffeur*, they would have clapped for over thirty minutes. The sad fact of Arab life is that they simply have always looked down on non-Arab Muslims. They consider themselves to be gods of the earth as the position of the Brahmins in the religion of

Hinduism. In fact, Indian Muslims also practiced the caste system and divided themselves into Ashrafs, Ajlafs, and Arzals. The Ashrafs are the descendants of the Arab, Persian, and Mogul invaders who brought the curse of Islam to the Indian subcontinent. Therefore, the Ashrafs claimed to be the direct descendants of the prophet Muhammad and looked at other Indian Muslims as Ajlafs and Arzals. The Arzals are like the untouchable Hindus and they are not allowed to enter the mosques for prayers or permitted to touch the Qur'an.

One of the judges out of hatred towards the Pakistani Muslims interrupted the old man and asked him a very revealing question. Neither the judge who asked the question nor the old man anticipated the ramifications or where the question would lead. The inquiry was a slippery slope that changed the whole direction of the trial and created a great division between the old Saudi and his faithful Pakistani chauffeur who had allegedly volunteered to be the wali of Iffat Khan. (Before that question was presented, the old man was planning to refer to the pseudo marriage of his former maidservant and his chauffer and then argues that Iffat became like a niece/daughter/close relative or whatever the hell Islam would define such a relationship between a stepdaughter and her stepfather. He knew that his Qur'an forbids adoption and hence he would not be allowed to say in a Shari'a court that Iffat Khan became a stepdaughter to his Pakistani chauffer). However, the judge saved him that trouble and asked him a direct and straightforward question. The judge wanted to know why Sheikh Ahmed did not convince his "faithful Pakistani chauffeur" to marry the small child and save himself all the trouble he caused himself by marrying her. The foolish old man could have easily answered that difficult question by saying that the Shari'a would not permit his Pakistani chauffeur to marry Iffat Khan because he had already married her mother, Rayhana Khan and consummated her marriage on the same day. Nevertheless, he couldn't use this defense because he inadvertently mentioned that he did harbor that thought and had in fact, talked to his Pakistani chauffeur about the possibility of marrying the daughter of his maidservant. However, his chauffeur refused to marry her for some personal reason. The judge wasn't satisfied with that vague of an answer and demanded to know precisely the personal issue that prevented the chauffeur from marrying the little girl. At this point in the trial, the old man still had a chance to escape from the messy trap he was setting for himself, but he missed the opportunity again. Instead of offering as a effective counterargument for his case, he said that his Pakistani pimp informed him that he did not have what other men had. The insistent judge asked Sheikh Ahmed to explain and speak plainly and clearly to the court exactly what his Pakistani chauffeur spoke to him.

The old man's memory lapsed and he forgot that his Pakistani chauffeur was present in the courtroom. He said his chauffeur told him that he was castrated when he was in Pakistan and hence he would not marry a woman and deny her what every wife should get from her husband. Confidently, Sheikh Ahmed made a request to the court to enter an exhibit into evidence and doing so, he made another absent-minded error. He took out of his suitcase, a medical report issued by a Pakistani doctor in Jeddah, which proved that Sabir Ibrahim Shah was a eunuch. All of the judges looked curiously at each other for a second and then all five judges spoke their minds in unison as if they were singing in a five-part harmony. *"Then how did your Pakistani chauffeur marry her mother and sleep with her?"* There was dead silence in the courtroom. Everyone was waiting for someone to speak, particularly Sheikh Ahmed. He was finally caught in his trap web of lies. When Sabir Ibrahim Shah heard for the first time that he was a castrated man, the mystery that had puzzled him for the last three years was solved. He remembered that on the day he married the beautiful Indian woman and slept with her in the same room, he tried to have sex with her, but couldn't. Even Rayhana invited him to have sex with her before the old man would come and sleep with her, but he could not for some reason. She tried everything he asked her to do to stimulate him, but he could not get an erection. He also remembered the same thing happened to him when his secret woman, Mrs. Ahmed, tried to have sex with him soon after that day and he could not do it with her either. He also remembered he tried several times to have sex with the little girl, Iffat Khan in the absence of his master, but failed. Finally, Sabir concluded that his Allah had cursed him and turned him into an impotent man because of the evils he did to Rayhana Khan and her child.

Only now, when the ruthless old man took out of his suitcase the medical report issued by a Pakistani doctor and showed it to the court, did Sabir know he had been castrated. He then understood why the old man trusted him whole-heartedly with Rayhana Khan and her daughter, Iffat. Why would his wicked master allow him to sleep with the young beautiful Indian woman in the same bedroom on the day of his secret marriage to her and why would he allow him to live with his child-bride in the same house in his absence. He knew that a Saudi man would never trust his own father or brother with his wife.

Sabir Shah was so angry that when he stood up he couldn't speak. It was like his lips were frozen in time. The judge asked him to tell the court what he wanted to say. When he opened his mouth, it was as if a bomb had been dropped and exploded all of a sudden inside the courtroom by a terrorist on a mission to kill and be killed. He let loose a stockpile of ammunition telling the court whatever the old man had said to the court was a pack of lies. He confessed that Sheikh Ahmed was the one who forced him to marry Rayhana Khan on paper because he wanted to sleep with her himself. He stated proudly, Sheikh Ahmed was the one who pressured him to convince Rayhana to become a kept-wife, which he did successfully after many attempts. He said Sheikh Ahmed was the one who spent truckloads of money to bring the beautiful Indian woman from Bombay because he was madly in love with her. He was the one who cheated him out of his manhood and sent him to the Pakistani doctor and had him castrated without his consent and knowledge. Then, the Pakistani man turned to Sheikh Ahmed's testimony about the little girl and began to rip it apart piece by piece.

Sabir narrated to the court the story of Rayhana Khan and her daughter from the time they arrived at the Jeddah International Airport until they found them at *the Filipino Beautiful Women Salon*. He admitted that he did not marry Rayhana Khan in reality. It was a fake marriage, which was merely on paper only. He admitted to the court that he was the one who helped Sheikh Ahmed's two sons smuggle a surveillance camera inside their house. He also said that he installed the camera in the women's bathroom for them. The two sons then videotaped Rayhana Khan while she was taking a bath bare-naked and used the video to blackmail her and have sex with her. Sabir told the court that he strongly believed the child that the Indian maidservant delivered in jail was the son of one of Sheikh Ahmed's two sons.

Then, Sabir narrated to the court the sad story of Iffat Khan. He narrated in tears, how the evil old man had raped her and imprisoned her in Asmara for three years. Sabir admitted that he had collaborated with the wicked old man in all his evils that he had committed against the young Indian child. He said that he had acted as a wali for Iffat and signed the marriage contract. He also informed the court that for three years he lived in the house of Sheikh Ahmed at Asmara and kept the young Muslim girl imprisoned within the confines of the house. His confession made the seven-member team of the CIA weep openly in court. Tears ran down their faces into their hands, as they tried to conceal their unprofessional behavior in the line of duty. With his admission to being an accessory to the crimes of his master, the audience stared at him in disgust. He had become to them as a bad taste in their mouths, but none of them said a word in response and none of them shed a single tear for Rayhana and her daughter nor had his testimony touched the hearts of the judges.

CHAPTER 11

THE RETRIAL OF RAYHANA

The retrial of Rayhana Khan took place shortly after the Jeddah Shari'a court dealt with the case of her daughter. Unfortunately, the confession of Sabir Ibrahim Shah did not convince the Islamic court to invalidate the marriage contract between Sheikh Ahmed and his child-wife, Iffat Khan. The five Islamic judges rejected Sabir's statement against his Saudi employer on the grounds that he took part in the marriage contract and volunteered himself to be the wali of Iffat Khan. He had also taken care of the wife in question for three years. Therefore, he was considered a *Shahood Zoor (False Witness)*. He was charged as *a False Testifier and Slanderer* who presented to the court oral communication of a false confession that was injurious to the reputation of a God's fearing Muslim. He was also convicted of providing false and malicious statements about his Saudi employer. According to the Qur'an, if a person gives a false statement about someone, he is prescribed eighty stripes and his testimony is never to be accepted again.

As was written in the laws of the country, Sabir Ibrahim Shah was sentenced to eighty whiplashes. In addition, the court ordered that he be deported back to his country of origin after sentencing. The court also banned him from visiting Saudi Arabia ever again, even if it was to perform the Islamic pilgrimage (the Hajj) in the holy cities of Mecca and Medina, to go around the House of Allah and stone the accursed Satan. Anyway, after sentencing Sabir, the court ruled in favor of his former employer, Sheikh Ahmed. His marriage to the female Indian child was considered valid and did not violate the Islamic Shari'a law in any way. Therefore, the court issued a verdict that the husband, Sheikh Faiz bin Ahmed, should be allowed to take his Indian wife Iffat Khan to another Muslim country of his own choice and continue his married life with her.

The trial of the child-bride and the old man had given the CIA team incidental clues that they were looking for in solving Rayhana's problem. First of all, they got a copy of the medical certificate that Sheikh Ahmed presented in the Shari'a court to prove that his Pakistani chauffeur had been medically castrated. This certificate would be critical in Rayhana's defense. It would prove to the court that the second marriage of Rayhana Khan was based on deception and hence it was illegal according to their laws. It would also prove that the marriage was never consummated. There was still the danger that the court might still convict her of having an illegitimate child. They learned that the pregnancy tests performed during her medical exam showed that the Indian maidservant was eight weeks pregnant before she was married to the Pakistani chauffeur of her employer. Obviously, based on the same medical report, the two sons of the Sheikh could not have fathered her child. They were inclined to believe Rayhana's story. She was pregnant because she was raped by two Saudi police officers upon her arrival in Saudi Arabia. For that reason, the CIA team decided to search for the Bedouin family that rescued Rayhana and saved her life when the two Saudi policemen brutally raped and attempted to murder her. That would convince the court that Rayhana was impregnated by her rapist and not conceived through adultery. Accordingly, the team employed fifteen young Arab men and began their search around the outskirts of Jeddah City. The search was difficult due to the huge numbers of Bedouin tents encircling the city like an ant farm. The team members knew that if they did not find and present the Bedouin family at her retrial, Rayhana Khan would be stoned to death.

In their search, the CIA team members used some of Rayhana's photos that they collected from the newspapers and magazines, which included articles about her simultaneous marriages. After two weeks of intensive searching, the Bedouin family was found near a small suburb at the outskirts to the east of Jeddah City. The kind Bedouin parents identified Rayhana's photos and narrated the entire story of her discovery and rescue. They began from the time they spotted the small daughter walking all alone on the rough desert road. At first, they thought that she was a satanic creature who had come to attack them. Therefore, they decided to beat her up if she came to their tent. However, the wife told her husband to read *the Verse of the Throne* first before he attacked the female creature and kill her. The Bedouin woman told her husband that if the creature did not disappear after hearing the verse of the throne then he shouldn't attack or kill her. In that way, the Bedouin man said he came to know the female creature was a human being instead of a satanic jinni because she did not vanish after he read aloud the verse of the throne from the Qur'an.

Then, the Bedouins narrated how the little girl directed them to the place where her mother lay half-dead in the desert. When they reached the place, they found the mother was half-naked because her rapists had torn off most of her clothes. They carried her on their shoulders and brought her to their tent. Her body was full of cuts and bruises. The Bedouin woman narrated how she used Dettol and hot water to treat her wounds. Then, she used cold water to revive her. Everything the Bedouins said was videotaped by the CIA team. The Bedouins mentioned that Rayhana and her daughter spent one month with them. After one month, the mother using sign language requested the Bedouin man take her with him to the city. Then, the Bedouins said that they took the mother and her daughter by donkeys and rode them to the nearest suburb and left them in front of a supermarket. The last time they saw them was where they had left them.

The statements of the Bedouin family were considered by the CIA team as good concrete evidence that Rayhana was kidnapped, beaten, and raped. However, the Bedouins did not see who had raped her and attempted to murder her. The Shari'a court might accept the testimony of the Bedouin family about the kidnap and murder attempt of Rayhana Khan, but it might reject the claim that Rayhana was raped and subsequently impregnated. To solidify their case, the CIA team tried to confirm that the two Saudi policemen who took Rayhana and her daughter from the Jeddah International Airport were the ones who in fact had kidnapped, raped, and attempted to kill her. If that missing piece of information were obtained, then the two culprits would be found and punished.

The CIA team went to the Saudi airlines and demanded to know what had happened to the two Indian passengers who managed to enter the Saudi plane and travel from Bombay to Jeddah without their passports. The airlines office found the report of the Saudi plane that brought Rayhana and her daughter from Bombay to Jeddah. The report showed that two Indian passengers by the names of Rayhana Khan and Iffat Khan had boarded the Saudi plane without their passports. It also mentioned that the two passengers were handed over to the airport police.

Based on these reports, the CIA team approached the Jeddah International Airport Authority and confirmed the arrest of the two Indian passengers who arrived from Bombay without their passports. The team got an official copy of the record and added it to their files. Then the team approached the airport police and demanded to know what had happened with the two Indian passengers who were arrested without their passports. The airport police confirmed the arrest and gave the names of the two police officers who came and took the Indian woman and her daughter to the Jeddah Jail For Women. Before informing the Jeddah police officials about the two policemen who had raped Rayhana Khan and dumped her unconscious body in the desert, the CIA team decided to confirm that the two arrested Indian passengers were not actually taken to jail. Therefore, after comparing evidence from the three different sources—the Saudi Airlines, the Jeddah International Airport, and the airport police, the CIA team approached the Central Prison for Women and confirmed that the two arrested Indian passengers who arrived in the country without passports were never received as inmates.

Once more, the team did not approach the Jeddah police to demand the arrest of the two Saudi policemen. The CIA team submitted the results of their investigation to the Royal family. It was to the royals that they made their demands that the two Saudi policemen be arrested and that DNA tests be conducted to determine the paternity of the child of the imprisoned Indian woman, Rayhana Khan. Although, the Kingdom of Saudi Arabia does not usually administer a DNA test in deciding the outcome in cases of adultery or other immoral crimes, the Royal family issued a decree for the detention of the two policemen and gave their consent for DNA and paternity tests to be done. A special medical team was brought in from the UK to conduct the tests.

The results of the DNA paternity tests confirmed that one of the two policemen had fathered the boy of Rayhana Khan. Confronted with overwhelming evidence against them, the two Saudi policemen confessed their crimes of kidnapping and raping the Indian woman on the day of her arrival in Jeddah and that they had left her and her daughter in the desert and returned to the city. As soon as the two culprits confessed their crimes and the DNA tests proved that the Indian maidservant had been raped, the Royal family issued a second decree and canceled the scheduled retrial of Rayhana Khan. The decree ordered the immediate release of the Indian woman with honor. Moreover, the King of Saudi Arabia decreed that Rayhana Khan should be compensated with a sum of 3,750,000 Saudi Riyals. It was a huge amount of money which equivalent to 1,000,000 US dollars (45,000,000 Indian Rupees).

In India, that amount was called *Four Crores and Fifty Lakhs* (i.e. 45,000,000). If Rayhana had worked for one thousand years as a maidservant in India, she would not have made 1% of what she was awarded in compensation for her imprisonment. Even if her former Saudi sponsor had employed her as his maidservant for one hundred years, she would not have made 10% of the wages for sin that the Saudi government paid to reward her for the evils committed against her. Although she was released with honor and her life snatched away from the jaws of death, and she was paid an immense amount of money in compensation, Rayhana's heart was sad. She was devastated when she came to know that her little daughter was forced into marrying the old Saudi and impregnated by him while she was only eleven years old. She cried and begged the Royal family to intervene and release her little girl from the old man, but her tears and pleadings fell on cold stone hearts. She was told that no power or authority on earth could release her daughter from her lawful Saudi husband unless he willingly agreed to divorce her without coercion.

The CIA team members understood that they had not fully accomplished their mission successfully. They could not convince the Shari'a court that Sheikh Ahmed had killed the wife of the son of Senator Peter Thomason. They also were not able to invalidate the marriage contract of the old man and the little Indian girl. They failed to force the Islamic court to convict Sheikh Ahmed of kidnapping, rapping, and imprisoning a young minor female. However, they felt that they had achieved a considerable victory by stopping the stoning of an innocent Indian woman from the slums. On the same day Rayhana Khan took an air Indian plane and flew back to her homeland, the seven members of the CIA team boarded their plane and began their trip back to the United States of America. They felt as if they were flying away from a society still living in a backward seventh century ancient religious system of the old Sahara to an advanced free society and the greatest nation and country in the world of the twenty-first century.

CHAPTER 12

TEARS OF THE HEART

Rayhana Khan arrived at the Mumbai Chhatrapati Shiviji International Airport at 11:28 am, local time. When she left India over three years ago, the city was called Bombay and its airport was known as the Sahara International Airport. In her absence, the Shev Sina Hindu political party had changed the name of every street and every local-train station in the city. Even the city did not escape the radical religious change. Even the one and a half century old Bombay University was changed to Mumbai University. The University of Bombay was established in 1857. The only thing that the Hindu party could not achieve yet was the changing of the name of the country from India to Hindustan.

The Shev Sina party was part of the national Hindu party known as Bhahartiya Janata Party (BJP). India in Hindi was called Bharata. I wish God would help them in changing the name of the country to Hindustan or Bharata. 150 million Muslims were living in India and yet they were more loyal to Pakistan than India. They always cheered for the Pakistani Cricket team and celebrated and rejoiced openly whenever it defeated the Indian Cricket team. I wonder how a person could live in a country but support another; one that is considered India's bitterest enemy. This problem is not only confined to the Muslims of India, but we notice it in many Western countries like Canada, Australia, and the UK and the USA. Many Muslims born in these countries and those who obtain their citizenship in these countries, do not integrate into mainstream society and hate their new homeland. They direct their hatred at a country that gives them a way to make a living and social liberties not available in their previous countries and sometimes they help plot out terrorist attacks against innocent citizens of their adopted nation.

Suffice to say, Rayhana left one country with her little girl, Iffat Khan, and returned with her baby boy, Irvan Khan. She boarded a plane as one of the poorest slum women and returned to it among one of the richest. Despite it all, she was miserable. The suffering, torture, and abuse she experienced in the so-called holy land left permanent painful scars on her heart, mind, and body that no amount of money could erase or alleviate. She felt despair for what the wicked old man had done and was still doing to her young daughter. She hated with passion and cursed the day she met him at the Gate of India. She regretted the very day she trusted him and took her daughter with her and traveled to his accursed country.

Before she left Saudi Arabia, Rayhana was invited by the CIA team to emigrate to the United States and start a new life among civilized and loving people. However, she thanked them and decided to return to India for the sake of her mother and sons. She left her poor family with what she figured was enough money to last them at least over a year. More than three years had passed since she took her only daughter and traveled to the rich land of the Arabs. She did not know how her old mother could have fed her children on the money that she had given her.

Rayhana was so scared going back to the slum of her family. She was afraid that she might find her mother had died and her sons become beggars or starved to death. She knew that she had not kept her promise to them. She told her mother that she would send money as soon as she started working. Her mother thanked her Allah a thousand times when she came to know that her daughter was traveling to the country of the rich Arabs where there was the shrine of the prophet Muhammad and the House of Allah. Rayhana promised her mother that she would return after two years with so much money and take her to visit the holy lands and fulfill the fifth pillar of Islam (i.e. the Hajj). Before she left, the loving daughter disclosed to her dear mother her secret treasure and told her to use the money inside her underground bank for buying food for the family.

Rayhana took a taxi from the international airport to the Dharavi slum area. Her heart was beating faster and louder every second that passed by. As she was riding inside the taxi, she felt as if her heart might jump out of her chest any moment. She began to sweat and shake when the taxi reached Dharavi. She did not recognize home. Instead of dirty and foul smelling slums, a fifteen-story building greeted her. She was confused and perplexed. At first, she thought that the long period she spent in the Jeddah jail had somehow twisted her memory. Approaching the nearest shop, she asked about her slum in Dharavi. The shopkeeper told her that where she was standing was part of Dharavi slums, but a builder bought the place she was inquiring about. The builder constructed a huge fifteen-story building in its place. When she asked him what had happened to the poor people who used to live there, he told her that the builder gave some of them apartments on the first floor and some he gave a few thousands rupees. However, those who rejected his offer and refused to leave, he used Gondas to kick them off the land.

The information gave Rayhana some ray of hope. She wished that her mother got some money from the builder and used it to take care of her family. Therefore, she left the shop and went to the tall building and began to inquire about her family. She found a few people who used to live near her slum. From them, she got conflicting information about her family. One woman told her that her mother died in the slum and the government of Bombay buried her body. Another woman confirmed the death of her mother, but said her children ran away from the slum and became beggars. One man also confirmed the death of the mother and described how she died. He said that her mother became so poor until her body wasted away. When her mother became destitute, her grandchildren forsook her and ran away and disappeared. They never returned again. She died shortly thereafter from starvation. Her body was found dead after three days when it decomposed and began to smell. No Muslim man or woman in the slum area was willing to take the decomposing body of her mother and bury it. Therefore, it was taken away by the government and burned to ashes.

Rayhana listened to the horrifying story of the death of her mother with tears falling unrestrained from her eyes. She prostrated on the ground and began to cry. She regretted that she had left her mother and let her die in such a horrific way. She hated herself and hated the day she was born. After overcoming her grief, she decided to search for her sons in every nook and corner of the cosmopolitan city. She wanted to find them and pick them up from the streets and hug them and give them the love that she denied them for three years. She carried her little baby boy and went and booked a room in a cheap motel. She told the front desk that she came from Pakistan to visit some of her relatives in Bombay. She said further that she could not stay in their chawl because it was too small and crowded and her relatives had too many children for her to stay with them. She decided not to tell anyone about what had happened to her in Saudi Arabia. Her appearance had changed quite a bit from the way she used to be and she disguised herself to hide her true identity. She put on a burqa and even hid her face. She was scared that if the Gondas came to know she was the one who received four crores and fifty lakhs rupees from the government of Saudi Arabia, they might kidnap her and blackmail her until they got all her money. She wanted to find her children. She had changed her mind about America. The CIA team had promised to assist her anytime she would like to move to the USA. She accepted their offer, but told them she would like to return to her country first and then she would contact them as soon as she found her family.

Rayhana Khan spent three months in that cheap motel. She searched every local train station and every street in Bombay without finding her children. She went to Churchgate and Colaba areas where there were thousands of beggars, but could not find her children among them. She went to the crowded train terminals such as VT Station and Bombay Central Station many times, but could not find her children. It was as if the earth had opened up and swallowed them. It was when she lost all hope that Rayhana remembered her lover. She hoped that she could find Jamaal Khan and marry him and take him with her to the USA. She stopped searching for her children and began to search for her lover. This time, her search did not take long. She learned from the police authority that Jamaal Khan was serving a long sentence at Thane Prison for robbing, raping, impregnating, and causing the death of a girl who used to work with him in a travel agency. Rayhana refused to believe that Jamaal Khan could do such terrible crimes. She remembered that she sat with him many times at the beach and tempted him in every way possible. If he were that kind of a man he would have taken her to a motel and slept with her. Instead, Jamaal did nothing to her except hug and kiss her.

When she found out where the prison was located, Rayhana went to Thane Jail and visited him. Jamaal Khan could not believe his eyes when he saw his beloved girlfriend had come after many years to visit him. Rayhana was afraid to tell him about what had happened to her in Saudi Arabia. She expected that her conversation with him might be recorded by the authorities at the jail. She just told him that she went to Saudi Arabia and worked as a maidservant for three years. Jamaal remembered that he was the one who began processing her papers. Somehow all the news of what had happened to her escaped his attention or he didn't connect the events with her. He thanked his Allah for giving his beloved his grace and leading her to Saudi Arabia and to a good job. Rayhana did not bring her little baby boy with her. She did not want Jamaal to think that she left him and married another man. She hired a baby sitter to keep him while she went out and made her daily searches.

Jamaal narrated his story to his beloved in tears. Rayhana wept bitterly when she learned that her lover was falsely accused and sentenced to fifteen years. She knew firsthand, how any person would feel when falsely accused and condemned for a crime that they had not committed. She recollected those days when she was dragged like an animal from the house of her Saudi sponsor and thrown behind bars. She cried and begged for her freedom, but no one gave heed to her tears. She understood that her lover had gone through the same pain and suffering. She wished that she could find honest, sincere, and caring people like those seven Americans who did not leave a stone unturned in order to free her from the dungeon of those wicked Arab people. They had tortured her endlessly and sentenced her to be stoned to death for a crime she had never committed. She knew that her country also was full of corrupt and evil lawmen. Working within the system, Rayhana decided to find a lawyer to reopen the case of her boyfriend and push for a retrial. She told her lover that she was going to appoint a good lawyer and request for him to apply for a new trial. Jamaal told his girlfriend not to waste her money on a retrial that might not have any success. He too knew the corrupt judicial system of his country intimately. Rayhana paid her lover no heed and affirmed that she would not allow him to spend another twelve years in jail for crimes he had not committed.

Decision made, Rayhana decided to move from the motel to a rented apartment. She knew that the retrial of her lover might take many months. She went to Bandara and rented an apartment in a beautiful colony. The colony was located in a rich area. It had many security guards. The building had an elevator. Her apartment was on the fifteenth floor. Rayhana hired a babysitter and three maidservants to work for her. She employed a babysitter, a wash woman, a housekeeper, and a cook. She remembered how she worked as a slave in the rich people's houses before she went to the rich land of the Arabs. In those days, she used to work from six o'clock in the morning until nine o'clock at night. Therefore, she decided not to enslave the poor girls she employed. She paid them very well. She did not force them to work for her more than eight hours a day. She invited them to eat in her apartment while they were working for her. She allowed them to use her washroom. She remembered how the rich people she worked for did not allow her to use their washrooms while she was working in their houses. She bought beautiful uniforms for her maidservants and gave them some of her spare clothes. It should come as no surprise that her maidservants loved her so much. They told her that no Indian woman would treat her maidservants the way she had treated them. Rayhana did not tell her workers that she was a maidservant before. She told them that she came from Pakistan to visit her Indian boyfriend who was in jail.

Rayhana retained a lawyer and discussed the case of her imprisoned lover with him. She told him that she was certain that her boyfriend was innocent. She asked him to apply for another trial. The lawyer accepted the case and promised to do his level best to get the case tried again. A week had passed when the lawyer phoned her and told her the court agreed to retry the case. He ended the conversation by asking her to come to his office because he wanted to discuss with her some important matters that he would rather not discuss over the phone. When they met, the lawyer explained that the evidence against her lover was overwhelming and no advocate in Bombay would be able to disprove this evidence. Nevertheless, if she would agree to pay a few lakhs to him and to the judge, the charges against her lover would be dropped. Rayhana agreed to pay the money, but with a condition. She said that she would pay only 10% of the bribe before the retrial and the remaining amount she would pay after her lover was released. The lawyer told her that he had to talk to the judge before he would be able to accept her stipulations. After a few weeks, the lawyer called her again on the phone and asked her to come to his office for discussing an important matter. When she reached his office, he said to her the judge wanted her to pay 25% of the amount before the retrial and 75% after her boyfriend was freed. Rayhana accepted the counter-offer. According to the new deal, she had to pay one lakh rupees to the judge and one lakh rupees to the lawyer before the retrial and three lakhs to each one after her imprisoned lover was set free. So, the total amount of the bribe was eight lakhs. It would be divided equally between the lawyer and the judge.

Rayhana paid the two lakhs and waited for six months before her lover reappeared again before His Majesty at the Churchgate High Court. The lawyer was able to somehow refute all the evidences against Jamaal Khan. First of all, the lawyer brought a young boy in the court and made him to swear under oath that he was the former boyfriend of the deceased Bulbola Sheikh. The boy brought letters and claimed that he received them from his late girlfriend before she died. In one of the letters, Bulbolah informed her boyfriend that she was impregnated by him and asked him to marry her. The boy admitted that he had sex with his ex-girlfriend Bulbolah Sheikh many times before she passed away. In another letter, Bulbolah threatened that she was going to kill herself if he would not marry her before her parents and neighbors found out about her pregnancy. (In reality the late Bulbolah Sheikh was impregnated by her evil boss, Muhammad Khan).

The boy was excellent actor and cried before His Majesty and the audience while he was reading the last letter that his beloved had sent to him before she committed suicide. He said that due to his poverty and lack of work, his parents did not allow him to marry his pregnant girlfriend. In keeping with this act, the boy wept and wept until he made everyone in the court weep along with him, none more than the judge and the lawyer who knew the truth of the matter, crocodile tears and all. At the end of the sad love story, the boy admitted to the court that he was the one who had impregnated Bulbolah Sheikh, which led her to commit suicide. In fact, the boy received five thousand rupees before he appeared in court and was promised ten thousand more rupees after the retrial was over. Of course, Rayhana paid an advance to the boy and promised to pay the rest of the money after the retrial and her lover was set free.

After destroying the rape charge, the lawyer began to dismantle the robbery charge. He produced enough evidence, which indicated that Bulbolah Sheikh came from a very poor family. Her family lived in a chawl. She worked in the Muhammad Tours and Travels Agency for a few months before taking her life. Then, he argued that it would be impossible for a poor girl like the late Bulbolah Sheikh to make so much money in such a short period of time to buy jewelry costing two lakhs rupees unless she herself had robbed someone. It's clear her boyfriend could not afford to buy them for her. The clever advocate contended that if Jamaal Khan had robbed and raped Bulbolah Sheikh, why didn't she inform the police immediately after she was robbed and raped. Why did she not report her rapist who had impregnated her and stolen her money? Why did she kill herself for being a victim of a crime and not seek justice from the law? It was her employer that made the complaint and not her.

After dismantling the robbery charge, the lawyer began to deal with the charge of theft. According to the complaint of the employer, after raping and robbing Bulbolah Sheikh, Jamaal had supposedly stolen three lakhs from the travel agency. The lawyer argued that the conviction was not backed by any substantial evidence. There were no fingerprints taken by the police or any pictures of the broken safe supplied by the employer. The employer neither informed the police at the time of the theft that he had discovered he had been robbed. Jamaal Khan was arrested a long time after the alleged robbery and rape took place. (By the way, the court could not summon his former employer, Muhammad Khan, for Jamaal's retrial because by that time he had lost his mind and was under restraints in a small cell in a mental asylum. After the tragedy of Black Sunday, the wicked boss remained in the hospital for several months in a full body cast. Physically he was able to regain control of some movement in his body and legs, but then lost his mind. He became like a madman and would attack anyone that came near him until they chained him to his bed. Shortly thereafter, he was diagnosed with paranoid schizophrenia and transferred to a mental hospital). Anyway, when Jamaal Khan was tried and convicted over three years ago, he had no defense attorney. His wicked employer had paid the prosecutor handsomely to try him and make the charges stick. At the end of the retrial, the judge dropped all the charges against Jamaal Khan and ordered he be released with honor. Instead of rejoicing, Rayhana Khan fell on her knees and began to weep. It was her lover who came and lifted her from off the floor and hugged her until her tears stopped flowing from her eyes…

BOOK IV

AMINA HYDER ALI

CHAPTER 1

SEVEN YEARS LATER

After the Jeddah Shari'a court ruled in his favor, the old man took his pregnant child-bride, emigrated to the Islamic Republic of Iran and settled there. As he did in Asmara, he bought a house in Tehran and kept his child-bride imprisoned within its four walls. He hired three Iranian maidservants and one security-guard. The security-guard was an Afghani man, licensed to carry a gun. He was a retired Taliban terrorist in his late sixties but still a very tough character and a dangerous man. He had no qualms about shooting anyone who might try to break in and free the imprisoned child-bride. He slept a few hours during the day and remained awake throughout the night. The three Iranian women served Iffat Khan around the clock. They had a huge room, which they used as a dormitory to sleep in and if any of them wanted to visit family, they got only one day off each week. Iffat was not allowed to do any work. Her only duty was to use the washroom and take a bath. She was not permitted to step out of the boundary of the house under any circumstances. If she fell sick, one of the maidservants would call a nurse to treat her. If her illness were serious, an Iranian doctor would be called in to diagnose her and treat her for her specific illness.

When Iffat delivered her first baby, she was a few months past the age of twelve. The old man called in an Iranian midwife for the delivery. The midwife found it difficult to guide Iffat through a normal delivery. She was afraid that the young girl might die. She also expected that Iffat might need a caesarean and strongly advised the old man to send his wife to the hospital. He refused saying that he would never allow any man to see the nakedness of his wife. Iffat was almost dead before the midwife managed to ease the baby out of her. Unfortunately, the baby died shortly after it was born. After that, the old man made Iffat use birth control pills to prevent his child-wife from getting pregnant again. He was afraid that if she conceived again she might die. His main concern was to enjoy her beautiful body that warmed his bed anytime he wanted. The old man believed as many mentally perverted Arab men believed that, marrying of underage an girl would restore to the old man his youth days.

Sheikh Ahmed had, by this time, totally neglected his other three Saudi wives and spent most of his time in Tehran with his child-bride. He began to do most of his business in Iran. He traveled once every two or three months to Saudi Arabia and spent a few weeks there. Sometimes, he traveled to other Asian and Arab countries and conducted business. His business flourished in Iran and he became quite wealthy many times over. He spent a lot of money on his child-bride; he bought her hundreds of dresses and adorned her with exquisite and expensive jewels that he bought on his many travels. He went out of his way to build a swimming pool for her inside his huge mansion and then he hired a young Iranian woman to teach Iffat to swim. Once his child bride had learned how to swim, the old man began to sit by the pool on an armchair and watch her swimming in her bikini. He also purchased very costly jewelry for her. He modified his former practice with her and began to allow her to watch Indian movies. When they were in Asmara and when she was under nine years old, he used to make her watch porn movies with him and then force her to do to him what she saw in the movies. He still continued this practice with her in Tehran, but began to allow her to watch other movies too. He bought a home theater system for her. Whatever she asked for, he bought for her; any kind of food she wanted to eat, he provided to her. The only thing he refused to allow her to do was to go out of the house. Although he treated her like a queen, Iffat did not love the old man. She always felt great relief whenever he went away for a few weeks. She hated sex with him. Sex for her always meant pain and torture—he made her to hate sex. She hated the nights because it always reminded her of her first year with him in Asmara, when he first started to rape her.

For eight years onward, the old man continually and repeatedly raped Iffat. She bound by her circumstances, simply resigned herself to the fact that she was going to be under his control forever. He made her believe that her mother had died. He repeatedly told her that her mother was arrested and sentenced to death by the Shari'a court because she committed heinous crimes. Iffat never tried to run away from the old man—there was nowhere to go. She had no money and also no idea how to buy a ticket to fly back to India where she knew that she had brothers and a grandmother in Bombay. In any case, her passport was locked inside a secure safe and the keys were always with the old man.

So Iffat accepted her fate in life and whatever little entertainment she was allowed was enough for her. She loved to watch Indian movies because she understood Hindi. She spoke three languages, Urdu, Hindi, and Persian. She had learned Persian from her maidservants who were living with her in the house. However, she could read nor write any of these languages; the old man did not provide her with tutors to teach her reading and writing—education for females was just not in his agenda. He decided to keep her illiterate like his other Arab women. The old man followed the advice of his prophet Muhammad and caliph Omar Ibn al-Khattab who commanded, "Prevent women from learning to write, adopt positions opposite those of women. There is great virtue in such opposition."

Iffat Khan spent seven years in Tehran imprisoned in the house of the old man. Her daily life varied little except when he traveled abroad. Whenever he went on his business trips or visited his other wives in Saudi Arabia, she would be completely free from his unpleasant presence. Whenever he was home, he would ask her to massage his body. Sex with him was the worst thing for her. During those seven years, the old man had never spent more than a few weeks at a time away from her. However, his last trip was prolonged beyond his usual schedule, until the maidservants began to complain to her about their monthly payments.

The old man went for a business trip to Pakistan and did not come back for many weeks. Iffat had no money nor did she know where the old man kept his money. Whenever the old man returned from his trips abroad, it was he who paid the maidservants and the security guard their wages. So she told the Iranian women that she had no money to give them. The women asked her to contact his wives in Saudi Arabia to find out whether he was still alive or if he was dead and to ask what was the delay in his return. Iffat told them that she had no phone numbers to any of his wives.

After three months had passed, the maidservants began to quarrel with Iffat. They had concluded that the old man was dead and buried in Pakistan. They asked Iffat to sell some of her gold and use the money to pay them for the three months they were due. They said that they wanted to go and seek other employment. Iffat feared that the angry Iranian women might get so angry, they would beat her up, steal all her jewelry, kill her and run away. To avoid that situation, she agreed to sell some of her gold jewelry and pay them. The maidservants tried to convince the security guard to allow Iffat to go to the market to sell some of her jewelry. The security guard refused to listen to them. He said he would shoot any one of them if they tried to help Iffat go out of the house or run away. He was the only one, at this point, who remained loyal to his master. After giving it some thought, Iffat settled the problem with the maidservants by giving each one of them some of her expensive clothes and some smaller pieces of her costly ornaments. The Iranian women took what she gave them and quit their jobs.

After her maidservants deserted her, Iffat was forced to do everything by herself. She was not used to any kind of manual labor. Out of necessity, she began washing her own clothes and cooking her own meals. She struggled with her chores and worried about her dwindling store of food. She had no money and knew that the unmovable security guard took his job seriously. He would never allow her to go out of the house, even if she had to starve to death. She was also under the impression that the old man had died. She tried many times to convince the security guard to allow her to go to the market to sell some of her gold and buy groceries and other things, but he always refused. Finally, after four months passed, a letter was sent to her written in Arabic. When the mysterious letter arrived, she succeeded in convincing the security guard to allow her to find someone to read it and tell her what was written on it. The security man told her that he would go to the market, find an Arabic translator and bring him to her. He locked her up in her bedroom, went to the market and brought back a translator.

Through the translator, Iffat came to know that the letter was written and sent to her by the old man himself. He stated that he was held up in a jail in India. He claimed that he was falsely accused of kidnapping and raping a young Indian girl and thrown inside a filthy prison in Bombay. In his letter, the old Saudi ordered Iffat to come to India and appoint a lawyer for him. He wanted her to sell some of her jewelry, purchase a ticket and come to Bombay as soon as possible. However, he strictly mentioned that she shouldn't come alone—his Afghani security guard who had faithfully served him for seven years should come with her and she was to buy a ticket for the security guard too. The Arabic translator read the letter in front of the Afghani security guard and after hearing the contents of the letter, the guard finally allowed Iffat to get out of her dungeon. He accompanied her to the market, concealing his rifle in his robe. He forewarned her before he allowed her to step out of the house that if she tried to run away at any time, he would not hesitate to shoot and kill her in front of the people.

In his letter, the old man also informed Iffat how and where she could find the key to the safe holding her Indian passport. The Afghani security guard had a valid Iranian passport. After selling some jewelry and obtaining enough money, the security guard took Iffat to the Indian Consulate and applied for his visa. His visa was issued after a week. After that, he took her with him to the Iranian airlines and made her purchase their tickets and booking their flight to Bombay. Although she was a little over eighteen, Iffat was like a child who needed someone to tell her what to do and how to do it. She had no experience of the outside world. For ten years, she had been imprisoned like a bird inside a golden cage and denied access to any form of social interaction.

The Afghani terrorist led her from place to place and made her do what he wanted her to do. He scared her with his gun, which he always kept hidden inside his clothes. It took a month before Iffat and the Afghani guard flew from Tehran to Bombay. People who saw the Afghani with Iffat naturally assumed him to be her grandfather. (Afghani women look like Indian women and Indians believe that Afghanistan was part of the subcontinent of India before the Arabs invaded it and infected it with their religious disease, which they forced it upon the Buddhist and Hindu countrymen. There was strong evidence, which proved that the Hindu Rig Veda was created in Afghanistan. Rig Veda is one of the four religious books of Hinduism known as the sacred Vedas).

The Taliban terrorist knew that he could not pass his gun through the checkpoint at the Tehran International Airport so he left it behind, however he managed to convince Iffat that he had somehow managed to smuggle the gun inside with him. Iffat followed him inside the airport with the docility of a prisoner accompanied by a guard. She would not even contemplate using the washroom without his express permission. When inside the plane she told him she wanted to go to the lavatory he allowed her to go, but he went with her and waited outside the lavatory. Some of the flying crew and passengers noticed the behavior of the Afghani man and the young girl with him, but they thought that as a fanatic male Muslim, he was simply protecting his granddaughter from being teased or harassed. Who would have guessed otherwise? So they let be, the dangerous Afghani terrorist and his young Indian captive, the product of ten years of abduction, rape and captivity.

Upon arrival at the Mumbai Chhatrapati Shiviji International Airport, anti-terrorist police routinely went through every passenger manifest and found that one of the Iranian flights was carrying one Bismillah Ali Altalbi, a Taliban terrorist. The police did not identify him through his fake Iranian nationality and name, (His passport carried the name Mustafa Ahmad Shakir), but through his passport photo which matched a computerized photo line-up, his name was tagged. The Indian police took him to a room and fingerprinted him. Computers matched his prints to Bismillah Ali Altalbi. He was arrested immediately and transferred to a maximum-security jail in Mumbai. The police did not know that Iffat Khan had come with him. She was after all, Indian with a valid passport and there was nothing to indicate that she was related to him in any way. Iffat did not know that her captor was arrested until she asked some of the Indian passengers who were traveling on the same plane. She was told that her grandfather was placed under arrest by the Bombay police. The passengers were surprised when they saw Iffat simply turn her back and walk away; she did not want to be arrested with that dangerous man who filled her heart with dread for so many years.

When Iffat came out of the airport, she did not know what to do or where to go. Although, she was free from her captor she was still controlled by fear of the old man. She was scared that if she did not go to him at the jail and do what he told her to do he might send some men to search for her and kill her. For ten years, the ferocious beast had frightened her and made her feel as helpless prey in his hands. He had made her believe from the age of eight that if she tried to run away from him he would send some of his men to find her and slaughter her. So, heeding her instincts, she took a taxi and asked the driver to take her to Arthur Road Jail. While the taxi was driving through the busy city, Iffat was shocked to see the huge crowds of people. Her memory of Bombay had grown dim over the years and she could only remember little glimpses of her slum. She remembered that she used to sleep on the ground with her five brothers. Her memory also recollected the poor food she used to eat. She compared her poor and miserable life when she was a child and the rich and comfortable life she lived with the old man. Reflecting back, she wished that she could have continued her miserable life in Bombay. Asmara and Tehran, with all the trappings of wealth held no attraction for her because of the tyranny of a dirty old man.

It was 12:50 p.m. when the taxi dropped Iffat off at the Arthur Road Jail. When asked to fill a visiting form she told the police authorities that she did not know how to read or write. One of the police officers asked her to give him some money if she wanted him to help her fill out the form. Iffat gave him a hundred dollar note. The guard felt as if she had given him a small fortune. His monthly salary was three thousand rupees. What Iffat had given him was the equivalent of four thousand five hundred rupees and if he exchanged it on the black-market he might get five thousand rupees. It was more than he made in a month. He asked her to come into his office and sit on a chair and he ordered her a cold drink. After she had finished her drink, the officer asked her the questions on the form and filled it in for her. He conversed with her in Hindi. Then he personally took the rich Indian girl to the place where she could meet the detainee…

CHAPTER 2

AMINA

Sheikh Ahmed had not returned to India for ten years. After his bad experience with his former Pakistani driver and Indian business client, Muhammad Khan, the old Saudi made an oath to Allah by placing his right hand on the Qur'an and swearing that he would never go back to the accursed land of the Hindu idolaters. He kept this oath for ten years. However, his lust for female children inevitably drew him back there. Someone in Tehran told him that there was a city in India called Hyderabad where there were Muslim Marriage Agencies. Those marriage agencies could supply him with a pretty young girl as young as eight or nine years old. The evil old man relished the memory of how he thighed Iffat at that age and how he took her virginity at nine. After sleeping with her for ten years, she was becoming an adult and had lost much of her sexual appeal as a child-bride. He wanted to start all over again with another child-bride. So he broke his oath to Allah and flew back to India and Hindustan. As was his habit, subterfuge was his rule of thumb. He lied to his Indian wife, Iffat, and her Iranian maidservants and his security guard and told them instead, he was flying to Pakistan for a business trip.

Hyderabad felt to the old Saudi much like any other poor Muslim country, like Sudan or Somalia in Africa. Everybody was a Muslim and the city itself was named after an ancient Muslim king. There were mosques on every street. Every man had a long beard and every woman walking on the street was covered in a black burqa. Everyone looked as though they had been buried in the ground and dug up; people were covered in dust and mud from head to toe. The streets were filthy and the buildings were dilapidated. There were no garbage containers and the garbage was carelessly and thoughtlessly strewn everywhere. If a visitor did not throw up on his arrival of that filthy city, he would never vomit again in his life.

The old man regretted he had ever come to that dirty Muslim town to advance his plans. He could not believe that in such a city he would ever be able to find a little damsel that he could marry and enjoy the rest of his life. He even doubted that anyone could find a healthy female among the decrepit poor women he saw walking on the streets. They looked like skeletons wrapped in black plastic garbage bags. However, since he was already there, the old man decided to see it through with the hope that he might find a young girl with the help of Allah, whatever her health condition. With the blessing of his Allah, he would take her to Tehran; nurse her back to health and then start his predatory way with her. With those devilish thoughts in mind, the evil old man spent a few hours resting in a hotel; then took a taxi and headed to one of the foremost marriage agencies.

The Dalal, or Pimp, who was running the marriage agency was known as Farooq Khan. He had a beard one meter long, and looked like an old dust broom. He had the **Black Mark** of prayer on his forehead, which resembled the Mark of the Beast 666. In his left hand he clutched a long rosary and in his right, a green copy of his holy Qur'an from which he was reciting verses when the old Saudi man walked into his office. Ironically, his copy of the holy Qur'an was Arabic, a language as foreign to him as Japanese. This is one of the miracles of the non-Arabic speaking Muslims, but it wasn't the right place to try to figure it out. Muslims all over the world are required to read the Qur'an and pray five times a day in Arabic, although the majority of them can neither read nor write, or even speak the language.

The Muslim Pimp, Farooq Khan proudly told the old man that he had been to his country and visited Mecca and Medina and done the Hajj three times. The old man praised him for his religious piety and asked Allah to bless his sons and daughters too. After a little chatting the old man revealed the purpose of his visit. He said plainly that he wanted to marry a very small girl no older than eight. Farooq Khan told him that he could supply a girl of that age, but he warned him that it would be too risky for both of them for him to take a girl of that age out of the country. He said further that while he could forge a birth certificate and get a passport issued to her as a seventeen-year-old maidservant, the officials at the Indian airport would probably see right through it. A young child at that age would look small and child-like, befitting her age. For that reason, Farooq Khan advised the old man to go for a small girl who had already had her first period, but was still a virgin. The old man said he would not accept a girl who had already started to menstruate. As an excuse, he said he would not trust such a girl, adding that anyone could have claimed her virginity before him without his knowledge. Eager to retain his obviously wealthy client, Farooq Khan suggested that the old man go for a thirteen-year-old girl who had not yet had her first period. The old man strongly rejected that suggestion and said that a thirteen-year-old girl would be too old for him.

After two hours of intense discussion and bantering, the two wicked men settled for an eleven-year-old girl. When the critical issue of age was finally decided upon, it took another hour of haggling to decide a price they could both agree upon. All the nitty-gritty concluded, Farooq Khan took the old man to a room where he could pick and choose. The Muslim marriage agency had many rooms; each room was designed for a specific age group. In one particular room, the old man found fifteen Indian Muslim girls aged eleven. The fifteen little girls looked like Barbie dolls dressed in burqas, but for the sake of the business, they had their faces uncovered. (By the way, in some Muslim countries, Barbie dolls must by law have hijabs or niqabs. The pro-Shari'a American Muslims are trying to push for the same).

The old man demanded that all the eleven-year-old girls be stripped of their burqas so that he could make good his choice and Farooq Khan ordered all the little girls to come out of their Islamic cocoons so that his rich Arab customer could make his selection. The small girls removed their black burqas and stood like dolls in their Indian Salwar Kameez. The old man further demanded that each girl remove her Salwar Kameez and remain in her bra and underwear only. Farooq Khan rejected that demand because it was *haram* in Islam for the man to see the body of a girl who wasn't his wife yet. However, when the old man insisted and threatened to cancel the deal and demand a refund, the pimp agreed to commit *haram* for the sake of money. Some of the little girls said they would not strip in front of each other. They said they would do so one at a time and behind the modesty afforded behind a curtain. The Dalal and the old man agreed to accommodate that moral request.

The old Saudi was asked to sit inside a small room much like a fitting room in a clothing store. Then, the fifteen small girls were ordered by the Dalal to enter that fitting room one after another and strip off her Salwar Kameez in front of the old man, then put her clothes back and then come out. Each girl was given a number—starting from Girl No. 1 to Girl No. 15. The old man was told by Farooq Khan to write down the number of the girl that won his heart. The nefarious old man touched the body of each girl as if he was buying a lamb. His hands wandered between their breasts and bums and did not spare the face and lips. He managed to kiss and hug some of them, but some resisted and refused to allow him to do *haram and faahisha* with them before marriage.

The wicked old man claimed to have made wrong choices three times. So, each girl was forced to enter behind the curtain and strip off before him three times. Finally, Girl No. 13 was chosen to be the wife of the wealthy Saudi. Her name was Amina Hyder Ali. As soon as he chose her, the old man took hold of her hand and began to walk her with him out of the fitting room, heading toward the door as if he bought a jaria from the slave market at the time of the prophet Muhammad. Farooq Khan stopped him and said to him he would not allow him to take her to his hotel unless the *Nikah* contract was performed. He said further that he could not allow him to commit *haram* acts with the girl without marrying her. The old man said he had already paid the agreed upon price. The Dalal said to him he was running a marriage agency and not a slave trade.

Unwillingly, the old man agreed to perform the Nikah contract. Then, the Dalal sent one of his boys to the lucky parents of the chosen girl to carry them the good news and bring the father of the girl to sign the Nikah contract of his daughter with her soon-to-be wealthy Saudi bridegroom. In less than half an hour, a man who looked like he had not eaten in days, came with the messenger of the good news. Shortly, afterward, the Mazoon of a nearby mosque was phoned and called in. The Mazoon came with two male witnesses and with the blessings of the father, the marriage contract between Sheikh Faiz bin Ahmed and Amina Hyder Ali was conducted according the Sunna of Allah and his Messenger. Then, and only then, was the old man allowed to take his bride to his hotel.

Before the newly wedded couple left the premises of that renowned Muslim Marriage Agency, the proprietor, Farooq Khan, took the bridegroom aside and gave him a piece of advice. He told him not to consummate his Nikah with the girl until they had safely reached his country. The word Nikah in Shari'a has various meanings; the widely known and most common use of the word meant legal fornication with any number of female slaves, lawful adultery with two, three, or four women at the same time, legalized rape with female children, and of course conventional marriage with one woman. However, the old man thought that Farooq Khan wanted to trick him and he rejected the advice and was determined in his wicked heart to consummate his marriage with his child-bride on the very same day he married her. He knew that Amina had already crossed the lawful prescribed age of nine years for Nikah.

When they reached the hotel, the old man raped the little girl and she was screaming at the top of her lungs. Since everyone in the hotel was a Muslim and the hotel management had seen the marriage contract between the Muslim Arab and the Muslim Indian girl, no one intervened or tried to save the girl from her rapist. From that day on, the old man raped the eleven-year-old girl and continued to rape her day and night until the marriage agency arranged her passport. The old man already had a maidservant visa with him, so one week from the day he arrived in the city he took his new child-bride to Hyderabad airport and headed to Tehran via Mumbai.

Before she got married to the eighty-year-old Saudi man, Amina was a virgin and had not yet had her menses. She was simply not ready in the slightest for sex. When the old man raped her on the day she was sold in marriage to him, she felt as if he was digging a hole inside her vagina. She bled profusely and experienced unbearable pain. On the following day, she experienced more pain than the first day. The old man caused many abrasions and tears in her privates. Therefore, the second rape was worse than the first one. Every day, the pain increased and her torture, undiminished. As was his plan all along, the old man continued to rape her day and night until her paperwork was completed. Amina wished for death before the old man could take her to his country and continue causing her anguish and pain. When her parents came to say goodbye to her at the airport she begged them to take her away from the old man. Her father shouted at her and told her that he would cut her throat if she said that again. Moreover, he told her not to tell anyone that the old man was her husband or try to run away from him. If anyone asked her, she should say he was her employer and she was his maidservant. Out of fear of her father, the little girl agreed to go with the old man to the airplane.

Inside the plane, Amina felt as if she was sitting beside a ferocious mountain lion. His old face and long beard reminded her of the story of Beauty and the Beast that her schoolteacher narrated to her. She was shaking and trembling in fear from the Hyderabad airport until their plane landed at Santacruz domestic airport in Mumbai. They were transferred by bus from the domestic airport to the international airport. When they had reached the departure hall, Amina knew that she was far enough away from her father where he could not slit her throat. She began to cry and resist when the old man tried to pull her with him and walk her to the plane. This drew the curiosity of the other passengers and some airport officials. One woman interfered and asked Amina in Hindi why she was crying. The old man shouted at the woman who began to talk to his wife. He talked to her in Arabic and ordered her not to talk to his *Khadamiah*. One Indian man understood the meaning of the word Khadamiah and told the Indian woman that the little girl was a Muslim maidservant to the old Arab man. However, Amina still resisting and putting up a fight, exposed the old man as a liar and told the woman adamantly why she was crying. She shouted out loudly that she wasn't his khadamiah, but his wife. The people who heard her words were shocked and stood in their steps with their mouths wide-open. When they learned that the old man old enough to be her great-grandfather was actually her husband, someone called the airport police immediately and the matter became an official complaint.

When the police arrived at the scene, the old Saudi man was placed under arrest. He was handcuffed, slapped, and kicked by a police officer in front of everyone. Some Indian women spat on the face of the old man and some men called him *Teri maa ki chute, teri bahan ki chute*. Some people pushed him and pinched him. Some very angry passengers even tried to choke him and kill him. The crowd would have killed the old man if not for the six tough police officers that surrounded him. After that, the old man was dragged out of the airport and thrown into a police truck. The little girl Amina was taken in a different police car and sent to the hospital for a rape exam. The tests proved that Amina had been brutally raped by the rapist and the hospital sent the results to the police. When she was questioned at the hospital, Amina revealed her real age to the police. The city of Mumbai was turned upside down when the Midday Newspapers published the headlines—"80-YEAR-OLD SAUDI MUSLIM WEDS 11-YEAR-OLD HYDERBADI GIRL".

Citizens of Mumbai demonstrated in thousands marching to police headquarters and demanding the old man be hanged until death. The main leaders of Shev Sina stood behind the wave of popular support and mirrored the call for capital punishment. There were a few organized Muslim marches and protests, which called for the immediate release of the old Muslim man and his young Muslim wife. Their religious leaders said that the marriage of the Saudi Muslim man and the Indian girl was valid because she was also a Muslim and according to their holy Qur'an and Sunna of their prophet, the marriage was in every way legal. They quoted the example of the 6-year-old Aisha and the 54-year-old prophet Muhammad.

The Mumbai police contacted the police of Hyderabad who then ordered the immediate arrest of Amina's father, Farooq Khan, the Mazoon, and the two male witnesses who signed the unlawful marriage contract. According to Indian Marriage law, a girl is not allowed to get married until she reaches eighteen and the boy twenty-one. The only exception to the rule is if a seventeen-year-old girl is wed, it must be with parental consent. Other than this, in India at least, an eighteen-year-old Indian girl has the right to legally marry regardless of her parents' wishes. The law is applicable to all Indian girls regardless of religion and caste. Sex with a girl below the age of seventeen is deemed to be statutory rape or rape of a minor. As provided for by the laws of the land, the old Saudi was arrested for rape, kidnapping, the attempt to smuggle a minor female out of the country for sexual purposes, violating child work laws and sex slave trade laws.

Under the persuasive methods of interrogation by the Indian police, Sheikh Faiz bin Ahmed admitted that he contracted the little girl in marriage and slept with her for seven days and seven nights. However, he tried to justify his marriage on the grounds that the marriage agency deceived him about the real age of the girl. The Mumbai police did not buy that line and they flogged the old man mercilessly, until he spoke the truth. After his interrogation, the old Saudi man was arraigned for trial. Amina was placed under the care of the Maharashtra State Government of India, which decided to place her in a foster home to await qualified adoptive parents. Given the publicity generated by her case, the government had to process in one month alone, half a million applications from wealthy people all over the country who wanted to adopt Amina Hyder Ali.

CHAPTER 3

THE DEAL

Iffat Khan was sitting on a bench waiting for the guards to bring her Saudi husband who had been arrested and jailed for more than four months. At that time, she was eighteen years old and her Arab husband was eighty years old. She had spent three years with him in Eritrea and seven years in Iran. For ten years, he had abused and subdued her; he had turned her into a robot. Even though he was in jail, he still continued to frighten and control her. He controlled her as if he had a wireless remote control in his hand that he could operate to move her from place to place and switch her on and off; she was like a wingless bird, which could only fly when given wings by him. While she was sitting waiting on the bench, Iffat suddenly saw the old man coming toward her guarded by two male jailers. He was chained from head to foot and dressed up in a prisoner's uniform. When he sat on the opposite side and faced her, she began to shake and sweat, her heart began to beat fast. When he greeted her in the Persian language, she could not talk, her voice failed her even though her mouth was open. He raised his voice and shouted at her and she was forced to reply to his greeting.

The first question the old man asked Iffat was about her Afghani security guard and she told him that he had been arrested at the Mumbai airport. This information filled the old man's heart with fear. The first thought that arose in his mind was that Iffat might run away without anyone to guard her. Concealing his fear, he began to instruct her what to do. First, he warned her that if she tried to run away, he had more than a thousand Indian Gondas who would find and cut her into pieces. Secondly, he told her not to tell anyone that she was his wife. Thirdly, he told her not to open her burqa or allow anyone to see her face; she had to be hidden inside her burqa even when she was inside her hotel room. After giving her those instructions, he began to tell her what to do.

The first assignment the old man gave to Iffat was to take a taxi, go to Churchgate and deliver a letter that he had written to the manager of the Abu Dhabi International Bank—the letter was written in Arabic. Like his maidservant, Iffat took a taxi and headed to the address written on the letter. When she reached the bank, she first showed the letter to a female employee of Indian descent, who then passed it on to a male employee of Arab descent. The Arab man read the letter and understood that it was addressed to the bank manager, so he directed Iffat to the manager of the bank. In the letter, the old man requested the manager of the bank send one of the bank employees with the necessary forms so that he could make a joint account with his Indian wife, Iffat Khan, who had brought the letter to him. He requested the bank not allow his Indian wife to withdraw more than one thousand rupees a day. The manager filled out the forms and asked Iffat Khan to affix her signature. When Iffat admitted she could not write, he suggested she simply use her thumbprint. After that, the manager asked one of his Arab employees to accompany the wife of their important Saudi client to the jail to get his signature.

Iffat Khan had to pay a couple hundred more dollars to the officer whom she had bribed before to allow her to revisit the old man for the second and the third time. According to the rules, the same person was not allowed to visit a prisoner more than once in a day. However, that day, Iffat visited her Saudi husband three times. After the old man signed the joint account forms, Iffat went back to the Abu Dhabi International Bank and got her debit card and account book. As instructed in the letter, the bank allowed her to withdraw only one thousand rupees. She was told by the manager she could use her debit card to eat in a restaurant, or to rent a room in a hotel. The manager also followed the instructions of the letter and took one thousand US dollars from Iffat Khan, which she had on her person from the sale of jewelry she sold in Iran. He exchanged it for forty five thousand Indian rupees;

Iffat then returned to visit her Saudi husband for the third time. The second assignment was appointing a lawyer. He told her to go to the Mumbai High Court and find the best lawyer and bring him to meet him at the jail. He said that the lawyer should be a Muslim. Since it was already evening, he told her to go to Colaba, find a small hotel and book a room to stay in. She was told not to stay in an expensive hotel because they would charge more than five hundred rupees per day. Iffat, like an obedient wife should, stopped a taxi and asked the driver to take her to any hotel at Colaba that charged five hundred rupees. The driver responded by saying he knew of no decent hotel that had rates that low, but Iffat had no intention of seeing the old man for the fourth time that day. So she told the driver just to take her to any nearby hotel that would charge her only five hundred rupees. The driver took her to a cheap hotel in Bombay Central. It charged four hundred and ninety-nine rupees a day for a room.

The last time Iffat had eaten was aboard the Iranian passenger jet. She was starving as she entered her room, but was so tired and exhausted she would have slept without food if the hotel front desk hadn't phoned her room to ask whether she wanted to order dinner from the hotel restaurant before it closed in less than an hour. So, she ordered a rushed meal before going to sleep. She fell asleep wearing the same clothes she had been wearing since she left Tehran. She came with a small travel handbag that held a couple of dresses and a few inner clothes. She had two black burqas and one pair of spare shoes; that was all. She had never traveled by herself and she was completely ignorant of the outside world. She was acting as if she was a Mowgli girl that raised in the jungle and this was her first time interacting with humans. The old man had succeeded in changing her from a human being into a domesticated animal with two legs and vagina.

As soon as she woke up from her sleep, Iffat left the hotel and took a taxi to the Mumbai High Court. Finding a lawyer in Mumbai is as easy as sighting a policeman on the street. Lawyers do not stay in their offices, they gather every day in the courtyard of the court and chase after people. As soon as you enter the courtyard, tens of advocates would come running toward you and offer to defend you and fight your case in court. They would charge you according to your case or your means. As soon as the lawyers saw the Muslim woman in a black burqa, she held court to fifteen of them. She heard them babbling in Hindi and in Urdu. All talking at the same time, some ventured that Iffat had come to ask for a divorce from her abusive Muslim husband. Some guessed that she wanted to marry her Hindu boyfriend without the consent of her parents. She brushed away both suggestions and asked for a Muslim lawyer to step forward. The crowd around her was now a group of five, out of which she chose the oldest one. The old man had told her to go for an old and experienced lawyer. Immediately the chosen *Wakeel* asked her to sit with him in a corner and tell him her problem and what she needed help with. He had a notebook, which he always carried around with him ready to take notes like he was a schoolboy. Iffat told him she did not have a problem, but that she had someone in the Arthur Road Jail who had a very serious case. She said that she could not tell him what the problem was herself, but that the one inside the jail would relate his situation.

At first, the Muslim lawyer thought that Iffat was just a playgirl who wanted to fool him and waste his valuable time. To make sure she was up and up, he asked her for an advance. Iffat agreed to give him a couple hundred rupees. He also said she would be liable for his traveling expenses and Iffat assured him that she would pay for his trips. Seeing no opposition from the burqa clad girl, he requested that lunch be on her if the case demanded more time than necessary. With Iffat agreeing to all his demands, he hailed a taxi and slid into the front seat. He motioned for Iffat to sit in the rear because it would be *haram* for him to sit near a young Muslim woman that wasn't his wife.

With the taxi racing down Beach Street of Marine Drive, the Muslim lawyer took the opportunity to ask Iffat all the questions that remained unanswered in his mind. He wanted to know whether the person in jail was her husband, boyfriend, father, brother, uncle, cousin, etc. Iffat answered no to all of his questions and that made him even more curious. He was puzzled as to the relationship between the Muslim girl and the Arthur Road detainee. He also wanted to know where she was living and what level of education she had reached; what her age was and if she was married, and if not, what were her plans in this regard? His questions were endless and Iffat breathed a sigh of relief when the taxi reached the jail.

The Muslim lawyer had mentally prepared himself to meet anyone in the world except the one he saw sitting inside the small visiting room. If he had seen Satan himself, he would not have been surprised, but what he saw was shockingly staring right at him, the embodiment of the devil in a man. The Muslim lawyer thought for a second he was stranded in the Sahara desert and seeing a mirage. He had seen his photo a million times before in the media these past few months, and he was more familiar with the case than the old man himself. He had discussed his case with his family at home and with other lawyers at the courthouse. He had read the details in the newspapers and watched all the news coverage on the TV stations. Yet again, this old man was making headlines and becoming a menace and laughing stock all around the world. The Muslim lawyer knew that he had just been dealt a high profile case. Iffat was now the translator between her Saudi husband, Sheikh Ahmed, and the Muslim lawyer. The old man spoke in Persian and his new lawyer in Urdu. Iffat translated everything as best she could except for the greeting, for which there was no need.

"First of all Sir, you must know that your case is a very difficult one to defend. There is a very strong case against you. The police have amassed more than enough proof to convict you. Upon conviction, you are probably looking at the hangman's noose or life imprisonment."

"I haven't called you here to tell me that. I want to know whether you will be able to release me from this cursed Hindu prison or not. You are a Muslim and you must know that according to the Qur'an and the Sunna of our gracious prophet Muhammad, peace and prayers of Allah be upon him, that I have done nothing wrong. I married an eleven-year-old girl, which is lawful in our blessed Shari'a. For your information in Surat Al-Talaq, verse four, the Qur'an allows every

Muslim man to marry a girl before she reaches puberty. Even our gracious prophet Muhammad had married our blessed mother, Aisha bint Abu Bakr when she was six years old and slept with her when she was nine years old. So, what kind of haram have I done when I married and slept with an eleven-year-old girl? Did she die when I f...ked her? Had I kidnapped her from her parents and married her? Did I not make the correct Nikah contract with her? Did I not pay her father her dowry?"

"Whatever you have done is absolutely lawful in our Shari'a and backed up with verses from our holy Qur'an and authentic hadiths from the Sunna of our prophet Muhammad (PBUH). However, this is not Saudi Arabia or Iran. This is a Hindu and secular country. It is the land of the Kofar [Infidels]. According to the laws of this country, what you have done with this Hyderabadi Muslim girl, Amina Hyder Ali, in their eyes, has made you a kidnapper, a rapist, and a slave trader. There is no lawyer can defend you if the case goes to court no dent made in it. We need to punch holes and weaken the state's case before the court renders a final decision regarding the charges against you."

"How can you make holes and weaken the case?"

"Money can weaken the case. You need to pay a lot of money to so many people. We need to bribe the judge, the police, and other people. I will not charge you as much as the police and judge might ask in return for leniency. We need to pay the Mumbai police and the Hyderabad police. We need to fill the pockets of the judge with so much money he won't give a second thought to convict you. We might even need to offer money to the mother, sisters, and brothers of the girl in question. And if it is possible, we might need to get hold of Amina herself and buy her silence. We can make her say that her father told her to lie to you and tell you she was seventeen years old."

"How much money do I need to pay?"

"Crores of rupees. I cannot give you the exact figures now. I must first talk to the judge and the police and contact other officials who are handling your case."

"If I agree to pay whatever they ask, what is my guarantee that I will win the case and be released from this filthy Hindu prison?"

"I will get the judge to sign a secret contract the same as anyone else who is involved."

"I will pay 10% of what they ask for and the rest after I am released."

"All judges and policemen in Mumbai charge fifty percent before the trial and fifty after."

"Can you tell me approximately how much this is going to cost?"

"Roughly ten crores." [10 crores are 100,000,000 rupees. One US Dollar is equal to 45 Indian Rupees at the time this case was going on in India].

"Ten crores is a lot of money."

"That is what I said from the beginning. You need to pay a lot of money to come out of this Kofar jail. Otherwise, you will lose your life or die inside this filthy place. Consider your advanced age. Would you like to die in the Muslim holy land among your Muslim wives and children, or starve and die like a criminal in the land of the Hindu idolaters?"

"Okay I am ready to pay the money, but try to reduce it to seven or eight crores."

"I will try my level best, but I can give you no guarantees. Hindus are very greedy people when it comes to money."

"Go and talk to the judge and other officials and bring to me the exact figures."

"Inshallah after two weeks I will come to you with some good news."

"Barka Allah feek ya akhi fi alislam" said the old man. (Iffat could not translate this Islamic phrase because it was spoken in Arabic. It means God bless you my brother in Islam).

"Before I accept the case officially, I will need my standard fee, and as a token of your intent, the sum of one lakh rupees."

"Why should I give you money before you talk to those people?"

"I need money to talk to them. I need to bribe their security guards and those close to them so that I can have access to them."

The old man talked to his wife in Persian before responding to the demand of the Muslim lawyer. He ordered her to go to the Abu Dhabi International Bank and pay one-lakh rupees to his lawyer. He said further that if the manager refused to issue the amount to him, then tell him to send someone from the bank to visit him at the jail so that he could provide authorization.

"Go with my maidservant Iffat Khan to the bank and get the money."

The Muslim lawyer remembered that he could not discern the relationship between the young Muslim woman and the prisoner, but now, the cat was out of the bag. He was awed and respectful of the devotion and loyalty this maidservant had for her Arab master. That day Iffat was compelled to visit the old man four times at the Arthur Road jail. Firstly, the bank refused to issue the one-lakh rupees without the signature of the old man. Secondly, the signature was rejected twice because the old man's hand was shaking and trembling and that altered his signature. The beating he had received during the harsh interrogation caused him to tremble for no reason. Finally, the bank sent one of its employees and confirmed that the old man wanted the Muslim lawyer to get the one-lakh rupees. After receiving the money, the lawyer took Iffat back to the prison and made the old man sign the required forms giving him the right to be his legal representative and to start the process. The old man not only give the Muslim man the right to represent him in court, but appointed him as the legal guard and guardian of his maidservant. He told Iffat not to go anywhere without the company of that good Muslim man. If he was not afraid he would succumb to his young and very beautiful wife, he would have asked the lawyer to stay with her inside her room in the hotel and watch her movements.

The good Muslim lawyer gave his business card to Iffat and accompanied her to her hotel. She had nothing to do after her new guard escorted her to the hotel. However, the new guard wasn't as watchful as the Afghani terrorist. As soon as he dropped Iffat off, he took the remainder of the day off and went to celebrate his windfall of one-lakh rupees with his family. Iffat was supposed to visit the old man everyday while he was incarcerated and do whatever he wanted her to do. That day she tot back to her hotel at 4:15 pm. She did not know what to do. She had a small TV in her room, not being connected to cable, it received only local news. It had only one channel. She wished she had a DVD player and an Indian movie to watch. She considered venturing out of the hotel, but decided that it would be prudent to stay inside in case the Muslim lawyer saw her and reported her to the old man, resulting in a beating or worse. After a while, boredom took hold and again she was tempted to go out. An idea came to her and she went down to the front desk and told them that she was looking for someone to help her get a DVD player and a new Indian movie. The girl at the front desk suggested that instead of spending so much money buying a DVD player for just one movie, she should go to the movie theater and watch it there. Iffat had never been to a movie theater in her life. She only knew of them from the movies she had watched in her Tehran prison-house. She wanted to go to the movie theater, but she was gripped by the fear of being caught and punished. The front desk girl wrote down the name of the movie theater nearby and gave it to her.

Iffat glanced at the paper but did not know what was written on it. The girl told her that it was the name of the movie theater that was playing the new popular Indian movie. Iffat returned to her room, opened the hotel window and scanned the street below for the Muslim lawyer. She spent one hour standing by the window looking for the lawyer. She felt as if she was searching for a coin among the hundreds of people walking by, below her self-imposed prison. Eventually she came up with a plan and decided to put it into action.

CHAPTER 4

MAHMUD KHAN

Mahmud Khan was the top film director in Bollywood, bar none. His movies were always huge hits. Every film actor or actress dreamed of a leading role in one of his movies. In a land that idolized movies, he was the highest paying director in India and he chose his actors very carefully. He would never give the main roles in his movies to new actors, but always targeted high profile girls such as Miss India, Miss World, or Miss Universe. His latest movie featured the former Miss World, Priyanka Chopra, and the movie before that starred the former Miss Universe, Sushmita Sen. The Queen of Bollywood and former Miss World, Aishwarya Rai was a favorite choice for many of his recent movies. Even the former Miss Universe, Lara Dutta had acted in some of his movies. His leading men were icons in the Indian Film Industry such as Shahrukh Khan, Salman Khan, Amir Khan, Saif Ali Khan, Akshay Kumar, Hrithik Roshan, Abhishek Bachchan, Johnny Abraham, etc.

Although, he was an extremely successful director, Mahmud Khan had serious women issues. He was a serial womanizer who targeted young girls. Every time a young beautiful girl would come to him and request a role in one of his films productions, he would stipulate one condition—if she wanted a role, she would have to sleep with him. If the girl continued to sleep with him, he would give her a second role. If she was very beautiful, she might act as a maidservant for the main heroine, who was supposed to tempt the hero and create a problem between him and his wife or girlfriend. She might also play a secretary to the hero and cause him to cheat on his wife or something of that sort. If she wasn't that beautiful then she might get a side role like dancing behind the main heroine, or a former school friend of the heroine who would appear for five minutes in the entire movie. If the girl continued to sleep with him, he would make her his mistress and gradually tempting her with more significant roles. However, he never gave any new girl a leading role in his movie no matter how smart she might be or how extremely beautiful.

Mahmud was a married man. He was sixty-six years old and rarely slept with his wife. He had many houses. His main house was in Juhu but he had other houses; a farmhouse, a hill-house, and a big hotel in the city of Lonavala. He also had a resort in Khandala. At the spare residences, is where he would bed his mistresses. Each house was equipped with high security and every modern means of convenience and entertainment. He had bars, swimming pools, and disco clubs in all his houses. In each house, he had many menservants and maidservants. He would never travel long distances by car or train; he had his own two private helicopters.

The latest Mahmud Khan production featured the King and the Queen of Bollywood; Shahrukh Khan and Priyanka Chopra. It was called *The International Gonda,* a remake of an old movie by the same name. Its original actors were the former King of Bollywood, Amitabh Bachchan, and the former Miss Asia and the Bollywood Sex Symbol of all time, Zeenat Aman. The new version was heralded a hundred times better than the old version. Karina Kapoor, who danced in the place of the former dancer, Helen, excelled in her role. It was no surprise that the movie was a must-see for everyone in Mumbai. The new version of "*The International Gonda*", was featured in four movie theaters across the city. Tickets were sold a month in advance and Black Market scalpers offered them for ten times their original price.

Mahmud Khan came to the opening of his hugely successful movie at the famous Eros Theater. Usually, he would send a representative to launch his new movie but the unprecedented success of this particular movie enticed him to make a personal appearance at the Eros. Unlike in western countries, the make or break factor for Bollywood movies is solely dependent on the songs and the actor lineup. It is normal for a movie be a hit if it features sweet and popular songs and if the hero and heroine dances well. Of course, the hero and heroine had to be on the A list of Bollywood.

Mahmud Khan spent only ten minutes in the theater before he got up and left. As he was leaving, he spotted the most beautiful Indian girl he had ever seen in his life. He could not believe that such a beautiful girl was living in Mumbai without being crowned Miss Bombay or Miss India, or appearing in any movie. He knew that if any director had seen her, he would have introduced her to the film industry or encouraged her to join the regional and national beauty pageants. For that reason, he concluded that the girl was a visitor to the city or new to India. He decided to talk to her and offer to introduce her to Bollywood. Moreover, he wanted to tempt her with a role, and take her to one of his houses and sleep with her.

Mahmud approached the girl and offered his hand to greet her. The girl refused to take his hand. He introduced himself and told her who he was and the offer he had in mind. The girl thanked him for the offer and told him she was not interested in acting in movies. The proud film director was shocked at the rejection. No girl had ever refused his offers. Thousands of young girls were lined up just for a three-minute scene. He asked the girl where she was living and where she was from. She refused to tell him anything about herself. He told her that if she did not want to appear in a movie, he could introduce her to the beauty pageants officials. The girl did not understand what he meant by that. The concept was totally alien to her. When she remained silent, he thought that she was considering his second offer. Therefore, he gave her his card and asked her to either visit his office or give him a phone call.

The girl accepted his card but remained silent and revealed nothing about her true identity. As he was leaving, Mahmud Khan instructed some of his assistants to follow the girl and find out who she was and where she was living. He not only wanted her to star in his movies and crown her as Miss India, but he had fallen in love with her at first sight. He had never felt such a feeling for any woman before. No young woman had ever captivated his heart as that young girl did in that instant. Although the girl had walked away, her magnificent beauty was engraved inside his mind and the shapeliness of her seductive body kindled an unquenchable desire inflaming his passions. No girl ever before had dominated and captivated his mind and made him feel things he had never felt before. He was overwrought with titillating sensations throughout his entire body. If it wasn't for his position, he would have followed her everywhere she went. Instead, three of his men began to follow her and gather information about her. He was determined in his heart to get her by all means and to make her his bed woman. While she was walking away he continued to stare at her…

Iffat Khan had decided to fool the Muslim lawyer and go see the latest Indian movie. She planned to go outside with her face and hair uncovered. She had never stepped foot outside in public before without her Islamic veil. She knew that no one had ever seen her face since she came to India. Therefore, she expected that the Muslim lawyer would not recognize her if he happened to see her without her black burqa. She put on her Salwar Kameez, spent a few minutes before the mirror and then left her room. Iffat was not aware of her fabulous looks and extraordinary beauty. She had lived most of her life excluded from the outside world and she had never before heard anyone praise her for the way she looked. However, that day, as soon as she stepped out of her room without her burqa, she began to notice the effect of her beauty on the onlookers. People were staring at her as if she was an angelic creature that had descended from the heavens. Some men stumbled onto others while staring at her. She ignored them, continuing her walk until she found a taxi. She asked the taxi driver to take her to the movie theater that the front desk girl had written on the piece of paper. When the taxi dropped her off in front of Eros Theater, she paid the driver and stepped out. As soon as she emerged out of the taxi, she saw a man coming towards her.

Iffat was so scared when she saw the man standing in front of her and offering his hand to her. She thought he was a spy sent by her husband and she would be punished severely or tortured and killed.

She was about to run away from him, but the man blocked her way. She began to shake in fear. The man smiled and introduced himself as the Bollywood director, Mahmud Khan. Then, he asked her what her name was and where she was staying. She refused to tell him her name and she also refused to reveal where she was staying. She was scared that he might recognize her and inform her husband. She knew that her husband would cut off her head if he came to know that she had stepped out of her hotel with her face and hair uncovered. The man told her that he was a film director and he would like to offer her a role in his movie. Iffat rejected the offer. He said to her if she was not interested in acting in the film industry he would love to introduce her to the beauty contestant officials. Iffat had no clue what he was talking about. When she remained silent he took out his card and offered it to her and asked her to visit his office or call him on the phone. Iffat accepted the card from his hand. After that, she walked away without uttering a word.

Iffat felt a great relief when the man did not follow her. She went inside the movie theater and was told that all the tickets were sold out for over a month and the movie had already started. Iffat felt so disappointed and decided to stop a taxi and return to her hotel. However, while she was walking away the same man stopped her and told her that he could get her inside the theater without a ticket if she wanted to see the new movie. He could get her a ticket for the next show. Iffat did not know what to do or say to the man. She just continued to look at the man without uttering a word. The man thought that she might be deaf and dumb. He repeated his offer three times before she responded. She told him she wanted to see the movie right away. The man took hold of her hand and walked her inside the theater without anyone stopping them. Then, he said to her *"enjoy the movie"* and left the theater. The man forgotten, Iffat immersed herself and began to enjoy the movie. It was her first experience of watching a movie on the silver screen and she was thrilled with the new experience.

When the movie was over, Iffat came out of the theater, stopped a taxi and returned to her hotel, tailed by three men. One of them followed her inside the hotel. He showed his card to the front desk and asked them to tell him about the girl who just walked in. He said that he was sent by the movie director, Mahmud Khan, to talk to the girl that had just returned back to the hotel and offer her a role in his next movie. He said further that he wanted to know her name and where she was from. The front desk girl was so excited when she realized that the secretary of the well renowned film director, Mahmud Khan, had come to offer a role to one of the hotel's guests. She told him the girl was called Iffat Khan and that she had recently come from Iran. When he requested her call the girl and ask her to come and talk to him, the receptionist immediately picked up the phone receiver and dialed the room number of Iffat Khan. When Iffat responded to the call, she told her that someone would like to talk to her. Iffat was very frightened when she learned that a man wanted to speak to her. She thought that someone had informed her husband that she had gone out of the hotel with her face and hair uncovered. She decided to deny that she had ever stepped out of her room. She put on her black burqa and came down to meet the man.

The man was shocked when he saw Iffat in a black burqa. He asked her whether she was the same girl who had just come from the movie theater. Iffat strongly denied it. The front desk girl was surprised when Iffat denied that she was the same girl. She knew that she was the one who went out without her burqa and just came in. She even handed her the key to her room when she came back. She was the very one who gave her the address of the Eros Theater. Regardless, the man knew that she was the one and tried to talk to her about the movie offer. She told him she did not live in India. She came from a foreign country and she would soon return to her country; for that reason, she wasn't interested in appearing in any movies. The secretary had to accept the realization that he had failed in getting Iffat to accept his boss' offer, but he felt satisfied with the information he had gathered thus far. He apologized to Iffat and thanked her for her time. When he came out of the hotel, he phoned his boss and conveyed the information he had obtained about her. Mahmud was crushed when he heard Iffat Khan was an N R I (i.e. Non-resident Indian). Nevertheless, he wanted to know more about her. He ordered his men to continue tailing her and find out why she was there and when she planned to leave the country.

For two weeks, Mahmud Khan's men followed Iffat Khan just about everywhere she went. They learned from their tailing of her that she went to the Arthur Road Jail daily to visit an eighty-year-old Saudi man who had been arrested on charges of rape and kidnapping. They asked the guards the relationship between her and the Saudi man. One of the guards said she was the maidservant of the Arab man. Yet another suspected that the girl might be a kept-wife or a real wife of the old Arab man. Mahmud Khan felt twisted up inside when he realized that the object of his adoration might be engaged in a sexual relationship with an eighty-year-old Saudi. Hope glistened when he remembered the case and the punishment that was probably going to be dispensed for the crimes the old man had committed against the Hyderabadi girl.

CHAPTER 5

THE JOINT ACCOUNT

For a full three weeks, Mahmud Khan's men followed Iffat Khan everywhere she went and gave her nightmares. She saw them following her everyday and she naturally assumed that they were sent by her terrorist husband to keep watch over her. She did not repeat her adventure of going out of her hotel with her face and head uncovered. In her mind, her husband's spies might take her picture and smuggle it to him inside the jail. She foresaw her dangerous husband might very well tell them to punish her in some awful way. To this end, she confined her movements to the hotel and the jail. She became like a soldier or a guard at a prison, whose duty was to guard herself inside her room without fail. Every morning she left her hotel and headed to the jail. She spent a few minutes listening to the instructions of her Saudi husband and then she took a taxi and returned to her hotel. Every day without fail, she was aware of the men following her and who shadowed her every move about the city. Whenever she reached her room, she would peep from her window and see the very same men loitering outside watching the hotel. The men would remain standing smoking their cigarettes until midnight and then they would disappear. Whenever she came out, she would see them again, either on the street or following her taxi. This went on for three weeks, without fail.

In the meantime, Mahmud Khan used every available tactic to convince Iffat Khan to accept his offers. He started writing love letters to her and sending them to her room at the hotel. He wrote his romantic epistles in Urdu, Hindi, and English. He sent many beautiful cards. He sent her many beautiful bouquets of flowers. He collected the loveliest poems he found and sent them to her. He sent her invitations to expensive restaurants in five star hotels such as Taj Mahal, Sea Rock, Oberoi, and Lielas. He went as far as to send her tickets for movies that were currently playing in the best movie theaters in town. He wanted her to come out of her ugly black Islamic cocoon and show her lovely face and sexy body again. Little did he know that Iffat did not respond nor understand any of his overtures because she could not read. She did not know why someone was sending her letters, cards, tickets, invitations, and many flowers. She had no idea who was sending them. She thought about but decided against showing these love messages to the front desk girls and ask them to translate them for her. She suspected that her cruel husband might have bribed the hotel management and told them to spy on her. Although, Iffat could speak three languages, she could read and write none of them. She was completely illiterate and that fact was absent to the renowned film director. Iffat thought it best she did away with all the mail she was collecting from a stranger.

Mahmud Khan remained determined to get to Iffat Khan by any means. He decided that if he could not get her attention through his various temptations, he would resort to kidnapping her and hiding her in one of his out-of-town houses. He did not want the outside world to know of her. Thinking it over, he decided to give her a month to respond to his advances, whereupon he would order his men to kidnap her and take her to his farmhouse if no response was forthcoming. While all this attention was flooding her room something extraordinary happened which changed the course of Iffat's movements.

The Muslim lawyer, Sheikh Barkattullah, worked extensively in his mission to fulfill his promise to the old Saudi. He talked to the Judge of the High Court handling the case and informed him about the bride. The Judge demanded four crores (i.e. 40,000,000 Indian rupees). The corrupt Judge promised that he would acquit the Old Saudi man with honor if he got two crores before the trial and two crores after his honorable release. Barkattullah also made contact with many top officials in the police departments of Mumbai and

Hyderabad. Each police commissioner demanded two crores. Sheikh Barkattullah worked hard to contact and convince many other people in Mumbai and Hyderabad to join the pact. He talked to the airport police officers who arrested the old man and promised to pay them lakhs of rupees if they would agree to change their statements. He also visited Hyderabad city and called in the mother, brothers, and sisters of Amina Hyder Ali. He promised to pay the family one lakh of rupees if they would all appear in Mumbai High Court and swear under oath by placing their right hands on the holy Qur'an and say that they met the Old Saudi man before he married Amina and lied to him about her age. Through the mother, the Muslim lawyer also succeeded in contacting Amina and made her promise to change her court statements. The mother told Amina that her father and she would not force her to go with the old man. She also promised her daughter that they would allow her to go back to school and finish her education.

After fifteen days, as promised, Sheikh Barkattullah came to the old man at Arthur Road Jail and broke the good news to him. He narrated to him everything he had done on his case and how much that was going to cost him. He informed him that the entire hush deal would cost him fourteen crores (i.e. 140,000,000 Indian rupees). Seven crores had to be paid before the trial and seven crores after his honorable release. The greedy and crooked Muslim lawyer decided to get the lion's share of the six crores himself. He was planning after the trial was over to quit his profession, leave the land of the Hindu idolaters, and immigrate to the Muslim land of Pakistan. The Old Saudi tried to reduce the amount to ten crores, but the Muslim lawyer insisted that his price of freedom would remain fourteen crores. Being a life or death situation, the old Saudi agreed to all the charges.

At first, Sheikh Ahmed thought to send his Indian wife to the Abu Dhabi International Bank and get the management to send him the necessary documents to transfer seven crores rupees from his account to the account of Sheikh Barkattullah. However, the Muslim lawyer stopped him and told him that he would not accept such a large amount of money from him directly. The money should go to someone else's account and that person should deposit the money in Sheikh Barkattullah's account. He explained to him, transferring such a large amount of money from Sheikh Ahmed directly, would expose their scheme and everyone involved would go to jail. It was, after all, an enormous amount and bound to raise suspicion once it was discovered that the transfer had taken place. In order to keep such a concealed from the prying eyes of the police, the media, and others, a third person should act as the middleman. The old man understood the risk that was involved if the money went directly from his account to his lawyer's account. However, the question that puzzled him was who would be the best person with whom he could trust with such a huge amount of money. It was Sheikh Barkattullah who suggested that the faithful Indian maidservant act as an in-between. He told the old man that Iffat Khan was the only person who was not known to the government and the public. The old man understood that no one in India knew that Iffat was related to him in any way. He balked when he considered the amount of money that he would have to place in her trust. She might very well get a notion to run off with the money. But, he knew he had no one else he could use in such a situation, except her. Moreover, he understood that he had already brainwashed her and made her compliant. He reasoned that if she had thought to run away, she wouldn't have come from the Mumbai International Airport after his Afghani guard was arrested. She came from the airport all alone to him and began to do everything he said and continued to visit him without fail everyday in the jail and follow his orders.

Sheikh Barkattullah outlined his plan and advised Sheikh Ahmed to transfer the entire sum of fourteen crores into Iffat's yet to be established account. Then, he would accompany her to Switzerland to ensure that the two secret accounts (his and hers) and the agreed upon first transfer was accomplished properly. As soon as the trial was over and Sheikh Ahmed was acquitted with honor, Iffat and his lawyer would make another trip to Switzerland and get the second installment transferred from her account to his. To make sure that the old man would not change his mind after his release, the crooked lawyer told him that the Judge of the High Court said that he would not release his passport and allow him to fly out of the country of India until the amount was fully paid off. He disclosed that thc Judge would withhold his passport under the premise that protesting parties be given a chance to appeal. This would satisfy both the court and the media. The old man was not feeling comfortable with any of these conditions; the withholding of his passport, further detention in India, and transferring fourteen crores to an overseas bank account in his wife's name, was a bit more than he could handle; but his Muslim lawyer told him he had no other choice.

The old man accepted the suggestion of his Muslim lawyer, but warned his Indian maidservant in front of Sheikh Barkattullah that he would send his spies to follow her to Switzerland and if she tried to cheat him or run away with his money, his men would shoot and kill her. Then, he lied to her and said his men were already following her everywhere she went and reporting to him her daily activities. Iffat Khan swore by her Allah that she would not ever take his money and run away or do anything to upset her Saudi master.

Nevertheless, the Old Saudi man added some conditions to the deal. He told Barkattullah, he would not pay the first installment unless he got it in writing and in voice recordings, guaranteed statements from him, the Judge of the High Court, the two police commissioners of Mumbai and Hyderabad that they were going to receive from him seven crores before the trial and seven crores after the trial for his release with honor. He said further that the recorded and written confessions should be given to his Indian maidservant. When Iffat Khan received the written and recorded acknowledgments, she would come and translate them to him in Persian. He would not be satisfied until he heard these declarations and his Indian maidservant had mailed them to his personal address in Tehran. Until then, he would not pay a single rupee. The old man knew he had no one to receive the mailed confessions when they reach Iran, but he wanted to make sure that the Muslim lawyer, the Judge of the High Court, the police commissioner of Mumbai, and the police commissioner of Hyderabad could not renege on their word and let him hang high and dry. Moreover, the old man had a nagging fear and some suspicion that the Muslim lawyer might convince his Indian wife to run away with him after getting such huge amount of money in their hands. Sheikh Barkattullah tried to convince his client to drop his preconditions and trust him, but the old man refused. Finally, the Muslim lawyer agreed to try and fulfill the conditions of the old man. He said that he needed at least two weeks to obtain the written and recorded statements of these VIP persons.

While Barkattullah was busy collecting the recorded and written confessions, Sheikh Ahmed sent his obedient Indian wife to the Abu Dhabi International Bank to request the manager come see him in person. When the manager visited the Saudi man in jail, he told him to create a second account for his Indian wife, Iffat Khan, and transfer from their joint account fourteen crores to her new account. The manager asked why he was transferring such a large sum of money to his Indian wife, but the old man said to him it was his money and he was free to do with it whatever he pleased. The manager apologized to him for interfering in his personal affairs. The manager of the bank was an Arab man from a small town in the Untitled Arab Emirates (UAE). He guessed that the Saudi man was planning to purchase his freedom with this large amount of money. However, he knew it wasn't his business to ask him or question him about this either. As instructed, the International Bank of Abu Dhabi opened a new account for Iffat Khan and transferred from the joint account to her new account fourteen crores (i.e. 140,000,000 Indian rupees).

CHAPTER 6

THE BIG FEAST

Sheikh Barkattullah was able to collect the recorded and written confessions from the Judge of the High Court, the police commissioner of Mumbai, and the police commissioner of Hyderabad. In addition, he prepared his own written and recorded confession as well. He went first to the hotel, met Iffat in a small conference room, and made her listen to the recorded confessions. After that, he took her with him to visit the Old Saudi uncomfortably anxious waiting in jail. Sheikh Ahmed asked Iffat to tell him what she heard. Iffat narrated to her Saudi husband whatever she remembered from the four-recorded confessions of the corrupt Indian lawmen. The old man asked her tens of questions before he was satisfied with the recorded statements. He also looked at the four written confessions without understanding what was written in them. All four confessions were written and signed in Hindi. After that, the old man gave the green light for his lawyer and his Indian wife to travel to Switzerland together in the same plane and complete the secret deal. He also ordered his Indian maidservant on the same day to mail the recorded and written confessions to the residence in Tehran.

Iffat Khan followed the order of her husband and went to the nearest post office and mailed the secret materials to Iran and returned to her hotel. The following day, the Muslim lawyer came to her hotel and asked her to accompany him to the Swiss Consulate. Sheikh Barkattullah had never been to any Western country before. It was his life's dream to see the Western world. In fact, the only foreign country he visited was Pakistan. However, after his Allah came down from heaven and showered blessings upon him, he felt like he was the luckiest man on earth. He had never dreamt of one day being a Crorepati (i.e. a person whose net worth was at least ten million rupees). Before luck knocked on his door, he never expected to ever fulfill his lifelong dream of visiting the West or immigrating to the Muslim country of Pakistan. Now, all his heart's desires were coming true after the blessed young Indian girl, Iffat Khan, was sent by his Allah to the High Court and came and picked him from the gaggle of fifteen lawyers. In fact, Sheikh Barkattullah liked the young Muslim girl so much so, that she became his symbol of good luck. He had never seen her face, but he believed that she would be so beautiful and her face would be so radiant and shining like the face of Fatima Al-Zahra, the daughter of the Prophet Muhammad. He also believed that such a blessed and holy Indian Muslim girl, so faithful and obedient to her Arab master would be most holy and pure. If this was the case, like the daughter of Muhammad, she would not have monthly periods. (Fatima, the daughter of the Prophet Muhammad was nicknamed Al-Zahra because she was believed to be so pure and holy that Allah did not inflict upon her the curse of Eve's monthly menstruation. Although, Fatima Al-Zahra had children from her husband Ali Ibn Abi Talib, still some Muslim historians claim that she never had a period in all her life).

Sheikh Barkattullah was astonished and puzzled by the honesty shown by Iffat Khan. He could not believe that a poor young Indian maidservant could be entrusted with such a huge amount of money and still not be tempted by Satan to run away with it all. If she was like any other young Indian woman, she would not hesitate for a second to run away and spend the rest of her life as a rich Maharani (i.e. The Queen of Queens, First Lady, and Wife of Maharaja / King of Kings). In the eyes of the Muslim lawyer, the blessed, honest, pure, holy, chaste, virtuous, and loyal Iffat Khan decided to remain a maidservant in her Arab master's employ rather than running away and becoming one of the richest women in India. Barkattullah wished in his heart that Allah would bless him with such a faithful daughter-in-law. He was determined in his heart that when he got hold of his seven crores, he would get Iffat Khan married to his first son, Maqsood Barkattullah. He had already mentioned her to his family and told his wife and children about her and how honest, humble, and blessed a maidservant she was. If Iffat agreed to marry his blessed son, Maqsood Barkattullah, they would take her to Pakistan and throw the biggest marriage celebration in the history of Lahore.

Barkattullah decided to leave the land of the accursed Hindu idol-worshippers, and immigrate to the blessed land of the Muslims and settle among one of the cities of Pakistan. He had distant relatives who were fed up fighting with Hindus in Ahmadabad, and immigrated to Pakistan and settled in Lahore. Barkattullah had already contacted his relatives in Lahore and requested they find him a big house in the richest area of the city and book it for him. He promised that he would come to Pakistan and pay off the entire sum of the house as soon as he returned from his business trip in Switzerland.

The Muslim lawyer promised his wife, nine children, and parents that he would take them all to the holy lands of Mecca and Medina to visit the tomb of the Prophet Muhammad and the House of Allah to perform the Hajj. Moreover, his five sons were told that there was no need for them to pursue their secular education any longer. As soon as he returned from his important business trip to Europe, he would give each one of them twenty-five lakhs of rupees so that they could start their own business. To his four daughters, he promised that he would find good Muslim husbands for them to marry and settle down. He admitted being dismayed at allowing them to continue their education at secular schools and the possibility of them falling in love with Hindu boys bringing great shame and a curse to his blessed and holy family. Barkattullah swore by his Allah that when he returned from the West, he would bring them back gifts and the best clothing he could afford to his wife and nine children. He also told his family that as soon as they relocated in Lahore, he would buy for them the most expensive cars on the market. (In India and Pakistan, a five-passenger-car can hold up to fifteen passengers). The only thing Sheikh Barkattullah did not share with his wife and children was that he was planning to find three young, beautiful, Allah-fearing Pakistani Muslim girls to marry.

He planned for each year, to find and wed one young beautiful Lahori Muslim girl until he completed the Sunna of the Prophet Muhammad and the holy Qur'an of having four wives at the same time. Their ages should be between twelve and fourteen. The second wife should be fourteen years old. However, the third wife should be thirteen and the fourth wife, twelve years old.

With those plans in mind, Sheikh Barkattullah took the blessed and holy Muslim Indian maidservant from the hotel to the Swiss Consulate to apply for visiting visas. To ensure that the Consulate would not reject their applications, Iffat claimed that Barkattullah was her mother's brother and she attached an official letter from the Abu Dhabi International Bank that showed her bank account balance. The Consulate could not believe such a young Indian girl could have that much money. Contacting the bank eliminated that doubt. The following day, the Consulate issued the two visas for the rich young Indian girl and her uncle. After that, Iffat and Barkattullah went to air India to purchase their tickets and book their flight. They were told that the nearest date for booking would be after one month. Nevertheless, they were told that if they wanted to fly immediately, they would have to pay more and purchase first class tickets.

Before purchasing first class airfares, Iffat and Barkattullah consulted the Old Saudi by traveling back to the jail. His consent obtained, they returned to the bank for additional funds and returned to the Air India office and bought first class tickets. Their trip was scheduled within a couple of days. When all was ready, the old man imposed more conditions for his two delegates. First of all, he ordered that the two tickets and passports should be kept with Iffat Khan. Secondly, Barkattullah was to show up at the Mumbai International Airport three hours before flight time. Thirdly, Iffat had to take a taxi from the hotel and travel to the Mumbai International Airport alone. Fourth, the two should not sit together in the plane or let anyone know they knew each other in any way. Fifth, when they arrived at Zurich, they should stay in the same hotel, but in separate rooms. Laying down the law, the old Saudi lifted up both his hands to the heavens and ordered Iffat and Barkattullah to both lift up their hands to give praise to Allah. Then, he recited loudly Surat Al-Fatiha;

> *"In the name of Allah, the most beneficent the most merciful. All praise is due to Allah, Lord of the worlds. The most beneficent, the most merciful. The lord of the Day of Judgment. Thee alone do we worship and thee alone we seek for help. Guide us to the right path. The path of those upon whom thou has bestowed favors [the Muslims], Not of those who thou has cursed [the Jews] nor of those who have gone astray [the Christians]."*

AMEEN said the three in unison. Then the Old Saudi sent his lawyer and Indian wife with the blessings and protection of Allah and his Messenger Muhammad (PBUH). Sheikh Barkattullah dropped Iffat Khan off at her hotel and gave her his blessings and promised to meet her at the Mumbai International Airport in forty-eight hours. He was in a great hurry that day. His wife and children had organized a big party for him. The family invited two hundred Muslim men and women plus an uncountable number of their children to the great feast. (Muslims in India are trying to produce as many as possible of children with the hope to outnumber Hindus. A single Muslim man in Bombay reached the highest record of having 75 children. So far in India there are 150 million Muslims and 850 million Hindus).

Barkattullah's family spent thirty-five thousand rupees preparing for the big feast. Everyone invited was told that the party was in honor of the successful business that Sheikh Barkattullah had started with a big international European company. The crooked lawyer lied to everyone even his own family that he had started an international import and export company. His trip to Switzerland was for the commencement of the business. He claimed that he had been invited by his European partners to come to Zurich for the inauguration ceremony of the business. With nodding heads of every Muslim around him, the corrupt lawyer swore by his Allah that he was going to quit working as a Wakeel. He argued that his Islamic conscience convicted him of the great sins he committed by working in a profession that was condemned by Shari'a law.

According to the Islamic Shari'a law, the profession of being an attorney is not an acceptable practice and hence it is haram in Islam to study secular law and become a lawyer or a secular judge. Only those who have attended a *bona fide* Islamic college and studied Shari'a law would be allowed to become judges in Shari'a courts. In fact, according to all schools of the Shari'a law, soliciting was not a part of the Islamic judicial system. It was an invention created by the Western secular judicial system, which is man-made and not divinely revealed as the Shari'a. And according to Islam, every new system not founded in the book of Allah and the Sunna of his Messenger is simply considered an innovation. Every innovation leads to hellfire. Therefore, Sheikh Barkattullah told everyone that he was planning to quit working as a solicitor in the secular Indian court system and start an acceptable business to his Allah of importing and exporting. He said further that his Prophet Muhammad before receiving his first revelation from his Allah used to work in the import and export trade of his first wife Khadijah bint Khuwaylid. (The three types of people that are *persona non grata* in the Islamic judicial system are a woman, a lawyer, and an infidel). In any case, Barkattullah had truly made up his mind to forsake the profession that he worked in for so many years and of which he had used this income to fill the mouths and stomachs of his wife, his children, and himself.

For the great feast, Sheikh Barkattullah slaughtered five goats and bought two hundred chickens to celebrate his new overseas business and to thank his Allah for the great treasure that he brought into his life. He was made to jump over each goat that was beheaded in front of the door of his house. (A Muslim was required to celebrate every blessing by slaughtering an animal as a Qurban to his Allah and jumping over its blood). That day, the Barkattullah family and their two hundred Muslim guests along with their many children celebrated the happy occasion with merry hearts. That day, everyone filled his/her stomach with delicious Mutton Biryani, Chicken Curry, Chicken Tandoori, and various kinds of Indian sweet dishes.

CHAPTER 7

THE GIRL IN A BLACK BURQA

The happy Barkattullah family came to the Mumbai Chhatrapati Shiviji International Airport accompanied by more than a hundred Muslim brethren. Half of the guests who celebrated and were present at the big feast came to the airport to see the blessed Muslim man, Sheikh Barkattullah off. In keeping with his new station in life, Barkattullah rented two buses for those who wanted to come to the airport and say good-bye to him. The two buses picked up all the guests from their houses and brought them to the airport. The Barkattullah clan, his wife, their nine children, and some very close Muslim relatives came to the airport in a third hired mini-bus. The wife and the four daughters were eager to meet the blessed and loyal Muslim girl, Iffat Khan. Barkattullah told his family that one of his Arab partners had a very faithful and holy Indian Muslim maidservant. He told his wife and daughters in particular that when they meet Iffat Khan, they should try to convince her to unveil herself and show them her face. Then, if her features pleased them, they should tell her about the proposal of his eldest son, Maqsood Barkattullah. If Iffat accepted the proposal, they would have a big wedding party and get Maqsood married to the blessed Muslim girl immediately upon their return.

That day, Sheikh Barkattullah was dashing in his distinguished look up to the point that people that had known him before might not have recognized him. If he claimed to be an Indian celebrity—a film star, a minister, or a big shot, no one would deny it. His sons also sported new attire. In keeping with the men, his wife and five daughters were dressed up in new Muslim burqas. Everyone in their social circle came to the airport that particular afternoon to talk to the man of the hour and get his blessings. The happy Wakeel was so uncharacteristically generous that day. He was distributing tens, fifties, and hundreds of Indian rupee notes like flowers. Everyone that shook hands with him got blessed with money. Barkattullah would place in the pocket of any man or the hand of any woman whatever note magically appeared from out of his pants or jacket. He was like a walking jackpot machine. Everyone received according to his or her luck. Some people got ten-rupee notes, some fifty notes, and some very lucky ones got notes for a hundred. He was not bothered if he finished all of the one-lakh rupees that he got as an advance from the old Saudi. He knew that in less than twenty-four hours he was going to receive 70,000,000 Indian rupees. He already counted himself as a Crorepati. His plan all along was to give his accomplices four crores and keep three crores for himself. The corrupt Judge of the High Court would get as a first installment two crores rupees and the two crooked police commissioners would receive one crore each and the remaining three crores would remain in the account of the happiest and the luckiest Muslim lawyer in the entire world.

The airport police officers who arrested the kidnapper and rapist of the eleven-year-old Indian girl would receive two lakhs each (i.e. 200,000 Indian rupees each). Amina's family would get fifty thousand rupees as a first payment. Barkattullah volunteered to pay the airport police officers and the victim's family from his lion's share. After the trial was successfully conducted and the old Arab man was released with honor, the same distribution process would be repeated again. Barkattullah promised to pay the airport police officers and Amina's family in cash. However, for the Judge and the two police commissioners he would transfer their shares into a secret foreign account of their choosing. It was up to each one of them which bank they would nominate, be it in an Arab or a Western country.

While Sheikh Barkattullah prepared everything, he forgot one critical thing. He reached the airport three hours prior to his flight as was decided by the Old Saudi. Iffat Khan was supposed to reach the airport at the same time and meet him outside the airport. Then, the plan required the two of them to proceed toward the departure hall and begin the process of their overseas flight. However, that particular afternoon Barkattullah waited one hour outside the airport without seeing Iffat Khan. He thought that the obedient and loyal Indian Muslim maidservant had come, and was unable to meet up with him because of his huge entourage of well-wishers. Shrugging this small matter off would change his fate. He bid his family and admirers farewell and proceeded inside the departure hall. His head was turning around like a table fan and searching for *the girl in the black burqa*. While he was searching, his heart was beating inside his chest like a Tabla (i.e. traditional flat India ceremonial drum). His search for Iffat grew more and more frantic and crazier every second as minutes passed by. With the passing of another nail biting half hour, when his accomplice in the *black burqa* who had, in the past few weeks, been like his shadow, failed to appear into his sight, he ran to the information office and paid for an urgent announcement. The information office announced the name of Iffat Khan all throughout the airport and requested she come as soon as possible to the inquiry office and meet her uncle Sheikh Barkattullah. The announcement was made three times over.

Barkattullah waited another half hour at the information office without seeing Iffat Khan. He left the information office and ran to another airport office to inquire about his and his niece's flight. The office confirmed their bookings, but said they had no clue whether his niece had arrived in the departure hall or if she had passed through the checkpoints to complete the process to board the Saudi plane or not. He was advised to rush to the security checkpoint before he missed his flight. The frantic man ran as if he was being chased by a wild cheetah. He could not feel his feet or his body. He stumbled over a passenger's luggage and fell awkwardly to the floor; ignored the pain and humiliation, got up quickly and resumed his panicked pace. At the departure hall entrance, airport security prevented his entry because he had neither a passport nor a ticket. He begged the attendants to allow him to pass onto the flight, but his pleadings fell on deaf ears. At this point, security threatened to arrest him and have him thrown behind bars if he continued to bother them. Barkattullah was almost crying when the airport police pushed him back. Blistering tears started to fall from his eyes. Then half an hour before takeoff, he heard the name of Iffat Khan and his name being heralded to Gate No. 14. The announcer urgently stressed that it was the last call for Zurich flight, 284. He once again presented himself at the boarding checkpoint. When he faced the airport personnel again for the second time, explaining that he was responding to the announcement, they once again requested his boarding pass and his passport. He stood still, pleading with them, until he was kicked out again.

Sheikh Barkattullah marched back and forth watching all entrances and exits hoping still for a glimpse of the girl in the *black burqa*. When the plane took off, Sheikh Barkattullah fell on his knees and began to weep. Some kind Indians waiting in the lobby for arrivals and departures came and helped him to stand on his feet. His feet which moments ago propelled him at breakneck speed, now became so feeble that he had to be helped to stand and assisted to a bench to sit. It took him a long time to come back to his senses. The first step he decided to take was to go to the hotel, find that stupid Indian girl, and kick her left and right for forgetting to come to the airport and for unnecessarily missing her flight. When he looked around, he found that all his family members and admirers had already gone. He abstractedly visualized the happy moment when all of them saw the airplane taking off, waving at him. He was not looking forward to the abject shock and sadness when his family members would learn that the rapture took place, but he was left behind.

With his small bag in his hand, Sheikh Barkattullah stopped a taxi and told him to take him to Bombay Central. It took him one hour to reach Iffat Khan's hotel. The ride was far from peaceful with his raging mood growing hotter by the second as the taxi driver did battle with the typical Mumbai traffic. When the taxi dropped him in front of the hotel, he felt like he was going to explode any moment. He ran inside the hotel and asked the front desk girl, in a tone that did not hide his indescribable anger, to summon the room of Iffat Khan and tell her to come immediately to meet her uncle, Sheikh Barkattullah.

She had missed her flight and they need to catch another one as soon as possible! She had forgotten to come to the Mumbai International Airport for their trip to Europe to conduct a very important business deal. The front desk girl said to him that Iffat Khan had not returned to the hotel for two days. Neither had she checked out. Her bag and her personal effects were still in her room. Barkattullah felt a slight fluttering in his heart. He fell on his knees once again and held his head. This time, he did not cry. He would if he could, but he lost some of his senses and his mouth was paralyzed.

When Sheikh Barkattullah somehow overcame this second rude awakening for the day, he tried to clear his mind, so he could unravel the mess. The first place he decided to go to was the Arthur Road Jail. Maybe he could find out what had happened to the accursed girl in the *black burqa* there. On his way in yet another taxi, he had the sinking feeling that if he could not find out where Iffat Khan went to, he would simply die of a major heart attack or lose his mind and end up in a mental hospital. He began to talk to himself as if he was a madman. He talked to his Allah and begged him to intervene before he committed suicide. This was now his third option, none of them particularly appealing. From the exultant and joyous mood in the airport, he was now suicidal. At the jail, he was told that visiting time was over for the day. He was advised to come back the following day. Barkattullah knew that his mental condition would not allow him to survive for twenty-four hours without knowing where Iffat Khan was. Therefore, he paid a bribe of two thousand rupees and convinced the jail authority to allow him to meet his client.

When the old man came out and was informed what had happened, he spit in the face of his lawyer ten times and called him every filthy Hindi word he had learnt in jail. He accused him of conspiring with his Indian maidservant. The first thought that erupted in the mind of the old man was that the Indian lawyer had convinced his Indian wife to double cross her Arab master and steal his money and divide it between them. For that reason, he spat on his lawyer and showered him with bad language. He also threatened that he would pay a huge amount of money to send some Gondas with whom he had become well acquainted with while in jail, to wipe out his entire family. With this threat looming over him firmly registering in the lawyer's face, Sheikh Ahmed gave him twenty-four hours to abandon his wicked scheme and bring his Indian maidservant to him; with the two of them on their knees, repentant and begging his forgiveness. If his maidservant refused to come with him, he would tell the Gondas to find her and gang rape her, and then kill her in the most cruel and brutal way possible. He even swore by his Allah that he would tell the Gondas to tie her legs up between two horses and split her body in two halves. (Sheikh Ahmed came to know of this inhumane and cruel punishment in the Islamic school, while studying the biography of his Prophet Muhammad. The old woman, Om Girfa, was killed for criticizing the alleged Prophet of Allah. The Prophet instructed her legs be tied to two camels and her body torn into two halves. Om Girfa was over a hundred years old when she was sentenced to meet a violent and gruesome death). In keeping with tradition, the furious and extremely incensed old man swore by his Allah that if his lawyer and his maidservant would not show up the following day, he would send some Gondas to kill them in exactly the same way.

After receiving the death threat, Sheikh Barkattullah returned again to the hotel and begged the management to supply him with any clues that might lead him to the whereabouts of Iffat Khan. He proposed to pay a few thousand rupees if anyone could give him any clues. The hotel staff apologized and explained that they had no idea where their hotel guest went. One front desk girl advised him to search for her at the hospitals in case she met with an accident or if she was in police lockup in case she ran into some trouble with the law. Barkattullah knew that there were hundreds of hospitals and many police lockups in Mumbai. He would have needed more than a month to go from hospital to hospital and from one police lockup to another. He no longer considered Iffat Khan the most holy and honest girl he had ever met. Now, she was no longer the angel-like Muslim girl. To him, the female was now some satanic creature that crossed his path bringing with her a bad omen. He hated her with a passion for turning his great joy and happiness overnight into chaos, panic, sorrow, and great misfortune. He abhorred her for snatching his life's opportunity from out of his hands and in its place; death threats to him and to members of his family. He knew that if the Old Saudi decided to carry out his threats, his family would meet a cruel end at the hands of the ruthless Mumbai Gondas within twenty-four hours.

Sheikh Barkattullah understood that he could not solve the problem of the missing maidservant alone. He decided to involve his accomplices in his search for the missing Indian maidservant of his Arab client. He wasted no time phoning the police commissioner of Mumbai and told him about the sad news and asked him to help him in locating the missing girl. The police commissioner was even more disturbed and troubled than the Muslim lawyer. More than just the one crore rupee was in the balance, this was a man who was not accustomed to being swindled. He told Barkattullah that he would mobilize the entire police department of Mumbai to search for the missing maidservant, Iffat Khan. He promised to find her within twenty-four hours. The citywide search hit its first hurdle when they realized that they had no photo of Iffat Khan. Coming in from Iran, the only clue of the eighteen-year-old's identity was a photocopy of her passport issued when she was eight. The police commissioner contacted Mumbai international and domestic airports. Both airports did not find a record of a girl by that name or description traveling out of the city. The police commissioner sent over fifty police officers to all the railway stations at Mumbai in search of the missing girl. They could neither confirm nor disprove that Iffat Khan left on a train. Every hospital and police lockup in the city was searched. In less than twenty-four hours, the city was searched inside and out. It was as if the earth had opened up and swallowed her whole. During the citywide search, Sheikh Barkattullah, rented a room in a hotel and spent the entire night on his knees crying to his Allah and begging him to intervene and save him and his family from the greatest catastrophe that he had ever encountered.

CHAPTER 8

IN A GOLDEN CAGE

If Sheikh Barkattullah had waited five minutes more in front of the hotel, he would have seen the men who had kidnapped Iffat Khan and the plate of the car they were in. That particular evening, the happy lawyer was in a great hurry, and his trained powers of observation and patience had deserted him. As soon as Iffat lit from her taxi, he told his taxi driver to hurry up and take him to his house "pronto!" A big feast and celebration planned in his honor was being prepared. Iffat crossed the road and headed towards her hotel. She did not see the two Indian men coming up behind her. They grabbed her waist and clamped her mouth. A third accomplice drove up in a big car just behind them. Her two kidnappers shoved Iffat into the car. Anyone looking would have just assumed that the three men had just picked up one of the hundreds of call girls on Bombay Central. Iffat's hotel was smack dab in the middle of one of the worst areas of Mumbai. It was part of the largest *red light prostitutes' center* on Farris Road. She was able to live over a month in that area without being kidnapped or raped because of her Islamic burqa that hid her physical assets. Yes, her burqa was a blessing in disguise sometimes. The one time she walked out without her burqa led to the film director, Mahmud Khan, falling head over heels for her. It was ironically the same one-sided love affair that her mother fell victim to many years ago with the Old Saudi man; changing the course of her life forever.

Mahmud Khan had tried every trick under the sun and failed. He already knew that she was an N.R.I., and would leave India and return to wherever she came from one day. That had the effect of increasing his determination and efforts to have her. It was when his assistants reported her movements with the Muslim lawyer of the Old Saudi that he understood she would be flying out of the country soon. Faced with the thought that he would never see her again, he knew he either had to 'detain' her or delay her departure. As a last resort, he gave his men the green light to kidnap her and bring her to his farmhouse. He did not intend to force himself on her, but rather to take his time and try to win her heart, housing her in what was to be yet another golden cage. Before the kidnapping, his men were warned not to harm her.

Iffat's entire life-long experience with men had heightened her fear of all men. She grew up thinking that men were somehow designed by nature to harm women. She had vivid memories of her mother's brutal rape by the two Saudi policemen. She clearly remembered the way the old man forced himself on her sexually when she was just a little girl. No, there was nothing in Iffat's life that led her to believe otherwise. Iffat simply thought that man was created by God to be like an animal and stronger than his mate, so he could have forced sex whenever he wanted. This idea was impressed upon her by the way she had observed some animals forcing other animals to stay still while they pushed themselves on top of them. As a child, she had witnessed a bloody fight between a pair of cats. Exercising his physical superiority, the boy cat forced the girl cat to submit. She had seen the same with a cock and a hen. Iffat concluded that sex equals pain. She had no concept of lovemaking. It was in this frame of mind she was dwelling, the day of her kidnapping. She fully expected her abductors to beat her up and brutally rape her. She thought that the men would kill her the same way the Saudi policemen had left her mother to die after raping her. Iffat was eighteen years old, but she had the social and cognitive skills of an eight year old. Her mind stopped growing from the time the old man took her to Asmara and imprisoned her in his mansion, raping her night and day.

The men took her to a place very far away. Their car only reached Mahmud Khan's farmhouse at midnight. Iffat's heightened fear denied her any sleep even though she was thoroughly tired and exhausted. When the men did not drag her or force her out of the car, Iffat obeyed their mild tone and respectful manner, for she was expecting a beating otherwise. One of them politely invited her out of the car and asked if she could follow them into the house. She entered the house into a huge room. She was surprised when she saw the marvelous beauty of the room she was standing in. The men were talking to her in Hindi. One of them told her that very soon she was going to have her dinner. He even apologized to her for serving her dinner at such a late hour. Then, he asked her whether she would prefer to have her food first or take a bath. When she understood that the men intended her no harm, Iffat began to talk to them. The first question she asked was why they had kidnapped her from the street in front of her hotel and brought her here.

Iffat was keenly aware that the house she was in was more opulent and better decorated than her previous two homes in Asmara and Tehran. One of the three men broached the subject carefully, gently breaking it to her that she was not being kidnapped. He explained that his boss loved her so much and wanted to make her a big film star and that was why he had asked them to bring her to his house. Iffat immediately remembered the man who met her in front of the movie theater and offered her a role in his next movie. She retorted that she was not interested in becoming a film star. Noting that they did not get angry, she requested to be taken back to her hotel because she was flying out of India in two days. The man apologized, and told her that decision was his boss' decision and not his to make. Iffat told them that she would be cruelly punished by her Saudi husband if she did not fly to Europe and do the work he told her to do. The three men were shocked that the eighty-year-old Saudi man who was under trial for kidnapping and raping an eleven-year-old Indian girl was her husband. They tried digging more information but Iffat fell silent. One of them asked her which kind of work she was going to do for her Saudi husband in Europe. She remained silent.

Before the three men could get further information from Iffat, someone walked in carrying the largest food tray she ever had seen. She recognized nothing on the serving platter but she was very hungry, not having eaten since that morning. In her hunger, she began eating with her hand, ignoring the fork and spoon, causing the men to gape at her and wonder. She stuffed herself with food, did not chew properly and grabbed continually at anything within her reach. Iffat simply ate the way she knew how. At one point, she was trying to stuff food into a mouth that could hold no more. The men forced themselves not to laugh, for fear of offending her. Iffat finished almost everything that was brought to her on the huge tray. One of the men said to her that he could ask the cook to bring her more food. She thanked him; refused the offer and said she was full.

After finishing her dinner, one of the men invited Iffat to go and take a bath. She said to him she did not want to take a bath. She reminded the man of her request. She begged him to take her back to her hotel so that she wouldn't miss her flight to Zurich. The man ignored her request and wished her good night. Then, he asked the other men to follow him, locking her in the room. She did not know whether they had left the house or were hiding somewhere. She remained seated on the huge bed in the middle of the room staring blankly ahead. She fully expected the men to come back at any moment and forcefully sleep with her. Sleep did not come easily to her. Eventually, fatigue won over fear and she fell asleep on the huge bed and soon began to snore.

Iffat Khan woke up at midday with no idea how long she had slept. Disoriented but fresh from her rest, she looked around her and found everything to be the same. Her heart beat faster when she remembered where she was supposed to be. She supposed to visit her Saudi husband and bid him goodbye. She jerked upright and ran to the door trying to open it. It was locked. She banged on the door and called for help, but no one responded. When she tired of knocking and shouting, she went back and sat on the edge of the bed. Looking around the room, she realized that someone had left a covered serving tray on a table across from the bed. With nothing else to do and curiosity mounting, she got up and lifted the cover off the tray. It was full of various food and fruits. There was a big pot of tea. Scanning the room and realizing she was completely alone, she started eating her breakfast standing up. The previous night's table manners returned. She ate with her hands and stuffed her mouth with food until crumbs littered the floor. The food met with her approval and when satiated, she poured herself a big cup of tea. Iffat wished that her Saudi husband would not find out that she had been kidnapped and spent the night in a house with three men. She also wished that the Muslim lawyer would not fly to Zurich without her. She looked idly at the two passports and tickets in her handbag and expected that the lawyer would surely go to her husband and complain about her absence. As she had been trained, she now knew that her husband would fly into a rage and send his men out searching for her.

While her mind was occupied with those unsettling thoughts, Iffat heard the door open and saw someone walking in. She recognized him immediately. She saw the man who had met and talked to her in front of the movie theater and had helped her get into the fully booked theater. The man smiled to her and sat across her in an armchair. Mahmud Khan told Iffat that he was responsible for her situation. He repeated what his men had already said to her. That he loved her and planned to make her a film star. Noting that she was alarmed, he assured her that he was not going to harm her nor allow anyone else to. Iffat repeated her plea to be released but Mahmud Khan told her that he would not allow any man to come near her. He added that her Saudi husband was not going to get out of jail anytime soon. Seeing her response, he added that her husband might be hanged to death by the Mumbai High Court for the hideous crimes that he had committed against the eleven-year-old Indian girl. Then, he narrated to her what her husband had done to the Hyderbadi girl.

Despite her situation, Mahmud Khan was able to convince Iffat Khan that she was going to be safe in his farmhouse. His tone and his body language subtly underlined his promise not to harm her or force her into anything she didn't want to do. All he seemed to want was her company. When Iffat was fully convinced that Mahmud was not going to beat or rape her, she opened up her heart and told him everything the old man had done to her in Asmara and Tehran. Mahmud was shocked to the core. He told her that such an evil man deserved to be punished severely by the Indian courts. He also assured her that as long as she was staying in his house, she would be under his protection and the Old Saudi man would not be able to reach her. Iffat believed Mahmud and decided to stay under his protection forever. For her, this was a far better option than returning to the old man who filled her heart with fear and abused her in every way possible for ten years. For the first time, Iffat felt secure. She innocently believed that her kidnapper wasn't going to proposition her for sex.

Mahmud Khan felt very sad when he discovered that his dream girl, Iffat, was illiterate. He promised to teach her to read and write in Hindi and English. Before he left, he told her to take a bath and change her clothes. He showed her a big cupboard filled with all manner of very beautiful female dresses. When he had left, Iffat entered the huge bathroom and took a bath with warm water. She changed her Islamic clothes and put on a modern dress. After her bath, a woman came to her room and showed her how to operate the home theater system. She also showed her a huge cupboard full of Indian movies. Iffat felt as if she was dug out of a dark dungeon and placed in a golden palace. She found it hard to believe that there was such a loving and caring man like Mahmud Khan. For her he appeared as an angel compared to her evil Saudi husband.

As he promised, Mahmud Khan immediately appointed a tutor to teach Iffat Khan. It did not take too long for Mahmud to discover that Iffat was not trained for anything in life. She talked and behaved as if she had lived all her life like a caged animal. She did not know anything about the world she lived in. She only knew the Old Saudi man and his evil ways of punishing her whenever she did something he did not like. The old man destroyed her personality and turned her into a robot. She became like a child who needed someone to protect and care for her the rest of her life.

CHAPTER 9

THE NEW DEAL

The Old Saudi waited a week for his Muslim lawyer and his Indian maidservant. Instead of twenty-four hours, he had given his lawyer seven more days. When Barkattullah did not show, the old man assumed that his crooked lawyer had taken Iffat out of Mumbai and hidden her somewhere in India. He lost no time in locating a few dangerous Gondas to search for his Indian maidservant and his crooked lawyer. He planned to tempt the Gondas with a huge amount of money to search for the kidnapper of his beloved wife and the robber of his fourteen crores of rupees. The first step he took was ask one of his inmates to connect him with the most dangerous Gondas in Mumbai. He proposed to pay ten thousand rupees to his inmate. That inmate was about to be released in a week's time. The inmate promised to supply him with the best Gondas in the city. Moreover, the Old Saudi gave the inmate a letter to take to the manager of his bank. In the letter, he requested the manager send someone with a checkbook so that he could pay the Indians he was hiring for his case.

When the bank received the letter, it sent someone to the jail and met with Mr. Sheikh Faiz bin Ahmed. The old man almost had a heart attack when the bank told him that he could not withdraw more than one thousand Indian rupees per day. His account was no longer his alone. What he did have was a joint account with his 'Indian wife', Iffat Khan. It was he himself who had stipulated this condition; neither party of the joint account was to withdraw more than one thousand rupees without the consent of the other. With this stipulation in place, the old man would now need Iffat Khan to approve any withdrawal exceeding one thousand rupees on any given day. Naturally, the bank refused to allow him to withdraw more than the agreed upon sum as a single signatory. The old man told the bank that his Indian wife had stolen fourteen crores from him and eloped with his Muslim lawyer. The bank informed him that this was a matter for the police and not them. The old man begged the bank to dissolve the joint account and create one account under his name. The bank said that the joint account could not be canceled without the consent of Iffat Khan. However, the bank did tactfully suggest that if one of signatories passed away, the surviving signatory would be entitled to the entire sum and the account would revert to a single account holder.

The Saudi business tycoon had more than four hundred crores of rupees in the joint account at the time when the Abu Dhabi International Bank imposed the withdrawal restrictions upon him. He felt like a man who was dying of thirst standing in the midst of a huge river and could not drink water unless he used a thimble. His final appearance in court before trial was scheduled to take place in a couple of months. He knew that if he could not find another lawyer and use him to purchase his freedom, he would go to the gallows and leave his wealth to his accursed Indian wife. The old man had already transferred all his properties in the Kingdom of Saudi Arabia to the name of Iffat Khan without her knowledge. Even his two houses in Asmara and Tehran were hers.

Sheikh Faiz bin Ahmed hated all his sons and daughters. He even hated his Saudi wives. He did not want any one of his wives to inherit the houses they were living in. At the time of his arrest in Mumbai, he still had two Saudi wives with his second wife passing away a long time ago. The disappearance of his Indian wife now created serious problems for him. Her disappearance was now a matter of life or death for the old Saudi. At first, he did not want to inform his families in Saudi Arabia about his arrest in Mumbai. He remembered that when he was arrested in Asmara with his eleven-year-old Indian child bride, all his wives, sons, and daughters stood against him because they saw it as an unconscionable shame for him to have married the daughter of an Indian maidservant. Even his surviving cousins, brothers, sisters and distant relatives disapproved his marriage. To them, Iffat was but a girl from a lowly Muslim background. None of his relatives, close or distant, came to court when he was on trial in Jeddah. And when the court cleared him of the charges that the CIA team tried to nail him with, none of his relatives had come to congratulate him on his victory. For that reason, Sheikh Ahmed decided to punish all his wives and children by cutting them off from inheriting any of his great wealth or property.

However, after his Indian wife supposedly left him and ran away with his Indian lawyer, the old man decided to bite the bullet and seek the help of one of his sons. He wrote a long letter to his favourite son and asked him to come as soon as possible and save him before the accursed Hindu idolaters sent him to the gallows. This son was much-loved by the old man because he was the only highly educated son among his many sons and daughters. He studied in the United States of America and became a medical doctor, at present practicing his profession at the Royal Hospital in the Jeddah city. He was the one who impregnated his American girlfriend and had a daughter with her out of the benefits of marriage. The daughter was the late Shama Abd Al-Bari Ahmed (Shama Thomson) who was killed by the Somali chauffeur of the old man under his orders and instigation.

In his letter, the old man requested his son not inform anyone about his second marriage to his second Indian wife and his arrest. His son was even more furious when he came to know that his father had once again married another low caste Muslim woman, this one from the Arzal tribe of India. (His first Indian wife, Iffat Khan was from the Ajlaf tribe). According to Barani, "Islamic Sharia laws allow for slavery and no Muslim will ever denounce Sharia. The Catholic Church did allow for slavery until 1888 and the Orthodox Church until 1863, but they modified their texts and banned slavery. In Islam, unlike every other religion, one cannot modify their texts due to new times and changed times, and is still stuck with slavery and many other ills." Besides the persistent slavery system in Muslim societies until today, there is the caste system between Muslims in India, Pakistan, Bangladesh, and Afghanistan. In fact, the caste system is practiced until today in many Muslim countries especially in Sudan and Somalia. In Sudan, the so-called Arab Muslims treat the African Muslims as slaves and dirt. The two civil wars in Darfur and South of Sudan are mainly result of this ugly racial discrimination.

The Muslims in India are three castes—Ashraf, Ajlaf, and Arzal. Ashraf is plural and its singular Shareef, which means highborn, high bred, noble, illustrious, eminent, distinguished, and high-ranking. Ajlaf is the plural of Jilf, which means boorish, rude, uncivil, ill-mannered, rough, fool. Finally, Arzal is the plural form of Razeel, meaning low, base, mean, and vile. According to Dr. B. R. Ambedkar, the Arzal Muslims are treated worse than the Hindu Untouchables or Hirijans. The Arzal Muslims are not allowed to touch the Qur'an or enter a mosque. Their jobs are same like those of the Noba Mountains' Muslims of Sudan, to carry human refuse and clean sewer and other low jobs. The words Ashraf, Ajlaf, and Arzal are socially discriminative Arabic terms, which use until today to distinguish people into castes. The Arab Muslims always look down upon non-Arab Muslims. Their superiority is summarized in Al-Tabari, "**Arabs are the most noble people in lineage, the most prominent, and the best in deeds.** We were the first to respond to the call of the Prophet. We are Allah's helpers and the viziers of His Messenger. We fight people until they believe in Allah. He who believes in Allah and His Messenger has protected his life and possessions from us. As for one who disbelieves, we will fight him forever in Allah's Cause. Killing him is a small matter to us," (Al-Tabari, Vol. 9, p. 69).

The prophet Muhammad owned slaves—males and females—and practiced slavery until he died. He used to exchange a white slave for two black slaves. Figh Alriq (i.e. The Science of Slavery) is part of every curriculum and taught until today in all Muslim schools and universities including the prestigious Islamic Institute of Learning of Al-Azhar Al-Shareef University. The prophet Muhammad hated **black color** even in human beings and animals. He said, the **black dog is devil,** if you dream of **a black woman is a bad omen**, if anyone said to you **the prophet is black kill him**, and for him **one white**

slave equals two black slaves. Muhammad believed that **the black man is Satan**, "I heard the Apostle say: 'Whoever wants to see Satan should look at Nabtal!' He was a black man with long flowing hair, inflamed eyes, and dark ruddy cheeks… Allah sent down concerning him: 'To those who annoy the Prophet there is a painful doom." [9: 61] "Gabriel came to Muhammad and said, 'If a black man comes to you his heart is more gross than a donkey's'" (Ishaq: 243).

Fearing the scandal that would result from his father's execution in Mumbai for marrying an eleven-year-old non-Saudi and non-Arab Muslim Indian girl, the son made plans to go to India and preserve the honor of his noble Saudi Arabian family. When the son arrived at Mumbai and visited his father in jail, he became more outraged when he found out his father had transferred all his money and properties to his low caste Indian wife. At first, he decided to forsake his father and leave him to die in the Indian jail. This however, would do nothing but leave the reputation of his noble family in the balance. He told his father his terms to rectify their relationship. Unless his father places his right hand on the holy Qur'an and his left hand on his head and swear by the name of his noble family that he would not repeat these disgraceful acts again, he could expect no help. The father obeyed his son and swore on the Qur'an that he would never ever marry an Indian woman again. Somehow, this did not satisfy his son. He asked his father to make a second solemn oath. This time, he asked his father to swear by *his penis and the Holy Ka'aba*. (Some Muslim Arab men considered the most important things in life for a man are his penis and the House of Allah). Therefore, the old man placed his left hand on his penis and he pointed his right hand towards the Qibla at Mecca and made a second oath to reassure his son of his future intentions. Then, and only then, did the son agree to find a good lawyer for his father and tempt him with money and purchase the freedom of his father.

The old man told his son about the secret deal that was made between him and the Judge and the two police commissioners. The son decided to renew the unfulfilled deal, but he told his father that he would not pay more than fifty lakhs each (i.e. 5,000,000 Indian rupees each). He was a medical doctor at Jeddah and did not have that much money in his account. Moreover, this son lived many years in the States and received an American education and that made him smart enough not to be easily cheated by Indian crooks of the law. Before appointing a new lawyer, the son contacted the Judge of the High Court and the two police commissioners and told them about the new offer. The two police commissioners agreed to the fifty lakhs before trial. However, they both demanded one crore after the father was released. The Judge of the High Court demanded seventy-five lakhs before the trial and two crores after the father was acquitted with honor. The son accepted the demands of the three men of law with the hope that his father would find a way after his release to get his frozen money released and pay off the rest of the funds. The Judge informed the son that if the father would not pay the rest of the money after his release he would be subjected to a retrial and convicted. The son accepted the condition.

This time, the first installments were paid off in a less complicated fashion. Instead of traveling to Zurich and opening secret accounts, the son wrote three checks and handed them over to the Judge and the two police commissioners. It was up to each one to decide whether he wanted to deposit his check in his own personal bank account or travel to one of the OAPEC countries and open secret accounts there to deposit their funds. After making the new deal with these corrupt lawmen, the son found another crooked lawyer and told him the plan. This lawyer as was the first, a Muslim Indian. However, the son misled the lawyer into thinking that he paid each party five lakhs and that he would pay each the same amount after the release of his father. The Muslim lawyer accepted the deal and thanked his Allah and prepared his client for trial. With the new deal in place, the son felt he had adequately done everything he could to try and salvage whatever was left of his noble family's honor, and his father, Sheikh Ahmed, breathed a small sigh of relief until his trial date.

CHAPTER 10

VIOLATION OF PRIVACY

Mahmud Khan could not keep his promise to Iffat Khan. For thirty days, he treated her like a princess and provided her with all kinds of entertainment. He visited her often and spent time talking to her. He did not rape her or try to force himself on her. However, he was too enticed by her beauty and voluptuous body for her to remain untouchable. He made her swim in a sexy bikini while he sat by and watched. He struggled to control his passion and desire thinking one day soon, she would fall in love with him and offer herself to him willingly. Unexpectedly, for Mahmud at least, Iffat turned out to be emotionally dead and asexual. She seemed to have no interest in men at all.

Mahmud Khan deceitfully installed a video camera in her bathroom so that he could watch her while she was undressing. Often times, while she was taking a bath, he would watch from another room and masturbate at her image on a large screen TV. It was the only way he could keep his urges in check. Mahmud knew that eventually he would need Iffat physically to fulfill his urges. He was still unwilling to rape her. He knew that if he forced himself on her, she would think of him as no different from her Saudi husband. His pity would not allow her to identify him with the Arab pedophile that took away her childhood. There was some pride in his ability to attract women, and have them fall at his feet. He wanted her to fall in love with him and come into his bed on her own accord. As the days rolled by, he began to feel disappointed and frustrated. She had no heart to love him or sexual desire. He observed her closely and intently for any clue of how she felt. Since the day his men kidnapped her and brought her to his farmhouse, he had not seen her masturbate. He kept four secret surveillance cameras in her bedroom and videotaped her movements day and night.

Mahmud Khan then decided he had to do something to induce within her a sexual desire for men. He changed all the Indian movies he kept in her bedroom and replaced them with porn movies. He expected watching them would stir her sexuality and help develop in her a healthy desire for men. That trick didn't work exactly the way he planned. Looking at his surveillance tapes, Iffat seemed to be unhappy watching her first porn movie in his farmhouse. She could not watch it for more than a few minutes. It reminded her of her bitter experiences enduring the savage behavior of her Saudi husband. Flashbacks of the old man and his coercive methods of starvation and beatings were associated with pornographic films, killing off any stimulation or curiosity that may have been evoked in a normal person. If anything, she felt glad she was no longer under the influence of that old evil Arab man. She just wished and hoped that no man would ever again force her to do to him what her Arab husband did.

Eventually, Iffat Khan discovered that all the movies in her cupboard were on the same subject and she was compelled to watch them for entertainment and enjoyment, having nothing else to do. She gradually began to be stimulated by the movies. She even started to imitate some of the sexual moves the actresses performed with their hands on their own breasts and private parts. Therefore, little by little Mahmud awoke in Iffat the concept of self-pleasure and opened her up to new possibilities. It did not please him that his plan to attract her to him did not bear fruit. Whenever he showed up in her room or met her somewhere in his huge mansion, she reverted into the asexual girl he was so familiar with. When his porn movies did not advance his plans, Mahmud resorted to another tactic. He decided that he would have to catch Iffat in the very act of masturbating. He expected that while she was aroused and feeling pleasurable, she would not be able to deny him any longer. He bid his time until the day she was taking a bath. He sneaked into her room and hid himself. He knew from watching her that her favorite time to watch blue movies was after taking her bath. Whenever she watched, she would close every window and door, sit on her bed, and participate.

Iffat had many activities during the day. She always started her day by having some tuition classes in Hindi and English. Her tutor was an old Indian man. Every day, she was made to spend a couple of hours with him learning to read and write in English and Hindi. After having her lunch, she would have three hours of free time. She could go and play in the swing in the garden. She would also go swimming in his swimming pool whenever she desired. Once ever so often, she would just sit in the beautiful garden and soak in all the colorful birds darting among the many lovely flowers and roses. After having her dinner, she could always be counted on to take a bath. Mahmud told her that she should take a bath every day after her daily activities. After taking a bath with warm water, Iffat always spent at least a couple of hours watching movies in the home theater she had in her bedroom.

That particular evening, Iffat spent a long time in the bathroom before she reappeared again in her nightdress. She was happy after she had a warm bubble bath in the spacious tub. She was singing an Indian song, which she learned from one of the movies she watched. Iffat began to love her new golden cage and was actually fond of her new master. By comparison, her old husband could not compare in the slightest to Mahmud Khan. Mahmud had never tried to harm her or starve her for withholding sex. She would have been content if life continued exactly the same way every day because for her it was bliss. Whatever she wanted, she got. She thought that paradise would be exactly like the beautiful palace she was living in now.

In a short time, Iffat became addicted to those blue movies. She thought that the good man who saved her from her cruel husband and brought her to his palace had added those movies to increase her enjoyment. Before this, she always thought that the function of sex was to give a man pleasure, but for the woman, unbearable pain. She had known no other way. The movies started to change her perspective on sex. It would seem that sex was somewhat pleasurable without the violence and the beatings she had come to associate it with.

Iffat closed all the windows and doors of her spacious bedroom and walked over to her home theater system and selected the movie she liked most and inserted it into the DVD player. She did not bother to shut off the lights. As soon as the movie began to play, she stripped off her nightdress and jumped on her huge bed and began to watch it, getting excited. She lay on her stomach, stretching out her legs as wide as she could. Her legs were long and evenly rounded. Her backside protruded upward slightly oversized. She kept her chin suspended upon her hands and her fully developed breasts peaked like pomegranates. Almost everything about her body could be seen by the man who was hiding in the room watching her as she lay bare her nakedness.

Her sexy posture ignited a fire in Mahmud Khan like kindling wood in a fireplace and aroused him beyond measure. His excitement reached the maximum limit and he knew that if he denied himself any longer, he would explode in frustration. Waiting for the right time, he continued to watch her, just a few feet away, with Iffat completely unaware. After twenty minutes of erotic footage, Iffat flipped over and began to rest on her right side. When she changed her posture, it exposed her full curvy figure to the man concealed and waiting for the right moment. She lifted her left leg and her right hand moved slowly down her abdomen to between her legs touching her vagina. She began to massage herself gently. Her left hand found her left breast and started to caress it. Her hand began deliberately moving from one breast to the other breast fondling them. Her fingers touched the top of each of her nipples making them firm and erect. She lifted each breast to her mouth and began sucking and squeezing them; making them swell in exaltation. The middle finger of her right hand was rubbing against her clitoris and before she could climax, it decided to make her wait a little bit longer and disappeared inside her vagina with the index finger. She liked feeling herself; humming and moaning in pleasure. She was breathing heavily as the room resonated with every voice and essence of her feminine sexuality. Her tongue was rhythmically licking her lips and she lost interest in the movie; closed her eyes, sighing and pretending she was the lady in the movie.

Mahmud Khan stared at her pleasing herself and imitated her wetting her lips…She eased onto her back spread-eagle; her legs folded at the knees and her feet wide apart as if she was getting ready for sex with an invisible partner. The right hand became more aggressive in its strokes; the roughness caused a slight pain but was overcome by the pleasure it brought. She became lost in an ecstasy of her own making; soaring and sighing in the indescribable exotic pleasure of making love to herself.

Mahmud Khan lost it. His conscious mind switched off and he became like an animal in mating season. He felt like a hungry beast with fresh meat within his reach. He came out of his hiding place and walked quickly to *the uncovered meat*. Iffat suddenly became aware of someone in her room. She opened her eyes and saw a man standing in front of her. First, she thought that she was hallucinating. However, she saw that the face was familiar to her. She knew it was the kind man who saved her from her cruel husband and brought her to his beautiful palace. She felt very shy and embarrassed. She changed her position quickly and gathered the bed sheet around her and covered her naked body. Her heart was beating so fast and her body began to sweat. She couldn't utter a word. She waited for the good man to shout at her and rebuke her for the bad thing she was doing in his house.

Instead, Iffat saw the man sitting beside her. She felt his hand touching her head. His hand began to shake when it felt the sweat on her forehead. When Iffat did not push his hand away, he concluded that his heart's desire was at last going to be fulfilled. He knew that beneath the white sheet was the sexiest female body he ever seen in his life. She was within his reach and she was for him and him alone. His hand moved from her forehead and traveled down to her cheek. Iffat did not resist yet but that had not convinced him she was yielding. His hand moved to her lips and began to feel them. No reaction still. He moved yet closer to her and took her in his arms. Iffat remained stationed in her position as if nothing was happening. However, when his hand moved gradually down to the side of her breasts, she pushed it away and retreated. He did not like the way she pushed away his hand. He tried to hug her again, but she prevented him. She used both hands and pushed him back from her.

Mahmud Khan waited for a few minutes and tired to approach her again. This time, he held her face with both his hands and began to kiss her in her mouth. She struggled to free her lips from this unwelcomed kiss. However, he overpowered her and held her arms holding them down over above her head. She began to kick with her feet. Nonetheless, all her efforts could not stop him from forcing himself on her and kissing her. When he let go of her lips and slid down the bed sheet from off her body. Iffat began to scream for help. Her screaming jolted him back from his temporary insanity. He knew that if he continued to force himself on her, whatever gains he had made in winning her over would vanish and she would hate him for raping her. He knew that if he raped her, he would never dream of ever wining her love. Therefore, he stopped and asked her to forgive him for his indiscretion.

Iffat stopped screaming and began to weep. After that, Mahmud Khan tried to convince her that she had tempted him through her actions. He justified his violation of her privacy by lying to her. He said that he had a spare key to her bedroom and he came in to look for something important. He found her naked and masturbating and that made him lose himself. He promised that he would not try to have sex with her against her wishes ever again. Iffat said nothing and continued to weep piercingly at her would be rapist and she felt ashamed she was caught in such a way. Mahmud Khan stood up and left the room leaving her alone.

CHAPTER 11

STINK NEWS

The trial of Sheikh Faiz bin Ahmed was conducted on a Friday afternoon at the Mumbai High Court. The day and the time were chosen purposely by the court to avoid a huge gathering of Muslims and prevent possible riots and clashes with Hindus. Nevertheless, Muslims gathered in hundreds outside the court and continued to shout and demand the release of the Saudi Muslim man. Many Muslims had gone to their mosques to perform their Friday Public Prayer and ask Allah to grant victory to their Arab brother who was "unjustly" held for "lawfully" marrying an 11-year-old Muslim girl and set him free from the hands of the Hindu polytheists. Inside the courtroom, Hindus sat calmly and waited for the verdict to be delivered. Everyone expected a verdict of guilty and the kidnapper and rapist of the eleven-year-old Indian girl to be punished to the fullest extent of the law. The judge was a Hindu and that gave the spectators reassurance that the wicked Old Saudi was going to be sent for a hanging. When the final hearing of the trial began, that assurance was shaken. The evidence presented in court astonished the audience. First of all, the Mumbai Chhatrapati Shiviji International Airport police changed their statements. They said that when they asked the girl about her age she said she was seventeen years old. Her passport also showed that her age was seventeen. However, they doubted her age and that is why they arrested the Old Saudi who claimed he was taking her to Iran as his maidservant.

Secondly, the Hyderabad police commissioner supplied evidence that the Marriage Agency and the family of Amina Hyder Ali had fooled the Saudi man. The corrupt police commissioner brought to court Amina's father, mother, brothers, and sisters. All of them testified under oath that they told the Old Saudi that their daughter was seventeen years old. Thirdly, the police commissioner of Mumbai produced Amina as a witness who then told the court she had told the Saudi she was seventeen. In fact, the Mumbai police commissioner was the one who had bribed the airport police and made them change their statements. Fourth, the only problem that faced the court was the maidservant visa. The Muslim lawyer was able to convince the court why the Saudi man decided to take Amina Hyder Ali to Tehran as his maidservant and not as his lawful wife. He argued that his client was advised by someone to take his Indian wife under a work visa because that would hasten the process of their travel. The lawyer said further that his client had a lot of work to do and had no time to waste in India waiting for the long process of getting an Indian wife out of the country.

At the end of the trial, the crooked Judge of the High Court nullified the marriage contract between Amina Hyder Ali and Sheikh Ahmed because it was based on deception and it was illegal in India to marry a girl below the age of seventeen. Additionally, he ruled that the Old Saudi was a victim of deception and conspiracy. He raised his voice above the rising murmurs of the courtroom and announced, *"Sheikh Faiz bin Ahmed is to be released with Honor."* The Hindu audience began to shout and protest and refused to leave the court. The police used their batons and emptied the courtroom. The Muslims began to rejoice and celebrate outside the courtyard when they heard the outcome of the trial. The outrageous Hindu crowd driven from the court met head to head with the celebrating Muslims outside the courthouse and fierce fighting erupted. Many people were beaten up and some were knocked down. The police had to use teargases to disperse the crowd.

The local and national media broadcast the results of the trial. People all over India received the news with shock. They were outraged when they came to know that a Muslim pedophile and child abuser walked out of the Mumbai High Court with honor. Many people believed that the wealthy Saudi business tycoon had bribed the Judge and the police commissioners. However, no one could prove it. Muslims all over India celebrated the release of the Saudi pedophile.

Nonetheless, the celebration of the Muslims in India and the elation of the eighty-year-old Saudi man was premature and only temporary. A news agency in Mumbai known as Stink News shocked the entire Indian nation when it broadcast a few hours later, the confessions of the High Court Judge and the Police Commissioners of Mumbai and Hyderabad. All three confessions were videotaped and handwritten so that the Judge and the two police commissioners could not deny them. The Home Ministry of New Delhi ordered immediately the arrest of the three Indian culprits. Sheikh Faiz bin Ahmed was rearrested. He was picked up from his hotel room at the Taj Mahal Hotel.

The question of the day was how did the Stink News outlet find out about those secret confessions. No one could believe that law enforcement and government officials would make such dangerous and foolish admissions and on videotape! In an interview that followed the broadcasting of the three confessions, the director of Stink News said that an anonymous person sent to him the confessions through the mail. He received them a week before the final trial. However, he decided to keep them hidden from the police and the public until the trial was over. He did not want the three corrupt men of the law to get away with the crores of rupees that they received from the Old Saudi to pervert justice.

Needless to say, the confessions were the very ones which the old man ordered his Indian wife to mail to his home residence in Tehran, Iran. Iffat Khan followed the orders of her Saudi husband and sent them registered mail. When the registered package reached the address, the Iranian postman found the house was locked and no one was there to sign and receive the registered mail for a signature. The postman made three attempts to deliver the mail, but each time, there was no response at the residence. In due course, the local post office returned the mail to the general post office and stamped it as undeliverable mail. The general post office at Tehran returned the mail to the sender in Mumbai. The undelivered mail returned to the hotel where Iffat

Khan used to stay before the men of Mahmud Khan kidnapped her. The hotel management kept the mail for a month. When no one came to claim it, they decided to get rid of it. However, out of curiosity one of the front desk girls opened the mail. She thought that she might find a nice video of a foreign film or some music CDs or DVDs. Therefore, she hid it in her handbag and smuggled it to her house. When she eventually played the tapes and read the papers, she was astonished at the contents.

The girl knew that if the police commissioner of Mumbai gained knowledge that she was in possession of such incriminating evidence, they would not hesitate to send someone to kill her or arrest her and charge her falsely for a crime. She talked to her boyfriend. The girl and her lover were Hindus and following the trial of the Old man and the Hayderabadi girl with great interest. Both of them wanted the Old Serpent to be convicted and sent to the gallows. Therefore, the boyfriend suggested that his girlfriend should send the confessions to Stink News. He knew that the Stink News' *raison d'être* was like no other news when unearthing scandals of high profile Indians. To avoid being involved in a conspiracy, the boyfriend told his girlfriend to send the materials as an anonymous person.

The Stink News closest twin would be the international non-profit organization of Wiki Leaks. A couple of days later, it also broadcast the confession of a Muslim lawyer who wasn't part of the trial. The new confession revealed that the Muslim lawyer admitted on tape and through writing that he was going to receive three crores of rupees prior to the trial and three crores after the trial. That indicated he was going to receive more money than the corrupt Judge and the two crooked police commissioners. The confession of Sheikh Barkatullah puzzled the police of Mumbai. When the police went to arrest him, they did not find him. They did not find any of his family members. From his neighbors, the police were informed that he sold his house a couple of months ago and left India and traveled to Pakistan. The police were also puzzled by the new Muslim lawyer who replaced Barkatullah. The Indian 'Wiki Leaks' had no information on him. Given the notoriety of the case, he was picked up, and crumbled under interrogation. He admitted to receiving a bribe from the son of the Old Saudi. The police were baffled as to his claim he received five lakhs prior to the trial. It was a mystery they could not solve. So, it just remained an unsolved inexplicable riddle that the former Muslim lawyer, who sold his house and escaped to Pakistan was promised six crores, whereas the new Muslim lawyer who replaced him, was only promised ten lakhs.

Sheikh Barkatullah was perhaps not the only person who managed to escape the grasp of the stink scandal just in time. The son of Sheikh Ahmed also left Mumbai the same night his father was rearrested in his room at the Taj Mahal Hotel. He flew out of Mumbai on the next flight out. Mumbai police issued another arrest warrant. This one against the person that mailed the secret confessions by registered mail to Iran. The sender was identified as an Indian Muslim maidservant of the Old Saudi. Her name was Iffat Khan. Her name was published in every newspaper in Mumbai with her photo. Again, the police did not have a recent photograph of her. Her passport was not renewed because it remained valid for ten years from the date of its issue by Worli Passport Office, Mumbai. The passport showed that she lived for a short time in Saudi Arabia. She lived three years in Asmara, Eritrea and six and a half years in Tehran, Iran. The police also guessed that she was sexually involved with the Old Saudi in some way. As before, the police could not trace her family in Mumbai. The address on her passport showed that she used to live with her family at Vakola Colony, which turned out to be fictitious. The residents of the colony were mostly Hindus and some foreign students. None of the residents of the colony claimed to have known a Muslim family by the name of Khan. The police were able to find the date she traveled to Saudi Arabia along with her mother, Rayhana Khan. Questions arose as to whether this was the Saudi's maidservant or the missing child-bride that was the center of an international controversy many years ago. What continued to puzzle the police were the variations in the dates in which her passport was issued and the date she traveled out of India from the Bombay International Airport. It appeared that her passport was reissued after she left India. This was another mystery that mystified the minds of all the police of Mumbai. Still, an arrest warrant was issued for her, as she was deemed to be a critical component of the complicity.

CHAPTER 12

THE LAST RESORT

Mahmud Khan was very disappointed and frustrated by Iffat's last refusal. He thought that no man in the world would find a young and beautiful girl like Iffat in that position and just walk away and leave her ravaging her body. Rape was steadily becoming his last option. He decided to give her one more chance to love him. If she would not allow him to have his way with her within the week, he would simply have no choice but to rape her. Visions of her naked body lying in bed masturbating tortured him day and night. He could not think of anything else except her body. It was not the easiest of times for a man used to having women fall all over him and giving in to his every request.

Mahmud Khan decided to blackmail Iffat Khan in a way that would bring her begging on her knees and doing whatever he wanted. He would tell her that unless she would agree to be his secret kept-wife, the film director would carry out his blackmailing scheme. He emptied her entire cupboard of porn movies and replaced them with only one single DVD. He expected that Iffat would play it and then watch in surprise. The DVD contained a secret recording of her while she was naked and masturbating. The recording also showed when he approached her and began touching her. After making her watch it, he decided he would approach her and tell her that he would send the DVD to her Saudi husband who was recently released from the Mumbai jail and was searching for her. Mahmud Khan knew that Iffat feared the Old Saudi more than she did the devil. Then, he would tell her that if she did not want to go back to the Old Saudi and be brutally punished by him for agreeing to be videotaped in that shameful manner, she would have to stay with him and be his mistress. He had some local newspapers on hand, with photos of the old Saudi after the Judge of the High Court declared him innocent and acquitted him with honor. Mahmud Khan decided to use the pictures and articles to mislead Iffat Khan into thinking that her Saudi husband was released from prison and was frantically searching for her.

Iffat Khan changed a lot after Mahmud Khan caught her masturbating in his house. She stopped watching porn. She retreated into her burqa, thinking that it would save her from the man who kidnapped her and imprisoned her in his house. Now she looked like a caterpillar in her cocoon. When Mahmud Khan brought her to his farmhouse, Iffat Khan had come out of her black cocoon and transformed herself from a proverbial chrysalis into a fluttering butterfly; just as she was taking flight, she reverted back into her cocoon. He tried to persuade her not to dress up in her burqa, but nothing he said would convince her to venture out again. She wrapped herself up and retreated like a vampire during the day and a phantom by night, not even coming out of her room. She refused to go swimming in the pool or visit the beautiful garden and enjoy the sweet sound of the birds or watch the colorful flowers and roses. She no longer played in the swing in the garden. She became very gloomy and distant. She behaved as if she was recently bereaved and had lost someone very dear to her. She locked herself up inside her room all the time. She did not remove her clothes except inside the bathroom. However, inside the bathroom she did not remove her clothes until she switched all the lights off. Like a black ghost in darkness, she quickly took shower and donned again her burqa. Her behavior brought great sadness in the heart of her kidnapper. He blamed himself for violating her privacy and breaking her wings. His plan to blackmail her again did not work because Iffat stopped watching any DVDs.

When all his tricks and secret plans did not work, finally Mahmud Khan made up his mind to have sex with Iffat Khan, forcibly if necessary. He hated the idea as it went against his character. So he came up with the idea of tranquilizing her and then raping her. He bought strong sleeping tablets and planned to hide them in her drink. He knew that Iffat loved to drink milk after her dinner. He dissolved the sleeping tablets in her milk and then asked his cook to take the dinner tray to his new actress. Mahmud Khan had already convinced all his menservants and maidservants that Iffat Khan was an Indian girl from Iran and he brought her to his farmhouse to teach her Hindi and English so that he could give her a leading role in his upcoming movie.

That particular evening Iffat ate her dinner and drank her milk as usual. As soon as her system digested the milk she fell asleep on the chair in front of the dining table in her room. Meanwhile, Mahmud Khan was sitting in another room and watching her through his surveillance cameras. He waited until he knew that she was completely under the influence of the drug. By then, Iffat had already slid out of her chair and was sprawled all over the floor. The wicked man came out of his room and like a thief in the night crept to her bedroom and unlocked the door. When he entered her bedroom, he found her lying unconscious on the floor. He took hold of her black veil and uncovered her face. Her face looked like the face of an innocent child who fell asleep and needed her loving mother to come and carry her and put her to bed. Mahmud Khan bent over her body and lifted her up, carrying her to the huge bed and lying her down in it. Beside himself with joy and expectation, he sat beside her body and began to look at her face. Her closed eyes deprived her face of half its marvelous beauty. Nevertheless, he bent over her and kissed her on the lips. He found her lips lifeless and cold. He stopped kissing her lips and started to touch her breasts. He uncovered her breasts and began to caress and fondle her nipples. He found her breasts cold and lifeless too. Not too concerned, he began to undress her. He stripped off her offensive black burqa. Then, he removed her Salwar Kameez. After that, he began to remove her inner clothes piece by piece until she lay bare.

Mahmud Khan began to explore her naked body and feel it everywhere. However, he found her unconscious body to be dead and void of sensation. There was no response to his lustful touches. He felt as if he was trying to arouse a corpse. He lost his mood and regretted putting her to sleep. He initially thought that he was going to enjoy himself but what he wanted was the girl he had seen on his camera, aroused and masturbating, deep in the throes of sexual gratification. Mahmud felt as if he had dug a body out of its grave and tried to rape it. He simply could not sleep with Iffat's unconscious body. He replaced all her clothes and left her asleep on the bed. Iffat remained under the effect of the strong sleeping pills for a very long time. When she woke up the following morning, she was feeling drowsy and her head ached. Feeling nauseous, she forced her unwilling body to the washroom and vomited. Her digestive system had not digested her food and she began to tremble, sweating profusely. She lost her strength and fell on the floor. Her head hit the edge of the tub on the way down, and left her bleeding on the floor.

Iffat Khan almost died that day. Her fate was intervened by the cook who came to serve her breakfast. When she did not find Iffat in the bedroom, she correctly assumed that she was in the washroom. She placed the tray on the table and knocked on the door of the washroom. She wanted to tell Iffat that she had brought her breakfast and to come eat before her food got cold. When Iffat did not answer her, she pushed open the door of the washroom. She became frightened when she saw Iffat lying on the floor with her face covered in blood and thought the new film actress had committed suicide. Too scared to touch her, she ran to her employer screaming and babbling what had happened. Mahmud Khan asked the cook to summon his personal doctor and ask him to come to the bedroom of his new film actress. Then, he ran to Iffat's bedroom and tended to her while waiting for his private doctor.

Mahmud Khan obviously did not tell his private doctor that he had put sleeping pills in Iffat's milk the night before. He said that she most likely had food poisoning since she had vomited in the washroom. However, the doctor knew that Iffat condition was a serious ailment caused by something entering her system and preventing her digestive system from functioning properly. The doctor was able to stop the bleeding and revive Iffat. Then, he prescribed some antibiotics for her and strongly advised Iffat to remain in bed until she was fully recovered. Mahmud Khan did not like how the situation was turning out. Not only had he failed to win her love, he had also made her distrustful of him. Given his need to have her aroused and responding during sex, he decided he would try another intoxicant... Alcohol.

He waited for a few days until Iffat was fully recovered. He knew that she always drank juice after her breakfast. So, he slipped, into her morning juice, some extra strong Indian liquor called Tharra. (Tharra is similar to Moonshine or hooch in North America. It was made by fermenting the mash of sugar cane juice and ground up pulp in large terracotta spherical containers. The fermented mash is distilled to near 90% alcohol or 180 proof. Good Tharra is comparable to Vodka. Unfortunately, hundreds of villagers die each year from copper formaldehyde poisoning induced during distilling). Iffat ate her breakfast and drank her juice without realizing what was in it. She had never tasted alcohol before. Given the potency of Thara, this first time drinker got drunk almost immediately. Everything in front of her was moving. She tried to sit up straight but slumped over the side of the chair and felt like she was falling off. She could not control her body to make it do what she wanted it to do. She decided to go to bed and maybe if she could sleep for a while, she would feel better. She thought that maybe she had once again contracted the same illness that caused her to bedridden for some days. She tried to stand on her feet, but could not. She crept on her knees until she reached the bed. Her body responded to the drug by completely doing the opposite of what was normal. She was totally out of her body and stiff as a stone. She managed to force her body onto the bed and fall over onto her stomach. After that, she could not move a limb. While she was sleeping on her stomach, she felt someone come and sit near her. She felt his hands take hold of her body and turn it over. Then, she saw her kidnapper sitting near her with a faint smile on his lips.

Mahmud Khan tried to talk to Iffat, but she did not respond to his words. She was altogether drunk and oblivious to the world. He reached with his right hand and removed the veil from off her face. She was sweating as if she had run a twenty-mile marathon or sat in the sauna for hours. Her breathing was laborious and hoarse. Mahmud began his seduction by massaging her left hand. She did not stop him. His hand traveled up her arm to her shoulder and slid slightly down and to the left of her breast. He began to gently press against her breasts to see if she would protest. She did not push his hand away. He bent over her and started kissing her lips. Her lips were moist and intoxicating and hotter than hot. Her entire body was extremely hot, and Mahmud felt she was now sexually ready for him to express his desire; but she wasn't sexually hot—she had a very high fever. Mahmud Khan stopped kissing her lips and began to remove her clothes.

Iffat still hadn't shown any objection or response. Although she could see him, she could not feel his hands touching her. Mahmud undressed the upper part of her body. Then, he started to fondle her fully exposed breasts. He expected her to respond to his touches. However, her hands and legs remained stationery in their positions as if she was paralyzed. He did not bother about her lack of response and continued to remove her clothing. She was lying on her back and every part of her body was gradually being exposed. The only thing that moved was her half moon-shaped eyes. Mahmud opened her legs apart and began feeling her, but she did not try to stop him then either. He thought she was enjoying his experience at pleasing a woman, but she could not show any response due to the effects of alcohol in her system. He went ahead and removed the last pieces of her clothing.

Before mounting over her half-conscious body, the lustful man heard Iffat snoring loudly. When he looked at her face, her eyes were closed and he could see that she was fast asleep. Mahmud, disgusted with the turn of events, wondered if he had given her too much alcohol. Seething with anger, he stormed out of her room, leaving her naked on the bed. Patience has a limit and Mahmud Khan had just reached his. Giving up on his lighter methods of coercion, he braced his mind to prepare to rape the lovely captive woman. He was determined that as soon as she became sober he would go into her bedroom and rape her.

So far, apart from the 'unlawful detention' there had been no rape or abuse. It was like the prophet who decided not to rape a six-year-old girl, but to thigh her up until she reached nine years of age. In the Qur'an, the man was allowed to do whatever he wanted with the woman except penetration. This is what is called in the Qur'an as the Al-Lamam (Qur'an Surat al-Najim 53: 32). A Muslim man one day came to the prophet Muhammad and told him that a woman came to his shop and he asked her to come inside for choosing the best dates he had. The woman believed his words and walked in his shop. He immediately seized the woman and began to rape her. Then he went to say, he hugged her, kissed her, undressed her, caressed her breasts, and fondled her privates. In short, he touched her bare-naked body everywhere, and did everything to her except penetrating her vagina. The prophet Muhammad ordered him to only wash himself. Therefore, in the Shari'a law hugging, kissing, fondling, and touching a woman everywhere by a man who wasn't her husband would not be considered adultery or fornication and hence there was no punishment for this type of activity. Even anal sex is not adultery. The sexual act of adultery is defined by penile penetration of the female vagina. Therefore, according to the Shari'a law (Islamic law), whatever Mahmud Khan had done thus far to Iffat Khan wasn't adultery or rape and hence he wasn't committing a crime according to the laws of Islam.

His last attempt had also failed miserably and there was nothing to do but wait for her to recover from the effects of alcohol poisoning. While Mahmud Khan was waiting for Iffat Khan to awaken, one of his men brought to his attention the case of the Old Saudi and the Hyderabdi girl, which involved his captive girl, Iffat Khan. The Bollywood director found Iffat's photo on the front pages of all the Mumbai newspapers. He read the articles under her photos and discovered that she was wanted by the Mumbai police for her involvement in the greatest scandal that ever rocked the Mumbai police department. He could see that he had saved her by kidnapping her at the right time. If she had been staying at the same hotel when the scandal broke, she would have been locked up behind bars. Although he was now her saviour, Mahmud Khan decided to use the situation to his advantage to blackmail his young victim.

Iffat had never been in a jail before. In her mind, jail meant a place where bad people were brutally beaten and tortured and killed. She remembered that her mother went to jail and never returned. Her Saudi husband told her that her mother was stoned to death for her bad deeds. Therefore, when she became sober and her captor showed her the newspapers, which published her photo on the front pages, he frightened the hell out of her. She thought that he was going to hand her over to the police. She cried and begged him not to inform the Mumbai police where she was. Mahmud Khan gave in to her pleas and agreed to keep her hiding place secret, but he put forth some conditions. He told her that if she did not want to go to jail then she had to agree to certain conditions. Firstly, she should stop wearing her burqa and just regular clothes. Secondly, she had to agree to marry him and remain his second wife. Therefore, as his wife, she should allow him to have sex with her anytime he wanted to, and whatever way he wanted to. Thirdly, as his second Muslim wife she should live with him in his beautiful house forever. He told her that in Islam the man is allowed by the Qur'an to have up to four wives at the same time (Surat al-Nissa 4: 3). Iffat Khan, out of the fear for her life agreed to fulfil the conditions of her captivity.

Mahmud Khan then followed the footsteps of the Old Saudi man who followed the "blessed" Sunna of his prophet Muhammad and brought a Muslim Mullah and two male witnesses, and conducted a marriage between him and his captive girl. Although the Old Saudi man imitated the tradition of his prophet and Aisha and married a female child of seven years of age, the Old Indian man likewise followed the example of Muhammad and his captive Jewish girl, Safiya bint Huaya and married his captive girl against her wish and without her wali (guardian). From that day forward, Iffat Khan allowed her new captor to abuse her body. While he was having sex with her for the first time, she felt like she was having an out of the body experience. It was like exploratory surgery without anaesthesia. She knew what to expect from her cruel Arab husband but this Indian husband made her feel like she was safe and yet misused her trust and deceived her. He had said he cared about her but only as long as he could use her. With her abusive Saudi husband, she didn't have to pretend like she liked it for he liked torturing her. With this new animal on top of her, he wanted her to say, "I like it" and "I want you" and pretend she wanted him to do what he was doing to her. While he was doing sex with her for the second time, she felt like the person who was undergoing harsh interrogation method. Her evil interrogator was using a whip and inflicting sever pain on her delicate body. And that was the way, the wolf in sheep clothing enjoyed doing it. She concluded a beast would not torture her as he did to her. She hated him with passion and understood that he was more cruel than her evil Saudi captor. Her two evil masters had all things in common. She just switched hands from Ahmed to Mahmud…to be continued in part two…

CPSIA information can be obtained at www.ICGtesting.com
Printed in the USA
BVOW071259310812

299273BV00002B/39/P

9 781462 672417